Daughter
of
York

ANNE EASTER SMITH

A Touchstone Book
PUBLISHED BY SIMON AND SCHUSTER
NEW YORK   LONDON   TORONTO   SYDNEY

 Touchstone
A Division of Simon & Schuster, Inc.
1230 Avenue of the Americas
New York, NY 10020

First Touchstone trade paperback edition February 2008

TOUCHSTONE and colophon are registered trademarks of Simon & Schuster, Inc.

For information about special discounts for bulk purchases, please contact Simon & Schuster
Special Sales at 1-800-456-6798 or business@simonandschuster.com.

Designed by Mary Austin Speaker

Manufactured in the United States of America

10 9 8 7 6 5 4

ISBN-13: 978-0-7432-7731-0
ISBN-10:   0-7432-7731-7

With love to my husband, Scott,
who encourages me every day to dream

Acknowledgments

*I*t is my great pleasure to acknowledge and thank several people for helping me tell Margaret of York's story. First and foremost, my friend Maryann Long, who agreed to accompany me on my journey to Belgium to follow Margaret's footsteps. She was Passepartout to my Phileas: carrying the maps, taking hundreds of photographs, acting as a sounding board as I plotted out the novel and saving my life as I blithely stepped off sidewalks onto busy Belgian boulevards thinking I was back in the fifteenth century. We discovered Burgundy together and shared many fascinating excursions. I must also thank my sister, Jill Phillips, who once again hosted me in London while I went to the British Library, the Public Record Office and other venues. Through her friend Jo Cottrell I was able to view the only medieval portion of Greenwich Palace (now the Royal Naval College), which is not generally open to the public. Thanks, too, to Ann Wroe, author of *The Perfect Prince* (entitled *Perkin* in UK), whose knowledge of Margaret was invaluable to my research and who gamely photocopied the entire Vander Linden's *Itinéraires de Charles, duc de Bourgogne, Marguerite d'York et Marie de Bourgogne* for me. Claire Denenberg, nurse practitioner extraordinaire, helped me with medical aspects of the book.

I would also like to acknowledge: Professor Marc Boone of the University of Ghent, who graciously gave me a crash course in Burgundian politics in just under two hours in his office; Professor Emeritus Walter Prevenier of the same university, who through an e-mail exchange pointed me in the direction of fifteenth-century buildings in Mechelen; medieval-history consultant Henk 't Jong of Dordrecht, Netherlands; my friend Kiek van Kempen for help with Dutch/Flemish; and Pamela Butler, membership chair of the U.S. branch of the Richard III Society, who kindly lent me Joseph Calmette's *Philip the Good* and *Charles the Bold* for more than a year even before she had read them herself.

My thanks to erstwhile singing partner and graphic artist Patrick Duniho of Plattsburgh, N.Y., for contributing his creative talent to the chart and map at the front of the book.

I would be remiss not to thank again my tireless agent, Kirsten Manges, and my overworked and brilliant editor, Trish Todd.

And finally, to my family for supporting my new career venture, all love and thanks.

Dramatis Personae

*Fictional Characters

ENGLAND

York family
see Plantagenet Family Tree

Lancaster family
see Plantagenet Family Tree

Woodville family
Sir Anthony (later Lord Scales and second Earl Rivers)
Eliza Scales, *his wife*
Elizabeth Grey (later Queen Elizabeth), *his eldest sister*
Jacquetta (formerly duchess of Bedford), *his mother*
Richard, first Earl Rivers, *his father*
Sir Edward, *his brother*
John, *his brother*
various brothers and sisters

Neville family
Cecily, duchess of York (see Genealogy chart)
Richard, earl of Warwick, *her nephew*
Countess Anne, *his wife*
Isabel (later duchess of Clarence), *Warwick's daughter* (see Genealogy chart)
Anne (later duchess of Gloucester), *her sister* (see Genealogy chart)
George Neville, *Warwick's brother, chancellor of England*

Miscellaneous
Anne of Caux, *the York family nursemaid*
*Jane Percy, *Margaret's attendant*
*Ann Herbert, *Margaret's attendant*
*Beatrice Metcalfe, *Margaret's attendant*
*Fortunata, *Margaret's attendant*
John Harper, *soldier and messenger in Edward's train*
William, Lord Hastings, *Edward's councilor and chamberlain*
John Howard (later Lord Howard and duke of Norfolk), *Edward's councilor*
John Tiptoft, Earl of Worcester, *Edward's councilor*
Jehan Le Sage and Richard L'Amoureux, *Edward's jesters*
Lady Eleanor Butler, *one of Edward's mistresses*
Isobel, countess of Essex, *lady-in-waiting to Duchess Cecily*
*Francis, *Anthony Woodville's squire*
*Brother Damian, *monk at Reading Abbey*
Dr. Fryse, *one of Edward's physicians*
Señor Martin Berenger, *emissary of the court of Aragon*
*Master Vaughan, *Margaret's steward*

Burgundy, (see Plantagenet Family Tree)
Charles, count of Charolais (later duke of Burgundy), *Margaret's husband*
Duke Philip, *his father*
Dowager Duchess Isabella, *his mother*
Countess Isabelle, *his first wife*
Mary, *his daughter*
Antoine, count de la Roche, the Grand Bastard of Burgundy, *his stepbrother*
Maximilian, *archduke of Austria and heir to the Holy Roman Empire*

Marie de Charny, *Charles's stepsister and Margaret's chief attendant*
Pierre de Bauffremont, count of Charny, *her husband*
Anne of Burgundy (later Lady Ravenstein), *Charles's stepsister*
Adolphe of Cleves, Lord Ravenstein, *Margaret's councilor*
Lord Louis of Gruuthuse, *merchant of Bruges and Margaret's councilor*
Guillaume de la Baume, Lord of Irlain, *Margaret's chevalier d'honneur*
Henriette de Longwy, *his wife*
Jeanne de Halewijn, *Mary's chief attendant*
Jehan de Mazilles, *young courtier*
Dr. Roelandts, *one of Margaret's physicians*
Olivier de Famars, *captain of Margaret's bodyguard under Guillaume de la
    Baume*
*Hugues, *one of Margaret's bodyguards*
William Caxton, *governor of merchant-adventurers at Bruges, later printer*
"Jehan Le Sage," *Margaret's ward or "secret boy"* (real name unknown)
*Frieda Warbeque, *his mother*
Madame de Beaugrand (Azize), *Mary of Burgundy's dwarf*
Chancellor Guillaume Hugonet
Guy de Brimeu, Lord of Humbercourt } *Charles the Bold's chief councilors*

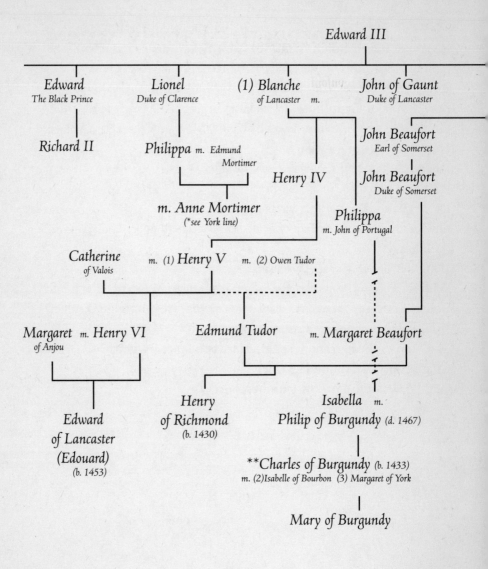

Edward III

Edward
The Black Prince

Richard II

Lionel
Duke of Clarence

Philippa m. Edmund
Mortimer

m. Anne Mortimer
*(*see York line)*

(1) Blanche
of Lancaster   m.

John of Gaunt
Duke of Lancaster

John Beaufort
Earl of Somerset

Henry IV

John Beaufort
Duke of Somerset

Philippa
m. John of Portugal

Catherine
of Valois   m. (1) Henry V   m. (2) Owen Tudor

Margaret m. Henry VI
of Anjou

Edmund Tudor   m. Margaret Beaufort

Edward
of Lancaster
(Edouard)
(b. 1453)

Henry
of Richmond
(b. 1430)

Isabella m.
Philip of Burgundy *(d. 1467)*

**Charles of Burgundy *(b. 1433)*
m. (2)Isabelle of Bourbon (3) Margaret of York

Mary of Burgundy

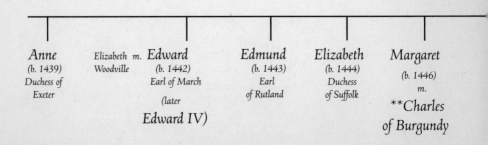

Anne
(b. 1439)
*Duchess of
Exeter*

Elizabeth m. Edward
Woodville   *(b. 1442)*
Earl of March

(later
Edward IV)

Edmund
(b. 1443)
*Earl
of Rutland*

Elizabeth
(b. 1444)
*Duchess
of Suffolk*

Margaret
(b. 1446)
m.
**Charles
of Burgundy

Plantagenet Family Tree

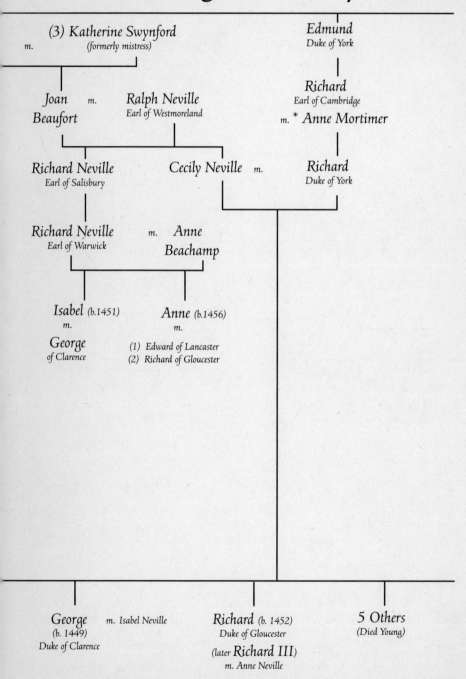

(3) Katherine Swynford
m. (formerly mistress)

Edmund
Duke of York

Joan Beaufort m. Ralph Neville
Earl of Westmoreland

Richard
Earl of Cambridge
m. * Anne Mortimer

Richard Neville
Earl of Salisbury

Cecily Neville m. Richard
Duke of York

Richard Neville
Earl of Warwick m. Anne Beachamp

Isabel (b.1451)
m.
George
of Clarence

Anne (b.1456)
m.
(1) Edward of Lancaster
(2) Richard of Gloucester

George
(b. 1449)
Duke of Clarence
m. Isabel Neville

Richard (b. 1452)
Duke of Gloucester
(later Richard III)
m. Anne Neville

5 Others
(Died Young)

NORTH
SEA

England &
The Burgundian
Low Countries
(1466-1480)

Ravenspur

• Fotheringhay

England

Ipswich

• St. Alban's
• Barnet

London
Greenwich
Canterbury •
Margate
Dover
Calais

THAMES

Middleburg

Utrecht

The Hague

LEK

MAAS

RHINE

Sluis
Male
Bruges
Ooidonk
Ghent
Antwerp
• Ter Elst

St. Omer
La Motte
LYS
Dendermonde
Malines
• Louvain

Aire
• Lille
Oudenaarde
Brussels

HOLY
ROMAN
EMPIRE

• Aachen

Tournai
Liege

Hesdin
CANCHE
Mons
Binche

Le Crotoy
SCHELDT
Cambrai
SAMBRE

SOMME
• Picquigny

France

Luxembourg

PART ONE

A Plantagenet Princess

1461–1468

1

1461

*T*he Micklegate towered above her, seeming to touch the lowering sky, as she knelt in the mud and stared at the gruesome objects decorating the battlement. Rudely thrust on spikes, several human heads kept watch from the crenellations, wisps of hair stirring in the breeze. A paper crown sat askew on one of the bloodied skulls and drooped over a socket now empty of the owner's dark gray eye. The flesh on the cheeks had been picked clean by birds, and there was no nose. Yet still Margaret recognized her father. She could not tear her eyes from him even as his lifeless lips began to stretch over his teeth into a hideous smile.

It was then Margaret screamed.

"Margaret! Wake up! 'Tis but a dream, my child." Cecily shook her daughter awake. She watched anxiously as Margaret's eyes flew open and looked around her with relief.

"Oh, Mother, dear Mother, I dreamed of Micklegate again! A terrible, ghastly dream. Why does it not go away? I cannot bear to imagine Father and Edmund like that!" Margaret sat up, threw her arms around her mother's neck and sobbed. "Oh, why did they have to die?"

Cecily held her daughter close and was silent for a moment. Why, indeed, she thought, fighting back her own tears. It was surely a mistake, a horrible mistake! If only she had stopped them venturing out that fateful New Year's eve. Christmas was supposed to be sacrosanct no matter how great the hatred between enemies—all retiring to hearths and homes to celebrate the birth of Jesus. The great hall at Sandal Castle had been decorated with boughs of holly and pine, the rafters ringing with the noise of men feasting and drinking. The Christmas fortnight was half spent, and thoughts of death had been put aside for the holy season. Cecily sat close to her beloved husband, Richard, duke of York, and their second son, Edmund, earl of Rutland, aware of the uneasy peace that lay around them, for the enemy army of Lancaster lay not ten miles hence at the royal castle of Pontefract. Then came the knocking at the great oak door and the unexpected entrance of more soldiers—but these were armed, disheveled, bloody. Richard upset a goblet of wine as he rose in alarm.

"Ambush!" cried the leader of the stragglers. "Trollope ambushed us as we foraged!"

The duke and seventeen-year-old Edmund called for their arms, and the cry was taken up by the rest of the company: "*Aux armes! A* York, *à* York!" Pandemonium broke out as servants ran to fetch weapons and armor, men donned breastplates, helmets and shields and ran out to the castle courtyard.

"My lord, my dearest lord, this is Christmas!" Cecily cried, taking Richard's face between her hands. "Surely Somerset would not break a Christmas truce! These men must have come upon a band of brigands, not an army of the king!"

"Perhaps you are right. Trust me, *mon amour*, we shall be home again in a little while. Keep faith, Cecily. I must go and avenge my comrades." Richard bent, kissed her hard on the mouth and grinned. "Just a little while, have no fear!"

"I beg of you, wait for Edward, my love! We know he is coming with his own army. Wait, for the love of God!" But she spoke to an empty hall. Her husband was gone, impetuously—and arrogantly—believing he could defeat any Lancastrian force. She had broken down and cried.

The scene faded, and Cecily stifled a sob in her daughter's blond hair. That had been exactly a month ago, but it seemed to her a lifetime of loneliness. Richard and Edmund had been killed that day at Wakefield along-side the great Yorkist lord, Richard, earl of Salisbury, who was Cecily's beloved brother. Two thousand men fell in the York ranks, trapped as they were by a far superior Lancastrian force, which lost a mere two hundred, so the messengers said. In an unwonted act of spite, the Lancastrian victors had taken the heads of the defeated Yorkist leaders and stuck them on the city of York's Micklegate, adorning Richard's brow with a paper crown. "See," they laughed, "he wanted to be king, this duke of York, and now he's king of his namesake city!"

"Richard, my Richard, why were you always so hasty—so rash?" Cecily muttered to herself unintelligibly. "If only you had been patient that day—waited for Edward—listened to me—you might be with me still." Her voice rose, "Oh, my dearest love . . ."

Margaret heard her mother's soft moan and immediately wiped her eyes. The girl was astonished by this uncharacteristic display of emotion from her mother. Cecily came from strong northern stock. Her family were Nevilles—after the royal princes, the most powerful nobles in England. Her father had been earl of Westmoreland, and she was a granddaughter of John of Gaunt on her mother's side. A noble line indeed—and one used to the vagaries of political fortune and the terrifying consequences of battle.

"Mother! I am so sorry. How you must be grieving, too! All this time you have allowed me to think . . . made me wonder . . ." She hesitated, embarrassed by such an intimate conversation with her usually imperturbable parent. Aloof, proud and stoic were words Margaret had heard whispered behind Cecily's back, and for the most part she agreed with them. But she had also been witness to Cecily's deep devotion for her husband and the recipient of a motherly protection as fierce as any lioness's. Margaret had known, as had her seven siblings, a mother's love from the day she was born.

Cecily allowed her tears to fall. "Aye, sweeting. You thought I had a heart of stone. Is that what you would say?" She attempted a wan smile. "Nay! My loss is so great I feel my heart is shattered in so many shards that they pierce my skin here," she tapped her breast, "and make me want to scream in agony!" And she sobbed again.

This time, it was Margaret who put her arms around Cecily and soothed her with gentle sounds. How glad she was to see a softer side of her mother. At fifteen, she had already formed her own shell and learned to hide inside to protect herself from hurt, but there were times when she ran into the garden and found a solitary place where she could cry or stamp her foot in anger—emotions that were frowned upon in Cecily's strict household.

"Hush, Mother. God has Father and Edmund in his care now. Let us pray together for their souls," Margaret cajoled, gentling the older woman away. She knew her mother would respond to a call for prayer; Cecily's piety was well known. The two women knelt by the bed, crossed themselves and intoned the ritual, "In the name of the Father and of the Son and of the Holy Ghost . . ." and then disappeared into silent memories of their lost dear ones.

Margaret shut her eyes tight, hoping the darkness behind them would erase the grisly dream. When that didn't work, she forced herself to think of her father as alive and well and dandling her on his knee when she was a child. She knew she was his favorite—the boys told her so constantly. Richard of York had not been a big man, but his body was sinewy and carried not an ounce of fat. He used to allow Margaret to test the solid muscle in his upper arm and try to wrap her hands around it. He'd laugh at her wide eyes and loudly kiss her fair head. All his children except the eldest, Anne, and the youngest, Richard, had inherited their mother's fair hair. Margaret and Richard, however, had their father's slate gray eyes. He had worn his thick, dark hair in the old-fashioned short cut—Margaret told him it looked as though his squire had stuck a bowl on his head and simply chopped off the hair that hung below. That would make him throw back his head and neigh with laughter. Margaret loved it when her father laughed. His whole body shook, and he would make little snorting sounds between the laughs. It would make everyone else laugh—even Cecily, who never found life very amusing.

Remembering his laughter now, Margaret found herself smiling and thanked the Virgin Mary for giving her a happy memory of her father to replace the nightmare.

DICKON AND GEORGE were fighting again. Margaret found the antics of her two brothers as tiresome as any elder sister would. She was too grown up now to jump into the fray—something she would have relished a few years ago.

There were three years between each of them, and nine-year-old Richard—nicknamed Dickon to distinguish him from his father—was the runt of York's litter. Small for his age, he had been sickly as a little boy but had survived those first five precarious years when so many children died and now was not loath to tackle his bigger brother, George, when the occasion arose. The three siblings were, in fact, firm friends. During these most tumultuous years, they had endured being dragged around the countryside with their parents or left in the care of others while Cecily followed her beloved husband wherever she could on his quest for the crown—very often into danger. The children frequently squabbled like dogs over a scrap, but woe betide anyone else who picked on one of them. The other two would rush to their sibling's aid and staunchly defend the victim, fists clenched. Cecily and duke Richard encouraged this behavior in their brood.

"Never forget your blood kin, children," their father would say. "The most important people in your world are right here in this house—the house of York."

Now, whenever someone referred to the proud lineage of her family name, Margaret would hold her head high, puff out her chest and brim with confidence.

As she idly watched her brothers laughing and tumbling—taller George with his fair hair and good looks and Richard, who was a miniature of their father—she wondered what would become of them. Would they, like Edmund, end up on a pike on top of a city gate? She shuddered.

And what of Edward, her godlike eldest brother? Where was he this cold February day? She turned to look out of the window and onto the courtyard of Baynard's Castle, the York family residence in London on the banks of the Thames. Mercifully, Edward—titled the earl of March—had been in Wales gathering forces for his father and not at Wakefield that fateful Christmas season. Margaret knew her mother was worried. Edward should have been marching to London with an army to head off King Henry and Queen Margaret's force. Whoever owned London owned the kingdom, she said. Fear akin to panic had greeted Cecily in every village when she rode posthaste to London after the loss on New Year's eve.

The people knew Queen Margaret was allowing her troops to loot and pillage the towns and villages as they marched south, intent on making London their own. London merchants shut up their shops in anticipation of her arrival; they had no love for the French woman.

Mother and daughter had taken a few minutes to rest one day following a rigorous session with the steward regarding the day's castle business. Margaret had begun to accompany the duchess on her errands around the castle—meeting with the steward, visiting ailing attendants, dispensing justice in petty disputes among the staff—and she sank gratefully into some cushions in a window embrasure overlooking the busy river. Cecily closed her eyes for a moment and fussed with the rosary at her belt.

"Pray tell me why our house," and Margaret involuntarily swelled with pride, "is fighting the king, Mother. Is that not treason?"

Cecily's eyes flew open. She frowned and glanced about her. "Enough talk of treason, Margaret. Come close and I will explain all. It all began more than three score years ago and involved my grandsire, John of Gaunt, duke of *Lancaster*."

Margaret's eyes widened and mouthed the hated "Lancaster" back to her mother. Cecily nodded and proceeded to regale Margaret with the beginnings of the civil strife between York and Lancaster. When she told how Gaunt's son had usurped the crown, Margaret could not but help blurt out, "Usurped? Mother, he was the grandsire of our present king. Oh, for sure that must be a treasonable thought. Have a care!"

"Do not dare to speak to me thus, daughter!" Cecily scolded her. "We are safe here, and besides I speak the truth. And the king knows it also, for he agreed to make Father his heir, denying his own son the crown. But 'tis Queen Margaret who holds King Henry's leading strings, for the poor man has bouts of madness and delusion, and she hates your father—and indeed all of us—for disinheriting her son. Understand this, Margaret, and understand it well. Your father had the right to the throne through his grandsire on his mother's side, the earl of March," she stated sternly. "He was descended from King Edward's second son."

Margaret had lowered her eyes at the reprimand and absorbed the information for a moment before her quick intelligence found a missing thread. "Then why was Father the duke of York and not the earl of March?"

Cecily was pleased. "You show much wit, my dear, which will help you greatly when you take your place as wife of some lord. 'Twas from his father's line, which descends from great Edward's fourth son, the duke of York, also named Edward. You see, Father had double the royal blood of any of Gaunt's descendants!" She finished triumphantly. "A pox on them!"

"But you just said you are one of his descendants, *ma mère*." Margaret could not resist and once again paid the price for a willful tongue.

"Enough of your cheek! Leave us now," Cecily ordered, and Margaret meekly obeyed until she closed the heavy door behind her, when she ran giggling to her apartments.

"York and Mortimer, Gaunt and March, Lancaster and Boling-broke—oh, a pox on them *all*," she cried, imitating Cecily beautifully and making her old nurse, Anne, chuckle indulgently.

Margaret smiled now as she remembered the scene that day, vaguely aware that the din behind her had quietened as George and Richard seemed to have come to a truce and were back at their Latin books. Her smile soon vanished as she saw a company of horsemen at the castle gate on Thames Street calling loudly for the portcullis to be raised.

"Boys, come and see what is happening below," Margaret called. "There are some soldiers riding into the courtyard with a herald."

The magic word "soldiers" had the boys scrambling to take a perch at the window. They opened it and leaned out dangerously far to hear what news the men brought. Margaret hauled Richard back by his jerkin, and he glared at her.

"You will not be any good to Edward dead, you idiot!" Margaret told him. "Have a care!"

"You're not my warden! You aren't even my nursemaid! Leave me be, you . . . you . . . whey-faced wench!" Richard sputtered at her and instantly regretted it. Cecily had entered the room at exactly the wrong moment, and she was shocked by his speech.

"Richard! Where have you learned such talk? Apologize to your sister at once and then you may go to bed without your supper. I am ashamed of you. To think your father has only been dead these five weeks! You children have lost all discipline." It was a common theme of Cecily's, and Margaret rolled her eyes at George behind Richard's back.

Characteristically, George jumped to Richard's defense by attempting to distract her. "But, Mother, something is happening in the courtyard. Come, see for yourself."

"'Tis true, Mother, look!" Margaret chimed in. Cecily waited in silence until Richard had slipped out of the room to obey her, and then she peered from the casement.

"What did you hear, George?"

"I heard Ned's name, but then Meg pulled Dickon in and they quarreled, so I couldn't hear any more." He scowled at his sister.

How unattractive he is when he does that, Margaret thought fleetingly, although no one had ever heard Margaret say an unkind word about George. That she preferred this good-looking boy to Richard was no secret to those close to the children. He was nearer in age, as willful as she, loved to dance and recite poetry, and they both enjoyed the luxuries and limelight that went along with being a duke's child. Richard was more serious and secretive, rarely putting a foot wrong, so needful he was of his parents' approval. You never knew what he was thinking, Margaret told George one day. And he preferred the outdoors to indoor pursuits, unlike her and George. But Dickon was fiercely loyal, she'd give him that.

"George, stay here. Margaret, come with me."

The scowl persisted. "But Mother—I am the man—I am the head of the family in Ned's absence. I should be by your side."

"When you look at me like that, George, all you show me is that you are still naught but a babe. Now, do as you are told!" Cecily took Margaret's arm and swept out of the room, followed by her ladies, who had been tittering in a corner at the family scene. Margaret turned at the last moment and gave George a helpless look.

"Bah!" sputtered George at the closing door.

By the time the ladies entered the great hall, the messenger was being attended to by a squire and had rid himself of his dirty cloak and tabard. He knelt as Cecily swept in.

"What news, master herald? Come you from my son?" Cecily went straight to the point.

"Aye, my lady. And I have to report a victory for Lord Edward seven days since!" A cheer rose from the assembled company. "At a place near Ludlow called Mortimer's Cross."

"I know that place," Cecily said eagerly, gripping Margaret's arm. "A victory you say. There was a battle? Who was there? How many were slain?"

"My lady, I would tell you all but I am in sore need of some refreshment . . . if it please you."

Cecily clapped her hands for some wine and bade her steward arrange refreshment in the armory for the rest of the troop. Margaret noted how her mother took charge of the situation, giving commands with an authority that was tempered with benevolence. The young woman was beginning to understand how to earn loyalty from the retainers and staff. Cecily treated each servant fairly, her nursemaid had told her young charge once. "'Tis why they would die for her, Margaret. She knows the name of every man, woman and child who serves the house of York here at Baynard's. Watch and learn," Anne of Caux advised.

The herald followed the duchess to her chair on the dais, where she sat flanked by Margaret on one side and her ladies on the other. She bade him to sit on a stool at her feet. He was a handsome young man with a twinkle in his hazel eyes, and he cast a few admiring glances Margaret's way that made her blush. She stood beside her mother and waited for his tale. After a long draught from a goblet, he began.

"My lord Edward was marching to meet with the earl of Warwick to stop the king's army from reaching London from the north when he heard that a large force was moving from Wales under Jasper Tudor to join the king. Lord Edward turned his army and chose to face this force in battle."

"His first as head of our house," Cecily reminded the company proudly.

"Aye, your grace," the messenger agreed. "He comported himself brilliantly! He knew the country well and chose Mortimer's Cross for its strategic benefits. There were those who doubted his choice of day, however. 'Twas the feast of Candlemas—a most holy day—and some were loath to fight upon it. But just before the battle began, a strange happening took place that convinced our troops Edward would be victorious."

Margaret was imagining her handsome giant of a brother in his armor rallying his men to battle. She leaned forward to hear more. The herald paused for effect and took another draught.

Cecily impatiently waved him on. "What strange happening? No riddles, sirrah, I pray you."

" 'Twas close to ten of the clock, and we were chafing at the bit waiting for the enemy to approach when we noticed three suns in the sky—"

"Three? Do not babble nonsense, man," Cecily snapped. "How can there be three suns?"

Others in the room crossed themselves in wonder and awe. It did seem a portent, an omen, and yet their lord was victorious. After the weeks of depression following the loss of their leader, York's supporters were in need of such good news.

"I know not how, lady. But I saw them with my own eyes. A hush came over the army, and then my lord Edward turned his horse to us and cried, ' 'Tis the symbol of the Trinity, God the Father, God the Son and God the Holy Ghost! It means God is on our side! 'Tis a sign.' And we believed him then. He was so sure and so brave, and the light from the three suns shone bright on his gold-brown head, making him look like . . . like a young god," he flattered the duchess, and Cecily nodded proudly. "We routed the Welsh rabble 'tis true, but in all three thousand were slain that day. Their leaders were executed, including that Welshman Tudor."

"Good riddance!" Cecily sneered. "I hope they put his head on a pike, like my husband's."

Margaret cringed, her dream remembered. Men are barbarous creatures, she thought.

"Aye, my lady, they did. 'Tis said a mad woman combed his hair and washed his face as it sat high upon the market cross."

"And now, herald? Where is my son now?" Cecily demanded.

"He gathers men from every village, field and manor to meet with my lord Neville, earl of Warwick, and defend London from the royal army. I know not where he is, in truth, for he sent me from Gloucester to bring these tidings to your grace."

"Warwick is still in London—at The Erber," Cecily frowned. "Does he know where to meet Edward?"

"Indeed, I was just now at that place afore I came here, your grace, and saw his lordship. My lord Edward has charged him to march his forces out of London, as the king's—or I should say, the queen's—army is still plundering what they will on the road south." He shook his head. " 'Twas folly for her not to have marched direct on London after Wakefield. But we are all the stronger for it."

"Aye, 'tis true, London would have fallen had she moved swiftly. And with the poor demented king housed safely at the Tower, she would have held all the power here. Herald, I thank you for your news. Gather your men and get you gone to The Erber, where you can help my lord of Warwick best. We are safe here for the time being."

The herald finished his wine and took his leave with a graceful bow, giving Margaret a brilliant smile.

Cecily turned to Margaret and frowned. "I hope you did not encourage that smile, daughter?"

"Certes, no!" Margaret said innocently, but secretly she knew she had. That night she went to bed and imagined herself being led out for a *basse danse* by the handsome herald. She reached out her hand under the covers and, pretending the other one was his, she squeezed her own fingers and murmured, "With pleasure, master herald." She frowned. She didn't even know his name. Before she could make one up, however, she drifted off to sleep.

MARGARET WAS BORED. Baynard's had been under a self-imposed curfew since the earl of Warwick had marched out of London from his residence on the twelfth day of February five days ago. Only those charged with provisioning the castle and its vast stables were permitted to venture into the streets. Cecily was taking no chances. The children were allowed to walk around the ramparts or in the extensive walled garden and exercise their horses by trotting round and round the courtyard. The boys, Margaret noted enviously, never tired of competing with each other at archery in the butts, tilting or with wooden weapons in swordplay, cheered on by idle squires and stable lads.

She had toiled over a tapestry for more than an hour that morning, attended Mass, and followed Cecily around dutifully as her mother oversaw the smooth running of the castle. She listened to the usual conversation with the steward, who told Cecily about everything from the birth of a child to a beating of an errant page. Then Cecily checked the account books with the comptroller and signed orders for provisions for the entire castle. Margaret did not have an aptitude for figures, but she knew that when she had her own household, she would be expected to oversee not only her own expenses but also those of her husband, should he be gone. But Cecily seemed to enjoy the responsibility, and Margaret marveled at how quickly it was all resolved every day.

Then she had played her lute until her fingertips were sore and practiced French with old Anne, the Norman nursemaid who had begun service with the York family at Edward's birth. Even her beloved books could not keep her mind occupied today. She longed to escape the confinement of her chamber and the castle walls. Cecily had even forbidden the daily outing along the river in the ducal barge—too dangerous in these times of uncertainty, she told the children. We cannot afford to lose any more York family members, she said. Not while your brother is staking his claim to the throne. Margaret's attendants Ann and Jane had tried to persuade her to play a game of hide and go seek that would include several of the pimply pages they flirted with incessantly, but Margaret found those two girls' company less than stimulating. They had been assigned to her by Cecily, who recognized her daughter needed companionship of her own age, but their simpering and obsession with clothes and jewels bored her.

And so that afternoon she escaped her own chambers and wandered through the maze of rooms in the vast castle, avoiding her mother's apartment, where she knew she would be immediately put to work on an embroidery Cecily had designed to honor Edward's victory at Mortimer's Cross. She found her way to the bridge room, a tiny space directly over the castle gate that had a window onto the world outside the castle. She had come here to cry those first few days after the news of Wakefield reached Baynard's. Although she still found herself close to tears many times a day, she was learning to hide them—like her mother. Cecily did not tolerate displays of emotion in public. "Those of our station must always be in control of our feelings, do you understand, Margaret? 'Tis a sign of weakness to be seen crying," she had told Margaret after another of Margaret's nightmares. "How will we deserve loyalty from our servants if we appear weak?"

Today, her visit to the bridge room was more to alleviate her boredom than to grieve. Perhaps she could watch ordinary townsfolk in their ordinary lives, something that intrigued the privileged young woman. The door was unlatched, so she pushed it open. Unaware of her presence, a young squire and a servant maid were enjoying a passionate embrace. Margaret stared fascinated at the sight. The young man's bare buttocks were thrusting back and forth at the young woman, who was standing spreadeagled against the wall, her skirt and shift lifted to her neck. "Harder, harder," moaned the girl, writhing in what seemed to Margaret to be pain. The squire obliged, and in a very few seconds, both lovers climaxed with a cry. As quietly as she had entered, Margaret left the room, her mind in a whirl.

At the onset of her courses not a year ago, Cecily had given Margaret a perfunctory explanation of the begetting of children, which had terrified her. But this scene did not seem so terrifying; in fact, it had made her pulse race, and she had experienced a strange physical yearning. She touched her breast and was surprised at the warm sensation she felt all the way to her thighs. At once she was ashamed and mumbled an Ave, feeling for the rosary she kept at her waist. Certes, I shall have to confess this when the priest hears me tomorrow, she thought, for if this feels so pleasurable, it cannot be good for the soul. Cecily's training had been well digested. She wished she had someone to talk to about the experience other than immature Ann and Jane, and she was sure old Anne would not ever have felt as she was now. Not for the first time, Margaret wished she had been born a boy. They have all the fun, she lamented.

The rattling noise of the portcullis being raised and the shouts of men interrupted her thoughts. She ran down the stairs, taking the narrow steps two at a time and stopping at the open balcony at the foot. Others were beginning to appear at windows and balconies all over the castle, watching as more and more bloodied men limped, hobbled or were borne by others into the courtyard. Cecily's steward, an imperious man with white hair and bright blue eyes, stood on the top step leading into the great hall, waiting for the herald to extricate himself from the melee and climb the steps. Margaret recognized the smiling man who had brought them news of Mortimer's Cross. He was not smiling now.

"I bring bad news to her grace, the duchess, sir," he addressed Sir Henry Heydon, the steward, loudly enough for all to hear. "My lord of Warwick has suffered a bitter defeat this day at the hands of the queen at St. Albans field. These few of us escaped to bring the news to London, so you can prepare for the advancing army."

Cecily appeared from the hall, and the messenger went down on one knee and doffed his bonnet.

"God keep you, sir herald. At St. Albans you say?" she asked, a tremor in her voice. "And what of my cousin of Warwick? God forbid he is not slain."

"Nay, your grace. The earl and the rest of our force who escaped the slaughter have fled west to find your son, Lord Edward."

"Praise be to the Virgin for that!" Cecily exclaimed.

"My lord of Warwick had taken the king with him to the battlefield, I know not why," the herald continued. "He is back with his queen now, as mad as ever. Some said they saw him at the edge of the battlefield sitting under a tree, laughing at his enemies."

"Sweet Jesu, he is indeed mad," whispered Cecily, crossing herself. Aloud to the company she cried, "Hear this, loyal friends of York. We are in danger here, and I would command all those who can walk and fight to join this herald and leave London as soon as they have had nourishment. Follow Warwick's trail and join with my son. Those too wounded to be moved will be looked after here. I do not believe the queen will harm me or those who cannot fight, so we must remain to defend Baynard's from her looting army. God help us! And may God bless the lord Edward!"

"God bless Lord Edward!" Margaret cheered along with the rest, and a thrill of pride went through her at the deafening sound of loyal voices echoing Cecily's prayer.

A few minutes later, Margaret joined her mother in the great hall. The duchess was in full command of the servants, who gathered around her, receiving orders. The deference they gave the proud, beautiful woman was not lost on Margaret. She longed to emulate her dignified mother—but not until I am much older, she thought timidly.

"Ah, Margaret, my dear, come here and help me. I want you to go up to your apartments and tell Nurse Anne to ready George and Richard for a journey. Tell her to pack their warmest clothes and one good doublet and bonnet each. I will be there anon."

"Where will they go, Mother?" Margaret asked, unfortunately.

"'Tis not your place to question me, Margaret," Cecily retorted. "Pray do as I tell you at once!" A few sympathetic eyes turned to Margaret upon hearing Cecily's sharp chiding.

Margaret blushed, ashamed that she had been reprimanded in front of so many people. Cecily relented and said less severely, "You will know in a little while. I simply do not have time to explain now."

Margaret, still smarting, curtseyed and hurried upstairs to the boys' chambers. Her brothers were appalled that they were to leave for parts unknown without her, for her mother had not told Margaret to prepare herself for a journey with them. It would be one of the rare times in their young lives that the siblings would be parted. Margaret gave the boys the news, and Anne began packing.

Richard was still crying when Cecily joined them half an hour later.

"Where is your York backbone, Richard?" she admonished him. "You are near ten years old and here you are crying like a baby. 'Tis not the first time you have been without me."

"But . . . but . . . Meg has always been with us. Why can't she come, too?" Richard tried to stop his lip quivering and tears from flowing, but he did not succeed.

It was Margaret who gathered him into her arms and cajoled him out of his fear. " 'Twill be an adventure, Dickon! George will be with you, and Nurse Anne, I expect."

"Aye, Anne will go with you. Although I expect George will not care for that! And your favorite squire, John Skelton, will also keep you company." Cecily knelt in front of her youngest and took him from Margaret, holding him close. "Hush, child. It will not be for long, I promise, for Edward will come and take London and all will be well."

At Edward's name, Richard brightened. "You think he will really come, Mother. I would dearly love to see Ned again!" He blinked back his tears and attempted a smile.

"That's better, child." Cecily stood up and drew George to her as well. "Now, would you like to know where you are going?"

"Aye, Mother," chorused the boys. "And why," added George.

" 'Tis for your own safety, George. If something should happen to Edward—pray God it does not"—they all crossed themselves—"then you and Richard are York's heirs. And therefore heirs to the crown."

Both boys looked nonplussed, and Cecily decided not to explain but fussed with the clothes Anne had laid on the bed. "I am sending you to our friend the duke of Burgundy, so you must remember your manners.

Aye," she said, nodding, as the boys' eyes widened, "you will have your first voyage on a ship!"

"A ship, Georgie!" Richard cried ecstatically, his tears forgotten. "We are going to sea, like the game we played yesterday!"

George was less enthusiastic, old enough to understand that he was to miss events at home that might carve out his future. But he put his arm about Richard's shoulders protectively, giving his mother's back a resentful stare. "Aye, Dickon. And I will protect you, never fear."

"I am not afraid, George!" Richard exclaimed. "I am a York. And us Yorks are never afraid!"

"There's a brave boy, Richard." Cecily turned, beaming. "Only it should be we Yorks, but no mind. Now, both of you say good-bye to Margaret and come with me."

Margaret watched, stunned, as the trio left the room, followed by Anne and a servant carrying the clothes chest. How could her life change so quickly? Only a few weeks ago, she had a father and another brother. Now they were gone. Then Edward had triumphed at Mortimer's Cross, giving Yorkists hope of winning the crown of England, and now the disastrous news of St. Albans had turned their world upside down again. She shook her head in disbelief. A mere hour ago, she had been relatively carefree and experiencing her first sensual thrill of womanhood. Now her world was falling apart, and as if the news weren't bad enough, her brothers were to be taken from her.

"George! Dickon!" she cried, "Wait for me!"

She picked up her skirts and ran down to the castle quay, where she was just in time to give both boys a last kiss. The boatmen dipped their heavy oars into the water and pulled away from the pier towards the scores of ships moored in the Pool on the other side of London Bridge. Cecily sat with her black fur-trimmed cloak wrapped around her frightened children as they huddled together for warmth against the damp February evening.

"I will be back with the tide, Margaret," Cecily called. "You must take care of everything until I return. You know what to do. You have learned well!"

Margaret nodded and waved, her eyes brimming with tears, as she watched the boat and the small figures of her brothers recede into the diminishing light. "God go with you, boys. Until we meet again!" she cried. Then she turned, held her head high and walked sedately up the stone steps and back into the castle. For the next few hours, she was in charge of the York household, giving orders—a little timorously, but still with enough authority—and presiding over the evening prayers. She prayed to St. Margaret to help her during Cecily's absence. She looked around at the expectant faces all waiting for her to dismiss them after the chaplain had intoned the blessing, and she realized in that moment that her childhood was over.

2

1461

*Q*ueen Margaret had missed her chance again. Instead of marching her victorious army the twenty miles into London immediately following the battle at St. Albans, she hesitated. For the next ten days she parlayed with the mayor and aldermen, attempting to negotiate an entry. The city elders were loath to resist the queen—fearing reprisals for having lent the preferred Yorkists vast sums to equip their army—and agreed to meet her to suggest that four of her deputies negotiate with the London magistrates, acting on behalf of its citizens, to allow only the royalist leaders into the city. The London elders, however, had reckoned without their fellow citizens. Londoners shut up their shops, hid their jewels and money and turned on the mayor, taking the keys of the city gates for themselves and refusing to let anyone in or out.

At Baynard's Castle, the York household held its breath and waited. Surely the lord Edward could not be far now. Cecily attempted to continue the daily routine of the castle, and she and Margaret spent time plying their needles, walking about the orchard and terraces, visiting the wounded and attending Mass. Margaret was relieved to know George and Richard had been taken on board a vessel bound for Burgundy, and Cecily assured her that Duke Philip would treat them kindly. Cecily had had to negotiate personally with the captains of two or three ships lying in the harbor before one going to the Low Countries agreed to her price. Her mother's bravery and resolve to protect her family even in the face of danger left an indelible mark on Margaret, and she hoped that when her turn came, she too would be as fearless.

She missed her brothers, even their squabbling, and kept expecting to see them as she went through the days. She had escaped a few times to the bridge room window—empty each time, although she did once see the servant girl hurrying down the corridor near the duchess's apartments. Over the thatched roofs across Thames Street, Margaret could see the lofty tower of St. Paul's Cathedral, a mere stone's throw from Baynard's and reputedly the tallest in all Europe. Thames Street had been seething with people the first day following the St. Albans battle: citizens scurrying in and out of houses, closing their shutters and their shops, fetching buckets of water from the conduit, carrying baskets of food from the market, calling to their children to go inside in anticipation of the queen's pillaging soldiers. Then came the calm, when the city gates were locked and people slowed to their usual gait, the shutters were unbolted and the children went out to play. Margaret never tired of watching life in the street and envied the commoners their freedom. She could not leave the castle yard without at least one lady companion and two retainers, and she was never permitted to talk to people or inspect the colorful offerings on market stalls. It did not occur to her that the townsfolk might envy her luxurious life behind the castle walls.

Today, as she watched, there seemed to be an excitement in the air. People nodded and smiled or stopped to talk to one another, pointing to the west. She looked towards the western wall of the city and thought she saw a metallic glint in the far distance. Then a little boy hared around the corner shouting, "Soldiers! Soldiers approaching the Ludgate!"

"At last!" cried a stout man in the boy's path. "'Tis Edward of York you see, boy, ain't it?"

"Aye, sir! And the earl of Warwick with him, they say! They are opening the gates!"

Margaret turned on her heel and ran to her mother's solar, bursting in unceremoniously and earning a frown from Cecily. "Walk, don't run, Margaret. 'Tis undignified."

"But Mother, Ned is come! I was watching from the bridge room, and I can see the army approaching from the west. May we go to the Ludgate and watch his entry?"

"Certes, you may not! We shall wait here until Edward calls for us," Cecily said, continuing to ply her needle as though Margaret had merely announced it was another cold day. Her mother's calm amazed Margaret, who was hopping from one foot to the other. But then she saw her mother wince and a drop of blood fall on her dress. Aha! she thought happily, Mother is as excited as I am!

Her mother caught her watching and said haughtily, "Go to your chamber and wait. I must make arrangements for Edward's arrival." She sucked on her pricked finger.

Margaret curtseyed and remembered to walk out of the room. "Go to my room and wait?" she muttered. "I shall not!"

She took off running down the corridor and up a short flight of stairs to what was known as the children's apartments. Her two young ladies-in-waiting were gossiping by the window of the solar that overlooked the river. They were unaware of events unfolding on the other side of the castle. They broke off their conversation and curtseyed as Margaret came in.

"Jane," she addressed the taller of the two, "help me off with my gown. And take off your own so that we can exchange clothes."

The women gawped at her. Margaret waved her hands impatiently. "Do not stare at me like beetle-headed clack-dishes! Jane, do as I say, and Ann, stand by the door and see that no one enters." She wasted no time unbelting her gown and backed towards Jane, who helped her with the heavy garment. Then Jane took off her plain woolen gown, and Margaret slipped it over her own head. Margaret was tall, like her mother, and she had small breasts that showed off the current high-waisted fashion to advantage. Jane's gown was a little short, she noted, but it would do. Jane, on the other hand, would be tripping over the hem of Margaret's dress, and she sent up a prayer that the duchess would not choose to visit the apartments any time soon.

"But what if someone comes? What if they notice I am wearing your dress? Oh, 'tis unfair, Lady Margaret," Jane whined, fluttering her hands and close to tears. Margaret scoffed at her dismay.

"Don't be such a goose! Ann, lock the door behind me, and if someone comes, say you are indisposed." Ann nodded conspiratorially, pleased that Margaret was entrusting her with the more important task of protecting her mistress. "Besides," Margaret continued happily. "Mother is far too busy to pay attention to us this afternoon. Ned is come!"

The news made the girls forget their concerns for a moment as they clapped their hands and squealed with excitement, causing Margaret to scold them for making so much noise. She went to the armoire built into the wall and selected as drab a cloak as she could find. Winding it around her and pulling the hood down over her face, she would pass muster as a merchant's daughter, she thought.

"If anyone asks, you do not know where I am. Do you understand?"

"But we do not know where you are going, Lady Margaret," Jane said, her face a picture of woe again.

"Then you will not have to lie, will you?" retorted Margaret and swept out as Jane collapsed on the bed sobbing and Ann ran to her to commiserate. "Ninnies!" Margaret muttered as she closed the door.

The news of Edward's coming had streamed through the castle like a welcome shaft of sunlight, and jubilant servants, squires, stable lads and pages were milling around the courtyard, some of them getting permission to run to the Ludgate to watch the entry. The main body of the army would camp outside the city, but Edward was coming home to Baynard's and would choose to enter at the Ludgate, she knew.

She slipped out unnoticed in a group and ran up Athelyng Street, past Knightridder Street and Carter Lane and into St. Paul's square. There she was lost among a throng of hundreds awaiting the White Rose of Rouen, as she heard men call her brother—after his birthplace, she assumed. She had never been this close to so many people before, and it frightened yet thrilled her. However, she had to admit that the smell of all these towns-folk was enough to curl her toes, and she regretted not having her bag of sweet lavender on her belt. Even her drabbest cloak received admiring looks from her neighbors, and she noticed most of theirs were of rough wool and patched. Many had none at all, and those unfortunates shivered, huddling close to one another for warmth. But the cold did not dampen their enthusiasm for the occasion, and several shouts of "Long live March! Long live York!" were taken up by others with such volume that Margaret could hardly hear herself think. Her chest again rose proudly at her family's name.

Something about her bearing made the crowd part for her as she edged her way to the front. She had no idea how conspicuous she was, but no one recognized the tall, attractive young woman with her hood clutched tightly around her face to keep out the wind. Finally, she saw Edward as he passed under the massive, fortified gate in the city's wall. Hundreds of exuberant Londoners thronged the short distance to St. Paul's, throwing their hats in the air and chanting his name. Edward wisely entered the city surrounded only by his closest advisers, including his mentor, Warwick. He rode his magnificent gray courser down Bower Row to towering St. Paul's, waving and grinning at the tumultuous welcome.

As he scanned the crowd, Edward's eye fell upon a familiar face radiantly smiling up at him from the throng, and he reined in his mount in astonishment. "Margaret!" he mouthed in disbelief and laughed out loud. "Does Proud Cis know you are here?" he shouted, but Margaret could not hear his words above the din.

Nudging his horse into a walk, he continued to the steps of the cathedral, where the bells had begun pealing. Margaret watched, her eyes shining with tears of happiness. How handsome he was, she thought. His six-foot-three-inch frame sat as if he had been born in the saddle, and he towered over the nobles riding beside him. His bare head was crowned by chin-length, red-gold hair, neatly turned under in the latest fashion, and his features were as beautiful in a masculine way as his mother's. Margaret fancied every woman in London must be in love with her eighteen-year-old brother, and she hugged herself with excitement, knowing she, as a York family member, was part of this demonstration of affection.

After Edward and the nobles in his train disappeared into the cathedral to give thanks, Margaret wended her way back through the crowd, exhilarated by her foray into London's everyday life. She ran down the hill to Baynard's, barely avoiding the contents of a piss pot that was being dumped out of an upstairs window.

"Bah!" she muttered, giving the waste a wide berth. Maybe she was better off at the castle, after all.

. . .

MARGARET DID NOT see much of Edward for the next few days. He was consumed by a whirlwind of activity from the moment he arrived. Meetings Edward held with his mother and with the earl of Warwick went far into the night. When he had first seen Margaret at supper the evening of the entry, Edward crushed his baby sister to him in a long embrace, almost knocking off her headdress, and told her, "You are receiving three hugs in one, for I do not have George and Richard here!" Then he whispered, "Your secret is safe with me, little Meg. But you are headstrong."

Margaret stood on tiptoe and kissed his freshly pumiced face. "Thank you, Ned!" she whispered back.

That had been two days ago, and during that time, Edward and his councilors decided on a resolution to the extraordinary dilemma that England could have two kings. It had been arranged that an "election by procedure" would take place, a custom that was used before William, called the Conqueror, had changed the ancient system of arranging the succession. Margaret joined her mother and brother in Cecily's comfortable solar and was told they were awaiting the result of this election. Edward was hoping the people would prefer him as king to Henry, Cecily said, but he wanted it to be legal.

"There is not enough time to call Parliament or a representative council," Edward explained to a puzzled Margaret. "It's those in command at hand in the city and others who give financial and moral support who can vote."

Chancellor George Neville, younger brother to the earl of Warwick, was addressing an assembly consisting of all peers currently in the city, the mayor, aldermen, merchants and anyone else wishing to participate in the election of the next king—Edward.

Margaret was not sure this was very fair, as, in the current climate in London, King Henry would not have a chance of being elected, but she nodded and held her tongue.

A few hours later, it was all over. George Neville had addressed the crowd as his brother had instructed: "Is King Henry fit to rule over us, as feeble as he is?"

The cry had been "Nay!"

"In his feebleness, the queen has all the power. Do you want to be ruled by her?"

"Nay!" was the emphatic reply.

"Will you take Edward, heir of Richard of York and rightful heir to the crown, as your king?"

"Yea!" was the overwhelming response from the people.

And so it was decided. Edward would be king. When Edward and his friend William Hastings arrived, Cecily rose and faced her son. "Your grace," she said, and sank into a deep reverence. Margaret quickly followed suit. Edward laughed, hauled his long body out of the chair and strode from the room, followed by Cecily and Will. Margaret stared after them, dumbfounded. Sweet Jesu, she thought incredulously, I will be a princess.

WHERE, IN ALL of this, was King Henry and his queen? Margaret wanted to know. Cecily was proud of Margaret's keen perception and the intelligent curiosity that had prompted the question. They both looked at Edward. He was relaxing for a few hours in front of the fire in his mother's solar with his favorite wolfhound lying on the tiled floor beside him, using Edward's foot as a pillow.

"The She-Wolf is on her way north, Meg. Turned on her tail, with Henry tied tightly to it, and went back north. Word has reached me of more devastation in her army's path as they retreat. I can never forgive her for her disregard for our people. In truth, what can you expect from a French woman! God's nails, but I hate her!" He hissed the last comment and drew a frown and a "Hush, Edward" from his mother.

"What happens now, Ned? Does England have two kings?" Margaret asked, innocently.

Edward grinned at her. " 'Twould appear so, my dear sister." Then he turned serious. "Nay, the business is not finished until one or other of us kings is defeated completely. The queen is not finished, I can promise you that. And," he paused, shifting his weight so the dog had to move, "neither am I!"

"More fighting then?" Margaret lamented. Edward nodded and reached for his wine.

IN THREE WEEKS, Edward's call to arms had brought thousands of new followers to London, who were eager to rid the realm of the hated Margaret of Anjou. Almost immediately after Edward's victory, Warwick had taken his force to the Midlands, intending to gather more men along the way. Messengers to Baynard's regularly came and went, keeping Edward informed of Warwick's progress and the whereabouts of Henry and his queen. Edward learned that the Lancastrians had now amassed a greater army in Yorkshire than the one they had taken to the gates of London, bolstered by the duke of Somerset rallying new troops to the cause.

On the thirteenth of March, Cecily and Margaret watched grimly as Edward led his personal meinie out of Baynard's courtyard. The tabors beat a slow march and the shawms alerted the citizens that York was on the move. Londoners gathered to cheer him out of the city as loudly as they had cheered him in. He twisted round in the saddle and waved to his mother and sister, looking every inch the young warrior on a crusade. He had ordered a new badge for his men, a blazing sun in splendor chosen because of the three suns phenomenon at Mortimer's Cross. All of them wore the badge proudly on their tunics.

"God speed, my son! And may He hold you safe!" Cecily called, drawing her sable cloak close to shield herself from the biting wind. "I pray, dear Mother of God, that he is safe," she whispered, her lip trembling.

"Have no fear, Mother," Margaret tried to sound cheerful. "How can Edward lose? Look at him!"

Cecily gave her a grateful look and turned back into the hall. How many times would they, as women, have to watch their men march off to do battle? Certes, she sighed, there must be another way!

Margaret left her mother's side and, under the pretext of using the garderobe, hurried to the bridge room, where she could catch a last glimpse of the cavalcade as it disappeared from view. She waited until she could no longer hear the shawms and tabors and then went back to her own apartments.

EDWARD MARCHED NORTH towards York, joining with Warwick's force along the way, and on Palm Sunday on a plateau known as Towton Field, the two armies finally faced each other. It was said that fifty thousand men were arrayed that day in the snow, with Edward's force two-thirds the size of Henry's.

· · ·

"NEAR TWENTY THOUSAND slain? 'Tis pitiable!" Cecily exclaimed, when she heard the news. "God rest their poor souls."

"Aye, God rest their souls," the messenger echoed, crossing himself, after Cecily had read the letter from Edward.

But even the dreadful toll could not dampen her joy at Edward's stunning victory. "You say the snow helped Edward in the fight, sir. How, pray?"

"'Twas the wind, your grace. When the Lancastrians let fly their arrows, the blizzard was in their faces and the arrows fell short. Our side picked them out of the ground and with the wind behind us shot them back with far more success."

Margaret's hand flew to her mouth. "Killed with their own arrows? 'Tis horrible."

"Nay, lady, when you are fighting, you do not think on such things. Why, in the snow, 'twas difficult to tell who was with who. Many of us may have slain those of our own side, I know not! Somerset was on the higher ground, but when the archers failed to breach York's ranks, they charged downhill to fight hand to hand. Arms and legs were hacked off, if you were fortunate. Heads, if you were not. When you thought you had broken through a line, another one was there. My lord Edward was our rallying point, never losing ground, always pressing forward and encouraging us loudly until his voice was hoarse. What was begun in the morning did not end until evening, when my lord of Norfolk arrived to reinforce us with his East Anglian force, God be praised. That is when things turned black for King Henry, for his weary men turned and ran, leaving pink snow in their wake. The pity of it was, the only place to run was down the steep sides of the other hill to the Cock Beck stream, full to bursting its banks. Many drowned in their heavy mail, and I saw others using the dead bodies to form a bridge over which they attempted to flee. The water ran red that day, your grace, red with the blood of good Englishmen. Their only fault was fighting for the wrong cause."

Margaret and Cecily sat in silence, transfixed by the scenes of carnage so vividly described by the messenger. Cecily, still clutching the letter, gripped the arms of her chair, her thoughts all of her late husband and how he, too, must have died thus. Margaret shuddered as she tried to imagine losing an arm or a leg—although growing up she had seen several of Baynard's soldiers with limbs, hands or feet missing.

"What happens to all those dead men?" she suddenly asked. "How do their families know if they are safe or killed? They cannot send messengers to every village."

"The wounded are cared for by the field surgeons, although butchers might be a better word, my lady," the man said, holding up his hand and showing the stumps of two fingers, still black with the tar used to cauterize the amputation. Margaret winced, and the man grinned. "But we have to dig pits for the dead. This time, it took nigh on two days before all were buried. 'Tis presumed if a man does not return to his home that he perished," the messenger said softly.

Everyone in the hall crossed themselves, and Cecily fingered her rosary. Then she asked, "Where are King Henry and Queen Margaret?"

"The king, queen and their son, the prince of Wales, are fled to Scotland, your grace, and their troops scattered. Many of the lords of Lancaster were slain that day, and those who are not dead or fled have asked pardon of the lord Edward and joined our ranks. 'Tis truly a victory for the house of York!"

"Aye, a great victory for York," Cecily pronounced proudly and called for wine for the assembled company.

"I charge you all to drink to"—she hesitated, savoring the thought—"to King Edward!"

"God save King Edward!" shouted the triumphant household as one.

Margaret felt the swell of pride again.

3

June 1461

*T*he palace of Shene was situated far from the city on a beautiful bend of the Thames, where islands thick with hazelnut and oak trees floated in the river. It was early June, and the field on the opposite bank was carpeted with buttercups. Yellow water lilies floated below Margaret's vantage point above the water, and she watched a pair of swans glide along, regally ignoring a family of coots chugging upstream. The blue wing of a kingfisher flashed from a willow as it neatly dived and speared a fish. Then a gray heron lifted out of the rushes as effortlessly as down and obligingly flew across the scene, making her smile with pleasure. How she loved it here!

Cecily had been instructed by Edward to leave Baynard's and make royal Shene their own. He would join her there. Built by Henry the Fifth, it was not a fortress but an elegant palace with high, timbered roofs and intricate spires. Overlooking the river and flanked by orchards and herb gardens, it afforded the king a haven from the heat and sickness of London in the summertime. One of the royal hunting parks, teeming with deer and other game for the king's pleasure, bordered the orchards.

One early morning the royal barge, hastily redecorated with the white rose of York, had conveyed Cecily, Margaret, and their attendants up the river, past Westminster and the villages of Chelsea and Kew and to the great bend that hid the palace from view. As the oarsmen pulled the boat to starboard and the three-story, gleaming white structure shimmered through the light mist rising from the water, the women gasped with delight. Only in a fairy tale could a palace be so beautiful, Margaret thought, staring at the many octagonal and round towers capped with pepperpot domes and turrets, which were graced by ornamental weathervanes and carvings.

Once inside, she ran from room to room, admiring the fluted ceilings, carved columns and colorful, tiled floors. Servants, who had accompanied the household baggage overland on huge carts, carried in furniture, chests and wall hangings brought from Baynard's. Cecily assigned Margaret the chamber overlooking the river where she now sat, and after a week she still had not tired of watching the wildlife teeming below her.

Today, however, was special. Edward was coming. She had chosen to stay out of the way all morning while her mother commanded the preparations for a royal welcome. Not long after Prime, boats had begun to arrive filled with barrels and sacks, boxes of animal carcasses, fowl and fish of all kinds, fruits and spices, and great hogsheads of wine. Neverending relays of servants carried the food from the dock into the kitchens behind the palace.

Now, later in the afternoon, Margaret heard music wafting softly on the wind. Ned must be coming, she thought, and checked her appearance in the polished silver mirror. She tucked a stray lock of hair under her short hennin, pulled her pointed sleeve cuffs over the backs of her hands and smoothed her gray mourning gown. Like her mother, who was known to outspend even Queen Margaret on her wardrobe, Margaret took great pains with her dress and made sure her seamstress kept her in the latest fashions. She lightly bit her lips to give them some color, checked that her eyebrows were exactly the right thinness and wished her cheeks weren't so plump.

The music was louder now; Margaret could distinguish viols, lutes and gemshorns. She heard voices, laughter and Ned booming, "Ho, there! Mother, Margaret, where are you?" Hurrying Ann and Jane along, she went down to the great hall to greet the king. Cecily had told her to curt-sey low, which she did, making a graceful picture as Edward strode in.

"As is befitting my status, Lady Margaret," he teased. "Nay, Meggie, rise and give your brother a kiss!" He gave her an appraising look as she stood back from their embrace. "That gown becomes you right well. You are all grown up, in truth! What do you think, friends? My little sister is growing into quite a beauty." He whispered, "But I would halt the growing part, Meg, or I shall have to find you a giant for a husband."

Margaret was stunned by this reception. Her mother had instructed her that etiquette at a royal court was very different from the more infor-mal way in their ducal household, and she had expected Edward to pay little attention to her in public. She found her tongue and managed, "I thank you," despite the hurt of his last comment, for she was sensitive about her inches. She put it from her and gave him her warm smile. "You are right welcome home, Ned."

"Ah, there you are, *ma mère*. Well met!" Edward greeted Cecily, who had not been waiting by the window for her son's arrival, as Margaret had, and thus was caught napping, literally. She hurried into the hall. Her widow's wimple was askew, and she had obviously slept in her overdress. Edward grinned and, picking her up as if she were a child, kissed her openmouthed astonishment.

"Really, Edward!" she admonished him as he set her down again, before she remembered his rank and sank to her knees. "I mean, your grace."

He raised her up. "Edward suits me well, Mother. It always has. I am not used to this new state, and until I am, I shall not expect my family to treat me any differently from before. Besides," he said, as he set her down and appraised her, "how can I take your lecture seriously when you come before your king in such disarray?"

Margaret gasped and expected Cecily to upbraid him again, but Cecily pretended not to have heard his last remark.

"Then I shall school you in the way things should be at court," Cecily retorted, rearranging the folds of her wimple. "You now are king of En-gland, and I shall expect you to behave like one!"

"*Oui, ma mère*," Edward said meekly, winking at Margaret. "But first, I have a gift for both of you."

"You are incorrigible, my son," Cecily replied, hiding a smile. Margaret made a note to ask her mother what the word meant; she liked the sound of it.

Edward whispered to his chamberlain, Will Hastings, who in turn sent a page running back outside. Everyone waited as Edward stood between his mother and sister, a sly grin on his face. Those closest to the door began to cheer as two small figures clothed in velvet doublets and bonnets entered the hall.

"George! Dickon!" squeaked Margaret, forgetting where she was and running the length of the hall to embrace them. Highly embarrassed, the boys forestalled the dreaded kissing that was sure to follow and both bowed low.

"Lady Margaret," George said, hoping to avert the inevitable. "Greetings."

But to no avail. In a trice, they were both bowled over by their sibling's exuberance, and Richard ended up on his backside. Tears streamed down Margaret's cheeks as she hugged George to her. She knew she had missed them, but until she had seen them again she had not realized how much. George extricated himself from her and straightened his bonnet, while Richard scrambled to his feet and ran past Margaret headlong into his mother's waiting arms. Edward stood by quietly, pleased his surprise had been so successful. George bowed to his mother and gravely kissed her hand.

Cecily smiled. "I see you have learned some nice manners with Duke Philip, George. Was he kind to you?"

"Aye, Mother," George said enthusiastically. "The court at Bruges was so magnificent and everyone was very kind. *Madame la duchesse* gave us these clothes when we left. She said she could not have the brothers of the king of England looking shabby upon their arrival home."

Edward laughed. "Aye, I fear we now owe Burgundy a favor for this kindness. Let me see, what can we send him? His son already has a wife or I'd offer him our Meg!" He chucked Margaret under the chin, and she was furious with herself for blushing.

"I shall stay in England, Ned. This is where I belong!" she told him firmly. "Anyway, I am much too young to be wed yet." She sent a prayer to the Virgin to delay the dreaded arranged marriage she knew was her lot in life and let her stay at home for many more years.

"Oh, no, you are not, my beauty! But I have other things on my mind at present"—he paused and grinned down at her—"like hunting in the park! Tell me, Anthony, have you hunted here?"

A hush came over Edward's companions, and all eyes turned to a newcomer about the same age as Edward. Margaret looked at the man curiously as he stepped forward. Sir Anthony Woodville and his father, Lord Rivers, had fought for the Lancastrians until not long after the battle of Towton, when, knowing their cause lost, they swore allegiance to Edward. Edward had not yet officially granted them pardons, but he felt safer having the two men in his train rather than at liberty to rejoin any Lancastrian faction still at large, should they decide to change their allegiance yet again. For his part, Anthony was understandably anxious in the new king's presence, and to be singled out like this because he must have known Shene under the old regime was unsettling.

"Well, Woodville, is the hunting good?" Edward repeated the question, but his tone was warm, and Anthony breathed more easily.

"Certes, your grace. There is a red deer for every man in London! I know there are wild boars, though none taken in my sight." Anthony turned in a circle as he spoke, including all in his view. "And as many hares"—he paused and looked at Edward, smiling—"as you have on your head, sire!"

Margaret involuntarily clapped her hands and laughed, the first to understand the joke. Anthony looked at her with interest but was interrupted by Edward's merry laughter, and he turned to acknowledge the compliment. Edward put his arm about Anthony's shoulders, and they moved towards the door. "Then let us to the hunt, my friends!" he cried, "and see what we can find for tomorrow's dinner."

Anthony looked back over his shoulder at the king's sister; his lively blue eyes met her equally intelligent gray ones. They both smiled, and Margaret's heart skipped a beat.

"WELL MET, MY lady," a young man murmured in Margaret's ear a few days later. "Have you placed a wager on anyone as yet?"

Margaret swung round and found herself eye to eye with the heraldmessenger who had brought them news of Towton and Mortimer's Cross. He bowed over her hand. "John Harper, if it please you, madam. And these ladies?"

"Well met, sir." She nodded at Ann and Jane, who curtseyed quickly. "Mistress Herbert and Mistress Percy." John Harper gave them a cursory glance and bowed.

Margaret was nervous. She was intrigued that he should seek her out, but she was taken aback by his audacity. It was not usual for one of his lower rank to thus address her. Although she knew she ought to rebuff him, she decided to answer his first question after checking to see her mother was nowhere in sight. Ann and Jane's presence provided her safety and a measure of courage. "I do not wager, Master Harper, but if I did, I would pick my brother to win the day."

He was standing very close to her, and she could smell a mix of sweat, horses and rosewater. Her pulse raced, and she found her palms were clammy. She held on tightly to the chaplet of flowers she and her ladies had woven earlier as a crown for the victor and tried to appear nonchalant. Calm down, Meg, she told herself, 'tis a man of no import and a bold one at that. But her senses were aroused, although she tried to concentrate on the sport taking place on the river. Tell him to leave, she admonished herself, he has no right to unnerve you thus! Go away, herald, oh, please go away! It did not help that Jane was fluttering her eyelashes at him. Margaret felt like slapping her.

As if he had sensed Margaret's plea, he said pleasantly, "Aye, the king has a fair chance, Lady Margaret, but my money is on Sir Anthony. I shall bother you no further. Farewell, ladies." And he bowed and walked away. Margaret experienced first disappointment and then the familiar twinge of shame about her height, putting the blame for his sudden departure squarely on her lack of desirability.

Ann and Jane twittered as they watched him go. "'Tis a pity he left so quickly, my lady," Jane whispered. "A handsome young man indeed!" agreed Ann.

"Jane!" Margaret retorted. "He was out of bounds, in truth. And I should not have answered him. But I grant you, he is handsome," she murmured, looking after him wistfully.

A fanfare of trumpets, shawms and sackbuts drew their attention from the herald to the impending competition. Edward had declared that a water tournament would be the sport of the day, and several contestants had stepped up to participate. A boat was anchored in the middle of the river with a wooden quintain target attached, and one by one the tilters would try their luck at hitting the target with their lances—long, dry sticks for this occasion. Margaret and her ladies found seats on a bench close to the riverbank and watched as the first tilter stepped into the small boat equipped with four oars. The boatmen were given the signal, and William Hastings, standing in the center of the boat, was propelled toward the target, lance poised. The crowd began to cheer and the tilter readied himself for the impact, making the boat wobble precariously. Loud laughter accompanied his failed attempt to hit the quintain. He gave a mock bow to the spectators and was rowed back to shore.

Next in line was Anthony Woodville. Edward encouraged the cheering for his new friend, and Anthony was helped into the boat by his father, a striking figure in green silk who gave him a few last-minute pointers. Margaret could see from whom the younger Woodville had his looks, and although not present to prove it, Anthony's mother, Jacquetta, was reputed to have been the most beautiful woman at court in her day. Anthony's chestnut hair gleamed in the sun, and, clothed only in hose and shirt, his physique was admired by all the ladies present, including Margaret. Ann nudged Jane. "Sweet Jesu, I have not seen so fair a man this many a month!" she exclaimed, and then remembered her place. "Excepting our lord Edward, of course." And she gave a nervous laugh.

Margaret patted her hand. Why do I feel so much older than these two? she asked herself for the hundredth time, and for the hundredth time she wished she had a sister. "No need to flatter me, Mistress Herbert. Sir Anthony is far fairer than my brother, in truth. Tut, tut, but you are fickle, Ann. Two minutes ago you were expounding on Master Harper's good looks. But we should not prattle on thus! Mother would not approve." They all laughed happily. After the winter of uncertainty, death and despair, it seemed the summer of that year would be a warm and carefree one indeed.

The signal was given, and Anthony's oarsmen pulled hard while he kept his balance in the middle of the boat. This time, the lance hit the quintain squarely in the middle, and the wooden stick crumpled in his hand. He weaved back and forth for a few seconds before recovering his stance, and the crowd threw flowers into the water and roared their approval. He waved his bonnet and blew kisses to the ladies. Margaret found herself clapping enthusiastically, raising an eyebrow from Ann. "My lady, surely you are for our lord, the king."

"Oh, aye, Ann. But 'twas nicely done, nonetheless!" Margaret tossed off.

Now it was Edward's turn. The musicians piped him on board his boat, and he shouted, "Sir Anthony, now you shall see some real tilting!" and the crowd cheered him on. Again the oarsmen rowed their erect passenger forward, and Edward stood like a sturdy oak, not wavering one inch. He approached the quintain and lifted his lance, thrusting it at the target. This time, the green branch did not break. The force of the hit threw Edward off balance, and he fell ungracefully into the river. A gasp of horror went up. The crowd was on its feet as he disappeared under the dark surface. A few seconds went by, and everyone held their breath while the oarsmen sat rigid, their oars up. One peered anxiously into the water where the king had fallen, and a moment later, the grinning Edward popped up on the other side of the boat, waving a handful of weeds. Margaret started the laughter that erupted after seeing their sovereign safe. She ran to the bank to where Edward was swimming and placed the chaplet of flowers on his dripping golden hair.

"You are naught but king of the water sprites today, Ned," she teased him. "And here is your scepter!" She plucked a bulrush from the bank and gave it to him, curtseying mockingly. The spectators applauded and bowed as well.

Edward was amused. This was a new side to his little sister. She had indeed matured in the two years he had been busy helping his family win the crown. "I have a good mind to pull you in with me, Meg!" he murmured, as she offered her hand and helped him gain his footing on the slippery slope.

"Ned! You would not dare!" she retorted, and promptly let go of him. Surprised, Edward slid back into the water. The onlookers gasped, expecting a torrent of fury from their soldier king, but Edward just laughed. "*Touché, ma soeur!* But see if I don't repay your courtesy," he said, winking at her.

By this time, George and Richard had run forward to help Edward, and the crowd looked on with admiration at the handsome family group.

"These Yorks stick together," one man told his neighbor. "It seems the family ties bind strongly."

"Aye, 'twould seem they have turned the disaster of six months ago into a triumph of courage. Certes, King Edward will serve us better than the addle-pated Henry and the French bitch, God save his simple soul."

EDWARD SPENT THE next two weeks planning his coronation and setting up his household. For one so young, he had assumed the mantle of kingship with an ease ascribed to men twice his age. He enjoyed having his family around him, and so Margaret found herself taking a keen interest in meetings she witnessed. She would sit quietly with her needlework and listen while Edward and his chief councilors discussed the merits of one man over another for a certain position at court. He asked Cecily's opinion on several occasions, and Margaret learned that a woman could wield quiet power from behind a veiled hennin.

When she grew bored with the details, she would excuse herself and take her book to sit by the water's edge. Kept clean in a velvet bag, *Sir Gawain and the Green Knight* was her constant companion. She loved the feel of the vellum under her fingers and would pore over the beautiful illuminations of the Arthurian story and marvel at the meticulous lettering. Mistress Nose-in-a-Book was what George often called her when he would come upon her reading. "Look, Dickon," he said once, "Meg's eyes are crossed and her nose is black from the hours she spends in books!" And he would laugh at her. Little Dickon, however, wasn't listening. He was busy turning the pages and gazing in wonder at the colorful illuminations.

Camelot must have looked just like this, Margaret mused, twiddling a grass stalk between her fingers and observing the scene around her. She was sorry to think that Edward could not compare to King Arthur. She had noticed in the last few days that Edward flirted with any passably pretty young woman he encountered. She had heard a rumor that he had a bastard daughter, and she hoped her mother hadn't heard it, too. King Arthur had been modest and chaste—so claimed all the stories about him—and had been betrayed by his beautiful queen Guinevere. No one had mentioned a bride for Edward as far as she knew, but Margaret pitied the poor woman, for she would have to keep a tight rein on her handsome bridegroom, she knew.

Her thoughts turned to her own burgeoning emotions. John Harper had danced with her one night, and she found his nearness tantalizing. When he had approached her after gaining Edward's permission, she had been sure he would change his mind once he got closer. She was, she estimated, two inches taller. But he had smiled into her eyes and asked for the honor of a dance. Her feet hardly touched the floor when she stepped out with him. Almost like her waking dream, he had kissed her fingers afterwards and run his thumb along her palm at the same time. She felt a warmth between her thighs, and she was sure the whole room knew her for a wanton.

"Good day, Lady Margaret," a pleasant voice interrupted her thoughts. "I hope I am not disturbing you?"

Margaret looked up into Anthony Woodville's smiling face and smiled back unconsciously. "Why, Sir Anthony, I am delighted to have company," she said, patting the grass. "I pray you sit down."

Anthony murmured his thanks and carefully eased his long limbs onto the ground. Margaret had not been this close to him before, and she appraised him at her leisure. Aye, he was possibly the handsomest man she had ever seen, but what she liked more was the openness of his expression. She saw no guile in the wide eyes and upward-turned mouth, simply confidence and a modicum of arrogance. She was also intrigued by the dimple that appeared in his left cheek as he smiled. Thank you, dear Mother of God, for letting me be seated, she thought. Perhaps he will not notice my height.

"I saw you with a book, my lady, and as books are my passion, I could not resist coming to see what you were so earnestly reading."

Margaret wondered vaguely if he was flattering her, but his tone was sincere, and so she offered the book to him.

"Ah, so you, too, are enthralled by Arthur and his knights," he said, turning the pages reverently. "Tell me, who is your preferred knight?"

"Galahad, sir. Certes, who could not favor a man who searches so long and valiantly for the Grail? And you, Sir Anthony?"

"I commend your choice, Lady Margaret. Mine is Lancelot du Lac for his gentleness, courtesy and courage. If I may be so forward as to tell you, my aim is to model myself upon him. You do know he was also the greatest fighter of all Arthur's knights, do you not?"

Margaret scrutinized his face for signs of falseness, but she was rewarded with a direct look and serious expression. "Aye, my lord," she answered him with equal directness, "although I cannot fathom why men have to prove themselves by fighting each other. But your goal is honorable and long may it continue. But"—she paused, and a small smile changed the tone of her response—"you must guard against falling in love with the queen—when my brother chooses one!"

"Ah, yes. Guinevere. But you see, I am married, and that is where Lancelot and I differ."

At the mention of his wife, Margaret was brought back to earth. How stupid she was not to have remembered! She lowered her eyes. "Aye, so I have heard. We have not yet had the pleasure of your lady wife's company at court. Will she be joining you here, sir?"

"Eliza's health has not been strong of late. She has been keeping to our estates in Norfolk much of the time," was all he would say. Baroness Scales was the only daughter of Thomas, Seventh Baron Scales, and had inherited the title when her Lancastrian father was murdered by boatmen on the Thames in the year of her marriage to Anthony in 1460. By rights and by marriage Anthony should have been granted the title of baron, but King Henry had more on his mind at that precarious juncture with the Yorkists than to spend time on granting this right to such an insignificant young man. He sighed and looked down at the book, running one immaculately manicured finger over the gold leaf of one of the illustrations. "This is beautiful, Lady Margaret. I can see why it is a favorite." Then he closed it and handed it to her. "Now I must go." He could see questions in Margaret's eyes and had no desire to go into details about his lack of title for fear of reminding Edward's sister of his recent Lancastrian leanings. He winced as he rose to leave.

Concerned, Margaret said, "Edward tells me you were wounded at Towton field, sir. I see it pains you still."

"'Tis nothing, in truth. A flesh wound to the leg, and it heals gradually." He grinned. "I am unused to sitting on the ground, 'tis all. You thought I was looking for sympathy from a lady, perhaps? I *am* a poet, 'tis true, but I have not tried my hand at mummery yet!"

Margaret laughed up at him. "Good day, my lord. I should like to read some of your verses." She added shyly, "Certes, if you share them."

"I would have to know you a good deal better before inflicting them on you, Lady Margaret," he murmured, bowing over her outstretched hand. "Good day to you."

Margaret was unprepared for the fire that ran up her arm to her heart as he kissed her fingers. She drew in a sharp breath but covered it with a cough. Anthony turned and walked away, his short cote swinging rhythmically around his knees and his head held high.

"Leave us!" Edward's shouted command was heard clearly in Margaret's chamber three doors away. It was not the first time she and her ladies had heard angry outbursts from the new king. Cecily informed her that the king of France had made good on a promise to aid Queen Margaret and had laid siege to one of the Channel Islands, and the news had reached Edward not long after his arrival at Shene. It was feared that an invasion of England would be France's next move. A few Lancastrian lords were thought to be inciting the West Country to insurrection against Edward, so Edward had sent troops to the area to resist the French—who never came.

Today, the messengers had brought news of an even more alarming nature. Queen Margaret and her son, Edouard, had led an army of Scots over the border to Carlisle, and after laying waste to the land, they threatened the city. Powerful Lancastrians in the north had rallied to her banner and were preparing to march south and reclaim the throne for Henry, left out of harm's way over the border in Scotland.

"Christ's nails! When will I be rid of that she-wolf," Edward growled later, when the family ate supper in the royal apartments. The atmosphere was tense, and Edward's attendants kept a respectful distance, talking with Cecily's ladies. "Where is Warwick when I need him?"

"Hush, my son," Cecily soothed. "My lord of Warwick gives you good service. You would not be where you are now without him. You know he is loyally serving you from Middleham. I warrant he is on the march now to rout the queen."

Edward grunted. "*Oui, ma mère*, you are probably right. But I cannot sit idly by while the bitch is snapping at our heels. I have given orders for my coronation to be brought forward, and we will postpone the parliament until November so I may join Warwick in the north."

Cecily raised an almost invisible eyebrow. "How soon do you propose to be crowned, Edward? I thought the Relic Sunday date was set. You will stretch the poor lord marshal to his breaking point, if you do not give him sufficient time to crown you with all due ceremony!"

"May he rot in hell!" Edward swore, and then apologized to his horrified mother. "Mowbray is a stalwart; he will be ready on the twenty-eighth."

"The twenty-eighth? Have you taken leave of your senses? That is no more than a sennight hence. How can we be ready so soon?"

"When have you cared how you look, mother?" Edward grinned at her. "You are the most beautiful woman at court, and you do not know it."

"Pah! Flatterer," Cecily retorted and then caught George twisting Richard's arm painfully over a sweetmeat. Richard's face was grim as he silently bore the torture, not wanting Edward to see him weak.

"Let Dickon be, George!" Cecily cried. "You deserve a whipping for that!"

"Nay, mother," piped up Richard, rubbing his arm. "It did not hurt, I promise you. And I will pay him back one, you see if I don't." He stuck his tongue out at George, snatched the sweetmeat and turned away. George put his thumb on his nose and waggled his fingers at Richard.

Edward frowned. "Do they squabble like this often?"

"All the time," Margaret said, looking up from her book. "It is tiresome, and I wish they would grow up!"

"Mistress Nose-in-a-Book, Nose-in-a-Book," the two boys chorused. Margaret flung a red damask cushion at them.

"Enough!" roared Edward, rising suddenly out of his chair. His siblings cringed, and the conversation at the back of the room stopped. "If we fight among ourselves like this, how do you think others will serve us? We must be united. Our father taught us to love and respect one another, and I will see his wishes carried out. 'Tis difficult enough to hold on to what we have earned through fighting others. We do not need to fight each other. Dickon and George, shake hands immediately! And Margaret, you are the eldest; you must set an example."

The boys meekly shook hands, and Margaret turned the color of the cushion.

Cecily rose, curtseyed to her son and stood on tiptoe to kiss him. "*Bonne nuit,* Edward, I will take these baggages away to bed and leave you in peace."

"A fair night to you, too, *ma chère mère*. Margaret, I pray you stay awhile. I would talk to you."

An usher opened the door for Cecily, and she shooed the boys out before her and was followed by her ladies. Margaret sat straight and still, wondering if she was to be punished for her cushion-throwing. Edward waved his attendants away after filling two cups with wine.

"Have them prepare the all-night, Jack," Edward called after Sir John Howard, the last to leave the room. "I shall not be long. And tell them to make sure the bread is fresher than last evening's!"

"Aye, your grace," Howard assented, bowing.

Edward handed Margaret one of the cups and sprawled his six-foot-three-inch body on a velvet settle, twirling his own cup between his big hands, causing a sapphire to flash in the candlelight. Edward's expression softened as he surveyed her, and Margaret relaxed a little.

"Do you like being a royal princess, Meggie?" he asked.

"I do not feel any different, Edward. How am I supposed to feel?"

"Proud! Proud our family has finally achieved what was rightfully ours all these years," he insisted. "But you are right to be modest, little sister."

"Not so little," retorted Margaret. "I am as tall as Mother, as you love to point out."

"Aye, you are, you are," chuckled Edward. "And though no one will ever hold a candle to her, you have your own beauty, Meg. 'Tis in your eyes and your spirit. I believe you are as intelligent as a woman can be!"

"Ned! Do you really believe men are always more intelligent than women? What of King Henry and his queen? From everything I have heard, I know which one is more boil-brained!" Margaret's ire was roused. "Besides, who has been talking to you about my intelligence?"

"Anthony Woodville, my dear." Edward let that sink in while he watched, amused, as Margaret colored. "Aye, he spoke highly of you the other day. I hope you have not been flirting with him, Meg. He's a married man, you know. Although," he muttered as an aside, "Eliza Scales sounds as dull as ditchwater and a sickly hag."

"I have no interest in Sir Anthony, Ned! We had a pleasant conversation about King Arthur, that was all," Margaret protested.

"Ho, ho! No interest, eh? Then why the blush, *ma soeur!*" He leaned forward conspiratorially. "Listen, Margaret, I have learned to take my pleasures as they are presented. I may die in battle or be murdered in my bed tomorrow. I love women and women love me. If you choose to dally with Sir Anthony and are discreet, you will not be rebuked by me!"

Margaret was shocked into dropping her jaw. Edward had obviously escaped Cecily's lectures about chastity and morality that she, George and Richard had been subjected to time and time again. Why, he must be in peril of his mortal soul! But he didn't look very worried about it, she admitted. She chose to say nothing but smiled back at him, hoping to elicit more confidences. She was awed and fascinated by the assured ease with which her big brother grasped life by the horns. She wanted so much to be like him, and yet . . .

"Just be careful, Meg. In truth, I will be needing you for some future marriage negotiations, and a virginal bride is usually part of the bargain."

"Ned!" was all Margaret could manage. She felt the familiar icy fingers of fear brush her heart with the mention of marriage. Why must I be used as a pawn, she wondered miserably. Surely it would not be so if I were a commoner.

She was startled from her thoughts by Edward's next statement. "I see you looking at men, Meg. I know you have carnal feelings like me. We are alike, you and I, so I am just asking you to be careful." He smiled at her embarrassment. "And I have a favor to ask of you."

Relieved that he was not asking her to admit to those carnal feelings, she nodded readily. "What favor, my lord? You have only to ask."

"Although Mother will still rule the roost"—the siblings grinned in unison—"she has no desire to act as my hostess until I take a wife. As soon as she feels you are ready to take her place, you will serve me in that capacity, and she will keep her court at Baynard's. You will have your own household when the time comes. We shall miss her, but she says she has lost interest in being my helpmate since Father died. Unless she knows I have need of her, she prefers to keep her own company."

Margaret was stunned. She had not envisioned life without Cecily at her elbow, showing her the way. "Certes, 'tis hard to believe, Ned," she exclaimed. "George, Dickon and I still need her. You cannot let her go. Edward, please!"

"Me, stop as stubborn a woman as Proud Cis? I may be able to win battles, Meg, but those are simple skirmishes compared with battling our lady mother! Nay, her mind is made up. With your sisters Anne and Elizabeth having ducal households of their own to manage, Mother and I believe you will, with their help, serve the court well—until I find myself a suitable bride, that is." He grimaced at the thought.

As Ann and Jane prepared her for bed a little while later, Margaret's mind was in a whirl. First lady at court! She would be a queen of sorts. *Holy Mother of God*, she panicked, *and I told him aye!* At her prayers that night, she begged the sweet Virgin to keep her mother from retiring until Edward found a queen. Then she allowed thoughts of Anthony Woodville to flit through her head as she snuggled into her feather pillow and breathed the scent of sweet herbs tucked into it. Anthony's face became confused with John Harper's, and a smile curled her mouth as she drifted into slumber.

THE SUN SHONE on Edward's triumphant entry into London on the last Friday of June. He started at Lambeth Palace, then rode across London Bridge and along Eastcheap and Tower Street to his royal apartments in the Tower of London. Then on Saturday afternoon, like every king of England before him, Edward, mounted on a richly caparisoned horse, wended his way from William the Conqueror's palace through the city streets to Westminster, accompanied by the newly dubbed knights of the Bath. Among the knights, clothed in blue gowns with white silk hoods, were the small figures of George and Richard. George strutted purposefully behind Edward, nodding graciously from left to right at the cheering crowds. Cecily, Margaret and her sisters watched from the canopied dais set up in Westminster Palace's courtyard in front of the great hall.

"I am assuming Edward has told George he is to be duke of Clarence," Cecily said. "Look at him, as proud as a peacock!" The description could have fitted his mother as her eyes followed George.

Margaret, too, had been watching George with affection. She thought he had never looked so handsome. He should always wear blue, she decided.

"Ah, but Dickon is more humbled by his knightly honor. See, he stares straight ahead with his hands in prayer. He's a solemn little boy, in truth, but I like him." Elizabeth, duchess of Suffolk, looked fondly at her youngest sibling. "He does not demand attention as George does. And he is kind-hearted."

A fanfare of trumpets caused Edward's horse to shy, but its master's hands expertly calmed it. The whole household was lined up to greet Edward, and the great bells of the abbey pealed over the acres of palace buildings and grounds and over the river beyond the walls. The noise was deafening, and Margaret shivered with excitement. Edward rode up to the steps of the dais, dismounted and bowed low to his mother, sweeping off his purple velvet bonnet. Cecily inclined her head, descended the stairs and took his arm to be led into the great hall.

The palace was abuzz with activity the morning of the coronation a day later, and those at Prime thanked God for another fair day. Margaret was given several responsibilities before she was finally able to dress for the ceremony. Edward had given her permission to come out of mourning for her father after six months, and she had chosen a shimmering blue cloth of silver for her gown, trimmed at hem and neckline with marten, the train of which trailed several feet behind her. Her butterfly hennin was sewn with pearls and draped with a silver veil. Edward had given each of his sisters a necklace for the occasion, and hers was graceful loops of sapphires and pearls that draped delicately at the nape of her neck. She decorated each finger with rings and stood back to study herself in the full-length polished copper mirror.

"Today you will rival even the beautiful Elizabeth Lucy, my lady!" Ann gushed, citing an acknowledged beauty at court and one of Edward's mistresses. Jane murmured agreement, but Margaret could see the girl was really admiring her own reflection over Margaret's shoulder. Margaret sighed. These two were respectful but silly, and she knew they were there only because they were the daughters of loyal friends of her father's, William Herbert and Robert Percy. I would so love to find a true friend to confide in, she thought yet again. Old Anne had been a gentle influence in her childhood, and she had had fun with George on many occasions, but in all the turmoil of her parents' lives during the past five years, Margaret's circle of friends had been limited to her mother's ladies and these two simpering girls. Let us hope they find husbands soon, she mused, but she smiled her thanks at them for their compliments.

Cecily bustled in, looking every inch a dowager queen in violet silk and ermine. She had refused to come out of mourning for her husband, but to humor Edward she had ordered a gown of violet, the other acceptable color for bereaved widows. Her wimple was crowned with a small diadem, and she looked so imposing that even Margaret sank into a deep reverence.

"Get up, child, and let me look at you," Cecily said impatiently. She walked slowly round her daughter, tweaking a sleeve, rearranging the long gossamer veil and removing one of the larger rings. "Too ostentatious, my dear. 'Tis quality, not quantity, that defines taste."

Margaret stoically subjected herself to the scrutiny of her imperious parent, which made her feel like a dowdy mouse. Finally Cecily was satisfied. "Very nice, my dear. You will do. Mayhap we can find a suitable bridegroom for you before long. You will be a credit to the York name, I have no doubt."

More talk of bridegrooms. Margaret inwardly groaned but smiled sweetly and said, "Aye, Mother. Thank you, Mother."

THE CORONATION WAS long and, depending where one sat, thrilling or tedious. Edward was imperious in royal purple and godlike when he removed all but a loincloth for his anointing. His muscular arms, livid with recent scars, his smooth, broad chest and shoulders and ringing responses to his vows gave those able to see him confidence that he had the strength of body and mind to rule them. Following the anointing with the holy chrism, Edward was garbed in cloth of gold and knelt at the high altar. Margaret held her breath as the Archbishop of Canterbury dramatically raised the crown from its proffered cushion and held it high. When he finally placed it on Edward's head, the organ and choir thundered an anthem, praising the Trinity and all the saints. George and Richard were kneeling across the aisle from her, and she tried to catch George's eye. He was too busy wiggling his hand to make the gemstone sparkle on the ring Edward had given him, and Margaret despaired of him. She glanced at Richard by his side and she was astonished to see tears of joy coursing down his face as he watched his brother rise as king. Margaret unexpectedly found herself also moved to tears by this expression of devotion.

After the king and his court had processed along the red carpet running between the abbey and the palace, Cecily tried to keep a close eye on her youngest during the ensuing feast. However, she was pulled in so many directions that she finally gave up.

"Watch those boys for me, Margaret, there's a good girl," she said, on her way to avert yet another crisis with the steward.

Margaret seethed. I'm nothing but a nursemaid, she pouted, knowing that trying to keep an eye on two boys amidst the hundreds of gorgeously arrayed guests who milled about in the great hall and rooms beyond would be a nightmare. She finally spotted them entering one of the antechambers and began to thread her way through the throng. She heard music coming from the room. A young, sweet voice rose over the onlookers around the door, and standing on tiptoe, she saw a small girl, no more than a dozen years, she guessed, entertaining the guests with her harp. She listened for a minute and then squeezed past a large woman with foul breath and tugged at Richard's sleeve.

"Richard!" she hissed. But Richard ignored her, gazing in awe at the girl with the harp on the stool, who seemingly had no fear of playing on her own. She was surprised to see he was with a strange boy, not George.

"You baggage!" she said in Richard's ear as the music ended. "Come with me at once! And where is George?" She glowered at the other boy, who shrank from the scowl and hid behind Richard.

"Rob, this is my sister Margaret," Richard said sulkily and added under his breath, "She likes to lord it over George and me. Take no notice."

"You come with me this instant, Dickon, or—" Margaret was cut off by a loud fanfare calling the guests to the feast, and Richard was spared telling tales on George. Fortunately George appeared at his seat and no one questioned his truancy.

While the ewerers solemnly tendered their silver basins of water in which the diners rinsed their fingers and trenchermen ran up and down the tables serving food, the royal party sat in silence on their platform, ministered to by the highest peers of the realm. Margaret had never seen such food. Peacocks in full feathers, whole suckling pigs, lambs, haunches of beef, herons, quails, cranes and capons were presented to Edward during the feast, along with eels, haddock, salmon and sardines. Pies, pasties, tarts and fritters followed by dessert, wafers and fruit were all washed down with wines from France and Spain.

Each course was ended with a subtlety of spun sugar or marchpane fashioned to represent characters from the Bible or mythology.

She was beginning to feel a little sick when George Neville, Edward's chancellor and brother of the earl of Warwick, stood to greet the company. The powerful earl was not at the coronation, an odd happenstance as it was he who had virtually helped Edward up the steps to the throne.

"He is keeping the north strong for Edward," her mother had told her earlier that week. "He and his brother, Sir John Neville, are Edward's finest generals. Warwick can never be king, and, in truth, I fear he may be a little envious of your brother's crowning. 'Tis well he remains where he is most needed."

Margaret now studied the youngest Neville, who appeared to have an intelligent face but none of the swagger of his brother about him. A plain man, she decided.

"My lords, ladies, pray silence for his grace, King Edward," he cried. As chancellor, the Great Seal of England was in his care, and he wore his office with honor, as befitted his noble family.

All eyes turned to the table on the dais. Edward pushed his chair back and stood towering over his chancellor. On his chin-length hair was a simple gold crown set with a huge amethyst. His fingers were covered with rings of every precious stone, and he wore an elaborate gold collar that hung from his broad shoulders. The guests rose as one and bowed from their benches. Edward waved them down.

"My loyal subjects, my friends! I greet you well and you are right welcome at our table. Tonight I honor my family: my mother, her grace, the duchess of York, to whom I give all obeisance and devotion!" He bowed low to Cecily.

"My dearest sisters, Anne, Elizabeth and Margaret, God be with you all!" He toasted them, grinning over his goblet. "I warrant Margaret will expect me to find a royal bed for her now I am king!" he said behind his hand, and the company roared, thumping the tables.

Margaret didn't hear what he said next, for her blood was boiling. She stared at her plate as Edward droned on, thanking this person and that, and when she finally raised her head, she looked straight into the sympathetic eyes of Anthony Woodville, seated at the next table. Her heart leaped into her throat, and, feeling herself blush, she cast her eyes down again.

Edward sat down amidst cheering. The chancellor stepped forward and raised his goblet. "God save the king!" he cried over the din. Benches scraped back as the company rose, cups were held high and the shout was taken up on all sides: "À York! God save the king! God save King Edward!"

It was done. Edward was crowned, and England now had two anointed kings.

4

1463

"Scotland? I don't want to go to Scotland!" Margaret cried. "There are savages in Scotland. I have heard you say so yourself. How could you promise me to King James, Ned? 'Tis not fair!"

Edward sat in his favorite chair, made especially for his large frame, and fixed his hooded blue eyes on his sister's distraught face. He let her rant. She was right, there were savages in Scotland, he agreed, but her marriage to James might tame them, he suggested. That really riled her, and she stamped her foot, unaware of the attention she had drawn to herself from the courtiers and foreign dignitaries at the other end of the long antechamber.

"*Taisez-vous, ma chère soeur,*" Edward commanded her with quiet authority. "We do not need the whole court to hear our business."

The French emissary was looking particularly interested, and a flicker of a smile flitted over Edward's face as he noticed. More loudly he called, "Lord Hastings, I pray you allow me some private time with my sister."

Hastings, Edward's chamberlain, bowed and herded everyone out of the audience chamber. Margaret plucked at her skirt nervously as she watched the courtiers give Edward reverence and leave. For two years she had enjoyed the life of a royal princess with no real responsibilities except to be the gracious hostess at Edward's table and court festivities. She had flirted with young courtiers, danced her feet off, availed herself of Edward's growing library and had almost forgotten that one day she would hear Edward's plan for her; and perhaps that day was come. For all that time, however, she had never put Anthony Woodville far from her thoughts, although the man had not often been at court. When he had, he had been solicitous, but they had never enjoyed another private conversation such as they had that summer day at Shene.

Will Hastings closed the door on the last two retainers, turned and grinned at Edward. "'Twas well done, your grace. The Frenchman most certainly took note. King Louis will hear of this within the week, I warrant."

Margaret frowned. "Hear of what, pray? My outburst? Why should he care?" She turned back to Edward. "I beg of you, Ned, do not make me go to Scotland! I promise never to shout at you again. I will pray for your eternal soul daily if you will not send me to Scotland. Besides," she begged, "you need me here. I've been a good sister-consort—or whatever it is I am—have I not these past two years? Please, please, listen to me, Ned."

Edward threw back his head and laughed. "Will, I pray you take note of the day and the time. My sister penitent is a rarity indeed, and I should remember it always!" He was rewarded by a reluctant smile from Margaret. "Aye, see, she knows 'tis unusual. Think, my dear, dutiful sister, you could become the second St. Margaret of Scotland!" At the mention of that queen's name, Margaret scowled and crossed herself. "Do not blaspheme, Ned. I am no saint, although 'tis no wonder the poor woman became one after having to live in that godforsaken land. I shall not follow suit. I'd rather cast myself from London Bridge!" Margaret was spluttering so vehemently that she failed to see Edward wink at Hastings.

Then Edward leaned forward and his tone became serious. "Meggie, I fear I have played a diabolical trick on you. You are right, I was jesting. But 'tis necessary for King Louis to think I have King James in my pocket so the frog cannot aid that she-wolf Margaret of Anjou again." He held up his hand to stop her interrupting. "By pretending to have made a marriage between you and James, we may avert more bloodshed on our northern borders. Queen Margaret is bound to ask her kinsman Louis for help, but he may be reluctant if he thinks she may not be welcome in Scotland."

Margaret stared in disbelief. "Diabolical trick? Pretend to marry me off? By the sweet Virgin, I am speechless, brother. What have I ever done to deserve such a trick, pray? You allowed me to make a spectacle of myself in front of everyone!" she cried.

"I told you I would think of something the day of the water tournament at Shene, remember?" he said, pleased with himself. "That day, you made *me* the spectacle! I had not forgotten, little Meg."

Margaret's jaw dropped, Hastings chuckled, and Edward rose to take the stupefied girl into his embrace. "Forgive me for discomfiting you, Meg. I suppose you will now not be praying for my eternal soul."

"Eternal damnation, more like!" came the muffled reply from the folds of his magnificent brocade doublet.

"I promise you, you will not hear of any marriage I make for you in such a public place. Will that make you feel better?" He felt her nod and set her from him. "That's better," he said as he saw her smile. " 'Tis what I like best about you, Meg. You are never sour-faced for long. Now, I must not keep my subjects outside waiting for the droppings from my royal mouth any longer."

Margaret gave him a deep reverence and stood aside to watch Hastings open the door. Edward settled back into his throne and for the next hour listened patiently while those who had bought or wormed their way into his presence petitioned him on one matter or another. Edward's hooded eyes never gave away his boredom or distaste, and he dispensed decisions with an ease that astonished Margaret.

Each time she was with Edward in public, her eyes would scan the groups of courtiers for Anthony Woodville. He was occasionally in attendance on Edward, but other than exchanging smiles or, on the rare occasion, when he was obliged to kiss her hand, she had only spoken to him in her dreams. She had tried to put him from her mind in the two years since Edward was crowned. When he was absent, Margaret hated the thought that he was probably in his wife's arms and unaware of her existence, but then she fancied a warmth in his touch or in his smile when he was present at court that buoyed her hopes until the next time. She had yet to set eyes on Eliza Scales, and she hoped she never would. Margaret sighed. No, Anthony was not here today, she realized disconsolately.

An hour into the audiences, she saw Edward sit up and the blue eyes snap open wide as a comely young woman stepped before him. Hastings announced, "The Lady Eleanor Butler, if it please you, your grace."

"It does, it does," Edward muttered, bestowing his most dazzling smile on Eleanor's bowed head. "Lady Eleanor, I pray you, rise and tell me what I can do for you."

What she can do for you, is more to the point, Margaret thought, suppressing a smile. She had become used to watching Edward seduce women young and old, and although she derided his morals in conversation with her ladies, she rather enjoyed watching her brother ensnare his prey and move in for the kill. If these women were so silly as to allow themselves to be toyed with, well, then, who could blame Edward? Men are so fortunate, she thought again. I hope I never make a fool of myself like one of Ned's conquests.

"Your grace, I thank you for hearing my plea," Eleanor said sweetly, her voice as light and airy as a dandelion seed blown on the wind. "I am the widow of Sir Thomas Butler and am come to beg your support in a matter of two manors that my father-in-law, Lord Sudeley, is attempting to wrest from me."

"Ah, yes," murmured Edward, who wasn't listening and had eyes only for the lovely face. "The widow's wimple, I should have noticed."

"My lord?" Eleanor leaned forward to hear him better and tripped on the hem of her gown, stumbling. Edward was out of his chair in a flash, steadying her.

"Have a care, lady, I pray you." Under his breath, he said, "But see, you have your king to support you, and he is at your service."

Eleanor dimpled prettily and attempted to pull her hand from his, but he held on fast, stroking her palm with his thumb. The ever watchful Hastings, seeing the way of things, began to talk loudly to a few of the courtiers and distract their attention from the seduction scene in front of them.

"So you will uphold my honor, your grace?" Eleanor tried again and this time succeeded in removing her hand.

"Certes, I will!" Edward pronounced to one and all, not having the faintest notion to what she was referring. "And gladly."

He will uphold far more than your honor, Lady Eleanor, Margaret wanted to tell her. Beware! But it seemed the Lady Eleanor was used to being flirted with. She looked Edward straight in the eye and said with more dandelion root than seed in her voice, "Then these kind ladies and gentlemen are my witnesses that your grace has agreed to restore my manors to me!"

Edward was taken aback. He had mistaken this lady's dainty appearance and was now faced with fait accompli without her having to shed as much as her hennin. He seemed gracious in defeat, Margaret noted, but his eyes were hungry as they followed Eleanor gliding to the door.

MARGARET SPENT MUCH of the year at Greenwich now. The royal palace had been a favorite of Margaret of Anjou, who had spent her honeymoon with young King Henry there. He had named it La Pleasaunce for its gentle architecture and charming setting on the Thames, with the wooded park rising high behind it to Blackheath. Unlike the fortress palaces of Windsor and the Tower, Greenwich had no battlements, fortified gate or curtain wall. It was as though the inhabitants never expected an enemy to dare disturb its bucolic peace. Margaret was content there, loving the millions of painted marguerites that decorated pillars and arches in honor of the former queen, but she still longed for the magical turrets of Shene.

She was lodged in the apartments behind the inner court, as were George and Richard, but whenever the river beckoned, she made her way through the royal private rooms along the inner court and to the king's apartments, where she could sit and watch the ships sail slowly up the Thames to London. Fine cloth from Burgundy, spices from Spain, wine from France, pomegranates from Italy, gems and perfumes from the east and ambergris from the Baltic all plied their way past the palace. She could only imagine the ports and cities the vessels had traveled from. Occasionally a ship would dock at the palace quay, and weather-beaten seamen swarmed up the masts to lower the sails. She recognized French, Italian and Spanish words, but Dutch sounded guttural to her ear and unintelligible. Richard and George had told her tales of the dazzling Burgundian court at Bruges, but she could not imagine anything as grand as

Edward's. He was generous with his siblings' household expenditures, and Margaret had a wardrobe fit for a queen.

Today, as sleet pitter-pattered on the window panes, she and George played chess while Richard watched quietly, occasionally digging George in the ribs if he thought his elder brother was making a bad move.

"'Tis unfair of you, Dickon," Margaret complained. "As soon as I have beaten George, I will take a turn with you. So let George make his own mistakes."

"George always makes his own mistakes," Richard remarked, getting up and wandering to the window. "And everybody just thinks he is charming and special. No one thinks I am. I don't understand it."

"I think you're special, Dickon." They hadn't heard Edward come into the room and now they jumped at the sound of his voice. Richard ran to him.

"You do, Ned, really?" His earnest little face was flushed as he gazed adoringly up at his brother.

George harrumphed loudly, moved his queen to a dangerous spot and fixed Margaret with a look of triumph. "Check!"

Margaret shook her head. "Oh, George, why don't you look ahead? You must always be at least two steps ahead of your adversary. Father taught us that."

Edward laughed. "Well said, Meggie. I always know I can count on you to remember what Father told us. George, you should learn from Meg. She is as sharp as the Devil's dagger. Now, let us see why Meg looks so smug. Ah, 'tis plain as the nose on your face, George. Your queen will die and Meg will take your bishop for checkmate!"

"God's bones, everyone is cleverer than me!" George shouted as he swept the pieces from the board. "One day I will show you. I'll show you all who's cleverer!"

Margaret and Richard held their breath as they watched Edward's face.

"Pick those pieces up—*now!*" Edward's anger was cold and menacing. "And apologize to your sister for your blasphemy. You have succeeded in irritating me, George."

George cowered before his king. He scurried around gathering the ornate pieces and glowered at Dickon, who came over to help. "I can do it," he growled, keeping one eye on Edward, who watched for a moment and then turned to go.

"Meg, follow me," Edward said, his tone more moderate. "I have something to discuss with you."

On their way to his privy chamber, Margaret begged him to be kinder to George. "He is jealous of you, Ned. He wants to be like you, but he is too young. And he misses Edmund." She knew mention of their lost brother would soften Edward, and it did.

"Aye, I suppose you are right. But the lad is shallow, Meg, and I know not why you cannot see it. He is charming and handsome, I grant you, but he needs to be charming and handsome inside as well as out. Young Dickon has more moral fiber in his little finger than George has in his whole body. But for your sake, Meg, I will always look after him, have no fear. But now I have a favor to ask," he said conspiratorially. "Anthony Woodville has paid us a visit unexpectedly, and I had something else in mind for this afternoon. You remember him, don't you? He spends too much time in Norfolk caring for his wife, and in truth I like his company, but"—he grinned at his sister—"not this afternoon. I hope you will not mind distracting him for me, Meggie." He glanced down at her and saw her telltale red cheeks. His eyes widened for a moment, and then he chuckled. "Ah, little sis, I see the task may not be as dull for you as I thought. I always love it when you blush!"

"I am *not* blushing, Ned!" Margaret muttered. "Let me be, I beg of you."

They arrived at the privy chamber, where two guards saluted the king and opened the studded oak door for him. Margaret followed Edward in, trying to compose herself and pressing her cool hands to her cheeks. Anthony Woodville was standing by the fire, deep in conversation with Hastings.

"Scales!" Edward was pleased recently to have granted Anthony full use of his wife's title in view of the man's loyalty. "I insist you entertain my sister while Will and I go over a tedious business matter," Edward said. Anthony and Will had bowed as Edward entered, and only now did Anthony see Margaret behind him. He bowed again in her direction.

"As you wish, your grace. Lady Margaret, I am right glad to see you," he said pleasantly, and he came forward to kiss her hand. He turned to Edward. "What do you propose we do?"

"Well, Margaret has recently made a fool of Clarence in a chess game, Anthony, so unless you wish to be made one too, I suggest you think of something else—something innocent, mind you!" He laughed, as did Will, but Margaret and Anthony were not amused.

"Perhaps you would like to read to me, my lady. What have you been reading lately?" Anthony offered Margaret his arm and they left the room. She heard Edward ask Will, "Where is Eleanor? Those two may do something innocent, but I am in the mood for a conquest."

For the next hour, Margaret and Anthony sat together on a high-backed settle in a small, cozy room overlooking the inner court, where Edward kept his small collection of books. Ann and Jane sat by themselves on two stools on the far side of the room with their needlework. The settle ensconced Margaret and Anthony in its soft cushions, and they lost themselves in the fantasy world that lay between the pages of the book. Anthony selected *Ipomedon,* and Margaret nodded her assent. She had not read this poem of courtly love and so begged Anthony to read the French masterpiece for her.

"A marriage was proposed between young Prince Ipomedon and the queen of Calabria, even though neither had set eyes on the other," he began, his rich voice filling the little room as the story unfolded. Ipomedon decides to woo and win the queen on his own merits. He appears at a tournament as an unknown knight and impresses her with his prowess in manly exploits, intriguing the young queen. Having piqued her interest, he leaves her court for no reason. Later he returns when he learns the queen is to be the prize in a tournament. He loudly derides jousting and announces his intention of hunting—considered a far less manly sport—all the days of the tournament. In fact, he goes to a hermitage, where he has all the accoutrements for jousting. Each day he competes anonymously in armor of a different color and wins every joust, leaving at the end without his prize.

Anthony closed the book at this point, and Margaret sighed. "I cannot believe the queen did not force him to reveal himself any of the days. And why would a man not claim his prize, especially such a beautiful one?"

"When you read the rest of the story, my lady, you will know. If I were a woman, I would be proud to know my intended would act so honorably.

He wanted to be sure he was accepted for his own sake and not because he was forced upon her." He allowed a grimace to flit across his face and then he was all smiles. "Do you think his grace, the king, has finished his . . . ah . . . business with William Hastings? This has been a pleasant hour, Lady Margaret, but I fear I am keeping you from your duties."

Margaret laughed. "Aye, my lord, my embroidery calls me, and I must go!"

Anthony chuckled, and he nonchalantly placed his hand over hers. "I do enjoy your humor."

Margaret stared at his hand as she felt the familiar crimson tide flood her face. She rose quickly and taking the book, placed it back on the shelf. "Thank you, sir," she murmured. "I enjoy your company equally. Ann, Jane, 'tis time to return to our own rooms. I give you a good day, Lord Anthony."

He bowed as she turned away, and he was aware of a loss of warmth in the room when she was gone.

TRAVELING IN FEBRUARY was a muddy ordeal. Despite the fur blankets, soft cushions and covered sides of their chariot, Margaret and Cecily shivered. The cumbersome vehicle lurched over the rutted road, jolting the women out of daydreaming about their soft beds in London. Every now and then, a wheel would stick in the mud, and their escort would need to heave their shoulders into it to free it, leaving them with mire up to their knees.

The royal cavalcade had left London two days before on their way to meet Edward at Fotheringhay Castle, the York family's chief seat, where the long overdue obit for the late duke and his son Edmund would be held. George and Richard had their own escort and had left London on horseback a few days earlier to learn their part in the ceremonies. Margaret watched them ride off enviously. She knew their journey would be far swifter than hers and that riding would keep them warmer than sitting still for hours in a draughty carriage, fur coverings or no fur coverings.

The women stayed the first night at Duke Richard's favorite country residence, Hunsdon House. "Your birthplace, Margaret," Cecily told her, before they rumbled into the tiny village of Hunsdon, where all twenty villagers turned out to wave and cheer the duchess and the princess Margaret.

"Mother, tell me the story again," Margaret begged.

"There is not much to tell, my child. Your father tried to take me home to Fotheringhay to birth you, which now seems foolish since I was so close to my time. We stopped first at the abbey at Waltham, where the brothers were all smiles and welcome. I rested well that night, I remember, but once we were on the road again, you must have objected to all the bumping and jolting, for we had only gone seven or eight miles before I knew I should have stayed at the abbey. I prayed to St. Anthony to keep me and my baby safe, and my ladies called to Richard to halt." She laughed. "When he saw the way of things, he did not hesitate. He picked me up and held me before him on his horse and galloped the three miles to Hunsdon. I was screaming by this time very regularly and then laughing at his ashen face. The children playing in the village scattered like chickens when he rode through calling for a midwife or anyone who could help. Poor old Tom, our caretaker steward, was not expecting us, of course, and he did his best to make me comfortable. And Richard, my dearest love"—her eyes sparkled and a tender smile lit up her face as she said the words, and Margaret knew then why Edward thought his mother the most beautiful woman in the world—"carried me to our chamber himself."

Margaret listened spellbound, imagining the scene and thrilling to the romance of it all.

"Two rather unkempt women ran into the room and shooed the men out, telling Tom to boil water. 'Twas too late for that. Five minutes later and I held you in my arms. A beautiful and healthy little girl!" Cecily's face clouded for a second, and Margaret knew she was also remembering the six children she had lost: Edmund in battle, and William, John, Henry, Thomas and baby Ursula, who had all died in infancy. Sweet Mother of God, I pray all my children are healthy and live to be a ripe old age, Margaret thought. She was yearning to be a mother, although she decided that Cecily's twelve were perhaps six too many.

Margaret looked about her with interest at Hunsdon, gazing at the big tester bed where she was born and touching the heavy damask curtains with reverence. Cecily was tired but watched Margaret at the bed, a soft smile playing around her mouth.

"Would you like to share my bed tonight, Margaret? Lady Isabel will not mind sharing with your ladies, will you Isabel?" Cecily asked a tart older woman sweetly.

Isabel, countess of Essex, Cecily's sister-in-law, raised a haughty eyebrow but bowed her assent. "As you wish, Cecily."

Margaret ran and hugged the countess and then her mother, who at once admonished her for such a show of emotion. "Really, Margaret, you must learn to restrain yourself! I pray you forgive her, Isabel, she lacks discipline still."

Isabel sniffed and, giving orders to Cecily's attendants to ready the duchess for bed, refrained from comment.

Later, snuggled in private behind the bed curtains, Margaret took advantage of the intimacy to ask Cecily about being a wife and mother. "Did you love Father very much?" she ventured. "We all thought you and Father were the happiest people in the world."

Cecily sighed. "Aye, Meg," and Margaret glowed at the unaccustomed use of her nickname by her mother. "Your father and I loved each other deeply, because we had known each other since children. Your father was a ward of my father's, as you know, and came to live with us at Raby when he was four. We were so fortunate. But I must caution you that it may not be so for you, my dear. When Richard was away, I felt as half a person, as though I were missing a limb or something akin. I foolishly risked myself and my children to be with him whenever I could. You should know, Margaret, that your children are the most precious things you have, and I beg of you, when you become a mother, do not imitate my folly. I might have lost George and Richard at Ludlow had I not insisted on staying with your father. You were safe at Fotheringhay then, but I took a chance that the queen would not harm a woman and two little boys when your father was betrayed and had to flee with his army, leaving me at the castle to face the enemy."

"You hate Margaret of Anjou a great deal, do you not, Mother? I almost wish I did not bear her name, for you and Edward speak it with such hatred."

"Aye, we should all hate her. 'Twas she who turned King Henry against us. I must tell you, though, that during the time when your father and Henry were on good terms and you were born, we thought it would flatter the young, beautiful queen to name you after her. To no avail. Now, because you are so very different from that she-wolf, when I say your name, it doesn't even sound the same as hers. So never believe I think of her when I say it."

"I long to have children, Mother," Margaret whispered. "But I am afraid of who Edward will choose for me. Suppose I hate him on sight?"

"You must always pray to the good Lord to give you strength for such eventualities. How do you think I have survived these two years without your father? My strength and my only comfort is my faith, and you would do well to spend more time reading your Bible and attending Mass than you do, my dear. I am not there to guide you in this every day, I understand, but instead of reading about King Arthur and Sir Gawain—aye, I have my spies, Meg—I would suggest you look to the writings of St. Catherine of Siena or St. Bridget of Sweden. Promise me you will."

"Aye, Mother," Margaret said, stifling a yawn.

"Now, let us say an Ave together for your father's and brother's souls."

Ave Maria, gratia plena
Dominicum tecum
Benedicta tu in mulieribus . . .

By then Margaret was asleep. Cecily, however, prayed on.

"FOTHERINGHAY HAS NEVER seemed so far," Cecily complained, peering out of the carriage over the flat, marshy fens. "I do not recall it taking this long. I hope we are on the right road."

"Mother! Ermine Street is the only road from London to Huntingdon, and we turned off to take the Corby road a few miles ago. We are not far now. 'Tis strange how I remember the road after all this time. I was not ten years old the last time I traveled it."

The wheels were stuck again, and while some of the servants attempted to move the heavy chariot, others chose to dismount, relieve themselves and let their horses chomp the coarse fenland grasses. The cold rain was turning to sleet, and Cecily was afraid they would have snow before reaching Fotheringhay.

Margaret poked her head through one of the side openings to watch the progress with the wheel and failed to notice a shadowy figure emerge from behind a tree some thirty paces from her and let loose an arrow. The thwack three feet from her head alarmed her, and when she saw the still quivering arrow, she screamed. All at once, several more men came running from the forest towards the royal group, waving sticks and knives. Margaret, Cecily and their ladies huddled in a corner of the chariot and listened to the skirmish outside. Shouts, groans and clanging of weapons behind the chariot told the occupants that their armed escort was valiantly defending them. Cecily led the women in prayer, telling her rosary and entreating the Virgin to spare them. When one knife-wielding ruffian peered into the dark interior of the vehicle, they all shrieked in terror.

"What 'ave we 'ere?" he snarled, his mouth curling into a menacing grin. "Oooh, tasty morsels! Pretties! Prizes!" He was reaching for Jane, who was the closest, when suddenly his filthy face contorted in pain. As the women watched in horror, he fell forward with an anguished grunt into Jane's lap, his lifeblood flowing from a sword wound in his back. Jane swooned, but Margaret didn't hesitate to move forward and heave the man off her attendant.

"Have a care, Margaret," Cecily cried. "He may still be alive!"

"I doubt it, your grace," a familiar voice came from the outside. "I ran the measle through from stem to stern." He pulled wide the curtained door. "Our men have run the vagabonds off, madam. You have no cause to be afraid any longer."

"John Harper!" Margaret laughed, relieved. "Mother, 'tis the messenger from Towton field."

Cecily had not the faintest recollection of the man, but whoever he was, he had saved them from certain death, she was sure. "Thanks be to God!" she said, and allowed John Harper to escort her out of the chariot.

"And to Master Harper!" Margaret called after her and could have bitten off her tongue.

"Don't be impertinent, Margaret," her mother scolded. "Certes, 'twas our prayers answered, and God led Master Harper to us!"

"Aye, Mother," Margaret said, meekly. "Thanks be to God."

She was next out of the carriage. John put his hands around her waist and lifted her down, lingering a second more than necessary. Margaret again smelled the scent of sweat and rosewater, and with her senses heightened from the adventure, his nearness intoxicated her. She allowed him to hold her longer than was seemly, but Cecily was already commending her soldiers for their bravery and did not notice Margaret's lapse of etiquette. John's tawny eyes looked admiringly at her, and Margaret felt her pulse race.

"I am at your service, my lady," he said graciously. He bowed over her hand and went to join the other retainers, calling one to remove the body from the chariot. Four outlaws, including the one inside, had been slain. Cecily commanded that they be buried right there in the woods. "Certes, this is where they belong. Surely they will rot in hell for their misdeeds eventually," she said. The two soldiers who had been killed were strapped onto their mounts to be buried at Fotheringhay.

Back in the bloodstained carriage, the wheels finally freed from the mud, the women chattered nervously for the rest of the journey. They all knew that England had become a dangerous place for innocent travelers after the second year of Edward's reign. The euphoria that had reigned for the handsome young king at his coronation had descended into discontent as Edward continued to tax the people to rid himself once and for all of the Lancastrian threats in the north. The taxes and benevolences he levied drove many into the forests to live as outlaws. Earlier that winter, Edward had started north to quell the uprisings and chase the old king and queen over the border into Scotland, but a case of the measles kept him bedridden while the Lancastrian border castles were surrendered to the earl of Warwick.

"Measles? Do you think he was too frightened to fight?" George asked Margaret maliciously. Margaret had told him to go to confession for his insult.

Cecily hoped her son would not return to his wanton ways of hunting, feasting and womanizing that she so deplored and that she feared would turn his subjects against him. She resolved to speak to him of this during the obit. Perhaps knowing that his mother and sister had been in peril of their lives might bring him to his senses.

An hour later, Margaret looked out through the lightly falling snow and called back to her companions, "I can see the castle keep! I can see Fotheringhay on the hill!"

"Home," breathed Cecily, contentedly. "I am home at last."

. . .

MARGARET'S KNEES WERE beginning to feel the effects of so many hours of prayer the family kept during those days at Fotheringhay. The beautiful church was filled with the sounds of chanting, voices lifted in memoriam for the slain duke and his son. Margaret tried to remember the faces of her father and brother as she prayed for their everlasting life in Heaven, but her memory of them had grown dim and only her father's words stayed with her.

"Never forget you are a York, Margaret. You have royal blood in your veins from both your mother and from me. Never be disloyal to your family, child. For me, there is no greater crime."

She glanced around at the others of her family, heads bowed and hands in prayer: Cecily telling her beads with tears flowing down her cheeks; Edward, his handsome face marked by a few lingering measles; her sisters, Anne and Elizabeth, who had arrived the day before with their ducal husbands and who were as strangers to her; and her two younger brothers, George of Clarence and Richard of Gloucester, the one admiring a ring on his thumb and the other mouthing a prayer. Aye, she thought, these are the only people in the world who matter to me. Father was right.

She sank back on her heels to relieve her sore knees and gazed at the magnificent stained glass windows all around her, the cobalt blues, ruby reds, golden yellows and tawny browns melting into a kaleidoscope of patterns, with here and there a figure—her ancestors, she surmised. One, clothed in full armor, was on his knees, just as she was. Something about the face reminded her of Anthony, and she felt a blush begin at the base of her throat. What was it about the man that so intrigued her? He had sent her a short poem with Edward, penned while besieging Alnwick Castle a few weeks before. But there was no romance about it. He had written of the dedication by Warwick's troops to take the fortress and that only God could show them the way. In the end, God had decided the fighting must desist, and the castle had surrendered before it was attacked. Despite the impersonal nature of the poem, she was excited because he had thought of her, and so she folded it carefully and placed it in her silver casket, where, among other treasures, she had a lock of baby Ursula's hair, a pilgrim's badge from her father, and her first lost baby tooth. She wondered when she would see Anthony again, and she began daydreaming of possible circumstances.

She caught Cecily's eye, who frowned at her to raise herself up again, and as she turned to see what her hem was snagged on, she was unnerved to find John Harper staring straight at her from his position at the back of the church. The essence of a smile crossed his face before he lowered his eyes. Margaret inadvertently smiled back. Mother of God, she panicked, forgive me! 'Twas not seemly of me. I pray he did not see. But she knew her plea was too late.

A splendid feast followed the final ceremonies. Edward invited the gentry among his neighbors to dine with the royal company. Cecily had suggested that he might gain support from the landowners in the surrounding region with the gesture and that word of his goodwill might spread. Edward loved a party. "The more the merrier," he had cried upon hearing the idea.

The large company overflowed into antechambers and the noise was deafening. Margaret could see the musicians blowing and bowing away on their instruments, but they were drowned out by the loud conversation. She had consumed one too many glasses of wine, and the din was giving her a headache. Despite the freezing temperature outside, she wanted some air and thought she would go up to the ramparts. She left the table when Cecily's head was turned and slipped past the arras that hid the staircase to the family's private chambers. The heavy tapestry instantly dulled the noise from the hall and she felt better. She mounted the circular stairway in the tower to an arrow loop where she could feel some fresh air through its narrow opening. She leaned into the deep sill of the loop and breathed deeply.

"I hope you are not ill, Lady Margaret." John Harper's voice held quiet concern. "I saw you leave and you looked pale. Forgive me if I intrude."

Margaret jumped at the sound of his voice. She saw him standing a few steps below her, the trailing train on her red velvet gown preventing him from coming nearer. His black, curly hair disappeared into the shadows behind him, and the torchlight flickering on his face gave it a ghostly look. They were alone, and Margaret was suddenly aware of all the implications of her action. She should have asked Jane or Ann to leave with her, she knew, but her need for air had caused her to be impetuous.

However, she reasoned, she did not fear harm from John Harper, and so she let down her guard a little.

"I thank you, Master Harper. I had need of some fresh air, but now I am feeling better, I would ask you to escort me back to the hall." She hoped she sounded as regal as her mother.

She lifted the train of her dress and draped it gracefully over her arm, revealing a white satin underdress embroidered with marguerites, her own special flower. She had put out her hand for him to help her descend the winding steps when her foot slipped. In a second, she was in his arms, feeling the strength in his shoulders as he stopped her from falling. Again the rosewater, and again her pulse raced. He had her captive, and she found she could not pull away. The urge to be kissed was too great. She closed her eyes and their lips met. Her fingers caressed his curls as she pulled his tongue deeper into her mouth. Somewhere in the back of her mind she wondered how she knew to do this, but the thought was lost in the wonderful sensation she was experiencing all through her body. Then, without warning, Cecily's face intruded on her brain, and shame suffused her. One of John's hands was fondling her breast and the other held her buttocks firmly against him. She could feel something hard through the layers of clothing pressing against her thigh, and his desire was mounting as surely as her panic. Then Edward's familiar, lazy voice pierced the moment.

"Why, Margaret, 'tis early in the evening for such sport. Our lady mother inquires after you. I do believe 'tis time to return to our guests."

John released his hold instantly and tried to bow awkwardly on the narrow circular stairs. On the landing below, Edward laughed. "'Tis John Harper, is it not?" John nodded, speechless. "You fought beside me at Towton and St. Albans, and I would not deny you a prize. But I fear my sister may be too high a one! Kiss her if you must, but I forbid anything further."

John gasped, and Margaret sank down on the step, her hand flying to her head to right her steepled hennin as she stammered, "'Twas my fault, Edward. Pray do not be angry with Master Harper." Margaret knew in her heart that she had encouraged the young man, and she did not want to add another sin to the list she must confess on the morrow by pretending she had not.

"Nay, Lady Margaret, the fault lies with me," John protested. "I confess I could not help myself. If I have offended you or your grace, I am heartily sorry. My loyalty to your house is unswerving, I swear. Punish me as you will, my lord." John had descended the few steps to the landing and was now kneeling before Edward, his hand on his heart.

"Punish you? Punish you for what, pray? Don't be such an addle-pate, sir. You have not offended me, and as I did not hear her screaming for help, my sister is quite obviously not offended either. I am correct, Margaret?" He saw her look of acquiescence and continued, "Who am I to gainsay young love? Come, Meg, we shall be missed. Good evening, Master Harper."

He offered his arm to Margaret, who carefully climbed down the last two steps to join him. They walked silently back to the great hall, leaving a mortified John Harper in their wake. As Edward held the arras aside for his sister, he turned, and John could have sworn his sovereign winked at him.

WHEN THE ROYAL entourage traveled back to London two days later, Margaret and her ladies were alone in the chariot. The time at Fotheringhay had convinced Cecily that it was where she belonged, and she had received permission from Edward to make it her principal residence. She happily settled in among the towering moated ramparts and fortified baileys, which made Fotheringhay one of the strongest castles in the Midlands of England. It was also one of the must luxurious. Cecily was overjoyed when Edward promised to send the rest of her wardrobe and household to her as soon as he returned to London. He loved his mother, but her disapproval of his lifestyle was a burr under his saddle. The farther away she was, the better, he thought.

Margaret had cried when she kissed Cecily good-bye on the steps of the inner bailey. Even though they had lived apart now for two years, Margaret at Greenwich and Cecily at Baynard's, and Margaret had been in control of her own little household, it was only an hour or two by boat between them, and her mother's proximity had been a comfort.

"I shall be in London from time to time, Margaret, never fear. And you will write to me, will you not? I will miss you, too, my child, but you are a woman now, and I have taught you well. 'Twill not be so bad. But you must see to it that George and Richard conduct themselves properly, my dear," Cecily advised her, and Margaret nodded dutifully.

George was to remain at Greenwich, but it had been decided during private conversations with Cecily's nephew, the earl of Warwick, that when Richard turned fourteen, he would be placed in the earl's care and undertake his knightly training at Warwick's castle of Middleham. But for now, the three siblings would spend much of their time in one another's company, with Edward keeping an eye on their activities and household expenditures.

If the truth be told, Margaret was none too happy with the arrangement. A fight was always simmering beneath the surface when the two brothers were together. George sensed Edward's partiality for Richard, and his jealousy was increasing. Despite being warned by Edward to remain calm, Richard would not take George's jabs and taunts lying down. He would bunch his hands into fists and threaten to take on the bigger George in a fight. George would laugh unkindly, which would inflame Richard's anger further until Edward or Cecily stepped in to take charge. Not long after such an incident, however, the two might be seen arm in arm wandering down to the butts to try their luck with a bow and arrow, fast friends again. Their behavior was perplexing to Cecily and simply annoying to Margaret.

During the journey back to Greenwich, however, Margaret was far too absorbed in herself to worry about her brothers. Time after exhilarating time, she had gone over the moments of her embrace with John Harper, trying to remember each exquisite sensation and making it last in her mind twice as long as it had. She had seen John once more after the incident, and they had but a brief exchange.

"I must thank you, my lady, for excusing me to his grace, the king. Certes, I was so surprised and overcome by his presence that I lost my tongue. Forgive me."

Seeing him so contrite, Margaret tried to make amends. "Nay, Master Harper. There is naught to forgive. I should not have put you in such a position. But," she said with a twinkle, trying to make light of the event, "I hope you enjoyed our moment together as much as I did."

The sensual smile that suffused his face told her that he had.

"'Tis enough then, sir, and so," she found herself saying, "until the next time."

His astonishment was extremely satisfying, she remembered, as she lay wrapped in furs and daydreaming on the cushions of the chariot.

· · ·

MARGARET LISTENED IN on a conversation between Sir John Howard and Will Hastings one evening after supper in the queen's watching chamber. She was presiding over the entertainment that night, and Edward had graciously accepted her invitation to visit his sister at Greenwich. He had arrived with some of his closest advisers in the royal barge from Westminster earlier in the day and spent some time with George and Richard before attending Margaret's entertainment. Edward's two councilors had begun their talk mundanely enough, commenting on the music as the dancers in front of them stepped to a stately *pavane*. Margaret liked Jack Howard for his forthrightness. His loyalty to the house of York was unquestioned, and Edward held his councilor in high esteem. Margaret appeared intent on the dancing, and they forgot about her as their talk became more political.

"The last few months have made for some strange bedfellows for his grace and Warwick, Jack," Will said, referring to the weeks of uncertainty for Edward along the Scottish border.

"Aye, my lord of Warwick is none too happy he has to consider Ralph Percy one of us now," Jack said, twirling his long black mustache. Margaret knew Warwick's Neville family, with royal connections through its Beaufort roots, had a running feud over lands with the other powerful lords of the north, the Percies. "In truth, I was suspicious when they told me he had sworn allegiance to Edward, when all these years he has worn Lancaster's colors. But he seems to be holding Dunstanburgh strong for the king after it fell into our hands, Will."

"Percy? Certes, that is strange, but stranger still is Somerset's obedience to his grace," Will replied. The young and handsome duke of Somerset, rumored to be Queen Margaret's lover and possibly the father of her son Edouard, had astounded all of Edward's councilors when he, too, swore allegiance to Edward following the siege of Alnwick Castle in December. With all the bothersome northern castles now in Yorkist hands, easygoing Edward had forgiven both these lords, and indeed Henry of Somerset was now among Edward's inner circle. "You should see the scowl on Warwick's face," Will said, chuckling. "'Twould send even the Devil scurrying back into Hell! The earl mislikes his protégé's pardonings, I warrant. But he wisely curbs his tongue for now."

"Perhaps his grace likes to keep his enemies where he can see them," Jack Howard remarked. "'Tis certain my lord Rivers and his son, Scales, have proven loyal."

At the mention of Anthony, Margaret startled the two men by remarking, "My lord Scales proved a worthy fighter in the north, Sir William, so my brother tells me. I wonder when we shall see him again at court."

"Forgive our indiscretion, my lady," Will apologized, recovering. "We were unaware you were within earshot. I hope we said nothing untoward. You must know our loyalties lie with your brother."

"Have no fear, Sir William, you have not disgraced yourself." Margaret smiled. "I was enjoying eavesdropping. I do not have enough news here at Greenwich, in truth. I feel as though I were in some backwater with only two squabbling brothers for entertainment. Lord Scales and I are acquainted, and I find his company pleasant. I would have news of him."

Jack laughed. "Anthony Woodville was heard to rue Warwick's decision not to attack Alnwick, Lady Margaret. A valiant soldier with no one to fight is a sad sight indeed!"

The conversation was halted abruptly as loud laughter erupted from one end of the hall. The three watched as Edward's jester, Jehan Le Sage, turned another cartwheel, lightly plucked a bonnet from an unsuspecting guest's head and leapt easily up onto a table, brandishing the cap on the end of his bell stick. Edward applauded loudly and threw Jehan a coin. He called to his sister: "Margaret, let us have dancing, I pray you. Jehan looks weary." Margaret nodded and the musicians tuned their instruments.

"I hope one day to have someone like Jehan to keep me company," Margaret said to Will and Jack. "He seems to know Edward's every humor and can adapt himself to any occasion. I warrant he is closer to my brother than any of you, sirs!" She laughed when she saw the consternation on their faces. "Fear not, I know your loyalty, too. 'Tis simply a different kind."

Jack's eyes twinkled as he went back to stroking his mustache and looked admiringly at her. He hoped Edward would find the lady a good match. She would make England proud.

Just then, John Harper stepped up to Margaret, extended his leg and bowed gracefully over it. "Lady Margaret, may I have the pleasure?" he asked, offering her his arm. "I pray you excuse us, sirs."

Margaret inclined her head and took John's arm, smiling an apology to the two councilors. Jack kissed her hand and moved away with Will to talk to Robert Stillington, the bishop of Bath and Wells and another of the king's councilors. They moved aside to allow the couple to join the other dancers in a slow *basse danse*. Margaret was in a dusky blue gown, the V-necked bodice turned back to show the creamy satin lining. The hemline was trimmed with ermine. She deftly gathered the train over her free arm and allowed John to lead her in the stately dance. She noticed his hand trembled slightly in hers, and she smiled to herself. The memory of their kiss at Fotheringhay came back in all its sensuousness, and she glanced over at him and wondered if he could feel her pulse beating. He caught her eye, and his expression told her he could. Immediately, a flush of scarlet flooded her cheeks and she turned her head away.

They processed down the room, their steps in perfect time to the beat of the tambourine, the recorders, gemshorns and viols. Turning inward and coming together face to face in the movement of the dance, their hands whispering together, John murmured, "Is this perhaps the next time, my lady?"

Margaret knew he was referring to her last and somewhat bold remark on the tower stairs. They moved away from each other again, and she was spared having to answer. How many times had she dreamed of that kiss? And how many times had she dreamed of repeating it she was ashamed she could not tell. A simple kiss, she thought, and Edward seems to expect it of me. Perhaps, later . . .

"I shall take a turn around the garden by the river after my brother has retired, Master Harper," she was brave enough to tell him the next time they were close enough for conversation. "Certes, I shall be accompanied by my ladies, but I would not find your company unwelcome should you happen upon us."

Now she saw him flush, and when he returned her to her seat, he kissed her fingers with as much meaning as he could without drawing attention. "I thank you, Lady Margaret," he said, "for the dance."

He walked away. Margaret watched his long, lazy stride, admiring the shapely thighs and calves encased in green and yellow chequered hose. Aye, she thought, perhaps 'tis the time.

She looked around for Edward and saw him in a window embrasure with Eleanor Butler. She briefly wondered how Eleanor happened to be at her entertainment, but then she knew that Edward had orchestrated it, and shrugged. The word was that Eleanor was proving a difficult conquest for her lusty brother, and she watched the two play the seduction game from her vantage point across the room. Eleanor was indeed a beauty, with translucent skin, a fine nose and dark sapphire eyes. A wisp of auburn hair had escaped from under her hennin, and Edward was playing with it and touching her neck delicately. Giving him license for a minute or two, Eleanor then firmly removed his hand and said something that made Edward laugh. Margaret saw her stifle a yawn, curtsey prettily and move towards the door. At that moment, Jack Howard claimed his attention, and Edward was unable to follow his heart's desire. Poor Edward, Margaret thought, I hear the lady is unwilling to be bedded.

An hour later, after bidding the last of her guests a good night, Margaret told Jane to fetch their cloaks for a short stroll in the night air. Jane hurried from the hall and pulled Ann with her. "Our mistress wants to walk in the garden," she said, making a face. " 'Tis freezing out there. What can she be thinking?"

Ann groaned. She had made some headway with a young squire in Edward's retinue and was hoping for some stolen kisses before she had to ready Margaret for bed. "We had better put on our pattens, too," she sighed, looking down at the long green points of her fashionable crakows peeping out from beneath her hem, "or these will be ruined. Do hurry, Jane. You are slower than a snail, I swear."

"But I long for my bed," the indolent young woman complained, but followed Ann out of the room.

Many of Edward's younger retainers were already curled up in their cloaks near the still roaring fire as Margaret's servants lowered the huge chandelier to extinguish the dozens of candles. Margaret left the hall on her steward's arm, and he escorted her back to her chambers. They wished each other good night, and the man bowed and left. As soon as the door closed, Margaret called to Jane, who hurried in with her mistress's cloak and pattens. Ann followed close behind. Without a word, Margaret crossed to descend the central stairway that led to the inner courtyard, and with the two bemused young women in her wake, glided under the archway in the west wing of the palace into the garden beyond. Less formal than the inner court's manicured lawn and low border hedges, it was a pleasant place with large trees, bushes and shrubs. In the summer it was a riot of colorful flowering plants, but now the leafless trees were ghostly in the March moonlight and made eerie shadows on the icy ground. Ann and Jane shivered, partly from cold and partly from fear.

"Do be sensible, ladies. There are guards at every entrance to the palace. Who do you think will attack us, pray?" Margaret teased them, picking her way carefully on the slippery path. "I know you think I have lost my mind, but I know what I am doing. I must ask you to be discreet and not divulge anything you may see. Do you understand?"

The women nodded, openmouthed. What was their mistress doing—except walking out in the middle of a cold night—that would be of any interest to anyone? And then they saw him, a man who stepped out of the shadow of a large yew bush and called, "Lady Margaret," in a hoarse whisper. The two ladies-in-waiting strained to see who could possibly be expecting their mistress, but he kept in the shadows. Margaret told them to stay where they were and keep up a quiet conversation. She walked the few dozen yards to where John Harper waited. He whisked her out of sight of the women, and his lips were on hers, his tongue filling her mouth so that she could not breathe.

"Master Harper, I pray you, give me air," she said, pulling away and laughing. "'Tis unchivalrous of you not to begin with some sweet words of love. Or to give me the respect due my rank!"

"Madam, you are cruel," John said, taking her hand and covering it with kisses. "If I declare my love for you, you know it must be unrequited, certes, because of your rank, and so what is the point? I have longed for you since our last meeting and did not dare to hope you would grant me such an interview. I might write poems about your eyes, your lips, your grace and your kindness, madam, but I am no poet, I am ashamed to say."

Again Anthony's face was conjured up, but she quickly banished it from her mind. This young man was here and now, and she enjoyed his kisses. He was part of Edward's household and as such was aware that his very fate was in her hands. He would not dare to tread where she did not wish to go. And what was the harm in a few kisses? But she was new to lovemaking and had no idea how urgent a man's desire became once aroused. She did not know she was toying with him, being naive in the ways of seduction.

"I do not need poems, John. I need you to *speak* to me of your passion. Your few words were a good start. Now tell me more about my eyes." She was coy, and John knew it. But he was in love, and if that was what she wanted, he would not deny her.

"Your eyes remind me of the light that comes between sundown and night. Dusky gray I would call them, and of such luster I cannot describe. I can only imagine your hair—'tis always hidden by those monstrous hennins—but in my dreams I feel it in my fingers, thick and soft like the finest silk cloth."

She pushed the voluminous hood of her cloak back from her headdress, lifted off the brocade pillbox hennin, unpinned the braid underneath and let her honey-colored hair tumble over her shoulders to her waist. It was too much for John. He took handfuls of the tresses and pressed them to his lips and then pulled her to him, their faces inches apart. He could just make out the smile that curved her mouth in the moonglow before he kissed her again, slowly. She could feel his hardness against her, and she was sorely pressed not to reach down and touch it. He seemed to be moving against her in a most erotic fashion, all the while kissing her more deeply. Suddenly he moaned in her mouth, and she remembered the scene in the bridge room at Baynard's. Now she understood! 'Twas pleasure, not pain, she had heard. She was puzzled that she did not feel moved to moan until she felt him lift her skirt and put his fingers where even she had never dared explore. An explosion rocked her and she gasped and groaned at the same time. Her eyes flew wide as the exquisite sensation lingered for several seconds, and she saw John watching and smiling triumphantly. He dropped her skirt and kissed her gently this time, holding her wilted body close.

"Now I believe we are both pleasured, my lady. I trust we have not frightened your ladies."

Margaret sprang away, her hand over her mouth. "Sweet Virgin! Ann and Jane! What must they be thinking? Do you think they heard?" She was so childlike in her confusion that he could not forbear taking her in his arms one last time, kissing away her embarrassment. "Nay, lady, you were very discreet, I can assure you! But now I must go before my master notices my absence."

"Aye, and I must away as well." Margaret tucked all her hair under her hood and hid her hennin under her cloak. "God speed, Master Harper. And . . . um . . ." She was at a loss whether to thank him or wish him good night as though they had merely danced again.

He spared her the decision. "Nay, thank *you*, my lady. In my dreams I could not be as content as I am at this moment."

And he was gone, leaving her to gather her wits and allow him enough time to disappear inside the palace. Then she strained to see Ann and Jane, who had their backs to her and were stamping their feet to keep warm and chattering much too fast. They turned at her approach and pretended not to notice her disheveled appearance. But Jane bent down surreptitiously and retrieved the trailing veil that had come away from the hennin and had dropped behind Margaret as she walked back to their lodgings.

Margaret glanced up at the king's private apartment and saw two figures facing each other illuminated by a single candle in a window. Edward was holding Eleanor's hand. Margaret thought she saw a third figure, hovering in the background, make the sign of the cross. It looked like Bishop Stillington.

Nay, she thought, I must be dreaming, and passed under the arch.

"NOT AGAIN!" MARGARET groaned when she heard the news that the Northumbrian castles had once more fallen into Lancastrian hands. "I suppose that means Edward will have to go north."

It was high summer, and Greenwich was dressed in its best. Emerald green grass carpeted the courtyards, flowers of every hue graced the gardens and the river sparkled in the sunshine. A peacock strutted on the lawn in the inner courtyard, its tail spread in a proud fan of teal, blue, gold and green. George and Richard had finished their studies for the day and had been told this news by their tutor.

"Aye, he has gone north," George grumbled, "and he did not ask me to go with him. Meggie, when will I be old enough to be considered a man?"

"Soon, George, I warrant. When you are sixteen." Margaret dragged her eyes from her latest passion, Geoffrey Chaucer's *Canterbury Tales,* to answer her disgruntled brother. "You have only a little more than a year to wait. Though 'tis a mystery to me why men hunger to fight. You could be killed or, even worse, maimed for life. Certes, I do not understand you."

"'Tis our duty to fight for our brother, the king," piped up Richard. "Just as it will be your duty to marry for him."

George guffawed, and Richard looked pleased with himself. Margaret glared at them, turned her back and put her nose back in the book. She pretended to be reading, and, thinking their sport with her was at an end, the boys chose another and ran off to the archery butts. Margaret breathed a sigh of relief. She applied herself again to Master Chaucer's words. She was reading the preamble to the tale told by the wife of Bath when she was startled by the lines:

> Or where commanded God virginity?
> I read as well as you no doubt have read
> The apostle when he speaks of maidenhead;
> He said, commandment of the Lord he'd none.

She looked around the room guiltily as though someone could see what she was reading, but her ladies were all occupied with their needle-work and gossip, and so she read on:

> Men may advise a woman to be one,
> But such advice is not commandment, no;
> He left the thing to our own judgment so.

Was this true? Saving one's maidenhood for the sanctity of marriage was as innate to her as breathing or sleeping. She had wondered if John Harper's wandering fingers counted, and she had whispered her confession of their tryst to the shadowy priest behind the grille in the confessional, praying he would not recognize her. She felt better afterwards, thinking God had pardoned her. She had worried she might be with child, having limited knowledge of how her body worked, and was relieved when her courses had reappeared later in the month. Now, if she understood the wife of Bath's implication—and if she could trust in Master Chaucer's knowledge of the Scriptures—losing one's maidenhead before marriage was not breaking God's law.

A bell rang the Terce and banished these thoughts. More by rote than by inclination, she picked up her rosary and ran through the empty king's apartments to the royal chapel and knelt on a tapestry-covered footstool before the altar. The chaplain smiled at her; she was never late for her prayers. As soon as she was joined by other members of her household, he began the service. Margaret prayed for her family, for the souls of her departed father and brother, and then she prayed for a quick end to any fighting in Northumbria and especially for Edward's safety. Finally she sneaked in a quick Ave for John—assuming he was with Edward—and for Anthony. She had learned that Anthony had been keeping his wife company in Norfolk during the spring, and she had been in the doldrums for a while upon hearing it. She did not know that he had departed for the north once more with a body of men to join the earl of Warwick, who had followed his brother, Lord Montagu, to reclaim those pesky Northumbrian castles.

"Lord God, keep them both in your loving care, and I pray you make an end to all the fighting."

It seemed God heard her and had acted quickly, for upon leaving the chapel, she was almost knocked down by Richard, who, intent on besting George with his bow and arrow, had not heeded the call to prayer as she had.

"The queen and her son are fled to Scotland! Montagu beat back their army! The castles are ours again," the boy cried, breathless. "Sir John Howard has come to tell us. We are safe from the She-Wolf, Meggie. Safe!"

Margaret smiled at his excitement, took his hand and allowed him to lead her to the privy chamber nearby where Jack was waiting.

"Lady Margaret." He smiled, doffing his bonnet and bowing over her hand. She noticed a circle of gray hair amid the black on the crown of his head. "I trust young Lord Richard here gave you the good news. 'Tis a week or two old, but I heard it aboard ship at Sandwich and came straightway to tell you. Nay, I was not involved in the fighting, my lady," he said, anticipating her next question. "Your brother, the king's grace, commanded I ready the fleet for possible war with the French. The earl of Warwick and his brother were victorious, it seems, and your brother and all his friends are now staying at Fotheringhay."

Margaret nodded absently, for her attention was riveted on a diminutive creature with a saturnine countenance cowering behind the chair

Jack had just vacated. She was dressed in a miniature gown of a style Margaret did not recognize. The embroidered bodice was laced up to a plain, modest neckline. Enormous pleated sleeves, which were a different color from her dress, ballooned over the dwarf's upper arms, making the shoulders appear disproportionately large. A piece of soft silk was pinned over her neatly braided black hair. Margaret saw that this little person was fastidious about her appearance, which surprised Margaret, for having never seen a dwarf before, she had preconceived notions that their ways were as abnormal as their bodies. She had always thought the condition was a cruel joke played by God.

And then she saw the eyes. Now wide with terror, as black as coal and framed in long, soft lashes, they were the girl's most arresting feature. Margaret held them in her gaze, and her heart melted at the fear she could plainly read in them. Forgetting her first distaste, she smiled. "Who is this, I pray, Sir John? I do not remember her accompanying you before."

Jack beamed, clapping his hat back on his head. "This, my lady, is Fortunata. She is a gift from me to you, if you will take her," he said with a flourish.

Margaret was taken aback. "For . . . for me? 'Tis gracious, Sir John, but why for me?"

"Ah, I see you do not recall our last meeting, when you expressed a wish to have your own Jehan Le Sage to keep you company and amused, Lady Margaret. Certes, when I encountered Fortunata, I straightway thought of you. I pray you honor this simple man and take his simple gift. She is Italian but speaks English quite well, I believe." John ushered Fortunata towards Margaret, hoping he would not have to answer any more questions. The dwarf, a grim expression set on her sallow face, made an awkward little bow.

"Fortunata," Margaret repeated the name slowly. "What a beautiful name. I fear it did not bring her good fortune, though. How old is she?"

"I fifteen years, *madonna*," the dwarf murmured, daring to look up at Margaret through those incredible lashes. "Plis."

"Plis?" Margaret frowned and then laughed. "Oh! Please, of course!"

"Fifteen?" blurted out Richard, who had been staring, fascinated, at Fortunata. "Why, she is smaller than me!"

"Dickon, hold your tongue!" Margaret rebuked him. "Please go and tell Ann where I am. Dickon! Are you listening? That's better, now go!"

Richard made a face behind his sister's back on his way out, and Jack hid a smile.

"Sir John, how long have you been hiding Fortunata, and how is it you are able to give her to me? Is she a servant of yours?" Margaret asked.

"Nay, my lady. She is mine to give, but I confess how I came by her is not fit for a lady's ears."

"Nonsense, Sir John! I am not so lily-livered I cannot hear your tale. Tell me you fought pirates to free her and I would be more than satisfied. Except then we should have to send her back fom whence she came," she mused, her mouth turning down.

"*Non, madonna, non, non!* Plis!" All of a sudden, Fortunata was on her knees, tears running down her face. Margaret and Jack stared in astonishment. "Not go back, plis! I burn!"

"Be calm, child," Jack commanded, "and listen to me. This lady is the sister of the king of England. Aye, you may look dumbfounded, but 'tis no lie. You will serve the Lady Margaret with respect."

Fortunata responded by kissing the hem of Margaret's gown.

"Sir John, what do you know about her?" Margaret persisted. "I command you tell me how she came to be with you, unless of course you won her in a game of chance—that I would not countenance! 'Twould be mortifying for her."

Jack covered his embarrassment with a cough, while Margaret bent and coaxed Fortunata to stand up. "Well, Sir John?" she asked again.

"'Twas not I but the captain of my vessel, the *Mary Talbot*, my lady," he explained. "Richard Outlaw is a good man, in truth, but he did indeed win Fortunata in a game."

Margaret frowned. "From whom did this Outlaw cruelly steal this poor thing, Sir John? I pray it was not from her father and mother, or I will have him horsewhipped." Her own anger surprised her, but her heart had gone out to this unfortunate creature. She was determined to make amends. God had obviously sent Fortunata to her as a test of her charity, and she knew already she would take the dwarf into her household, if Edward would countenance an extra mouth for her to feed. She was dependent upon Edward's bounty for every gold noble she spent, and so far he had been generous.

She sat down in the chair, holding Fortunata's hand all the while, and waited for Jack to speak.

"I swear I know not where she came from. I only know Outlaw was taken with her skills upon seeing her perform in a traveling circus with her magician master. Later, after a few drinks I suppose, he and the master fell in together, and Outlaw suggested they throw dice. The man lost all his money that night and begged to try and win it back. Richard took pity on him and offered the money back in exchange for Fortunata, and he accepted. I came aboard a day later and found Fortunata cleaning Richard's quarters and without much ado extracted the story from him." He saw Margaret's dark look and hurried on. "Certes, I railed at him for a goodly few minutes but could do no more than pay him the money he had given. 'Twas only then I realized I now had Fortunata's fate in *my* hands. And then I thought of you, Lady Margaret."

"Poor child," Margaret murmured and then told Sir John, "I like not that your man was playing for a human life, sir, but perhaps she has been sent to me for a reason. You may be sure I will look after her." She added more kindly, "I am indeed grateful that you thought of me, Sir John. I am glad you did not consider my wish a foolish one that evening in March! You are a good man, I am sure, and Edward shall hear of your kindness."

"Thank you, my lady. May I have your leave to return to my ship? I have to continue to London."

"Go, sir." Margaret held out her hand for him to kiss. "And God speed."

Without a backward glance at Fortunata, he strode quickly from the hall, his dark blue houppelande flapping around his ankles.

5

1463

Margaret stared after Jack, her mind in a whirl. What was she thinking? Who was this little woman whom she had agreed to absorb into her household? Could she be a spy? Was she a witch? This last question concerned her deeply. Her superstitious nature and strict religious upbringing had taught her to be wary of anyone with physical deformities. Even a birthmark could be a message from the Devil. And if she was a witch, she was doomed to the flames of Hell.

"Burn! 'Tis what you tried to say," Margaret said suddenly, startling Fortunata. "Is that what happened to you where you came from? Did they try to burn you?"

Fortunata crossed herself, pulled a rosary from a fold in her gown and nodded. "I not witch, *madonna*. I good girl. Love God, love *la Sancta Madonna* . . ."

"Aye, I believe you do." Margaret rose, and Fortunata scrambled to her feet. "But we must be sure everyone else believes it, too. Now, what are the skills you have—tricks, you understand—that so impressed Captain Outlaw? Magic?" Margaret waved her hands dramatically.

Fortunata cocked her head, watching her new mistress, and then nodded. "I show you, *madonna.*" She took a black wand from her belt, turned
around three times and threw it in the air. When it came down it was
naught but a silk kerchief. Margaret clapped her hands in delight. "Good,
good, Fortunata!" she cried, and the smile of gratitude she received transformed the grim features of the girl's face into a semblance of beauty.
Margaret was charmed.

Ann came hurrying through the door and stopped in her tracks. "Lord
Richard told us"—she saw Margaret frown, and she faltered—"he told us
you wanted to see me."

"This is Fortunata. She is Italian but she speaks some English. She
will be joining us, Ann, and I will brook no unkindness towards her, do
you understand?" Margaret attempted to sound as commanding as her
mother, and, watching Ann curtsey and demur, she knew she had succeeded. She turned to Fortunata, who was again hiding behind the chair,
and beckoned to her. "Come here, child. This is Mistress Ann Herbert.
You must call her Mistress Ann. Do you understand? Mistress Ann."

"Sì, *madonna.* Mistress Anna." Fortunata looked up shyly at Ann, studying her. Ann's haughty stare made her inch closer to Margaret, trusting
her new mistress to protect her.

An enormous wolfhound bounded into the room, dragging George
behind it, and Fortunata screamed in terror and ran to the safety of the
chair again. Her fear was a magnet for the dog, which lunged as far as its
leash would allow at the small person who had clambered onto the heavy
wooden seat.

"George! Call Alaris off at once!" Margaret ordered, standing in
front of the terrified Fortunata. Alaris was barking, Fortunata screaming and George shouting, "Down, boy! Down!" to his hound. Curious
servants began peering in at the scene, whispering and pointing at
Fortunata, who was trying to climb onto Margaret's back to escape
Alaris's bared teeth. The steward arrived on the scene, flushed and
puffing from taking the stairs two at a time, and threw up his hands at
the pandemonium. Richard ran into the room, followed closely by Jane
and Margaret's other ladies, and soon the whole wing of the palace was
in an uproar. Richard finally calmed the dog and then took the leash
from George and spoke something into the hound's ear. It immedi-

ately whined and sat back on its haunches. "Good dog," said Richard, patting its enormous head, and Alaris washed the boy's face with one sweep of its tongue.

"My lady, what has happened here?" cried the white-haired steward, asserting his position as overseer of the royal brothers' and sister's households. "Certes, it sounded as though there had been murder done!"

Margaret was extricating herself from Fortunata's surprisingly strong grip on her neck and succeeded in calming the girl sufficiently to respond with a little dignity.

"All is well, Sir Walter, I thank you. 'Twas my lord of Clarence's dog that set upon my new servant, Fortunata, here. She was justly afraid. 'Tis over now, and you may go about your business. Pray forgive us for disturbing you, sir."

The steward had only now spotted Fortunata, and his eyebrows disappeared under his hastily donned bonnet. "Who is this mon—"

"Young woman, Sir Walter? Is that what you were about to say?" Margaret smiled sweetly at him, and he did not dare to gainsay her in front of the household. He nodded, and Margaret enlightened him. "She joined my household this afternoon as a gift from Sir John Howard, to whom I am most grateful."

She looked around and saw that a goodly number of the household had gathered in the doorway and others were craning their necks over them to see into the room. She spoke so that everyone could hear. "This unfortunate girl has been persecuted in her native land for her lack of inches, and she has been bought and sold like a slave by wicked men who hoped to make their fortune from her want of growth. 'Tis monstrous. I know you would all agree." She looked at them all intently, and many nodded or crossed themselves. "She has learned some wondrous magic tricks, which will amuse us all on cold winter evenings, and I have no doubt my brother, the king, will be envious of my good fortune. Jehan Le Sage may have a rival!" she finished triumphantly. "Fortunata means good luck in the Italian tongue, and I believe she brings good fortune to us all! Now who will carry her to my own apartments?"

The astonished Fortunata found herself being swept up in the air and borne aloft to Margaret's apartments by several smiling squires, followed by an exuberant Margaret and less enthusiastic ladies-in-waiting.

The steward bowed as Margaret passed, but she heard his "Tch, tch" as she left the room. Oh, dear, she thought, this would certainly reach Mother's ears before long. But her heart lifted at her own courage.

It was late September. Fortunata was no longer stared at nor was she the talk of the Greenwich court. She followed Margaret wherever she went, becoming invisible behind chairs or pillars and even hiding under the table. Margaret didn't mind; in fact, it amused her. The dwarf was now simply part of Margaret, and Margaret's attendants could not remember a time when Fortunata had not been there. She had an uncanny knack for knowing exactly how Margaret was feeling and could fetch a cloak or a drink without being asked or turn a cartwheel to jog Margaret out of an ill humor. What Margaret admired the most about her new servant was her quickness of mind and how soon her English became fluent. The accent would always be there, of course, but it lent the dwarf a charm that transcended her unusual appearance.

Of all Margaret's ladies, Ann was the unhappiest about the addition to their small group. She had imagined she was Margaret's friend and favorite companion, but Fortunata was quickly taking that corner of Margaret's heart. Lazy Jane told Ann to be glad someone else would fetch and carry, and what did it matter? Both of them had been found husbands by their fathers and would soon leave Margaret's service. But Ann continued to sulk, and she slyly pinched Fortunata when she had the chance or tripped her up so that she looked ridiculous. But the little woman would turn the tumble into a comical act and make Margaret laugh, which caused more black looks from Ann.

So life went on as usual, although the rift between George and Richard was deepening. Margaret felt sorry for George, for by now the son of a duke should be in another noble household, learning the responsibilities of his rank. Edward seemed to have forgotten him, just as he had forgotten to find a suitable husband for her. With four years between George and Richard, the elder boy was chafing to shed his minor status and join Edward's court, while Richard, who was still enjoying boyhood, had the promise of knightly training with Warwick.

"'Tis not fair!" became George's cry, and often Margaret would not even lift her eyes from her book.

"What is it this time, George?" she asked on one occasion not long after Fortunata had arrived.

"Richard's new doublet is finer than mine," George complained. "And he's my baby brother. Why does Edward favor him so?"

"George, I do understand that you would rather be far from here, but you must not take your impatience out on Richard. Edward sent you equally handsome jackets. Now be glad he remembers you." She kept her mouth closed on her next comment, which would have been "I did not receive anything from Edward," and said instead, "'Tis in your imagination that Edward favors Richard. Besides, I favor you; doesn't that count for something?"

And George had given her his most charming smile and kissed her cheek fondly. "Aye, Meggie, I know you love me. I hope you always will."

"And why should I not, pray? No matter where I have to go, I will *never* forget my family," she said vehemently, even though it seemed Edward had forgotten her.

SHE WAS RIGHT. Edward had international relations on his mind that autumn. His ally in Europe, Philip of Burgundy, had finally succeeded in arranging a meeting between Edward's ambassadors and the new king of France, Louis. With King Henry's and Queen Margaret's Lancastrian cause seemingly finished, the wily Louis, who at one point had promised the queen he would always have her best interests at heart, realized it would be provident to cease hostilities with Edward, and thus the two countries signed a year-long truce at St. Omer, promising to meet at a peace conference the following April.

"The terms of the agreement dictate that neither party may give succor to the other's enemies, which means Louis cannot give Queen Margaret aid, God be praised," said Jack Howard, who had stopped at Greenwich pier on the way to his town house at Stepney to pay his respects and to see if Fortunata was pleasing Margaret. He was delighted to see the change in the dwarf since rescuing her from his captain. The scowl had gone, and although she would never be described as fair, her long countenance was not unattractive thanks to those liquid eyes. Margaret had given her a new gown, and it was more flattering to her short body. Margaret allowed Fortunata to sit at her feet during their interview, and Jack noticed the girl paid rapt attention to the conversation, which he found somewhat unsettling. He, too, wondered if she were a spy.

"But I thought Burgundy and France were enemies," Margaret said, puzzled. "Why would the duke want Louis to sign a truce with England? 'Tis all very confusing."

"Certes! 'Tis even more confusing than you think, madam. As you know, Philip of Burgundy was close to death last summer, and his hot-headed son Charles was poised to succeed him. He and his father do not see eye to eye," Jack chuckled, "and that is an understatement!

"When Louis took the throne, he saw that the Burgundian lands stopped only a few leagues from Paris, and he has been trying to persuade Philip to sell him back the towns along the Somme that Louis' father ceded thirty years ago. Philip, for his part, is looking to ease his mortal soul into a happy eternity and so would dearly love to finance a crusade. Louis' money would pay for that, but Philip knows Charles does not want to give up one acre of his inheritance, and so they quarreled again, 'tis said."

"In truth, this Charles seems a disrespectful son, Sir John. I cannot imagine Edward disputing any of my father's decisions," Margaret said, smiling at the thought. " 'Twould have been unthinkable!"

Having spent time with the late duke of York, Jack had to nod in agreement.

Margaret changed the subject. "The news you bring is happy, sir, but when does my brother return to London? I confess I am weary of this solitary life in Greenwich."

Jack kept a straight face as his dark eyes swept the room with its many attendants. Margaret did not miss the glance and defended herself. "With only my lords of Clarence and Gloucester for company, I mean."

"Ah, I see your point, my lady. Brothers, and especially younger brothers, can be a trial," Jack sympathized. "As for the king's grace, he is busy in the north, but he will come back to London soon, I warrant. Perhaps you were not aware that he went to Dover to talk to his ambassadors last month. He was there but a day or two before returning north."

Jack had heard rumors that Edward spent much of his time hunting and feasting with members of his immediate circle at Fotheringhay. It appeared there was a lady nearby he was pursuing as well, although he said nothing of this to Margaret. It was his turn to change the subject.

"Would you care to step aboard my new ship, my lady? I am right proud of her, and I think you will approve of her name."

Margaret's eyes lit up. A chance to do something different, she thought. Damn Edward! He must have passed close by here and yet did not stop. She dismissed her uncharitable thought and turned to Jack.

"Aye, Sir John, I would go with you gladly. I have never been on a ship before," she said as she rose to her feet. Jack eased his stocky frame out of his chair and took her hand. He smiled as Fortunata rose from her footstool and attached herself to Margaret like a shadow. "*Et tu, Fortunata*," he said, hoping his Latin was close enough to Italian.

Several attendants followed the trio down the long waiting chamber, past the musicians' gallery that looked over the great hall and down the stairs of the king's tower to the watergate. A chill October wind was blowing, and a man ran past chasing his fashionable high-crowned hat before it fell into the river. Margaret was happy she was wearing her turbaned headdress and not a hennin. She welcomed the fresh air after hours in the stale, overly perfumed rooms inside. A caravel was tied up to the wharf, its streamer showing the cross of St. George fluttering from the main mast. The Howard red and white badge on a standard graced the forecastle. And painted in gold letters on the side of the bow was her name, *Margaret*.

Margaret was delighted and turned to her entourage, pointing and smiling.

"I confess 'twas another Margaret I had in mind, my lady," Jack said. "My mother was Margaret Mowbray, and she dearly loved the sea. 'Twas she who took me to Dunwich when I was but a boy, and I have had a love for ships and sailing ever since."

He hurried on ahead and had some of his crew form the semblance of an honor guard in front of the gangplank. The wind was making waves on the river, and the ship lurched backwards and forwards against the dock, giving Margaret second thoughts about boarding her. Even Fortunata had widened the customary proximity to her mistress; her memories of being at sea were not happy ones. Her servant's timidity and Jack's easy striding onto the wobbling plank convinced Margaret that she must show fortitude, and she took his outstretched hand and walked up the wooden board and onto the ship. Several seamen stood about, staring at her, their hats in their hands, and she favored them with a smile. Jack showed her the cramped cabin that he shared with the ship's master, its porthole set in the stern, and as they walked along the decks, he explained the rigging and how they stowed the cargo and pointed out the small cannon tied fast to the deck. Margaret was fascinated by it all and regaled him with questions.

"I wonder if I will ever sail in such a ship, Sir John," she mused. "The *mal de mer*, by all accounts, is hard to stomach!"

Jack laughed, appreciating her play on words. "Nay, my lady. Some of us never feel it, so perhaps you will be the same. 'Tis possible you will sail to a new home one of these days," he said, and, seeing her frown, thought he had overstepped the bounds of familiarity. "I beg your pardon, 'twas forward of me."

"You are forgiven, sir." Margaret was polite. "Now let us return to dry land."

She thanked him heartily for his pains, but her mood had darkened. She let him bow over her hand and without a word left the dock with the little group processing behind her. Jack Howard was left to wonder if he had truly offended her.

But Margaret was thinking, confound Edward, will he leave me here in Greenwich forever?

THAT WEEK, MARGARET was confined to her chamber with the onset of her monthly courses and whiled away the time reading and teaching Fortunata English. During a quiet moment after dinner, when her ladies were dozing and she lay on her richly decorated bed with half of the velvet curtains drawn, she patted the bed and invited the girl to sit with her. She put her finger to her lips so that the attendants would not be disturbed. Fortunata fetched a stool to climb onto the high bed. For one who was disfigured, Fortunata was exceptionally nimble and her body was as pliant as dough. Her acrobatics had drawn gasps from guests at Margaret's dinner table, and her sturdy little legs could propel her into the air in amazing leaps and tumbles, earning many a groat for her skill.

Hidden behind the heavy drapes, Margaret encouraged Fortunata to continue the fascinating tale of her life. She had learned of the girl's abandonment on the steps of the university at Padua and how a kindly doctor had put the baby in the care of an elderly servant there. The woman and her husband, a stonemason, were childless and had taken her in as their own, even when, upon unswaddling the baby, they saw she was malformed. The doctor had decided the child must be the luckiest little girl in the world and had named her Fortunata. The foster mother, Tomasina, carried the child on her back as she worked until Fortunata was able to walk. The doctors were good to the bright child, and her original mentor exploited the chance to study her growth, keeping her with him during the day as he tutored students and consulted with his colleagues. So it was that as she grew up, Fortunata spent many hours in the presence of some of the greatest minds in all of Europe.

Margaret had listened entranced, envious of the girl's knowledge. It was only then, a few weeks after Fortunata entered her household, that Margaret realized what a treasure she had been given. I will keep her by me always, she thought, for she brings more than good luck to my house. She brings an ancient wisdom.

"Papa Giorgio died." Fortunata picked up her story where she had left off the last time, and Margaret nodded. When Fortunata was nine, he had fallen from the scaffolding of a building he was working on and was killed instantly.

"And Tomasina could not feed both of you, so she asked the good doctor to take you as his servant," Margaret remembered, massaging her tender belly with a smooth, warmed stone.

"*Si, madonna.* The doctor was a good man. I work for him *tre*"—she held up three fingers—"years. Then he died." Her eyes were sad as she crossed herself. "*Benedictus deus. Fiat volutas tua!*"

"Amen," murmured Margaret, also signing.

"I thought my life was finished," Fortunata said dramatically, "and I cried many tears. I knew I must leave *dell'università.* I had no money, I had no home."

"The other doctors would not give you work? No? 'Twas shameful of them. Where did you go? What did you do?" Margaret could not imagine being without a home or wealth. She was horrified. "You poor child."

"*Madonna mia,* I am not a child," Fortunata said indignantly. "I am fifteen—a lady!"

"In truth, I confess I look at you as a child because—" Margaret broke off, knowing her next words would be insensitive. The other ladies had remarked on the fact that Fortunata had not begun her courses yet: another reason to look on the dwarf with suspicion.

"I am only small. I am not a child!" Fortunata retorted. "I am a lady as you. You see," she said, pointing to her small breasts.

Margaret laughed. "You are right, mistress. You are a woman. Pray forgive me. Now, tell me more. More of your story—of your life."

Even in the dim light, the anguish showed in Fortunata's face as she told the next episode. She was cast out on the streets of Padua to fend for herself. A few of the doctors had taken up a collection, and the money had lasted a few weeks, but now she found herself begging in the market-place and sleeping under the archways of the Palazzo della Ragione with other vagrants. In her broken English, she told Margaret how she learned to pick pockets as a thief's assistant. Her eyes clouded, and she whispered a prayer of supplication to the Virgin for her sins. "I must eat, *madonna*," she said, "so I stole food."

Margaret nodded and gazed with a mixture of awe and sadness at the dejected figure in front of her. "God will understand, Fortunata. You had to eat."

"But I learn much, *Madonna* Margherita. Many people have bad troubles with *corpo*—you know, body—like me, but worse. One lady had only one eye, one man no leg, one other man a big head like this." Her ever-moving hands illustrated its size. "Many people *pazzo*," she put her finger to her temple and twisted it back and forth indicating madness. "I was not so strange. I learn and it make me strong. I am not stupid, I am *furbo*—how do you say—clever."

"Aye, Fortunata, you are clever, for you have bewitched your mistress, 'tis certain." Margaret smiled at Fortunata's puzzled look and cocked head. "'Tis of no import, I promise. You must be clever to end up in a palace after living among thieves and vagabonds."

Now Fortunata was completely lost. "*Perdone me, madonna*. I do not understand."

Margaret patted her hand and gently stroked her cheek. "Certes, what a wretched life you have had! Tell me, how did you happen to be on Captain Outlaw's ship?"

The absentminded caress astonished Fortunata, who had forgotten what it was like to be touched by a loving hand since Tomasina died. She took Margaret's hand and kissed it, a tear splashing on to it. Margaret was touched but gently withdrew her fingers from the girl's grasp.

"Captain Outlaw?" she insisted.

"*Si*, the captain." Fortunata brushed away her tears and sat erect again. "One day there was a *festa* in *piazza, carnevale . . .*"

"Ah, carnival, you mean?" Margaret asked. Fortunata nodded eagerly.

"*Si*, it is correct. I went to see." Fortunata tried to tell Margaret about the clowns, the theatrical depictions of biblical scenes, the food and gewgaws for sale, and the number of dropped coins she was able to scrounge, but it was all a babble to Margaret, mostly in Italian. She laughed at Fortunata's excitement and waving hands.

"I understand, 'twas a fair, just as we have in many towns here in England. But what has it to do with you?"

"A man was making magic and I went to see. He made a ball go away under a cup," she said. "I stayed many hours. But I am so small, he did not see me watching. I saw what he did."

"Is that how you learned your tricks? By watching him and others at the street fairs?" Margaret asked.

Fortunata nodded. "One day an Englishman comes. His name is Giovanni . . . John . . . Hawkins. He see me watching. He made me go to the table and he take a *denari* from my ear. Then he asked me to choose a ball under the cups. I choose the correct ball, and he was not happy!" She illustrated his anger by shaking her fist and glaring at Margaret, who chuckled.

After people had wandered away, John Hawkins saw Fortunata begging nearby and noticed several stopped to give her a coin, pointing back at him and laughing. She was obviously a crowd-pleaser, he explained to her later, after he had offered her the chance to travel with him in the circus and learn to be his assistant.

"I was so happy—I am *fortunata!*" she said, but her face did not register happiness. "He was not a good man. Not good to me. He beat me many times."

"Beat you. Why? Did you steal from him? Or were you lazy?" Margaret was curious but not shocked. Servants at the palace were regularly beaten for indolence or insolence.

"*Non, madonna*. He liked to drink—plenty. All the money pay for drink every time. When he drank, he beat me. Then he laughed when I cried. He was cruel. I helped with . . . how you do say, treeks?" She cocked her head to see if Margaret understood.

"Tricks, aye." Margaret nodded.

Fortunata also learned tumbling from another performer in the traveling circus. Her deformity, acrobatics and magic skills brought Hawkins larger and larger audiences, and he raked in the money. He made her cook, wash their clothes, take care of the two donkeys and fetch and carry for him.

"I ate, *si*, and I rode the ass, *si*, but he did not give me any money. I had nothing."

"More of a slave than an assistant, 'tis true," Margaret agreed, "but Master Hawkins taught you English, and that is worth much. He should not have beaten you if you did not deserve it, but he rescued you from the gutter, Fortunata. And now you are here. God be thanked for Master Hawkins!"

Fortunata understood most of Margaret's words, but she shook her head violently at the end. "*Che sciocco!*" she spat, balling her fists and assuming her mistress would not understand the obscenity but not caring if she did. "Do not thank Hawkins. He *sold* me! He is a bad man. Sorry for the bad word, *madonna*," she said sheepishly.

As the vulgarity meant nothing to her, Margaret laughed. "In truth, I believe John Hawkins was relieved to have lost you. You have quite a temper, Mistress Frown-face!"

A few days later, as Margaret was attempting a new tune on the recorder, there was a knock at the door, and one of the gentlewomen rose from her stool and padded across the floor to open it. A squire stood on the threshold and announced, "My master, Lord Scales, is recently arrived, madam. He craves pardon of the Lady Margaret for disturbing her but wonders if he might have an audience at her convenience. My master is traveling to his estate in Kent and is here on the king's business."

"Anthony, here!" Margaret gulped, making Fortunata curious. Then more loudly she called, "Tell your master I will be with him anon."

The man bowed and left the room. As soon as the door closed,

Margaret jumped up and sent Ann to fetch her favorite dove-gray silk gown. Jane set to brushing through the waves of waist-long fair hair as Margaret sat on a cushioned stool and chose earbobs, rings and a necklace from a mother-of-pearl-inlaid box offered her by another lady-in-waiting. Jane finished braiding Margaret's hair and tucked it under a cap while Fortunata readied an elaborate butterfly hennin to place over it. There were shoes to match the gown, their points peeking out from beneath the vair-fur hem. Jane touched her mistress's cheeks with a rouge made from dried berry skins and used her wooden tweezers to pluck away a few regrown eyebrow hairs. Plucked foreheads and a minimum of eyebrow was the look all high-born ladies aspired to, Margaret had told Fortunata one day, who was now watching Margaret's toilet with a critical eye.

"Certes! We shall have to soften Fortunata's brow, ladies. Then perhaps her frown would not be so fearsome," Margaret said. Jane nodded, Ann smirked and Fortunata unconsciously proved Margaret's case with a scowl. "But now, are we finished? And am I presentable to meet Lord Scales?"

The women stood back and smiled their approval.

"You are beautiful, *madonna. Non, non! Bellisima!*" Fortunata exclaimed, clapping her hands and turning an exuberant somersault. Ann clucked her disapproval as all glimpsed skin under the flurry of petticoats, but the dwarf was so fast that no one could swear to what they actually saw. Margaret admired herself in the silver mirror one last time before beckoning Fortunata and Jane to accompany her. Ann was crushed to be left out, and she glared after the trio, her resentment of Fortunata growing.

Margaret's serene entrance into the king's antechamber by the river belied her sweating palms and racing pulse. *Absolutely nothing has passed between us, so why am I so nervous*, she thought, as she walked towards a smiling Anthony, who bowed low over his shapely outstretched leg and swept off his tall, coned-shaped hat. He wore a short green doublet, its padding and tight waist accentuating his well-proportioned torso, and he came forward to take her hand.

"Well met, Lady Margaret," he said, brushing her fingers with his lips. "I trust I find you well."

Again his touch sent pleasant vibrations through her. She inclined her head and tried to sound nonchalant. "Well enough, my lord." Lowering her voice she added, "And better for seeing you."

Anthony was taken aback. They were not alone, and Margaret was most certainly flirting with him. He was amused and flattered. He took in all of her long, lithe form in a sideways glance as he led her to the heavy oak chairs facing the window. She would have been happy to know the dove-gray gown did not go unnoticed, for his approving look registered acknowledgment of her exquisite taste.

Margaret brought Fortunata forward, and for the first time at Greenwich, the dwarf was accorded nothing more than a nod of the head and a friendly "Good day, mistress" from the newcomer as though she looked like everyone else, and it made Fortunata Anthony's devoted slave. She perched on her customary footstool beside Margaret's chair and surreptitiously observed him. She was curious about a man who had made her mistress catch her breath upon hearing his name.

Surrounded by courtiers, the princess and the baron made polite conversation about the weather and Anthony's journey from Fotheringhay. Soon, some drifted away in search of refreshment or talked among themselves, and Margaret began a more personal discourse about her new favorite work, the tales of the Canterbury pilgrims that Master Geoffrey Chaucer had so eloquently penned. Needless to say, she did not mention the particular passage in the wife of Bath's tale that had surprised her, although she was sorely tempted. There was something about Anthony that made her want to tell him everything, but Cecily's lessons in courtly etiquette forbade her to cross intimate boundaries. Instead she praised Chaucer's poetry and ability to make a character come to life on the page.

" 'Tis a pity more people cannot enjoy his work, my lord. I am told the common folk have not the means to own such a book, and it is lamentable how few can read," Margaret said, regret in her voice. "It takes many weeks to complete one book, I understand, and the scribe must be paid, the parchment purchased and the powders ground for the paints and inks. Why, they even take my favorite lapis stone and grind it up for the brilliant blue that so pleases me. And do not forget the gold leaf and then the leather binding. 'Tis no wonder the ordinary man cannot afford such a treasure!"

"I am inspired by your concern for the common man, Lady Margaret," Anthony answered cynically. He had never given the less fortunate much thought. He was who he was, and they were who they were, and there was not much he could do about it. He looked around the room and called to his squire, who hurried over the marble flagstones to his lord. "Fetch my small saddlebag, Francis. I have something for the lady Margaret from her brother."

Margaret was delighted. "From Ned for me? I thought he had forgotten all about me!"

Anthony smiled. "Nay, lady, you are too modest. When Francis returns, will you not walk with me apace? I will tell you news of him."

Margaret was intrigued. Anthony must have some private information to pass on, she thought. She nodded and then tapped Fortunata on the shoulder.

"Show Lord Scales your magic trick with the cups while we wait, Fortunata. She is a woman of many skills, Sir Anthony, as you will see."

The court gathered closer, always entertained by the dwarf, and a page ran forward with a small table and three cups. They had seen this trick before. Fortunata picked a polished pebble from a pouch at her waist, placed it under one of the downturned cups and told Anthony to watch that cup carefully. Then she moved the cups around slowly and deliberately at first, stopping every now and then to cock her head at Anthony and make sure he was still watching the correct cup. He grinned and pointed to it each time, and she lifted it up to confirm that he was right. Faster and faster her hands moved, and finally she stopped and stood back.

"*E ora?* Now, my lord?" she asked, smiling and spreading her hands. "Where is the stone?"

Anthony leaned forward and confidently upturned the cup. His face was a picture of astonishment when he saw the empty space on the table. The company clapped and laughed at his expense, and his expression registered chagrin. Fortunata stood by proudly, her hands on her hips.

"But I was certain!" Anthony cried. "I never took my eyes from it. Ah, perhaps you did not even put one underneath a cup, mistress," he added with a sly smile. "Perhaps I have guessed your trick."

"Ha!" exulted Margaret. "You are wrong, my lord. Fortunata, show him the stone."

"Here!" her servant replied, and lifted the correct cup to reveal the pebble.

Anthony made her perform the trick all over again, quite certain he would not err this time. But he did—and took it in good sport. Margaret sat back and quietly observed him, noticing for the first time that his left ear was disfigured. A battle scar, she assumed, and it reminded her that he was more than a courteous and literate gentleman: He had killed and maimed others. She shivered and hoped she would never have to see that side of him. But now Anthony the courtier was turning to her, and the soldier had disappeared. He offered her his arm, and she rose and laid her fingers on it. A different shiver ran through both of their bodies simultaneously, and both looked down at her hand as though it had magical powers. Their eyes met in an instance of recognition, and Margaret could not control her blush. Sweet Virgin, let no one notice, she panicked.

If anyone had, it was not apparent, for Fortunata had chosen the moment to turn several cartwheels and leaps, drawing all eyes off the couple. Her black eyes had seen her mistress's blush begin, and she had taken immediate action. By the time Margaret and Anthony had processed to the door, she was waiting there, making her courtesy. Anthony raised her up, reached into his saddlebag and pressed a half-angel into her palm. Fortunata's eyes nearly popped out of her head when she saw the gold coin.

"Thank you, milord," she stammered and followed them out into the late September afternoon.

As they walked, Anthony glanced back at Margaret's faithful shadow from time to time and lowered his voice to ask about Fortunata. Margaret told him the short version of the tale; she was far more interested in what he had to say about Edward. She eyed the finely tooled saddlebag he was swinging with his free hand as he strolled through the gardens with her and resisted the urge to ask what was in it. Jane and Ann, who had joined them, followed a few lengths behind with Francis and another member of Anthony's small retinue. Oh, to be alone, Margaret thought resentfully.

She purposely steered him away from the archway that led into the setting of her tryst with John Harper and instead passed through the gateway under her own apartments into the seclusion of the orchard behind. A grass-covered excedra had been built near the recently harvested fruit trees, and Anthony and Margaret sat down on it with their backs to the palace. Their retainers kept a discreet distance, amusing themselves by picking up dropped apples. Margaret uncharacteristically sent Fortunata to join them and was rewarded by a lowered brow and downturned mouth. But Margaret was firm and shooed her away.

"May I see what Ned sent for me, my lord?" Margaret asked, when the dwarf was out of earshot. "You have been very secretive about it."

Anthony laughed, and opened the bag. He gave her something well wrapped in oiled canvas and a letter. "I hope nothing spilled in the ride here, my lady. Nay, I see it is still whole."

Margaret squealed with delight when she revealed an earthenware pot tightly sealed and read the contents written on the cork stopper. "Rose-petal jam! My favorite! How sweet of Ned to remember," she exclaimed, pulling up the small knife that was tied on a long cord to her belt and prying the lid open. She dipped her finger unceremoniously into the jar and licked off the sticky preserve. "Mmm," she extolled. "But I forget myself, Lord Anthony, would you like some?"

Anthony put his finger into the pink jam and then stuck it into his mouth, nodding his approval. They looked at each other like mischievous children and were convulsed with laughter, checking over their shoulders to see if their companions had seen the act. Margaret wiped her finger on the grass, picked up her knife again and broke open Edward's enormous royal seal. Anthony left her alone to read.

"*Right well beloved sister, we greet you.*" Margaret skipped over the rest of Edward's standard opening line.

"I have sent Lord Scales to you with a small token that I hope will be to your taste. I could think of no better messenger to send. He will apprise you of what is keeping me here at Fotheringhay longer than anticipated, and you are to keep your peace on it. I demand your promise on this, Meg. Do not delay Anthony's departure for too long, petite soeur, he is on my business in Kent and then must return with all speed. Enjoy him while you may!"

Certes! He would push me into Anthony's bed, Margaret thought drily. We do not all have the morals of a lecher like you, Ned. She read on.

"You also have my permission to go to the Wardrobe at the time of All Souls. It will be warmer in the winter than at Greenwich. From there I trust you to make

arrangements for Richard to join you. Mother is at Baynard's. I will see you there anon and I shall be calling on you to help me with the entertainment at Yuletide.

Your faithful brother, Edward."

The Royal Wardrobe! It was a few steps from Baynard's and hard by the friary off Carter Lane. She would be in the center of things again and could hardly wait until November to move there. She called to Anthony, who was munching on an apple. He picked up a second and came back to his seat, holding it out to her.

"I trust your brother had good news for you, my lady," he said, knowing full well what Edward had written.

"Oh, do stop calling me my lady. If I may call you Anthony, I would prefer you call me Margaret," she said, teasing. "I know not if the news is good, for Ned has asked you to tell it!"

Anthony's eyes twinkled. "Ah, has he now. Well . . . Margaret. Nay, I must tell you I always think of you as Marguerite. Like the dog-daisy in a summer meadow, you stand tall and independent, your skin as white as a swan's feather, and there is something golden at the heart of you, a generosity of spirit that cannot be denied."

"Flatterer! You do not know me well enough to know whether or not I am generous." Margaret's eyes were on the ground; her head was in the clouds.

"Well enough to see how kind you are to that unfortunate dwarf, who obviously worships you. Well enough to mark how you consider the plight of the poor. And I have heard you visit your sickly servants unheeding of your own health. Nay, I do not flatter you, Marguerite, I speak the truth." As he concluded his compliment, he took her hand in his and raised it to his lips. "Dare I presume that I am fortunate enough to be called your friend?"

"Aye, Anthony. I thank God for your friendship daily," she murmured, letting his hold on her hand linger. "You are always in my prayers. But now," she said, replacing her hand in her lap, "you must tell me what you know. Is Ned well? Is he in danger? I think not, for he would not have sent one of his best soldiers from his side."

She, too, could flatter, she thought happily.

Anthony was serious. "Aye, he is in danger," he said slowly, but grinned when he saw her anxiety. "He is in danger of falling in love with my sister! And Elizabeth is no simpering wench waiting to be bedded, let me tell you. And I fear Edward will not rest—or leave Northampton—until he has lain with her."

Margaret's hand flew to her mouth. "Anthony! Such talk. Did Ned allow you to say this to me?"

Anthony was at once contrite. "I have shocked you, Marguerite. Forgive me, but the king told me you would understand plain speaking."

Margaret removed her hand to show a wide grin. "I am teasing you, sir. But tell me more of your sister. Does she know about Eleanor Butler? The last I saw of Edward he was pursuing her ruthlessly."

"Aye, I believe the lady capitulated," Anthony said. "I was surprised, as she was not shy about rejecting the king's advances for many weeks. In truth, I admired her spirit and her morals greatly. But I fear your brother has a charm that cannot be denied, and eventually he has his own way."

He did not tell Margaret that Elizabeth had informed him of Edward's attempt to bed her at knife point one day. Margaret might truly be shocked by that, he decided. He had been aghast when Edward had laughingly recounted the episode but did not think it prudent to challenge the king as an outraged brother.

"Aye, and the crown on his head may also have something to do with it," Margaret admitted, almost to herself. "And 'twill be so with your sister, you think?"

Anthony shrugged. "I know not, Marguerite. But I will confide in you that my mother hopes Edward will marry Bess."

Now Margaret was dumbfounded. "Marriage! Why, of course he cannot marry her, 'twould be folly!" Again her hand covered her mouth. "I am so sorry, Anthony, I forgot to whom I was speaking. I did not mean to insinuate that your sister . . ."

She looked so miserable that he took her chin in his hand and turned her face to his. "I understand completely, Marguerite. 'Tis indeed folly for a king to marry with a widow of no import. Although," he admitted, "my mother was married to the duke of Bedford before she wed my father. She is the daughter of a count. My grandfather was count of St. Pol in Luxembourg, and my father was knighted by King Henry at the very same time as your father, you know."

Margaret nodded. She knew all about Anthony's parents. The old duke of Bedford had taken seventeen-year-old Jacquetta as his bride and died two years later. The young widow had fallen in love, probably before the duke's death, with Sir Richard Woodville, son of lesser-known gentry of Grafton in Northamptonshire, a soldier in the duke's service. King Henry had returned her dower to her at the time of the duke's death provided that she remarried only with the king's assent. His anger had been great when the beautiful Jacquetta finally confessed that she and her lieutenant—then called the handsomest man in all England—had married in secret. She paid a hefty fine and forfeited some manors to win her Woodville knight. It sounded to Margaret as though history might repeat itself, but at what cost? Edward should look to an alliance with another royal family; he should shore up allies that he sorely needed. I pray he would not be so foolish, she thought.

Instead she said, "I admire your sister's courage in face of such an assault on her virtue. Ned is incorrigible, and I understand your dilemma. But I hope you will steer him right, Anthony. I fear Will Hastings is not a good influence, for I see a look of lust in his eyes also."

Anthony was too diplomatic to agree with her. Will Hastings was Edward's closest adviser—although the earl of Warwick would be surprised to know his position had been usurped—and Anthony would not dare come between them. Margaret was forgetting that Anthony had no reason to push Edward away from Elizabeth; as a man of the times, he would benefit greatly from such a match with his family.

"I must write to Ned and tell him to beware of acting with such reckless abandon," Margaret went on. "I am sure your sister is delightful, and 'tis certain she is beautiful, but if our mother should hear of this, I fear for Ned's safety." She gave a nervous laugh. "You know my mother, Anthony. She would not countenance such a match. Nay, Ned will just have to satisfy himself elsewhere. What happened to the Butler woman?"

"I believe he tired of her once she—" he broke off. This was no subject to be discussing with a lady.

"Once she capitulated. Is that what you were going to say?"

Anthony looked sheepish. "Aye, it is."

Margaret laughed at him. "I do not shock so easily, Anthony. 'Tis the ignorance and folly of folk that shocks me, not their . . . natural inclinations," she finished delicately.

"In truth, the king has much on his mind at present, not the least of which is a possible *détente* with King Louis through—" He stopped when he saw Margaret nodding vigorously.

"Philip of Burgundy," she ended for him. "Sir John Howard explained it all to me not long ago, you see. I am happy to know that the *rapprochement* is almost achieved. Is that the king's business you are on, Anthony?"

"Aye. Some of the negotiators are lodged at my manor in Kent, and I have messages from the king for them. My wife is there to serve their needs in truth, but 'tis better if I am there, too."

He did not notice Margaret flinch at the mention of his wife, for his eye had been drawn to Fortunata, who had boldly climbed into a tree and was trying to pick a rosy red apple that had been missed and was just out of reach.

"Wait, Fortunata, I will get it for you," he called. And before Margaret knew he had left her side, he was also climbing the tree.

"Anthony! Have a care!" she cried. "Those branches do not look sturdy."

Somehow, even with her cumbersome skirts, Fortunata effected an acrobatic exit from her branch by hanging upside down on it and turning a circle in the air before landing on her feet. She stood grinning up at Anthony, who was now regretting his gallantry. He plucked the apple and threw it down to her. Then he reluctantly called to Francis to come and offer his shoulder for a step down. Margaret and the others gathered round him laughing. Once safely on the ground, Anthony gave them a good-natured bow and walked Margaret back to her seat.

"Why do you complain of the boredom at Greenwich, my lady? With Fortunata in tow, there can be never a dull moment."

Margaret looked back fondly at her servant and nodded. "'Tis true, she contents me well. But what more of Ned? Rumor has it he is much taken with our cousin of Somerset, now that he swears allegiance to the white rose. Can we truly be sure of him, Anthony? After all, he is a Beaufort."

Anthony cleared his throat. He was on delicate ground, having effected exactly the same turnabout after Towton. It was obvious that Margaret had forgotten this and now trusted him implicitly. "Aye, the rumor is true," he said. "And nay, we cannot be sure of him."

"Certes! And it was his father who was so . . . close to the queen, wasn't it?" Margaret raised an eyebrow.

Anthony nodded. "You have it right, Marguerite. She was distraught when he died at the first St. Albans. She took young Henry under her wing like a son. 'Tis why I cannot think he is true to Edward. I know him as a hotheaded, violent man steeped in his Lancaster heritage, but I could not convince your brother of it. The king is too trusting, in truth. I fear we have not seen the last of Beaufort, but perhaps I am wrong."

They sat in silence for several minutes, each acutely aware of the other's nearness. He saw her consternation and changed the subject. "The shadows are lengthening. Come, let me see you safely inside." He called out to the others, "Walk on with the ladies, Francis. I shall return Lady Margaret to her apartment in a few minutes."

The small group processed back under the gateway with Fortunata trailing reluctantly behind them while Margaret replaced the stopper in the jam pot and carefully wrapped the oil cloth around it. She was trembling a little. Anthony had commanded they be alone and she was unsure what to expect. She glanced up at the palace windows; surely someone would see them unchaperoned. But Anthony casually picked up his saddlebag and offered to carry the jar and letter back to the palace. Margaret breathed a sigh of relief and walked sedately along the path with him.

Then under the archway, where no prying eyes could see them, he stopped and pulled her to him. All she could see was the shape of his head silhouetted against the opening until the light was obscured as he bent and kissed her waiting lips. Such sweetness she had never dreamed of flooded her whole being. This was not the lustful kiss of a John Harper; Anthony did not touch any intimate part of her but her mouth. Margaret was keenly aware of the difference in her response to this kiss. How she wished her head did not get in the way of her heart so much! Why was she even thinking such thoughts at so precious a moment? She squeezed her eyes shut. Go away, she wanted to tell the chattering brain, and let me savor this fully. Before she could touch his hair with her free hand, Anthony abruptly released her.

"Sweet lady, forgive me. I know not what you must think of me or what came over me," he whispered bitterly. "Dear God, I have a wife to whom I owe all honor! What was I thinking? I pray you, Marguerite, forgive me.

I break all rules of courtesy." Margaret could hear he was truly contrite, although she could not see his expression, for he faced the dark.

She tossed her head to show it meant nothing to her. "Certes, Anthony! I do not need to forgive you, for I gave myself fully. You have done nothing wrong but to give a lonely lady solace for no more than—say—a shake of a lamb's tail!" she said flippantly. "I took it as a kiss of friendship, that is all." She hoped he could not see her expression either, or he would know she was lying. "Now let us hurry after the others. Then you must be on your way to Kent."

She picked up her train and ran into the garden from the darkness, hoping he could not see her tears. The kiss meant nothing to him, she thought miserably, nothing! You addle-pate, Meg, slow down or he will know you care. She forced herself to a walk, used her veil to wipe her face and held her head high.

Puzzled, Anthony stared after her.

6

1464

Anthony had been right about Henry Beaufort, duke of Somerset. He turned traitor that Yuletide season while seemingly safe with Edward's supporters in Wales and bolted to join other Lancastrian lords at Bamburgh Castle, although not before almost being apprehended at Newcastle. Edward spent an uneasy Christmas in York, knowing his enemies were once again threatening north of him.

Margaret, on the other hand, spent Christmas in London. Cecily was at Baynard's Castle, complaining that Fotheringhay was too cold at this time of year, and as Edward had commanded, Margaret and Richard were lodged at the Wardrobe. It was the first time the three younger siblings had not been together for the season.

Not long before they all removed to London, George had burst into Margaret's apartments at Greenwich, waving a letter.

"Meggie, Edward has called for me!" he shouted, causing several of Margaret's ladies to stab themselves with their needles and Jane's recorder to hit an unnaturally high note.

"Sweet Mother of God, George, calm yourself. Lady Ann almost fell off her stool!" Margaret laughed, as Ann grumbled and clutched at her headdress. "Come, sit down beside me and explain."

Margaret made room for him on her padded bench and gave him her attention, again admiring his handsome profile. She briefly wondered whom he would wed, and the thought made her frown. *I should be wed before George! What am I thinking?*

"I am not to spend my time with you and Richard any longer," George said, grinning. "Isn't it wonderful!"

"Why, thank you, brother, for the compliment. I warrant Richard and I will be glad to be rid of you, too," Margaret retorted. But then she smiled; she knew this was what George had been waiting a year to hear. "When must you leave, George, and where will you go?"

"I am to join Ned in York for the winter, beginning at Martinmas, and then I will be at court with him until he finds a use for me. Do you hear? I shall be at court!" He included all the ladies in his statement, and they nodded and smiled at his exuberance. "I am to have new clothes and my own chamberlain. As the king's brother, I will have influence and power! 'Tis what I dreamed, why I prayed nightly to all the saints. They heard my prayer, Meggie, God be praised!" And he rapidly signed himself.

Resentment that these same saints had not heard her own prayer to change her life was stifled by her pleasure at seeing George so happy. She called to the trio of musicians at the far end of the room to play something more lively, pulled George to his feet and swept him a curtsey. "Aye, my lord duke, I would be honored to dance with you," she simpered, pretending to be a smitten young woman. George never missed a chance to show off his prowess in the dance and offered her his hand.

Fortunata clapped her hands in time to the *estampie* as the brother and sister trod the flagstone floor in perfect unison. No one had noticed Richard sidle into the room and stand behind the high-backed chair to watch his siblings, his face blotched from crying and his mouth downturned. He knew that George's leaving would mean their lives would take different paths and that they might never again share the same close companionship.

A DECORATED LITTER carried Margaret from the Wardrobe to visit her mother at Baynard's a few minutes away. It had been a rainy April, and the streets were puddled and thick with muck and mire. Margaret was relieved the litter-bearers were slopping through it, allowing her to keep her shoes and stockings clean and dry.

A few children gaped at the luxurious canopied chair as it was borne down Athelyng Street to the castle gate on Thames Street, and Margaret felt guilty when she noticed the holes and tears in their mud-spattered hose and skirts. Edward was in debt up to his ears, and his people were constantly taxed to fund his attempts to stay on the throne. Insurrections were commonplace, and he was even now on his way north yet again to help put one down that, rumor had it, was instigated by the traitor Somerset. Margaret vaguely wondered if these children had been reduced to stealing, and she was reminded of Fortunata's early life in Padua. She reached into the pouch at her waist and threw them a few pennies she kept there for such occasions. Sadly she watched them scrabbling in the mud for the coins, fighting each other off for the treasure.

"Who is Bona of Savoy, pray?" she asked Cecily, once she was ensconced in her mother's cheery solar overlooking the terraced garden. Cecily had sent for Margaret to bid farewell a few days before the duchess's departure for a summer at Fotheringhay.

"She is naught but King Louis' sister-in-law!" Cecily scoffed. "He first offered his own daughter, but I told Edward 'twas folly to negotiate a marriage with a child. He needs an heir quickly or he will never make the throne secure for our house. But Savoy? In truth, Savoy is naught but a duchy and not worthy of a York prince. If Louis thinks to weaken Edward's friendship with Philip of Burgundy through this alliance, he should think again."

Cecily's blue eyes were hard as she stared out of the window contemplating this unfavorable match. Margaret didn't like her mother at these moments. Her naked ambition and haughty pride lent an ugliness to the beautiful face that made Margaret cringe. She tried to change the subject.

"Cousin Richard is said to be in London, Mother. Jane saw several men-at-arms with the badge of the Ragged Staff in the Chepe the day before yesterday. Do you know his business?"

"Aye, my nephew Warwick has already been here to see me. 'Twas from him I learned of the proposed Savoy match. He sets much stock by it, in truth, but he is more concerned that Edward heeds his advice less and less. Such folly, when we owe the throne to the man. Ned appears bent on thwarting him at every turn. Warwick is here to meet with the French envoys, but I know not if it is concerning the marriage idea. I cannot think he is wanting Ned to make a French alliance—Neville has always been for Burgundy. But 'twould be just like our Ned to gainsay him and do something rash. Foolish boy!" She gazed out of the window.

Sweet Jesu, she thinks of nothing but politics, Margaret said to herself, but smiled and nodded politely. "Something rash, aye," she repeated, picking up an apple from a bowl and polishing it. She glanced over at Cecily before blurting out, "Mother, shall I ever have a bridegroom?" causing Cecily to blink at the non sequitur and turn back.

"Oh, don't be so impatient, Margaret. Of course you will. I daresay it will happen very soon. In the meantime, you should learn to curb that tongue of yours, in truth. I shall speak to your tutor, for you must have learned your boldness at your lessons. Certes, you have not learned it from me! 'Twould not do to speak thus in some foreign court where etiquette is stricter."

"Stricter than here?" groaned Margaret, suppressing her urge to point out her mother's own forthrightness. "Where is it stricter than here?" She took a bite of apple.

"I hear the court at Bruges is run with the Portuguese customs of formality. The duke's wife, Isabella, is a stickler." Cecily did not mention that the duke himself was less strict with his own morals and had had several mistresses. "But don't looked so worried, my child; Philip's son, Charles, already has a wife!"

Margaret blushed. "I will go where I am told, Mother, have no fear. I just hope Edward finds me someone kind. And handsome. And intelligent." She stared off into space, chewing on the piece of apple, and imagined the paragon with whom she would have many sweet children.

"Pah!" Cecily retorted. "There isn't a man in Europe that fits that description. But"—her voice softened—"your father came close. For now, child, apply yourself to your studies and think less about the male of the species. Don't think I have not noticed the way you look at young men. You are as bad as Edward, may God forgive you."

Margaret almost choked on the apple.

· · ·

MARGARET LOVED MAY Day. Despite Cecily's piety and religious fervor, she turned a blind eye to the gaiety of the old pagan holiday. Nurse Anne had told Margaret of the traditions in her native Normandy, and Margaret begged her mother to let Anne take her to the village outside Fotheringhay Castle when she was a child. Cecily had agreed, and Anne had taken her to watch the villagers spend the day dancing and singing around the tall maypole. A beautiful young woman was chosen from among them, crowned with a garland of flowers and conveyed on a flower-laden cart to a makeshift throne set up on the green. There she ruled over the proceedings, smiling and waving, and Margaret had dreamed of being Queen of the May for years afterwards.

This May Day eve, Margaret's restlessness made her reckless. She was free of her mother's presence as Cecily had already left for Fotheringhay. When Fortunata described an Italian May Day custom, Margaret made up her mind.

"The girl who washes her face in . . . the water on grass in the morning, you know?" Fortunata looked from one face to another.

"Water on grass? Rainwater, Fortunata?" Margaret asked.

"*Non, non!* Every day, in the early morning there is water on grass . . ."

"Dew," squeaked Jane. "She means dew."

"*Si,* d'you. If you wash your face in d'you on this day, you may marry the man you love," she declared.

Margaret felt her palms moisten. "Marry the man you love," she repeated under her breath. "Is this true, Fortunata?"

Fortunata nodded her head vigorously. "It is true, *madonna,*" she said, crossing her heart.

Margaret went into action. She told Fortunata, Ann and Jane that they would test Fortunata's tradition and then secretly participate in the day's festivities at Smithfield. Fortunata turned a somersault, Jane giggled and Ann grumbled.

"Certes! We shall be caught, and then what?" Ann said, biting her nails. It was a habit Margaret loathed, and she slapped Ann's hand from her mouth. "I am sorry, madam," she muttered.

Margaret glared at her. "Very well, Mistress Spoil Sport, you do not have to come. You can stay here and sew with the old ladies they have saddled me with. But if you breathe a word to anyone of this, 'tis the dungeon for you! I mean it!" Ann's chagrin was so great that Margaret could not keep a straight face. "By all that is holy, Ann, you cannot believe I was serious."

Margaret went to her silver coffer and took out some coins. She gave them to Ann and said, "You are excused from coming if you do two things. First, you will put it about the house tomorrow that I am unwell and will not see anyone but Fortunata and Jane. Second, you will find a squire you can bribe to accompany us. Do we have an agreement?"

Ann nodded. "Aye, madam. I know just the one." She winked at Jane and left the room.

Fortunata was sent off to find suitable disguises for the three truants and the squire, and Margaret did not want to know how she obtained them.

"I did not steal, *madonna,* I borrowed," she said with a laugh. And borrow she did.

Before dawn, Fortunata woke her mistress, and by the time they were dressed in their new clothes, a gentle knock was heard at the door. Ann crept in followed by Henry, a young squire from Richard's household. He vanished into the garderobe and reappeared in a groom's chemise, hood, and leather jerkin. Using the secret door in Margaret's chamber, the foursome felt their way down a dusty spiral staircase in the dark and out into the garden. The dew had fallen heavily, and while Henry gathered a few flowers, as was the tradition at the dawning of this day, Margaret and Jane knelt down, ceremoniously wetting their hands in the grass and rubbing the soft water on their faces.

"Good," said Fortunata. "You close your eyes, and you will see the man you love."

The two women closed their eyes, and Anthony Woodville's face filled Margaret's mind. She put her hand to her mouth to suppress an exclamation.

"I do not see anyone," Jane said, disappointed. "I know who I shall marry, but I do not love him."

The sky was rosy. Fortunata nodded. "It is better before the sun comes," she said. "It is strong magic. You see a man, *madonna?*" she asked Margaret anxiously.

Margaret crossed herself. "Magic?" she whispered. "Is this sorcery?"

She was suddenly afraid and looked about for the Devil. She thought she saw a shadow under the high wall and whispered to Henry, "Is that a guard? I had not thought about a guard." Henry froze. They all waited, standing like statues. Silence. Margaret had taken Fortunata's hand and was walking forward a few paces, certain she had seen something, when Anthony Woodville stepped out of the darkness.

"Who goes there?" he asked in a low voice.

Margaret gasped and crossed herself. Her May Day vision stood in front of her. What sort of an omen was this? She bent her head, hoping he could not see her face in the faint light. She was momentarily stunned by the coincidence.

Anthony walked towards the group, one hand on his short sword. Before he could accost them, the squire leaped in front of Margaret and reached for his dagger, which, dressed as he was as a groom, he did not have. More embarrassing, he was holding flowers. He quickly hid them behind his back.

Thankfully, Anthony had not recognized Margaret, but knowing Fortunata might give them away, Margaret pulled the dwarf behind her and held her there. Fortunata had the sense not to move or make a sound.

"You are trespassing, sirrah," Anthony said to Henry, just making out the figures of two women behind the young man in the predawn light. "Do you know you are on the grounds of the royal Wardrobe, and the king would have you arrested if he knew you were here?"

Margaret bit her tongue. She knew he would surely recognize her voice if she said anything more, although she dearly wanted to point out that he, too, was trespassing. She bent her head to make herself seem smaller and allowed Henry to answer.

"We be sorry, master, it be my fault. I thought we were in St. Andrew's churchyard." Margaret was impressed. Dickon has a clever squire, she thought. But Henry hadn't finished. He brought out the flowers from behind his back. "My sister and me come to lay these on our mother's grave. 'Twas her special day today."

Margaret heard Jane gasp at this lie, and she sent a prayer heavenward that Henry would be forgiven. The sky was brightening, and she knew that if they were there much longer, Anthony would discover the lie, so she pretended to weep.

"Forgive us, your lordship, we meant no harm," she sobbed in a voice Anthony could never know. "We be on our way to the churchyard and then the maypole at Smithfield and in the dark we lost our way. I beg of you, let us go now."

Anthony grunted an assent. "Get you gone! And close the gate behind you. St. Andrew's is down towards the river."

He watched as the trio, with what looked to be a child, gratefully scurried down the path to the garden door. He then took his own posy of flowers from behind his back and walked through the arch into the main courtyard, hoping for a meeting with Margaret. He heard laughter coming from behind the high garden wall and frowned. He hoped he had not been duped by those peasants, but why would they laugh on their way to put flowers on a grave? But his preoccupation with his own thoughts overtook his instinct to follow them. His journey to London was something of an escape, and he could think of nothing else.

Edward was pursuing Elizabeth still, and he would not take no for an answer. It was flattering, of course, but how honorable his intentions were Anthony could not be sure. His sense of honor railed at Edward bedding his sister for lust, but being newly enfolded in the Yorkist camp, his family could not afford to offend the king. And surely the king would not be interested in a mere Woodville for wife? Anthony had finally confided his anger to his mother, Jacquetta, who had merely smiled and shrugged. "Why should he not wed Bess, Anthony?" was all she would offer. "If he wants her badly enough." Anthony could think of many reasons, the strongest of which was that a king of England needed to make a strong alliance with a foreign power. No, Mother must be daydreaming, he decided. Edward only wants Elizabeth's body. Afraid he might say something to Edward that he would regret, he chose to absent himself from the family and so made an excuse that he had urgent business at The Mote, his manor in Kent, and would catch up with Edward in the north in a few days. On his way to London, he concluded that the one sympathetic ear he could count on was Margaret's and so resolved to pay her his respects on the way to Kent.

He had ridden hard the day before and arrived at the Newgate after curfew. He spent the night in a tavern near the prison and had been unable to sleep for the noise and the smell of the place. Just before dawn, he left his sleeping squires and waited by the gate into the city. Forgetting it was May Day, he was surprised by the number of young people who flocked past him on their way out of London to gather branches and flowers for the holiday. He made his way to the Wardrobe on Carter Lane but surmising he was somewhat early, chose to avoid the guards at the main entrance and, finding the garden door unlocked, slipped in unseen to gather a few gillyflowers for Margaret at the bottom of the garden. He had been so engrossed in his task and contemplating his meeting with Margaret that he did not hear the ivy-covered hidden door open to discharge the would-be revelers from the house. He only knew he was not alone when he had heard the sotto voce question.

He mounted the stone steps to the Wardrobe's weighty door and commanded a sentry to announce him.

Once safely outside the garden gate, Margaret could not contain herself. She was bent double and shaking with mirth. Jane giggled nervously and Henry stood by, grinning. Fortunata had not really understood the exchange in the garden from her hiding place in the thick folds of Margaret's coarse kersey gown. But she saw that her mistress was happy and so she was happy too. She let loose a peal of laughter that Margaret immediately silenced with a hand over her servant's mouth.

"Ssh! We do not want to arouse Lord Anthony's suspicions. Be quiet, Fortunata. And let us away from this place before he changes his mind about us."

Soon they were mingling with hundreds of other excited merrymakers singing and dancing their way towards the Smithfield marketplace, where the permanent maypole stood. Fortunata was used to pushing her way through crowds, and she suggested Margaret take hold of her belt and Jane take hold of Margaret's, so they would not lose each other. Then she barreled in among the young men's brawny legs and the drab linen skirts of the women and pulled Margaret and Jane behind her. Henry kept up as best he could and lent an elbow or a fist to protect Margaret when necessary.

The music of pipes and tabors accompanied the sounds of the throng, and Margaret was more exhilarated than she could ever remember. Soon she found herself swept into a ring of young girls holding onto ribbons from the maypole. The men took the alternate strands facing the women, and the human chain began to wind its way around the tall tree, making a braid of brightly colored ribbons as they wove in and out, up and down. When the knot was formed and the ribbon ran out, each man gave the woman standing in front of him a kiss.

Jane was in front of a giant of a man with a hairy face and merry eyes. He picked her up and swung her round before planting a wet kiss on her button mouth. She found herself set down again and blushing before she had time to object. She turned to express her indignation to Margaret and was astonished to see her mistress, her golden hair sweeping the ground, bent backwards and half hidden under a bold apprentice, who had straddled her and was taking his time with a kiss.

"My lady!" Jane exclaimed, and then clapped her hand over her mouth. Too late, she groaned to herself, for the youth heard her cry of dismay and lifted his handsome face from Margaret's, his eyes wide with surprise.

"Lady?" he asked, looking down at Margaret trapped in his embrace. "Then you shall have two kisses!" And without more ado, he set his lips on Margaret's open mouth before she could say a word. This time she struggled and was beginning to make headway with the lad when a small whirlwind came flying out of nowhere and landed on his back. He promptly let go of Margaret to deal with the flailing fists and sharp heels of the fiend that clung to him like a limpet.

"*Bastardo, figlio di puttana! Basta!*" Fortunata screamed in his ear, forgetting her English. "*Lascia la stare.* Leave her alone!"

The youth's friends ran to help him and succeeded in prying Fortunata from his back, still kicking and shouting Italian obscenities. Seeing the crowd staring curiously and the assaulted youth looking angrily at the dwarf, Margaret stepped forward and took his arm.

"That was thirsty work, by all that is holy," she said in the coarsest tone she could. "Be kind enough to find me a cup of ale. Fortunata, you silly girl, follow me!"

The young man bowed awkwardly, giving her a lopsided grin. "Wiv pleasure, my lady," he said sarcastically. "You bain't really a lady, be you?"

Margaret went off into loud laughter. "Me, a lady. Whatever gave you that idea? My name is Meg. But you can call me Lady Meg!"

She turned and glared at Jane, who hung her head and looked to Henry for sympathy.

"I'll meet you back home, Jane. I'm going for some ale. Henry, tell Mother that Fortunata and I'll be late."

Margaret had the satisfaction of seeing Henry's jaw drop before she stalked off with her new beau. Fortunata trailed behind, shaking her head. Now how was her mistress to find her way back without Henry to escort them? She looked about her, and deciding that fiestas were fiestas wherever you were, she thought Margaret was probably in no more danger among these people than she would have been in Padua on May Day.

BACK IN HER own chamber that night, the damask curtains drawn around her, Margaret gloried in her escapade. She had been among the common people and had been happy to be thought of as one of them for a few hours.

Always curious, she had asked many questions of Tom, her companion, and listened to complaints about life as a dyer in the largest city in England. There was an unpleasant odor of piss about him, not surprising from his trade. She had wrinkled her nose when he told her, "Woad is a delicate dye, Meg, and it needs the strongest piss to make it fast. One of my jobs is to collect the fullers' jars—piss buckets, in truth—on street corners to use on our cloth."

Margaret had affected nonchalance, but inwardly she cringed. She had never had to handle a piss pot or jakes in her life, and at the Wardrobe, she had a privy with a padded seat. She never thought much about how the waste was disposed of, even though she had heard about the gong farmers, who raked the muck from the streets and privies and carted it outside the city walls, but she never dreamed some of it ended up in her clothes. She pulled the damask to her and sniffed it deeply. It smelled of lavender and sage, she was relieved to discover.

As she snuggled down in her feather bed, Jane fast asleep next to her, she dared to think back on her early morning encounter with Anthony. She was certain he had not known her, for which she was grateful. She was convinced he would not have approved of such wanton behavior, and she resolved never to breathe a word of her day to anyone, not even to George. Certes, Jane would gossip with Ann and the other ladies, she knew, but she hoped she could trust them not to allow it to get back to Ned or—heaven help her—Cecily.

Why had Anthony come? She had not thought much about it during the fun-filled morning. She and Fortunata had made their way back to the Wardrobe without incident and let themselves in through the secret door. Jane and Ann were waiting for her in the chamber, and true to her word, Ann had let it be known that Margaret was unwell and did not require her ladies that day.

"My lady, Lord Scales requested an audience early this morning," Ann had told her. "He left these flowers." She indicated the white and pink gillyflowers in a pewter jug on the table next to the bed.

Now Margaret pulled aside the curtain to touch them lovingly. That must have been why he was in the garden, she surmised, and she hugged herself. But it still did not explain his visit. She knew Anthony had been with Edward when the king had left London to go north not four days since. Perhaps he brought her news of George. Could it be that he had come because he longed to see her? She could not guess, and she did not much care. He had come!

The question of most significance was what conclusion should she draw from the vision she had while washing in the dew and seeing that same beloved face in the flesh immediately afterwards. We are destined for each other, she hoped. But he had a wife. That could not be denied. And why would Edward give his royal sister to a nobody in marriage, even if Anthony were free? Her questions turned into prayers to the Virgin, to St. Anthony of Padua, to St. Valentine, the patron saint of lovers, until she finally fell asleep.

" 'TIS WHY you came?" Margaret exclaimed, her face a picture of dismay. She had still hoped when she saw him that he had come because of her. Her heart had leapt when he was announced, but when he was admitted to her presence, he was all business, and the kiss at Greenwich seemingly a figment of her imagination. "To tell me that Edward is wooing Elizabeth? You told me this at Greenwich. I am sorry for you that he still has his eye on your sister, and I know he is reprehensible when it comes to his lusty conquests, but I do not think I can deter him. Is that what you were thinking?" she asked, her laugh sounding bitter.

"What I did not tell you, Marguerite, is that my mother is determined your brother will marry Bess. And for all I know, 'tis done already," Anthony said quietly, twirling the silver stem of his goblet between his strong fingers. He glanced over his shoulder again to make sure no one was within earshot. "I do not think you know my mother, madam, but she is perhaps more ambitious than your own—nay, I mean that in a good way," he assured her as she turned to frown at him. "That our mothers have their children's best interests at heart is all I am saying."

Margaret nodded her acknowledgment of this truth. Her mind was reeling. Edward marry the beautiful widow, eldest child of Jacquetta and her handsome knight, Richard Woodville? It was unthinkable!

"I cannot believe he would do this, Anthony. When you left Grafton—two days ago, you say—your mother and Elizabeth were only talking of the possibility of marriage. You are certain a contract had not been made?"

Anthony shook his head. " 'Tis true, I was only visiting on estate business for a few days and was supposed to join Edward on his way to Northumberland. Somerset is gaining ground with the other Lancastrian lords, and the king must halt them," he explained as an aside. "I do not know why I felt I must come to you, Marguerite, but I fear that if Edward's council—Warwick in particular—was made aware of Edward's desire, my family will be ridiculed in the end. I hoped you might see a way out of this, that you might deter him."

Margaret was disappointed. She wanted to hear that he had come to her because of his feelings for her. Now she knew it was only because of her influence with Ned. She was peeved. "Why would you not rejoice in the marriage? You will have so much more influence at court. Your family would be elevated to the highest level in the land." Despite her burgeoning feelings for him, she was wary. She was well versed in the ways of ambitious men. She had been surrounded by them her whole life.

Anthony was taken aback by her sharp rebuke and mistook it for a question about his motives. He thought carefully before he spoke. "I do not believe Edward will marry Elizabeth, but if she does not capitulate, I fear it will not go well for us. Certes, if he married her, I would be foolish not to rejoice for my family." He walked to the window and stared out on the knot garden below. "In truth, I would like to believe you know I do not seek power and glory. I am content the way I am. His grace, the king, has shown me a friendship I never dared to hope for, and my father is on his council. My mother and my siblings have more than enough ambition for the family. I want to serve my king, read my books, write my poetry and occasionally show off my jousting skills." He paused, looking round to see if she was accepting this. "Certes, a good joust has not been seen in London these many moons. Edward has been away from the city more than he has been here in the past six months. And most of that time, it appears, he has spent wooing my sister!"

"Hush, Anthony, someone may hear," Margaret admonished him, putting her finger to her lips. It was her turn to pause. She wanted to believe him and had watched him closely during his speech. She saw no signs of dissembling and so decided she would trust him. After all, he was the only one with anything to lose if he were lying. "Let us imagine that Ned has come to his senses. Besides, Mother told me there are negotiations with Louis for a match with his sister-in-law, Bona. My lord of Warwick was meeting with emissaries here in London not a fortnight ago. He, too, has gone north, so we know nothing of the outcome of the negotiations. But I cannot think Edward would offend the king of France or Warwick by marrying Elizabeth. If Mother ever found out . . ." She shook her wrist and clucked her tongue.

"I expect you are right." Anthony nodded, somewhat mollified by her friendlier attitude. He took a chance. "To change the subject, may I say that you look the picture of health today. 'Twould seem the indisposition of yesterday was quickly healed."

Margaret had the grace to blush. Her spirits lifted. "Aye, thank you. And thank you for the flowers, they cheered me greatly. Shall we walk, Anthony? Look!" she cried, pointing above them where a red-winged kite hung as if suspended in the sky, ready to pounce on some unsuspecting rodent. They watched the bird with admiration as it soared and glided on currents of air until it disappeared behind St. Andrew's church spire.

MARGARET DID NOT see Anthony privately again for many months. Her eighteenth birthday came and went with only Richard to raise a cup and toast it. She missed George, who would have called for dancing to celebrate, unlike Richard, who suggested a game of chess. She indulged him that day and was taken aback when he beat her three times.

"Certes, Dickon, is this all you do to while away your time here? Play chess with your gentlemen? I have seen you in the courtyard tilting and learning swordplay. What else do you do?" she asked him, as they settled back into their cushions while servants ran in and out preparing a private supper for the two of them. It had poured with rain all day, and Margaret had ordered that the windows of the solar covered with heavy tapestries to keep out the damp. She even had a fire made up, and after Mass, she and her ladies spent the day reading to each other, playing music and trying new dance steps.

"No work today, ladies," Margaret had said as she sat on the edge of her bed that morning ready to be dressed. "Put away your needlework, your spinning wheels and looms, let us keep our hands idle but our minds busy. It is my special day, and I would have you each read a favorite passage to me. Fortunata, you will show us some of your tricks, and this time we *shall* win the three-cup game."

And thus they had forgotten the dreary day outside and Margaret had been indulged. She invited Richard to join them later in the afternoon, and the ladies had fussed around him, embarrassing the quiet youth. Margaret observed him as he discussed a piece of prose with Jane. A strong nose and jutting chin dominated his face, which was handsome enough, Margaret decided, although not in an obvious way like George's. She saw a kindness in it, perhaps emanating from the deep-set, slate gray eyes, as his mouth was rather thin and straight. He turned when he felt her studying him.

" 'Tis rude to stare, Meggie," he said, grinning. "What do you look for, pray? I am no dissembler. What you see is who I am."

And much too astute for your fourteen years, my lad, Margaret wanted to say, but instead she said, "I do not see you often enough, Dickon. I was thinking we should remedy that. I am astonished at how you have grown right under my nose. You have always just been my little brother."

"And so I still am, my lady. How would you like to play chess with me? You would only play with George, and how I used to wish you would deign to play with me."

Margaret instantly felt ashamed. She had indeed dismissed Richard so many times during those years together with George.

"Come," she invited, "let us see how you have progressed."

She quickly found out and laughed away her defeats with a great deal of pleasure in Richard's prowess. As she wished him good night, she said in a moment of intuition, "I predict you will go far, Dickon. Farther even than George." He looked puzzled, and she shrugged. "In truth, why I said that, heaven only knows! You are only the third son, after all."

As he left the room, Master Vaughan appeared and beckoned to Fortunata. Margaret looked enquiringly at her steward, who bowed and said that Fortunata was wanted downstairs. Margaret nodded and waved them away.

A few minutes later, Fortunata nonchalantly walked into the chamber where the other ladies were readying Margaret for bed and put her finger to her lips when she caught Margaret's eye. As the curtains were drawn around the big bed, Fortunata tucked something under the pillow and whispered, "It is for you. I will leave the light to read it, *madonna*."

"I give you good night, ladies. May God keep you safe," Margaret called, and her women chorused good night before all except Beatrice, the oldest of her ladies, and Fortunata filed out. She heard the door click shut and Fortunata and Beatrice preparing their truckle beds before she reached under the pillow and pulled out the letter.

> *"I greet you on your birthday, dearest Elaine. I hope you have not forgotten your knight, who pines for you.*
>
> *Lancelot."*

Under the elegant signature, Anthony had translated one of the sayings by the writer Christine de Pisan:

> *"True gentleness can be no other thing*
> *But the place where honor is dwelling."*

Margaret ran her fingertips over the parchment as if to absorb Anthony's essence from it. She put it to her nose and inhaled deeply, hoping to smell something of his scent. Then she kissed it, tucked it under her chemise next to her heart and blew out the candle.

. . .

THREE WEEKS LATER, a dusty rider made his way to Carter Lane and the Wardrobe bearing news of a crushing defeat for the Lancastrian rebels in Northumberland. Margaret and Richard sat together to listen as the messenger from the earl of Warwick spoke.

"My lord's brother, the lord Montagu, was given intelligence that the rebels were encamped in the Tyne valley, much farther south than was comfortable for us. Although the main royal army was still in Leicester, Montagu deliberately chose to attack the rebels at Hexham. I presume, my lord, my lady, you know the duke of Somerset had turned his coat and was now among the rebels." Margaret and Richard nodded. "'Twas his last time to turn his coat, in truth"—his voice rose triumphantly—"for he and four others were executed that very day." He paused as he waited for their reaction.

"Somerset dead?" Margaret exclaimed. "Why, that is the best news for Ned, Dickon. The man was a traitor to his master, Henry, and then was traitor to Edward, who had shown him naught but kindness." She turned back to the messenger. "You say others were executed. Who, pray?"

The man shrugged, "I know not their names, my lady, but two days later, Lord Roos and Lord Hungerford were among five others who met the same fate at Newcastle. The day I left my master at Middleham to bring you the news, as many as seven more were to be chopped." He grinned, dragging his finger gleefully across his throat. Margaret shuddered.

"And Henry, King Henry," Richard asked, bending forward. "Was he captured?"

"Not as far as I know, my lord duke. He was not on the battlefield but nearby, as I heard tell."

"God's nails!" Richard exclaimed, causing Margaret to gasp at his uncharacteristic blasphemy. "We need to capture that madman before the She-Wolf finds him. He will be a danger to Ned until we do. If we have him safe, then she is powerless."

Margaret was surprised by Richard's grasp of the situation. She frowned. "But would it not be better for Ned if Henry had been killed? Then he would not be a threat at all."

"Certes, but Edouard would be, Meg. Do not forget Margaret's cub, Edouard," Richard pronounced the French name with disdain. "I warrant she would be happier to fight for her son's crown than her addle-pated husband's. We are better off with Henry alive and captured than Henry dead with Edouard on the rampage. The son has a stabler banner for Lancastrians to rally around than his father's."

Again Margaret was impressed by Richard's assessment. She nodded and then dismissed the messenger, thanking him for his pains and sending him off with the steward for lodging.

Later, as the brother and sister walked arm in arm over the private bridge from the Wardrobe to the priory next door to give thanks to God for Montagu's victory, Richard stated, "'Tis my belief the rebels are finished once and for all, Meg, provided Ned joins the northern forces and pushes the rest of their broken army back into Scotland."

Edward must have read Richard's mind, for at the end of June came news of the surrender of the final rebel castle at Bamburgh—not to Edward, though, who had remained in York, but again to Montagu—and the beaten Lancastrians slunk back over the Scottish border pursued by the royal army. Brave Montagu was rewarded with the earldom of Northumberland. Pitiful Henry, abandoned by his followers, was left to wander and hide in the northern hills all alone for many months to come.

MARGARET AND RICHARD were chafing at their long sojourn at the dull Wardrobe until one day in early July, when a kitchen boy came running back from the fish market near London Bridge.

"Plague!" he cried as he ran headlong into the head cook. "There be plague, master!"

Margaret and her steward made a quick decision, and within a day of hearing the dreaded word, a letter was on its way north to Edward, requesting permission to remove the household to Greenwich.

"Greenwich," groaned Margaret to Richard. "'Tis so dull there! But safer to be away from the city with plague, in truth."

"I like Greenwich," Richard replied. "I can hunt and fish, and it smells sweeter. But I'd rather be with my brothers in the north."

"Soon enough, Dickon," Margaret replied. "You will be living at Middleham soon enough."

They waited ten days for a response from Edward, and during that time the little kitchen boy died. Several other servants were showing symptoms: the black buboes, sweating, bloody flux and high fever. Fortunata told Margaret that she had recovered from the plague when she was ten, thanks to a less virulent case and the care from her physician mentors. They had assured her that she now had God's grace and might be free of it for the rest of her life. Even so, she managed to convey to her mistress that when *la peste* had revisited Padua, she had remembered how the physicians wrapped their fingers in muslin and tied cloths around their faces when they treated patients, protecting themselves from *la miasma,* as they called the poisonous vapors that came from the plague victims. So she stayed as isolated as she could under the archways of the *palazzo* and had torn off a piece of her skirt to tie about her mouth and nose. She was taking no chances, God's grace or not. She also prayed fervently to St. Sebastian and told Margaret that she was convinced the saint's intervention had much to do with her salvation.

During the next few frightening days at the Wardrobe, Fortunata became a familiar figure in the servants' quarters, her dark eyes peering kindly over her gag and her gloved hands stroking hot heads and feeling for swollen armpits and groins. She knew to quarantine healthy folk from ill, and soon Margaret and her ladies were helping to fill the gaps left by ailing servants. Ann was disgusted that she was expected to dispose of the piss pot shared by the waiting women in Margaret's chamber each day, a job Margaret assigned her when Ann turned up her nose at removing the leftover food from the table.

"Too lowly a task for you, Lady Ann?" Margaret asked, smiling sweetly. "Then we will ask Beatrice to do it. You may take her daily duty, Mistress Nose-in-the-Air!"

"B-b-but Lady Beatrice cleans the . . ."

"Piss pot? Aye, she does, and without complaint. Certes, she will be happy to take your terrible task, my dear Ann. Now, pray, leave me! 'Tis enough that my household is dying before my eyes. I do not have time for milk-livered babies. Go!"

Ann had run from the room in tears, Margaret staring sadly after her. How she missed the stoic Fortunata during these frightening days and nights! It was as though her right hand had been struck from her. Jane tried to take Fortunata's place but she could not read Margaret's moods as Fortunata did. A window had opened when Fortunata had come into Margaret's life. She had recognized an old soul in the dwarf and was immediately drawn to her, especially when she discovered they had something in common. One day, while at her prayers, Margaret had whispered her usual plea that she might wake up dainty and pretty like other girls at court.

"Why do you wish to be small like me, *madonna*," Fortunata had whispered back. "Everybody stares at me, not you. You are beautiful and tall like a queen. I cannot see from a window, I cannot see the faces of people. All I see is their chin and nose above me. I cannot see their eyes. I do not know if they are honest or not."

Margaret had not realized she had spoken out loud, and she turned and looked curiously at her servant. So she does care, she thought. The dwarf had such an air of confidence about her that Margaret had been convinced Fortunata did not mind her odd appearance.

"Aye, I can see where that would be a disadvantage." Margaret still believed her plight was worse, however, and was determined to prove it. "'Tis humiliating when your brother tells you most men would prefer a small, plump creature in their bed than a lanky woman like me," she grumbled.

"No man will ever want me in bed," Fortunata whispered, her dark lashes wet with a few unashamed tears. "I will never have love and I will never bear a child. I know this. So I pray to St. John every night to make me tall like you," she said fervently. "He is the tallest apostle, you know."

"I did not know that, *pochina*," Margaret replied. "Who is the shortest? Certes, perhaps I should petition him." The ridiculousness of this struck them both simultaneously, and both suppressed laughter. In that moment, an unspoken bond was sealed between them.

MARGARET HAD PROTESTED when Fortunata told her she would stay with the sick and not reappear until the plague was over. Margaret had clasped the dwarf to her, begging her to stay, afraid the girl might die with the others, but Fortunata was adamant that she would not attend the sick and Margaret at the same time.

"*Non, madonna.* If I stay away, you will not get sick. It is right," she said, stroking her mistress's hand and fixing Margaret with her huge black eyes that were all anyone could see of her now. "I am going now, and you must stay here."

Margaret picked up her silver coffer and beckoned Fortunata to follow her. They went into a tiny antechamber, where Margaret's private prie-dieu was set up, a purple satin cushion on the wooden kneeler and her precious book of hours open on the shelf. A tiny window gave them some light, as did a dozen candles Margaret kept lit day and night to the memory of her father. She opened the lid of a chest and searched among her jewels until she found the ring she was looking for. The ruby winked in the light of the candles, and the tiny filigree leaves that decorated the rest of the rosy gold shone with a warm glow. Margaret held it out to the servant, who pulled her kerchief from her mouth and gasped, "*Non, madonna* Margherita. This cannot be for me. Is too rich!"

"Too precious for the best servant a woman could ever ask for? No, Fortunata, you deserve it. If something should happen to me, I want to know you will not have to beg on the streets again. Now hang it around your neck on this—under your clothes, you understand," she said and pulled out a long gold chain from the box. "If God blesses us and we come through this safely, and if you are ever in trouble, you have only to send it back to me and I will help you. Do you understand?"

Fortunata searched Margaret's face for any signs of dissembling, and when she was satisfied Margaret was serious, she tentatively took the gift. She sank into a curtsey and kissed the hem of Margaret's gown.

"Thank you, *madonna*. God bless you."

"And now, let us pray to our Lord Jesus Christ and all the saints to keep you safe, to keep us all safe until we may leave this place." Margaret knelt on the cushion and Fortunata on the stone floor, holding their peace in silent prayer.

SEVEN IN MARGARET's household died during the next few days, including one of her older ladies-in-waiting. When the messenger arrived bearing Edward's permission for his two siblings to move to Greenwich, the latest victim of that July plague was being carted from the Wardrobe to be thrown into the communal pit and covered with lime for quick disintegration of the infected flesh.

It took Margaret many hours of planning with her steward to ready the two small households to move to the country. Rather than wind their way through the streets and risk more infection, Margaret sent to Baynard's to ready the barges for the next day's journey. Cartloads of furnishings, coffers and chests rumbled down Athelyng Street to the Yorkist castle on the river, and once Margaret received word the baggage had been loaded onto the boats, she climbed into her litter, drew the curtains around her and was whisked down to the water's edge. Holding her nose against the stench of rotting flesh, she then gratefully stepped into the luxurious barge with twenty of her illness-free retinue. Only Fortunata was missing. Margaret had not seen her masked face gazing glumly from an attic window as the litter was borne away. The faithful servant had turned back sadly to attend to a dying laundry woman.

Margaret's barge led the convoy, Richard following closely, and others piled with the trappings of a royal household on the move bringing up the rear. They could hear the bells of the more than a hundred churches and monasteries in London tolling for departed souls, priests and friars chanting the last rites, the weeping of wives and mothers, and the carters jingling their little bells and calling, "Bring out your dead!"

When they approached London Bridge, the water bucked and chopped as it prepared to shoot through the many arches of the stone structure. Margaret always held her breath at this point, watching as the oarsmen lifted their oars in unison at the command of the captain to keep them safe from the slimy bridge walls and the sturdy man at the rudder steered them expertly into the rapids.

As they were about to pass under the bridge, a body in a crude shroud was tipped from the window of a house directly above them into the river below. The captain bellowed, "Heave to! Heave to!" and shook his fist at the disappearing figures in the window who had thus divested the house of a plague victim. The women cried out in alarm, but the rudderman deftly evaded the missile, and within a few seconds, the party had navigated the dangerous passage and shot through to the other side, leaving the weed-covered walls behind.

Calm water in London's wide Pool was greeted with smiles and a smattering of applause for the crew as the boatmen again took up the chant of "rumbelow, furbelow" to regain their rhythm. Margaret breathed a sigh of relief as the towers and spires of London receded behind her and the watermen expertly avoided the many tall-masted ships and their anchor lines as they pulled for the marshy flats of the Isle of Dogs on the left side of the river and the wooded banks of Greenwich on the other. Her thoughts were all of her faithful dwarf left behind to care for the sick. She had sent a message to Fortunata commanding her to stay until it was safe for her to join the rest of the household.

"I believe you do have God's grace, my little friend," she had written. "I shall see you again anon, have no fear. God stay with you."

But she was by no means certain she would see Fortunata again, and as the boatmen kept up their long, lazy rhythm, Margaret slipped into a melancholic doze.

EVEN THE INVIGORATING air at Greenwich could not seem to bring Margaret out of her lassitude. She spent hours at her prie-dieu surrounded by candles, and her ladies could hear her weeping.

" 'Tis not right to be so devoted to a servant, and a malformed servant at that," Ann remarked to Beatrice one day in early August. They were walking along the river, having left Margaret seated under a huge beech tree, her back against the smooth bark, her book unopened on her lap and her eyes closed. She did not want anyone near her, and for the first time in her service, her ladies feared her tongue. Once comfortable under the tree, she had shooed the women away. It worried her that she had fits of melancholy that she could not control. Often they began with a head-ache, and then a black humor would descend and stay with her for hours. She gazed through the rustling leaves to the flower garden beyond, and self-pity overcame her.

Ann and Beatrice strolled through the stone arch in the garden wall to the quay that ran the length of the palace grounds. A flotilla of ships was slowly making its way past them up the river to London, passing the slower shouts, laden with cargoes of stone, grain and timber. The standard flying on the lead vessel bore the unmistakable Ragged Staff badge of the earl of Warwick. "Coming from Calais," conjectured Beatrice. The women waved, and a few of the soldiers leaning over the gunwales shouted greet-ings. They watched the convoy's progress for a few more minutes before turning back to their path.

"It has been four weeks since we left the city, Ann. It would seem to me Fortunata would have come if she were still alive. The pestilence has run its course, so one of the boatmen told me. Lady Margaret must believe she is dead and so is mourning her friend. You should not be so spiteful, mistress."

Beatrice Metcalfe was a spinster from a knight's family near Raby, where Cecily Neville had grown up. Cecily had offered Beatrice, who was about her own age, the opportunity to leave her father's draughty hall in the dales of Yorkshire to serve the young Margaret. Beatrice kept a motherly eye on her charge, although as an older woman, she was not a confidante. She was grateful for the chance to serve the great York family and kept her own counsel among the much younger ladies-in-waiting. If Margaret did but know it, Beatrice was as devoted to her mistress as Fortunata, but she chose to keep in the background. Cecily received letters from her periodically, keeping Cecily informed of Margaret's comings and goings.

"I doubt my lady would grieve this much for you or me," Ann retorted. "I wish the precious little thing had never come here, in truth!"

"Aye, Ann, you do not need to tell me this, for you wear your heart upon your sleeve. You should beware if you would keep your position. Lady Margaret is as sharp as a needle, and I have no doubt she knows exactly how you feel."

"Pah!" Ann scoffed. "I am to be married shortly and shall soon be gone from this stifling life. I shall have my own household and, God willing, soon hold my own babes." She stopped to look back at the receding ships and put up her hand to shade her eyes. "But look, there is a boat pulling for the pier." She pointed at a small boat with one oarsman ferrying a single passenger making for the palace. "Let us go and see who visits us from London. At least it will be a change of pace."

The two women hurried along the stone walk to the jetty and waited for the boat to pull alongside. Crouched in the middle of the boat, her face gaunt and her coif askew, sat Fortunata.

"Speak of the Devil," muttered Ann under her breath, crossing herself for conjuring him up.

"Fortunata!" cried Beatrice, hurrying forward. "Oh, Fortunata, we thought you were dead."

The dwarf sat up when she heard her name, and her expression brightened when she saw Beatrice.

"Beatrice, Beatrice," she said, almost falling out of the boat in her hurry to exit the hated craft. "I am so happy to see you."

Beatrice embraced the younger woman, who was now a good deal thinner, and called to Ann to come and greet Fortunata. Ann grudgingly gave her a smile and a greeting, but Fortunata was already asking for Margaret.

"Your mistress is under the big tree in the garden." Beatrice pointed back the way she and Ann had come. "Oh, Fortunata, she will be so glad to see you."

Her words were lost to Fortunata, who was running towards the garden.

"*Madonna, Madonna* Margherita! Where are you?" she called as she ran.

"Fortunata?" Margaret jumped to her feet when she heard the familiar voice from the other side of the wall. "Fortunata, is that really you?"

The two women ran into each other's arms between the rose bushes and the hollyhocks, crying and laughing at the same time.

"I thought you were dead, *pochina*," Margaret said, using her new nickname for Fortunata when she found out the Italian word for "tiny bit."

"*Non, madonna, quasi*—but almost." She unwound the scarf from her neck and pointed to where an ugly sore was visible but healing. "I prayed—*tanto*—as you told me, and now I am here, safe with you!"

"Aye, you are lucky, like your name," Margaret said, her black depression lifting. "Come, we must fatten you up again, my small friend. Ah, here are Ann and Beatrice. Do you see, ladies? Fortunata is restored to us."

"We are so glad, are we not, Ann?" Beatrice said, digging her companion in the ribs with her elbow.

"Aye, that we are, my lady. Fortunata, welcome back," Ann said with as much enthusiasm as she could muster.

Fortunata inclined her head in acknowledgment, but as she turned to walk with Margaret, she arched a skeptical brow.

7

1464–1465

$\mathcal{M}$argaret was overjoyed to receive Edward's summons to meet him at Westminster before he journeyed to Reading Abbey for a meeting of Parliament.

"Come with but a few of your attendants, Meg. I have made provision for you to stay at the abbott's house, where I shall also be. The abbey will be filled with members of the parliament, and the town will also need to host a great many. Richard is to remain at Greenwich this time. He will have many chances to take his seat with the peers when he is older."

She had broken the news to Richard, who accepted his fate with his usual calm. Unlike George, he was not one to make a fuss, Margaret thought, watching his expression change from interest in the missive to resignation to the content. "Certes, Ned must have good reason to leave me here," he said, a tinge of disappointment in his voice. "You will have to tell me all when you return, Meggie."

He had been at the wharf to see her off, promising to keep an eye on her other ladies while she was gone. "Gladly." He had grinned at her. "How close an eye?"

"Why, Dickon, you are still but a boy and much too young to flirt yet!" Margaret retorted, but she winked at him as she stepped into the barge. "Farewell, and may God keep you safe."

"And you, Meg," he called, as the boat was pushed away from the dock and the oarsmen began their rhythmic stroke.

She watched the swans glide by and saw a heron rise from the bulrushes on the Essex side of the river as her thoughts returned to Edward's letter. She was intrigued; Ned had been mysterious.

"The reason for this summons will become clear to you when we meet," he wrote, giving her no clue. He ended abruptly with,

"God speed, little sister, until I see you at Westminster on the tenth day of September.

Edward R."

There was only one reason, she decided. He had found her a bridegroom. She had lain awake for two nights imagining who the man could be, and she vacillated between trepidation and curiosity. One moment he was a handsome Englishman with a face not unlike Anthony Woodville's, and the next he was a fearsome foreigner with black eyes, stout frame and stubby legs. Aye, he might free her from the monotony of life in Greenwich and offer her the joys of motherhood, but at what price? She sighed, settled back into her comfortable cushions and fell asleep. Fortunata curled up under Margaret's cloak at her feet and tried to forget she was once again in *un battello molto brutto,* which loosely translated to "beastly boat."

"Well met, well met, my dearly beloved sister," Edward enthused from the steps of the dais as if he had not seen her for years. He came forward to raise her from a deep curtsey and almost tripped in his haste. "By the rood!" he exclaimed with an overly loud laugh. "I shall have the cordwainer's guts for garters, I swear." He pointed to the long points on his blue leather ankle boots. "How I detest this fashion!"

"Then change it, Ned," Margaret retorted as she went into his arms and received two smacking kisses on her cheeks. "'Tis glad I am to see you, too. And in such good spirits."

"Well met," he said again.

"And I you, your grace," Margaret said, smiling at his unusual excitement. "I thought you had forgotten me in my backwater. Dickon and I were plotting some mischief to relieve our boredom when your letter came. 'Twas perfect timing."

Edward gave a shout of exuberant laughter. Margaret was not sure how to react. 'Twas not that amusing, she thought. She was spared the effort when Edward's eye fell on Fortunata, still prostrate on the floor next to Jane.

"Ah, this must be the unfortunate Fortunata," he said, chuckling at his own wit. "Some saint must have been looking after you, mistress, when you were rescued by Jack Howard. Jack!" he bellowed to the group of gentlemen gathered below his throne. Jack turned warily at the king's raised voice. "I commend your charity in charging Margaret with such an unusual gift." He pointed to the dwarf. "You shall be rewarded in Heaven, I have no doubt!"

Jack Howard laughed, relieved, and bowed his thanks. "If I ever get there, my liege!" he exclaimed. The company laughed heartily, and Will Hastings thumped him on the back.

Fortunata had not dared look at the king when he graciously offered his hand to raise her from her knees. Towering above her, he made her feel even smaller than she was, and she stared at the ground, quaking in her shoes. She dared herself to look at his feet and almost uttered an amazed *madre mia!* Why, she could have sailed all the way home to Italy in one of his long, pointed shoes. This amusing fancy made her less afraid, and she gradually lifted her head as he chatted to Margaret and found her eyes only came on a level with—*madre mia!* she thought again—his rather substantial codpiece. Despite her olive complexion, her face reddened.

"Aye, this is Fortunata, and later she will give your Jehan some competition. *Pochina,* show the king how you can tumble," Margaret said, rolling her arms to illustrate. The dwarf ran a few steps and then executed a dazzling assortment of leaps, somersaults and cartwheels, landing deftly in Jack Howard's arms. The company applauded. Edward cheered the loudest of all. Margaret glanced at him, again puzzled.

"Ned, what ails you?" she whispered over the din.

"*Patience, ma petite!*" He grinned sheepishly at her. "Attend me later privately. But now come and sit. Tell me about Dickon."

Margaret sat on a cushioned stool next to him on the dais and sent Jane to see to her wardrobe. She motioned to Fortunata to sit on the floor next to her, and the dwarf settled herself out of sight of the company, hidden by Margaret's sumptuous gown. She had learned to be invisible in the physicians' consulting chambers at the university, and she was quickly forgotten by those who came to talk to her mistress. Out of sight, out of mind, her doctor mentor had told her. "You can learn much, *piccolina* Fortunata." She observed the other members of Edward's retinue, noting the hearty laugh and long, drooping mustache of her savior, Jack Howard; the handsome but aging features of Richard Woodville, Lord Rivers; and the large nose and wandering eye of Edward's chamberlain, Will Hastings. She guessed Will was at least ten years his master's senior, but it was clear the man was devoted to Edward and—judging from the winks Edward shared with Will—was also held in the highest regard by the king.

"Is Anthony here?" Margaret finally had the courage to ask softly after answering Edward's many questions. She watched as he nervously pulled on and off an enormous ring she had not seen before. She thought he wasn't paying attention, so she tried again. "Lord Scales, Ned? Is he here?"

"Aye, Meg, I heard you the first time," he answered. "He is here. You will see him anon, have no fear. But I will warn you, little sister, so is his wife. In fact, it seems his whole family is here."

"To go with you to Reading, Ned? My lords Scales and Rivers must needs be at the council, I see that. Who else? Anthony has many brothers and sisters."

Edward jammed the ring back on his finger and stood suddenly. "You will see. Now I must talk with Hastings and Howard. Your pardon, Meg." And he almost fell down the steps to the floor in his hurry to leave her. "Come to me at supper. I will have Jack accompany you."

Margaret stared after him as he strode down the length of the presence chamber, gathering his councilors in a colorful procession behind him. He had been so distracted, she had not dared ask him the most important question: Whom was she to marry?

JACK HOWARD WAS admitted to Margaret's apartments a few hours later and bowed over her hand, his mustache tickling her fingers. He stood up and again found himself eye to eye with the princess, something he found reassuring. Certainly her intelligence would serve England well when Edward came to find a bridegroom for her, but her height and bearing added a confidence that would be an asset at any foreign prince's court. His frank expression must have told Margaret that she had chosen her wardrobe well, for she smiled and said, "Thank you, Sir John."

His black eyebrows shot up in surprise. "Forgive me, my lady, I was unaware I had spoken. Certes, scarlet is dear to my heart as it is one of the Howard colors! May I say you wear it well."

"Sir John, if you flatter me any more I shall outgrow this monstrous confection," she said with a laugh, pointing up to her butterfly hennin, its starched gauze protruding a foot from her head. Her fingers glittered with rings of every precious stone as she turned and swept the mink-trimmed train of her gown behind her and out of her path. Fortunata kept her distance as the small group wended its way through several antechambers until they reached the king's private rooms. An usher sprang to open the heavy wooden door and announced them in ringing tones.

Edward was conferring with Will Hastings. A number of scrolls were scattered over the table and a tawny greyhound was lying beneath it. The dog eased itself off the floor and tentatively wagged its tail as Jack went forward to bow to the king.

"Ambergris!" squeaked Margaret when she saw the hound, and upon hearing its name, the dog loped over to her, sat down and offered a long, elegant paw.

"See, he remembers!" Margaret exclaimed. "I taught him that, Ned, when we were all at Baynard's. What a sweet dog!" She put her arms about its neck and Ambergris licked her nose.

Behind her, Fortunata drew in her breath. "Holy Mother, you are sure to die, *madonna!*" she whispered, fear in her voice.

"Nay, Fortunata, there is naught poisonous about a dog's wet kiss," Edward said, going to greet Margaret and hearing the dwarf's frightened exclamation. "No more than our own, in truth." Fortunata was already on the floor in an obeisance but allowed herself to look up at Edward this time. "Come, child, let me show you not to be afraid."

Margaret was impressed by Edward's kindness. She watched with delight as he led Ambergris to Fortunata, made the dog lie down and gently placed Fortunata's hand on the dog's soft head. The tail batted the floor happily, and Edward nodded. "Certes, he likes you."

The dog's nonchalance calmed Fortunata, and she smiled as she lightly stroked its head. But then it decided to lick her hand, and she squeaked and backed away again. Everyone laughed, and Ambergris wagged his tail harder. He rose and went to get some more petting from his new friend, and as Fortunata was now backed up against the arras on the wall, she raised her hand in fear. To her amazement, instead of eating her alive, the dog sat down and offered her his paw again.

"That is the signal, *pochina*! See, he obeys you. He is now your friend," Margaret exclaimed. She turned back to talk to Edward as Fortunata cautiously put out her hand to touch the dog.

"God's greeting to you, Will," she said, smiling at Hastings, who bowed over her outstretched hand. "I trust you are taking care of my brother when I am not there to keep him in hand."

Will laughed. "Aye, my lady, we go on well enough without you."

"But now, good sirs, I would spend time alone with my sister. I bid you both a pleasant evening," Edward said and acknowledged their bows as the two men left the room. "Is it safe to talk in front of Fortunata?" he murmured as he led Margaret to a chair. "What I am about to tell you must not leave this room."

Margaret stiffened, her expression full of concern. "Fortunata is my faithful servant, Ned. She knows all my secrets, and I would trust her with my life." She began to doubt the mystery had anything to do with a bridegroom for her.

"Very well. I think I am going to shock you when I tell you the news. But I think it will be more shocking to my councilors, especially my lord of Warwick."

Margaret frowned. "Shocked, Ned? What can be so shocking that you cannot even share it with Will?" And then she knew. "Oh, no!" she cried involuntarily.

Edward was already speaking. "I am married, Meggie. I married Dame Elizabeth Grey—Woodville that was—and I have told no one."

"Oh, no!" she cried again. "Anthony was right! He thought you were contemplating this. How could you, Ned? How could you marry a nobody?"

Edward reacted angrily. He rose, kicked over a stool and slammed his hand on the table, sending scrolls all over the floor. Ambergris retreated hurriedly under the table, taking Fortunata with him.

"How dare you question your king, Lady Margaret?" he barked. " 'Tis not your place, in truth!" He began to pace, controlling his anger and lowering his voice, knowing full well there were curious ears pressed to the door. "You do not know my lady! She is good and kind and . . . I . . . love her," he finished quietly, now looking shamefaced. "Meggie, I am telling you because I thought you would understand. You are like me, I know. And besides"—he sulked, staring out of the window into the darkening sky—"she is not a nobody. Her mother used to be the duchess of Bedford."

Margaret took a deep breath and went to him, gently taking his arm. She turned him to her and looked up into his eyes. "Forgive me, Ned, I should not have spoken thus. 'Tis such a shock, in truth. We—nay, all England—had hopes of a great alliance for you. You will dash many people's hopes and perhaps even make some new enemies. And"—she paused, her eyes widening—"I dread to think how Mother will take this." She finished on a chuckle, which made Edward laugh, too, albeit nervously.

Margaret settled him back in his chair and poured them both some wine. She noticed Fortunata under the table, her arms around the dog, and touched Edward's leg with her shoe, silently pointing to the scene. Edward relaxed and nodded, quaffing his drink in a single swallow.

"Now, tell me how this came about, Ned. I promise I will not chide you further, at least not this evening."

"You are a born diplomat, Meg. I know I can count on you to be silent until the time comes to reveal all, which surely must be soon."

"Aye, how long have you been"—she swallowed hard—"married?"

"Since May Day," Edward said, grinning shamefacedly. "Elizabeth and I married at dawn on May Day at Rivers' home in Grafton Regis, with only her mother and two ladies as witness. Oh, and a whey-faced lad who sang for the priest. Poor Bess, she has not seen much of me since then, I must confess. That is why she is here now."

"Who else knows, Ned? And why not Will? He is your best friend and councilor. Ah," she thought out loud. "Perhaps he would have stopped you. Is that it?"

"Only the elder Woodvilles and Anthony know. I could not tell Will, Meg, because there is bad blood between him and Anthony. I have to confess I am pleased with Scales. He has kept his peace honorably," Edward said.

"Anthony told me—sweet Jesu, now I realize he told me the day after your wedding day—that you might do this, but I thought he had lost his wits." She caught herself. "Oh, sorry, Ned, I said I would not comment again. There are so many questions, the first of which is how will you face our cousin of Warwick? He has been negotiating for an alliance with Bona of Savoy, has he not? Certes, this could ruin your relationship with Louis."

"You know too much, little sister. Aye, Warwick will be angered, but he thinks he can use me like a cat's paw." He frowned. "Edward do this, Edward do that—God's bones, but I am sick of his high-handed way with me! I care not what he thinks. I am the king, and he is not."

"Have a care, Ned. He is a powerful man. You do not want him as your enemy. In truth, this will challenge his reputation in France, and he will not take this news quietly." She sighed and shook her head. Seeing him despondent, she changed the subject. "But what of Elizabeth? Shall I like her as well as I like her brother? And her family, I hear it is large."

"You will love Bess as soon as you see her, and, aye, Rivers and Jacquetta have enjoyed each other enough to have fifteen children, although two died as babes. In truth, they are more like lovers than husband and wife. Like mother, like daughter, I say! Bess and I—" He broke off, his hooded eyes unable to hide his desire, and a small secret smile played around his mouth. "But I talk too much. Pour me some more wine, Meg," he said, holding out his cup. Before Margaret had time to gather her skirts, Fortunata had filled his goblet. "God's nails, the woman must have read my mind," he said, inclining his head in thanks. She bowed and disappeared behind Margaret's chair.

"When will you reveal this information, Ned? In truth, you are compromising Elizabeth, are you not?"

Edward sighed and sipped his wine. "I know, I know, as she reminds me each time I see her. When I get her with child, I must own up, I suppose. But can you keep my secret, Meg?"

"You know I can, Edward. But I will extract a promise as reward. You will not leave me to languish in Greenwich until my dotage, and you will please find me a good English husband! I am getting old, brother, and I dearly want children." She leaned back disconsolately. "And to think I thought your cryptic letter meant you had found *me* a mate, not you!"

"Pshaw! Old? You are but eighteen. I'm sorry I have disappointed you, Meg, and you have my word I will find a husband for you before the year is over. But I doubt he will be English, my dear."

Margaret's heart sank. Her sisters had married Englishmen, why not her? She sat up straight as a thought occurred to her. "Now that you have raised Elizabeth to a royal state, Anthony would be eligible to woo me, would he not?" she asked eagerly.

"You addle-pate. Anthony is married, as you well know. You cannot have him!" Edward chuckled. "And I think Warwick would be doubly displeased with me if I instigated a divorce and married you off to Anthony. Nay, Meggie, we must look higher for you."

"'Tis not fair, Ned!" Margaret pouted. "You may do as you please, but I may not."

"Life is not fair, little sister, have you not learned that by now? As compensation, you can sit back and watch gleefully whenever I am rebuked for my rash May Day act. But now I want to tell you why you are here. The marriage news was but a beginning. I want you to meet her. In a little while, we will be joined by my wife, her mother and father, and so that you feel comfortable, by Anthony. I fear Will will be much offended he is not included, but I cannot risk telling him yet. And though she may also be offended, I must ask Fortunata to leave the room before Elizabeth comes. She will not understand, Meg."

Margaret snapped her fingers, and Fortunata was at her feet in a second.

"Did you hear his grace, *pochina?* You must go back to our apartments and wait for me there. Go now and say nothing to anyone of what you have heard."

Fortunata knew she had no choice and backed as gracefully as she could out of their presence, closing the door behind her.

"Amusing little person, Meggie. She must be a comfort to you." He rose and went to a smaller door at the other end of the chamber and knocked softly. A woman's voice called, "Come," and Edward opened the door. A vision in white taffeta trimmed with ermine stood on the threshold.

Margaret noted the fur before the lady decked out in it. It was reserved for the royal family and nobles, and she knew at once Edward had indeed taken Elizabeth for his queen or Elizabeth would not have dared to wear it. She curtseyed as Elizabeth took Edward's arm but was not willing to give her new sister-in-law more courtesy than was necessary. She rose and went to greet the lovely woman at whom Edward was gazing adoringly. Elizabeth was no coy maiden, Margaret noted. She was a few years older than Edward, and experience emanated from her, forming an invisible wall between her and any who approached her. Despite her royal blood, Margaret was intimidated.

"Bess, this is Margaret, my dearly beloved sister. The two of you will become fast friends in no time, I am certain," he said, eager to please both women.

Elizabeth smiled and Margaret could see at once why Edward had been smitten by the English rose in front of her. She had porcelain skin, high cheekbones, a dainty nose, eyes the color of sky after rain and a cherubic mouth. An unkind person might have pointed out that her ears were too big, but that was the only flaw Margaret could see. She smiled in return and was relieved her first impression may have been wrong.

Elizabeth was surprised by Margaret's height; she found it disconcerting to have to look up to her younger sister-in-law. But she recognized the smile of greeting was genuine and relaxed.

"Elizabeth—your grace," Margaret corrected herself. "God's greeting to you. Ned has been telling me all about you," she lied, mentally crossing herself, and she was glad to see out of the corner of her eye that Edward was guiltily studying the floor.

Elizabeth allowed herself to be embraced and responded, "God's greeting, my lady. For my part, 'tis Anthony who has told me all about you."

Before Margaret could embarrass herself with a blush, a small, dynamic woman bustled into the room, followed by Lord Rivers. This must be Jacquetta, she guessed. Rivers bowed and kissed Margaret's hand as the dowager duchess of Bedford, which was how Jacquetta was styled rather than mere Lady Rivers, made Margaret obeisance.

"Rise, your grace, I pray you," Margaret said. "Come, let us all sit."

Edward took pains to settle Elizabeth into his luxurious chair, while Richard Woodville saw to his wife's comfort. Margaret took care of herself, but not before being able to whisper to her brother, "So you promised me Anthony. Where is he?"

Edward shrugged his shoulders and looked sheepish. When she realized she had been duped, she scowled at him. But her face was all smiles when she turned back to the handsome trio who were now part of her family—they and twelve others.

THE ROYAL BARGE left the pier of the sumptuous palace of Westminster early the next morning and, like a ghost, disappeared into the rising mist, followed by several others. The journey up the Thames to the fork where its tributary, the Kennet, began at Reading took several days. Autumn was in the air, although the September sun was still warm during the afternoon. Margaret loved traveling by water: It was peaceful, smooth and afforded beautiful aspects at every bend.

By midmorning on the first day, the sun had burned off the haze and a dazzling blue sky put the royal party in a spirited mood. The leaves were beginning to lose their summer brilliance and a few were turning brown and gold. Blackbirds, thrushes and warblers sang out from the yellow willow branches that drooped gracefully onto the water, while moorhens and coots chugged upstream. When one of the many barges came too close, the terrified birds scooted towards the shore for safety. As the river narrowed, Margaret recognized the purple water mint, the yellow flower of fleabane (good for loose bowels, she remembered) and the abundant starry-flowered purple loosestrife growing on the banks. Once she saw an otter before it disappeared beneath the dark water; another time a pheasant flew from one side of the river to the other; often, jewel-colored kingfishers flashed from trees to spear unsuspecting fish; and a large herd of fallow deer lifted their heads from the mossy grass as the boats passed by.

"Where is my bow when I need it," shouted Edward, pointing at the deer, who were startled by his cry and bounded away on fragile legs.

"He is still such a boy, is he not, Lady Margaret," Elizabeth murmured in Margaret's ear, startling her. It was the first time Elizabeth had spoken.

The ladies of the company were in their own barge, which was decked with flowers and ribbons, and Elizabeth sat with Jacquetta, Margaret, Margaret's elder sister the duchess of Suffolk, Lady Hastings and several other ladies of rank. Elizabeth was looked at askance when the party boarded, but Margaret, on Edward's command, told them all airily that she had invited her to travel in their barge because her good friend Lord Scales had asked her particularly to look after his sister. The ladies had accepted the fact graciously. Despite earlier Lancastrian leanings, as one of the noblest ladies in England, Jacquetta had a right to ride with Margaret and her sister, but Elizabeth was another matter. Soon Jacquetta and Lady Hastings, who was sister to the earl of Warwick, were conversing happily, and Elizabeth was forgotten as she sat quietly next to Margaret, her aloofness mistaken by the others for shyness and awe at being with the king's sister.

"I have to take Elizabeth with me to Reading," Ned had told Margaret the night before. "I fear I am to be pressured into accepting Louis' match with the beautiful Bona. If so, I shall have no choice but to present Elizabeth. Having you there too will lend reasonableness to her presence among my retinue. 'Tis known by all that Anthony is a good friend to both of us, and it will not seem unnatural if you accompany Elizabeth as a favor to him. Say you will sit by her, Meggie, for my sake," Edward had pleaded with her, his expression as earnest as a little boy's. "I could command you, but I will not."

"Aye, he is still such a boy," Margaret reiterated in a whisper to Ned's new wife, chuckling. "Sometimes I think *I* am the older one!"

Elizabeth smiled. "He thinks you are the most capable of his family, did you know that, Lady Margaret?"

Margaret's expression made Elizabeth laugh, a high, tinkling sound that wafted over the water and was picked up by Edward's sharp ears. He stood up and waved at them, blowing a kiss their way. She waved back, glancing at Elizabeth, who must surely know the kiss was meant for her, but her lovely face was impassive. In another boat, she could see George, handsome and proud, seated under a canopy, surrounded by his gentlemen and enjoying his newfound importance at court. He had greeted Margaret exuberantly after her audience with Edward the night before, but she could tell he was not aware of the change in Ned's marital status. She smiled inwardly, treasuring the confidence her oldest brother placed in her.

Standing up, she searched the other boats for Fortunata and spotted her huddled in the back of the one behind George's, staring longingly at the shore. She sighed, missing her *pochina*, but Ned had not thought Elizabeth would relish sharing anything she might say to Margaret with the little creature until she was used to Fortunata. Margaret felt a little ashamed that she had not stood up for herself and insisted Fortunata travel in her boat, but Edward was in one of his stubborn moods, and she had no wish to rile him again. However, she had seen the look of disdain on Elizabeth's face when Elizabeth first saw the dwarf on the pier that morning. Margaret felt herself flush slightly with anger at the snub but decided to say nothing until the moment was right, and this was it, she decided.

"My poor servant, Fortunata, is a little green around the gills in the next boat," she said to Elizabeth as she sat down again. "She was violently ill on her voyage from Italy and ever since cannot bear being on the water."

"I am surprised you care so much about a servant, Lady Margaret. Which one is Fortunata?" Elizabeth glanced over at the boat in question.

Margaret bristled. "You may have seen her earlier, Dame Grey," she said, delighting in the use of Elizabeth's former married name, agreed upon so not to arouse suspicion. "She had the misfortune to be born a dwarf, but I have the fortune to have the most devoted and dare I say cleverest servant a person could wish for." Her expression and tone of voice brooked no rejection of her dear *pochina*, and Elizabeth wisely smiled and merely said, "Ah. I did see her."

THE WHARVES AT Reading teemed with people of all ranks: the urchin who ran filthy-footed in and out of the crowd, the rough-and-ready dockers who hauled on the lines thrown to them from the boats, the merchants haggling with ships' masters, the tavern workers rolling tuns of wine and barrels of ale up the hill to the town, and the servants sporting their masters' colors elbowing others aside to help their noble employers out of the arriving barges. But the people scurrying about their important business looked like so many ants beneath Reading Abbey, a mass of Caen limestone and English greystone climbing to a tower pinnacle that seemed to scrape the clouds.

Reading Abbey had been home to a Benedictine order for three centuries, and the town had grown up around it once it became a regular site for important events and Great Council meetings. The abbey church, which was larger than Westminster's, had been consecrated by Thomas à Becket himself and had seen the wedding of Edward III's son John of Gaunt to his first wife, Blanche of Lancaster, beneath its soaring Gothic arches and slate roof. Gardens and cloisters, the community's own mill, a hospitium for pilgrims and other guests as well as the chapter house, refectory and dormitory and the many other red-tiled buildings that housed this secluded order were set on thirty acres within a great stone wall.

All activity on the wharves stopped when a fanfare from a barge of musicians announced the arrival of the king. A column of guards formed a barrier between the king and his subjects as more townspeople came running from their houses to watch the royal procession move past the lime-washed warehouses strung along the shore.

The canopy over Edward, decorated with his Sun in Splendor insignia and the lions of England, was carried by four men as he walked, waving this way and that. His golden-brown hair was encircled by a simple crown, and his purple mantle sat on his broad shoulders magnificently as only it could on a man of his stature. His subjects gawped at him, a few shouting "God save the king," and Margaret felt the familiar lifting of her chest as she took her place and processed through the enormous wooden gates and into the quiet of the abbey grounds beyond. How proud she was of Ned! How natural that he should be king, she thought.

The abbot met the royal party at the gate and escorted them to their guest quarters. Margaret looked around her with interest. She noticed that the monks had servants—townsfolk, who, she was told, toiled in the gardens, cooked and laundered for the order, as well as kept the account books and helped in the infirmary. Hers and Elizabeth's escort, a tall, friendly monk named Brother Damian, told his charges that many of the order were employed in the scriptorium morning, noon and night, copying manuscripts, and that this work was of such importance that they had no time to spend on the running of the abbey. He promised to show Margaret some of the completed work, but as this was a silent order, the monks at their desks were not allowed to talk, and so visitors were discouraged. Margaret looked so disappointed that he offered to get her special permission from the abbot if he could.

"My thanks, Brother Damian," she cried. "I should like to see the work above anything." She pulled out her book of hours from the bag she always carried at her waist. "I have a passion for books, you see."

Elizabeth looked on, amused, as the brother bowed, showing his shiny tonsure, and left them in their comfortable quarters. "I hope you will show as much passion for whomever Edward chooses for you, my dear," she said. "The man will be very fortunate." She looked over Margaret's shoulder, and her eyes lit up as Anthony stepped onto the threshold. "Anthony! There you are. I now know why you find Lady Margaret so interesting. The two of you must bore each other to tears with your talk of books! That poor brother has had to promise to take her to see the scriptorium. She would brook no refusal!"

Margaret spun round when she heard Elizabeth say Anthony's name. She was happy that dusk was settling in and no one could see the blush that she could feel all over her.

"Lord Scales, God's greeting to you, sir," she murmured, putting out her hand for him to kiss. "I had not seen you with so many on the river. I am happy to meet you again."

Anthony went along with her formality, kissed her hand and said that he, too, was glad of the meeting. Then he embraced his sister. He looked at the women quizzically. "Well?" was all he said.

"Aye, brother, Lady Margaret is apprised. I felt certain Mother or Father would have told you of the meeting with her at Westminster the other evening. She and I have become friends, have we not, Margaret?" She kept hold of Anthony's hand and picked up Margaret's. "Let us all three be friends. Edward would like that."

"Why, Elizabeth, Mar—Lady Margaret and I are already friends, and I shall be escorting her to the scriptorium with the good brother, if she will allow." Anthony smiled at one and then the other, and Margaret felt him press her hand slightly. "But first, I must see to my wife, who seems to have lost her baggage. I told her she should not come, for such a journey takes a toll on her, but she insisted." He looked mournfully at Margaret before loosing both their hands and turning to go.

"Eliza is a bore, Anthony. You should have made her stay at home! Now Lady Margaret and I will have to look after her." Looking as though she had a nasty odor under her nose, she said to Margaret, "Wait until you meet her. You will wonder how Anthony spends more than an hour with her."

"How unkind, Bessie," Anthony responded, although without much vehemence. "She is prone to sickness and not particularly interesting, I grant you, but in truth, she is a dutiful wife to me, and you have no right to deride her thus." He murmured his farewells and left, leaving Elizabeth staring after him.

Margaret looked away to hide her dismay. Eliza Scales here? Aye, she knew Anthony was married. She had always known he was married. But it was quite another thing actually to see him with his wife. She walked to the window and fiddled with the casement latch.

"'Tis odd, Margaret—I may call you Margaret, may I not?" the queen asked and knowing Margaret could not refuse, did not wait for a reply. "Anthony has never cared for Eliza, although he is kind to her, more than she deserves, I am bold to say. They have no children, and he often tells me how he envies me my two boys. How he has longed to have a son."

Margaret turned back, determined to show nonchalance. "'Tis odd, Elizabeth"—she matched Elizabeth's disregard for politesse—"but in all our conversations, Lord Scales has never talked to me of his wife. We were always talking of other matters, such as books." And we have kissed, she would love to have told the cool Elizabeth, but instead she changed the subject abruptly. "Where in heaven's name is Fortunata? Jane!" she called out, and her lady-in-waiting hurried in. "Where is Fortunata? I need something for my headache."

MARGARET AND ELIZABETH listened spellbound as Edward recounted what happened at the Great Council. Ned loved telling stories and heaved his six-foot-three-inch frame from his chair to present the unfolding drama to his wife and sister.

"Warwick was already testy when several of my councilors, Anthony included, questioned Louis' real intentions. It seems no one trusts the man"—he thumped his chest—"least of all *me*. Margaret of Anjou's favorite, de Brézé, is still at Louis' side, and I do not want a rift with Burgundy. Our wool trade depends on it. Warwick laughed at everyone and assured us Louis' motives were pure. Ha! That spider weaves such a web, even the tiniest midge could not escape its sticky traces. But his words consoled the others, who decided to add Bona to the discussion, saying they were eager for me to make a great alliance with France. And would I not like to be married?"

Elizabeth chuckled, and Edward smiled his adoration. Margaret cleared her throat loudly. "So what did you say, Ned?"

Edward dragged his eyes from Elizabeth. "Ah, yes, what did I say? I said, 'I will be glad to be married and hope you will be happy with my choice,' and they looked mightily puzzled. 'This sounds as though you have made one,' Will said. And I said, 'Indeed I have. In fact, I am already married.'"

The two women looked at each other and burst out laughing.

"Just like that, Ned?" Margaret spluttered.

"Oh, Edward, you are brazen. Come here, my love, and let me kiss that mischievous mouth," Elizabeth said, beckoning. Edward acquiesced without a moment's hesitation, and Margaret interrupted them impatiently.

"I beg of you, Ned, save your affection for later. I need to know. What did Warwick say?"

"Nothing. He said nothing and nor did anyone else. They stood in silence staring at me like puny clodpoles, so I repeated my statement—politely, certes! 'My lords and trusted councilors, I say again, I am already married.' Warwick finally found his tongue, and he was cool, I'll give him that." Edward grinned as he remembered and struck a pose that might have come from the earl's repertoire. "'Your grace, my liege, I beg of you explain this nonsense. How can you be married without our permission,'" Edward imitated the earl's stentorian baritone well. "I replied, 'Your permission, my lord? Since when has a king needed permission from an earl?'"

"Ned, how could you?" Margaret bemoaned his immaturity. "He is our cousin, and he helped you to the throne."

"He is a power-hungry pest, Margaret. He needs to learn his place!" Edward leveled his angry gaze at her, and she flushed.

Elizabeth patted her hand in the first sisterly gesture she had made. "Edward, do not speak to Margaret thus. She is quite right. You should not make an enemy of Warwick. He could spell trouble for you."

Edward was at once contrite. Margaret was awed to see how Elizabeth calmed him. Perhaps this was not such a bad match after all, she thought. Ned needs a level head by him. Will Hastings was his closest friend and adviser, but he was not always circumspect and seemed to spend much of his time enjoying wine, food and women when the politics of the day were ended. Edward often went along for the ride, George had told her. And

George, trained as she and Richard had been in Cecily's school of morals, did not approve.

"What did my lord of Warwick say then?" Elizabeth asked.

Margaret could imagine the man's fury—everything he had worked for over the past year with the French seemingly in ruins. Louis was even now awaiting word from him, she knew. She shivered for her brother.

"He did not have the chance to respond," Ned said. "Will stepped up and asked me who it was I had wed, and"—he paused and looked contrite—"I have to admit I felt guilty Will had been excluded from our secret, Bess. He is a good man and true. Why did you not allow me to tell him? He looked betrayed."

Margaret was again astonished by Ned's deference. 'Twas Elizabeth Grey who had forbidden the king to tell his closest adviser. Hers was a serious influence indeed. She fleetingly wondered if Jacquetta had bewitched Ned into falling in love with her daughter. After all, Jacquetta was descended from that siren Melusine, half woman, half sea serpent, and more than one rumor had circulated around the court that she was not above sorcery.

"Bah! He will get over it, Edward." Elizabeth dismissed Will Hastings with a wave of her delicate hand. "Go on, my love, tell us what you said next."

Edward's expression changed to one of amusement. "I told them, ' 'Tis true, my friends, I have taken a wife. On May Day, I was married in all solemnity to Dame Elizabeth Grey—Woodville that was. And there is an end to it.' Warwick had the gall to guffaw, and I was chagrined to see several others, including Howard, hiding laughter behind their hands. They did not believe me!"

Elizabeth was appalled. "Why ever not, by the sweet Virgin? Had not their king just told them so?"

How could Edward tell his wife that the greatest men in England had then upbraided him for his foolish choice? He turned away so that she could not see the truth in his eyes.

"Aye, Bess. And so I told them again in no uncertain terms. They believed me then."

Elizabeth jumped up and ran into his arms. "You told them, you told them! You have made me your queen, Edward, and I am so happy."

Edward was unprepared for this show of emotion, and Margaret decided she was redundant, so she curtseyed low and backed out of the room without saying another word. The lovers were oblivious, their lips locked in a kiss that bespoke a lust Margaret had not yet experienced. But the scene and its probable consequence again aroused her. How she longed to have such intimacy!

MARGARET STOOD BACK from the squint in the Treasury wall that gave her full view of the choir of the church, including Edward's throne, and took a deep breath. Then she bent forward again to peer through the holes in the wall, there for visiting ladies to participate in a Mass from which they were excluded. Today it was not a Mass but the meeting of the Great Council from which they were banned. Edward was to announce to the world that he had chosen a queen. The nave was full of nobles, prelates, gentry and county officers from all over the realm who were gathered for the meeting, all dwarfed by the massive stone columns that rose high above them to the glory of God.

Elizabeth had her eyes glued to the other set of holes, and Margaret took her hand to give her courage. Gratefully Elizabeth squeezed her sister-in-law's fingers and held on tightly. She was dressed in sky-blue cloth of silver, a gown Edward had had made for her for such an occasion. Its motifs were intertwined letter Es and the Sun in Splendor, and the train, trimmed with fur, stretching eight feet behind her. Her steeple hennin was two feet high, sewn with freshwater pearls and trimmed with white fur. Around her neck was a collar of enameled white roses, the emblem of the house of York; at the center of each was a precious stone of a different color. Her fingers glittered with gold and gems, and huge pearls hung from her ears. Margaret had to admit that despite her lowly rank, Elizabeth looked every inch a queen. Her downy skin was tinged with excited pink, and her large blue eyes glittered with anticipation of this defining moment in her life.

In the abbey, many topics had been discussed, when at last the French alliance was brought up. Edward's eyes flicked upward to where he knew Elizabeth was watching and sent her a tiny signal. They saw him rise and hold up his hand for silence.

"'Tis time, Margaret," Elizabeth said, with a nervous smile. "I do not think I have ever been so frightened in my life."

"Courage, Elizabeth. How can they fail to accept you? You will dazzle them, believe me!" Margaret picked up Elizabeth's train, and together with Jacquetta they made their way down the stairs to the cloister and through the door to the chapel in the south transept of the church. The noise that greeted them was not for Elizabeth but a reaction to Edward's pronouncement. Once inside the chapel, George and the earl of Warwick each took one of Elizabeth's hands and with Margaret and Jacquetta bearing her train led her forward towards Edward, who received her and turned to the waiting company.

"I would present to you my wife, Elizabeth, now your queen," he said simply. "May God bless Queen Elizabeth."

His subjects managed a weak "God save the Queen" in response, which seemed to satisfy Edward.

Later Margaret was to describe the gaping assembly "like a stewpond of fish waiting for food to be thrown upon the waters."

THE REFECTORY WAS given over to a feast the abbey had not seen the like of since John of Gaunt's marriage almost a century before. Edward and Elizabeth sat in splendor on a hastily expanded dais and were served by none other than the lords Rivers and Scales, Elizabeth's father and brother, in a public gesture of acceptance of all the Woodville clan. Jacquetta, in her scarlet houppelande, refused to be left out and hovered all evening like a mother hen, making sure her daughter wanted for nothing. Margaret sat next to her sister at her table, and watched George across the room, who was deep in conversation with the earl of Warwick. She thought back to a moment earlier in the day when she was on her way to meet Anthony and Brother Damian for a visit to the scriptorium.

George had cornered Margaret as she came out into the sunshine from her guest quarters, her shadow the usual three paces behind her, and asked how long had she been in on the secret. Margaret pleaded innocence, but George took hold of her arm roughly, demanding to know.

"You must have known before the announcement, Meg, or you would not have been at the ready to carry Elizabeth's train. Tell me, when did Ned tell you?" he growled. "He only told me minutes before I led Elizabeth down the aisle. I was the last to know!"

"Why is it of import to you, George? And you are hurting me," Margaret exclaimed, pulling her arm from his grip.

"I'm sorry, Meg." George was contrite but persistent. "Why did Ned not trust *me* with the secret? He told me a few minutes ago that Anthony knew. It seems he trusts his new brother-in-law more than he trusts me, his own brother. What is more, I am next in line to the throne!"

Margaret drew in her breath. Aye, so he is, she thought, not having dwelled on such a possibility until George mentioned it. But what a disastrous king he would make with his petty jealousies and black humors. The favoritism she had shown this handsome young brother may have been misplaced, although 'twas perhaps not his fault, she acknowledged. He had been spoiled by everyone for his charm and good looks. It had given him high-flown ideas about his own importance, and now he was looking at himself as the next king. Ah, now I see why he is angered! Edward has a wife, a beauty whom he obviously adores and who has already shown she is not barren, and a child must result ere long. A boy would displace George in line for the crown. Poor George. She felt sorry for him: The brother of the king could only secretly aspire to the crown while having no true place in the world but by the king's side as a royal duke. Loyalty was not George's strong point, she knew, but she did not wish to hurt the sulky boy in front of her by saying, "Perhaps Ned thought he could not trust you to keep his secret." Her mind flashed back to Greenwich and to young Richard waiting patiently for his turn to enter court life. There is a boy who understands loyalty, she thought.

Then George smiled one of his dazzling, face-changing smiles, and her heart melted, just as it always had when he wanted to please her. "Ah, well, Meg. I should not expect you to explain the mysterious ways of our big brother, should I? 'Twas unfair of me. Do you forgive me?"

Margaret was relieved. "Certes!" she said gaily, saved by one of his mercurial mood changes. "Although I will own up to fears for Edward's rash choice of bride. If it makes you feel any better, just think of the agony of guilt Ned has endured for six months since May Day!"

George grinned. "Aye, in truth. Serves him right for marrying so foolishly. I shall never let my heart rule my head, of that you can be certain—or my prick," he muttered.

"I believe you, George. We have been too well versed in our duty by our mother ever to behave like Ned." Margaret laughed, moving away from him. "But now I am late for my meeting with Brother Damian. Be of good cheer, George. You could have been born a peasant," she called.

She instantly regretted her choice of phrase, for Fortunata was staring accusingly at her. "Forgive me, *pochina*, but he is such a silly boy. I have to talk to him like that. If you want to know a secret, in truth, there are many times I wish I could be a peasant!"

Fortunata shook her head. "*Non, madonna*. You would be a very bad peasant." And they both laughed.

Her thoughts of George were interrupted by the next course, several platters of roasted meats still steaming from the abbey kitchens. Margaret turned to look for Fortunata and was not surprised to find her servant right behind her holding her wand and three cups.

"I think we need a little entertainment, *pochina*. Are you ready to show your skills to these people?"

Fortunata needed no prompting. She loved performing and immediately began turning cartwheels and tumbling around the room in the new jester's regalia Margaret had had made especially for her. The hood ended in two long points that protruded over both ears, each with a bell sewn on the end. The loose tabard was multicolored and belted, with long points hanging down her arms, also sporting bells. She wore this over a white chemise and hose. It was impossible to tell if she was man or woman, but as most of the company had seen the dwarf with Margaret during the abbey visit, they knew her.

Fortunata kept the company laughing and gasping at her tricks, while Margaret retreated into her reverie again. She returned to her walk along the path after leaving George, past the refectory and to the south-east entrance of the cloister. She admired the beautiful covered walkway, with its rounded arches from another time elaborately painted with scenes from the Bible and the decorated cream and brown tiled floor. An immaculately kept lawn gave a pleasing sense of space to the square within the cloister, and she leaned over the coping to admire some gillyflowers planted along the edge of the grass. She could hear the heart-melting sounds of chanting coming from the abbey, and she sighed with pleasure.

"Lord Anthony, *madonna*. He is coming," Fortunata whispered, awed by this sacred place. Margaret turned to watch Anthony and Brother Damian walking silently along the south cloister towards her, past the entrance to the refectory, the hand basins outside and the rows of neatly hung towels.

The monk bowed and gave her a quiet blessing, and both women crossed themselves, Fortunata sinking into a deep curtsey. Anthony took Margaret's hand and kissed it briefly. He bent and whispered, "*Buongiorno,* Fortunata," and smiled when the dwarf's astonished mouth formed "*Grazie,* lord."

The visitors knew that a vow of silence was enforced on the monks who lived at Reading Abbey, except in cases like this, when several of the more senior brothers served as guides. Brother Damian cautioned them against speaking unnecessarily but indicated that a question or two would be permitted. Margaret noticed the north side of the cloister was the only one with windows, and the reason for them became evident when Brother Damian took them into the scriptorium. Both Anthony and Margaret were hypnotized by the astonishing scene. Rows of monks, some standing at their work and others seated at tables, were bent over books, pens and inks carefully placed far enough away so as not to spill the liquid onto the precious pages. Some of the older monks, their soft white hair sprouting around their tonsures, had their noses inches from the pages as they scratched out the words, so bad was their eyesight after decades of copying.

Brother Damian took them to a lectern and invited them with a gesture to look at the book upon it. Margaret gingerly opened the heavy volume to a page of meticulously copied Latin text, the beginning letter of the chapter richly decorated in gold leaf, azure and emerald. Their heads bent together to examine the work, Margaret was distracted by Anthony's closeness. She could see the stitches on his slashed sleeve, smell his perfume—what was it, musk, perhaps?—and feel his leg touching her gown. She forced herself to look at the book and was grateful when Anthony whispered a question to their host and they moved apart. He, too, must have sensed the uncomfortable intimacy, and he did not go too near her again.

Shelf upon shelf of books lined the walls, and Brother Damian told them they had recently added a library elsewhere in the abbey to house others. They were astounded to learn that the abbey had a collection of more than three hundred books, all produced by the monks over the past two hundred years. Margaret was particularly taken with the music that was shown her. She recognized one of her favorite songs, "*Sumer is icumen in*," with its neum notes for voice, and touched the two-hundred-year-old manuscript reverently.

Anthony walked her back to her quarters following the visit, and they talked about what they had witnessed.

"Not long ago, I was told by a visiting ambassador that in Germany a man has devised a way of copying text with woodcuts and a wine press. Have you heard of this, Anthony?" Margaret asked. "Someone must bring the invention here and relieve those poor old brothers. I suspect some must die at their desks, their fingers forever curled around their pens! Did you see their backs? To be so bent in one position for so many hours, sweet Jesu, it must be painful. But the books, the books." She sighed. "Oh, so beautiful, were they not?"

"Aye, they were. And, no, I have not heard of such a device as you describe. Are you certain the ambassador was not dreaming, Marguerite?"

Hearing his pet name for her after all this time again made her heart flutter, and she was about to touch his arm to acknowledge it when he called out, "Eliza, I am here!" to a tiny woman in green and her companion coming along the path from the physic garden.

Eliza Scales hurried to them, a plain, scrawny woman with a pronounced overbite, and when she saw Margaret, she dropped into a low obeisance. Margaret panicked. What does one say to the wife of the man one loves? Someone who clearly has no idea that the woman in front of her wants to claw her eyes out? But Margaret's strict training allowed her graciously to ask Lady Scales to rise and greet her warmly. Anthony kissed his wife's hand, taking her arm and tucking it under his.

Margaret's smile was sickly sweet, and she hated her own hypocrisy. "I am glad to meet you at last, my lady. Anthony has told me much about you," she lied twice in the same breath. "And I am sorry you have not been well enough to travel with him lately. He and I have a passion"—she paused for effect, but the mouse was listening politely with no sign of understanding the innuendo—"for books," she finished, not daring to look at Anthony, whose mouth was twitching with amusement at her audacity.

"Aye, my dear lord does enjoy his books," Lady Scales said, and Margaret thought she heard a hint of sarcasm, "far more than he enjoys his wife, I sometimes think." And she began a false, high-pitched laugh that made Anthony wince. Margaret was embarrassed for him as Eliza continued to laugh until she was overcome by coughing.

"Lady Margaret, the air is too cold for Eliza. I beg you to excuse us while I take her inside. I hope we may resume our discussion soon," Anthony said, his eyes telling her he would far prefer talking with her than accompanying his wife to her chamber.

Margaret inclined her head in the affirmative and wished them both a pleasant day. Lady Scales dropped a hasty curtsey, stared at Fortunata and trotted along obediently beside her husband.

Aye, Elizabeth was right, Eliza Scales is a bore, Margaret thought, as she walked towards the physic garden. A bore with a marriage contract.

THE ROYAL PARTY lingered for several weeks, enjoying the peace and quiet of the abbey and the abbot's fine table and by the time the barges left the Reading wharf in late October, Edward had already promised his bride the betrothal of the first of her many siblings to one of the noble families of England. However, before he approved this marriage of Elizabeth's next sister to Lord Maltravers, the heir of the earl of Arundel, he made sure that Maltravers' uncle, the earl of Warwick, was out of the country. Angering the earl twice in a month was, Margaret told Ned, imprudent to say the least.

"Meggie, you think too much," Ned replied. " 'Tis time you spread your wings and enjoyed life. Anthony is a bad influence. He, too, is always spouting philosophy around me. Where is young Harper? He would give you something else to think about, eh, Meggie." He laughed, but, seeing her serious face, he remembered to add, "I know, I know, I have not forgotten my promise to find you a husband soon, but in the meantime, why not let the harper play your strings?"

"Edward!" Margaret cried, trying hard not to laugh. "You are incorrigible!"

8

1465–1466

*M*argaret did not return to Greenwich from Reading. She moved directly back into the Wardrobe but was often at Elizabeth's side at Westminster Palace or at the queen's town house on Knightridder Street close to the Newgate outside the city wall. The new queen found Margaret's presence reassuring, she told Edward, and gradually Margaret grew to admire her sister-in-law for her dignity and courage in the face of the court's disappointment with Edward's choice. However, no one but Edward ever became the queen's intimate. She was pleasant to her ladies but never betrayed her emotions to them. Her own household was run to a strict moral code, and the curious pondered on her resignation to Edward's immoral one. Margaret saw that her brother adored his wife, and she knew Edward spent many nights in his wife's bed—unusual for most married couples of rank—but she also heard the rumors that other women shared his attentions in his own apartments at Westminster.

Although the royal circle disdained his choice of bride, Edward's decision to wed an Englishwoman of lower rank endeared him to his subjects, who it seemed had adopted an aversion to things foreign since English lands in France were lost to them under Henry's unstable rule. For a time their frustration with the young king's many taxes was buried as they relished the thought of an English queen.

Fortunata, who enjoyed slipping anonymously through the London streets whenever she could, had heard Edward praised for his courage in wedding a mere dame. But there were those who could not resist making fun of him. She was regaling Margaret and her ladies with stories of her exploits one evening after Vespers when she remembered a particular incident.

"One man, *madonna,* who was very drunk, called the queen 'the king's Grey mare.' Many people laughed. What is a 'mare'?"

Some of her ladies giggled, others gasped in horror, and Margaret stifled a chuckle. She could not allow Fortunata or the women to repeat this disparaging remark in the household, as it was certain to get back to Elizabeth somehow. These rumors always did.

"I command all of you to keep the story inside this room, ladies. Fortunata, you do not need to know what the man meant. 'Twas cruel is all you need to understand," she said sternly.

The women nodded and bent their heads over their needlework, hiding their smiles. Beatrice resolved to keep a closer eye on Fortunata's comings and goings. But she was so small and so good at disappearing, it would be a difficult task. Margaret had no such misgivings about her *pochina.* She encouraged Fortunata to tell her what she saw and heard in the streets. How else would one know what is really happening in the realm? And she alone knew Fortunata was able to fend for herself after her squalid life in Padua.

Margaret changed the topic and told her ladies that she had been summoned to accompany the king and queen to Shene for the weeks before the queen's coronation and that they should ready her things for the stay. The buzz of excited conversation took their minds off the unkind remark about Elizabeth, as Margaret hoped it would. Inwardly she fretted over Ned's choices, for following the betrothal of Elizabeth's sister in October, the queen had been the target of more snide remarks when Edward gave her nineteen-year-old brother John Woodville in marriage to the sixty-five-year-old dowager duchess of Norfolk—Warwick's aunt. Edward seemed bent on antagonizing the earl, she worried. The Woodville marriage had also been viewed on the Continent as a slap in the face for the earl, who was working hard for a treaty with Louis of France against Burgundy. Not only did Edward eschew the offer of marriage from Louis, but by marrying a descendant of the counts of St. Pol in Luxembourg, Edward could be perceived as allying himself with Burgundy.

SHENE WAS AS she remembered it, except that now it was early spring and even more enchanting than when she had been there in June four years before. As a child, Margaret loved the season that coincided with her birthday, and she thought God was giving her his special blessing every year with the return of warmer weather. She dubbed April God's golden month, when the fields, hills, woods and streams burst forth in the yellows of buttercups, marsh marigolds, cowslips, broom, daffodils and her favorite spring flower, the primrose. Even the new leaves on the willows, birches, aspens and hazels had a pale yellow tinge to them before the summer sun lent a depth to the green.

England never looks more beautiful than now, she thought, meandering by the river between the palace and the orchard. She hoped she would never have to leave it, though she guessed she probably would. She bent and gathered several buttercups, examining their burnished petals and jagged dark green leaf fronds. She stopped and turned to Fortunata, who she knew would be right behind her, and held one of the blossoms directly under her chin. Fortunata frowned. "*Madonna?*" she questioned.

"I am seeing if you like butter, *pochina*. And I see that you do," Margaret told her.

"What?"

"Not 'what' but 'forgive me' or 'I beg your pardon'," Margaret corrected her. She bent over, gave Fortunata the flower and told her to hold it no more than an inch from under her chin. "Can you see the yellow reflected on my skin?"

"*Si, madonna.* Very yellow!" Fortunata cried, fascinated. "Do you like butter, too?"

Margaret laughed. "Aye, I do."

Fortunata ran back to the other ladies, who were also gathering flowers to tuck in their bodices. She tested each one, much to everyone's amusement, and Margaret watched her fondly. No one could have predicted the friendship that had grown between the tall princess and her dwarf, but with her quick intelligence and ability to read her mistress's every humor, Fortunata was firmly established as Margaret's favorite companion.

"A silver penny for your thoughts, my lady," a familiar voice from her past murmured behind her. She swung round to face John Harper, his yellow-brown eyes smiling into hers. She had forgotten how handsome he was.

"Master Harper, you startled me," she said, smiling back. "God's greeting, sir. I do not remember how long ago it was when . . ." She tailed off, remembering exactly when it was he had given her that moment of ecstasy.

He picked up her hand that still held a buttercup and kissed it. "Ah, my lady, but I do. Would you like to know how many days I have counted since then?" His tone was seductive, and Margaret was tempted to flirt with him. But knowing how many eyes were upon them from her immediate circle to others who might be at the dozens of windows in the palace, she resisted the temptation. Perhaps Anthony was among those observing this little scene, she thought. Besides, she realized somewhat regretfully, she had no desire for John anymore. His desire for her, however, seemed to be as strong as ever.

"Dare I hope I have been as much in your mind as you have in mine, my lady? When I saw you among the queen's party arriving from London, my heart stopped beating." He was still holding her hand, so she gently but firmly disengaged herself from him.

"Master Harper, I am flattered by your declaration, but I was young when we first met, and I must ask your forgiveness that I behaved as I did with you. Please tell me you forgive me, and that this must be an end to our . . ." She didn't quite know what the correct word was.

"*Affaire de coeur,* madam," the crushed young man finished for her. "Ah, lady, then I must leave you with my broken heart." He bowed curtly and strode over the grass to the palace. Margaret sighed. He was indeed appealing, but she knew she was destined for greater things. She hoped she had not been too cruel.

WHEN SHE SAW Anthony dancing with his wife, her thoughts flew back to the meeting in the garden. If she had not rebuffed John and could be flirting with him now, she might have been able to give Anthony cause for jealousy. She was surprised by the resentment she harbored for Eliza Scales. The woman was quite obviously unaware of the magnificent man she had for a husband, for she hardly looked at him during the intricate steps of the *basse danse*. Certes, Margaret knew dance decorum ruled that a woman was not supposed to lift her eyes to her partner's face, but tedium was written all over Eliza's countenance. She was plainly bored with the dance, with her partner and with the whole court. Margaret wondered how she had taken the news that she was to be one of Elizabeth's ladies-in-waiting, an enormous honor for Anthony's wife.

Anthony was constantly by Edward's side these days, much to the chagrin of Will Hastings, who was, however, still the king's right-hand man. Through the years, there had been some bad blood over a land dispute between the Hastings and Woodville families, but Edward seemed oblivious to the hostility and trusted both men implicitly, making them uncomfortable bedfellows among his closest advisers.

Margaret grimaced watching the couple now. How she longed to have Anthony drop his wife's hands, take Eliza to a chair and come and invite her to dance in Eliza's stead. She and George had spent hours with their dancing master at Greenwich and had become accomplished dancers, and she knew she would make Anthony a better partner.

George must have thought about those lessons at precisely the same time, for there he was, exquisitely dressed in a peacock-blue doublet and spotless white hose, to ask for a dance. He tucked the trailing ends of his long sleeves in his belt behind his back and executed a graceful bow. Margaret draped the train of her skirt over her arm, showing off the brilliant blue silk underdress. The minstrels picked up their pace, the recorders, crumhorns, rebecs and tambourines striking up a lively *saltarello*, which allowed the dancers' feet to leave the ground. Even though George was not as tall as Margaret, they were well matched in skill, and all eyes were on them as they made their way nimbly around the hall, her cream satin gown swirling gracefully behind her.

Edward, already in his cups, applauded loudly as they made their bow to each other at the end of the dance. George basked in Edward's admiration and slowly and deliberately led Margaret to the throne, where they both made their obeisance.

"Why don't you ask Bess to dance, George? I think she is every whit as good as Meg here. Go, my love," he said to his wife, "I would see you dance."

Elizabeth rose, curtseyed to Edward and took George's arm. Edward patted her vacant seat. "I have seen your Harper friend here tonight, Meggie. He seems down in the mouth. Why don't you cheer him up?" Edward muttered behind his hand. "'Tis no good pining for Anthony— aye, I have seen you staring lovelorn at him. You need a good romp in the hay with a lusty young man who has no wife!"

"Ned! Will you stop tempting me to risk my maidenhead," Margaret said, also behind her hand. "I am in control of my behavior, which is more than I can say for you. You have been married but a year, and I have seen you make sheep's eyes at several ladies in that time. And the rumors! 'Tis even said you have a bastard, and I cannot doubt it," she tut-tutted teasingly. "How will Elizabeth put up with you? Does she know about Eleanor Butler, for example?"

Margaret was not prepared for the reaction to this name from the past, simply the first name that came into her mind. She saw Edward grip his chair until his knuckles were white, the color of his face when he turned and leveled his furious gaze on her. Had they been alone, she might have expected him to hit her.

"What do you know about Eleanor Butler?" he hissed under his breath, so angry that she was truly afraid of him.

"N-nothing, Ned, I swear. I only . . . Oh, I am so s-sorry . . ." She could not go on for the tears that welled up. She was grateful that they were set apart from the rest of the company so that no one could see her humiliation.

"You swear you know naught of Eleanor?" he said again, a little more gently. "Why did you mention her then?" His blue eyes bored through her, and the fear in them surprised her back to her rational self. Why, he is afraid of the Butler woman, she thought. Why? She had not seen Eleanor at court for more than two years, and everyone surmised Edward had grown tired of her.

"I know naught of her, I swear to you, Ned. Her name sprang into my mind, 'tis all. Did you cast her aside unkindly?" She waited, but Edward was sullenly silent. "Ah, perhaps 'twas she who cast you aside," she said, certain she had hit on the truth. "Is that why you are so angry? Fear not, brother, for I did the same thing today in the garden with Master John Harper." She was cajoling him to let go of his black humor, and when she saw his complexion regain its natural color and his full mouth turn up at the corners, she knew she had succeeded.

"Oh, well, Meggie, more's the pity. The young man might have given you a good deal of pleasure!" Edward chose not to answer her question about Eleanor, and he called to an attendant for more wine. Margaret sat back thankfully, her fear of him abating, and she vowed not to cross him again.

A few days later, when seasonal showers were keeping everyone indoors, Elizabeth summoned Margaret to her privy chamber. Margaret still had difficulty acknowledging Elizabeth's superiority after so many years as the highest-ranked lady at Edward's court after Cecily, who was rarely in attendance there. However, dutifully she hurried to her sister-in-law's side, Fortunata and Beatrice in her wake. Margaret had not been sorry to say good-bye to Ann, whose new husband had begged to be allowed to take his bride to live on his estates a few months previously. Jane was in seclusion with her monthly courses and regretfully relinquished her place to Beatrice.

Margaret found Elizabeth at her most animated when she arrived, curtseyed and sat in the other high-backed chair. Lady Alice Fogge brought her a footstool and was clearly offended when Margaret did not use it but tucked it beside her chair for Fortunata to sit on. Margaret took no notice of Lady Alice's stuck-up nose but gave her a brilliant smile, shaming the woman into a curtsey and a "by your leave, my lady." Elizabeth, too, eyed Fortunata with mild annoyance, but Margaret had to admit the queen had never again questioned the presence of the dwarf since that day on the river. Today, Elizabeth was too keyed up to pay the servant much mind, as she was eager to impart her plan to Margaret.

"I am so glad you are come, Margaret. I have conceived of a delightful *divertissement* that I read about in a book Anthony gave me, a chronicle of chivalric exploits. I have no doubt you have read it from end to end, if what I hear about you is true," she said, her distinctive tinkling laugh lending her a warmth that was not always present. Edward must have

constantly made her laugh during their courtship, Margaret had uncharitably decided early in her acquaintance with Elizabeth. It lit up her face
and transformed her.

Margaret smiled. "Was it perhaps Froissart's *Chronicles,* Elizabeth? And,
yes, I have indeed read them. They are inspiring, don't you think?"

"Aye," Elizabeth dismissed them. "'Twas one exploit that took my fancy,
and I have received permission from Edward to re-create it now," she went
on excitedly. "Pray tell me what you think. It involves my brother and a
flower of sovenance."

TWO DAYS LATER, after High Mass, Anthony answered a command to
visit the apartments of his sister the queen. He arrived and was surprised
to see so many ladies in attendance, including a smiling Margaret, dressed
in a gown that would have put the buttercup's golden glory to shame. He
extended his leg and bowed low in the midst of them, sweeping off his
soft velvet bonnet.

"My sovereign lady," he murmured, kneeling in front of Elizabeth. "I
am your humble servant. How may I serve you?"

"My Lord Scales, we have called you here for a special purpose," Elizabeth said, enigmatically.

Anthony looked up at her quizzically and dared to glance at Margaret despite the presence of his wife on Elizabeth's other side. Margaret continued to smile and on a signal from Elizabeth slowly rose as
another lady stepped forward to present her with a cushion on which
lay an exquisite garter of gold garnished with pearls in the form of a
flower. Before Anthony knew what was happening, Margaret was fas-
tening the garter around his muscular thigh just above the soft cuffs of
his leather boots. At the same time, his wife slipped a piece of parchment tied with gold thread into his hat. They all stood back to see their
handiwork.

Anthony put his hand on his heart and thanked them all for this flower
of sovenance, perfectly understanding that in the paper was the manner
of his emprise, or adventure, and that he must now seek the king's consent to carry it out. He rose, kissed Elizabeth's hand, bowed to Margaret
and took his leave, carrying his hat and parchment with him.

The clucking and twittering broke out as soon as the door shut behind him and the ladies were alone. After enduring the unattractive din for a few moments, Elizabeth stood and held up her hand to silence it.

"Lady Margaret and I have charged Lord Scales to enter the lists in a two-day tournament in London with a knight of equal valor, the emprise being arranged within the year. The jeweled garter will be the prize for the winner. For those of you who may not already know, my brother is a master of the art of jousting, and I could not have a more admirable champion. We can all look forward to this special event." Elizabeth was at her most charming, and Margaret found herself applauding with the rest as the queen sat down.

Margaret did not know that her name would be forever linked to the challenge that was given to Anthony, Lord Scales, that day.

WITH EDWARD'S CONSENT, Anthony sent the Chester Herald to Brussels to offer the challenge—and the garter prize—to another Anthony, called Antoine in his native Burgundy. He was the illegitimate son of Duke Philip and was known to be the duke's favorite son, especially since the duke's falling out with his heir, Charles, count of Charolais. Within the month, the challenge was accepted by the Bastard in front of his senile father the duke and his half brother, Charles, as well as the great lords of Burgundy. After receiving many gifts, Chester Herald arrived back in England a few days before Elizabeth's crowning, returned the garter and gave Edward and Anthony the Bastard's assurance that he would be in England within the year as stipulated in the emprise.

And in yet another overt sign to Warwick that Edward's friendship with Burgundy would not be tested, the king had invited to the coronation a delegation from the Burgundian court that would include Elizabeth's St. Pol kin on her mother's side. The invitation was ostensibly to lend weight to Elizabeth's claim to a distinguished lineage, but when Jacques de Luxembourg arrived at the English court to take part in the celebrations, he also came with an alliance offer from Count Charles. Now reconciled with his doddering father, Charles—sometimes nicknamed the Bold for his exploits on the battlefield—had decided to forsake his former Lancastrian leanings and hoped an alliance with Edward would help him fend off the unwanted attentions of Louis. However, Edward had not tipped his hand one way or the other, and so the earl of Warwick and William Hastings were dispatched to Calais on a commission to see what Edward could gain from both sides at once.

Margaret gleaned all of this from Anthony one early morning at Greenwich the day before Chester Herald's reappearance in England. The situation was so complex that she wished she hadn't asked him for the news, although her quick mind was always eager to understand everything that would keep her brother on the throne. She always wrote diligently to her mother of what she learned, and Cecily's letters to her were full of questions but also praise for her grasp of politics. Her latest showed Margaret that Cecily had her own spies.

> *"You do know, my dear, that Charolais and Francis of Brittany were conspiring to attack Louis at the same time, which would be most inconvenient for the Spider, squeezed as he is between the two duchies. And just when Louis thought he had won both of them over. Why is it that men do not see treachery when it is under their noses? Edward does well not to commit to anyone, but it seems to me our commerce is all tied up with Burgundy's and keeping the trading lines open will bring England more stability and wealth than anything France can offer. I have never liked Louis, Margaret, and more to the point, I do not trust him. I pray the earl, my nephew, will effect an accord with all parties, and we may all live in peace. It is my daily prayer.*
>
> *"In other news, I have not been well these past weeks. A malaise of some kind, but nothing that rest and good Fotheringhay air will not cure, but I fear it will keep me from the coronation. I am not unhappy about that for you know all too well what I think about Edward's foolish marriage."*

Aye, mother, you let us all know quite emphatically how you felt about it, Margaret chuckled to herself.

> *"God keep you well, my child. Your loving mother, Cecily."*

"What do you know about the count of Charolais, Anthony?" Margaret asked, curious about a man who would so oppose his father and who now appeared to have had a change of heart. "He is called *Le Téméraire*—the Bold—is he not?"

Anthony confessed he had never met the man, but from everything he had heard, he was more at home in a tent than in a solar. "His father is known for his penchant for pretty women. Charles has a penchant for war. In truth, I have heard he has only one child, a daughter, Mary, and that his mother, Isabella, holds great sway over him. 'Twas she who helped reconcile father and son. But more I cannot tell you. I have, on the other hand, knowledge that his half brother, the Bastard, is a far gentler, wiser man than Charles. I am proud he has accepted my challenge, and I shall look forward to tilting with him, for he is a worthy opponent."

Margaret turned anxious eyes on him. "I shall be afraid for you, Anthony. But I shall not worry yet, for 'tis a long way off."

Anthony answered by taking her hand, turning it up and kissing her palm. She was thrilled and shocked at once. With her thumb she stroked his cheek, and he lifted his eyes to meet hers in a moment of quiet understanding.

"I would be yours if you asked me," she whispered. "I think I would forsake all for your love, if you were free." She could hardly believe her daring. She could not conceive from what shameless part of her this had been unearthed. She held her breath, expecting him to be shocked. A slight tension in his jaw was all she could discern, but he did not leave and he was not angry. He looked intently at her hand, but he did not drop it. He said simply, "Ah, but I am not free, Marguerite, and 'tis my cross to bear every time I am with you. By the sweet Virgin, if I could—" he stopped, seeing her expression change to one of warning. A movement among the flower beds had caught her eye, and she saw Eliza Scales approaching. She sucked in her breath and quickly removed her hand from his. She and Anthony were virtually unaccompanied, unless one counted Fortunata, who was making a daisy chain at a discreet distance from the bench, and Francis, who was intently studying a pale-blue iris with his back to them.

"Your wife, Anthony," she murmured and rose to take her leave, pretending she had not seen Eliza. In a louder voice she said, "I would be delighted to borrow the book, Lord Scales. I shall send Fortunata to fetch it later this morning. I thank you. Good day."

Before Anthony could rise, bow or kiss her hand, she was gone, Fortunata running behind her to keep up with her mistress's long strides.

Damn that woman, Margaret thought, she must be spying on us. But her frustration was fleeting as her heart and mind tried to wrap themselves around those last few precious moments. By all that was holy, she knew now that Anthony loved her, and her whole being was suffused with pleasure. But the few seconds of ecstasy were soon replaced by despair. She knew they could never consummate their love unless they were both free.

And with Eliza Scales very much alive, Anthony would never break his marriage vow, she knew that.

THERE WAS NO time to ponder her hopes and dreams. The palace was in a frenzy during the last days before the coronation. Edward rode to London on Thursday, the twenty-third of May, and created more than forty knights of the Bath in honor of his queen.

Margaret, together with her sisters, joined the queen and her ladies on the barge that transported them to London the next day. There, the mayor and aldermen gathered to escort Elizabeth to the royal apartments in the Tower for one night before she was carried through the banner-festooned streets that were strewn with flowers to Westminster Palace. Margaret had never seen London more crowded. Everyone flocked to the procession route along Tower Street to Eastcheap, past St. Paul's massive Gothic facade and through the Ludgate to the Strand and Westminster beyond. The citizens' cheers, the horses' hooves clattering on the cobblestones and the dozens of musicians blowing their lungs out were barely distinguishable above the hundreds of pealing church bells all over the city.

Merchants and their wives, apprentices, journeymen, hawkers, beggars, prostitutes and priests all strained to catch a glimpse of the fair Elizabeth as she passed by. Petals rained down on them as if from heaven. Margaret saw hundreds of spectators hanging precariously from windows holding baskets from which they flung the flowers. She thought her heart would burst with pride. These were Edward's subjects—York's subjects, she thought, wishing her father could have witnessed this—and they welcomed his new queen with affection. She thought it must be the throngs of people so closely packed together and the sun on her head that made her perspire more than usual. She wiped her brow with the back of her sleeve, a heaviness behind her eyes. Aye, the air was oppressive.

The next day, following her coronation, with a closed crown upon her head and her silver hair streaming down her back to below her waist,

Elizabeth processed from Westminster Abbey to Westminster Hall. She wore robes of a traditional cotehardie with sideless gown of vermilion cloth, the entire front of which was of ermine. The white fur trimmed the hem of the gown and lined the deep blue velvet cloak bordered at the neck with gold filament. She carried the heavy orb in one hand and the scepter in the other. She was greeted by more cheering as she stepped out into the May sunlight.

"God save the queen!" the people cried, dazzled by the sumptuously robed beauty who stood acknowledging their homage to her.

Margaret, in cloth of crimson gold with the golden gauze of her butterfly hennin creating a halo around her, held Elizabeth's train with her two elder sisters. Edward greeted his wife at the steps of the hall and escorted her to the feast. There she sat on a dais in solitary splendor and ate from dishes of gold and silver. Unlike Edward's boisterous and merry coronation feast, as ordained by Elizabeth, the feast was to be conducted in total silence, an old etiquette that Edward had eschewed. Margaret and her sisters, as the highest born ladies at the feast, were her honored servers that day, much of which they spent on their knees waiting for a signal from the queen that she required something. When Margaret's sister from Suffolk, nicknamed Lizzie by her family, was told what her place would be at the banquet, she had raised her head and let forth the well-known neigh of laughter that reminded Margaret of her father. "Tell me 'tis not true, Meg. This upstart demands that I, a duchess, spend the entire feast at her beck and call on my knees!" she cried in disbelief.

When Margaret nodded, she neighed again but without humor this time and stalked off to find Edward. In no more than half an hour, she returned chastised and grimacing. "Aye, 'tis the Grey Mare's wish. Meg spoke the truth," she reported and sighed, "I think my days at court are waning fast, sisters. John does not stand on ceremony and will be glad for us to retire to Wingfield, where we can be ourselves."

Anne, duchess of Exeter, was the oldest of the York children. She had been three when Edward had arrived and had since doted on her baby brother. Despite her husband's position as one of the leading Lancastrian lords now in exile, Edward had allowed his sister to be at court with him. Everyone knew she was in love with Thomas St. Leger and turned a blind eye to her affair. She was amused that Ned had picked a bride older than she was. "He needs mothering," she told her sisters. "I, for one, am happy he chose someone mature. Although I wish I looked as good."

Lizzie did not answer, for indeed there was no comparison. Anne had not inherited their mother's looks but was a smaller version of her strong-featured father. If she had not been forced to wear a gown, many might have mistaken her for a man. Margaret, though, immediately became the diplomat in situations with her sisters.

"Anne, none of us can compare with Elizabeth, in truth. 'Tis foolish to even try!" she said, making Lizzie chuckle.

Besides Cecily, the most notable absentees at the crowning of Elizabeth Woodville that day were Richard Neville, earl of Warwick, and William, Lord Hastings. Margaret had not been surprised when Ned sent both men to Calais on a commission to meet with Louis of France, the count of Charolais and the duke of Brittany to forge a truce among them all at this particular time. Certes, a great deal rested on a truce among those enemies, but Margaret also concluded that Warwick and Hastings were the least pleased by their sovereign's choice of consort and were well out of the way when Elizabeth would be so feted. She knew Will was a good enough friend to Ned and that his affability would in the end overcome his jealousy of the Woodvilles. However, the high and mighty earl of War-wick, who liked to boast he had made Edward king, was another matter entirely. She had begun to think of this growing schism between the king and his kingmaker as her Warwick worry.

She and Lizzie gave their knees a rest that night and instead sat on the edge of their shared bed to say their prayers. Margaret chose not to tell her sister that twice during the feasting she thought she would swoon. Certes, it does a body no good to stay that long on one's knees, she told herself. They said a Paternoster together after several minutes of private meditation, and Lizzie was asleep before the candles were extinguished.

Margaret's mind was too busy with the sights and sounds of the day to close her eyes, and besides, her head was pounding. When she finally fell into a fretful sleep, she had the nightmare she had had after Wakefield, only this time the blackened head that grinned down at her from the castle gate was Anthony's. She awoke in a panic, her side of the bed wet with sweat, and it was then she knew she had a fever.

. . .

FACES CAME AND went through her unfocused vision, although Fortunata's was never far from her side, while Margaret wrestled for three days with her illness. Edward sent one of his own physicians to tend her, and as no rashes or other outward signs of serious disease were apparent, the doctor supposed a simple humor imbalance had left her open to illness. He prescribed bloodletting to correct the harmful excess of humors, several potions—which Fortunata tasted first to make sure this crow of a man was not trying to poison her *madonna*—and a daily cold bath. In her delirium, Margaret fought all three remedies, and Master Fryse, a dour little German, clucked around her and threw up his hands in despair.

"She must haf *der bad,* ladies!" he shouted at Beatrice and Jane. "I vill tell der king, I cannot treat her more. She is impossible. You see, she is hot *und* dry; haf too much choler!" he said, referring to the yellow-bile humor that caused agitation. He turned to find Fortunata at his elbow. "Mistress, you understand, *ja?* Lady Margaret must haf *bad?*"

Fortunata nodded. She knew he was right, but observing her mistress's flailing arms and angry cries, she wondered how they could accomplish the task. The German shook his head, clucked some more and stomped off angrily. He did not return.

Elizabeth came to see her and felt the burning forehead, a worried frown on her face. Jane and Beatrice were on the floor in a deep obeisance.

"Do not leave me now, Margaret, just as we have become friends," she said, in an impulsive show of emotion. She leaned closer to her sister-in-law. "And Anthony is asking after you. Shall I tell him you are not obeying Edward's physician? He told me to tell you he had a new book to show you, but only if you are obedient and agree to take the doctor's medicine."

Anthony's name seemed to calm Margaret. She turned her too-bright eyes on Elizabeth. "He said that? Truly?"

Elizabeth smiled and nodded. "Aye, he did. That's better. Now I pray you let your ladies carry you to your bath."

The women watched in astonishment as Margaret sat up and allowed herself to be helped out of bed and to the copper bathtub. How had the promise of a silly book made her comply with the doctor's orders? She squealed as her heated body slipped beneath the frigid water, her already

clammy nightgown clinging to her burning skin, and only her turbaned
head above the surface. She tried to extricate herself immediately, but
Jane and Beatrice held her shoulders down at the end of the bath and
Elizabeth stood guarding her feet. Fortunata, her sleeves rolled up to her
shoulders, proceeded to sponge her mistress's neck and face with the cool,
scented water. As Margaret became accustomed to the cold, she smiled
sheepishly up at Elizabeth.

"You may tell Lord Scales that as soon as I am well he can send me that
book," she said. "Elizabeth, I thank you heartily for taking the time to come
and see me. I know you would not have permitted me to kneel for so long
at the feast if you had had an inkling that I was ill." She could not resist
the reproach but was concentrating so hard to sound coherent that she did
not catch the fleeting expression of hurt on Elizabeth's face. "In truth, you
must have other duties where you are needed more. I shall endeavor to give
these ladies no more cause for complaint." She saw Elizabeth's eyebrow rise
skeptically and added, "I am not promising, but I shall try."

The tinkling laugh floated back to those around the bath long after
Elizabeth had left the room.

It took a few weeks before Margaret was hale again, and she was dismayed that some of her gowns needed to be taken in.

"I look like Ambergris, in truth," she groaned, staring at herself in the
polished silver mirror.

She was still at Westminster enjoying the luxurious apartments set
aside for her recuperation. The walls were covered in rich tapestries. Her
bed had a high canopy above it under which the damask curtains were
looped up and out of the way. One had only to loose the string, and they
spread around the bed as if by magic. As a bachelor, Edward had never
paid much attention to his surroundings, although he was not above
spending huge sums on his personal wardrobe, but Elizabeth's presence
spelled many changes. She insisted on clean rushes on the floors every
day, was extravagant in the use of candles and would not tolerate dogs in
her solar for fear of fleas. She imposed strict etiquette on all the court,
which caused Beatrice to remark to Jane one day that the queen was
behaving just as she would have expected from a member of the gentry
who had come up in the world.

Today Margaret was confined, not because of her illness, but because of her monthly courses. She sat by the window, a view of the abbey framed in it, and opened the richly illustrated book Anthony had promised.

Her heart had jumped into her throat when she saw what he had chosen for her. Master Chaucer's *Troilus and Criseyde* was a love story of infinite beauty and tragedy. It was not among her mother's books, and after a few stanzas, Margaret quickly knew why. The story of the love between a prince of Troy and a beautiful widow and how the lady's uncle helped them consummate their love was full of powerful descriptions of desire. The book would certainly not have fitted in with Cecily's library of treatises and writings of holy women, Margaret smiled to herself. She was fond of *The Canterbury Tales,* but this work thrilled her with the poet's ability to write so perfectly about love, from Troilus's first glimpse of Criseyde:

> *"And from her look, in him there drew the quick*
> *of such desire and such affection*
> *that in his heart's bottom began to stick*
> *of her his fixed and deep impression . . .*
> *he was glad now his horns in to shrink:*
> *he hardly knew how to look or wink."*

to the night of passion they shared before Criseyde betrayed him with another. Margaret hardly dared read the words, they stirred so much in her:

> *"Her slender arms, her back straight and soft,*
> *her long flanks, fleshly smooth and white,*
> *he began to stroke, and blessed full oft*
> *her snowy throat, her breasts round and slight.*
> *Thus in his heaven he started to take delight,*
> *and with that a thousand times he kissed her too:*
> *so that for joy he scarce knew what to do."*

Nay, Cecily would never have allowed such a book in her collection. Margaret could not put the volume down, and she didn't dare to guess why Anthony had chosen to send her this. Tears filled her eyes as she lifted her head from the pages. Did she weep for Troilus in his agony of betrayal or did she weep for the intimacy she could never have with Anthony?

. . .

MARGARET RETURNED TO Greenwich for the summer of 1465, but Edward didn't let her rest there for long.

He sent a barge for her, and this time he also called for Richard to attend him. Brother and sister chatted amiably about the reason for Ned's command. Margaret guessed Edward was ready for Richard to go north to Middleham for his knight apprenticeship with Warwick. Richard's face lit up at her conjecture, and Margaret was charmed by his sweet smile.

"Certes, Dickon, I have foretold the reason for your journey, 'tis only fair you should guess the reason for mine," Margaret said, fanning herself in the heat of the early July day. "I wager Elizabeth has something to do with it, although I can't imagine what I can accomplish that her other ladies or her formidable mother cannot."

Richard was unfamiliar with both ladies and murmured a vague assent. He was deep in thought about how his life was about to change forever. Margaret's prediction turned out to be correct, and following his short audience with Edward, he was seen running along the wide terrace overlooking the river whooping for joy and throwing his bonnet in the air.

Later, Margaret was ushered into the king's presence chamber, where Edward and Elizabeth sat on thrones surrounded by a goodly number of courtiers. It was not the private scene she had imagined, and for a moment she worried that she had displeased the king somehow. When she saw Elizabeth's smile, she was relieved. She gave them both obeisance.

"My dear sister, God's greeting to you," Ned said affably. "I told you I would not forget you."

A marriage proposal, Margaret realized in that instant. She had waited so long for this, but now that the moment had arrived, she had butterflies in her stomach and her mouth was dry. Chin up, my girl, she told herself, and then sent a prayer to St. Catherine—the saint of unmarried girls— that Edward had found her a pleasant young husband. In her trepidation, she forgot Edward had promised a few years ago not to surprise her with this news in public.

The king nodded to his chancellor, who ushered a small, haughty man with an olive complexion and a great beak of a nose to the dais.

"Martyn Berenger, knight of Catalonia, emissary of Dom Pedro of Aragon, if it please your graces," Chancellor Neville announced.

The man, who was dressed in the Spanish manner, swept off his high velvet hat and bowed low first to Edward, then to Elizabeth and finally to Margaret, who bowed her head in acknowledgment.

"Margaret, Señor Berenger is sent to us from Dom Pedro of Aragon, nephew to the duchess of Burgundy. I am considering his offer for your hand in marriage. Thank you, señor, I would have further discussions in private with my sister. I will have my councilors review the proposal and send you home with our response."

Señor Berenger stepped forward and kissed Margaret's hand. The top of his balding head only reached Margaret's nose, and he was plainly taken aback by her stature. She found herself blushing as the knight studied her from the top of her gold silk hennin to the long-toed points of her fashionable crakows as if to commit to memory a description that would please his master. She was glad she had told Jane to loop a small lock of hair on her forehead when she had chosen her wardrobe for her audience with Edward, so the Catalonian could see she had fair hair, but she hoped he would disregard her too-large nose and stubborn chin. She also prayed Dom Pedro was taller than his compatriot, or they would indeed make a mismatched couple.

But the emissary's admiration showed in his satisfied expression, and he turned to his servant, who ran forward carrying a small ebony box decorated with carved roses and daisies. Margaret gave a little cry of delight as she accepted it. Señor Berenger smiled for the first time and revealed four missing teeth. He helped her to open the box, and inside, nestled in green velvet, was an exquisitely painted miniature of her bridegroom.

"I pray you convey my thanks to your master, señor, and tell him I will treasure this until we meet in person," Margaret said, closing the lid quickly. Neither her smile nor her tone betrayed the desperation she felt after seeing the likeness of her intended. He was not in the first bloom of youth and appeared to have inherited his looks from a bullfrog she had once tried to catch at Greenwich.

Señor Berenger bowed to her again, murmuring, "Milady Margarita," turned and bent almost double, backed away from the king. Margaret, painfully aware that she was the focus of attention in the middle of the room, could hear whisperings all around her and was unsure of what to do next. The moment seemed like an age before Edward whispered something to Elizabeth, stood and stepped down from the dais to enfold her in an embrace. The queen rose, nodded to her ladies and returned to her chambers.

Edward tucked her arm in his. "I am pleased with the offer, Meggie. What is more, Señor Berenger assures me Dom Pedro is young, handsome and very kind. I think I remembered your wishes correctly?" Ned grinned, leading her away from the assembly and to his antechamber.

"Aye, Ned, I thank you," Margaret said meekly, quite sure Edward had not seen Dom Pedro's miniature. She was still in a daze.

"I wanted to tell you before Bess and I take a pilgrimage to Canterbury next week, 'Tis not set in stone yet, Meg, but you may trust me to do what is best for you—and England," he said. "And let me tell you why this offer is good for England."

Margaret, her eyes glazed and her back stiff as a pikestaff, only lent half an ear to his explanation about alliances with Castile and Catalonia against Louis as they walked towards Edward's privy chamber. For once her usual quest for knowledge was focused on one question.

"When?" she asked the man who held her fate in his hands.

"'Tis early days yet, Meg," Edward answered, blithely. "Take heart!"

EDWARD AND ELIZABETH accompanied Margaret and Richard back to Greenwich by boat and then set out on the road to Canterbury. They had not been gone five days when Edward learned of the capture of poor mad King Henry in the wilds of Lancashire. After the Northumbrian castles had fallen the summer before, he had first taken refuge in Scotland and then had wandered alone and friendless in the north of England, taking shelter in the houses of Lancastrian supporters and, for a time, disguised in a monastery. Finally, a so-called friend had betrayed him to his enemies, and after escaping from the man's house, he was eventually run to earth near Bungerly Hippinstones across the River Ribble. The king and queen announced the news to the citizens of Canterbury inside the cathedral and processed to give thanks at Thomas à Becket's tomb.

Margaret heard the news from Jack Howard, who, as a king's councilor, was sent by Edward to report to Greenwich. She received him in her chambers and invited him to dine privately with her. Once again, the forty-year-old Howard found himself in awe of this young woman's grasp of state affairs.

" 'Tis good for Edward that Henry is captive, Sir John, but I fear he is only the face of Lancaster. 'Tis his wife who is the brain behind the face. He cannot rule with his wits so addled, I know, but he is still a danger while Queen Margaret and young Edouard are still abroad scheming for him."

Jack nodded. "You are right, Lady Margaret, as always. It did not hurt our cause for the people to see him so pathetically conveyed to the Tower by my Lord of Warwick. He was in plain cloth on a meager mount with his feet bound to the stirrups with strips of leather. 'Twas hard to believe he had once been king of England and ruled us for thirty-seven years." He shook his head sadly. "And all the while he looked to the heavens and said prayers. He is comfortable at the Tower, and the king has ordered he be accorded respect and gentleness, but even so he must know he is imprisoned. In truth, a sad end."

Margaret liked Jack Howard all the more for his direct speech and kindness. "A sad end, indeed, Sir John," she replied. "But is it the end? My sister Anne's husband is abroad with his Lancastrian friends, Edmund Beaufort for instance. She tells me John is with Charolais in Burgundy. Can Queen Margaret be far behind? And if the old duke dies, will his son turn against Edward? Already he is in control there. What news of the League of the Public Weal?" she asked referring to the conspiracy of the dukes of Burgundy, Alençon, Berri, Bourbon, Brittany and Lorraine to stop their overlord, King Louis, from encroaching on their territories and weakening their independence. There was talk that the rebellious dukes would divide France up among themselves and place the weak duc de Berri on the throne. Charles, count of Charolais, and Francis of Brittany had been the main instigators of the conspiracy.

Jack Howard chuckled. "You are indeed starved of news here, Lady Margaret. We know the different armies of the League were closing in on Louis, but in the end the royal army was engaged by the impatient Charles alone, who could not wait for his allies. There was a bloody battle at Montlhéri—nay, I do not know where it is, my lady, but 'tis far from Charles's home in the Low Country—and although Louis was forced to run back to Paris, nevertheless the Burgundians suffered terrible losses."

He gave a quiet snort of derision. "However, I doubt not Charles will be swaggering back to Bruges, lending much prestige to his reputation among the other dukes. He is a warmonger, Lady Margaret. I pity his wife, for I wager he wears his spurs to bed!"

Margaret laughed outright. "Aye, Sir John, I, too, pity her." She paused as she contemplated what she had recently learned of her prospective bridegroom, Dom Pedro. He, too, was in constant conflict with the other king of Aragon—another country with two kings, she thought. And as it did every time she thought of her possible marriage, her stomach heaved. "So the war of the League is not yet over?" she continued bravely. "These wars are tedious, in truth. I am much relieved we live in a time of peace at home now," she said, holding her thumb up between her fore and middle fingers to make the sign of the cross. "I am certain your lady wife is of the same mind, Sir John. I do not recall having met her yet," she said, aiming to turn the subject away from Burgundy. "You keep her hidden away in . . . Suffolk, is it?"

"Aye, you have it right, my lady. My dear wife, Catherine, is, I am glad to say, as fond of Tendring Hall as I am. 'Tis an honor to serve the king's grace, and I do it willingly and humbly, but I confess I am never happier than when hunting on my own land, fishing in my own streams or overseeing the building of a new ship in my yard at Ipswich. You are gracious to ask, but it distresses me to tell you that my wife is ailing at present, and I shall be returning to her as soon as his grace, the king, regains London and gives me leave."

"I wish I had the authority, Sir John. I would send you home immediately. But selfishly, I beg a little more of your time, for there is more I need to know."

Jack found his hour with Margaret invigorating and the time flew by. If she hadn't been surrounded by her ladies—all busy sewing and uninterested in talk of taxes and turmoil—he might have forgotten she was not a man. Her clear gray eyes brooked no dissembling, and he did not mince his words or hold information back from her. She learned he was concerned about the rise in the fortunes of the Woodville family, although he was diplomatically uncritical of Edward. As well as the ludicrous marriage of Elizabeth's nineteen-year-old brother to his elderly duchess, Edward had bestowed enormous sums of money for the new queen's household and wardrobe as well as giving her the palaces of Greenwich and Shene, all of which pragmatic Jack Howard disapproved.

By the time their conversation had come to an end, Jack was wishing Margaret could also sit on Edward's council. Before he left her, Margaret insisted Fortunata show him her newest trick of the disappearing coin. The conjurer showed them a silver penny, placed it on the back of her hand and proceeded to rub it into her skin until it had vanished. She then turned her palm up and the coin was nestled in it. After he had asked her to repeat the trick three times and still could not fathom how she accomplished it, he laughed and tossed her a coin from his money pouch. Fortunata tested it between her teeth, drawing a reprimand from Margaret and a chuckle from Jack.

"Nay, she has a right to try it—'tis a new angelet and one of the monies his grace ordered issued to help with the shortage of bullion. We have yet to see if the new mintings will keep more gold at home," Jack said, nodding and smiling at Fortunata when her cocked head asked if she could keep the coin. "But, my lady Margaret, that is for another conversation. I need to catch the tide back to my house in Stepney, by your leave. As always, it has been a pleasure to be in your company."

He bowed low and kissed Margaret's hand before signaling to his squire, Tom, to refrain from flirting with a dainty young woman with eyes the size of rose nobles and follow him. His mustache, now flecked with gray, twitched as he watched the young man ardently press the lady's hand to his lips and obey his master. Jack left the room with his characteristic short but determined strides.

ELIZABETH WAS PREGNANT and all England awaited an heir to Edward's crown. Elizabeth was uncomfortable and unpleasant during the months before her confinement, although her physician, Domenico de Sirego, foresaw few problems since two healthy boys had been born to her as Elizabeth Grey. Margaret sent Fortunata to entertain her, and she even visited the queen at her town house, Ormond's Inn, to sit and talk or read to her. The two women gradually developed a friendship that pleased Edward greatly. Margaret's initial reluctance to attend the queen came more from hostility to her lady-in-waiting, Eliza Scales, than to Elizabeth. She was reminded of Anthony every time she saw the woman, and it was only her good breeding that prevented her from showing Eliza anything but civility.

One afternoon in December, in front of a roaring fire, Margaret read Elizabeth *Troilus and Criseyde*. She could not resist telling the company that "my Lord Scales was generous enough to present me with this volume, and I trust your grace will enjoy the beautiful poem." She was gleeful when she saw Eliza's fashionably invisible eyebrows shoot heavenward.

She relished reciting the passionate prose. Towards the end, as Criseyde was about to betray Troilus, she was touched to see tears falling freely down Elizabeth's face.

"Are you unwell, Elizabeth?" Margaret asked anxiously, putting the book down and kneeling by her side. "Is it the babe?"

Elizabeth brushed the tears away impatiently. "Nay, sister, I am quite well, thank you." She hesitated before looking into Margaret's kind eyes and telling the truth. "The poem is moving, certes, but my mind is on Edward at present. Forgive me."

"Ned? Why, he is hale and safe on his throne, my dear. He tells everyone he is impatient to be a father," Margaret assured her, although there was talk that Edward had already sired a daughter with one of his conquests. "What could possibly make you cry?"

"Look at me, Margaret," Elizabeth muttered miserably, tapping her distended belly with disgust. "I am hideous, and Edward does not look at me. I know he is at Westminster with one of his . . . whores," she cried, causing her ladies to look anxiously at her. "Every night, 'tis someone new. He has not come to me for a month. Certes, I fear he no longer loves me."

She finished with a wail that took Margaret aback. Elizabeth was always the model of cool control, haughty and confident, and until she reddened her eyes with crying, more radiant and lovely in her pregnancy than she was before it. Her alabaster skin glowed, her breasts were full and soft, and her eyes less cold. Margaret saw her own shortcomings in that lovely face, and, if the truth be told, she was jealous of Elizabeth's motherhood. Negotiations with Dom Pedro dragged on, and she was no nearer to being wed or a mother than she had been six months earlier, although she was still not looking forward to leaving home.

As she tried to coax Elizabeth out of her melancholy, she was aware of a commotion in the courtyard but paid no heed as she patted the dejected queen's hand and soothed her. "Such foolishness, Elizabeth. Edward adores you." She silently cursed her brother for his blatant infidelities. "And . . ." She did not finish. The object of their discussion was being announced with a flourish at Elizabeth's solar door.

"Your grace," intoned implaccable chamberlain, Lord Berners, "The king requests an audience. Will you receive him here?"

Before Elizabeth had a chance to straighten her simple coif and veil, wipe her nose or dab rosewater on her breast, Edward strode in.

"Bessie, my sweet wife, you look magnificent!" he said, sweeping her out of her chair and planting a kiss on her astonished mouth. "I have never seen a more beautiful woman. We shall have to keep you with child always, my love."

The company was still giving him full obeisance when he raised Margaret up next and folded her into an embrace. "You, too, Meg, are looking magnificent," he said, grinning from ear to ear. "But not for the same reason, I hope. Ha!" he laughed, seeing Margaret's eyebrows shoot up. "Come, Bess, may we have some privacy? I have been searching London for my sister all day, and how happy I am to find the two of you together, the best of friends."

He was clearly in a good mood, Margaret thought, relieved. And Elizabeth's unhappy mood was chased off by his cheerful presence and loving words. She waved her ladies away and they bowed their way from the room. Lord Berners stood at a discreet distance, eyeing Fortunata, who did not include herself in Elizabeth's dismissal. As if by her own magic, she made herself invisible in the folds of Margaret's gown.

"Oh, Edward, I am right glad to see you," Elizabeth exclaimed, her sad mood chased away. " 'Tis a fortnight since you were last here." She did her best not to accuse, but Edward looked sheepish anyway.

"Aye, my love. I confess time caught me by surprise. But there is a good reason, and as you may infer, Meg is part of the reason."

"Me? How can I be blamed for the neglect of your poor wife, Ned?" Margaret was indignant but intrigued.

"Because I have been in more negotiations for your hand, dear sister. Now there are two dukes vying for your hand, and I could not be more pleased," Edward crowed.

Margaret was speechless.

"Aye, eloquent Margaret, I have taken your breath away, I can see." He winked at Elizabeth. "Bess, I knew I could *count* on you to keep the cat in the bag."

Elizabeth's eyes grew wide and a smile curved her perfect mouth. "So that is the way the wind blows, in truth. From the east this time. Pray do not test your sister's patience any longer, my love. Tell her."

"Tell me what? Ned—Elizabeth—do not taunt me so!" Margaret implored. Her hands were clammy and her breath shallow with fear. The bullfrog did not entice her, but she had spent many months learning about Catalonia, Aragon and her prospective husband's Portuguese lineage. She had even begun to learn a little Spanish, although the letters Dom Pedro had sent her had been written in perfect French. There had also been a promise of a fabulous diamond betrothal ring, although nothing yet had been forthcoming.

"Who are you bartering me off to this time, Ned? I am flattered to be so desirable," she said, her tongue finding its bite again as she tried to sound flippant while fighting back panic. "I can only be in one place at a time, in truth, no matter how clever you think me!"

"Have a care, Meggie." Edward was smiling but his eyes were glittering. "You are at my command, and you will go where I tell you. Because I know you well, I spared you the other possible matches I could have made for you."

Margaret's eyes widened in disbelief as Edward continued relentlessly, "Aye, Louis had his own ideas—certes, he has no wish to see me ally with Burgundy, whom he looks on as his rebellious vassal—so he gave me an array of eligibles to choose from: his brother-in-law, Philip of Bresse; René, count of Alençon; his nephew, Philibert of Savoy; and, last but not least, the Italian, Sforza, duke of Milan," he gloated, knowing he had taken her breath away. "It seems you are a desirable partner, my dear."

"Hush, Edward, there is no need to frighten your sister." Elizabeth jumped to Margaret's defense and Margaret shot a grateful glance her way. "You forget, my dear, you made your own choice. Women are not always so fortunate. Be gentle, Edward," she cajoled with a seductive smile. "I know how you can be."

Margaret could see Edward had a hard time resisting that smile. He reached out and stroked his wife's face, cupping her chin in his big hand and running his thumb along her bottom lip. Margaret cleared her throat in an attempt to distract him, and Edward turned his attention back to her.

"I wanted the best for you, Meg, and so I rejected Louis' offers." He did not need to add that these choices were only rejected because he had no intention of being caught in the French king's web; it was as clear to Margaret as spring water that Edward cared nothing for her feelings in the matter. "But now," he continued, "it seems we do have a choice, Meg. Dom Pedro is still very anxious to have you, but he is now a small fish compared to the other duke."

Recovering her composure, Margaret's curiosity got the better of her. "Two dukes, Ned? There is only one of any import to the east of us, and that is Philip of Burgundy, who I am told is not much longer for this world, 'tis true, but his duchess is very much alive. I know this because Dom Pedro is her nephew and, prolific letter writer that he is, he would have told me of her death."

"'Tis true, Duke Philip is the only duke to the east of us, and he and his wife are still living, but you may not know that their son, Count Charles, was widowed not two months ago. I have been approached by Philip on behalf of his son, Meg. You could be duchess of Burgundy one day and the richest woman in Europe!"

"Charolais?" gasped Margaret, her hand over her mouth. "But Ned, Sir John Howard told me he goes to bed in his spurs! In truth, I would rather have the frog!" She was so stupefied, she thought she might swoon. She grasped the arms of the chair for strength and stared dejectedly at the flames licking their way hungrily around the logs in the fireplace.

"But he is a frog, Meg," Edward laughed, pleased at his joke and insensible to her feelings. "He is a Valois duke, and thus French through and through. Except for the English on his grandmother's side and Portuguese on his mother's," he remembered. "But sweet Meg," he went on, trying to coax her out of her dejection, "we have only just begun to talk. These things take time, as you have seen with Dom Pedro, and we shall not show our hand one way or the other until an agreement is signed, until you have consented and all parties are content. 'Tis said Charolais is not as set on an English marriage as his father is. It may come to naught, but

I thought I must tell you. Be of good cheer, Meg. We have the Yuletide season to look forward to and our first child," he said, taking Elizabeth's hand again. "And now, why do I not have wine? Lord Berners, you run too sober a household. I pray you fetch us some wine. We need to drink to Lady Margaret's good health, she is looking a little green!"

Margaret, feeling the bile rise in her throat, jumped up from her chair and ran from the room.

9

1466–1467

*E*lizabeth delivered a lusty daughter on the eleventh day of February, and if Edward was disappointed not have a male heir, he did not show it. In fact, to prove his love for his queen and disavow any rumors that he was displeased, he named the baby Elizabeth.

"Elizabeth is a fine name for a queen, and it may be we have another Elizabeth to reign over us, eh, my pretty?" Edward was lounging on his wife's bed, holding the baby and smothering the tiny face with kisses. Elizabeth was clothed in a blue silk damask bed robe, her hair cascading down around her from under a tiny jeweled coif. Margaret and George had been invited to meet the newborn in the privacy of Elizabeth's chamber, and when it was Margaret's turn to hold the baby, she thought her heart would burst. The dark blue eyes stared vacantly up at her as if taking in her aunt's purple overdress and the flimsy gauze covering the black velvet pillbox. Margaret rocked the child as she slowly walked around the room and was rewarded when her niece closed her eyes and slept.

"She is beautiful, Elizabeth," Margaret told the queen. As she turned to give the child to the nurse, she felt a tug on her dress. Fortunata, who had been given permission by the queen to attend Margaret, was standing on tiptoe to get a glimpse of the child. Margaret bent down to present the bundle and saw Fortunata close her eyes and sway for a few seconds. A slow smile spread over her saturnine features, and when she opened her eyes again, she touched the baby's cheek.

"She will be a great lady, *madonna*. Aye, she will be a queen," she pronounced, and scurried back to her place behind the tall oak chair. The king and queen crossed themselves, and Edward looked pleased.

"Mayhap she will be queen of France!" he cried. "But she cannot be queen of England, because Bess and I plan to have many more children, and there is bound to be a boy among them somewhere. Forgive me, George, I know you of all people are content we have a girl and your place as my heir is secure," Edward teased, throwing the remark over his shoulder, "but I cannot think your luck will hold."

Elizabeth's mouth turned down, deciding Edward must be truly disappointed with a girl, and Margaret glared at her brother for his insensitivity. Turning to look at George, she was puzzled to see him standing by the fire gazing at the crackling logs with his hand gripping his dagger so tightly his knuckles gleamed white.

• • •

"My lord of Warwick placed me not among the guests at the Archbishop's board for the feast following his enthronement at York Minster, but as the only man of rank with the ladies of his household, to wit, the Countess Anne and her two daughters, Isabel and Anne, as well as our sister, Elizabeth of Suffolk, and our aunt of Westmoreland. My lord of Warwick, who was steward at the feast, gave me the singular honor of sitting at the head table in the chamber of estate. The banquet was the most sumptuous I have ever seen—but pray do not tell Ned this, he would not think kindly on the Nevilles if he thought they were trying to outdo him!"

How true, Margaret thought, raising her eyes from Richard's letter and focusing them on the exquisite new arras from Brussels on the opposite wall. Ned does not need any more reasons to drive a wedge between him and the earl. She read on.

"'Tis said my lord archbishop employed sixty-two cooks to provide food for us, and such food, Meg, as would feed a thousand. More than a hundred oxen, a thousand sheep, three hundred veals, two thousand pigs, hundreds of stags and

a dozen porpoises were served along with a hundred peacocks, thousands of geese,
chickens, quails and pigeons, all washed down with a hundred tuns of wine, and
three hundred tuns of ale. I must have eaten a great deal, for I could not move for
hours following, and my horse complained when I sat him next."

Margaret's mouth watered while her eyes popped out of her head at
the details. She chuckled at his last remark. He writes as he speaks, she
thought, missing her earnest younger brother in that moment. The last
time she had seen Warwick, he had complimented Richard on his ability
with the short sword and mace. Margaret had smiled politely, but she
would rather have heard that his reading and dancing had improved. Now
she could see that his writing certainly had. He would spend another year
or two under the earl's mentorship, she guessed. She hoped there would
not come a time when Richard would have to choose between his master
and his brother. The schism was growing daily, it seemed. She sighed,
folded the letter and put it in her silver coffer along with those from her
intended, Dom Pedro. The Warwick worry was still there.

EDWARD'S PREDICTION TO her in December was proved correct. None
of the marriage negotiations had moved forward by June, and Margaret
still had not seen the promised betrothal ring from Aragon. There were
whole days when she was able to forget she would have to leave England,
and these were her favorite times. Then the day came when she knew she
would never see the ring or her bullfrog bridegroom.

Will Hastings caught up to her one cloudless June morning as she was
enjoying a stroll in the Wardrobe gardens.

"God's greeting to you," he said, after bowing low. "I regret I bring bad
tidings, Lady Margaret. Dom Pedro is dead."

Margaret stood stock-still, thoughts tumbling in her head, her emotions raw. Relief, disappointment, frustration and sorrow crowded her
heart. She tried to sort out the emotions, but a desire to sit down won
the day, and she looked around for an excedra. Will stood quietly as he
watched her process the news. Her face betrayed nothing, and he was
afraid she had not heard him correctly. But then he noticed the busy fingers pulling apart a daisy she had plucked from the grassy wall she had
sunk down on, and he realized she was indeed thinking hard about what
the information meant to her.

Margaret had begun to like Dom Pedro for his neat turn of phrase and down-to-earth wooing in his letters. She had prayed to her own feast-day saints, St. James and St. Philip, to St. Monica, patron saint of wives, and even her own St. Margaret to guide Edward's negotiations in the direction of Aragon. It would be the better of two evils, she believed. Everything she had learned thus far of Charles of Burgundy was enough to turn even a stout-hearted woman's stomach, she thought, let alone someone as sensitive as she. She hoped she would experience with a lifelong mate at least a little of the pleasure John Harper and Anthony had aroused in her. She had witnessed the love between her mother and father, who hated being apart and fell into each other's arms when in private, even in front of their children. She had seen the grief in Jack Howard's face when his wife had died the previous year. Now she was witnessing the fulfillment of desire between her brother and his wife. She knew it was possible, but how could it be possible with a man happier on a horse in battle than in bed with her? A pox on Dom Pedro, she thought resentfully, and then was immediately contrite.

Will Hastings waited patiently for her response. Margaret had almost forgotten he was there except for his heavy breathing.

"Dead, my lord? How can he be dead? He was only thirty-eight. He was to have married me. I received a letter from him only last month, and he said nothing of sickness or dying. God rest his soul," she ended, crossing herself.

"We know not how he died, my lady. 'Twas a shock for all of us. Your brother sent me here as soon as we had the news. I am sorry for you. You have been anticipating your formal betrothal to him for almost a year— eagerly I must believe."

"Aye, my lord, I was," she lied, and held her thumb between her fingers for it. "But my grief must pale beside his family's. It cannot have been expected." She rose suddenly when she knew what she must do. "If you would be kind enough to escort me over the bridge to the good friars next door, I would be grateful. I am given leave by the abbot to pray in the little chapel when I need. I must light a candle and beg indulgences for Dom Pedro's soul through Purgatory."

"With all my heart, Lady Margaret," he said, offering his arm.

They walked along comfortably enough, and she pointed out flowers and plants of particular beauty to him while her mind sorted through her feelings. Beatrice and Fortunata followed a few paces behind them, and as they processed to the Grey Friars, Margaret glanced sideways at Will. His many pleasures in life—eating, drinking and philandering—had done little to keep him in fine fettle, Margaret had thought many times. The fashionable padded jacket added to his girth, despite the narrowing of the garment at the waistline. The king had legislated that no man under the status of lord could dress to draw attention to his privy parts, and thus, unfortunately, the new regulations set by Edward for dress in England allowed this overweight nobleman to wear the short cotehardie, exposing his rather large buttocks and exaggerated codpiece. 'Tis unflattering, Lord Hastings, Margaret had wanted to tell him on more than one occasion, but today she simply found the councilor a large, comforting presence. She could think of nothing but her deceased fiancé and the abrupt change in her fortune. She suddenly felt very cold and alone.

WHILE EDWARD TOOK his time about deciding Margaret's future, he had wasted none in elevating his parvenu Woodville relations.

In March, he had given the profitable office of Treasurer to Lord Rivers, who was then created Earl Rivers in May. By August the new earl, already a king's councilor, was named Constable of England for life, and his annual income exceeded one thousand pounds. But it was the marriages that rankled with the old nobility and especially with Richard Neville, earl of Warwick, who had two eligible daughters of his own to provide for. Elizabeth's sister, Katharine, was married to Henry Stafford, heir of the duke of Buckingham; Anne took William, Viscount Bourchier, heir to the earl of Essex; and Eleanor was given to the heir of the earl of Kent. In September, Mary Woodville was betrothed to the son of William Herbert, and Edward gave him the title of Lord Dunster. Elizabeth paid a handsome sum for Anne Holland, daughter of Edward's sister, the duchess of Exeter, for her oldest son, Thomas Grey. This was the last straw for Warwick, for Anne had been promised to his brother, Lord Montagu's son, who would become earl of Northumberland one day.

"My lord of Warwick did all but blow steam from his nostrils when he heard of the Holland purchase," George told Margaret as they sat together at Baynard's, awaiting their mother's arrival from a visit with

Edward. "And who could blame him, in truth? Elizabeth has learned her greedy ways from her father and mother. Rivers is the worst bootlicking, power-grasping parasite it has been my misfortune to know. 'Tis all because Edward is besotted with the Woodville woman, and I hate her."

"Soft, George, someone may hear you. Why do you rail so against her? She is only protecting her family. It cannot affect you, so why put hatred in your heart when there is no need. You must learn to keep your temper, my dear George, and you should not question Ned's decisions or speak your mind so openly or 'twill land you in hot water. Heed what I say. Ned is dangerous when he is crossed. Believe me, I know."

She glanced around the ducal waiting chamber, but other than Fortunata, who was seated in her usual spot, no one was paying them much heed.

"Aye, you are right, Meg, but I think I know Warwick now even better than Ned does. I have made it my business to be in his company and seek his advice. I am determined to marry well, and now that Mary of Burgundy has been denied me, I need the earl on my side." He declined to reveal that the earl had filled his head with ideas of a marriage with his elder daughter, Isabel, and that as heir-male to the throne, it was prudent to ally himself with the most powerful lord in the realm. Perhaps together they could set Edward against the Woodvilles and bring him back into Warwick's fold. Margaret would have been deeply concerned to know how easily the earl had turned George's handsome head.

"Imagine my happiness if you and I could have been together in Burgundy," Margaret replied. "In truth, I wish the negotiators for my marriage with Charles would all drown in a butt of malmsey!" she whispered, forgetting for a moment she was wishing Anthony would drown with them, as he was now the chief negotiator. "I am so frightened I will have to wed him."

George laughed. "Why, Meg, you would be the richest woman in Europe once the old dodderer daddy dies. Charles cannot be as bad as you paint, although 'tis certain he has put two wives in the ground already, and he is not even forty."

Margaret groaned. "Don't speak of him anymore, George. It sends me to the depths of despair."

"Very well, my lady. I am yours to command," he cajoled. "Cheer up,

my dear Meg. Let us speak instead of malmsey," George cried, motioning
to a squire. "Wine, sirrah, if you please!"

Later, she and Fortunata knelt together at the prie-dieu and prayed
first for Dom Pedro's soul and then for strength to face a possible future
with Charolais. Despite wanting the negotiations to fail, she sadly admitted that the English merchants needed an alliance with Burgundy to rally
the economy. Duke Philip's restrictions on English exports were hurting
everyone's pockets. As they often did, her thoughts turned to Anthony,
who was now so closely involved with her future. She hoped he knew she
did not want this betrothal because it would take her away from him.

And without warning or truly knowing why, Margaret began to cry.
At first a few tears hung on her long eyelashes and then slowly rolled
down her cheeks, but once they were released after months of damming,
more and more followed, until she was weeping as though her heart
would break. Fortunata quietly got up and went to find Beatrice. She had
not seen her mistress cry before and for once was at a loss how to help
her. There was something motherly about Beatrice that was comforting,
Fortunata knew, as more than once the older woman had put her arm
around the dwarf when an unkind taunt from another lady or squire had
wounded her. Beatrice was in the next room, readying Margaret's bed for
the night, and she came hurrying in at Fortunata's request.

"My lady, what ails you?" she asked gently, her hands resting lightly
on Margaret's shaking shoulders. Hearing the sympathy in Beatrice's
voice made matters worse, and Margaret found she could not control her
sobs.

"Oh, Beatrice, I am . . . so-so-sor-sorry," she managed to say. "I know
not what has come over me, truly I don't."

Beatrice raised her mistress from the kneeling cushion and took her
in her arms. There was nothing she would not do for this lovely young
woman. She is the best of mistresses, she had told Cecily in a letter, kind,
caring and dutiful. It was her honor and pleasure to serve her, she had
written. Cecily! Certes, the poor girl needs her mother, Beatrice decided,
and sent a page running to the duchess's apartments to fetch her.

Cecily came hurrying through the draughty rooms, a velvet bed robe
wrapped against the early-winter chill, and took charge when she saw the
scene in Margaret's solar.

"Come along, child. Stop weeping. Why, crying is for babies! You have naught to cry about, Margaret. Now let me see what we can do about your face." There was no disparagement in her tone, but the sensible words sank in, and Beatrice could see Margaret responding to them immediately. Cecily had always been calm in a crisis, it was true, and Beatrice had seen much of her mother in Margaret over the years. Dabbing at her daughter's eyes with a lawn kerchief and making her blow her nose on it, Cecily fussed around her, bringing Margaret's sobs to an end. But it was clear that a deep melancholy had overtaken her. Cecily shooed everyone from the room, and even Fortunata dared not disobey. Then mother and daughter sat down on the bed, their arms around each other, and Cecily rocked Margaret back and forth as she had been wont to do in years past.

"You are a little old for this, my dear. But it has been a while since I have held you in my arms, and I confess some of this is for me."

This made Margaret laugh, and she pulled away, shamefaced.

"Oh, Mother, I am so glad you are here. I know not what came over me. One minute I was praying and the next minute . . ." She was horrified to find herself crying again. "What is the matter with me, Mam," she sniffed, using the old nickname for the first time in ten years.

" 'Tis naught but an ill humor, I warrant. But I will tell you, Margaret, that in a life like ours there will be more tears. Your life is in an unsettled place today, but you must trust in God to show you the way to the next stage of it. I have come from Edward, who tells me all is not right yet for the Burgundy offer, and Warwick is still angling for one with France, so it appears you are safe for a spell, my dear. Now, dry your eyes and think on the entertainments Edward has in store for us this Yuletide season. I am invited, so we may have more time to talk about being a wife and mother. I am certain this is what is confusing and upsetting you. Am I right?"

Margaret could not tell her about Anthony, so she nodded and blew her nose loudly enough to cover a "Forgive me, Lord" for her lie, although, she admitted to herself, becoming the wife of a stranger did fill her with trepidation.

IT WAS NO good. God and his Son and all his saints were unable to give Margaret comfort or sensible advice. She spent hours at her prie-dieu trying to keep her melancholy in check and seeking answers from the luminous Virgin and Child who stared out of the painting in front of her. As she concentrated on the work of art, she found herself wishing the Virgin could speak. 'Tis always I who speak to you, sweet Mary, but I want someone to speak back to me. I am always so alone. She heard two of her ladies whispering together on the other side of the room and felt Fortunata move her position on her cushion next to her, and she almost laughed aloud. Alone? I am never alone!

She tried to read her prayer book and hoped the words would give her courage and focus her love on God. But it was no good; Anthony's face floated behind her eyes and filled her with longing. She snapped the book closed, causing Fortunata to jump from her cushion and pick up the trailing end of her mistress's dress.

"I know why you cried, *madonna,*" Fortunata whispered to Margaret's surprise.

"Don't be impertinent, Fortunata. You cannot possibly know, because I do not know myself," Margaret retorted. "I pray you, fetch my cloak and inform Master Vaughan that I wish my litter to be readied. We shall be visiting St. Bartholomew's hospital today."

Fortunata curtseyed and was gone.

A few flakes of snow were drifting down from the heavy sky when Margaret was helped into her litter by Steward Vaughan and the burly bearers picked up the chair as if it were nothing but a basket of cherries. They began their rhythmic stride out of the Wardrobe courtyard and into Carter Lane, and Margaret settled back on the cushions with Fortunata at her feet. The dwarf had thoughtfully tucked a copper footwarmer in among the fur covers, and the coals gave off a delicious warmth in the enclosed space.

"I pray you take the Newgate way today, Master Bull. The smell of the ditch beside the Old Bailey was most unpleasant last week," she called out to the lead bearer as she held her tussie-mussie to her nose and inhaled its sweet scents.

Fortunata glowed with pride that her mistress knew all the servants by name. She was also proud that Margaret never forgot to visit the sick at the priory hospital near Smithfield Market every week. If the truth be told, Fortunata thought the hospital far inferior to the one she had grown up at in Padua. Most of the sick and infirm were crammed sometimes four to a bed, the floors were swept daily by the monks, but still the wards smelled of human waste, and how anyone left there alive Fortunata could not understand. She kept her thoughts to herself, though, when Margaret traveled from cot to cot dispensing fresh water and words of comfort and prayers during her visits.

Margaret tapped Fortunata on the shoulder, startling the servant, who had been peering through the curtains to watch the citizens of London go about their business. "Now, *pochina*, let us return to your audacious state-ment that you know why I cry," Margaret said. She had not been able to think of anything else since. She didn't really care about the stink of the ditch—the stench in the wards was far worse, in truth, and she suffered that weekly—she wanted to go the longest route today, so she could quiz Fortunata on her confident remark.

"Auda—? What did you say, *madonna?* I did not understand," Fortunata frowned.

"Ah, yes, perhaps a rather advanced word for you yet. Bold, daring, impertinent. You understand now?" Seeing the nod, Margaret went on. "Why do you think I am sad?"

Fortunata plucked at the fur coverlet nervously and then raised her dark eyes to her mistress. "Because you love milord Scales, *madonna*. I see it every time when he is with you. You smile always, and always you . . . shine," she said, happy with her choice of word. "Aye, shine— from here," and she touched her heart. "Your brother wants to send you away. He wants you to marry a stranger. You do not want to leave your family. You do not want to leave London. But more than this, you do not want to leave your Anthony. *Allora,* it is simple—you cry!"

Anxiously, Margaret probed her further. "Does everyone notice that I . . . shine? Does *he* notice? Is it that obvious? Please say no or I shall not be able to face Anthony again."

"I watch you all the time, milady. Forgive me, but I know what you think all the time. I know you do not like the queen, that you do not trust my lord Warwick, and that you hate the Bold one of Burgundy. I know you love your brothers King Edward and Lord Richard. But you love Lord George more. And," she said expansively, lifting her chest, "I know you love your *pochina* the best of all!" She ended her little speech by kissing the tips of her fingers to the wind. Then she cocked her head and waited for Margaret's reaction.

Margaret sat gazing at her prodigious little servant and knew the Virgin in the painting had sent her an answer after all. She had found her confidante, and she knew she could face anything as long as she had this wise young woman to talk to. She crossed herself and marveled.

THE WINTER WAS cold and snowy and took a toll on the poor and sick. Margaret spent Christmas at Windsor with Edward, Elizabeth and Cecily. George and Richard were invited to accompany the Neville family to their estates in Cambridge, and Edward, though uncomfortable with the arrangement, saw little reason to deny Warwick's request. However, when it became obvious that the earl was allowing the king's two brothers to become more acquainted with his daughters, Edward recalled the pair to his side. Both denied emphatically that Warwick had mentioned marriage to either of them, although Margaret knew from her conversations with George that the earl had already discussed it with him. Edward was adamant, declaring angrily for all to hear that neither brother would ever wed a Neville and that he wanted to hear no more on the subject. Margaret had seen George's sulky face when he sought her out to commiserate after his audience with Ned, but for once she refrained from saying anything. "I told you he was dangerous" was on her lips, but she kept her eyes on her book as he stalked from the room.

On her return to London in March, Margaret and her ladies rode in her carriage to the Tower for an unusual viewing there. The Patriarch of Antioch had visited Edward in December and had brought with him as a gift to the king of England: camels from his native land. The menagerie at the Tower already boasted several lions and leopards, but no one had ever seen a camel in England before. Margaret and Fortunata were entranced by the creatures. " 'Tis higher than a horse, *pochina*. Certes, you would be afraid up there," Margaret said, and Fortunata nodded vigorously. " 'Tis truly one of God's little jests. How does one ride such an animal? And yet, I hear the people use them like horses in their country. Strange indeed."

When spring arrived, the negotiations for Margaret's marriage were still in flux. Margaret decided Edward would never make up his mind between France and Burgundy and she would die an old maid in her own bed at the Wardrobe, especially after her twenty-first birthday came and went without a contract. She dreamed one night, after a particularly trying day with Elizabeth, that Eliza Scales fell off a camel. She dreamed that she laughed and Eliza sat up and screamed abuse at her before sinking down in the grass and expiring. She awoke just as Anthony was putting out his hand to take hers over his wife's dead body. God help me! she thought, feeling sick. They do say the truth is revealed in your dreams. Sweet Mother of God, I do not wish for Eliza's death, I swear it! The next time she saw Anthony, she could not look him in the eye, for she was certain he must know she would burn in the hellfires for her wicked thoughts.

Margaret was not at Windsor when the Burgundian herald arrived to announce the Bastard was now anxious to fulfill his bargain in the flower of sovenance challenge. He had gladly been granted a stay by Edward when he had started out on a Crusade the year before on orders from his father. But that had come to nothing. He was now ready. Margaret's heart sank when the news reached her in London, for she was convinced the visit was also intended as part of the marriage negotiations. But as if Ned didn't want her to become too complacent, he had once again sent Warwick to France to see what he might negotiate with Louis. If it weren't so nerve-racking, she might have laughed about it.

Fortunata was puzzled by the constant reference to the Bastard of Burgundy. "I know it is not a good word, *madonna*. It means the father and mother did not wed. It is the same word in Italian, *bastardo*. Bastard Antoine does not care about this?" Fortunata seemed to have forgotten she was one, too.

Margaret chuckled. "Aye, 'tis an insult to be called thus, unless you are of noble blood, so it would seem. Even if one is baseborn of a noble, one is still noble. Count Antoine de la Roche—that is his proper name, *pochina*,—is Duke Philip's favorite son. He is the half brother of Charles, but a much better man, Anthony tells me. He cannot inherit the duchy from his father, certes, but he is nevertheless very powerful. 'Tis an honor to receive him at our court and an honor for Anthony to compete in the lists with him."

There were two reasons Margaret feared the upcoming tournament. It could mean the signing of her long-awaited contract and it could also result in Anthony's injury or, in a cruel stroke of bad luck, his death. Tournaments were not supposed to end fatally, but Margaret knew many a widow who could disprove that supposition. Anthony was one of the finest jousters in Europe, but so was the count de la Roche. She could not imagine why she had agreed to plan the challenge with Elizabeth two years ago. But two years ago, she was unaware of the depth of her feelings for Anthony.

A little more than a month later, the countryside was awash in color. The old Saxon saying "Ne'er cast a clout 'til the may is out" was pertinent that cold, wet month, but June began in sunshine. Now the blushing hawthorn was in full bloom in the hedgerows and corners of fields, mingling with the sweet, rose-tipped apple blossoms, the last heady-scented bluebells and, higher on the hills, the blazing yellow broom. Margaret hoped the party from Burgundy would notice how beautiful her native land was, and once again she chafed at the thought of leaving it.

London would be mobbed for the tournament, Margaret knew, but she thrilled to the pageantry of it and could not imagine a city that knew how to celebrate more festively than London. Lists were being prepared at West Smithfield, and Fortunata reported to Margaret that she had seen cartloads of gravel and sand trundled towards the marketplace to spread over the ground. Soon the repetitive sound of hammering penetrated the daily noise of London as temporary stages and seating were erected on either side of the jousting field. And then London waited.

One evening, Margaret took her candle and with Fortunata trailing behind her, climbed the tower stairs to a tiny chamber that must have been a watchman's haunt in times past. She often went up there during the day, for it gave her a bird's eye view over the thatched and shingled roofs all the way to the Tower to the east, to Baynard's and the river to the south, the city gates to the west and St. Paul's to the north. She could name many of the hundred church steeples in the city and recognize their chimes. Compline had rung at seven o'clock, and now all was quiet but for the occasional sounds of laughter and singing floating up to her from the Paul's Head tavern on Wharf Hill. Like the stars in the sky, pinpoints of light were visible from candles and oil and rush lamps in hundreds of houses, and she wondered what the townspeople could do by their weak beams before retiring. On the river, lights bobbed up and down in lanterns at the front of boats ferrying passengers home in time for the curfew. Here and there a dog barked only to be yelled at by its owner, and a baby cried for its mother in a house directly below her. She imagined she could feel the pulse of this great city and that she was a tiny part of its lifeblood.

"'Tis so beautiful, is it not, Fortunata," she murmured to her companion, who was standing on a stool to reach the window. "I love this place, and I know not how I shall bear to leave it." It seemed inevitable that she would and that France or Burgundy would be her home. Even losing her language weighed on her, although she had an easy facility with spoken French. In her parents' time, the court spoke French more than English, but gradually English had become the preferred conversational language, she was happy to say. She took one more long look at the scene in front of her and sighed.

"'Tis time for sleep, *pochina*. Who knows what tomorrow will bring?"

IT BROUGHT THE Bastard of Burgundy at last. Accompanied by Garter King-of-Arms, Antoine de la Roche sailed to Blackwall from Gravesend where, despite the fact that the king was still at his hunting lodge in Kingston, he was given a grand reception by a large party of lords that included one of Edward's most trusted advisers, John Tiptoft, earl of Worcester. Word of the arrival whistled along the streets and alleys, and when Margaret was told, she sent Fortunata off to witness the event. It was at times like these that her lofty station chafed at her.

"You will run all the way there and remember every detail, you understand. I want to know what he looks like, who was there, what language did they speak. Everything, *pochina*. I will be waiting," Margaret said, shooing Fortunata out of the room.

Later, with Margaret's closest women around her, Fortunata told how the barge carrying the visiting dignitaries arrived at Billingsgate wharf and how the group had to make its way through the fish market to Eastcheap, Watling Street, the Ludgate and to the Bishop of Salisbury's magnificent town house, which was at the disposal of the Bastard for his visit. Fortunata followed the procession.

"Make way, make way for my lord Anthony of Burgundy!" A voice rang above the cheering crowds, and a swathe was cut for the party to pass through. Fortunata immediately recognized Sir John Howard, striding ahead of the challenger from Bruges, the English knight's velvet-trimmed scarlet gown and elaborately rolled hat setting off his graying hair and black eyes. She spoke warmly of the earl of Worcester, the king's close councilor, describing his emerald short houppelande, large soft hat and liripipe and his many jewels so minutely that Margaret became impatient.

"'Tis enough about the earl, Fortunata. I know you admire him because he speaks your language, but we are more disposed to hear what the Bastard wore, are we not, ladies?"

"Aye!" was the unanimous response. Fortunata looked crestfallen until Margaret patted her hand and encouraged her to continue.

The Bastard, it seems, was even more magnificent than the English lords, and his jewels larger and more profuse. He wore an elaborate collar from which hung a gold and enameled medallion representing a sheepskin, "The order of the Golden Fleece," explained Margaret, and Fortunata looked blankly at her. "'Tis like our order of the Garter, *pochina*. A very great honor for a knight to receive. But go on. Is he handsome?" Margaret was anxiously awaiting a description of the man she thought might give a clue to his half brother Charles's looks.

"*Si*, very handsome. Not as young as milord Scales, *madonna*. Ten years older maybe. He has long hair to here," she said, touching her shoulders, "and brown like mine. Not as tall as the king, but big here." She indicated her chest. "Strong, you see."

Margaret suddenly felt cold. This is the man who could hurt Anthony, she thought. The women were surprised by her change in tone when she brought the conversation to a halt. "Enough, Fortunata. Ladies, apply yourselves to your books, please, we have heard enough!" she commanded.

THREE DAYS LATER, Edward and his retinue entered the city with heralds, clarions and trumpets preceding the colorful cavalcade. As king's champion, Anthony rode in front of his sovereign and received the accolades of the excited citizenry. He and Edward dismounted at St. Paul's and went inside to make an offering. Margaret was in her litter, surrounded by her pikemen in the York murrey and blue, watching the scene from in front of a chandler's shop, its gaily painted signboard swinging above her. Women leaned from casements on the second floor of the houses opposite St. Paul's and waved scarves and kerchiefs when the king came out on the steps leading to the courtyard, a small gold circlet on his shining hair. He was still the most striking man in the entourage that followed him out, Margaret thought, although Anthony was the more handsome. Ned saw her across the street and lifted his hand in greeting, placing it on his heart. She smiled and waved back.

At that moment the Bastard of Burgundy's group joined the throng at the entrance to the courtyard. A hush came over the crowd. Back in his saddle and swinging his great mount round to lead the procession with Edward, Anthony wondered at the silence, and when the reason for it was pointed out to him, he saw his antagonist for the first time. The two men locked gazes for a moment, and the Londoners watched with interest. The Englishman unsheathed his sword, kissed the hilt and saluted the Burgundian, who smiled briefly and bent in an elegant bow. The mounted company regrouped behind Edward and Anthony, and with fanfares and the beating of tabors moved off towards Ludgate, Fleet Street and on to Westminster.

LONDON BUZZED WITH tournament gossip and every inn, tavern and lodging house was full to bursting. A tournament was a treat for the hard-working citizens. It was a sporting event carried out with meticulous rules, and although injuries and even death could occur, the sport was in the skill of the jousters, not in bloodshed.

On one side of the Smithfield lists, a canopied section of seats was raised for the royal party, and on the opposite, a smaller stage for the mayor and aldermen. Count Antoine had an audience with the king and attended the opening of Parliament in the Painted Chamber at Westminster as part of his official visit to England. Two days later, Lord Scales made another grand entrance, from the river this time, coming up from Greenwich by barge to St. Katherine's Wharf just east of the massive outer Tower wall. John Howard, acting on behalf of his patron, the duke of Norfolk, Earl Marshal of England, escorted the queen's brother to the Bishop of Ely's palace at Holborn, where he would lodge until the tournament.

And so the citizens waited and waited. For six more days they waited.

ANTHONY WAS ANNOUNCED, much to the astonishment of the steward, who hurried to Margaret's solar to tell her of Lord Scales's visit.

"Such an honor, my lady. In this time of preparation that he should seek you out is a singular honor."

Margaret was fond of the old man and she did not point out that to the contrary, it was an honor for Anthony to be accorded an audience with the king's sister. Instead she smiled and asked for Anthony to be admitted. "We will have wine, Master Vaughan. I pray you find a good one," and, seeing the man's white eyebrows lower in a frown, for he watched over the household spending with a thrifty eye, she teased, "for such an honored guest, sir."

It happened that she was accompanied only by Jane and Fortunata when Master Vaughan ushered Anthony in. He swept off his high hat to make her obeisance. "My lady," he said. "Lady Jane, Mistress Fortunata, I give you good day."

The steward fussed around him, beaming, and pulled a chair forward.

"God's greeting, my lord. We are indeed honored by your visit." Margaret smiled, catching a satisfied look on Master Vaughan's face. "You may leave us, master steward, and send up some wine, as we discussed."

Master Vaughan bowed first to Margaret and then to Anthony and continued bowing as he backed out of the room, his face pink with pleasure.

"What have I done to deserve that?" Anthony laughed, putting the chair closer to her and sitting down.

"All London is at your feet. Certes, do not dissemble, sir. You must know it. Poor Master Vaughan is quite overcome with pride that you should choose our humble house to set your magnificent foot in." Margaret chuckled. Then she turned serious. "But I am glad you came, Anthony. I have had nightmares about the tournament and I fear for your life."

"Faint-hearted Marguerite. Have you no faith in me? I trounced your brother at Eltham in April, do you not remember? I live for the chance to use this God-given talent to all who challenge me. If I fight in His name, I cannot lose. If my heart is pure, I cannot lose. Have faith, sweet lady. I will accomplish my emprise and receive the flower of sovenance, you will see."

"If you say so, Anthony," Margaret said, meekly. She had observed the fire in his eyes when he talked of his passion for the joust and wished it could be directed at her. "But do not think ill of me if you see me with my hands over my eyes. I do not understand the need for men to prove themselves by fighting. I think God would prefer we use our tongues to resolve our differences."

"I cannot explain a man's desire, Marguerite. It is in our nature to fight, I believe, and is another cross God asks us to bear. All I know is that I will fight as fair and true as God gives me strength and courage to do."

"Like Sir Lancelot," Margaret said, nodding. "I remember."

A page entered with wine, and Fortunata took the jug and told him to go. Then she served them in the silver goblets and drew Jane to the window on the other side of the room. Anthony watched her, silently praising the clever servant.

"Aye, like Lancelot," he repeated. " 'Twas our first meeting by the river at Shene," Anthony said quietly, looking at her over the brim of his cup. "I was entranced by your eyes, Marguerite. Their color is mysterious, changing with your moods. But most of all they are filled with wit and kindness and mirror who you are. I wanted to know all about you from the moment I met you." He put the wine down and leaned close. "I still do."

Observant Fortunata opened the window wide and pointed something out to Jane in the garden below. Anthony seized the moment and took Margaret's face in his hands and kissed her on the mouth. Margaret could taste the sweet wine on his lips and closed her eyes. This time she allowed herself no interference from her head as she let his tongue lightly play between her lips. All she prayed was that the moment would last for ever.

Of course, it did not, and he sat back in his chair just as Jane turned her head and said, "Lady Margaret, there is a sweet pup lost in the garden. May I go down and rescue it?"

Margaret jumped at the sound of her voice. For a second, she had thought she and Anthony were completely alone. How had Jane not seen Anthony's kiss? She turned and saw Fortunata's innocent gaze on the ceiling and knew the dwarf must have diverted the other woman's attention. She laughed, her heart filled with gratitude for Fortunata and love for Anthony. She had no doubt she must be—in Fortunata's word—shining at this moment.

"Aye, Jane. Bring the little thing here. I wonder whose it can be?" She heard her own voice but knew not what she said. She dared not look at Anthony, but she was certain he understood her even better now, although she did not understand him. Their first kiss had elicited immediate regret and contrition, but this time, he appeared not to have been affected. Why the change? she wondered. She had no qualms about kissing him, although she knew she would have to confess it on the morrow. It was worth it to experience the sensual thrill his touch gave her. Touch me again, she wanted to say, touch my breast, my . . . She dared not name where else she wanted to be touched.

She held her hands tightly in her lap and forced herself to look at Jane. Anthony rose and drained his cup as Jane skipped out of the room. He began pacing, watched intently by Fortunata from the window. She wanted her mistress to be happy, and although she liked Anthony, she did not know yet whether she trusted him.

"I thought you might like a dog of your own, Marguerite," Anthony said, his voice betraying none of the emotion of the kiss. "This little pup is from Norfolk. My wolfhound, Tarquin, sired a litter two months ago, and I kept the prize of it for you. Say you will take him in."

The precious moment of passion was over, Margaret realized, and taking her cue from Anthony, she clapped her hands with delight. "Thank you, my lord, with all my heart. I shall name him something that will remind me of you. Let me see," she thought for a few moments and then her eyes lit up. "Astolat! That shall be his name."

Anthony looked puzzled. "Astolat. I cannot think why I know that name."

"Remember? Elaine of Astolat fell in love with Sir Lancelot, but he did not return her love. She died of a broken heart and floated down to Camelot on a flower-strewn barge, carrying a love letter to him."

"Aye, now I remember." Anthony was pensive. " 'Tis a sad story." He leaned over and whispered, "Do I make you sad, Marguerite?"

"When you are not with me, my lord," she murmured, "and there are times when I believe I shall die for love of you."

"Nay, do not say such things," Anthony said, harshly. "Or God will punish us for certain." He glanced at Fortunata, who was now standing on a stool to look out of the window.

"Does he punish us for what we think, Anthony?" Margaret asked, her eyes sad. "I cannot control my thoughts, and they are constantly of you. There have been times when I have been present at court that you appear to ignore me, making me think you do not care."

He took a deep breath and sat down again. "Do you think 'tis easy for me to see you day after day at court and watch you from afar?" he whispered. "I have no wish to hurt or shame Eliza, and so simply to see you there must satisfy me. I do not dare pay you more attention than is correct. But never doubt I care," he swore into her eyes. "If you think it would ease your mind, I will pen my devotion to you and write to you as Elaine." Margaret's eyes widened with pleasure, giving him his answer. "But," he repeated, "I swear that I care." Then louder he said, "Where is Lady Jane with the pup?"

Margaret's sunny tone told him she believed him as she answered, "Perhaps she is having trouble catching the dog. I could not wish for a more precious gift, Anthony, except perhaps a book. And," she called out purposely, "perhaps Fortunata will lose her fear of dogs."

Fortunata turned and stepped down from her stool. She looked skeptical, but she lifted her chin and declared, "I am not frightened anymore." Anthony and Margaret laughed.

It was a good time to change the subject. "'Tis much on my mind, as you must know, but what of my future, Anthony?" She watched him color. He had conveniently forgotten in that sweet, brief moment that he was chief negotiator with Burgundy in arranging Margaret's future. "Warwick has been sent to France to see Louis. I believe I am a subject of their discussion," Margaret continued. "And by chance—or not by chance—Burgundy sends his favorite son at exactly the same time. Should I take heed of this, my lord? I have waited nigh on two years for my brother to make up his mind. Can you tell me if this tournament has aught to do with my marriage?"

Anthony sighed. "You have the measure of it, my lady. Your brother is more disposed towards Burgundy than France, and in that he differs entirely from my lord of Warwick. One reason why the tournament has been postponed these six days is so that the king can deal more closely with a member of Philip's family. The Bastard has put forward a very favorable proposition. I fear Warwick is on a wild-goose chase, and he will not be happy when he returns."

Margaret set her cup down sharply, spilling some of its contents on the colorful Turkey carpet. "I feel like a prisoner on the rack being torn in opposite directions. I know not how long my poor heart can resist before my spirit is broken. Tell me, Anthony, is there no one suitable in England for me? 'Tis leaving England that I fear most."

Her anguish moved him deeply, and he did not know how to comfort her. For the first time in all their meetings, an awkward silence fell between them. It was broken by Jane returning carrying the wolfhound pup, which was already almost as large as Elizabeth's fully grown Italian greyhound. Margaret put out her arms, and Jane set the wriggling animal into her lap. Its wiry hair matched the color of her eyes, its bony tail waved happily and its legs were too long for its immature body. She laughed at its awkwardness, and it proceeded to slobber her face with affection. For the time being, her marriage was forgotten, and she smiled gratefully at Anthony. She set the pup down, and it immediately began to chase its tail, making Jane and Fortunata laugh.

"In exchange for your gift, my lord, I must give you something. Fetch my silver coffer, *pochina*," Margaret commanded. The dwarf left Jane playing with the dog and brought the chest to Margaret, who rose and drew an exquisite cloth of silver scarf from it. Anthony immediately stood and allowed Margaret to tuck it into his voluminous sleeve, a question in his eyes.

"Wear this when you joust, Anthony. I would give you more protection if I could, but know I shall be with you every step of the way." She took his hand and pressed it to her heart. "God keep you, my lord," she murmured and turned away.

"To accomplish and perform the acts comprised in articles set out by him unto the Bastard of Burgundy sent, I command thee to enter and do reverence," Edward cried to his champion and brother-in-law, Lord Scales, who halted at the list bars first, as was customary, and declared his intentions to the constable and earl marshal.

The crowd roared as Anthony was permitted to enter the field. He was preceded by the duke of Clarence and another of Queen Elizabeth's relatives, the earl of Arundel, both carrying Anthony's crested helmets. Behind them, bearing spears and swords, rode the duke of Buckingham, the earl of Kent and the Lords Herbert and Stafford. Scales bowed low before the king and then withdrew to his blue satin pavilion at one end of the field.

Good-natured jeers greeted the well-beloved bastard son of Philip of Burgundy as he, too, rode to salute Edward after identifying himself to the constable.

A proclamation was then made at each corner of the field as to the rules of the joust. The final words were aimed at the spectators. "No man must approach the lists without good cause, or make any undue noise or movement that would either trouble or comfort the combatants unless they wish to risk imprisonment, fine and ransom at the king's pleasure."

Margaret sat with Elizabeth and the queen's ladies in a canopied box set apart from the king's stage. She felt hemmed in and hot, and Eliza Scales's presence nearby added to her discomfort. Although it had rained the previous day and the tournament field was muddy, this day was warm, and the sun glinted on the armor of the jousters and their horses. Maybe if she swooned now, she would not have to witness any carnage, although Anthony had assured her that both he and the Bastard were far too important for the king to allow a fight to the death. That had made her smile. Besides which, he had reminded her, the weapons were blunted for such a tournament. It was too late now. The trumpeters were calling the jousters to their places.

Margaret could see Fortunata had squeezed her way through the crowd immediately below her box and had a knee-high view of the horses, which were so elaborately caparisoned and armored that it was hard to imagine they would not collapse with the weight of the regalia, the steel cranet protecting their necks and a fully armed man in the saddle.

The first day's jousting was to be on horseback in a free course. Gone were the wooden barriers that characterized jousts in bygone days. The combatants that day were to use lances and swords to unseat their rival.

Once in the saddle, Anthony reached down and took his crested helmet from his squire, and pulling Margaret's scarf from its hiding place behind his shield, he tied it to the saracen's scimitar that was his crest. Margaret felt herself flush as Eliza Scales sat bolt upright and gave a little cry of dismay, knowing she had not given the token to Anthony. Elizabeth, guessing it was Margaret's, gave a delighted laugh. "My brother has not forgotten he is *my* champion today," she gushed and waved at him gaily.

Margaret's jaw dropped, certain Elizabeth was lying to protect her. She placed her hand over the queen's and squeezed it lightly. Eliza was satisfied and smiled proudly as she watched her husband place the helm over his chain mail hood and affix it to his shoulder armor. He lowered the hinged *bavière* so that all but a narrow slit for his eyes protected his head and face. Both knights reined in their mounts at either end of the field, their lances couched, and the crowd held its breath.

"*Laissez aller!*" cried the herald. The two coursers sat back on their haunches, their riders precariously balanced in the heavy armor, and pawed the air with their front legs before being spurred to leap forward into a gallop full tilt at each other. Halfway down the field, hooves thudding and dirt flying, the men couched their spears, settled them under their arms and lowered their heads for the best view through the visor. Impatient for the inevitable clash of arms, the horses did not run true and veered away from each other, causing no score. A groan of disappointment came from the spectators, but Margaret closed her eyes and thanked St. George, the patron saint of soldiers, to whom she had prayed the night before.

At the ends of the lists, the knights slowed their mounts and came to a standstill. Anthony turned and removed his *bavière* and arm guard to be ready for the next course, which was to be fought with swords. The Bastard similarly prepared himself and grasped the sword offered him on a golden cushion. Once again the horses were spurred into action, and this time it seemed the two knights would clash directly in front of the king. Closer and closer they came, swords raised. Seconds later, they met with a loud clash of steel upon steel. Anthony's sword looked to have dealt a deadly blow to the Bastard's throat, but the Bastard's young, excitable horse had run headlong into Anthony's saddle and leg armor, crushing its own armor into its head. It emitted a ghastly scream, reared up and then came crashing down. Blood gushed from the wound, and the beast toppled to the ground, bringing the heavily weighted knight under it. A gasp of horror went up as the horse died, its lifeblood spouting in scarlet torrents.

Edward was on his feet and commanded that Antoine be helped from under his horse. The knight's face was like thunder when he was finally back on his feet, and he accused Anthony of harmful and unfair trappings on his mount. Anthony rode straight to the king, dismounted and allowed his horse to be examined to prove no hidden device could have killed the other animal, a practice strictly prohibited in jousting. Nothing untoward was found, and it was decided that an unlucky movement of the horse's head at just the wrong moment during the first clash of the riders had caused its death. The Burgundian was offered the chance to use one of the other twelve horses he had brought with him but, shaken and saddened by the demise of his favorite destrier, he declined, and the disappointed spectators were told there would be no more fighting that day.

"But it has only just begun," Fortunata groused to Margaret, as they watched the poor horse being dragged off the field by ropes and climbed back into the litter. "I will not find such a good place again tomorrow!"

Margaret said nothing. She had been horrified by the horse's death, and to think there might be human blood shed before this was all over made her feel sick. She had been proud of Anthony's behavior after the Burgundian's accusations. Antoine had declined the use of another horse, and after hearing many viewpoints, took back his harsh accusations and asked to be excused for the day. Anthony had walked the length of the lists side by side with his opponent to see him safely to his tent. There they were seen to exchange some friendly words and a handshake before Anthony turned and walked back to his own pavilion amid flowers and cheers from his admiring countrymen.

The next day, the trumpets sounded bright and sharp. The king's party once again took their places on the stage, and the ladies in their box. Margaret had chosen a pale blue silk gown, cut low to allow the breeze to cool her skin, and her hair was coiled in braids around her head and covered with a flimsy gauze veil. Next to her, Elizabeth was once again magnificent in purple silk with gold trim, a jeweled crown encircling her steepled hennin. Margaret knew no one would notice her while she sat next to such a beautiful creature, so she sank back in her chair and wished she was a hundred leagues away.

Lucky Dickon, she thought. He chose not to come from Middleham to witness this. "I learn the skill of arms, Meg," he had told her on a recent visit, "and I am good at it, but I would rather use what I know in the defense of Edward and England, not for sport." Always the little diplomat, Margaret smiled, remembering. I pray he never has to use those skills. She was jolted from her reverie by the trumpet fanfare and the reading of the rules again.

Today, the duelling would be on foot, and this was where Anthony would be in the most danger. The Bastard was broader, stronger and had a longer reach. However, it was well known that Anthony's skill hand to hand was unmatched in England, and he was faster and nimbler than his older opponent. No one had seen Antoine in action, so he was an unknown.

Margaret was relieved when Edward declared one of the weapons— the casting spear—right dangerous and refused his permission for it to be used. This left battle-axes and daggers.

"For St. George!" Scales shouted, somewhat muffled from inside his helmet. His armor jangling as he walked towards his foe, he raised his battle-ax above his head and attempted to bring it down on Burgundy's head. His opponent evaded the blow and brought his ax around in a sweeping motion, striking Scales in the side. Anthony bent double, clutching his side, and staggered back. Margaret half rose in her chair, a cry on her lips, but seeing Anthony nod to his opponent that he was able to continue, she inched down into her seat again. His heavily padded aketon and chain mail had protected him. The stroke had sent him off balance but no more. The crowd breathed a collective sigh of relief.

On foot, the two men were hampered by their heavy armor. The helmets with their high, fashioned crests sat awkwardly on neck and shoulders, the slit across the eyes only allowing limited vision. Time and time again the now weary fighters lunged at each other, the blunted blades occasionally causing a bruising blow but mostly clanging harmlessly on a raised shield. Sweating profusely in the sun inside their metal casing, both men were staggering with fatigue as they raised the fearsome axes with one hand and carried their heavy shields in the other and rained blow upon blow on each other. On and on they came, most missing their mark, as wielding the weighty weapons took all of the combatants' strength each time. Margaret winced at every clank, silently begging Edward to end her misery by stopping the fight, for it seemed no one could win. People had started to drift away, their interest waning.

Elizabeth, who was pregnant, was as anxious as Margaret to leave by this time, and she sent her page to Edward to beg him to bring the fight to a close. He listened to the boy and turned to look at the ladies' box. Elizabeth was white, and Margaret's hand was over her eyes. He grinned but did not act.

It was as though Anthony had also had his fill, for after evading Burgundy's next stroke, he swung his ax in a high circle and brought it down with all his force on the Bastard's helm, cutting through it as though it were a blade of grass and bringing the knight to his knees, one side of his perspiring face exposed. The ladies were on their feet now, crying to Edward to stop the fight. Anthony circled his foe, his movements menacing, but as if he had just begun the day, the Bastard jumped up and ran towards Anthony with a loud war whoop. Their interest renewed, the spectators screamed encouragement, and Margaret, sure she was about to see Anthony killed, ran from her place to the stairs at the back of the box and vomited as delicately as she could onto the ground below.

"Enough!" the king suddenly commanded, getting up from his throne and throwing the staff he was holding onto the field. With the deafening sounds of metal on metal ringing inside their helmets, the jousters did not hear him. Then an officer ran forward and put his pike between them, only to have it sliced in two by one of the axes. Edward cried again, "Whoa! 'Tis enough, I say. Enough!" This time, his voice penetrated both combatants' helmets, and they immediately put up their weapons and took off their helmets. They eyed each other with respect before walking slowly to the king.

Edward commended their bravery and skill and then commanded them to shake hands. "Love each other as brothers in arms, my friends," he said, smiling at them. "You have fought well today, but we want no bloodshed. You may both carry your weapons back to your pavilions, for 'tis not clear which of you is the winner." He leaned forward and chuckled. Jerking his thumb towards Elizabeth and Margaret, he muttered, "Now go before the ladies all swoon away."

The two exhausted men clasped arms in friendship and swore never to cross swords again. Anthony strode back to his pavilion, great gashes visible in his armor. He stopped and bowed to Elizabeth and Margaret, who had taken her seat again, and he was followed by loud applause for his knightly exploits. Later, the day was awarded to Anthony, and thus he claimed his jeweled-flower prize.

After two more days of jousting and feasting, the tournament came to an unexpected close. "Make way, make way for the king's messenger!" the cry rang out. The sea of people parted to allow a dust-covered rider and his equally filthy steed to gallop up to the royal dais.

"Your grace, I beg leave to give you bad tidings." The breathless messenger slid from the saddle and onto his knee in front of his sovereign in one graceful motion. The drifting masses regrouped behind him and listened expectantly. The king stiffened and nodded curtly.

" 'Tis news for the Maréchal of Burgundy," the man hurried on. "Duke Philip, his father, is dead, and he is required to return immediately to the court at Dijon!"

Within an hour, the mournful tolling of bells filled the air, making very different music for the city. The festivities were indeed over.

WITH DUKE PHILIP dead, it became more expedient for the widower Charles to take a wife, as he had no male heir, and thus Margaret began to look more and more appealing to him. He might be able to put aside his aversion for the house of York, especially if he were able to persuade Edward as part of the bargain to lift the ban on imports of Burgundian goods into England. This Edward did on Michaelmas Day, sealing Margaret's fate once and for all.

"Oh, Fortunata, we are to go to Burgundy," Margaret told her servant miserably that evening. Edward had summoned her to his hunting lodge at Kingston-on-Thames during a meeting of the Great Council to determine the terms of the marriage contract. Margaret had been demure in front of her brother when he told her the news, but now, with her ladies withdrawn and the silk curtains around the bed closed against the world, she wept. Fortunata let her cry. She alternated between stroking her mistress's beautiful golden hair and massaging her feet. She hummed a tune she remembered from her childhood, and the repetitive round eventually calmed Margaret, who wiped her nose on her fine lawn chemise, climbed out of bed and onto her knees on the red and blue Turkey carpet.

"Holy Mary, Mother of God, pray for me, a poor sinner. Help me be the princess my brother wants me to be and help me serve England to the best of my ability. And dear St. Monica, help me be the wife I should be to this man, who, if the truth be told, I cannot like. I ask that there be the joy of children for me and that I do my duty to my husband and my new country. All this I ask, Lord, in Your dear Son's name, Amen."

As she crossed herself, she felt a cold nose snuffling her bare feet.

"Astolat! You are tickling me," she said, reluctantly chuckling and gathering the dog into her arms, her tears momentarily forgotten. "I am at prayer, my sweet hound. You should not disturb me, but how can I resist you when your very presence daily reminds me of Anthony. I hope Duke Charles likes dogs, my pet, for you shall be with me wherever I go. You and Fortunata."

THE NEXT DAY, a page delivered a letter to Margaret; she fancied she could smell Anthony on the fine vellum. Dismissing the young man with thanks, she walked to the window for more light before breaking the seal. There was no greeting, only a simple poem.

> *"Love winged my hopes and taught me how to fly;*
> *Far from base earth but not to mount hie*
> *For thy true pleasure*
> *Loves in measure*
> *Which, if men forsake,*
> *Blinded they into folly run and grief for pleasure to take."*

"Ah, Anthony, 'tis folly indeed," she whispered, sadly. "And I do grieve."

TWO DAYS LATER, the Great Council was impressed by the entrance of the mature young woman on her brother George's arm. Her assent to this great marriage between England and Burgundy was eagerly anticipated.

"Magnificent," murmured Jack Howard, catching Margaret's eye as she swept past him on her way to the dais. "God keep you, Lady Margaret."

Margaret smiled at him but said nothing. She stood at the steps of Edward's dais and made him a graceful curtsey. "Your grace, you summoned me?" she said.

Edward bade her stand with him on the steps and in a loud voice asked if she gave her assent to the marriage he and his councilors had arranged for her.

"No, I do not!" she wanted to shout. "How dare you send me away!" Instead she held her head high and said quite clearly, "I do, my liege and my lords. And I do it happily for England."

A roar of approval went up, and the councilors gave her three cheers. Edward then presented her with Charles's ring as a betrothal gift, which Antoine had carried with him from Burgundy and left in Edward's care.

The first to congratulate her was George, his wardrobe so elaborate that he outshone the king himself. Margaret often wondered why Ned indulged his brother in this way, but Ned explained that if it kept George happy and close by him, then he could forgive his sartorial impudence. When Edward was present, no one could outshine his larger than life personality, magnificent physique—although Margaret noticed his girth was growing steadily—and genuine charm, not even popinjay George. George still had not forgiven Edward for refusing to allow him Isabel Neville's hand, and Margaret had warned Edward that George was headstrong enough to defy his sovereign. Edward had scoffed at her fears, saying George was empty-headed and cared only for his looks.

"The trouble with an empty head, my dear brother, is that it can so easily be filled with other people's ideas and ambitions," she had told Edward one day. "I trust you have noted the friendship between George and our cousin Warwick? When you have finally found me a willing husband and I am out of reach, who will be close enough to warn you then? But you are right to keep George close by you. 'Tis when he is out of earshot of your wisdom that he may heed the wrong man's counsel."

"Meggie, I am going to miss you," Edward had told her, giving her a smacking kiss. "I pray your husband, whoever he is, appreciates your wisdom,"—he winked at her—"as well as your other charms, *naturellement*. Never fear, I shall watch George."

She thought of that conversation as the earl of Warwick took her hand and told her he had no doubt she was the finest export England could offer. She was surprised at the warmth and sincerity in his voice and eyes. "I fear you flatter me, my lord. But I will try and live up to your kind compliment," she replied. "It is particularly important to me that I have your approbation for this marriage. Know that I am forever grateful for the work you have done on my behalf that did not bear fruit. Your loyalty to my father and brother will keep you always in my prayers."

Warwick gazed into Margaret's eyes and knew he could do no less than give her marriage his complete approval. Her honesty and diplomacy took his breath away, and he took her hand again and pressed it to his lips. "As I said, Lady Margaret, England's finest export," he murmured and bowed low to her.

Margaret could not help noticing the chill between him and Ned as he

then gave the king a curt bow. He was plainly angry, and she knew that
he had been embarrassed by Edward after his return from France with
French envoys in tow and offers of new negotiations, to which Edward
had given short shrift. He was convinced Edward's Woodville family were
causing the rift between him and his king, and his hatred of them was
barely concealed when he deigned to visit the court. He had disappeared
up to his northern estates soon after Elizabeth was delivered of another
daughter in August, and George had followed close behind. However, he
could not refuse the command to attend the Great Council, and so he had
returned, bringing his enmity with him. Margaret watched him go sadly.
He had such an overpowering magnetism, and she was dismayed that a
man so powerful and fiercely loyal to her father's and brother's cause had
now turned his back on them. The earl's burning ambition to rule his
protégé, Edward, from behind the throne was now patently obvious.

Edward introduced her to the two chief negotiators from Burgundy,
and she avised them both for a few minutes, committing to memory
the long, aquiline nose and sheep's eye of Lodewijk van Gruuthuse, also
known as Lord of Bruges, and Lord Halewijn's jowls and bad teeth. These
two lords would be part of Charles's council and thus very much part of
her life when she arrived in Burgundy. They, too, avised her for themselves, noting her height, the clear, gray eyes, generous mouth and loop
of blond hair on her forehead. She was lovelier than they had been led
to believe by other foreign envoys who passed through Bruges from the
English court. Perhaps they had not been this close to her flawless English
skin. The mutual scrutiny was not unusual, and both parties subjected
themselves to it unperturbed.

The other councilors filed past her now, bowing and kissing her hand.
Edward stood by proudly as each had a word for her: Will Hastings, who
took her hand in both of his and thanked her; John Tiptoft, who told
her Duke Charles was a lucky man; Jack Howard, who promised to give
her knowledge of the court at Burgundy if it would help her; Chancellor
Neville, recently restored to his office after some questionable dealings,
who gravely wished her well; and the other Neville brother, George, archbishop of York, who gave her a blessing.

And then Anthony stood in front of her, and their eyes met in a silent
moment of understanding and sadness. *Whatever has been between us*

must be forgotten, his eyes tried to tell her. But he did not read the same message in hers. I will love you always, Anthony, they said. He bowed over her hand, and she resisted the temptation to turn it over and feel his lips on her palm. The other councilors passed by in a blur, but all were clearly awed by the tall, graceful princess, who seemed to be accepting her fate with perfect equanimity. They could not see her knocking knees or the perspiration streaming down her sides. They certainly did not guess she had cried herself to sleep the two previous nights, except for Anthony, who received a one-line response to his poem.

"I shall grieve for you forever. Elaine."

MUCH OF MARGARET's daily routine after Michaelmas comprised learning about Burgundy. Even though Duke Charles had not yet signed a contract, it was presumed this was only a matter of time—and a dispensation from the pope. She learned that her future husband had always leaned to Lancaster to flout his father's preference for York and uphold his mother's heritage as a granddaughter of Lancaster. She also learned that unlike England, which was ruled by a king and a parliament with London as its capital, Burgundy was a hodgepodge of city states and territories, each of which had been autonomous until the Valois dukes of Burgundy had seized them during the previous hundred years. What was even more surprising to Margaret and a little hard to understand was that the duke was a vassal of the king of France and the Habsburg emperor of the Holy Roman Empire.

"Much of Burgundy's lands once belonged to France or the empire," John Tiptoft told her. "The dukes became so powerful that not even their two liege lords could stop them from acquiring more territory."

"And yet the dukes owed allegiance to those two rulers, my lord?" Margaret repeated, to make sure she understood. Tiptoft nodded and Margaret shook her head in disbelief. "What good is a king or an emperor if a mere duke can snatch land from him? It could not happen here. The king is all-powerful."

The councilor said nothing. It would not be politic to tell the king's sister that many people thought the earl of Warwick capable of it. There were rumors that he had treated with Louis of France during the June meetings and might even form a devilish alliance with the She-Wolf of Anjou in exchange for owning territories in Holland and Zeeland. But it was only rumors, and no loyal subject of Edward's could possibly believe in such a tale. Instead, he went on to explain to Margaret that the lands now ruled by Duke Charles encompassed a vast area that included the counties of Charolais, Artois and Flanders, the duchies of Burgundy, Hainault, Holland, Zeeland and Brabant, and boasted the extremely wealthy cities of Bruges, Ghent and Brussels. Upon her marriage, Tiptoft told her smiling, Margaret's titles would far exceed those of her brother, the king of England.

"But my fiancé's true allegiance should be with the king of France. And what happens if I do not marry Duke Charles or do not produce an heir, my lord? Charles has but one daughter from his two previous marriages. Can she inherit a duchy?"

"Aye, in principle, but should anything happen to Charles and young Mary has no husband to protect her, I cannot imagine that Louis and the Emperor Frederick would not swoop in to reclaim what they consider theirs." The astute politician saw the fleeting look of fear that crossed Margaret's face. "But, my lady, do not dwell on this. You are from a prolific line and will bear the duke a son, we all have no doubt."

Margaret inadvertently shivered. "I pray you are right, my lord."

That night, she prayed to the patron saint of barren women, Felicitas, to protect her.

MEANWHILE, THE ILL will between the Woodvilles and Warwick became too acrid for even easygoing Edward to tolerate, and in January of 1468, he called a meeting of his council at his castle in Coventry during which he commanded that Earl Rivers and the earl of Warwick make an attempt at a reconciliation in public.

" 'Twas a sour potion for the earl to swallow, Meg," Richard told his sister a few weeks later. "My lord is not accustomed to stooping to apologize to one as low as Rivers. His jaw was set for days following, and I blame him not."

"Certes, Dickon, but Ned needs to keep the peace between the two. He owes Warwick his throne and Woodville his wife. I do not envy him," Margaret told him. "Your lord is a greedy man, and by all that is holy, Ned has rewarded him well, but he needs to know who is king, in my view."

"Do not think I am disloyal to Ned!" Dickon cried anxiously. "I am torn by my duty to my liege lord Warwick, who has me under his roof, and my brother and sovereign lord, to whom I owe everything."

"You have but one allegiance, Dickon, and that is to your family. Never forget that. I shall never forget I am a York and a princess of England when—if—I go to Burgundy."

Richard nodded, understanding her well. Then he lowered his eyes and said softly, "I fear George needs to be reminded, Meg. He is constantly in Warwick's company and talks of Isabel interminably. I do not think he will rest until he has her."

"Ned will never sanction it. And besides, she is too close in kin by far. I am told Charles had his troubles with a dispensation for us to wed—and I wish it had been denied," she sighed, "and we are far more distant than George and Isabel."

Richard grinned. "But you will love Bruges, Meg. Duchess Isabella— the older one—was so kind to George and me. You will live like a queen there."

"I live like a queen here, Dickon. What can you mean?" Margaret retorted.

"Aye, we live well, but not half so well as the duke. You will see. But," he said in a quieter tone, a faraway look in his eyes, "I do not think having so many riches is as important as being happy, do you?"

Margaret heard a warmth in his voice she had not heard before and looked at him intently. Was it possible? she thought. After all, he is fifteen now. She smiled, her own woes forgotten. "Why, Dickon, I do believe you are in love! Who is the lady? Someone in the north? Do I know her?"

Richard was all business once more. He laughed a little too heartily, rose and evaded her questions. He was such a private young man, she often did not understand him, but she appreciated he was being loyal to whomever had taken his fancy and so did not press him further. Nonetheless, she was intrigued and so convinced he had fallen in love that she asked Fortunata to ferret out any information she could about Richard's paramour. Fortunata came up emptyhanded, but one foggy day in late February, while Edward was still haggling over her contract, Margaret herself found out a little more.

Jack Howard was back at court after many weeks of recuperation from a nasty hunting accident in Suffolk, where he was gored by a charging wild boar, and he had volunteered to give her his impressions of his many visits to Flanders. Margaret insisted on improving her French in preparation for her new life, and Jack found himself floundering in front of her fluency. His mistakes led to much laughter, and they spent a merry afternoon in conversation.

"I was sorry to hear about your accident, Sir John," Margaret said, pointing to his still bandaged leg. "I believe there is nothing more ferocious than a wild boar when it is cornered."

"Aye, the creature is courageous in the face of death, I grant you, and I liked not the look in his eye as he came at me. Your brother, Gloucester, has decided upon the boar for his device, he told me during his visit to Nayland a fortnight ago. 'Tis a noble animal indeed and a good choice."

"Dickon was with you, Sir John?" Margaret asked, innocently. " 'Tis strange he did not mention it the other day when we talked."

Jack unexpectedly colored and stammered, " 'Twas but a short visit, my lady, and he has much to occupy him these days. He had no reason to tell you of it." He thought quickly and rushed on, "And now, let me talk to you of the merchant adventurers in Bruges, with whom you are sure to have discourse as they are the English merchant representatives there."

Margaret did not miss the flush and fluster in his voice. Aha! she thought, whoever Dickon is dallying with has a connection to Howard. For his part, Jack cursed himself, because, as Margaret had correctly guessed, Richard had met a young woman at Tendring Hall, had sworn him and Lady Howard to secrecy, and Jack had almost let the cat out of the bag.

" 'TIS FINALLY signed, Meg," Edward told his sister on the afternoon of the fourteenth day of March. "I have ratified the treaty with Charles and you will marry him in early May at Bruges."

He observed her as the news sank in. Her back was long and straight as a Roman road, her hands were clasped in her lap, and her eyes stared unblinking at the red and gold tapestry in front of her. "Aye, your grace," she eventually whispered and crossed herself. "As you wish."

Edward chuckled. "You look as though you were about to be put on the rack. Come now, Meg, marriage is not so bad. Bess and I are very happy together, as are her mother and father, and I can give you other examples, including our own parents. Certes, Jack Howard and his new wife, Margaret, dote on each other.

"You have spent time with Antoine of Burgundy, and you told me you liked him. Why should you think his half brother will be any different? For one so intelligent, you are being addle-pated about this, Margaret. Now, smile for me; I cannot send you to Bruges looking so sour-faced." He clapped his hands, startling her out of her trance and silencing the buzz of conversation at the other side of the room. Edward called for music, the soft notes from lutes and viols broke the tension and the court-iers resumed their quiet talking.

Margaret lifted her head and smiled sweetly at her brother, though tears shone on her lashes. "Will this do?" she asked. "I can keep this up for as long as you like. But you cannot prevent the pain in my heart, Ned. 'Tis not a fear exactly, 'tis a deep melancholy I have in here"—she touched her heart—"that I will leave all that is near and dear to me for ever."

"Your tears are wasted on me, Margaret. I am fast losing patience—"

Edward was interrupted by a scuffle at the far end of the room, and they both turned to see all four of Astolat's gangly legs flailing wildly as he tried to release Fortunata's grip on the tether that was keeping him from reaching Margaret's side. Finally gaining a footing on the slippery flagstones, with rushes flying, the dog achieved his goal by simply drag-ging the poor Fortunata on her rump along the floor behind him. Brother and sister forgot their disagreement and laughed at the scene, and when the dwarf saw her mistress in merrier spirits, she encouraged the dog to go faster by picking up a long rush and using it as a whip.

"That's better, Meggie," Edward whispered as the courtiers cheered the dog on. "I am counting on you to win Charles over to the York cause. 'Tis vital for England."

10

Spring and Summer 1468

Margaret's favorite green and gold spring came and went so quickly that she hardly had time to savor it, as preparations for her marriage took up most of her days. Despite the problems Edward had in raising the first fifty thousand crowns Charles had demanded as dowry, he could not let his sister arrive in Burgundy—the most cultural and fashionable province in Europe—with an inadequate trousseau. Gowns of cloth of silver and gold, underdresses of damask, satin and silk, velvet mantles lined with fur, hennins adorned with pearls and jewels and shoes of every color had to be measured and made for her.

Edward had told her at the time of the signing in March that there was a problem with the dispensation for her and Charles to marry, and it was still wanting. The couple were related in the third and fourth degrees of consanguinity, and somewhere in the application process, Charles had made an error.

"Christ's nails!" roared Edward, when he had heard of yet another delay at the end of April. He swung around to face his council, and his eye rested on Anthony Woodville. "Scales, go and find my sister and tell her she will not be wed on the fourth of May. I warrant your shoulder is as good as anyone's for her to cry on. Duke Charles fears Louis may have had something to do with this, and if he has, I shall flay him alive—next time I see him. Now, let us choose another date for the marriage. I cannot believe the pope will make us wait more than a month, so I propose the twenty-fourth of June. Aye, tell Lady Margaret she has a reprieve until then, Anthony." And he waved his brother-in-law away.

Anthony hurried through the halls of Westminster Palace to where Margaret had her apartments. Master Vaughan greeted him warmly in the waiting room. Margaret had told Anthony after the tournament that her steward now held him in higher esteem than Edward, at which Anthony had laughed and called her a flatterer.

"I must see the Lady Margaret at once, Master Vaughan, I have a message from the king. Pray announce me without delay," Anthony commanded, clapping the old man on the shoulder as he would a friend.

"I regret, my lord, but the Lady Margaret is unable to give an audience at this moment," the steward replied. Then he leaned in and whispered conspiratorially, "For she is in her bath!"

"Then please send Fortunata to me, sir, so I may ascertain how long I must wait."

Within a few minutes, Fortunata slipped through the door and curtseyed to Anthony, who was inspecting a large tapestry that was strewn with tiny flowers. In a low voice so the steward could not hear, she said, "*Madonna* Margaret will let you come in and speak to her, but you cannot see her, milord." To the steward she said brightly, "Master Von, my mistress is ready to see Lord Scales. Thank you and farewell."

Vaughan bowed to Anthony and stomped off down the hall, his head jutting forward and his hands clasped behind his back. Anthony entered Margaret's chamber, and Fortunata announced him. Several of her ladies were hovering around a silk-covered screen, one holding a large steaming pot and another waiting with drying cloths. Fortunata scurried around the screen and told Margaret that Anthony was there.

"Good morning, Anthony," Margaret called. "Forgive my nonappearance, but the steward told me you had important news to give me. Beatrice, Fortunata, stay with me. The rest of you may go."

Anthony remembered that Jane was no longer with Margaret, having been wed several months ago and taken up her new residence with her husband in Lincolnshire. He was sorry. He liked Jane and told Margaret he thought Beatrice was a dragon. He had to admit the older woman obviously adored her mistress, and perhaps, Margaret had countered his unkind moniker, she was simply being protective when Anthony was near.

"The news can wait if this is awkward, my lady. Certes, 'tis not easy to speak to a voice behind a curtain." He chuckled. He could hear the water splashing as Fortunata sponged her mistress. Just then, the sun came out from behind a cloud, and the window behind the screen revealed the three women in silhouette just as Margaret stood up to be dried. He could clearly see the outline of her small breasts and the slight swell of her belly projected on the screen before the women wrapped her in towels. He felt the familiar ache he would experience when he had imagined her in his arms, and he instantly regretted he was wearing a doublet and hose and not a concealing gown.

"Nay, you may tell me, Anthony. It takes too long to clothe me and I am impatient to know." And without warning, she came out from behind the screen, a white silk wrap clinging to her damp body and her glorious fair hair falling to her waist. He gasped. He had never seen her hair uncovered before, and it gave her face a softer, more vulnerable look. He could not speak as he gazed at her, and only his rigid upbringing and moral fiber stopped him from taking the few strides into her arms. It was Beatrice's disapproving eyes on his telltale codpiece that made him lower his eyes from Margaret's lithe body, bow and turn discreetly to the window.

"The king's grace sent me," he began in a voice that was not his own. He cleared his throat and tried again. "Your brother has received word that the papal dispensation is still not given. Your marriage must therefore be postponed, my lady. I am sorry to be the bearer of this bad news. However, the king has named a new date. June twenty-fourth."

He heard a sound and swung round to see Margaret crumple to the floor. He was there before Beatrice could move, picking up her limp body and cradling it to his chest. Fortunata, who had been hanging the towels behind the screen, cried out when she saw Margaret and ran to pull back the bed curtains so that Anthony could lay Margaret down. Beatrice hurried to the door, calling for a page to fetch the physician.

"There is never anyone when you want them," she grumbled, looking up and down the long waiting room. "I suppose I shall have to go myself. Lord Scales, you must leave," she called back over her shoulder.

Anthony ignored her and instead sat on the bed beside Margaret, patting her hand and imploring her to open her eyes. Fortunata fetched wine and tried to make her drink it, but then crouched down out of sight on the other side of the bed, giving Anthony precious time with her mistress. It was only a matter of seconds before Margaret fluttered her eyelids and looked up into Anthony's anxious face.

"Praise be to God, Marguerite, you frightened us all," he whispered so close to her that his lips brushed her cheek.

"What happened?" she asked, putting up her free hand and touching his hair. Sweet Mary, how soft it is, she thought. She dragged her attention back to her circumstances and sat up in a panic, pulling her skimpy robe around her. "Why am I in bed? And why are we alone? Oh!" she exclaimed, "now I remember. You came to tell me news, Anthony."

"You are not alone, *madonna,* I am here!" cried the dwarf, popping up from her hiding place. "I am a good chaperon, no?" she asked Anthony, who smiled and nodded.

"You are right, Marguerite, I came to tell you about the postponement of your marriage, and you fainted clean away. Beatrice has gone to fetch the doctor."

Margaret gave a moan of helplessness. "Wed this one, wed that one! Wed this day, wed that day! Why can't they just leave me alone? Maybe I should go to a nunnery, and then I would never have to leave England and"—she impulsively took his face between her hands—"you, my lord . . . nay," she whispered, "my love."

Anthony could not help himself. He crushed her to him, not heeding Fortunata's openmouthed stare, and kissed her waiting lips, forcing his tongue deep into her mouth. Now her moan was one of pleasure, and they were able to control their longings only because Fortunata began shaking Margaret's shoulders roughly. "*Madonna,* Beatrice and the doctor are coming!" The lovers sprang apart, and Anthony strode to the window and pretended to be looking out as several hurrying feet could be heard approaching the room. Margaret was sitting on the farther edge of the bed, her back to Anthony, when Beatrice, the doctor and some of her other ladies entered. They all stopped as one, stared at Margaret on the bed and then all turned to look at Anthony, who acknowledged their presence with an innocent smile and a bow.

"You see, Master Fryse and ladies, your mistress is quite recovered," he said, cheerfully. "'Twas the bad news that her marriage has been postponed that disheartened her. 'Twas a simple swoon, 'tis all. And now, I must bid you all a good day. My lady." He bowed to Margaret and strode from the room.

The doctor gazed after him and did not miss the blush on Margaret's cheek when he turned back to look at her. So the rumors are correct, he told himself, the princess Margaret has her brother's profligate tendencies and may not be going to her marriage bed a virgin. He tee-heed to himself and could not wait to repeat what he had seen to his colleagues.

By the time the dispensation was finally given, it was late May, and Edward had again changed the date for the wedding. This time, he promised Margaret, it would take place on July third. Her two-month reprieve was over. At this point, Margaret was resigned to her fate and just knowing Anthony returned her love gave her the tranquility she needed to accept it with equanimity.

Cheapside, London's largest thoroughfare, was ablaze with color from the rooftops to the cobbled street with garlands of flowers, tapestries, banners, streamers, and pennants of York murrey and blue, royal scarlet and gold, and merchant guilds' colors draped from windows and doors of a city ready to bid farewell to a beloved princess, a princess who had lived among them at Baynard's Castle and the Royal Wardrobe for many of her twenty-two years. The tall young woman was well known in the hospitals and almshouses as she had gone about dispensing cheer, money and prayers to the sick and poor.

"She be one of us," one old woman remarked to a group near Mercers' Hall, who waited for the royal cavalcade to arrive from the Wardrobe at the Market Cross in front of Goldsmiths' Row. "Margaret is a Londoner. We must see her off right." Her companions nodded in agreement. "God bless the Princess Margaret!" By the time the procession came into view from St. Paul's, the cheer had been taken up the length and breadth of the wide street, past the waiting rows of merchants, aldermen and the mayor, and swelled to a roar that drenched Margaret in its support and devotion.

Riding pillion behind the earl of Warwick on his magnificent black destrier, whose trappings rivaled those of its riders, Margaret was overcome by the reception on that eighteenth day of June. In a shimmering gown of scarlet cloth of gold, the train of which was spread over Saladin's back, she smiled through tears of joy and waved to her countrymen until she felt her arm would surely drop off.

The incongruity of the king's choosing the earl to escort his sister was not lost on the canny Londoners. It was whispered in the taverns and the stews that no love was lost between the two these days, but nevertheless they cheered the earl and pretended all was well for the sake of the young woman riding with him today. Behind them, equally magnificent, rode some of the most powerful earls and barons in the land. By this show, Edward proclaimed how significant this alliance with Burgundy was to him.

At the Cross, the earl reined in Saladin and allowed Margaret to face the mayor and aldermen, who presented her with a gift of silver basins containing a hundred pounds of gold. The mayor and several merchants gave warm, flowery speeches, making Margaret blush and the people cheer with every compliment and good wish. Finally, Warwick put up his hand for Margaret to speak and a fanfare sounded. Turning as far around as she could while sitting sidesaddle to include as many as possible, she cried, "Loyal subjects of my brother and your sovereign, Edward, I thank you for this gift and most of all for your love. I will go to Flanders a true Englishwoman and carry this day in my heart always. God bless you all," she ended, choking on a sob.

"God bless Margaret, God bless Princess Margaret!" The people cheered again and showered her with flower petals that fluttered to earth around her, mingling with her tears.

EDWARD AND ELIZABETH greeted Margaret affectionately at the entrance to the great abbey at Stratford Langthorne, a half-day's journey into Essex from the Aldgate. It was here Margaret's family would celebrate with her before their valediction.

"Greetings, Meg! I trust Richard Neville saw you through London," Edward said, after she was helped from her litter into which she had gratefully subsided after leaving London. Fortunata hopped out and curtseyed low to the king and queen.

"Aye, Ned," she answered, accepting his warm embrace. "My lord of Warwick was the model of chivalry and none would suspect his smile was naught but the gritting of his teeth," she whispered.

Edward sighed and stood back from her to greet others who were wearily dismounting and entering the abbey.

"George," he called. "Clarence, *viens!* Margaret has need of your arm. Pray escort your sister to her quarters, and she can tell you of the Londoners' farewell. My spies tell me she was fairly feted." He then winked at George. "But we will not tell her how many bribes it took to encourage people to cheer."

"Brother, I shall not miss your attempts at wit. Not one whit!" Margaret retorted. "Elizabeth, I know not how you put up with him," she said, tongue firmly in cheek. "Now, George, what lowly monk's cell is he able to afford for me to make up for all those bribes he so generously paid on my behalf?"

She and George moved inside followed by Edward's laughter. As they made their way through the maze of corridors to the abbot's lodgings, to which the king's party had been consigned, she took the opportunity to give him some advice about his growing friendship with Richard Neville, earl of Warwick.

"Ned will not countenance it much further, George. You must know the two of them are headed for a rift, if it has not already occurred. You must come back into Edward's good graces, or you will rue the day. I know not why you are so unhappy—nay, do not deny it, my dear brother. 'Tis in your face and your eyes, for I know you all too well, don't forget. Wait, let me finish, I pray you," she said quickly, seeing him ready to interrupt. "Is it because Ned will not let you marry Isabel? Or is there something less plain and simple?"

"Who told you about Isabel?" Clarence rounded on her. He lowered his voice when he realized her entourage of ladies had all come to a standstill, too. "There is no one who knows, except—*Dickon!* Certes, 'tis Dickon who has tattled. You do not have to defend him, I know. Allow me to tell you something now, Meg. Dickon has his eye on Anne Neville, I know it. But it seems Ned will not let either of us have a Neville daughter." He turned his blue eyes on her, eyes she always had trouble resisting: "I love Isabel, Meg. And she loves me. 'Tis unfair that Ned can wed where he may, and I cannot."

Margaret set her jaw. Despite her unwillingness to leave her family, she hoped she would never have to hear George declare life unfair ever again. It was tedious. Instead she patted his hand, walked on and told him, "When you are sent away from your home and family to wed someone you have never even set eyes on, I will listen to what is fair and unfair, George. Until then, let us just enjoy these last hours in each other's company. I plan on feasting and dancing until I fall into a stupor and am carried on board ship bound for Burgundy."

George took her hand and kissed it as they arrived at her chamber. "Forgive me for a churl, Meggie. You have greater cause to be angry with Ned than I."

"But in truth, George, this is where we differ. I have no anger for Ned. 'Tis our place in life to do what is right for our family and what is right for England. That is why I caution you to stay away from my lord of Warwick. I will say no more on it, I promise." She kissed him lightly on the mouth and swept through the open door, her ladies tripping along behind her. George took a deep breath, scowled and stalked off to find Dickon.

AFTER THE FIRST night's feasting, Margaret pleaded weariness, and Edward rose to end the festivities early.

Edward motioned to Jack Howard, who had the honor of serving the king that night, to stop the music. Then he stood, and the company scraped back benches to stand in deferential silence.

"My lords, ladies and gentle sirs, my sister is tired and I warrant so are most of you. We shall hunt on the morrow, and all are invited to join us in the courtyard following Mass. And now, to bed! We wish you all God's good night." He took Elizabeth's arm, wrapped it around his and looked for George to escort Margaret. He frowned when he saw George in close proximity to Warwick. Damn them, he thought, with a heavy heart.

George hurried to the dais and helped Margaret down the steps in her heavy golden gown. Fortunata and Beatrice picked up the train, and the royal party processed out of the room, the guests in reverence as they passed.

DRESSED IN GREEN, a jaunty soft hat upon her head, Margaret ran down the stairs to her waiting horse the next morning. She had spent an hour on her knees at the prie-dieu in the chamber, which had been hung with draught-excluding tapestries for the king's visit. Then she spent another hour getting ready to ride to the hunt. Dickon had taught her to use a gerfalcon at Greenwich, and she loved the sport.

Yelping hounds and whinnying horses greeted her as she breathed in the flower-scented air at the top of the steps. The monks had an extensive herb garden, which was in full bloom, and the fragrances floated on the warm summer air, stimulating her senses. One of Margaret's squires helped her mount into the cumbersome saddle, and she hooked her leg around the horn and settled into a comfortable position before being handed her hawk. She wound the leather thong of her glove around the hooded hawk's leg, and it sat there, immobile. Astolat gamboled around her, his long tail waving in anticipation of the hunt. Riders jostled one another, she heard Edward call to Will Hastings and saw Richard's eager young face ready for the ride. He sidled his horse over to join her and adjusted her glove so that the bird sat more comfortably.

"Stay near me, Meggie. There are too many riders, and I would not wish your mount to be compromised," he said. At that moment, George appeared and looked scornfully over at Richard.

"I am Meg's escort here, Dickon. She has no need of a tattle-tale to protect her."

As Dickon's face reddened, Margaret snapped. "Enough, little brothers, I want to hear you laugh. Very soon I shall be gone, and if you will quarrel then, I cannot stop you, but now, I want to remember you both happy. I pray you, can do this for me?"

"I wager I will win every sport with you, Dickon, while we are here. Are you game?" George's mercurial temper turned, and he grinned over at his brother. Richard, not wanting another dressing-down from George, was relieved and nodded gladly. "What are the stakes, George?" he asked.

A horn signaled the start of the hunt, and George spurred his horse forward, shouting back, "I shall tell you when I've won!"

. . .

AFTER THE FEAST later that day, Margaret watched as Jack Howard approached the dais. Again she was seated with Edward and Elizabeth, both gorgeously arrayed in purple silk with ermine trim, who were engrossed in each other. She watched enviously as Edward's hand moved up Elizabeth's thigh. Would she could be in the same position with Anthony! Enough foolishness, Meg, she berated herself, but she stole a glance at her beloved seated at a table nearby. Edward's jester, Jehan Le Sage, and Fortunata were seated on the steps beneath their master and mistress, ready to entertain when commanded.

"Your graces, my lady," Jack Howard addressed the magnificent trio, and Edward removed his hand from Elizabeth's leg. "I would offer a divertissement for the Lady Margaret, if you will allow."

Edward raised his eyebrow at Margaret. "Well, Meg, shall we see what this gammy-legged treasurer of mine has to offer?" he teased Jack. Howard's wound still caused him trouble, and he could not conceal a limp. His mustache twitched above a smile as he waited for Margaret's response. She leaned forward and asked, "What do you have in mind, Sir John?"

"My dear wife's good friend Dame Katherine Haute has a voice to rival the angels. I think with some effort I could persuade her to sing for the company. Would that please you, my lady?" He looked at Edward. "Your grace?"

Edward waved his assent and Margaret thanked him. A few minutes later, a young woman of no mean beauty was propelled forward by Jack Howard. She clutched a harp to her bosom as if her life depended upon it and sank into a deep, graceful curtsey at the dais. A stool was brought for her, and she sat alone facing the king and settled the harp in her lap. With a practiced hand, she swept the first chords of her song and then began to sing. Margaret was spellbound. The song was an eerie tale of two sisters who fall in love with the same man. The younger is promised to him, and the jealous elder sister lures her to the edge of the river and pushes her in. Her body is found in his dam by a miller, and he is so moved by her beauty that he makes himself a harp from her breastbone and uses the beautiful hair to make the strings. The harp then takes on a life of its own, and in the last scene, the miller takes it to the castle where the young man lives now with his wife, the elder sister. And the harp sings all by itself, recognizing her father, the king, her mother, the queen and her sweet William. But then, in a denunciation of her murderer, the harp turns to William's wife and sings:

"And woe to my sister, the false Helen . . ."

The superstitious, including Margaret, crossed themselves. As she gazed down at the talented girl sitting quietly on the stool watching Edward with more than a little awe, something made her glance at Richard, and she gasped when she saw the look on his face. Such love she could recognize in her own gray eyes when she dared to look at Anthony! It was as plain as a pikestaff, she thought gleefully, here is Richard's paramour. And as if to confirm her suspicion, he left his seat and graciously went to raise Dame Haute from her stool and present her to her appreciative audience.

"Methinks Dickon has found himself a mistress," Edward whispered to Margaret, who nodded. "He has good taste."

Margaret frowned at him for his clumsy remark, not blaming Elizabeth for clicking her tongue and turning away. Edward's smile vanished. "'Twas well done, Dame Haute," he said loudly and then called to Howard, who was returning the woman to her seat, "Jack, you were right. She sings like an angel."

Later, when they were dancing, Margaret teased Richard. "Dickon, you should learn not to wear your heart on your sleeve. Do not deny you are in love with Katherine Haute. And if I am not mistaken, she looks to be with child. Yours, I presume."

Richard was so taken aback that he simply flushed, giving himself away. Margaret chuckled.

Anthony was next to claim a dance. As their hands touched, a quiver of excitement passed through them, and Margaret had to keep her eyes firmly glued to the floor to avoid those blue eyes.

"How now, my sweet Marguerite," he murmured as the steps brought them close. "Do you know how beautiful you are tonight?"

They danced apart, but he saw the deep flush on her cheeks and was satisfied. Every eye was upon the bride that night, and no one must ever guess what was between them. Only Edward watched them both with empathy. To be so close yet not to own was excruciating, he knew all too well. Then, rising, he turned to his beautiful wife. "Bess, come dance with me. And then we shall to bed!" he said, a gleam in his eye.

CECILY JOINED THE festivities on the final day, watching as George and Richard competed at archery, wrestling and swordplay. George never revealed the promised wager, because Richard was the winner in every instance except wrestling. Even at the hunt, Richard's skill with his falcon had won the praise of all who rode that day, most of all from Edward, turning George inwards and worrying Margaret more. Why does Ned not see the chasm opening between them, she thought woefully. He is not stupid, and yet his life of hedonistic adventure with wine, food and women must addle his wits, she concluded. What will happen when I am not here? She sent a prayer to St. Joseph to be a father to her family and guide them through these dangerous times. All royal men came into the world knowing that by their very rank they courted an early death, Cecily had told her. "Be thankful you were born a woman, Margaret," she said, while still in mourning for her husband.

Richard unexpectedly bested George in the sword fight. Margaret watched her favorite brother walk away without acknowledging Richard's win, and once again her heart went out to him. He can't win even against Dickon, she thought sadly. Poor George.

CECILY HAD PLEADED tiredness and begged to be excused from the journey into Kent, so Margaret's first farewell was to her mother, who had taught her everything. Cecily was standing in front of her still tall and regal, her blue eyes shining with pride in her daughter. "Go with a mother's blessing, my child. You are from a proud house, Margaret. Never forget your ancestry and teach your children well. Your father would have been so pleased with you. He never doubted your promise." As always when Cecily talked of her husband, the love in her eyes never failed to inspire Margaret.

"Mother . . ." She hesitated but then plunged on, knowing this might be her last chance of intimacy with Cecily. "I do not remember Father very well now. Am I a bad child? I only remember the feeling of warmth and safety. But I cannot see his eyes or hear his voice. Only sometimes I have the terrible nightmare, but there is no face on that hideous skull anymore." She paused, certain Cecily would stop this sudden flow of feeling. But Cecily's eyes tenderly told her to continue. "I am afraid that by going so far away, I will also forget your face—and Ned's, and George's." She broke down and wept. "More than this," she sobbed, "I fear I shall never see any of you again."

And then Cecily's protective arms were round her, making her feel like a little girl again, and they clung to each other for several minutes. "There, there," the mother soothed her child. "God will give you strength to bear whatever fate has in store. Have faith, Margaret."

Her mother's love and strength gave Margaret the confidence to stop crying and compose herself. She inhaled the familiar scent of lavender and oranges, as if trying to imprint it on her memory forever. Cecily gently untangled Margaret's fingers from her gown and softly kissed her on the forehead. "There, 'tis done. Remember, you are to be a duchess— and mother to young Mary. You cannot behave thus with her. You must be her model, just as I was yours." Nodding, Margaret wiped her eyes and nose.

"Do your duty by me and write often," Cecily said, becoming the stoic noblewoman once more. "Beatrice will be with you, and I shall hear about you from her, I have no doubt. And before long, I shall hear that you are to be a mother. God and his saints keep you safe. Farewell, Margaret."

She put out her hand stiffly for her daughter to kiss, and Margaret sank into a deep curtsey as she touched her mother's fingers to her lips, the familiar formality buoying her. Then with Fortunata and Astolat in tow, she held her head high and, without a backward glance, she left her mother alone in the room.

Thus, no one saw Cecily crumple to the ground as her last drop of courage dissolved into a stream of shameless tears.

HER ESCORT STRETCHED out for half a mile as the colorful cavalcade left the abbey courtyard. Lords and ladies, knights and soldiers on horseback, in carriages, on carts and on foot picked their way across the marshes of Essex to Tilbury, where they took boats across to Gravesend and continued on land to Canterbury along the Pilgrim's Way. Many seeking to salve their souls at Canterbury stood by the wayside, allowing the royal procession through, and Margaret thought back fondly on Chaucer's amusing tales.

The cathedral rose out of the summer mist, the lack of a tower giving it an odd appearance. Margaret learned the old tower had been pulled down thirty years before and the new tower was under construction. It was Margaret's first time at the cathedral that was considered the pinnacle of Gothic architecture in southern England, and she stood in the nave and marveled at its fluted arches soaring, as it were, to heaven. She lit candles at St. Thomas à Becket's tomb to her father and brother and made her confession for the last time on English soil.

"*Ignosce mihi, Pater, quia peccavi.* Forgive me, Father, for I have sinned . . ."

The priest behind the curtain heard the young woman confess that she was to be married to a man she already hated in her heart because she could not have the one she loved.

"Have you fornicated with the second man, my child?"

"Nay, Father, he is married, and I am a virgin before God."

The priest smiled. "Then, my child, your mortal soul is not in danger. Go in peace and say the rosary with Christ and His mother in the chapel of St. Anselm's, where you will not be disturbed. Pray to St. Monica for guidance in your marriage, and she will help heal the hate in you." He had seen the king's sister enter with her ladies to light candles at St. Thomas's tomb and was well aware to whom he was speaking. He wondered briefly who was the object of Margaret's love. A quiet click told him she had left the confessional, and he let the black velvet curtain over the dividing screen fall back into place.

Margaret spent another hour on her knees, praying and listening to the choir practice. The music reached down to her deepest core and filled her with a golden glow as she told her beads and stared up at one of the exquisite stained glass windows. She felt God's presence all around her, and it gave her courage to go to Charles with peace in her heart.

She heard a gown swish along the stone floor behind her, and then Fortunata was tugging at her skirt. "*Madonna, madonna.* I must talk to you."

Margaret frowned at the interruption, but when she saw Fortunata's worried face, she hastily crossed herself and rose from the kneeler. "What is it, *pochina?*"

Her other ladies began to close their prayer books and get up off their aching knees, but Margaret stayed them. "Nay, ladies, you must remain for a little longer and pray for our journey across the sea. Fortunata and I will be back at my chambers when you have finished." As soon as she exited the church, the others gratefully stood and stretched.

"Something has happened, milady. I think I must tell you," Fortunata said urgently. They made their way to a wooden bench under a huge beech tree and sat down. Fortunata spread her skirts carefully with her hands before launching into her tale.

"Jehan and me, we are friends, you know?" she began. Margaret nodded. "Jehan knows the king like I know you, you understand. He told me something I think will interest you. But I promised not to say anything." She looked around a little anxiously for the Devil.

"Fortunata, do not tease me thus. Either you will break your promise to Jehan or I will break your neck!" Margaret said, chuckling. "Nay, come back here, *pochina,* I am only jesting. But you cannot leave me hanging like a fish on a hook."

"A fish?" Fortunata sat back down, confused.

"Never mind, just tell me!" Margaret said, exasperated for once.

The dwarf took a deep breath and crossed herself for good measure. "The king has received news of a lady's death. An important lady to him, Jehan told me. Eleanor . . . but I forget her other name. She was a nun."

Margaret furrowed her brow, trying to think who this important lady was. She shook her head. "Did Jehan say why she was important? And what did Edward do when he heard?"

"Jehan said the king was very happy she is dead, because she could be big trouble for him. I am sorry, but he did not say what trouble."

Suddenly Margaret was transported back to the night in the garden with John Harper, when she had seen Eleanor Butler and Edward facing each other in the window, their hands clasped together.

"Sweet Jesu, it cannot be," she muttered. Surely Ned would not have promised himself to Eleanor just to bed her. It would mean his marriage to Elizabeth was . . . Dear God, I hope I am wrong. I must be wrong.

But then she recalled Edward's anger when she innocently mentioned Eleanor's name that evening at Shene when she had rejected poor John Harper. Her heart sank. Oh, foolish, lustful boy—aye, boy— for when it came to satisfying his pleasures, Ned acted like a spoiled one, she admitted finally. How she wished he would take his kingship a little more seriously, especially now. Several alarming events had occurred throughout the kingdom in the past weeks that should have given Edward pause for thought, she knew, not least of which was the growing schism between Edward and their cousin of Warwick. Margaret of Anjou was still a threat somewhere in Europe, with her Lancastrian adherents never far away. In fact, shortly before the festivities at Stratford Langthorne, a man had been captured carrying treasonable letters from Queen Margaret.

"*Pochina,* you must swear not to tell another living soul. I know not the significance now, but 'tis well to keep this a secret between you and me. Swear to it!" Margaret watched as Fortunata crossed her heart and promised on Giorgio and Tomasina of Padua's graves. Her face was so earnest and her eyes so guileless as she gave her mistress her promise that Margaret had to smile. She was remembering those first days at Greenwich when she wondered whether Fortunata was a spy. She knew without a shadow of a doubt that the dwarf was more loyal than any of the English servants. She knew she could trust Fortunata with her life.

Margaret sat under the airy branches of the majestic beech tree and contemplated the state of her beloved England at this troublesome time, knowing that in a few days she would be powerless to help Ned weather the brewing storms. And now, the fate of a beautiful young woman, who must have turned to Christ after Edward tired of her, seemed insignificant beside the fate of England. And yet instinctively Margaret knew she was significant all the same.

A magpie hopped into view, and Margaret looked about her for a second bird. "One for sorrow, two for joy," she muttered. "Oh, magpie, where is your mate?" But there was none.

ONE BY ONE, the family said their private farewells in the archbishop's palace, where they had been housed. Dickon pressed a small book into her hands. "'Tis a book of prayer for your journey, Meg. I will miss you," he said simply. As he embraced her, he whispered, "You will keep my Kate a secret, won't you?"

"Certes," she whispered back. As she stepped back from him, she said, "Thank you, I will treasure this, Dickon, and I shall miss you, too. Perhaps we shall see each other in Burgundy ere long."

Then she was in George's arms. Neither could speak, Margaret for her tears and George for those he was fighting with all his might to hold back. They stood, arms around each other, looking into each other's eyes in a silent au revoir. Margaret could feel his fingers digging into her skin through her satin sleeves, and she knew that of all her family, George, for all his weaknesses—or perhaps because of his weaknesses—would be the one she would miss the most.

George gave a tiny resentful cry as Elizabeth gently pulled them apart. "'Tis my turn, George. You cannot have Margaret all to yourself." The queen kissed Margaret on both cheeks, wiping the tears from them with her kerchief. She, too, pressed a gift into Margaret's hand. "So you will never forget," she said, as Margaret looked down on an exquisite enameled white rose brooch, a ruby at its center. "I regret if I have ever offended you, Margaret. And know that I love you in my own way. I pray you will be as fortunate as I in your husband."

Margaret was taken aback by this speech, and, her tears spent, she smiled and thanked Elizabeth graciously, allowing Edward to pin the brooch to her gown. Then he enveloped her in his big arms and swayed her gently from side to side, her nose crushed on his massive chest.

"I thank you for your tireless work on my behalf, and I promise to put England first if I have any influence with my husband, Ned. In return, I beg of you to honor your promise of my dowry in timely fashion, so that I am not embarrassed," she said meaningfully. She knew Edward had had difficulty in raising the first portion of her dowry and was afraid, once she was not there to remind him, that he would "forget" to pay the rest. "And now that you have sent me off so magnificently, I pray you look to yourself and to your crown. God keep you, Ned, until we meet again." She had decided it was useless to advise him further.

"And may God go with you, too, Meggie." Edward looked down at her oval face and marked the strong nose and chin, sensuous lower lip and intelligent gray eyes. She was not beautiful like his Bess, but she was every inch a princess. Then he said in her ear, "I hope you are pleased I'm sending Anthony as your escort. 'Twas the least I could do."

"Hush, Ned, please!" she murmured into his thickly padded pourpoint, "but thank you—I think."

Edward led Margaret out to the courtyard, where the rest of her escort was mounted and waiting to cover the sixteen miles to the fleet at Margate. He settled her in her carriage with the beautiful duchess of Norfolk, Eliza Scales and their own attendants and then stood with Elizabeth, George and Richard as the procession moved away. She saw her three brothers whispering together for a second, and then they all shouted after her in unison, "Adieu, Mistress Nose-in-a-Book!" Despite her sadness, she smiled and waved.

As soon as Margaret was out of sight and the music that had accompanied the departure had faded away, Edward, grim-faced, turned on his heel and returned to his chamber to prepare for the journey back to London—and trouble.

Through the villages along the Roman road to Margate, the people stood awed as the richly decorated carriages, horsemen in multihued clothes and pikemen in the royal colors wended their way to the port. A little girl, her flaxen hair tousled and her kirtle torn and grass-stained, ran to the carriage and reached up to give Margaret a nosegay of white meadowsweet, purple corn cockles and rosy ragged robin. Margaret thanked her, called to one of the escort to give the child a penny and was rewarded by the girl's look of astonishment as the man bent down to give it to her. She scampered back to her mother, who curtseyed as Margaret passed by.

"God bless you, Lady Margaret," she called. "We be wishing you happiness."

Not long after being ferried across the marshy Wantsum Channel to the Isle of Thanet, which formed the tip of Kent, the carriage trundled up a rise in the road. Anthony trotted alongside and directed the ladies' attention to their left as the sea came into view. Margaret had never seen the sea before. She had lived close by the watery fens of Huntingdonshire at Fotheringhay and along the River Teme at Ludlow, and of course at Greenwich, Shene, Windsor and Westminster on the Thames, but she had never looked over a body of water and not been able to see the other side. There was nothing on the horizon, which struck fear in her heart, and her hand flew to her mouth.

"When we lose sight of England, how shall we know if we are going in the right direction, my lord?" she asked. "And what if there is a storm?"

Anthony saw her consternation and so refrained from laughing. "The ships' masters have been plying these waters all their lives, my lady, and in the *Ellen* you will be in good hands. They have a device called an astrolabe that helps them navigate by heavenly bodies, and in the day they use the cross-staff that can measure the sun's height from the horizon. Rest assured, we shall be across in no time, unless we are unlucky enough to run into pirates."

"Pirates!" Margaret squeaked. "Dear God, what am I doing?"

"Take no notice of him, Lady Margaret," Eliza Scales piped up, having said very little the entire journey. "Anthony, you are cruel to frighten us thus, in truth. I beg you to leave us and ride on."

Nay, Margaret wanted to contradict, let him stay! But she turned her head to gaze out over the green water and trusted that with enough company to fill fourteen ships, they would surely be too daunting for pirates to attack. The sun low in the west now cast an amber glow on the rippling waves, and she found the unfamiliar salt air invigorating. By the time they descended the slight incline into Margate harbor and glimpsed the proud ships that were to carry the wedding party at anchor in the sheltered bay, she was almost excited about her first sea voyage.

Margaret spent a restless night in the house of Margate's wealthiest shipowner. By the time she went aboard the *New Ellen,* all the cargo had been loaded and the ships crowded with mariners and passengers. On board her three-masted carrack were, among others, Elizabeth, duchess of Norfolk, Sir Edward Woodville, Anthony and Eliza, and, at Margaret's request, Sir John Howard. Quarters had to be made for all on the small ships, for the crossing to Flanders could take up to four days, depending on the weather. Others aboard the many other carracks and caravels included Lord Wenlock, Lord Dacre, and Sir John Paston and his wife. One ship carried the horses and all the trappings of those knights who would be competing in the Tournament of the Golden Tree, as well as the entourage's baggage.

With Astolat by her side, Margaret stood on the poop deck, the royal standard flying proudly in the wind, and watched the mariners ready the vessel for sail. Men swarmed up the masts like monkeys, readying lines, untying the heavy canvas as they obeyed the commands from below. She saw Jehan Le Sage and Edward's other jester, Richard L'Amoureux, talking and laughing together. Ned had insisted they go with her "in case you are sad, Meggie. I have commanded them to keep you smiling," he told her. "Besides, I think your little Fortunata has been flirting with Jehan from what I have observed, and she will feel at home if they are there with you." Margaret was astonished by her brother's thoughtfulness, and the thought of him now brought the tears back behind her eyes and a lump to her throat. Steady, Margaret, she told herself, I forbid you to cry again.

A rasping sound from the front of the ship made her take notice, and the master told her the anchor was being hauled in. The command to unfurl the sails was given and she watched as little by little the great canvas on the mid-mast began to fill. Shouts of farewell came to her from the people waving from the harbor piers, hanging from second-story windows and from the small boats that clustered around the fleet. Margaret felt the ship creak beneath her feet as the wind pushed it inch by inch away from the shore. A rising panic filled her, and she turned to look over the stern. Standing alone, her back straight and proud, she gritted her teeth bravely as she watched the land she loved get smaller as it slipped farther and farther away in the twilight.

The lump in her throat grew so that it engulfed her whole chest and evolved into an anguished sob that was mercifully lost in the wind. She knew with sad certainty that a door in her life was closing.

PART TWO

A Bride for Burgundy

1468–1470

11

Summer 1468

Margaret turned away from the view of the distant shore of her homeland and looked for Fortunata in the knot of passengers on the deck. Fortunata was usually attached to her skirts—or keeping Jehan company of late—and Margaret was concerned because she was nowhere to be seen.

"Beatrice, where is Fortunata?" she called to her lady-in-waiting, one of the few who would be allowed to remain with her in Burgundy. "She did come on board, I know, because she was in my rowing boat."

Beatrice laughed, climbing the steps to join her. "Aye, my lady, and she no sooner stepped on board than she ran to the other side of the ship and was"—she lowered her voice—"sick over the gunwale. I sent her down to your stateroom to sleep."

"Poor little thing," Margaret said. "I hear the *mal de mer* is a terrible affliction. Praise God, I feel nothing."

Three hours later, Margaret thought she was going to die.

The wind was fair and the seas calm when they stood out from the harbor. And when Anthony came to stand with her, she was elated. They spoke for only a few minutes, Anthony showing her the astrolabe and cross-staff. As the navigator, whose eyes had been reduced to mere pinpricks in his face from squinting at the sun for so many years, demonstrated his skill for her, the waves began to grow steadily off shore. Jack Howard waved at her from the deck below, his smile wide as he swayed with practiced ease in rhythm with the rolling ship.

"Sir John loves the sea, his lady wife told me," Margaret said, as she smiled and waved back. "But she was not willing to endure the rigors of the voyage to come with him. This is a pleasant sensation, and I think I was born to it."

Margaret groaned now as she remembered those words. After their conversation on the poop deck, Anthony had escorted her to the captain's table, where she sat with Eliza and the duchess and other ladies. They feasted on cold meat and fish, bread and cheese, all washed down with some strong ale. It was then, in the stuffy interior of the cabin, that Margaret's stomach began to turn somersaults. She begged the captain's pardon and tried to rise to seek her own bed, but a wave of nausea forced her to sit down again. Recognizing the signs, the captain gently helped her up again and half carried her to the stateroom, which he had given up to her. A bucket was found quickly, and soon Margaret was making full use of it. Fortunata had crawled under the bed as soon as she had come aboard and had already emptied her stomach several times. Beatrice hovered over her mistress, seemingly immune to the seasickness, and gave her sips of water whenever Margaret could bear to sit up. It seemed to Margaret that the cabin walls were closing in on her, the ceiling was revolving and the bed was tossing her up and down. She passed the night in fitful sleep and puking.

"My lady," the captain called through the door to her the next morning. "May I suggest you try and take some fresh air? 'Twill do you the world of good, and now the sun is up and the sea calmer, I recommend you stay on deck so that you can focus your eyes on the horizon. 'Twill help your discomfort, I promise."

The idea of even trying to stand up caused Margaret to retch again, but with Beatrice's help, she managed to sit on the side of the bed and allow herself to be washed. Her hair was matted with the foul-smelling remains of her supper, but once Beatrice had cleaned her up, put on a fresh gown and tied her hair up under a coif, she was ready to put her feet on the ground and try to stand. She was astounded by how weak she felt. Her legs wobbled and she was light-headed. But believing the captain knew his business, she staggered to the door and climbed the companion-way to the deck. The North Sea wind slapped at her face and blew under her skirts, dragging her forward to a group of courtiers, who bowed when they saw her. Jack Howard took her arm, and she leaned gratefully on his sturdy frame. He could see she was in no mood for trite conversation, so he guided her silently around the main deck until she felt stronger.

"It may be of consolation to hear that half of the company spent the night in the same manner as you, Lady Margaret," he said, and then whispered, "including my Lord Scales, but he would not like that put about."

That made Margaret chuckle, and she sucked in the fresh air, stared at the horizon and began to feel a little better. She sensed the familiar movement behind her and turned to see Fortunata, her face as green as her gown, bravely standing sentinel, and the seated Astolat's head as high as hers.

"Good girl, *pochina*," she murmured. "Together we shall beat this. 'Tis too undignified for ladies to be thus afflicted."

It was Jack's turn to chuckle. "Perhaps you know now why my own dear Margaret would not join me, my lady. I took her on my favorite ship out of Ipswich—the one you saw at Greenwich—and she, too, turned the color of Fortunata's gown. And we were still moored at the wharf." He threw back his head and laughed merrily. "She will be cheered to hear she keeps good company."

Later in the day, the wind died completely, and the ships drifted help-lessly until the following morning, when creaking timbers and flapping sails moved the crew into action. All fourteen ships had managed to stay together overnight, and the passengers cheered as the canvas billowed out again in a west wind, and they felt the ship's forward movement.

Anthony had finally recovered and walked with Eliza up and down the crowded deck, giving Margaret pangs of jealousy, especially when she heard Eliza's high-pitched whinny. Once in a while, Anthony's eyes met hers, and a silent greeting passed between them, giving her some solace. She had her sea legs now and, to pass the time, she conversed with the master about all the ports he had visited.

"Of all the places I have been, my lady, Bruges is one of the most beautiful," he declared, a steady hand on the tiller. " 'Tis named the Venice of the north, in truth. I have a friend there who is the governor of the English merchant-adventurers. William Caxton is his name."

"I presume he is a wool merchant, Master Cooke, if he is the merchant-adventurers' chief. I have been told of these merchants of England who represent the many trades abroad. He must indeed be a fine man and experienced merchant to take the governorship of them all."

"Aye, he is, although he seems to be more taken with books and reading, in truth, which I cannot think will bring him fame and fortune, can you, my lady? Far better to stick to selling wool."

Margaret smiled. "You are addressing the wrong person, sir. Books are a passion of mine—"

"And mine," said a voice that always set her pulses racing. "And why were you talking of books with Master Cooke, Lady Margaret? I warrant 'tis not a subject he can wax poetic on, am I right, Master Cooke?" Anthony teased, joining them—alone. Margaret could see Eliza standing with a group being entertained by Jehan the jester. "He is far too busy sailing damoiselles to their weddings and keeping a true course."

The captain bowed and smiled ruefully. "Aye, my lord, I fear my skill at reading allows me to follow charts, 'tis all. And you are right, I should set my mind on the swiftest course for Sluis, or we shall be late for that wedding."

"Then let me relieve you of a distraction, sir," Anthony said, taking Margaret's arm and walking her the length of the deck to the prow, where the proud figurehead fixed her eyes on the horizon. As her official escort, Anthony had a reasonable claim to Margaret's exclusive attention, and in view of so many witnesses, including his wife, everything appeared circumspect. In fact, the two had an hour of uninterrupted time together that not even Eliza could gainsay. Only Fortunata, standing guard behind them, could hear the passion in Anthony's voice as he ended the tête-à-tête.

"I have wrestled with Satan over my desire for you, Marguerite. That day in your chamber, he almost won. I am ashamed to say I wish he had." Margaret clutched the rail, staring at the water below, as Anthony continued, "I wish I knew what it was like to feel your skin next to mine, to let your hair cover us both as we pleasure each other." Margaret drew in a sharp breath. Surely I am dreaming, she thought, but he continued, "I am consumed by love for you, and it comes from my mind as well as my heart. I love the way you think, I love that you always have the right word for the right time, I love your generosity, your caring and your piety. Most of all, I love that you love me."

"I do, Anthony," was all Margaret could whisper back.

"In a few days, you will belong to another—another man, who will know you as I cannot. Already I hate this man, and I fear God's wrath for even thinking such thoughts, let alone saying them out loud." Margaret crossed herself, knowing he was indeed tempting the Devil. She did not look at him for fear he would stop, and she didn't want him to stop.

"I have met this man, and it grieves me sore that although he is a duke, he is not good enough for you, my love," Anthony said. "You and I were destined to meet, but we were not destined to be together. Both of us must pray to God the Father, God the Holy Ghost and our Savior Jesu Christ to help us accept this destiny and live our lives in His way. If ever there comes a time when you and I are free of the bonds of marriage, I promise you I will come to you if you so desire. I pray you send me word of you whenever you can—as Elaine to Lancelot. Here is an address where you may send me letters without fear of discovery." He gave her a scrap of parchment, which she pushed into the pouch she carried. "I shall instruct my contact that anything addressed to Lancelot is for me. He is a good friend and will not ask questions.

"When you are comfortable, find a safe place for me to send mine. But let us vow to destroy these letters. Do you agree?" He saw her nod. "'Twas cruel of Edward to make me your escort. He tried to please you because he thought, like him, you enjoyed a passing fancy. He has no notion of our true natures or how painful this is for both of us. We do not need anyone else to know, except for Fortunata here"—he turned to the dwarf, who tried to look the innocent but crossed her heart to reassure him of her silence—"and now I beg of you, my love, laugh heartily at this speech, so all present will know I am but entertaining you on this voyage of Hell."

So Margaret laughed. She laughed and laughed until the tears flowed down her cheeks and blew behind her in the wind.

• • •

"Ships ahoy, starboard," cried the boy in the crow's nest, pointing south. He had carefully counted all fourteen in his flotilla and thus knew three new ships were bearing down on them at a run.

Sweet Jesu, pirates! Margaret thought, her heart in her mouth. As the crew and passengers watched anxiously, the new ships drew ever closer.

"'Tis the French, not pirates!" Jack Howard cried first. "God's bones! How did Louis know where to find us? Surely they would not attack so close to port and to sundown."

He hurried to the stern and climbed the steps to speak to the captain, advising him to thread their ship with its precious royal cargo through her sister ships and evade a possible skirmish. The French ships were taking a risk by threatening to attack such a large fleet, but Jack had weathered many a naval fight with the French and knew they were not cowards.

"Ladies, go below!" bellowed the captain, who was now on the fore-deck, sizing up the situation. "Close the shutters tight and lock the doors. Master-at-arms, ready weapons for the crew and any others prepared to fight."

Margaret found herself on her knees, her ladies around her, staring out to sea and at the advancing ships. She heard the captain, but she had to pray first. "St. Brendan, I beg you to protect these good people, who are only following the king's command. Preserve us from harm and let us find our harbor in peace," she cried out.

Anthony heard her and sighed. Marguerite, where is your common sense, he silently asked her. Running to where she knelt, he hoisted her up none too kindly and sternly told her to "obey the captain and go below, for mercy's sake!"

An arrow thudded a few feet from them. Beatrice screamed. A few more followed as the women scrambled, tripped and fell down the companionway in their frenzy to reach the safety of the stateroom. Anthony closed all the shutters and admonished them to be quiet so that if they were boarded, the Frenchmen would not know they had Margaret of York aboard. He left the room to find his sword, leaving the group of women in a state of terror.

Through a chink in a shutter, Margaret saw one of the French ships so close to the *Mary* that those men armed with pikes could almost impale the enemy. But the English captain had anticipated the ramming and already his ship was responding to his "Hard a-lee!" The French ship missed them completely.

The *New Ellen* was now far out of range. Another cry went up from the lookout: "Harbor lights ahead!" In the evening twilight, the French, who were not willing to follow the fleet into Burgundian waters in the dark, gave up the fight. They had no wish to repeat the defeat of their fleet by the English in Sluis harbor on that very same day a century before.

The English ships sailed away without injury to anyone aboard and into the wide bay before Sluis as the light faded. The ladies went back to their knees to offer thanks for their escape.

MARGARET WAS NOT prepared for the reception that greeted her in the harbor. Torches, beacons and lanterns were lit to guide the ships in, the little town was festooned with banners and garlands, and even though it was dark, townsfolk lined the wharves and hung from windows to greet the English princess. Margaret went below, and for the next hour, her ladies dressed her and decked her in jewels to satisfy the Burgundians that she was indeed a royal princess and show she was grateful for their tribute. She briefly wondered who would be greeting her, and she felt her stomach lurch. No one had told her what to expect, and she was arriving many days ahead of the third of July wedding date. But if the people of Sluis were ready to receive her, then perhaps Charles was there, too. It had already been explained to Margaret, however, that according to the strict court etiquette, she would not see her bridegroom immediately, which at once relieved and unnerved her. The longer he was absent, the more terrifying he grew in her imagination.

There was a knock on the door, and Anthony called out that a barge was approaching their vessel and perhaps she should be ready for an audience. "I know not who, my lady, but, judging from the trumpeting, 'tis people of importance. I will bring them to you as soon as they come aboard," he said.

Fortunata opened the door a crack, curtseyed and said with enough authority to make Anthony's mouth turn up, "Milady Margaret is almost ready, milord," and closed the door again. A few minutes later, a scraping on the side of the ship and sounds of people coming aboard were heard in the cabin. Arranging the skirts of her crimson gown trimmed in black and purple—the three Burgundian colors—and coaxing the veil on her jeweled headdress into perfection, Margaret's ladies stood back to admire their handiwork and nodded happily.

"Beautiful, my lady," Beatrice said for them all. Margaret managed a small smile, but her knees were knocking as she waited to meet the first of her new subjects. She fingered the white rose brooch pinned on the ermine trim of her bodice between her breasts for courage. She thought of her York heritage and felt the familiar swell.

"*Et maintenant, mes chères dames de compagnie, tout en français dès ce moment,*" she said. Fortunata cocked her head and nodded. She had never been far from Margaret's side during the months Margaret was improving her French, and as an Italian, she found the new language easier to understand than English. They would have to get used to speaking French now.

They were joined by the duchess of Norfolk, the bishop of Salisbury and others to wait for the ducal party to be presented. Anthony knocked again and once bidden to enter, stood on the threshold in a magnificent velvet gown trimmed with marten, his plumed hat in the very latest fashion. Blue eyes gazed into gray in a moment of mutual appreciation. They did not need to communicate; each knew what the other was thinking. Margaret's hand fluttered for a second in a secret salute before Anthony bowed.

"My lady, I have the honor to present to you his grace Duke Charles's esteemed chamberlain, Seigneur de Montigny," he said in French and stepped aside, a playful smile on his lips that she did not miss. Then she knew why.

It took all of her control to not laugh when the lord made his entrance. He had to turn sideways to fit his enormous frame through the cabin doorway, and the foot-high hat that perched precariously above his flabby face hit the low lintel and fell to the floor. The bailiff of Sluis, who followed him in, snatched it up, hiding it behind his back. Montigny's greasy brown-gray hair swung limply in front of his face as he executed as low a bow as his larded body would allow. Margaret was, however, impressed by his clothes, the many jewels on his fingers and the heavy gold collar around his shoulders. His piggy eyes regarded her solemnly as he straightened up, and, with relief, she saw admiration in them. He took her slim hand in his massive paw and kissed it with reverence.

"Princess Margaret, God's greeting to you. I am sent by his grace, Duke Charles, your fiancé, to bid you most welcome into Burgundy."

The comical scene broke Margaret's reserve and she gave him a brilliant smile. In a voice—to those who knew her—tinged with laughter, she responded, "God's greeting to you, Messire Montigny. I will be happy to finally set foot in your country and off this rocking ship. May I now present." She introduced the other members of her train. Her first duty was over, and she had to admit, it had been easier than she'd expected.

As Anthony handed her into the barge for the short way to shore, he whispered, "Your control was admirable, Marguerite. I am glad to see you still have your sense of humor. Remember, I am here—officially—whenever you need me."

"And unofficially?" she murmured. He shook his head. "'Tis not possible."

Once on land, she was greeted by two of Duke Philip's twenty-five illegitimate offspring, the Bishop of Utrecht, who intoned a blessing for the princess's safe crossing, and the Countess Marie de Charny. Both bore a resemblance to Antoine, their elder half brother who had fought at Smithfield, Margaret noted, although Charny's forty-year-old face was harder.

She gripped Anthony's arm as they made their way through the cheering crowd along streets that had been carpeted for her comfort. She tried to picture Edward sending his bastards, Arthur and Elizabeth, albeit still children, to meet a future queen, but she could not. It was as well Jack Howard had told her in what high esteem all of Philip's illegitimate children were held, or she might have been offended. She knew that yet another, Anne of Burgundy, was in charge of Charles's only daughter's education. She could not imagine what the dowager Duchess Isabella must think of all these reminders of her late husband's infidelities being in positions of power around her. It made her wonder whether Charles might have similar leanings, and she inadvertently shivered at the thought of him touching her.

The countess was alarmed. "Are you cold, my lady? We will soon be inside," she promised.

A stage had been set up in front of the rich merchant's house where she was to spend her first few nights in Flanders, and every day a new pageant was performed for her enjoyment. As the duke's third wife, Margaret had not been expecting her arrival to generate much interest, and the lengths to which the little town of Sluis had gone to make her welcome touched her heart. She made a point of walking out every day, passing by the tableaux and complimenting the players.

The day after her arrival was Sunday, and Margaret insisted on attending Mass in the quaint stone church with her English entourage. Townspeople once again lined the street to stare at the tall young woman on the arm of one of the handsomest men they had ever seen, a dwarf on the end of an enormous wolfhound's leash following behind. However, as their Flemish language was incomprehensible to her, Margaret did not know if they were complimenting or insulting her. She resolved to learn a few phrases once she settled in.

It was drizzling when they returned from church and hurried up the narrow stairs to the front door of the house. Margaret was glad to wrap her fingers around a steaming cup of hot mulled wine. She was now surrounded by ladies and gentlemen of both the English and the Burgundian courts, and the rooms in the modest house were full to overflowing. How she longed for some privacy! But upon skimming the formidable manual of etiquette written by one of Isabella's ladies that Countess de Charny had thrust on her the night before, she knew the more relaxed ways of the English court were behind her forever and she would never enjoy that luxury. She resolved to make it a game that she and Fortunata would play.

Shouting was heard in the street below and then cheering, and Margaret got to her feet to go to the window. Even that was not allowed, it seemed, as Charny tut-tutted through her pursed lips and wagged her finger at Beatrice, who was already peering out.

"Such improper behavior!" she said. "My lady, do you permit your servants to gape out of windows like fishwives?"

Margaret hurriedly sat down and begged Beatrice to behave herself. Beatrice was affronted, but sensing her mistress's dilemma, she curtseyed and demurred. When Charny's back was turned, Margaret winked at her faithful lady, and Beatrice smiled gratefully.

A kerfuffle was heard at the door as word reached the solar that her grace the dowager duchess and her granddaughter, Mary, were slowly processing along the road from Bruges to visit the English princess. Her heart beating so loudly that she felt sure everyone in the room could hear it, Margaret rose and instructed Fortunata to fetch the little gift she had brought for eleven-year-old Mary. Beatrice and Eliza Scales hovered around Margaret, tweaking the gossamer gauze covering her butterfly hennin and smoothing the skirts on her blue damask gown decorated with marguerites. Again Margaret touched the rose brooch at her bosom and sent a prayer to her own patron saint to help her through this next step of her new life.

The old duchess was nearing seventy, and Margaret was surprised with what agility Isabella was able to negotiate the steep staircase to the front door. The two women met on the threshold and each knelt before the other in observance of court etiquette. The courtiers remained silent as the dowager duchess and the duchess-in-waiting avised each other for several minutes. Then Isabella smiled out of her long, wizened face and looked to her escort to raise her off her knees, nodding to Margaret to do the same. Anthony came forward, bowed and took Margaret's arm possessively as a sign that he was her official escort.

"Madame Margaret, God be with you and welcome to Burgundy." Isabella spoke French with a hint of a Portuguese accent. "Lord Scales, commend us to your sovereign, for he has sent us a beauty," she said graciously, tilting her head and eyeing Margaret with a twinkle. "My grandfather, John of Gaunt, was a tall Plantagenet, and I see you are indeed a descendant," she said, intending to be kind. Instead, she realized she was referring to the patriarch of the hated Lancastrian line, and her smile faded in a moment of elderly confusion.

"Madame, I beg your . . . ," she began, but Margaret took a tiny step forward and gently interrupted her. "'Tis of no import, your grace. I believe your grandfather was a great man and a true Englishman. I am proud you think I am like him."

Anthony moved his arm so slightly that only Margaret was aware of his approbation. It gave her reassurance, and when Isabella chose the moment to embrace her future daughter-in-law, Margaret knew she had made a friend. It was only then that she noticed the young girl waiting patiently on a lower step, her bright gray eyes taking in every detail of the scene above her, and her button mouth trembling on the verge of a smile.

Margaret lifted her hand from Isabella's shoulder and wiggled her fingers at the girl in a secret wave. The smile broke free, and Mary ran up the steps to her grandmother's side.

"I think you must be Mary," Margaret said, as Isabella released her to turn to the girl. "I am so pleased to meet you, my dear. It seems you and I will see much of each other now. I hope we may be friends."

Mary was unprepared for such a down-to-earth greeting and could only respond with "Aye, my lady" and a deep reverence. Margaret thought she heard a "tut-tut" from the usual source behind her but ignored it. The child had been separated from her mother as soon as Margaret's predecessor had been diagnosed with the wasting sickness. It had taken Isabelle of Valois a year to die, and that had been three years ago. Margaret saw a sadness about the child, and her motherly instincts refused to be suppressed by the formality of the occasion.

"Come, my child, I think we can do better than that," Margaret said, and bent down to give Mary a kiss on each cheek. Duchess Isabella smiled broadly, took Margaret's hand and together they walked into the house, courtiers and ladies bowing before them, and Mary skipping along behind.

Margaret had passed her second test with flying colors. The third, she knew, would not be as easy.

CHARLES CAME UNANNOUNCED the next day, cantering up to the house with a small escort. He took the stairs to the second floor two at a time, and Margaret's chamberlain only had time to cram on his hat and make a hurried bow before flinging open the solar door to announce him. Charles strode past him to see Margaret standing alone in the middle of the room while her small entourage bowed low to the visitor. She held her head high for a second and looked him straight in the eye before sinking into a deep reverence.

Charles swept off his high hat and made her a low bow in return. Then he raised her up and to her astonishment kissed her on the lips. An audible sigh of relief was heard from the English courtiers.

Margaret gazed on her fiancé and he on her for a full minute. Her fears of a monster were unfounded. In his mid-thirties, he was broad-shouldered with a thick neck and a strong head of dark, curly hair. His piercing blue eyes dominated his broad, handsome face as he took stock of his intended, and his full, sensuous mouth curved into a smile. He leaned toward her, having to stand on tiptoe to reach her ear, and whispered, "*Maman* was right, you are tall."

All Margaret's adolescent insecurities about her physique came rushing back, and her confidence crumpled. "Do I displease you, my lord duke?" she stammered, also in a whisper.

Having no idea his crude remark might have disturbed her or knowing he should reassure her, he laughed and turned his attention to the others, leaving her bewildered. He had learned from his ambassadors that the English kissed everyone and often, and so he set about kissing all the ladies present before turning back to Margaret, who had regained her composure. He does not care about women, she surmised in a moment of intuition. He does not know how to behave around them. Poor Isabelle, she thought, and poor Mary.

"I hope you are treated well here, Lady Margaret," he said, when he returned to her side. "I assure you, the people of Burgundy are ready to accept you and have planned magnificent wedding festivities for you. I think you will be pleased."

"I expect nothing, your grace. But I have been treated with kindness here in Sluis from the moment I stepped ashore." He is trying, Margaret thought, and she smiled at him for the first time since his entrance. Having no notion how a smile softened her face, she wondered why his expression changed as he picked up her hand and kissed it more pleasurably.

"Then I am content, madame," he murmured. Still holding her hand, he turned to Anthony and said, "We have business to transact, I believe, Lord Scales."

Margaret cast her eyes down to the hand that held hers, its tapered fingers adorned with surprisingly long nails. She could not look at her love, as it pained her that he must witness this. Anthony suggested the betrothal take place in the garden because the chamber was too small to accommodate so many.

"My lord bishops," Charles addressed the prelates from Salisbury, Utrecht and Tournai in the pleasant garden at the back of the house, "you may begin."

Salisbury moved forward with a parchment and solemnly read the formal betrothal. Margaret and Charles affirmed their willingness to be wed and signed the document in front of the witnesses.

Without more ado, the duke bowed to Margaret, and she was surprised to realize he was preparing to leave. Margaret observed his confident stride on short muscular legs bowed to fit a saddle as he walked through the garden to the gate. On the threshold he stopped, thought for a moment and then called back to her: "My compliments, madame, your French is very good."

Then in a clatter of hooves and flying mud he and his escort were gone.

Now she was addressed as "your grace" and "duchess," for the betrothal contract was as formal for the couple as the civil ceremony would be. Duchess Isabella and Mary visited her every day during the week as the region waited for the wedding day. Mary was enthralled by her stepmother and then clapped her hands with glee when Fortunata was presented to her.

"I, too, have a little person to wait on me at Ten Waele Palace," she cried. "They will become the best of friends, I am certain. Madame de Beaugrand is from Constantinople, but she is not pretty like Fortunata."

Fortunata flashed one of her sweet smiles. "Thank you, milady," she said, and promptly produced a flower from behind Mary's ear and presented it to the astonished girl.

"Tell me about Edward, my dear," Isabella said, while pinching Mary's cheek. Margaret noticed the adoration in the old woman's face when she watched her granddaughter. Having a child and then a grandchild must be one of the joys of being a woman, she thought. But for her, having children meant bedding Charles, and although the fear of him had diminished since his few visits during the week, the dread of intimacy still weighed heavily on her.

She told Duchess Isabella about all her brothers, and Isabella saw the wistfulness in Margaret's face when she came to describe George.

"He is your favorite, I can tell, madame. I remember him and Richard when they were here as boys. But we hear he makes Edward angry."

"Aye, your grace, he is a vain boy, in truth. And he is too much in my cousin of Warwick's company to please Edward." Margaret sighed, and Isabella tactfully changed the subject. She was remembering her own arrival at Sluis as a young bride-to-be all those years ago and how homesick she felt. She recognized the look now on Margaret's face and patted her hand kindly.

By the time Margaret and her little court removed to Damme, a tiny port at the head of the waterway leading to Bruges, the three women had grown closer, and Isabella was grateful that Margaret was so taken with Mary. She knew she was not long for this world and was afraid for Mary, an only child and the female heir of the huge wealthy territory that was Burgundy. She had no wish to see Mary disinherited, but she nightly prayed that Margaret of York had her mother's ability to bear healthy children. Charles needed a son if he was to continue his rash military campaigns to win himself more and more land. She had no doubt his dangerous luck would run out one day.

The dowager loved her son, but she was wise enough to know that Philip had neglected him in favor of many of his bastard children, and so Charles had grown up bitter and autocratic. At the end, he had so hated his father that he had sworn to live his life as differently as possible. Where Philip had loved women, Charles rejected them. Where Philip had loved personal finery, Charles eschewed it, except on state occasions, and wore somber black and brown, albeit of the finest velvet and silk, and only a small gold chain around his neck on which hung the order of the Golden Fleece. Philip had favored the York house in England, Charles had supported the Lancastrians. Isabella wondered what Margaret would think had she known Queen Margaret of Anjou's most trusted lords were only now being asked to leave Bruges, where they had been living on Charles's charity. What worried Isabella most of all was that Charles scoffed at diplomacy, at which Philip had been a master, and favored going to war.

Isabella listened politely to Margaret's discourse about her family and England and was daily more and more intrigued by the young woman's intelligence. Margaret's predecessor had been a sweet person but even in good health had been ineffectual in matters of state and would not have made Charles a useful duchess. The dowager well knew the rigors of maintaining order in this diverse group of conquered nations, duchies and city states, and she had worked tirelessly and traveled independently to keep a constant ducal presence in the spread-out dukedom. Isabella had pushed Charles for this Yorkist alliance and now congratulated herself on Burgundy's good fortune.

"How will I ever learn all the names and faces here, Fortunata?" Margaret asked the rhetorical question at their daily prie-dieu ritual. "I smile and greet each one, but some of the names are so difficult and it seems everyone is named Jehan or Jean." She sighed. "There must be a way."

"When I was a little girl at the university, there were too many doctors, *professores,* so I played a game. Each person reminded me of some animal or a thing. I remembered faces by the thing they looked like, sometimes the name, too, and so the person."

Margaret chuckled under her breath. "You mean like Lord Ravenstein. He looks like a bird, so his name is like his face. And Lord Montigny is as big as a mountain—*mont.* How clever, *pochina!*"

Fortunata's face lit up with a happy smile. Then, aware they were being watched by the other ladies on their knees, she cast her eyes down and slipped her rosary through her fingers. Margaret intoned an Ave aloud and a chorus of amens confirmed that the group was paying her close attention. I cannot even pray without a gaggle looking on, she thought resentfully.

Early in their stay in Sluis, she told Fortunata, "You must be my eyes and ears here in Burgundy, *pochina,* and I am pleased with your progress in French," Margaret whispered at the prie-dieu. "I fear my days of freedom in England are over." She held up her copy of *Les Honneurs de la Cour.* "This book by Madame de Poitiers—you know, the lady with the hairs on her chin—is truly frightening. 'Tis written that the duchess may never be without at least three ladies in attendance at all times during the day and night except when the duke commands it." She groaned. "I shall make sure you are one of those ladies, Fortunata, and that Beatrice is another. I hope Duke Charles assigns me at least one pleasant Burgundian lady and not the countess de Charny as the third."

"*Madonna.* May I ask, do you like the duke?" Fortunata said timidly, knowing she might be crossing a boundary with her mistress. But Margaret had long ceased to look upon Fortunata as merely a servant and had no compunction about responding honestly.

"I do not fear him now, *pochina.* I think he is a man who is uncomfortable with women and prefers riding his horse," she said, chuckling. "I think perhaps if I can show him I can think like a man, he will give me respect. I do not think he is capable of love, and as I have no love to give him, he may be relieved and we will rub along well enough."

She could not bring herself to talk of the intimacy that would be her duty to endure after Sunday. The dread sat like a little imp on her shoulder every day, and she was ashamed to admit she had been counting down the hours with dread until her wedding day. She had been dismayed when she was told Charles had given Marie de Charny the honor of being in charge of her twelve maids of honor and three ladies-in-waiting. Anyone but her, she wanted to say, but instead she had smiled and acquiesced. Pierre de Bauffremont, the count of Charny, was another of Charles's councilors and had been married to Duke Philip's bastard daughter in 1447 when she was twenty-one years old. She stalked the palace halls like a bird of prey, talons ready to pounce on any unsuspecting servant in the dereliction of duty. Still dressed in black from head to toe in mourning for her beloved father, Marie de Charny was nicknamed *la corbine* by the servants, which also referred to her caw-caw of a laugh, though she rarely laughed.

Margaret learned all this from her stepdaughter, who, during the week at Sluis, had forged a strong bond with her. Mary was a mine of information, and nothing escaped her eyes and ears despite her docile expression and impeccable manners. Margaret did not tell Mary that Charny more nearly resembled a vulture.

"You will love Madame Jeanne, *belle-mère,*" she had said a few days after their first meeting. "She will come soon with my little Jacquotte. Grandmother gave her to me after my mother . . ." She paused, and Margaret pressed her hand in sympathy. "After *maman* died. She is very naughty, but she is my dearest friend."

"Jacquotte?" Margaret asked.

"My monkey," Mary said. "Do you not have a pet monkey, *belle-mère?*"

"Nay, little one, but I have Astolat." Margaret clicked her fingers, and the huge dog loped over to her mistress, its tail swaying to and fro. "Mary, this is my friend Astolat. Astolat, sit and shake hands," she commanded in English. The dog promptly sat and lifted its massive paw, and Mary squealed with delight.

"Shake hands, Astolat," she cried, trying to imitate Margaret's deep voice and English words. And the dog obeyed the little girl, who threw her arms about its hairy neck, causing Duchess Isabella to look up in alarm from her needlework.

Margaret smiled to herself. The best surprise of her short time in Burgundy was the instant affection both she and Mary had felt for each other. The child was a joy, she decided, and she reveled in the knowledge that she would be able to help in her maturing process.

After a short barge trip to Damme, she found herself the guest in another wealthy merchant's house on the eve of her wedding day. That night, as she lay in the tester bed, the heavy curtains shutting out the late northern daylight, and listened to the unfamiliar creaks of the beams and scuttling mice in the walls, she shed a few last tears for her English life. She painstakingly conjured up the face of each member of her beloved family and wondered if they were even giving her a passing thought on this, the most important day of her life. Then she tried to put names to the dozens of new faces she had encountered in her first week. Before she fell asleep, she whispered a prayer to the Virgin to help her through the next twenty-four hours and then asked God's forgiveness for her illicit love for Anthony.

It seemed she had been asleep for only a few minutes when she heard Beatrice calling softly to her through the curtains. "'Tis time to wake, your grace. The duke will be here soon."

The velvet was drawn back and Margaret sat up yawning. "Certes, 'tis still dark, Beatrice. It cannot be time."

But on seeing all her ladies already dressed in their finest clothes, she was grateful they had let her sleep so long. They had bathed her and washed her hair the evening before, and now they clothed her in a fresh chemise and began the long ritual of dressing her. The white cloth of gold gown shimmered in the candlelight as it was put over her head, its wide sleeves turned back to show the close-fitting sleeves of the crimson underdress. Long-toed, red silk shoes were slipped over the white silk hose and a gold belt gathered in the folds of the high-waisted skirt. Charles had given her a ruby ring on their betrothal day, and she wore it on her index finger as well as rings on all her fingers and thumbs. She insisted on wearing her white rose brooch, although the countess de Charny thought it a paltry piece of jewelry to wear upon such a magnificent gown.

Margaret stared down on her. "Madame," she said. "I am Margaret of York, and I will wear the badge of my family proudly."

For once the haughty woman was cowed. She colored and inclined her head. "I beg your pardon, your grace."

Sweet Jesu, Margaret thought, I hope I have not already made an enemy.

It had taken six women an hour and a half to ready Margaret for her marriage, and it was a little after five o'clock when the English nobles and prelates arrived and were admitted. Margaret was waiting in the hall, the early-morning sun weakly filtering through the glass window-panes. Her long, loose hair melted into the gold of her gown, and when Anthony was announced and gave her obeisance, he thought she looked like a golden statue of an ancient goddess. His head bowed, he smiled to himself, remembering the last time he had seen Margaret with her hair unbound. It seemed to him she was looking right through him as though he were invisible, but he knew her well enough to know it was her way of trying to forget he was anything but her presenter on this important day. He grimaced when he thought of Charles holding her long, slender body, as he surely would that night.

Charles arrived a few minutes later with his entourage. Margaret was astonished to see the duke so magnificently dressed. He looked more impos-ing than he had during all the visits he had made to her, and the little imp groaned in her ear. Charles, on his part, stared at length at the vision in front of him. If Margaret had known how intimidated he felt in front of this golden amazon, she might have dismissed the imp. But immediately he was all business and motioned to the bishops of Tournai and Salisbury to get on with the matrimonial blessing, which they did, intoning God's blessing on the happy couple and effecting the exchange of rings. Margaret tried to feel blessed; certes, she tried to feel something, but could summon no emotion through her numbness. I am a married woman, she told herself; I should feel elation. This is what every woman craves, in truth. What is wrong with me? As Charles kissed her solemnly, she caught Anthony's eye and he winked at her. And then the feeling of elation was there, and it warmed her from the top of her head to the tips of those crimson toes.

As soon as Mass was sung, Charles departed for Bruges, leaving his new bride the customary honor of a joyous entry into the city alone.

. . .

"Une joyeuse entrée" was the perfect description for what happened that day.

Conveyed on a gilded litter that was draped with crimson cloth of gold, Margaret sat on golden cushions, her crimson mantle with ermine trim flowing around her and a tiny but beautifully decorated gold coronet upon her head, a gift from Edward for this occasion. Slowly the carriage, pulled by matching white stallions, processed the last four miles of her long journey from London along the waterway and to the gates of Bruges itself. She was escorted by Anthony on Pegasus and all the nobles who had accompanied her from England as well as all the great lords of Burgundy and the knights of the Golden Fleece, their horses caparisoned from head to hoof in flowing silks that matched their owners' heraldic jupons. Minstrels playing trumpets, clarions and tambourines walked beside her litter. The crowds lining the route tossed flowers and garlands onto the litter as she passed, and she smiled and waved, hardly believing all this was for her.

She was humbled by her new subjects' ecstatic greeting. It had been different in London. There she was one of them, but here she was a stranger. She remembered Cecily telling her once when she made a sour face at her mother that if the wind should happen to change then, her face would freeze in that expression. Now she wondered if she would spend her life in a permanent grin.

She glanced up at the leaden sky and wondered how long the rain would hold off. She closed her eyes and prayed to St. Barbara, one of her favorite saints and who protected the faithful from thunderstorms, that the storm would hold off until everyone was safely indoors. But God and his saints had other plans, and soon great drops of rain began to fall, and the wind blew unhindered from the North Sea along the flat canal paths, lifting the veils and gowns of the ladies, making cloaks and silks flap around the horsemen and standing the banners, flags and pennants straight out from their poles. Yet still the procession moved forward until it reached the gate of the Holy Cross, its slated twin towers now shiny with rain. Her carriage rolled through the century-old gate and over another canal into the red-roofed city and finally came to a halt.

A fanfare sounded, and the crowds craned their necks to see what was happening. The first of four additional processions made their way to her. The mayor, magistrates and aldermen—called burghers—dressed in black were arrayed for her viewing, accompanied by more musicians. The mayor approached the litter and bowed low.

"Our great city of Bruges," he shouted to the crowd, "welcomes Margaret, the most high and mighty duchess of Burgundy, of Lotharingia, of Brabant, Limbourg and Luxembourg, countess of Flanders and of Artois, of Burgundy, Hainault, Holland, Zeeland and Namur, marchioness of the Holy Roman Empire, Lady of Friesland . . ." He droned on in his accented French, losing Margaret in the list of her new dominions. She wanted to giggle. How will I ever remember all my titles? she thought. I am glad George and Dickon aren't here to witness this, they would tease me for ever! Then, to her dismay, thoughts of them caused a wave of homesickness that threatened to overwhelm her, and tears pricked behind her eyes. Pull yourself together, Meg, she told herself, you are twenty-two years old and not a babe. And so she was able to bow solemnly and acknowledge the cheers.

Another man she guessed was a judge presented her with an intricate gold vase filled to the brim with gold coins as well as an enameled statue of her own saint, Margaret of Antioch. This group then moved on to become the head of the procession. They were quickly followed by more than a hundred and fifty bishops and abbots from throughout Burgundy, some carrying high, elaborate crosses. Margaret signed herself as they passed, and the bishop of Utrecht nodded to her.

Behind them the foreign merchants drew gasps of awe. The magnificent and colorful group was all mounted, except for the Scots, who marched proudly on foot, carefully avoiding the manure dropped by the horses in front. All of the merchants were clothed in the finest silks, brocades, velvets and wool, and the representative of each nation wore his country's colors. The English merchant-adventurers, led by a man Margaret guessed was William Caxton, were clad in their violet livery. With them were Italians from Venice, Florence, Lucca, Genoa; the German Hansards; the Portuguese and the Spanish. The Florentines presented Margaret with four beautiful white horses, worth a fortune, which astonished her. She was yet to know the extent of the riches in her new country, but she was beginning to have an idea. As they moved behind the disappearing backs of the bishops, Margaret guessed there must have been five hundred merchants, and that was not counting the pages and musicians who walked alongside. What next? she thought. Surely that is the end? But it wasn't.

The last to join the now fifteen hundred men wending their way through the streets, the Burg and the Market Square to the Prinsenhof Palace were the members of the ducal household themselves. Margaret was awed. I thought they were all with me, she thought. She gazed at the small, rotund man who headed up this group, wondering who he was.

Anthony, who was never far away and had anticipated her question, leaned over Pegasus' neck and said, " 'Tis Olivier de la Marche, your grace. We met this week to go over some of the events they are planning. He has orchestrated everything you will be seeing. Do not underestimate him. He has an agility of mind and predilection for detail that would make you giddy." Margaret nodded her thanks and stared after the man with interest. She thought she might enjoy meeting him.

As soon as the last of the purple-, crimson- and black-liveried servants had filed past, Margaret's carriage was moved forward to follow them. And thus, as torrents of rain pelted the open-sided chariot, she entered Bruges, gazed at by hundreds of spectators hanging from garlanded windows, seated on hastily constructed stands along the sides of the canal or hoisted up on parents' shoulders, all unconcerned by the weather.

Margaret felt sorry for the gorgeously arrayed cavalcade, which was not protected from the elements as she was. Some of the dyes in the men's hats were running down their faces, staining their cheeks. Along the route, the carriage would stop at wooden stages, where players would present a colorful pageant for her. Their themes were mostly biblical, such as Solomon and Sheba, Adam and Eve and the Marriage at Canaan. By the tenth, Margaret's stomach was grumbling, and she had a desperate need for the jakes. She hoped they would reach the palace before long.

She was disappointed that her first view of this beautiful city was marred by the lowering clouds and hampered by the waving mass of people. She caught glimpses of the magnificent houses of the merchants, the exquisite Gothic town hall in the Burg, St. Donatian's cathedral and the tall belfry watchtower in the Market Square before they finally reached the palace.

Sculpted archers set in the doorway to the courtyard spouted red and white wine from their bows, and on the limb of an artificial tree, a great golden pelican spurted sweet hippocras from its breast. Margaret was handed a cup to taste, and she gratefully swallowed the honeyed drink and ate a few wafers from the proffered plate as she admired the fanciful pelican.

Her mother-in-law greeted her graciously, and took her hand and led the way into the palace, which was grander even than Westminster, every inch of it painted in the colors and arms of Burgundy and hung with enormous tapestries woven from silk, wool, golden and silver thread. At last she came to her own rooms, all freshly painted with her own marguerites, and walls covered with more tapestries. There Isabella left her to rest before dinner.

Margaret allowed her ladies to remove her mantle, crown and shoes and then collapsed, not very gracefully, onto the biggest bed she had ever seen. She could not sleep for the myriad sights and sounds she had experienced this extraordinary day. She wondered if Edward would hear of it and smiled, imagining his wide eyes at the lavishness of the occasion. *Certes, there has been nothing in England to rival what I have seen today,* she told herself. She did not know that Burgundy had never seen anything like it before either—or would again. Charles had taken this occasion to show his people for the first time since he had become duke that he was every bit as capable as Philip of mounting an extravagant show of pomp and ceremony. But there he hoped all comparisons with his dead father ceased. Not the least of which was Philip's fondness for women.

STILL IN HER shining white cloth of gold gown, Margaret made her entrance at the first banquet of the nine days of wedding festivities.

Adolphe of Cleves, Lord Ravenstein, and after Charles, Burgundy's most important noble, accompanied her to her place at the high dais. He told her much of the hall had been made in Brussels and brought by river and canal to Bruges that spring for the Golden Fleece chapter meeting. She was not expecting the temporary hall to be much more than hurriedly constructed scaffolding, and so she gasped when she first saw it. It was graced on the outside by turrets, had glass windows and boasted two upper galleries, where guests were already ensconced. More gorgeous tapestries hung above her richly decorated throne, one in gold and silver silk telling the story of Jason and the Golden Fleece, and the tables were covered in cloth of gold. The ceiling was draped with blue and white cloth. Margaret felt diminutive in the magnificent space.

"Duke Charles will not join you for dinner, your grace," Ravenstein told her, his grave face reminding Margaret of a lugubrious statue of a long-dead abbot she had seen in a church somewhere. His hawk nose jutted out from his face, and his close-set eagle eyes under hooded lids never seemed to blink. Somewhere in his forties, he was one of Charles's councilors and brother of the duke of Cleves, also a vassal of Charles's. Despite his austere countenance, Margaret thought the man seemed trustworthy and was possibly kinder than he looked.

The company dazzled her eyes as she walked between their bowing figures, and she imagined she had arrived in some earthly paradise. Never in her life had she seen such a display of wealth as she had that day, and it was only half spent!

The noblest persons from England and Burgundy were seated at two tables on the first dais that she mounted. Her table was upon a third level. Isabella and Mary graced either end, standing and bowing to her as she reached her throne. As wife of Margaret's presenter, Eliza Scales had been given the honor of serving her that night, the irony of which was not lost on Margaret, and for the Burgundians, the other place was given to Marie de Charny.

Once on her throne, she could now marvel at the ingenuity of the decorations. At either end of the hall was a rocky mountain on which perched a beautifully constructed castle, the tower of which served as an enormous candleholder. Around the mountain paths were models of men and women on foot or on horseback, farm and wild animals, trees, flowers and shrubs.

The banquet was a feast for the eyes as well as the stomach. Roast swan and peacock, egret and pheasant were borne in on huge silver platters by servants dressed in the Burgundian crimson and black. Venison, beef and mutton followed great carp and bream wrapped in gold foil and then came decorated jellies and custards. Margaret was happy to nibble at a salat, and she marveled at this mixture of cress, lettuce, nasturtium, leek, fennel and herbs all covered with flowers.

And the entremets, or between courses, entertained her as she digested each delicacy before being served another. Huge, intricately carved mechanical animals magically rolled through the hall; live animals burst from inside enormous pies; dozens of monkeys raced up and down a tall tower; and the faces of black bears simultaneously appeared at every window, making the women cry out in fear and wonderment.

Fortunata, who was seated at the bottom of the dais steps, clapped excitedly at each marvel, and when a dwarf dressed to look like the Queen of Sheba rode in on a gilded lion, she rose to her feet and gleefully pointed her out to Margaret. Fortunata found it difficult to maintain silence, which seemed to be the way the court preferred to feast except for music on lutes and viols, but Margaret nodded and smiled at Fortunata, mouthing, "She's the lady Mary's" to her. Margaret's stomach had stopped grumbling, but her head was beginning to pound. She motioned to Lord Ravenstein, who hurried up the stairs to her.

"I wish to address the company, messire. I trust it will not be breaking with court etiquette?" she asked.

She saw the softening that she had been certain lay underneath the aloof exterior. I was not wrong, she thought, pleased.

"Your grace, you make the court etiquette today. I will arrange it. And perhaps you should know, the duke will join you soon to lead you to the tournament for the first day of jousting." He saw a hint of a grimace flit across her face, but then she was all smiles. He made a note. *The new duchess is not enamored of jousting.*

"Of course, my lord. The tournament of the Golden Tree. His grace did tell me. I shall look forward to it," she murmured, wishing her headache would go away. Ravenstein bowed, took her hand and led her to the edge of the dais. Then he motioned to the trumpeters, who blew a short fanfare. All eyes turned to the tall young duchess, standing so confidently before them.

"I am humbled by your gracious hospitality and welcome in Bruges, *messires et mesdames.* I know I can speak for all of my countrymen here today when I say thank you from the bottom of my heart. I shall endeavor to be as wise and kind a duchess as the dowager has been to Burgundy and earn the honor you have done me today. May God give you all his blessing and to my husband, Duke Charles." Her clear voice rang out across the hall as she raised her goblet, and a thousand voices answered her: "May God bless you, *Madame la duchesse*."

It was the signal to rise and move to the tournament. As Fortunata followed Margaret out, she slipped through the crowd to find Madame de Beaugrand, the other dwarf.

Charles was at the viewing stand to greet his bride, putting in his first appearance at the occasion after graciously allowing Margaret all the glory. Margaret hardly recognized him. His clothes were made of gold and covered with pearls and jewels. On his hat shone the largest ruby she had ever seen, which she was to learn had a name: the Ballas of Flanders. Despite her lovely gown, fashioned by the best tailors in London, she felt dowdy and insignificant next to him.

Her hand shook as she took his to be presented to the jubilant spectators and the splendid array of knights lined up in front of them on the muddy ground. One by one they were announced and stepped forward to kneel to the duke and the duchess before walking stiffly in their armor back to the gaily colored pavilions set up around the edge of the field. Anthony bowed his head, holding his helmet under his arm, and she almost gasped when she saw the torn silver scarf fluttering from it. He must have kept it from the Smithfield tournament, she thought with a thrill. As her official escort, Margaret decided Anthony warranted a special word.

"God's greeting to you, Lord Scales. May fortune be with you this day. All England is counting on you!" she called coolly.

Anthony bowed gravely, a small smile on his lips. "We are honored to represent our sovereign lord—and you, your grace. With God's help, we shall not let you down on this auspicious day. Surely, my lord duke," he said, now addressing Charles, "what we are witnessing today"—and he swept his arm to encompass the city—"is as close to Camelot as it can come." A thrill went through Margaret, knowing he was speaking directly to her. A small smile told him she understood and made him bolder. "And rest assured, Lady Margaret, that we will carry you in our hearts as we fight—and back to England with us," he said into her eyes.

Charles nodded, his generous mouth curved in a smile, but then he waved his hands impatiently. "Well said, milord. But now I pray you no more pretty speeches. Let us witness your skill." He would not fight today, but he was anxious to show off his prowess to Margaret later in the week, he told her. "God be with you all," he cried, and signaled for the first joust to begin.

As Anthony strode to his tent, Margaret heard one of her new ladies whisper: "Sweet Jesu, but he is handsome."

FORTUNATA COULD NOT wait to talk to Margaret later that night as the ladies were readying their mistress for her marriage bed. No one dared approach Margaret at the prie-dieu. Her English women were used to Fortunata always at her side there, and so they had explained this to the fierce Marie de Charny, who on the first night in Sluis had attempted to remove Fortunata. Margaret deduced this was going to be the only time in her crowded life when she could have a private conversation with her confidante, and she used it as often as she could. Consequently, the Burgundian ladies were impressed by the new duchess's piety.

"What?" Margaret whispered, incredulously. "Who said such a thing?"

"Madame de Beaugrand told me this, milady. She does not lie. Everybody has heard about it. I told her it was not true, and maybe she will tell others. I hope." Fortunata shrugged. Margaret bowed over her rosary, but her mind was not on her prayers. She could not believe her ears. It seemed a rumor had been started after the marriage contract was signed that she was not coming to Charles's marriage bed a virgin! The rumor went further. It was common knowledge at the English court that Margaret had had a child. Sweet Jesu, she panicked, how can I face Charles now? She took heart knowing that as soon as he bedded her, he would know she was in fact a virgin, but it did not lessen her worry. In her anxiety, she forgot the civil way he had greeted her every day in Sluis, even kissing her each time and conversing quite amicably. What must he think? She was mortified.

Fortunata was tugging at her skirt. "*Madonna*, you are not listening to me. There is more."

Margaret lifted her head and stared at the exquisite diptych in front of her. "Go on," she murmured disconsolately. "It cannot get worse, in truth."

"Nay, milady, this is better." Fortunata's eyes twinkled. "Madame de

Beaugrand said Duke Charles was so angry when he heard the rumor, he shouted that if anyone said it again he would throw them in the river." She finished triumphantly, "Maybe your husband is not so bad, *madonna*."

Maybe he believed it and that was why he became so angry, Margaret thought miserably. And for the next hour, as she was bathed, perfumed and dressed in a silk chemise, she wondered how she could face him. She was exhausted, homesick and unnerved by so many strange women fussing about her, touching her, stroking her hair.

Suddenly, Cecily's face appeared to her, and Margaret almost cried out in anguish for her mother. She gritted her teeth, held back her tears and called for wine. Fortunata was there in a flash with a goblet. Margaret was vaguely aware that the vessel was encrusted with jewels, but her mind was unable to absorb any more luxury after everything she had seen that day. It was all one golden blur.

The wine revived her a little, and she allowed herself to be put into bed, which was draped in the Burgundian colors, elaborate entwined letters of C and M embroidered upon them, and made up with sheets of the finest lawn scented with lavender and rose petals. The rich velvet bedspread was trimmed with ermine, and she almost called for her crown, because she felt underdressed lying there.

And then they waited. And they waited. Margaret could no longer keep her eyes open, and she whispered to Fortunata she was going to take a nap and to make sure she gave fair warning of the duke's arrival.

An hour later, with Margaret fast asleep and her ladies dozing on whatever seat they could find in the chamber, the sound of male voices alerted the vigilant Fortunata.

"*Madonna, madonna,* wake up. He is coming. Your husband is coming. Oh, please wake up!" she urged.

Margaret's eyes flew open and she sat up, allowing Countess de Charny to arrange her hair on the satin pillows. The door was flung open, and Charles and some of his squires strode in, seemingly the worse for drink.

"Out, out!" he said, waving the women away, his head jutting forward from his thick, muscular shoulders. They all turned to look at Margaret, who nodded, thanked them and watched them leave the room.

Fortunata was the last to go, her huge eyes expressing compassion.

Charles was undressed in the small chamber beyond amid whispers and ribald laughter. Finally he appeared in his chemise, his heavy, hairy legs visible from the knees. He stared at Margaret propped up on the pillows and managed an awkward little bow. He closed the door on his servants, blew out several candles and carried a candelabrum to the table near the bed, spilling wax on his hand and cursing.

"I pray you, my lord, will you not extinguish them all?" Margaret said, annoyed that her voice squeaked.

Charles gave a short laugh. "Nay, I have paid handsomely for you, my lady. I would see what I have paid for."

Margaret gasped at his indelicacy but chose to ignore it, putting it down to too much wine. Perhaps he is nervous, too, she thought magnanimously, and the drink gave him courage. She frantically tried to think of something to say to prolong the conversation—and put off the agony. As Fortunata's story was foremost in her mind, it came tumbling out. "Before we begin our marriage proper, Charles, I swear to you that I am a virgin and anything you may have heard to the contrary is a lie!" The strength in her voice surprised even her.

Charles blinked. "Did I hear correctly?" he asked incredulously. "You are acknowledging that you are a virgin? I expected nothing less, my lady, or I would not have signed the contract."

Margaret plucked nervously at the ermine trim. "But . . . the rumors, Charles. You must have heard the rumors."

"Rumors!" Charles bellowed, standing over her, his blue eyes bulging and his spittle landing on her hand. "When does a prince listen to rumors." Seeing her wince, he moderated his tone. "Have no fear, from everything I have witnessed this past week, I have no doubt of your virtue, Lady Margaret. You have exceeded my expectations in every way." He paused and looked away. "And what of me? I hope I do not displease you?"

He sat on the bed and began to blow out the candles one by one, relieving Margaret greatly, although the glowing embers of the fire made a grotesque shadow of him on the wall.

"I am well content, Charles," she answered, softly. "How could I not be after the day I have experienced. There are no words to tell you how honored and humbled I feel. I can only express my heartfelt thanks—" She was cut off by his rough, fleshy mouth on hers.

"Enough talking, madame," he rasped, "I would do my duty by you, and by Christ I am almost too tired to accomplish it."

You could not prove it by me, Margaret thought, enduring Charles's callused hands on her breasts. Sweet Mary, they are not dough, she wanted to tell him, wincing as he kneaded her and pinched her nipples through the flimsy gown. He had pulled back the bedclothes and heaved himself on top of her. She squeezed her eyes shut. He smelled of horses, but unlike John Harper, there was no counterscent of rosewater. He just smelled of horses and wine. I suppose I can bear this, she was just thinking, when her legs were pushed apart and he entered her, gently at first until he was resisted and then with a force that caused Margaret to cry out in pain. Charles grunted and bore down on her, his muscular buttocks driving farther and farther into her until she thought he had pierced not only her maidenhead but her womb as well. Tears of pain rolled down her cheeks, and she was glad there was no light. His grip on her outstretched arms tightened as he neared his climax and she maneuvered her hips into a less agonizing position. This only seemed to increase his pleasure, and finally with a noise somewhere between a bark and a whinny, he gave in to his need. Spent, he lay on her, breathing heavily for several minutes. Margaret was not sure what to do, so she tentatively put her hand on his back and stroked him.

Charles roused himself and rolled onto his side. "You spoke the truth, Margaret. I regret if I hurt you, but 'tis the nature of the marriage bed." He chuckled. "I would like to know how you knew to move yourself in that delicious way. I could almost believe you were practiced."

Margaret laughed. Now that it was all over, she had to admit it wasn't as dreadful as she had imagined. "Nay, Charles. I was merely making myself more comfortable, in truth."

Charles liked her honest response and said so. "And in the interest of honesty, Margaret, I must tell you that you will not have to endure my advances very often. I do not need a woman as my father did. If you are happy to be left alone, then I shall have no quarrel with that. I am advised to beget a male heir, however, so you may see me from time to time in your bed."

Margaret mouthed a round "Oh." She could not believe her ears or her good fortune.

With that, Charles called loudly to his squires, who were so ready to do his bidding—and, thought Margaret bitterly, so close to the door as to have heard everything—that they almost fell into the room in their eagerness to answer his call. Shunning the light of the men's candles, Margaret turned away, drawing the covers around her head as Charles jumped out of bed, wished her a good night and led the men from the room, leaving her in the darkness.

She lay perfectly still for several minutes before once again her room was invaded, this time by Marie and her other ladies.

"What is the meaning of this?" she demanded. "I did not call for you, countess. I wish you to leave me alone. All but Fortunata may go."

The authority in her voice left Marie no choice but to usher everyone from the room, but not before Margaret heard the now-familiar "Tut-tut."

She watched Fortunata scurry around the room in the flickering firelight, pouring some warm water from the jug near the fire into a bowl and taking it to the bed table.

"Are you hurt, *madonna*? Did he hurt you?" the dwarf asked, her brown eyes searching Margaret's face. "*Si*, I see you are crying. Poor *madonna*."

She wrung out a cloth and wiped Margaret's face, and then turned her back as Margaret washed the telltale blood from her thigh.

"In truth, 'twas not so bad, *pochina*. You should not be anxious on my account. I am no green girl, and I knew what to expect," she said more bravely than she felt. Did I know what to expect? Her moment of pleasure with John Harper had led her to believe she would experience the same sensation with any man. She had been sadly mistaken. She had not even been aroused by Charles. She knelt by the bed and said her prayers for the second time that night. A sadness overcame her as she realized her virginity was lost forever. Try as she might, she could not put Anthony's face from her mind.

For nine more days the festivities continued, each day bringing new evidence of the artistic and economic wealth of her new land. Margaret saw the work of artists such as Hans Memling, Jan van Eyck and Rogier van der Weyden, heard the music of Dufay and Binchois and wore creations from the workshops of Bruges goldsmiths and jewelers, who were the finest in Europe.

For her wedding gift, Charles gave her a magnificent necklace consisting of two gold chains three inches apart separated by golden knots and red and white enameled roses studded with pearls. From the lower chain hung the letters C and M in gold and enamel. By this time, she was realizing that the finery she had brought with her from England was a little old-fashioned and of lesser quality. Her own steepled hennins were dwarfed by the three-feet-high ones worn by Isabella and Marie de Charny. She told Fortunata that if she was to adopt the monstrosities, she would have difficulty going through doorways.

The tournament was the mainstay of the week, which Margaret guessed was planned more for Charles's enjoyment than hers. At one point during the sixth interminable day of it, the fighting between six knights became so fierce, albeit with blunt swords, that Margaret rose to her feet, waved her kerchief and begged them to stop. The only pleasure the tournament gave her was that it required the English retinue to stay until the end. And how proud she was that an Englishman—Anthony's twenty-three-year-old brother, John—was declared Prince of the Tournament when the last lance was shattered and the final axe blow had been struck.

The feast following outdid the rest, and afterwards the company danced until they dropped. Charles led Margaret out for a *basse danse,* and in the line she saw Anthony partnering an excited Mary. The girl was graceful and full of poise, her dove-gray eyes shining with pleasure, and Anthony gravely treated her as if she were a fully grown woman. Margaret caught his eye when she dared and sent him a tender look of gratitude. Charles was not light on his feet, and Margaret could tell he was only doing his duty as a dance partner, much like his duty to her in bed. Those visits had numbered three since their marriage, and although there had been no more pain for Margaret, neither had there been any passion in the act. She hoped she would find herself pregnant in no time.

"I regret I must leave you tomorrow, Margaret," Charles told her as they returned to the dais. "I have assigned you a competent knight of honor in Guillaume de la Baume. I trust he will be agreeable and serve you well. My sister Marie seems to have your ladies in hand." He winked at her. "In truth, she is bit of a dragon, is she not!"

Margaret nodded, diplomatically refusing to tell him the woman resembled quite another species of winged creature entirely.

"How do you like my daughter?" he asked. "I regret my skill as a father does not allow me confidences with her. She was so close to her mother, 'tis true, but *ma mère* tells me she is not unhappy with my choice of step-mother for her."

This was the longest conversation they had had so far, and Margaret was encouraged by Charles's attempts at friendship. He was not so bad, she thought, as she thanked him for the compliment and told him she had already formed an attachment to Mary.

" 'Tis happy news, Margaret, for you and she will be together constantly now. Those are my orders. I hope she grows to be as gracious as you. She will be duchess one day, and she needs someone strong to guide her."

Margaret's stomach lurched. Was Charles not expecting her to bear him a son? This was a shock, and her face must have registered a change, for he asked if she was unwell. She was spared the lie of a response as Lord Ravenstein, managing as much of a smile as his grave face could handle, approached them, bowed and requested permission to present the governor of the English merchant-adventurers to the duchess.

A short, neatly dressed man stood at Ravenstein's elbow, bowing. Margaret guessed him to be in his mid-forties. His thick curly hair was graying and his full beard more so. When he straightened up, Margaret looked into a pair of intelligent brown eyes that observed her from under beetling brows, the more surprising because they were still black, and over a fine, aquiline nose. She knew instantly she had found a friend in Bruges and smiled her pleasure at meeting him. Charles greeted him cursorily, excused himself—to avail himself of the garderobe, Margaret guessed—and was followed from the hall by all of his squires. Ravenstein watched him go with an eagle eye but remained behind with Margaret.

"We have a mutual friend, Master Caxton," she said in English. "My brother's loyal councilor, Sir John Howard, has told me of you. God's greeting to you."

William Caxton grinned, glad to be conversing with her in his native tongue. "Aye, your grace, Sir John has had some discourse with me here, in truth, and it is my honor to serve you. I bring you hearty greetings from all the English merchants. They are proud to welcome our sovereign's sister to these shores, especially"—he lowered his voice—"a daughter of York."

Margaret glanced quickly at Ravenstein, but realizing he did not speak English, she was relieved to see him yawn discreetly while watching for Charles's return. "I thank you, sir," she acknowledged his emphasis on York. She knew the English merchants favored her house over Lancaster because of the good relations between Duke Philip and her brother.

"You have my word I will do what I can for you with regard to trade, sir," she murmured. "My brother has charged me with the task of keeping the negotiations in process on an even keel. I pray you attend me in my quarters while I am still at Bruges, and we will talk more on it."

She held her hand out for him to kiss and was gratified to see his look of astonishment at her forthrightness and perspicacity. She could see he was not expecting her to be much more than a pretty pawn in this Burgundian alliance.

"'Twill be my honor, your grace," he answered, bowing and backing away from her. He turned and walked back to the group of English guests, and Margaret saw Jack Howard clap him on the shoulder and share a few words. Charles had not returned, and Margaret felt sorry for Ravenstein, standing first on one leg and then the other. She tried to engage him in conversation about the day's jousting, but he was taciturn, and she gave up. She watched as a new group of dancers took the floor, the musicians retuning their instruments before launching into a lively *saltarello*, her favorite dance. As the dancers began to form groups of six, she bent down to say something to Fortunata, who was seated on her customary footstool behind Margaret's skirts. She had to say the dwarf's name twice before Fortunata pulled her eyes off the receding figure of William Caxton and responded to her mistress, stammering, "Forgive me, *madonna*. I did not hear you." Margaret followed Fortunata's gaze and was intrigued to see it was directed at the stocky merchant. She was about to ask her servant to explain the love-lorn look when a familiar voice made her heart leap into her throat and Fortunata was forgotten.

"Would her grace the duchess of Burgundy favor me with this dance? There is a group in need of a third couple." Anthony stood before her, bowing first to Ravenstein before extending his leg and giving Margaret deep obeisance. "Is it permitted, my lady?" he asked again, not giving Ravenstein any inkling that his motive was not merely a formality.

"Is it permitted, messire?" Margaret asked the stiff Burgundian. "Can you sanction my dancing with Lord Scales without my husband's permission?" Margaret was only half serious, but she was unprepared for Marie de Charny's intrusion and was taken aback when the countess superseded any answer Ravenstein may have had.

"Certes, your grace. No one would think it untoward if you accepted a dance with one of such nobility as Lord Scales." And she gave Anthony a low curtsey, as Ravenstein gritted his teeth and stalked away.

"Marguerite, I fear I leave you here in severe hands. I know not who is more peevish, Ravenstein or Charny. But for the next few precious moments, let us think of no one but ourselves."

"As you wish, Anthony. I shall not gainsay you," Margaret said quietly. "There is nothing I would deny you, I hope you know."

Their hands met as the dance began, and Margaret, casting her eyes down as was customary, felt their love flow freely one to the other through their fingers.

"Never forget that I love you, Marguerite, although you are lost to me now."

He moved away with the dance but saw her nod imperceptibly. For the next few minutes, as the hundreds of guests watched the English princess and her handsome partner with admiration, she frantically sought for a way to see him alone before the English contingent set sail for home the next day. She glanced up and saw Charles back on the dais, his large eyes fixed on her, and she quickly looked down again. He looked none too pleased, she noted, and from the sulky look on Marie's face, she could see he had given his sister a dressing-down.

The dance came to an end all too soon, and she looked up at Anthony, who bowed solemnly and muttered under his breath, "Send Fortunata to me." Then he escorted her back to her seat, cheerfully greeting Charles with: "My lord duke, I am deeply grateful. I could not return to England without allowing your countrymen to witness the finest proponent of the *saltarello* in Christendom! 'Twas a pleasure, Lady Margaret," he said. "Your grace, I shall look forward to our appointed meeting on the morrow, and now, with a long day ahead, I wish you both a good night."

Before Charles could object, he was gone.

• • •

Margaret was melancholy for days after watching the departure of her beloved compatriots. Even Fortunata's successful meeting with Anthony just after Mass on the final morning and the resulting gift of a belt ornament fashioned into a marguerite did not lift her spirits. She took to her bed early every night and cried herself to sleep while reliving those last moments over and over.

She had kissed the duchess of Norfolk tearfully, instructing her to give Ned a good account of her reception in Burgundy, and then had a few words with several members of the company, asking them to pray for her and wishing them a safe voyage home.

"No more French attacks, I hope, Sir John," she said to Jack Howard, smiling fondly at him. "And I hope if you visit us here again, you will bring your delightful wife with you. In the meantime, I must thank you for commending me to Master Caxton. I think we have much to talk about and I shall seek his counsel when I am homesick. 'Twill be a comfort to speak English with him. Now go, sir, before I embarrass myself and cry."

Jack held her hand in both of his before he respectfully kissed it. "As I have said before, your grace, magnificent. You are truly magnificent."

She managed a smile as she accepted Anthony's farewell, thanking him graciously for his support as her escort. She took a small velvet pouch from her wide sleeve and, with Charles and the lords and ladies looking on, offered it to him. " 'Tis but a small token, my lord, but I shall never forget how you brought me into Burgundy and unto my lord, the duke. God speed to you and to all the company," she said. She had not felt guilty in prying off a gold and enamel M from her wedding necklace to give him as it might easily have fallen off during one of the many days of dressing and dancing. Anthony bowed and slipped the pouch into the bag at his waist. He read in Margaret's eyes not to open it there.

Then, with Charles, Duchess Isabella and little Mary beside her, she stood as if in a stupor and watched the love of her life mount his beautiful Pegasus and turn and wave one more time before trotting off at the head of the procession back to Sluis.

Margaret felt a small hand take hers in the folds of her silk brocade gown. She looked down to see Mary smiling shyly up at her.

"*Courage, belle-mère. Je suis là,*" the girl said. "You have me to love you now."

12

Late summer 1468

The following day, Margaret waved good-bye to Charles, who set off north to Zeeland and Holland to see to state affairs in those lowlands of marshes and peat bogs. He had kissed Margaret soundly on the lips before leaving, a practice he kept up with all the English ladies every time he saw them. It was the only endearing thing about Charles that Margaret could find in those first days as his wife. He had a violent temper, which he had certainly not turned on her yet, but some of his retainers were still smarting from something he had thrown at them in her presence.

With his household of more than two hundred gone from the Prinsenhof, the palace seemed empty and quiet. But her days were far from empty and quiet. Lord Ravenstein immediately began instructing her in the expectations Charles had of her as duchess, including how to manage her own household of more than one hundred and forty people. For days she sat in the lavishly decorated audience chamber with Ravenstein and her chevalier by her side and tried to remember names and faces of maids of honor, maîtres d'hôtel, ushers, sommeliers or housekeepers, provisioners, seamstresses, laundresses and all the kitchen staff. Then there were her priests, her doctors and surgeons, not forgetting the stable boys, farriers and falconers who would look after her dogs, horses and hunting birds. She was told not all of them would be on duty at once. They would work in three- or six-month shifts, and some of the lesser members would come from the local area surrounding each palace she would live in.

Used to moving a few times a year in England but mostly from the Wardrobe to Greenwich, Westminster or Shene, Margaret pricked up her ears. "How many residences are there, messire," Margaret asked Ravenstein.

"I could not say, your grace. Let me see, there is this one and Male, Mons, Ten Waele in Ghent, Aire, Oudenaarde, Dendermonde, Hesdin, Cassel, La Motte, Brussels, Binche, Ter Elst near Antwerp, Bellemotte, St. Josse ten Noode—"

"Enough, messire! You are making my head spin," she laughed. "I understand the duchy is well endowed with estates, but, certes, I need only know about those I shall be residing in."

Ravenstein eyed her with something akin to pity. "I hope you like traveling, madame, because you will never be in one place for very long."

Margaret sighed. She was beginning to lose faith in her ability to win over this humorless man, and she could see he was irked by having to play tutor to her when he should have been with Charles. She rose and said brightly, "Come, messire, if you must spend time in my company teaching me my duties—which I am certain is tedious for you—let us enjoy the garden. I need to stretch my legs after this morning's work."

Ravenstein quickly assured her he was honored to be her guide. He was disconcerted yet impressed that the duchess had seen right through him, as he prided himself on his unfailing civility no matter the circumstance. He bowed and offered her his arm with a little more enthusiasm now.

Immediately Margaret's ladies sprang into action. She was beginning to find some humor in constantly being trailed by ten or twelve people, and as Fortunata twitched her mistress's train behind her, Margaret winked at the dwarf. She loved it when a smile brightened Fortunata's sallow face as though the sun had suddenly come from behind a dark cloud. The little procession walked into the sunlight and through a rose-covered arbor to an immaculately kept lawn and flower garden beyond. 'Twas a pity we did not have a day like today for my entry into Bruges, Margaret thought, remembering the downpour.

She watched a team of gardeners with small razor-sharp scythes expertly cut the grass to an inch high, creating a soft emerald carpet for them to walk upon. Ravenstein led her to a horeshoe-shaped excedra, planted with grass and gillyflowers, and she sat down on it. Her ladies arranged themselves prettily around her feet, their skirts and mantles creating a tableau of vivid colors on a green background—like a tapestry from Tournai, Margaret mused. Just then, a thrush chose to show off his lilting voice, and the repetitive song, the smell of the roses, the cloudless sky and the peaceful garden gave Margaret her most pleasurable moment since leaving England.

She turned such a sweet smile on Lord Ravenstein that he was momentarily taken aback. He had not properly studied his master's new wife, so taken up was he with his duties to the duke. Now he perceived the duchess had good looks as well as a good pedigree, and he temporarily forgot the resentment he had harbored earlier for being left behind to tend to her. He brightened and, appreciating her pertinent and perceptive questions about the government of such a diverse state as Burgundy, over the next few days he soon became one of her most ardent admirers.

Before she left Bruges for Brussels, Margaret received a visit from William Caxton. It was raining again, so they sat in an antechamber in the presence of her *chevalier* and, as usual, her ladies. She watched him walk across the tiled floor and noted his slight limp before he knelt before her, as was court custom, until Margaret had avised him for several minutes and given him permission to rise. She also noticed that his right eyebrow seemed caught in a permanent arch, lending an appealing cynicism to his expression. She was curious as to why his short, strong fingers were stained black, and, so, after discussing the English wool trade and the new agreement Charles was considering, she asked, "Forgive the non sequitur, Master Caxton, but is it the wool that dyes your hands black?"

William was taken aback. He could not believe a lady of her rank would notice, much less ask about, his stained fingers. He tried to hide them under the bonnet he was holding and answered her equally directly, his voice carrying the hint of a Kentish accent. "I like to think I have a way with pen and ink, your grace. But much of it seems to end up on my fingers."

Then Margaret remembered the captain's disparaging remark about his friend Caxton's interest in books, and she smiled. "So 'tis true what I have heard about you, good sir. I, too, enjoy books more than anything. We shall have to talk more on this whenever I am in Bruges again. I have been told Duke Philip's library is unmatched in Europe. In truth, when I go to Brussels, I shall feel as though I am in a paradise."

"I envy you, my lady. I have acquired but three books, but I hope to copy a few more in my spare time for my own pleasure," he said. "I am particularly fond of the *recueil*—the history of Troy by Monsieur Lefevre— and I am making a modest attempt at translating it into English."

"One day you must show it to me, Master Caxton. I think it is a splendid endeavor," Margaret said. She was liking this industrious, plain-speaking man more and more, and by the time his hour-long audience with her was at an end, she had made up her mind to trust him.

"Walk with me, Master Caxton," she commanded, rising from her chair and putting out her hand for his arm, which he readily offered. She snapped her fingers and called to Astolat to accompany them, and the dog loped over, sniffing Caxton's crotch much to the merchant's embar-rassment. "He needs to know you are my friend, sir," Margaret said as straight-faced as she could, watching him attempt to protect his codpiece from the dog's huge mouth. " 'Tis a particular trait of the breed, I am told," she lied. "Here, Astolat! Fortunata, I pray you, control him while I talk to Master Caxton." She was astonished to see Fortunata give William one of her brightest smiles. I must ask her about this, Margaret thought, amused. Sadly, she doubted William Caxton would look on the dwarf with anything more than indifferent kindness.

As soon as she had risen from her chair, her entourage surrounded them and followed them up and down the long gallery that led from her antechamber and was beautifully hung with tapestries of the hunt of a mythical creature. She doubted she would ever get used to the constant procession that shadowed her all day. However, she had trained Fortunata to walk between her and the rest of the company, so she knew no one would hear her next words to Caxton, even if someone was conversant with English.

"Master Caxton, I have an enterprise that I need your help and discretion with. Can I trust you?" she began. "Fear not, 'tis not a hanging matter, but some torture could ensue should you be caught."

William heard the smile in her voice and returned the solemn tone. "I would be happy to be stretched on the rack for you, your grace. You have but to ask. The thumbscrews, however, may need a little more negotiation."

"We understand each other very well, sir," Margaret replied with a chuckle. "I believe you will be my saving grace here. I have a friend at my brother's court with whom I would like to correspond privately. 'Tis the only way I may still feel the pulse of events at home. I fear my correspondence here may not be for my eyes only, and in order to serve my country and"—she turned and indicated him—"my countrymen to the best of my ability, I must know what is transpiring in a timely way. Do you understand?" She hoped her new friend would not guess the real motivation for the letters, but when he nodded gravely and said he would be honored to do all in his power to serve England's interests abroad, she was satisfied.

"May I use your address in this enterprise, sir?" Seeing him nod, she continued, "Before I leave Bruges, I will send Fortunata to find you at the Waterhall with my first letter to an address of a goldsmith in Cheapside. I trust you will put it on the next ship to England. And do not wonder at the name that will appear on the letters, sir. My correspondent and I have a particular fondness for Camelot and all its tales. You will know 'tis for me when you see Dame Elaine Astolat written. Mine will be addressed to Lancelot Dulac."

Caxton smiled as if he perfectly understood this code. "Ah, Astolat, I understand," he murmured, and Margaret was pleased again with this well-read man. "I will do as you wish, your grace. I thank you for this audience, and I shall report on our discussion about trade with my fellow adventurers." He bowed respectfully over her hand and limped away, his long-toed leather boots slap-slapping unevenly on the colorful tiled floor.

"*My love,*" she began, her quill scratching on the parchment. She tickled her nose with the feather as she thought, not knowing it was a habit her brothers would always remember her for.

What to say? she wondered, staring at the tapestry on the wall in front of her. She was aware of several pairs of eyes boring into her back as she sat at the desk in her room. She had made her servants place the table in front of the wall the first day she had come so that she could read and write with a modicum of privacy, but she still felt ill at ease. She had written to her mother-in-law, who had returned to her castle at La Motte, thanking her for her kind support during the wedding festivities and giving her news of Mary, and she had written to George, telling him her first impressions of Bruges and Charles.

Now she was ready to write to Anthony, and she knew her ladies were busy with their needlework and idle chatter. She permitted them to talk among themselves in her presence, although Marie had duly pointed out that Madame de Poitiers would not have approved.

"She is not here, countess, and I am. This is my household, and as far as I know, 'tis my decision whether or not there is silence in my presence. I will let you know when I require it," Margaret had told her chief lady-in-waiting. She saw the glint of anger in Marie's eyes, but she refused to back down. She had turned and asked one of the others to play on her lute.

"*My love.*" She looked at her large, free-flowing script, trying to put the words on paper that would convey her yearning for him.

> *"As you see, I have found a way to begin our correspondence. I shall not name my kind messenger for fear this falls into the wrong hands, but rest assured he is to be trusted. You will be instructed where to respond when you receive this.*
>
> *"I trust all arrived safely after the voyage and that you found my brothers well. As for me, I have not been able to wipe the memory of our last meeting from my mind. How I wanted you to take me in your arms, throw me onto the saddle and ride off with me—anywhere. Foolish, I know! I wonder where you are, what you are doing, and most of all I wonder if you think of me.*
>
> *"Write to me soon, Lancelot, with any news of England. I sorely miss you all, but you above everyone. And pray for me as I do for you every day and every night, my dearest love.*
>
> *Your Elaine."*

She had trouble fighting back the urge to cry as she wrote. One tear did escape and lent an effective emphasis to her name, almost blotting it out entirely. She quickly sprinkled sand on the missive, folded it and dropped hot wax to seal it. Disguising her handwriting, she wrote Lancelot Dulac and the address in London on the front. Then she beckoned to Fortunata and whispered instructions in her ear, annoying Marie further.

" 'Tis for Master Caxton and no one else, understand, *pochina*? In truth, I believe you will not find this mission too irksome." Fortunata's eyes widened innocently, but her mouth curled into a secret smile. "Ah, I see I am right. The good William has taken your fancy. Be careful, *pochina*. You are naive in the ways of men, and I would not want you hurt."

Fortunata tossed her head. "I do not care about him," she said in a whisper. "You do not need to worry about me." She concealed the letter in the pocket where she kept her cups and pebbles and waited for more information.

Margaret sighed, sorry Fortunata would not confide in her yet. "You will find Master Caxton at the house of the merchant-adventurers. 'Tis the Waterhall on Engelstraat near the wharf. Be careful, *pochina,* and talk to no one unless you have to." A frown creased her perfectly plucked brow. Under her breath she said, "Perhaps 'tis better that you go as a man."

Fortunata had nodded, curtseyed and run out before Marie could inquire where she was going.

FROM HER BROWN wool tunic, its hem skirting her knees and the front buttoned up to the high collar, to the green hose in low, soft boots, with a simple cap on her head, Fortunata could pass for a man in any town in Europe.

The memorized Flemish street name ready on her lips at every corner, she was able to find her way through the narrow cobbled streets to the Market Square—jumping in panic as the carillon in the Belfort tower suddenly rang out the half hour—and on to the quays. She passed several streets named for the nationality of the merchants who dwelled there. The wharves were teeming with merchants, hand carters, wains, sailors and sea captains, all busy loading and unloading the many ships and small boats that filled the harbor. The sounds of pulleys squeaking, cartwheels rumbling on cobblestones, sails flapping and anchor chains rasping and rattling mingled with the smell of spices, raw wool, timber, fruit, and the hot pies, roasted meats and other refreshments hawked to the working men by street vendors.

Ships and shipping were a man's world, and for a moment Fortunata felt distinctly out of place until she remembered she was not in women's clothes. So she sauntered through the throng, her Paduan street-wise wiles about her, asking for Engelstraat, until she finally fell into it. The Waterhall was the largest building on the street, a two-story building housing the merchant-adventurers of England with dormitories above several common rooms, a cloth market and a covered dock underneath. Engelstraat, she thought, certes, street of the English.

She inquired for William Caxton in that tongue and was relieved when one burly man grunted and nodded, pointing her in the direction of one of the stalls. She recognized William talking to another merchant, and she inched up to him without attracting any attention.

"Pssst," she hissed behind him. "Master Caxton, please."

Caxton turned round and saw no one, frowned and turned back. Then he felt a tug on his gown. He turned again, and this time he looked down into Fortunata's upturned face. Recognizing the duchess's dwarf, he quickly excused himself from his colleague and gave her his full attention. "Come, Fortu—I mean sir," he said, amused. "I am thirsty. Let us go inside for some ale."

The other merchant looked curiously at the little person but then shrugged, bade his farewells to William and walked off. William steered Fortunata into an alehouse across the street and ordered them both a cup. His eyes twinkled as he watched her try to imitate a man quaffing ale, smacking her lips and wiping her mouth with her sleeve. When she was sure no one was watching them, she pulled the letter from the pouch at her waist and, concealing it under her hand, slid it across the table. Humoring the loyal servant, he checked over his shoulder and then surreptitiously walked his fingers over to hers and took over the concealment, slipping the missive quickly into the top of his boot.

Fortunata beamed at him. "That is good, Master Caxton." She looked at him impishly from under her long lashes, and he had the distinct impression she was flirting with him.

"You have a wife?" she asked.

Now he was sure she was, and he was amused but intrigued. "Nay, sir. 'Tis forbidden for merchant-adventurers to be married. We all live in that house across the street. We eat together, must keep a strict curfew, and we sleep in one big dormitory. Women are not allowed in the living quarters, but"—he leaned over and whispered to her—"some of the men have lady friends, and I have heard women's voices downstairs at night."

"Like monks?" Fortunata's eyes were wide. "Why you do that, Master Caxton? You do not like women?"

"Aye, I like women very much. And one day, if I go home to London, I may take myself a wife. But for now, I am content." He watched as this information sank in. She could have been striking, he thought, but for her deformity. He briefly wondered how it would be to bed a dwarf but dismissed the thought just as quickly. "Now you must return to your mistress. And tell her she can count on me to deliver the letter safely." He swallowed the last of his ale, threw some money on the table and prepared to leave.

Fortunata plucked up her courage as she too clambered off her stool, shaking off a stray cat that was trying to sharpen its claws on her boots. "Do you like me, Master Caxton?" She looked at him again from under her lashes.

William was astonished. He wanted to laugh, but instead he clapped her on the shoulder as he would a male comrade and said, "Why, I like you well enough, *sir*," he emphasized. "But I have taken a vow of celibacy as an adventurer, and as their governor, I am not above the law," he said solemnly. He did not want to offend the duchess's favorite servant. He scratched his curly beard, which he took immense pains to keep neat and free of lice. "Now I really must return to work. A ship is unloading some English wool, and I must be there. Can I send someone to escort you back to the—" He almost said palace, but corrected himself in case anyone was listening. "To your quarters?"

Fortunata tossed her head at the obvious rejection. "Nay, Master Caxton, I am safe by myself," she said defiantly. "I am sorry you do not like me."

She swaggered off with what she believed to be a manly gait, almost making William guffaw. He sighed and went back to the Waterhall, Margaret's letter now tucked into his tunic.

Walking back through the Market Square, Fortunata could not resist stopping and taking in the sights. A hanging had taken place the day before, and the rigid body was still swinging from the high scaffold, birds pecking at its eyes. A woman was tied to a stool next to the victim, an iron band tight about her head, its special device forcing open her mouth so that her tongue would hang out, preventing speech. Several towns-people pelted her with rotten food, and as the wind swung the hanged man's excrement-covered feet into her face, the laughing, pointing crowd shouted, "Liar! Liar!" Fortunata had seen sights like this in Padua, but it seemed a lifetime ago, so she stood and stared for a good many minutes, feeling sorry for the prisoner, who was being punished for lying.

Soon she found herself drawn to a group of men throwing dice, and her spirits rose. She knew she should return immediately to the Prinsen-hof, but she could not resist drawing the men into her cup game, the tools of which were always with her. It did not take long before she had amassed a tidy sum of money for her trick, until one drunken knave decided the dwarf was cheating him and lunged for her. His clumsy blow hit her on the mouth, splitting open her lip and making her nose gush blood. Her hat flew off, and the braid that had been wound tightly underneath fell down, unmasking her. The drunk stared as the other men backed away, not wanting to be involved in this odd scene.

Fortunata lay in the dirt, dazed and frightened. A kindly older man picked her up, gave her back her cups and stone and propelled her away from the drunkard, who was beginning to make juicy noises with his mouth and finger his codpiece. "Let me put this stone in your cup, wench!" he rasped, lurching forward. Fortunata did not understand the Flemish words but she certainly understood the gestures and fled for her life.

"POCHINA, I AM so sorry you have been hurt on my account," Margaret said bitterly, when she saw Fortunata's bruised face and bloodied clothes. "Before you tell me all about it, go down to the bathhouse and clean your-self ere Marie sees you. We do not want to have to explain why you are in such a plight. I will keep her occupied until you do and shall think of something to say, never fear. Now, go down the back stair."

They were in the garderobe, where Margaret had discovered Fortunata hiding amongst the gowns when she went to relieve herself. A tiny stair-case had been built as an escape in case of fire or danger, and Fortunata made use of it, descending dejectedly and in pain to the cesspit below and thence to the palace bathhouse.

Margaret returned to Mary and her women and for the third time that afternoon wondered aloud what had kept Fortunata from joining them. Marie de Charny looked smug, hoping Margaret would give the impudent servant a tongue-lashing when she did appear. She had taken a dislike to Fortunata from the minute she saw the dwarf standing so possessively beside Margaret at Sluis. She could not believe someone of Margaret's lineage would be seen in the company of one so lowborn, let alone share confidences with the menial. Daily she became more outraged at the thought and vowed to get the dwarf dismissed as soon as she could.

While Marie plotted Fortunata's downfall, Margaret's brain was desperately trying to concoct a story that would excuse her injuries. She was forgetting her wily *pochina*'s wits, which had got her out of trouble many times during her days as a pickpocket. The door to the hall suddenly flew open and Fortunata walked in, dragging a sheepish wolfhound behind her. She was back in her gown, which was now bloodied, and her cap sat askew on her head with half her hair tumbling out. One of her eyes was swollen shut, but the other blazed with anger.

"*Madonna* Margherita, Astolat is a bad dog," she cried, once she knew she had everyone's attention. "He pulled me down the staircase. Look, I am bleeding. I tried to clean it a little, but it hurts too much. And see," she said to the fascinated spectators, pointing to her split lip and reverting to pidgin English to gain sympathy, "Dog break mouth."

Gasps and whispers followed the declaration as those who understood English translated for their neighbors. Marie was for once at a loss for words as she took in Fortunata's disheveled appearance. Margaret, feigning shock and surprise, hurried forward, and poor Astolat found himself confronted by an angry mistress, who admonished him forcefully with "Bad dog! Go and lie down!" The dog hung its head, cast soulful eyes at the guilt-ridden Margaret, and slunk off to do her bidding. Then Margaret knelt down to Fortunata and gingerly touched her blackened eye. The dwarf winced and winked at the same time.

"Master Roelandts," Margaret called to one of her physicians. "I pray you take poor Fortunata and apply a soothing poultice to her face. No doubt she will tell you what potions she needs for her mouth."

"No doubt," the doctor agreed grimly. In the short time since the English contingent had arrived, he had suffered through several discussions with Fortunata on the correct way to treat an ailment.

As Margaret watched the two leave the room, she thanked God Fortunata had not been found lying unconscious on the street, raising questions as to why she was there and why she was wearing men's garb. There must be an easier way to communicate secretly with Anthony, she thought sadly, but for the moment she could think of none.

MARGARET HAD NEVER seen so much baggage. Carts, carriages, horses, soldiers, squires, servants and stable boys filled the Prinsenhof's large courtyard as she stood by the window of her chamber watching the scene below. She traced her finger along the crisscross of the leaded panes, admiring the clear glass. Only Westminster could compare in modern amenities to this sumptuous palace, she knew. She wondered what she would find in Brussels, the next residence she and Mary were to travel to. Ravenstein had told her that only three or four of the royal residences were large enough to accommodate both the duke's and the duchess's households at one time, and she was not surprised.

It would take them four days to make the fifty-mile journey to Brussels, staying at Charles's castles or estates along the way. Each stop would require the housing and feeding of her more than one hundred retainers, and the logistics made her head spin. She was glad she did not have to supervise the packing up of the household. Her chamberlain and stewards would see to that.

It was a hot and humid day. A thunderstorm overnight had not cleared the air, and the sun was making steam rise from the steep slate roofs of the tall, step-gabled houses. She was high enough to see over most of the city, and the scene took her back to the Wardrobe watchtower that evening when she had stood with Fortunata, looking out over London. London! A lump came to her throat, but she forced her eyes downwards to the courtyard and watched her chevalier stride over to her own carriage to see if all was in order.

He was a blond giant, this Guillaume de la Baume. His ruddy complexion, handsome face and blue eyes turned many a female head, she had noticed. He was supposed to be her escort—a substitute for Charles at public occasions—and her bodyguard. She had no doubt that he would vanquish anyone who might be foolish enough to attack her, but his intelligence did not match his physique, and Margaret found him impossible to converse with.

"How different from Anthony," she murmured, a painful stab to her heart reminding her of her love. She turned from the window and sighed.

"*Madonna*, it is time to go. All is prepared," Fortunata said, coming to her side. "It is hot to ride today, *non?*"

"Aye, *pochina*. Have you told them to put wet cloths in a basin for me for the journey? I shall need them in the stuffy carriage."

Fortunata nodded and gave her mistress a sweet-smelling tussie-mussie on a ribbon for her to carry. Margaret lifted the pomander to her nose and inhaled the aroma of the herbs and cloves inside.

"Then let us go and find Mary. I am happy to have some quiet time with her on the road to Brussels. In truth, I am sorry to leave Bruges, for I had just become comfortable here. I pray we will stay in Brussels a long time, for these journeys look to be tiresome."

By the time the cavalcade arrived at the Flanders Gate in the city wall of Brussels, the sun was setting on the fourth day. The noise of a large city was penetrating the padded interior of the carriage. Mary poked her head out of the window.

"See, *belle-mère*, the towers of Coudenberg," she cried, pointing up the steep Coudenberg hill to the ancient and immense palace that crowned it. Margaret's face joined Mary's at the carriage window, and she followed Mary's finger to catch the first glimpse of her seventh residence since arriving in Burgundy only a month before.

The city was sprawled over the hillside and down to the banks of the little river Senne. As they wended their way through the dirty streets, Margaret was glad to know London wasn't the only city with a refuse problem. Rotting vegetables, animal entrails and human waste assailed her nostrils as they trundled by the trench around the city wall that served as a dungheap. She held her tussie-mussie to her nose and looked about her with interest. Already she was becoming accustomed to the windmills and tall, step-gabled brick houses that had been prevalent in Bruges and the countryside through which they had traveled.

They passed a windmill next to the bread market, and she watched carters packing up their wares as the evening drew in. Close to the central market place, she admired the new town hall, its glorious bell tower reaching to the sky. The twin towers of the impressive church of St. Michael and St. Gudule were also visible beyond the newly built merchant houses around the market. Bells pealed from the many steeples in the city, and hundreds of people stopped what they were doing to get a glimpse of the new duchess. Even though she was travel-worn and in no mood to be gracious, she raised the curtains and waved.

"May God bless your grace," several cried, bowing to her as the carriage rolled past, "and may God bless our little Mary."

The horses began their final climb to the castle on the hill, and Margaret and Mary braced themselves against the seatback. Facing them and clinging to the edge of their seats were Marie de Charny and Mary's chief lady-in-waiting, Jeanne de Halewijn. Jeanne had joined them at Ghent, where Margaret had spent her second night after leaving Bruges. They had arrived in the political center of Burgundy at dusk, and although they left in daylight the next day, she had seen very little of the largest city in Europe after Paris other than the towering and sinister Castle of the Counts that straddled a river.

"Gravensteen is where Papa does his governing of the people," Mary had said solemnly, making Margaret smile. "And the biggest building is the courts of justice, where he passes judgment. I have been told there are horribly deep dungeons and torture chambers in there." The girl shivered. "*Belle-mère,* why do people have to be tortured?"

"'Tis only those who have been very, very bad, sweeting. Those who have perhaps tried to harm your father or you. But I am certain they use the dungeons rarely, as who would wish to harm you, Mary?" Margaret reassured her.

"But you are wrong, your grace," Jeanne de Halewijn was quick to comment. "The prison is full of Ghent scum who tried to rebel against our lord duke last year. We daily thank God Duke Charles is a strong leader and is not afraid to punish treasonable men. Lord Hugonet, too, knew just how to deal with them. And now they hate him for it," she scoffed.

Margaret felt Mary stiffen beside her, and she put her arm around her. She was acutely aware of Jeanne de Halewijn's unfriendly eyes on her, and she regretted this first meeting with Mary's favorite lady was not going well. The diminutive woman was but a few years Margaret's senior, and not long after their arrival at the Ten Waele palace, Margaret recognized jealousy in those pale blue eyes. Mary had thrown herself into Jeanne's waiting arms, and Margaret could see there was genuine love between them. You will have to tread carefully here, Meg, she thought, and so had shown Jeanne a mixture of gentle authority and respect during that first evening.

"You and I have something in common, madame," Margaret had said pleasantly, after they dined on cold pheasant. She had thought an informal supper in her chamber might be a chance to break the ice. After all, she and Mary would rarely be apart now, and she needed Jeanne's help in looking after her stepdaughter. To be suddenly thrust into motherhood was a little daunting, she admitted.

Jeanne raised an eyebrow politely. "We do?" she responded.

"Certes. Both of us have to be separated from our husbands for long periods, in truth." Margaret knew it was a lame beginning, but she hoped Jeanne would recognize she was trying.

Again the arched brow. "Ah, 'tis true, your grace." And that was the end of the conversation.

"I understand your husband is high steward of Flanders, madame, and is Flemish born. I would like to learn Dutch, and 'twould be delightful if you would teach me," Margaret persisted.

Before Jeanne could answer, Mary, unaware of this adult awkwardness, cried, "Oh, *belle-mère*, I shall teach you Dutch!"

"Mary, you must not interrupt a grown-up conversation. How many times must I tell you," Jeanne gently admonished her. She turned back to Margaret with a slight smile, "You have your teacher, your grace. Mary speaks Dutch far better than I, in truth. I, as you must know, am French."

Margaret inclined her head in acknowledgment and smiled at Mary. "Then you shall teach me, sweetheart. Perhaps we can start on the journey tomorrow. I will point to things and you can tell me the Dutch words."

"Papa said I must learn English, madame. Will you teach me?" Mary was eager.

Jeanne patted her hand possessively. "You have much to learn, my pop-pet. You cannot impose on your stepmother like this. And now 'tis time for your prayers and bed. We have a long day tomorrow."

Margaret was dismayed she was making no headway with Jeanne, but she signaled to the steward to pull back her chair and she stood up to say good night. At the Prinsenhof, Mary had kissed her on both cheeks before retiring, but Jeanne ushered her charge out as soon as she and Mary had made their obeisances. *Of course, she does not know Mary and I have already become friends,* Margaret thought with her usual charity, but her eyes were clouded by disappointment as they followed Mary out.

That was three nights ago, and although Jeanne had warmed a little to Margaret's cordial overtures, it had become clear to Margaret that Jeanne looked on her as a rival for Mary's love. She decided to approach the woman as soon as they were settled at Coudenberg.

Her gaze shifted to Marie de Charny, sitting ramrod-straight beside Jeanne. The proud woman had not unbent as much as her little finger in her rigidity towards the ladies in Margaret's train. She had relegated Beatrice to third lady-in-waiting, behind one of her own young proté-gées, and Margaret had no say in the matter. She chafed at the rules of court that gave her so little freedom, even to the choice of her own servants, and she resolved to talk to Charles about it whenever they were together again.

THE LARGEST OF the duke's palaces was also in the most beautiful setting. The undulating Warende park stretched for miles in front of Margaret as she slowly made her way through the immaculate beds of roses, holly-hocks, lilies and lupins en route to the wilder Forest of Soignes beyond. As usual, she was accompanied by the chevalier de la Baume, one of the few people she knew who was taller than she, and she had to acknowledge she enjoyed the feeling of daintiness that being with Guillaume gave her. In a way, he reminded her of Ned, and it comforted her.

She was daydreaming about her family and absently plucked a blossom from a gillyflower to twirl in her fingers. She missed them so badly. The night before, she had rocked herself to sleep thinking of her mother. She wondered if Anthony had received her letter, and she cursed her stupidity for not forming a plan for Master Caxton to follow now she was no longer in Bruges. There might be a letter waiting for her there with no means for her to receive it.

The tranquility of the morning stroll was suddenly interrupted by screams coming from some bushes farther down the walk.

"Guillaume, I pray you go and help that poor woman!" Margaret commanded. "I cannot think what is happening." The man took off at a run, his chaperon flying off his head and onto the grass. "Guards! Guards!" Margaret cried, as her ladies gathered around her and Mary clung to her skirts.

But the guards were not needed. A minute later, Guillaume appeared from behind a bush with Fortunata and Madame de Beaugrand suspended from each musclebound arm. The two women were still flailing at each other and screaming, one in Turkish and one in Italian, and a monkey was screeching at them from a tree branch above. Margaret could not help but laugh.

"Put them down, chevalier, I beg of you," she called, walking to the two disheveled dwarfs. "What is all this, pray? Fortunata, tell me what has occurred to make you behave in such a disgraceful way." Guillaume let them fall none too gently, annoyed that his duties to the duchess included such unmanly tasks.

Margaret recognized the mulish look on Fortunata's face, which she knew meant no explanation would be forthcoming. But she knew Charny was watching carefully, and not wanting to further aggravate the woman's ill-feeling for Fortunata, she leveled her most ferocious stare at her servant and asked her again, "Tell me what happened here, Fortunata, or I shall have no recourse but to beat you."

Fortunata let out a shriek. She had never known Margaret to beat any of her servants, even though it was common practice among the nobility. She hung her head and muttered, "I tried to take her monkey. That was all. I am very sorry, *madonna.*"

"Azize, is this correct?" Margaret asked the larger of the two dwarfs. She had discovered that Madame de Beaugrand was the name given her by the French count who had bought her from a Romany camp because he thought the name was appropriately ridiculous for such a small, ugly creature. Her Turkish given name rolled far more easily off the tongue, Margaret decided, and had addressed her thus since. Azize fell on her knees, swearing loyalty and devotion, and Margaret felt sorry for her.

"Fortunata, you will apologize to Azize immediately and go to my chamber. I will deal with you later." She turned to Guillaume, "Can you reach the monkey?"

Rolling his eyes so that only the twittering ladies could see, he muttered an affirmative and coaxed the still-chattering monkey into his hands. The little creature ran straight into Azize's arms, clutching onto her for dear life.

Later, Margaret demanded to be left alone with Fortunata and berated her loudly for her transgressions, knowing full well Marie would be listening at the door.

"You deserve a beating, Fortunata," Margaret cried. "You should know better." Then she picked up a leather strap and raised her arm. Fortunata screamed just as Margaret brought the strap down on the back of a chair in three quick successive strokes. "There, now go to your quarters. I do not want to see you until prayers," she said, winking at the astonished Fortunata. Under her breath she said in English, "Start crying and run from the room quickly."

Fortunata needed no second bidding. She feigned some heart-wrenching sobs, flung open the door and ran.

Margaret was puzzled that Fortunata did not appear for the customary evening prayers and beckoned to Beatrice to ask where she was.

"Why, your grace, she is confined to her bed with bandaged hands from her punishment. I could not persuade her to come when I went to find her a few minutes ago. Her eyes are swollen from crying and she appears to be in pain."

Margaret remarked on Beatrice's cold tone. Oh, *pochina*, you should not prolong the mummery, she thought. She looked across at Marie de Charny, who for once would not meet her eye. Why? she wondered. She shrugged and asked Marie to join her at her side at the prie-dieu. Full of smiles now, the older woman hurried to Margaret's side.

Charles came to Brussels at the beginning of August. Seated in her favorite solar overlooking the Warende, Margaret was playing chess with Mary when she heard the shawms, pibcorns and tabors faintly in the distance. Mary was on her feet, an anxious look on her face, and ran to the window.

"Papa is coming!" she cried. "Come, *belle-mère,* we must be ready and waiting for him on the staircase outside. He will not be pleased if we are not there."

Margaret's stomach had somersaulted when she had been told the day before that the duke was expected. She was beginning to enjoy her daily routine, which included an audience with Ravenstein, a walk or a ride with Mary, time with her chamberlain, and music or conversation with Mary in the afternoon. She had written letters to her mother, to Ned and to George, but as yet had heard nothing from her family across the North Sea. They have forgotten me already, she thought gloomily, whereas I long for them.

Now the routine would be broken, and she knew, because she had helped plan them, there would be elaborate banquets and hunting expeditions for Charles. She prayed to St. Andrew the Apostle to grant her wish to be with child, should he choose to share her bed, and then she begged her own St. Margaret to spare her her greatest fear: barrenness.

"Madame de Halewijn, I pray you make Mary as pretty as a picture for her father," Margaret said to Jeanne with more eagerness than she felt. "Let him be proud of his little girl, as we all are."

Mary beamed, a new confidence creeping into her eyes. She was terrified of her father, who showed her little affection, thus giving her the impression she must be stupid and unattractive. "Can I wear the orange dress, *belle-mère,* please?"

Margaret saw her chance, for she noticed Jeanne looking at her with something akin to respect. " 'Tis for madame to decide, sweeting. She is the best judge of that."

Jeanne's bright smile and deep obeisance told Margaret that she had perhaps turned the tide, and she watched, relieved, as Mary skipped off to change her gown. One down, the other to go, she thought, glancing at Marie. She smoothed her skirts, fluffed out the veil on her jeweled heart-shaped headdress and started the long walk through the many rooms and staircases of the enormous palace to the courtyard below.

Fortunata had given her place to Marie in the little procession, but Margaret was too wrapped up in her own thoughts to notice. What would she say to Charles? Now that they were well and truly married, would he treat her civilly? Fortunata had told her tales she had heard about Charles's temper, his lack of interest in women, and his autocratic nature.

On the other hand, she had heard he was a hard worker, something she admired in a leader and something she knew was lacking in her brother Edward. "He never stops working, your grace," Ravenstein had told her. "He has more energy than a team of hounds after a hare. They call him *le travailleur,* and it suits him well."

Margaret thought the Worker was considerably more flattering than the Rash and added it to her rapidly growing knowledge of her husband's character.

The courtyard was crowded when she arrived at the enormous wooden front door, which was standing wide. Guards and retainers were forming columns as far as the eye could see to salute the arrival of the duke, some on horseback and others on foot, all in the Burgundian black, purple and crimson; musicians were hurrying with their instruments to their places on an open balcony; grooms were lined up to take charge of the horses; and several noisy and excited dogs were being chased aside for the duke's entry. The sun shone down on the proceedings as the church of St. Jacques rang out a welcome.

"God's greeting, my lady. I trust I find you well," Charles said cheerfully upon mounting the steps to her side. His fanciful jeweled hat was a little out of place with full armor, Margaret thought, but he was a magnificent sight as she sank in a deep obeisance with Mary by her side. He raised Margaret up and kissed her on the mouth, a gesture Margaret had hoped he would discard after the English retinue left. She had discovered he believed all Englishwomen expected to be kissed thus, but she found it embarrassing and hoped one day she would be forward enough to tell him. Not today, though, she thought. Besides, she had Mary to worry about. Charles had given his daughter a cursory glance and a "How are you, child?" before taking Margaret's arm in readiness for their processing inside the gleaming white Magna Aula, the marble addition to the centuries-old palace. Margaret, however, stood rooted to the spot, and Charles frowned.

"What is it, my dear?" he asked.

Margaret smiled sweetly. Charles did not know her well enough to recognize the determination in that smile. "I believe you forgot to kiss Mary, my lord. And she has dressed in her favorite gown for your approval. Certes, you must agree she looks delightful, no?"

She heard not only Mary but Jeanne and Marie draw in their collective breath. Antoine, who was standing just behind his brother, arched his brow, and several others looked shocked. Only Lord Ravenstein's eyes shouted "Brava!" She felt Charles's arm stiffen under her hand for a second, but then he turned to Mary, who was trembling in her little crakows, and raised her face with his other hand and kissed her on the lips as well.

"Your gown is well chosen, daughter. Your mother would have been proud." If he had hoped to slight Margaret with this mention of Isabelle, he had not taken the measure of Margaret's self-worth.

"Indeed she would, Mary," Margaret cried. "I expect she is looking down from heaven and glowing with pride, sweetheart."

Charles harrumphed and almost dragged Margaret through the doorway and into the palace beyond. Margaret sent up a prayer to the Virgin to protect her later from Charles's famous temper.

HE CAME TO her that night after three hours of banquet, music and dancing.

"Out! Out!" he bellowed to Margaret's women when he burst into the room with a few of his squires. Margaret was already propped up on the silk pillows, her golden hair loose about her shoulders and a cap tied under her chin.

"Good luck, *madonna*," Fortunata whispered as she smoothed the embroidered, fur-lined satin bedspread one more time. "I will be near if you need me." More loudly she said, "Good night, your graces. May God bless you both."

She curtseyed first to Margaret, then to Charles, and with a last disdainful sniff at one of the squires holding the door for her, stalked out. Margaret covered a laugh with a cough. Charles had hardly noticed the attendant. He lolled in a chair while his boots were removed and points untied, sipping a glass of wine. He was amiable with his gentlemen and even threw a genial comment her way now and again. Margaret breathed more easily. All is well, she decided.

Finally they were alone. Hardly had the door closed behind the last squire when Charles flung back the bedcovers and pulled Margaret out of bed. She cried out as his cruel grasp pinched her wrist. Before she could protest his treatment of her, he crushed her to him, grinding his hips into hers and gripping her buttocks under the fine lawn chemise. She thought he would eat her tongue and mouth and knew he had bitten her when she tasted blood. She was enraged and terrified at once. There was no denying his lust; she could feel it hard between her thighs. Her extra inches made it easy for him to lower his mouth to her breast, which he sucked at noisily through the cloth.

"Charles . . . my lord . . . you . . . are h-hurting me," she stammered, her eyes full of tears.

"Quiet, wife! It seems you need to know who is lord here. I am about to show you!" he growled, taking her hand and forcing her to touch him under his shirt. "When you are alone, you may do as you please, but when I am here, I am master. Do you understand?"

Rage overcame the terror and she let go of his prick and slapped him hard across the face. "How dare you treat me like a whore!" she hissed, guessing there were several ears pressed to the door. "I am a Plantagenet and just as royal as you—"

She got no further. Fighting with him did nothing more than inflame his desire for her. A military machine, he was all muscle and sinew, and she was dismayed with what ease he picked her up, pinned her legs around his waist and slammed her against the wall. She could not have conceived of such a coupling in her worst nightmares, and as he forced her down upon him, she felt as though he would tear her apart. With a few lusty thrusts, he loosed his desire into her with his usual bark of pleasure and, sated, leaned panting against her. Then surprisingly gently he lowered her body to the ground.

"'Twas your fault, Margaret," he apologized. "Your boldness at the door today aroused my anger—and my lust. I trust you are not hurt."

Margaret lay crumpled on the floor, her thighs still trembling, her tears flowing freely. Anthony, she wanted to cry, how did I come to this? Why did you let me wed this beast? Oh, God, maybe all men are like this. Maybe Anthony . . . But she refused to believe it. She was aware that Charles was speaking to her quietly, as though nothing had passed between them. He knelt down, stroked her hair and begged her to get into bed.

"I shall leave you to your rest, Margaret. And I believe I need to bathe my cheek with cowslip water. What will the servants think if they see your fingers imprinted on it tomorrow?" He was chuckling as he helped her across the room and between the soft sheets. "May God keep you safe until the morrow. I am looking forward to showing you the Forest of Soignes, *ma mie*. The hunting is superb."

She could not believe her ears. He had just violated her in a most despicable manner, and now he was talking about hunting and calling her his love. She could not speak but lay there with her eyes closed, wishing him far from her.

"Ah, I see you are tired. You need to rest for tomorrow's sport." He bent and kissed her forehead before padding quietly from the room.

Margaret slipped her hand beneath the covers and gingerly felt herself for any signs of bleeding. She jumped when the door opened again but breathed a sigh of relief when she saw Fortunata slip into the room with a copper ewer. Margaret was sure the whole palace had heard their bestial fornicating, so she was not surprised the dwarf was there to help her expunge the evidence.

During the ablutions, Fortunata kept up a patter of inane gossip, hoping to keep Margaret from sinking into melancholy. She fed Margaret a hot posset she had prepared and made her drink it all. Gradually, as Fortunata sat quietly at her feet, patting her hand, Margaret pulled herself together. She invited her servant to kneel and pray with her again before she allowed herself to be tucked into bed and the candles to be extinguished.

"Thank you, *pochina*," Margaret whispered, as Fortunata slipped out of the room. "A thousand thanks."

Then she fell into a deep slumber, brought on by Fortunata's potion of henbane, skullcap and lemon balm.

The old dream of the fleshless head on top of the Micklegate returned to her that night, and this time it was Charles grimacing in agony. It failed to disturb her sleep.

13

Autumn 1468

"I think I am with child, *pochina*," Margaret whispered to the dwarf at prayers one day in September.

"I think you are right, *madonna*," Fortunata replied. "I knew before you did."

Margaret smiled and shook her head. "You are incorrigible," she murmured.

Fortunata bent closer. "In what, *madonna*. I did not understand."

"I will explain later. Now pray to the Virgin for me, Fortunata, that I bear a healthy child." She raised her voice so the others could join in. "*Ave Maria, gratia plena . . .*"

Margaret bowed her head and prayed that the memory of the night she must have conceived be washed from her mind forever. She was afraid she would look at her child and only remember the pain. As the comforting prayers she uttered gave her peace, the joy in knowing she was to be a mother buoyed her spirits, and she resolved to let God guide her through the next eight months.

• • •

HER JOY WAS short-lived. Margaret's and Mary's households were on the move again, and her morning sickness was not helped by the trundling along rutted roads for a week to reach Aire in Artois province. By the time her carriage pulled into the enclosed courtyard of the palace, she was cursing the growing seed inside her. She barely noticed her new surroundings, although she had remarked on the beautiful aspect of the towering castle on the banks of the pretty river Lys as they approached.

Soon the nausea that began as a morning annoyance erupted into violent vomiting, and the palace was abuzz with the news that the new duchess was ill. Margaret and Fortunata had kept the secret of the pregnancy to themselves for a time, although both Beatrice and Marie were convinced Margaret was pregnant. Margaret had trouble keeping anything in her stomach, and she spent days lying in her huge bed in a darkened room, wondering why God was punishing her thus. Fortunata finally persuaded her to tell the doctors of her condition, and they congregated in a corner of the room to discuss the situation.

"'Tis worse than the *mal de mer*," Margaret told them when they returned.

The learned men shook their gray beards over her bed, calling for bloodletting to realign her humors, and one consulted an astrological chart. Fortunata had seen this extreme nausea once before at the university in Padua, and she knew the bloodletting her mentor had performed on the patient had done nothing to alleviate it. The woman had continued to vomit for many days, but she had recovered and eventually given birth to a large boy with monstrous deformities. Marie had scoffed at the story and told Fortunata to hold her tongue, but she did not protest when Fortunata took charge of the slop bucket and would not leave Margaret's side. The dwarf shook her head when Master Roelandts approached with basin and knife, but he glared at her and insisted on bleeding Margaret.

"She is carrying Duke Charles's heir, mistress. She must be in our hands alone now. No more of your potions, do you understand?" Roelandts told Fortunata sternly.

He did not recognize the mulish glint in Fortunata's eyes, but she moved away to allow him to prepare Margaret's arm.

"We should get word to the duke as soon as possible," the physician said to the others. "This is great news for Burgundy."

At that Margaret sat up and heaved once again. "Not yet, Master Roelandts, I beg of you. Wait until I am well again." The Dutchman grunted an assent and hoped Charles would not blame him for delaying the news.

Three days later, just before Michaelmas, a strange comet appeared in the western sky, and Margaret prayed it was a sign from God, like the star that had settled over Bethlehem long ago to signal the advent of a child. She had been ten when another such phenomenon had appeared in the heavens, trailing a tail of light. At first, it seemed as though her prayer was answered. The vomiting subsided, leaving her frail and dehydrated but elated. Behind the physicians' backs, she had taken Fortunata's medicine diligently after the bloodletting, trusting more in her servant than the doctors.

During the third night she awoke with strong familiar monthly pain. She called out to be helped to the garderobe. Marie was horrified to see the blood on Margaret's chemise and the silken sheets, and by the time she and Beatrice had helped their mistress onto the wooden seat over the latrine, she knew the tiny life inside Margaret was lost.

THE PHYSICIANS WERE dismayed and prayed they would not be blamed. They insisted Margaret remain in bed and not go outdoors. Fortunata grumbled about the bloodletting but otherwise went about her tasks quietly. Marie became suspicious when the dwarf lost her tongue and determined she would get to the bottom of her silence.

Jeanne de Halewijn and Mary visited her every day, and Mary amused Margaret by bringing a different one of her pets with her. Dogs, monkeys and birds made their way into Margaret's chamber, and Jeanne whispered to her that she was lucky she had not fallen ill at Ten Waele, where Mary had a pet giraffe. Margaret's eyes widened with surprise. "I have never seen one, Jeanne. Is Mary not afraid?" She was delighted that Mary's chief attendant had finally conquered her jealousy and was now becoming a charming companion.

"It is very tall, your grace, but they are gentle creatures," Jeanne replied.

While her ladies, physicians and Mary constantly attended her all day and her chamberlain visited for his instructions, Margaret was able to keep up a semblance of cheerfulness. But at night, as soon as the dark green velvet curtains were drawn around her bed, she cried into her pillow for the loss of her first child. She begged St. Anthony of Padua to protect her from barrenness, and then merely whispering the name conjured up her own Anthony, consuming her with guilt. Please, dear God, do not punish me for what I cannot help. I have done my duty as a wife and endured an ignominious experience as part of it. I understand that as a woman I have no right to complain, but how could You end the innocent life of an unborn child just to punish me? Ah, she acknowledged sadly, but we are taught the sins of the father shall be visited upon the child, and I forgot that lesson. She buried her head into the sweet-smelling mattress and pulled the pillow over her head to muffle her sobs.

"Perhaps 'twas God's way of ending your misery, my lady," Jeanne said to Margaret one day, referring to the prolonged bouts of vomiting, as they finally took a turn about the pleasant gardens with the usual attendants in tow. Margaret's murrey damask gown hung limply from her shoulders, her breasts having temporarily lost their roundness. " 'Twas cruel, but who are we to question His ways?"

"Aye, Jeanne, perhaps. Certes, I do not understand it, for I was feeling better. I atrributed it to Fortunata's genius with infusions and potions," she said. "But I doubt Master Roelandts would give her any credit."

Marie's ears pricked up. So, the little monster had disobeyed the doctor and administered her own medicine. She resolved to visit the dispensary and see if she could ascertain what infusion the dwarf had concocted. And then she went straight to Master Roelandts.

Margaret was frantic. Fortunata had disappeared. No one had seen her for two days. Margaret asked Guillaume to do some investigating on her behalf. Beatrice was in tears. She had become very fond of the little woman; they often shared memories of London as they went about their tasks or plied their needles during the quiet afternoons. She was quite convinced Fortunata had been kidnapped.

"She left everything behind, your grace," she told Margaret. "I share the bed with her, and I know she would not go anywhere without the rosary you gave her upon our arrival in Burgundy. I found it under her pillow." She pulled it from her bodice and gave it to Margaret.

Margaret stared down at the pearl and onyx chain with its delicate silver crucifix and then raised frightened eyes to Beatrice's face. "Kidnapped, you say?" she whispered, tears starting behind her eyes. "Why?"

"'Tis but conjecture on my part, my lady," Beatrice soothed, trying to sound more confident than she felt. "But I do not think Fortunata has run away. Perhaps she has fallen somewhere and has not been found yet. Oh, no, I did not—" She stopped as Margaret gave a little scream and clutched at her heart. She turned and called to Marie, who was deadheading some late daisies. "Come and comfort her grace, Madame de Charny. You were the last to see Fortunata, were you not?"

At the mention of Fortunata's name, Marie went pale, which did not escape Margaret's notice. "Is this true, Marie?" Margaret used the first name to emphasize her superiority. "Why did you not volunteer this information? Where exactly did you see her?"

Margaret took the older woman's arm none too gently and made her walk alongside her. Her mind was racing. Marie hated Fortunata, but surely she would not harm the dwarf? In her short time in Burgundy, Margaret had learned that whereas torture and cruelty were exceptions in England, they were rife here. She had heard Charles praise the captain of his guards for punishing a prisoner on the rack until he talked. She had even heard of red-hot irons being used to loosen a young woman's tongue. She had questioned Charles about such methods, and he laughed at her.

"Perhaps your brother would not have so many rebellions to deal with if he used his power as I do. Traitors, assassins, spies, rebels—they all need to know who is their master, and I find torture a very effective way of teaching them, my dear. It keeps the peasants in their place."

Margaret had been shocked by this, but had calmly told him, "Do the scriptures not teach us to turn the other cheek, Charles? And our Savior himself said, 'All they that take the sword shall perish by the sword.'"

Again her husband laughed. Seeing her dismay, he tempered his response. "This is the way we govern so many divergent territories and people, and I need to know you can handle my affairs when I am away defending them. Tell me that you can."

Margaret nodded. "Certes, messire. 'Tis my duty to serve you," she said meekly. "But I still believe there are kinder ways to rule," she said under her breath.

She thought back to that conversation as she steered Marie de Charny to a bench set in a copse of hazelnut and birch trees.

"Leave us," she told Guillaume and the attendants. "Beatrice, stay close in case I need you."

Marie sat straight as one of the white birch trunks and stared at the river through the trees. She did not fear her new sister-in-law with her unfashionable clothes and accented French. She knew she had Charles's love—and his ear.

"Let me remind you that I am the duchess, Marie," Margaret began politely enough. "But do not forget you are an attendant on my person and are only such because you have some of Duke Philip's blood in your veins. I could dismiss you like that" —she snapped her fingers at the poker-faced woman—"should I so desire. Do I make myself clear? Good, now tell me where you last saw Fortunata."

"I saw her talking to Heer Roelandts after Matins two days ago, your grace," Marie said, furious that her bastardy had been alluded to. "They were near the dispensary and they were arguing. 'Tis all I can tell you." She clasped her hands tightly in her lap, controlling an urge to slap the younger woman and tell her that her influence with Charles was far greater than Margaret's would ever be. "You should interrogate the good doctor, not me, madame. He believes Fortunata is a witch," she added snidely, knowing Margaret had forbidden the word be associated with the dwarf in her presence.

Margaret stiffened, and Marie wondered if the duchess might strike her. But in a tone as cold as ice, Margaret merely said, "And so I shall. Thank you, Marie. You may go. Send Beatrice to me." She watched the countess leave with a mounting suspicion that the woman knew more than she was saying. Marie turned once, her facial lines pinched with anger, and then tossed her head and minced onto the lawn to Beatrice. Nay, *pochina*, you were wrong, Margaret thought. Not everyone resembles an animal. This one looks like a prune. A little sob caught in her throat as she remembered the conversation. Fortunata! What has become of you?

Heer Roelandts pleaded ignorance when Margaret questioned him later that morning. She could not tell if the question had caught him by surprise or not, but his story matched Marie's. However, his answers seemed a little too glib, and so she dismissed him with her thanks and immediately called her faithful chevalier to her presence chamber.

"I want you to watch Heer Roelandts carefully, Guillaume. I believe he knows more about Fortunata's disappearance than he is telling me." A thought occurred to her, and her hand flew to her mouth. She wondered if it were true that Roelandts believed the little servant was a witch. "I hope he has not poisoned her!" she cried.

"'Twould make no sense, your grace," he reasoned. "Never fear, I shall find her for you." He bowed and left the room, several pairs of admiring eyes following his perfectly formed figure.

Beatrice tried to comfort Margaret, assuring her that Fortunata had probably gone off to try her cup game on the townspeople and would come back with a cartload of coins. Margaret attempted a weak smile, but her chin trembled, and she finally could hold her frightened tears in check no longer. Beatrice put her arms around her, and Astolat padded over and put his whiskered snout in her lap in sympathy.

"Astolat!" Margaret cried, jumping to her feet and almost upending poor Beatrice. Astolat gave a deep, throaty bark and began gamboling around her. "Certes! He could find Fortunata. Quick, get his long leash and something of Fortunata's for him to sniff. And pray fetch back Guillaume. We are going hunting!"

As Margaret had given all her instructions to Beatrice in English, the three others present did not know what had transformed their mistress from despondency into a woman of purpose. Whatever it was, they were glad of it. They sprang into action when she asked for a cloak and a more practical headdress than the butterfly hennin with its enormous starched veil. They deduced she would be going outdoors, but that was all.

Guillaume and Beatrice joined her shortly afterwards, and with Astolat in Guillaume's strong grasp, they began their search. The wolfhound was not trained to follow a scent, but Astolat had smelt Fortunata's jester's cap with its jangling bells that Beatrice had thrust at him and, with tail wagging eagerly, he pulled forward on the leash, leading the procession on a merry chase through the palace and to the garden outside. At the end of an hour, Margaret was just beginning to give up when the dog started to jump at a small door in the castle wall directly under the great hall.

"'Tis where they store the ice, your grace," Guillaume said. "If the duke is here in the spring, the blocks of ice from winter keep the game cold. But no one goes in there in the summer and autumn."

"Open it, chevalier!" Margaret commanded excitedly. Astolat was sniffing under the heavy oak door, which did not look as though it had been opened for months, judging from the weeds and clinging ivy. Indeed, Guillaume had to use all his strength to heave it open.

The shaft of light illuminated a cellar that reeked of mold and damp from the old straw that had been tamped around the ice to slow its thawing. There was also a strong smell of urine.

"How Astolat can smell anything else but that I cannot imagine," Margaret said, holding her nose. Spiders' webs hung from the ceiling over the few stairs down, and a rat scuttled across the floor of the cellar, making Astolat leap out of Beatrice's grip on the leash and dash down to follow it.

"Is there anything else down there?" Margaret whispered, nervously. "'Tis too dark. We need a light."

A dusty oil lamp sat in a niche at the top of the staircase, and taking the flint from a tinderbox in a pouch at his waist, Guillaume expertly struck it on the stone doorway. The spark ignited the oiled cloth in the box, and he used it to light the lamp. Leading the way down the stairs, he held the lamp high for Margaret to see. Astolat was now visible in the far corner of the dank space, whining and worrying a bundle on the floor. Muffled sounds came from within the blanket. Horrified, Margaret knew it was Fortunata. Treading gingerly across the slippery floor, she knelt down and lifted the cloth to reveal her servant, gagged and her hands tied behind her back. On a low ledge beside her, the dim light of the lamp revealed a plate of crumbs and some ale. Fortunata's swollen eyes filled with tears when she saw her mistress kneeling beside her.

"Hurry, Guillaume, use your knife on these knots," Margaret ordered, gently removing the cloth from Fortunata's mouth.

"*Madonna* Margherita, I am so happy to see you. I was very frightened," she whimpered, standing up so that Guillaume could better cut through the rough rope that tied her hands. She grabbed the ale and gulped it down. "Please, I just want to leave now. I am cold and dirty. I am sorry that I am so much trouble for you." Her face puckered, and she looked so dejected that Margaret put her arms around her, knowing

Guillaume would be shocked at the breach in etiquette. But the man had a soft heart, and he too felt sorry for the dwarf, although he would not deign to soil his clothes as Margaret was doing. Astolat was busy snuffling up cheese crumbs when Fortunata fell upon the dog's neck and muttered Italian endearments into his ear.

"Clever dog, Astolat!" Margaret cried, patting him. Astolat enjoyed the attention. His tail wagged, and he sat and offered his paw. The little gesture gave them all a much-needed smile, and then Guillaume ushered them up the stairs and into the sunlight. When Fortunata appeared in the doorway, Beatrice cried "Thank God!" and the other ladies encircled the little woman, plying her with questions. Margaret looked around for Marie de Charny, but she was nowhere to be seen.

FORTUNATA SWORE SHE did not know who had imprisoned her for two and a half days. After talking to Heer Roelandts—she refused to say she was arguing with him—about the bloodletting, she had gone into the dispensary to make the usual potion for Margaret, and the next thing she knew, she was in the ice cellar.

"Why, *pochina?*" Margaret shook her head. "Who would want to harm you? Have you made an enemy in my household other than Madame de Charny? But she is with me morning, noon and night, it would seem. Besides she is not strong enough to carry you all the way to the ice cellar, and somebody would have seen her. Who brought you the food, do you know?"

The servant shook her head. "A man with a big cloak and hood, so I did not see his face. He came once and took the scarf from my mouth and let me eat, but he told me not to scream or he would kill me. He called me a witch. I was very afraid, *madonna*. It was so dark, and I felt rats run on my feet. It was horrible. I prayed many hours to every saint I know and to St. Margaret to bring you to me!" She finished, earnestly, "Praise God, she heard me."

"I can imagine how frightened you were. 'Twas cruel, and by our sweet Virgin Mary, I cannot think who would have done this."

Fortunata said nothing. Margaret paced up and down, thinking. Finally, she sank down in her chair and said, "'Tis better we forget this incident. 'Twill only make things harder on you if I persist in finding the culprit. You were not hurt, just frightened. I do not want the duke to know, for he will put people to the torturing machines if he did. I am trying to establish myself with my own household, and I do not want them to think I bear any of them rancor, do you understand, *pochina*? Will you forgive me if I do not pursue this further?"

"Aye, *madonna*. I understand," Fortunata said, breathing a sigh of relief, which Margaret did not notice. In fact, had Margaret not been so agitated by the incident, she might have asked some uncomfortable questions of her *pochina* that could well have shed some light on the mystery.

"If we find him, certes, I will punish him. But I beg of you, do not do anything to anger Madame de Charny, promise me. I do not trust her, but that is not enough to dismiss her. I am sure she has had a hand in this matter."

Fortunata promised to be circumspect. But Margaret noticed that every time she mentioned Marie's name, Fortunata jumped.

As soon as Fortunata left, the other courtiers flocked back into the audience chamber, and Margaret resumed her administrative duties. For the time being, she thought, I must put this strange incident aside.

RAVENSTEIN ENJOYED HIS daily audience with the duchess. He found Margaret well versed in English politics, and her passion for reading intrigued him.

Late in October, he brought news of a tactical victory Charles had achieved over his overlord and archenemy Louis of France. The result had been humiliation for Louis, and in a treaty at Péronne, where Louis had found himself cornered, he had reluctantly been forced to agree to recognition of the Anglo-Burgundian alliance, territorial concessions and an agreement to help Charles punish the city of Liège for rebelling against the duke.

"However, I regret to say, Madame la duchesse, as a concession to his overlord, Duke Charles had to promise to render no aid to the proposed English invasion of France." Ravenstein paused. He did not tell this intelligent and virtuous young woman how badly her husband had behaved when at first he believed Louis had tricked him by coming to Péronne, where Charles was encamped with an eye to a truce. News had come that Charles's other ally, the duke of Brittany, had broken his word and entered into a treaty with Louis. Charles had flown into a rage and planned a dreadful revenge on Louis' person. It had taken all his councilors' diplomatic reasoning to calm the duke down for his meeting with Louis. Loyal as he was to the house of Burgundy, Ravenstein was not one of Charles's greatest admirers, and Margaret added the incident to the list of her husband's shortcomings.

"Your brother had already outfitted a small fleet for the invasion, with our friend Lord Scales as its captain," Ravenstein went on. "However, with this news about Brittany and Charles's retraction of help with it, Lord Anthony had to abandon the effort."

Margaret felt herself color at the mention of Anthony's name, and so she put her hand up to the velvet headband under her hennin and pretended to secure it, thus hiding her face.

"I feel so helpless, messire. I have not seen the duke for two months now, and whereas I am happy he has scored a success over Louis, I cannot help but be perturbed by my brother's, and thus England's, dilemma."

"Tell me about Richard Neville, earl of Warwick, your grace."

Margaret was puzzled by this apparent non sequitur. "He is our mother's cousin, Messire Ravenstein, and a great man," Margaret hedged. "What did you want to know of him?"

"We believe he still intends to betray your brother's alliance with Burgundy in favor of Louis of France. We have intelligence that he was responsible for stirring Londoners against the Flemish artisans there in the late summer. He has effectively ruined trade with the Hanseatic League and has made English shipping ripe for attack and capture by those Germans. It seems the earl has set himself against the throne, and with his power we fear for King Edward and our alliance. Although with this new agreement with Louis, an invasion by England would be—" He wasn't allowed to finish.

"You have been misinformed, messire," Margaret interrupted him bluntly. "Certes, Warwick's power and influence were instrumental in securing the throne for our family, but he is not the king. My brother keeps his own counsel, let me assure you. If you want to deal with England, you must deal with Edward. His subjects will not rise against him," she said, although a wisp of hesitation crept into her voice. She had not heard these pieces of news before, but as she did not want to betray her dismay to the astute councilor, she stated firmly, "And certainly not in favor of my lord of Warwick."

Ravenstein was not so sure, but he kept his mouth shut.

"Let us speak of more mundane and pleasant matters, your grace. I would tell you about the palace of Hesdin, where we shall be going in a few days. You will find it most amusing."

THAT NIGHT, MARGARET could not sleep. The mere mention of Anthony's name had caused her to toss and turn, reliving his every word and gesture to her during their few precious moments alone during the wedding festivities. She loved the way his dimple appeared when he laughed, the silky sheen of his hair, and most of all the expression in his eyes when he looked at her. Ravenstein's news told her why Anthony had not written to her. Assuredly, he had not yet received her letter, if he had been plying the seas over the past several weeks. She yearned for a word from him, but just knowing he was fulfilling important missions for Edward warmed her. She had to smile to herself when she thought of him green at the rail of a ship again. *Perhaps it is something one gets over,* she decided.

Mother of God, I have been lying awake here for hours, it seems. She could hear Beatrice's and Fortunata's steady breathing across the room. *How difficult would it be for me to take a midnight walk? If I can persuade the guards outside the door that I am just going to the great hall and back to stretch my legs, they might let me go alone.*

She put on her woolen bed robe and hugged the sable lining to her against the chilly late-October air. Tying up her hose above her knees, she slipped out of bed. She gently pulled the bed curtain aside and, glad of the Turkey carpet to muffle her footsteps, quietly unlatched the door and stepped out into the torchlit antechamber, where two sleepy guards at once rose to attention. She put her finger to her lips as she closed the door quietly behind her.

"I cannot sleep, and so I will be grateful if you would keep your posts here and let me stretch my legs. I shall be but a few minutes. I will call if I need you."

The guards looked skeptically at each other. They had strict orders to keep watch over the duchess all night and make sure none but her ladies went in and out. They had not been confronted by the duchess herself before and were unsure what to do.

"You shall not be punished, I promise you. Take pity on me." She gave them a dazzling smile. "I never have time to myself."

The guards were smitten and grinned back. One of them gave her a lantern, its horn sides giving out enough light for her as she walked along the cold tiled floor. She wished she had worn her shoes. She heard the guards' whispered discussion receding and despite the darkness in front of her, she was unafraid.

She climbed the spiral stone steps to the ramparts and shivered in the cold wind that greeted her. To one side of the roof was the little town of Aire, nestled in the safety of the fortified wall encircling it, and Margaret could see the three watchtowers' braziers keeping the guards warm. Other than those beacons in the night, as she looked over the river side of the castle, it was the pitch black of a moonless night. She heard an owl off in the distance and then the howl of a wolf. She had never seen a wolf—they had more or less died out in England—but Ravenstein had told her they were often seen in the Forest of Soignes outside Brussels. She shivered again. Such a lonely sound, she thought.

Looking out into the void at that moment, she felt as though there was no one else in the world but her. "I wish I could howl my loneliness," she cried in the wind. She recalled telling Jack Howard all those years ago about feeling alone at Greenwich. Thinking of Jack, she smiled. His pragmatism and directness always reassured her. He was someone you could trust, she thought, and Edward is lucky to have him.

Thinking of Edward conjured up other conversations: when he had told her she might go to Scotland; or when he whispered of his love for Elizabeth and that he had secretly married the widow Grey, and when he had audaciously encouraged her to flirt with Anthony. Anthony! For the thousandth time she wondered if he had received her letter, if he loved her still and if she would ever see him again. She wrapped her arms around herself and moved her body from side to side, trying to recall every word he had spoken to her on the *New Ellen*.

"We were destined to meet, but we were not destined to be together. Both of us must pray to God the Father, God the Holy Ghost and our Savior Jesu Christ to help us accept this destiny and live our lives in His way.

If ever there comes a time when you and I are free of the bonds of marriage, I promise you, I will come . . ." She whispered again the wonderful
words. "Ah, Anthony, would you could keep your promise!"

"Twelve of the clock and all is well!" called the nightwatchman in the
town below, rousing Margaret from her reverie. Sweet Mary, she was still
not tired, but she acknowledged she was very cold.

She held the lantern high to light her way down the stair, but instead
of turning back to her chamber at the bottom of it, she went farther into
the palace. Outside a small chamber that Marie de Charny shared with
one of the other attendants, she noticed a glimmer of light under the
door and a man's voice, albeit hushed, coming from inside. She frowned.
Marie's elderly husband, Pierre, was with Charles, and she briefly wondered if Marie was in danger. *She deserves whatever fate has in store for
her* was her immediate unkind reaction, but when she heard the sound of
a smack to bare skin and Marie's tiny scream, she waited no longer. Not
heeding the danger she might put herself in, she put down her lantern,
lifted the hasp slowly and pushed open the door.

Marie was on her hands and knees, her graying hair loose over her
face and her bare buttocks raised high to take Guillaume's thrusting prick.
He brought his hand down hard on one of her cheeks, and again the
little scream—but now Margaret recognized pleasure—emanated from
Marie, who had her chemise around her neck, allowing her rather wizened breasts to swing free.

Neither saw the duchess standing there, her eyes wide with horror,
as she watched her two most prominent retainers in their act of carnal
passion. Suddenly Guillaume realized they were not alone, and when his
glance fell on the dimly lit figure in the doorway and in shock recognized
Margaret, he dropped Marie's backside and attempted to cover his swollen privates with his hands. His mouth opened and shut a few times, but
no words came.

Sprawled on the floor, Marie complained, "Chevalier, ride me some
more, I beg of you! Why do you not—" She twisted her head to look up
at him and then followed his gaze. When she saw Margaret, she gave a
real scream. "*Croix de dieu, Madame la duchesse!*" and scrambled on all fours
to hide under the blanket.

Margaret advanced into the room, every nerve in her body tensed.

Her mind was racing. Yes, she was angry that these two trusted servants of noble families would shamelessly act on some lustful urge right under her nose. Surprising and disquieting, she also found the scene titillating, although she did not know why. A forty-year-old woman being ravished by a young god of a man in a manner that suggested animal behavior must surely have repelled any sensitive and proper person's sensibilities, and yet, as well as being repelled, she was excited by it on some primitive level.

"Chevalier, cover yourself and leave the room immediately! I will attend to you tomorrow," she commanded. She turned away as he hurriedly grabbed up his doublet, hose and shoes and scurried—as ably as a six-foot-four-inch giant could scurry—out of her sight, executing a ridiculous bow as he went. She purposefully closed the door behind him and came to Marie, who was cowering at the foot of the bed and fighting with her chemise. Margaret knew triumphantly that she finally had power over this mean-spirited woman, whose fate was in her hands.

She was scornful. "I am ashamed of you, countess," she said, watching Marie squirm. "Your disgusting lust for my young chevalier does your noble blood no service. You are supposed to uphold the morality of the ladies at court and serve as model to them. And here you are, the wife of one of the most chivalrous and beloved men of Burgundy, fornicating with an innocent young man. What do you have to say for yourself?"

Marie looked so woebegone that Margaret almost laughed, but the woman did not deny she had coerced the artless Guillaume into a dalliance. Here's an apple that did not fall far from the tree, Margaret thought, remembering Duke Philip's lustiness.

"A million pardons, your grace," Marie began, climbing off the bed and effecting a passable obeisance. "How should I be punished?" she stammered from the floor. Then she looked up, afraid. "I pray you, nay, I beg of you, do not tell my husband—or," she added hastily, "my brother, your husband. I could not bear the disgrace." She had taken Margaret's hand and was pressing it to her cheek as she pleaded for mercy. But Margaret had made up her mind. She pulled her hand from Marie's grasp and walked slowly to a chair. She did not ask but assumed that Marie had persuaded her underling bedmate to share another attendant's bed that night to allow intimacy with Guillaume. She wondered how many times it had happened. It was all too degrading, and she decided she would rather not know the details.

"I will not say a word to anyone, Marie. But I shall request that your husband be assigned to my household so that you cannot repeat this behavior. And for my silence, I demand to know the truth about Fortunata's disappearance. Do not deny you were involved."

Marie gasped. She had not expected the accusation, and her face gave her away. She got to her feet, attempted to tidy her straggly hair and smoothed her kirtle. "I shall not deny it, your grace." When she saw the shock and anger in Margaret's eyes, she rushed on, "but I did it to protect you, Madame la duchesse, I swear. Fortunata gave you potions that caused you to lose your child." Now she had Margaret's attention. "When I heard you tell Jeanne de Halewijn that you had been given them every night, I was suspicious. I went to the dispensary where Heer Roelandts helped me discover what Fortunata was brewing." She paused for effect. Margaret had one hand on her belly as though to protect the life that had been in it, and the other was over her mouth. "We could not find anything, but we were both convinced she had poisoned you."

"'Tis an outrageous suggestion!" Margaret cried, leaping to her feet. "I would trust Fortunata with my life. So what did you intend to do? Torture her in that ice cellar until she confessed to this lie? Starve her to death? What, pray?"

Marie had the grace to look shamefaced. "'Twas my idea to frighten her a little into admitting her guilt. But you found her before we could—"

"Enough! I have heard enough! 'Twas barbaric what you and the good doctor conspired to do. Tomorrow I shall conduct my own interrogation of all three of you and find out the truth. Until then, you will remain in this room until I call for you, do you understand?"

Margaret strode to the door, took the key from it and held it up for Marie to see. She exited the room, picked up her lantern and locked the door. She heard Marie collapse in tears on the other side.

Now she was tired, nay, exhausted. This had been one of the most dramatic half hours of her life. Even so, she could not sleep. She spent much of the rest of the night on her knees, praying for guidance to anyone in God's heaven who would listen. *Fortunata poison me? Why, after all we have been through together? 'Tis unconscionable.* But Marie seemed quite sincere for once. And 'twas true, *pochina* did give me potions against the doctor's wishes. Certes, it did ease the puking, but did it cause the miscarriage? Ah, dear God, who should I believe? She begged St. Jude, St. Benedict, St. Anne and even the patron saint of the falsely accused, Raymond Nonnatus, to help her. But in the end, it was Cecily's face she saw and Cecily's voice she heard.

"Trust your heart, my child. 'Twas always your greatest strength," her mother seemed to say. "Trust in Fortunata. She loves you the best."

When she finally rose to her feet to climb into bed, she was surprised to see that Fortunata was kneeling behind her. The servant's eyes sparkled with tears in the candlelight, and she sagged down dejectedly onto her heels.

"*Madonna*, I have something I must tell you. I do not want to lie to you. It is difficult for me to say, you understand," she whispered. Beatrice stirred in her sleep for a second but then resumed her gentle snoring from the truckle bed. Fortunata shivered, and Margaret took off her warm robe, raised the dwarf from the floor and wrapped her in it.

"Aye, *pochina*, I cannot bear to have you lie to me. Tell me this bad thing." Margaret could not believe that her prayers had been answered so soon. She got into bed, keeping her stockings on for warmth, and waited.

"The medicine I gave you . . ." Fortunata hesitated, then crossed herself and hurried on. "It was many things, but also . . ." She hesitated again. "Pennyroyal."

"Pennyroyal?" Margaret was aghast. "Why did you give me that, you wicked girl? 'Tis well known it rids a woman of an unwanted child." She wrung her hands and stared in disbelief at the contrite young woman before her. "But I wanted that child, Fortunata! What were you thinking?" she whispered as loudly as she dared, angry tears welling. "You killed my child!"

Fortunata sank down on her knees again. "*Perdonne me, madonna,*" she whispered, retreating into her native tongue. "I did it for love. You must believe me. In Padua, I saw the same sickness you had take hold of a woman at the university. My master could not help her. He did try bleeding her, but . . ." She shrugged. "The woman left, and later when she had the child, it was a monster, *madonna*. Big, big head, no nose, and no eye coverings." She pointed to her own eyelids. "The head was too heavy for the little body, and it died soon after." She was crying now, and as Margaret absorbed this sad tale, she understood.

"Certes, you thought the same thing would happen to me. Is that right, Fortunata?"

The dwarf bowed her head in shame. "*Si, madonna.* You are right. I was wrong, yes?" she asked in utter dejection.

"Aye, Fortunata, you were wrong. May God forgive you for your act. I must think about what to do with you, so leave me to myself. I think you know I can never accept another potion from you as long as you remain in my service," Margaret said sadly, knowing that this would hurt Fortunata deeply. She was stern but not as angry as she had been. Fortunata kissed her hand.

"And you know who put you in the cellar, do you not? No more lies, *pochina,* I want the truth."

"It was Heer Roelandts," the dwarf whispered finally. "He said he had something to show me and took me to the cellar through the kitchen. Then he tied me, and when I tried and call out, he put a cloth in my mouth. He asked me about the medicine for you, but I did not tell him anything. He came three times, gave me food and asked again. I said nothing."

"I am happy to hear he did not go through with his threat to kill you, and he does not appear to have harmed you." She paused. "And you think he acted alone?"

Fortunata rolled her eyes and shrugged her shoulders, a gesture that Margaret had learned meant perhaps yes, perhaps no.

"I am waiting, Fortunata. The truth now."

But the dwarf had nothing more to say. "I am sorry, *madonna.* Please let me sleep now."

Margaret sighed and nodded. She had to admire Fortunata's integrity in not denouncing Marie, or perhaps the servant truly did not know that the woman had instigated her abduction. This was the most difficult problem she had had to deal with personally, and even though she fought it now, sleep overcame her before she had resolved how to handle the two different situations.

. . .

"MARIE, YOU WERE correct." Margaret's tone was cold as ice the next morning in her private audience chamber. "Fortunata has confessed all to me, and I am sending her away from me for a few weeks to pray for forgiveness. However, you are not blameless in this business, and for participating in the heinous kidnapping of my servant, I am depriving you of your status as head of my ladies for a month. Beatrice will take your place while you mull over what you have done with regard to both Fortunata and Guillaume."

Marie's face showed no emotion, but she was beginning to understand the new duchess's mettle, and she sank into a low curtsey. "Aye, your grace. I thank you, your grace." She did not dare ask whether her husband would be spared the details of either of her indiscretions, but she hoped the duchess's word of the night before was good. Her punishment was not so bad, and her feelings about Margaret were ameliorated somewhat, especially upon hearing that the dwarf would be sent away.

Margaret waved her aside and asked that Heer Roelandts be admitted to the audience chamber. His bloodletting cup and knife swinging from his belt, the ruddy-faced Dutchman entered as Marie was leaving. Neither looked at each other, and Margaret was pleased to see Marie's humility.

Roelandts was relegated to attending the sick among the kitchen staff and stable boys for a month, and nothing more was said about the matter. Guillaume could not look Margaret in the eye when he was called in. He knelt before her, his felt bonnet in one hand and the other over his heart.

"Forgive me, your grace," was all he could say, but Margaret heard the contrition in his voice and told him to rise.

"Perhaps we need to find you a wife, Guillaume," she said. "Then perhaps you would not be putting your pestle where it does not belong."

He could have sworn he saw her wink at him.

14

Winter 1469

Margaret could not remember when she had laughed so much. Guillaume was teaching her to skate on the frozen lake in the Hesdin castle park, and it was a painful beginning.

She had watched Londoners strap sharpened animal bones to their boots and glide along the ice on the Thames one particularly cold winter. It looked so easy and so exhilarating. She and George had begged Cecily for the chance to try their skill, but Cecily had raised an eyebrow and stated, "'Tis a sport for peasants, children. How would it seem if they saw a duke's child upended on his arse?" And the brother and sister had giggled at hearing their mother use such a coarse word. But dutifully, they returned to their perch high above the river in the warm solar and watched from the window.

Margaret had been delighted to know that everyone in Flanders knew how to skate, and ever willing to be accepted as one of them, she had agreed eagerly to Guillaume's suggestion that she learn the art.

Instead of bones she wore sharpened metal blades strapped tightly to her little boots when she gingerly stepped out onto the ice, the hood of her short fur-lined cloak keeping the wind from her face. She stood there, not daring to move, but with her ladies' encouragement, she attempted a step forward. She could not believe how swiftly the skate slid out from under her. Trying desperately to gain her balance with the other foot, she shrieked as she sat down ungracefully, her heavy skirts protecting her. She could not help but laugh, remembering Cecily's prediction. Guillaume was there in a flash to help her to her feet, and this time he suggested she hold tightly to his arm and let him guide her until she got a measure of balance. This proved to be a lengthy process, but Margaret was determined to traverse the pond once on her own before the lesson was over. Mary and Jeanne were laughing and applauding her progress, and Margaret watched with wonder as little Mary flew over the ice and even skated backwards for her.

In the meantime, Margaret watched as Guillaume gave one of her younger ladies a skating lesson, too. Henriette de Longwy was from an old Franche-Comté family, and Margaret could see the girl was hanging on Guillaume's every word. Aha, she thought, I think I will foster this. It would give her pleasure to arrange a match that would have a better chance of happiness than her own.

Mary flew across the ice to her. "Come, *belle-mère*, I will take one arm and Madame de Halewijn the other. Now follow what we do." Mary's eyes were shining. She was never happier than when outdoors, and as well as mastering this slippery art, she was the best horsewoman Margaret had ever seen.

During Fortunata's two months' absence at the convent and hospital of St. John's in Bruges, Margaret had found herself more and more in Mary's apartments or the girl in hers. Jeanne was no longer jealous, and after a busy morning with administrative duties, Margaret liked nothing better than to listen to Mary play her lute or challenge her to a game of trictrac. Margaret was also teaching her chess, "so you can play with your father when he comes, sweeting. 'Tis a way to pass the time with him." A pinched look always crossed Mary's face when her father was mentioned, and Margaret's heart ached for her. She was virtually an orphan, and so Margaret gave her as much love and attention as she could.

They had all spent Christmas in this favorite of Duke Philip's castles, and she was accepting of Charles's absence. In fact, she was much happier without him. She still missed her family, but her homesickness had dissipated somewhat over the months. Two letters had brought the feeling rushing back, however. The first was received a few days after the feast of the Epiphany. Margaret's eager fingers made short work of the familiar seal.

"*Christmas greetings to you, Margaret, from Windsor,*" her mother wrote in her flowery script.

> "*Edward and Elizabeth are gracious hosts, and we have kept the feast of Our Lord cheerfully. You were remembered in our Christmas Mass and in Edward's toast at the feasting each day. You would not recognize St. George's chapel now: Edward's masons must be inspired by God as they enlarge and beautify it.*
>
> "*I worry that my nephew Warwick has too much influence on George, but if he is given a choice, I have no doubt George will follow Edward. 'Tis not a happy situation. The rumor that Louis of France is helping that other queen does not bode well for us.*"

She knew her mother could not bring herself to write the She-Wolf's name, although in a happier time Cecily had thought to honor the queen by naming Margaret for her.

> "*But I daily pray her threat to invade comes to naught and your influence on your husband will lend us his aid in preventing it.*"

As 'tis the first time I have heard the rumor and as I never see Charles, I doubt I can have any influence, Margaret sighed. In truth, I have seen him on only twenty-one occasions in six months of marriage.

> "*I hope you keep my counsel, child, and daily read the good works of St. Bridget.*"

"Aye, mother," Margaret said aloud, smiling to herself. She still thinks on me as a child.

> "*And I pray to hear news that you are with child. Motherhood has been the joy of my life, and I would wish you to know it also.*"

So do I, Mother, oh, so do I.

> "*Write more often, Margaret, I would know if you have found your heart's desire.*"

Margaret smirked as she read the last sentence, knowing her mother was referring to the night she shared her dreams of a husband in her mother's bed at Hunsdon House on the way to Fotheringhay. I would hardly call Charles my heart's desire—far from it.

Cecily ended the letter with: *"Do not forget Proverbs, verse 11: A virtuous woman is a crown to her husband,"* at which Margaret rolled her eyes. "Aye, Mother," she repeated. Then she read the letter all over again before folding it carefully and setting it aside to answer.

Her hand had shaken when the second letter was given to her by a much chastened Fortunata, who had returned from the good sisters of St. John in time for the feast of Candlemas.

"From Master Caxton, *madonna*," Fortunata said conspiratorially. "I saw him many times." She longed to tell Margaret of one night beneath the Waterhall, when William had given in to her flirtations and given the dwarf her first taste of a man's mouth and of the lust it evoked. The encounter had gone no further that night, but it had left Fortunata ecstatic that someone found her desirable.

Margaret was too flustered by the letter to admonish Fortunata for escaping the convent, in secret she assumed, or notice the glow upon the servant's cheeks as she pronounced Caxton's name. Margaret broke the merchant-adventurer's seal open impatiently. As she surmised, a smaller letter was enclosed, and seeing *Dame Elaine Astolat* written on it, she thanked Fortunata and walked to the window to read it. Fortunata curtseyed and withdrew into her own world of lustful awakenings.

Snow was falling over the hillsides and covering the rooftops below in its soft mantle. One of her ladies was playing a recorder, and Margaret recognized the French ditty: *Ah, si mon moine voulait danser*. She felt like dancing around the room to the sprightly tune, waving her letter from Anthony and behaving like a lovelorn milkmaid instead of a demure duchess. Instead, she carefully broke the seal and opened the missive. A carefully pressed white marguerite slipped out of it, the tips of its snowy white petals turning brown. A lump came into her throat as she began to read.

"My beloved Elaine, I greet you well. Why does six months feel like six years? Your letter found me in the Isle of Wight after the failure of our fleet to find our enemies. You will be glad to know that the mal de mer did not affect me so much in those weeks at sea, and I began to believe it was mal de coeur I was experiencing on

the Ellen in its stead. My heart still hurts for you, and I beg of you, never doubt its devotion to you.

"There is much unrest in England, my love, and I wish your oldest brother had your wise counsel to guide him through this morass with the earl."

Margaret knew he was talking of Warwick.

"I fear they will never be reconciled and I fear he will soon be caught in a web of his own making—or of the spider over the water."

Louis of France, Margaret thought. How clever Anthony has been to disguise the names in the letter in case it fell into unfriendly hands.

"Your young brothers are well, but the older's loyalties concern us all."

George, George, did you not heed my words last summer?

"'Tis rumored the younger is a father, but doubtless he fears your mother's wrath and so keeps his peace."

Dickon a father, 'tis hard to believe. She smiled, remembering the young woman with the beautiful voice. She did not blame Dickon for keeping his peace with Cecily, whom she had overheard rail at Edward when his little bastard Arthur was born and acknowledged.

"As for myself, I yearn to travel and go on a pilgrimage, but your brother has much work for me, so I will have to wait. Would my travels took me to you, my love, but in the meantime,

> *I am your devoted, Lancelot."*

The letter with the daisy was now tucked inside her bodice, rumpled and tear-stained from so many readings. She knew she should burn it as agreed, but she could not bring herself to part with it just yet.

THE VILLAGE OF Hesdin was situated at the confluence of the Canche and Ternoise rivers. Its castle, in earlier centuries a stronghold with high walls and ramparts impregnable from the valley below, rose sentinel over the town like an extension of the strategic hill it sat upon.

When they first arrived in November, Mary could not wait for Margaret to experience the surprises at the castle. Duke Philip was a man with an impish sense of humor, Lord Ravenstein had told her before they journeyed there.

"But I will not spoil it for you, your grace," he said, his grave face belying the twinkle in his eyes. He was wearing a chaperon of such enormous proportions that Margaret wondered how his head could support it. He was a stiff-necked man at the best of times, but that day he had to turn his whole torso to summon a waiting page and ask for wine. Margaret imagined a whole nest of mice might happily reside in the hat's many folds.

"I hope they are pleasant surprises, messire," Margaret said, unwittingly, "like the delightful mechanical animals that carried in the dishes at my wedding banquet."

"Aye," Ravenstein nodded. "But these mechanical contraptions are less visible. Just do not believe everything you see there, 'tis all I will say."

Margaret thought back to that statement as she stood in the exquisite great hall at Hesdin with Mary by her side, gazing up at the wooden vaulted ceiling painted in brilliant azure and studded with stars of gold leaf. The paneled walls were polished like burnished chestnuts and the wall hangings were even more beautiful than the ones at the Coudenberg.

"Mary, where are the surprises I was told about?" she asked, looking about her and seeing nothing unusual. Mary grinned and with a grand gesture entreated Margaret to go ahead of her.

"Come, Fortunata, let us see what no one dares tell us about," Margaret called to the dwarf, who tiptoed behind her mistress, suspicious of every chair and stool. One of the ladies had told her about the tricks at Hesdin, and she was ready for anything.

They walked through the hall, eying every nook and cranny as though ghosts would jump out at them, to the threshold of a gallery beyond. Again Margaret was struck by the beauty of the painted walls and ceiling. Six statues stood on either side of the gallery, and as she walked through the doorway to admire them, she suddenly felt icy water spurt up under her dress. As she looked down in dismay, one of the statues squirted water from its mouth, its spout hitting her in the arm. She shrieked and ran to a lectern on which rested a magnificent book. Fortunata had not avoided the water spouts from the floor either, and she ran helter-skelter into the center of the gallery, wiping her legs with her petticoats, and was then confronted by a mirror that distorted her poor stunted body into that of a four-feet-wide and two-feet-tall midget. Curious, she stepped forward to touch the strange mirror, which triggered a small bag of soot that she had not noticed above her to empty its contents onto her head. She screamed and turned to see Mary still outside the room, now creased over with laughter. When Mary looked up, she saw Margaret about to turn a page of the book and too late cried out to her not to touch it. A white cloud of flour was puffed into Margaret's unsuspecting face and she jumped back with another cry of dismay.

Fortunata seeing her mistress's white face could not forbear to laugh. "You look like a dead woman, *madonna*," she said.

Margaret laughed. "And you look like a Moor, *pochina*. Come, let us go quickly before anything else befalls us." Taking hands, they made for a door at the other end of the gallery. But Duke Philip had not finished with them. Thunder and lightning suddenly erupted overhead and water rained down on them from the ceiling as they reached the door and pushed it open. Something padded thwacked Margaret on her backside and then hit Fortunata on the head before they emerged into another chamber to face an anxious group of courtiers whom Mary had made sure would be there. Seeing their faces, and knowing Mary had meant no harm, Margaret, who was now drenched from head to toe and had flour dripping like glue down her face, began to laugh. Relieved, the company laughed with her, while Jeanne ran forward with a dry cloak to wrap around Margaret's shivering body.

"Wait until I get my hands on young Mary," Margaret said, hurrying up the stairs with Jeanne and leaving a water trail behind her. "Certes, I am thinking up a few surprises of my own for her."

Jeanne might have been worried for her charge but for the chuckle she heard from Margaret as they reached the door to her chamber.

AT THE END of February, Charles came to Hesdin. He made an effort to spend time with both his wife and his daughter, but only after the business of the day was ended. He invited Margaret to sit with him one morning as he heard petition after petition from his subjects, who came in an unending stream while he dispensed decisions arbitrarily.

For her part, Margaret was slowly beginning to understand the magnitude of Charles's ambition for himself. She learned how ruthlessly he had amassed territory in his short time as duke and that he was intent on joining the northern part of his duchy with the south and east, even if it meant taking large parts of the Habsburg empire or France. Making war was his *raison d'être*, Ravenstein had confided in her, and Margaret had heard the disapproval in his voice. Ravenstein had acknowledged that although Charles was a hard worker, he insisted on being in control of all facets of the government: judicial, financial, secular and most of all the military.

"As he has done, you must learn to adapt to each city's and province's culture and political traditions when you are representing your husband. Of course, you will have help from those the duke has left in charge, but each place has a different way of doing things—running their economies, their armies—and then you have the difficulty of language. I am pleased, your grace, that your Flemish is improving with Madame Mary's help. It will be invaluable to you, especially with the Gantois, the people of Ghent, who are proud and tend to be the duke's most rebellious subjects. 'Tis why Madame Mary must remain here so often, and you, too, will be in Ghent more than any other city. 'Tis most necessary to have a ducal presence there often." He sighed and returned to his concern about his overlord.

"I believe the duke thinks he can conquer the world, your grace. I think 'tis a vain hope, and perhaps you can persuade him to end these military exploits, which cost us dearly in men and money, and be content to govern the land he has."

"Messire Ravenstein, you are gracious to trust me with this knowledge of my husband. I know you do so out of love and devotion to Burgundy and the former duke. Certes, your integrity is unquestioned by me, and if I feel I can have the slightest influence on my husband, you have my word I will try and steer him to a more peaceful course. I have a horror of war—my family has been embroiled in it for most of my life—and you may count on me."

Ravenstein smiled. "I have no doubt, madame." Under his breath he said, "Burgundy does not need a caesar."

Margaret looked at him quizzically, but he was already bowing and walking away.

Now she understood. As she sat in the great hall with Charles, she was astonished and dismayed to hear the number of comparisons her husband made of himself to the great leaders of the past in his long, meandering diatribes: Julius Caesar, Hannibal, Charlemagne and his favorite, Alexander the Great.

"Like me, Alexander had a father named Philip," he pronounced to one petitioner, who had been kept kneeling on the marble floor for almost half an hour. "And like me, Alexander devoted his life to expanding his territories. I shall succeed in joining our northern territories to our southern ones, and I shall be known one day as the most glorious leader of Burgundy"—he paused, scanning the room—"nay, of all Europe." He lowered his gaze from the courtiers to the kneeling figure in front of him. "Mark this, sirrah," he bellowed. "There are only three lords in the world: God, Lucifer and me." The man stared balefully at his lord and crossed himself. "And now, out of the goodness of my heart, I will grant you what you have asked. Hugonet, see that my wishes are carried out," he shouted to his chancellor. "Next!"

The courtiers were restless, Margaret could see. She was grateful that Charles allowed her to sit on a throne next to him. No one else was allowed to sit in his presence, and she guessed they had been there three hours. Charles's head jutted forward on his bull neck and shoulders, scanning the company for signs of lack of interest, but everyone appeared to be giving him rapt attention. Satisfied, he rubbed his hands together, waited for the next petitioner to be announced and prepared his next oration.

DURING ONE OF the private times Margaret had with him, she asked that Marie's husband be assigned to her household.

"Marie frets when he is not close, Charles," she lied, hoping she was not risking hellfire for it. "I believe she will be happier if he is with us, in truth. Can you spare him?"

Charles was feeling magnanimous. It was a mild March day, and a passing shower had left diamond droplets on the primroses that bordered the path where they were walking. He was pleased with Margaret's grasp of her duties and had had an excellent report of her from Ravenstein. He was also relieved that his daughter had taken to his new wife, which alleviated his guilt with regard to his lack of attention to the child.

"Marie pining for her husband?" Charles guffawed, taking her arm and walking through a garden to a path that girded the castle wall. "I think you must be mistaken, Margaret. Pierre is a courageous soldier and loyal, but he is almost in his dotage now, and I cannot think Marie craves his attentions. But if you believe this is so and it would please you, then I shall spare him. What is he to do for you?"

"Aye, Charles, it would please me. And I am grateful. Do you think the count would chafe as captain of my knights of honor?"

"He will do as he is told, Margaret. It surprises me that you should even ask the question. I will have the papers drawn up. Were you aware that Pierre fought in one of the most famous jousts of our age?" Charles's eyes lit up whenever fighting was in question, and Margaret let him describe it to her in gory detail. He was looking at her, but she was quite sure he did not see her or he would have noted the look of tedium in her face. She waited patiently until he had finished, smiling and making little noises of exclamation wherever she could. However, her ears pricked up when he began to talk of his father. She was quite convinced she would have preferred being married to a profligate patron of the arts than to this bellicose bore.

"I hated my father, Margaret," Charles began quietly. "I hated what he did to humiliate my mother first and foremost, and I made a solemn vow that I would be everything he was not. If he liked white, I liked black; if he laughed, I scowled. He liked your house, I was all for Lancaster—although now I see he was right to distrust France and ally with England." He saw the fleeting expression of dismay on her face, and qualified his remark. "It has nothing to do with you, my dear. Nothing, I promise.

"I hated that he gave Louis, as Dauphin, sanctuary here for so many years just because Louis could not get along with his own father. Louis made me squirm with his obsequiousness, always bowing and scraping to my father but secretly spying on us. You know that I left the court and went north while Louis was here? While he fawned and smiled, he was learning our ways and how he could defeat us," he spat. He picked up a stone from the path and flung it over the castle wall near which they were walking. "Now he is king and thinks I will lick his boots. Never!" he shouted, startling Margaret and causing Mary beside her to cringe.

"I do not think it is wise to cross him, Charles. Pray calm yourself, for you are frightening Mary," she chided him. Mary had indeed let go of Margaret's hand and had fallen back to take Jeanne's.

"Watch your step, Margaret," Charles warned, avoiding a large puddle and leaving Margaret to wonder if he meant the puddle or her admonishment. She drew herself up to her full height, which meant she had to look down on him when she next spoke. It gave her courage.

"Mary is a sensitive little thing, Charles. You forget she is almost exclusively in the company of women, and your outbursts are unpredictable and thus frightening to her." She paused and was pleased to see his expression matched the baleful one on the sheep that represented the order of the Golden Fleece he always wore about his neck. "I am sorry you hated your father. 'Tis incomprehensible to me. All of us loved and admired both our father and our mother, although Mother has been known to beat George and Dickon herself if they warranted it," she chuckled.

"My mother is a saint!" exclaimed Charles. "And although I love my siblings, I have to remind them from time to time that they are all my father's bastards. Marie is no exception. I hope she is giving you good service, Margaret."

"Aye, good enough," Margaret murmured. "But let us talk of my family, I beg of you. What is the news from England?"

"Ah, I wish I knew. Methinks my lord of Warwick still plays your brother for a fool, for I have heard he is in Calais and is in secret dealings with Louis while he is on a mission from Edward."

"I pray you are wrong. My lord of Warwick is Captain of Calais, so perhaps he is making an assessment of the garrison there for Edward."

Charles gave a short bark of laughter. "Aye, and I am the queen of Sheba. Nay, he is to visit us here on a diplomatic mission from Edward, so the messenger tells me. I shall be curious to see him again. I doubt he knows how much I dislike him. He is a dangerous man, and I fear he will bring Edward down, my dear. Mark my words." He seems to like that expression, Margaret thought.

"Then stop him, Charles," she begged. "Swear on our marriage vows that you will help Edward should he need you. Is that not what this union is all about?" Her voice was raised—as was one of Charles's eyebrows. She quieted down. " 'Tis for the good of Burgundy that we help Edward, is it not? He hates Louis as much as you do. Both of you can be strong against Louis if Edward is on the throne. Warwick has always been a friend of France. If he has the power in England, then you will regret it."

Charles looked astonished at this outburst. Ravenstein is right, he thought, she is well versed in politics.

"Never fear, I will help Edward if he will help me," he said, patting a spot next to him on a bench and inviting her to sit. Their retinue had stopped at a respectful distance and conversed among themselves, while Jeanne helped Mary gather primroses. Margaret took the seat and settled her hands in her lap as Charles continued, "In the meantime, we must prepare to receive the earl and his lady wife here in a matter of days."

"Here at Hesdin?" Margaret exclaimed, rising up again. "Sweet Mother of God, why did you not tell me before? I must make preparations. Does he come alone? How long will he stay? We must fete him with all honor." Despite her misgivings about Warwick, the prospect of seeing one so close to her family again was exhilarating.

Charles pulled her down and watched her face closely. Her eyes were sparkling and her cheeks tinged with excited pink. He suddenly leaned forward and kissed her full on the mouth, cupping her breast in his hand. Margaret was too stunned to move, but even with their mouths locked in a kiss, their eyes were wide open, avising each other. You are mine to do with as I will, his seemed to tell her. I am a princess of England and not to be trifled with, hers told him. They pulled apart, and Margaret put her hand up and straightened her turbaned headdress, with the ever-present rose brooch pinned to the front.

Charles studied her. "Have I told you how that shade of blue becomes you?"

It was Margaret's turn to be astonished. Charles had not once paid her a compliment since they had met, except for that first night, when he had praised her unintentional movements in bed. Although, she acknowledged, that was hardly flattering.

She blushed. "Why, thank you, Charles," she said spontaneously and could have kicked herself for sounding so coy. More boldly, and as they were out of earshot of the others, she said, "May I ask if you intend to visit my chamber while you are here?" Charles's eyebrow lifted again, but she hurried on. "These nine months have told me we will not be a daily part of each other's lives, and I must point out that if you have wed me with the intention of siring an heir . . ."

Charles's eyes bulged. "Margaret, you presume too much," he said coldly. "I already have an heir, my daughter, Mary, in case you have forgotten."

Stinging from the reproach, Margaret was scornful. "It seems to me, Charles, that you have not thought things through very clearly. You are intent on making war with whoever gets in your way of glory—no, pray let me finish—and having lost a father and a brother in this way, I know there is a good chance you may be killed before you grow to be an old man. With only a girl, and one as young, vulnerable and unmarried as Mary, to inherit this duchy, all you are working to achieve will be torn apart by your enemies and"—she spread her hands—"where is your glory then? If I give you a son, a son whose uncle is the king of England, for your good subjects to rally around, Burgundy might be saved." She sighed. "I see you are angry with me, but you are an intelligent man, Charles. Can you not acknowledge I am right?"

Charles leapt to his feet and began to pace. A vein stood out danger-ously on his forehead, his face was red and from the look in his eye, Mar-garet was afraid he might approach and strike her. His fists were clenched and his mouth grim. But he said nothing; he merely continued to pace with short, deliberate steps. She sat there awaiting his ire, but it did not come. Slowly he unclenched his hands, and the vein receded. He blinked a few times, and she thought she could hear his mind working.

Finally he turned to her and in a calm, even voice that surprised her said, "It has never occurred to me to want a son, Margaret. I believe I am destined for glory, and when the time comes, Mary will have a husband who will look after my—I mean, her—interests." He paused for a full minute, fingering the golden sheep and unnerving her with his steady gaze. "It has, however, occurred to me on more than one occasion that I have married a political equal. 'Tis your brain, not your birth, that pre-vents me from chastising you for your outburst." Then his tone turned pleasant, surprising her yet again. "However, your logic is hard to argue with, my dear. Therefore I shall indeed come to your bed tonight."

Her emotions strung out by this man's bizarre behavior, Margaret watched him stride away, his retainers hurrying to keep up with him. She trembled. She had won a small victory, she knew, and perhaps it might lead her to the joy of motherhood. But she did not relish the act that would achieve it.

She was pleasantly surprised, however, when Charles joined her in the sumptuous bed in her brightly lit chamber that night and treated her with the utmost respect. She had still never climaxed again since John Harper showed her the way in the garden at Greenwich, but hers and Charles's lovemaking was not without its pleasure, and she fell asleep with a happy assurance she had conceived.

"I BRING YOU messages of love and devotion from your family, your grace, with especial greetings from my aunt, your mother," the earl of Warwick said, bowing over Margaret's hand before the banquet in his honor at Hesdin a few days later. Huntsmen and fishermen, falconers and fewterers had used their skills for three days to provide a feast for the noble English guests, and the aromas wafting from the huge kitchens under the great hall were making Margaret's stomach rumble.

"Pray tell me more, my lord!" Margaret said eagerly, thinking that her cousin had aged in the year since she had seen him. One eyelid drooped markedly and gave her the impression he was winking at her. His noble profile and ready smile that mostly reached his eyes were still the same, but at age forty, his hair was sparse and gray and his shoulders stooped. He turned and beckoned to his squire, who stepped forward bearing a small carved chest with a silver lock.

"I was instructed to put this directly into your hands, Lady Margaret. Your brother George insisted upon it. I was so afraid it might have been damaged by the rough seas en route to Calais that I carried it with me day and night." Again that wink—or was it a wink?

Margaret held out her hands. "I fear you tease me, my lord. I cannot imagine what George has sent me." She took the box, stroked the silver tracings with her fingers and then turned the key. Inside were three jars of her favorite rose-petal jam. Instantly she was back in the little orchard at Greenwich with Anthony, licking the sticky delicacy off her fingers. She closed the lid quickly and smiled gratefully at Warwick. "George spoils me," she said. "Tell him thank you for me."

Anne Neville, Warwick's wife and mother of his two daughters, Isabel and Anne, was next presented to Charles. It was through her that Warwick had inherited his title, and Margaret was impressed that the middle-aged countess gave Charles just the obeisance due his ducal title but told the world she was the daughter of an earl. Margaret recognized the same indomitable spirit in Anne that she admired in Cecily, and she went forward to kiss the countess with genuine affection. When Anne smiled briefly, Margaret saw she had lost many of her teeth, and having already had one pulled at the back of her own mouth, prayed she would not be as unlucky as the countess.

It was Anne's first visit to Hesdin, and she gazed around her in wonder at the rich wall hangings, the velvet canopy above the ducal seat emblazoned with the arms of Burgundy and the brightly painted ceiling. It paled beside her castles of Middleham and Warwick.

"You look magnificent, your grace," Anne whispered to Margaret as they processed from the presence chamber to the great hall for the banquet. "I feel like a plain mouse beside you."

"You do yourself a disservice, countess. But thank you for the compliment."

In her new purple gown trimmed with ermine, the tightly fitted bodice sewn all over with seed pearls, and her heart-shaped headdress trimmed with gold, Margaret eclipsed every woman in the room. She wore her wedding necklace—its lost M since replaced—and her fingers were heavy with rings. Anne was immensely proud of her countrywoman, and she noticed the deference with which Charles treated his wife. A queen could not have been more regal than Margaret that night.

Warwick was charming, flattering and diplomatic throughout the twenty courses that were brought in, each more elaborate than the next. Charles was ready to show this powerful noble how wealthy he was. Indeed, he had greeted Warwick on the steps of the castle wearing a hat encrusted with so many jewels that he complained of a stiff neck the first time he wore it.

When the feast ended and the tables were pushed aside, Warwick led Margaret out for the first dance. It was a stately *basse danse,* and much of it allowed for conversation to take place. As was customary, Margaret's eyes were cast down, but Warwick found her very far from demure.

"There is talk, my lord, of an imminent invasion of France by my brother. Can this be true?"

She felt Warwick's fingers in hers tighten slightly, but his tone was light. "I do not believe Edward will attempt such a thing, your grace. Although it may be to your husband's benefit if he did, Edward has more domestic matters to attend to. And besides, until Duke Charles repeals the edicts against our cloth, Edward is not well disposed to helping him."

"Domestic matters, my lord? Are you meaning his family—*my* family?" Margaret knew all too well the earl was referring to the little rebellions that had festered throughout the autumn months, which had been quelled easily, but she feigned innocence. She was unprepared for the vehemence in Warwick's response.

"The Woodvilles, aye," he hissed. "Upstarts and ladder climbers, all of them. Your brother did himself and the country a disservice when he married into that family, your grace. Surely you must agree."

" 'Tis not for us to judge the king's decisions, my lord. I believe that is called treason," Margaret murmured, wondering how far the earl's obvious hatred was leading him. "But I will forgive you, as, certes, you are a loyal Englishman and devoted to our house. Your close friendship with George is proof of that." Her meaning was clear. "And he is intent on wedding your Isabel, is he not?—against Edward's wishes."

Warwick missed a beat in the steps and almost stumbled. Only Margaret noticed. "Have a care, duchess. 'Tis not a woman's place to meddle in politics."

"Ah, but these are family matters, my lord, not politics," she said coyly. And for a second she lifted her head and gave him her most disarming smile. How she wished she could entice him to walk through Duke Philip's mechanical chamber. She almost laughed imagining him soaked through and covered in soot.

WARWICK VISITED CHARLES several times in April and early May while at Calais, and when news came later that summer of more serious rebellions in England, no one except Margaret imagined the affable earl had anything to do with them. On the thirteenth of May, Charles was honored by proxy with membership in the order of the Garter in Warwick's presence, and it was said Edward once again sought Warwick's advice. Why should Edward have suspected him?

MARGARET KNEW BY the time her twenty-third birthday came and went that she was not with child. She could not believe her prayers had gone unanswered and found herself melancholy for several weeks afterwards. Every night, Fortunata held her mistress's head on her short lap and comforted her. The dwarf was back in Margaret's good graces, and even Marie no longer tried to come between them. Although she still helped other servants with their ailments, she accepted her punishment and had not attempted to prescribe for Margaret since her return from Bruges.

Spring was turning to summer, and on a beautiful late May day, Margaret was given a *joyeuse entrée* into Ghent, the political center of Burgundy, with Mary by her side. She chose to wear her scarlet cloth of gold mantle and the little gold crown Edward had had made for her wedding. Until they saw the towers of Ghent and the enormous twelfth-century castle that dominated the landscape come into view, Margaret and Mary had traveled on horseback.

Now her chariot was brought to the front of the cavalcade, and Marie and Beatrice put her mantle around her and settled her onto the upholstered chair, Mary on cushions beside her. The gilded and silk-draped chariot framing the two young women seated in it received the acclaim of the more than fifty thousand citizens of Ghent as they traveled along the River Lys and into the port, where ships unloaded wheat onto the Korenlei quay or vegetables and herbs onto the Graslei on the other side. The massive castle of Gravensteen had been visible for at least a mile, and now they stopped on St. Michael's Bridge so that Margaret could see straight up the river to the fortress that was the judicial seat of the city.

"I am happy that is not to be our home. 'Tis rather forbidding," she said to Mary, who nodded. Any more conversation was drowned out by hundreds of musicians and singers who welcomed Margaret into their midst by singing the song of Burgundy, which Margaret was beginning to tire of because Charles insisted it begin and end every ceremonial occasion.

> "Long live Burgundy is our cry,
> So be it in thought and deed,
> none other shall we have, for thus we feel,
> And thus we wish it ever to be . . .
> All together, we pray you, let us sing
> To this great and joyous entry. Long live Burgundy."

But she smiled and waved to the cheering crowds on either side of the river. A stage had been set up and a play was enacted, the three tall spires of Ghent visible in a line behind the stage: the Belfort, St. Bavo's Cathedral and St. Nicholas's Church. Margaret looked about her and admired the step-gabled houses along the quays reflected in the still, dark water, the long low Butchers' Hall just visible at the bend in the river.

A huge procession of merchants, guilds, priests and city dignitaries accompanied her out of the bustle of the thriving center and to the gate of the Ten Waele Palace on the outer edge of the city. There she was honored with speeches and gifts from the burghers and mayor before her chariot and household disappeared through the porticoed gatehouse.

Once inside the palace wall, Margaret asked to leave her vehicle and stretch her legs for the final entry into the palace. Guillaume handed her out onto the wide walkway that bordered the moat. The graceful three-story palace rose out of the water beyond. She walked slowly over the little wooden bridge and admired the island with its hexagonal formal garden on the southern side of the palace. Indeed, the whole palace seemed to be floating in the lake, its crenelations of step-gabled facades reflected in the dark waters that were home to dozens of swans and flocks of geese and ducks.

"I think I shall like being here, Mary," she said to her stepdaughter, who was holding her hand and looking expectantly up into her face.

"Aye, belle-mère, I know you will. And see over there"—she pointed to a group of buildings at the far end of the palace walk—"that is where we keep the wild animals. My pet giraffe is there and lions."

"Lions!" Margaret cried. "We have lions here? I shall have to keep Astolat by my side always. But later, when we are rested, ma chérie, we will go and visit the lions."

"And my giraffe, belle-mère," Mary enthused. "I have missed Raffi."

Margaret suddenly laughed and turned to seek out Fortunata, but she need not have worried. Her shadow was there. "Oh, pochina, you remember our game? Perhaps I shall add my own name to the list—Mistress Longneck. I think I must look like a giraffe. Especially with this spire on my head." She tapped the two-foot-high hennin anchored securely to the black velvet band that covered the front of her hair. She continued to laugh at her own joke as she processed through another gate and into the inner courtyard.

"At last, Beatrice, our mistress is losing her melancholia," Fortunata whispered in English to the older woman, and Beatrice crossed herself and nodded thankfully.

CHARLES EVENTUALLY JOINED her in Ghent, and soon they had another visit from Warwick. This time, though, the earl wanted to speak with Margaret alone. They took a turn about the wide, white-stoned walkway, both acutely aware that the other was wary.

"I could not let this anniversary of your marriage last year go by without congratulating you, your grace. From all accounts it was a splendid affair, was it not?"

"Aye, my lord, it was. I had not expected such a celebration, especially knowing that Charles had no love for the house of York," she acknowledged. "But I doubt you have come to talk to me of my wedding day. Am I right?"

Warwick drew in a deep breath. "You are, Lady Margaret. What I have to say is difficult, but I shall attempt to allay your suspicions." He felt her stiffen. "Nay, pray allow me to finish, if you would be so kind." He paused, and Margaret felt her palm sweating atop his silk sleeve. They walked along in step, the earl seemingly comfortable and at ease, despite the awkwardness of his overly long boot points. She did remark, however, that he spoke English with her and he glanced warily over his shoulder before continuing. "I want to assure you that my loyalties are wholly with York, no matter what you hear. What I do from this time forward is for England and no other reason."

Margaret stopped still and took her hand from his arm. "And what exactly are you planning to do, my lord, that would require this protestation of loyalty? Does this involve my husband? Are you come to break off the alliance with England?"

She hoped she sounded calmer than she felt, and she took out her kerchief and wiped her hands to occupy herself. The afternoon was hot, and she was perspiring even in her lightest silk gown and thin cambric chemise.

Warwick stroked his chin and stared at the ground before he spoke. "There is too much unrest in England, and it is almost all due to the power of those upstart Woodvilles. Surely you must agree." He did not await a reply. "I fear for your brother's safety, your grace, and for the throne. Your brother George is with me in this. Therefore it is my intent to return and try to put some distance between the king and his wife's relatives. I am hoping you might influence your husband to support me in this—for the good of England," he said again.

Margaret's mind was racing. So that was it. Warwick wants to take back power, she thought, but surely he cannot think to use force in overpowering Edward and bending him to his will. More than fearing for Edward she was concerned for Anthony. What form of distance would Warwick stoop to, she wondered, to rid himself of Woodvilles? Certes, he would not dare kill—or would he? She suddenly was aware that her mouth must have dropped open, as she saw Warwick scrutinizing her.

She took a step back and said in a measured, icy tone, "I am going to pretend I did not hear you say anything, my lord. But before I do, I would give you two pieces of advice. Do not underestimate Edward's love for his wife; and do not come between Edward and George. You will rue the day if you do. If you believe I am a mere woman with no influence, you should think again. I may be just as dangerous as my brother. But given our kinship and your friendship with my father, I will try to forget this conversation. And now, if you will excuse me, I have letters to write."

She turned and walked sedately back over the bridge and into the palace, her ladies and Guillaume hurrying behind her. Her heart was pounding and perspiration dripped down her back; she was glad Warwick could not see how unnerved she was. How could she get a message to Edward? Should she go to Charles?

Stay, Meg, she admonished herself. I must have read the situation all wrong. The earl must have informed me of his idea simply to keep my good opinion. Then again, if I am right, surely he would know I would pass on this information. No, his intentions must be honorable, she concluded; he would not be so stupid. She shook her head to get the confusing thoughts out of it, took off her straw sun hat and hurried up to her chamber to change out of her sweaty gown.

The earl of Warwick stared after her, his eyes hard and his mouth a thin line. Then he called for his horse and within the hour was galloping back to Calais.

At her desk, Margaret scribbled hurriedly.

"My dearest Lancelot, my mother's nephew was here today and I liked not the way of things with him. My heart tells me the man plans mischief so I beg of you to warn my brother.

"A year ago today, I was lost to you forever. 'Tis hard to believe how my life has changed. Know that I keep you in my heart and in my prayers daily—my love, my all. On this third day of July,

ever your Elaine."

THE VERY NEXT day, the duke and duchess moved on to Bruges, where Margaret had another visitor.

"Master Caxton, I am pleased to see you again," Margaret said, extending her hand for him to kiss as he knelt before her. As he looked up at her after brushing her fingertips with his lips, she made a mental note: a badger! With his black and white streaked beard and curly hair, he looked like a badger. She felt a movement beside her and thought, I must tell Fortunata tonight. The dwarf stepped forward, executing a little curtsey. "And I think I am not the only one pleased to see you," Margaret said, remembering Fortunata had seen Master Caxton on more than one occasion during her stay at St. John's. "Fortunata, give Master Caxton greeting."

Fortunata curtseyed again, and Margaret was puzzled to see the dwarf look shyly at the floor. "Good day, Master Caxton," she said, coloring.

Margaret was intrigued, no less because William also seemed at a loss for words. What is this all about, she wondered?

Finally he replied, "God's greeting, your grace. And you, Mistress Fortunata." Kneeling still, he was looking eye to eye with Fortunata, a smile hovering on his lips.

"Rise, Master Caxton, and join me in some wine," Margaret said, determined to worm the explanation for this little scene from her servant later. "I would know how your translation of the history of Troy is progressing."

Although he was impressed that the duchess had remembered his little enterprise, William's face fell. "I regret it has not progressed very far, your grace. My work as governor of the adventurers does not allow me much time for leisure pursuits. Would that it could, but it can't," he said sadly. "I have but five or six quires completed."

"I would see them, sir, if I may be so bold. To have such a collection of stories translated to English is an important undertaking, and you must pursue it." She was pensive for a moment as she chose her words carefully. William quaffed his wine, marveling at its quality and admiring the silver goblet. Fortunata was on the stool at her mistress's feet, and Caxton watched her over his drink. She was looking quite attractive in a black and white patterned dress, the emerald green plastron at her breast complementing her dark looks. In all ways but one she was his ideal of a beautiful woman. She had intelligence of expression, gentle yet humorous eyes and lustrous dark hair that she had allowed him to touch that night under the merchant's hall when he had given in to an urge to kiss her. She was ripe for the plucking . . .

"So what think you, Master Caxton?"

Startled, William almost spilled his wine on his best blue jacket. He had not heard a word as he thought on the memories of his dalliance with Fortunata. Christ's nails, he grimaced, women will be my downfall!

"Your pardon, my lady. I do not think I heard you correctly. A defect in my left ear, you know," he lied frantically. "I should like to answer you as succinctly as I can, if only you would be so kind as . . ."

"I am sorry about your hearing loss, sir," Margaret said, not believing him for a moment, as she had seen him ogling Fortunata. "Let me try again." She raised her voice so much that the others in the room stopped talking, and William had to control an urge to put his finger to his lips. "I offered you a position in my household that would allow you to continue with your writing, Master Caxton. Did you hear me this time?"

Caxton stared at Margaret in disbelief. "I-I did, your grace. Th-thank you, your grace," he stuttered. "But how . . . I mean why . . . no, I mean . . . what would I do? The adventurers?"

Margaret laughed. "Why, I do believe I have rendered you speechless, sir. The adventurers will find another governor, perhaps not as adept as you, but they will nominate someone competent, have no fear. I have need of your advice in all things commercial, Master Caxton, and I would have that advice in English, so I can better serve my subjects here—and our own English merchants. You will be granted time to work on the *recueil*, and I shall be here to help you. Your French, if I may say so upon listening to you last year, is not as good as mine."

"Nay, certes, it is not," William said unabashedly. "But I thought 'twas fair enough for translation. Perhaps not. I should be delighted to show you the work, Lady Margaret." He went down on one knee again, his hand on his heart. "Your grace, how do I deserve this privilege—nay, this honor—to serve you? 'Twould be the crowning of my career."

"Do I understand you are accepting the position, sir?" Margaret's eyes were merry, knowing poor Caxton in fact had no choice in the matter. But she was content that the change in his fortune was not displeasing to him and rose to end the audience. Using the movement to take a letter from her sleeve, she slipped it to him as he kissed her hand. "Then as soon as you can put your affairs in order, I would have you join me in Ghent next month. God go with you, Master Caxton."

William quickly put the letter into his hat as he bowed his way out of her presence. Then he hurried back to the Engelstraat to boast of his good fortune to his fellow merchants. All his life he had worked in the cloth trade. He was apprenticed at sixteen to a silk mercer in London and was then sent to trade in Bruges, where, at the age of thirty, he was finally admitted to the powerful Mercers Company. As governor of the English nation—as the company of merchant-adventurers in Burgundy was called—he was the wool trade's negotiator for commercial treaties with the duke, and he had been on several diplomatic missions to England during his tenure. Now it seemed he was to embark upon a new career, and the prospect made his spirits soar as high as St. Donatian's spire in the Market Square.

One niggling thought spoiled his enthusiasm, however. He would have to put his lust for Fortunata out of his mind. His new mistress would not condone a dalliance in that direction, he was sure.

IT DID NOT take Margaret long to get the truth from Fortunata. The dwarf was mortified that her mistress had guessed something had transpired between her and the merchant and expected another punishment.

"Aye, I should put you out on the street where you belong," Margaret scolded her. "Did you know the merchant-adventurers are supposed to be celibate, Fortunata? Did you perhaps think Master Caxton would take you to wife?"

"Wife? *Non, non, madonna*. I will never leave you." Then she glanced up at Margaret under her thick lashes and smirked. "But William and me had a nice evening kissing at the Waterhall. A lot of kissing."

Aye, and more, if the look in Caxton's eye had told her anything, but she just shook her head and clucked her tongue as if she disapproved. And now she had invited the man to come and be under her roof. How would she keep the two apart? It would be the talk of the court. Then she was contrite. What a hypocrite I am, she thought. I would do the same with Anthony, if I had the chance.

"Do you love Master Caxton?" she asked carefully. "Once he comes here, he will be free to marry."

Fortunata was taken aback by the question. She had not really thought about love. She enjoyed the feeling she had when she was with the man, and he was the first one she had been in any way intimate with. She was thankful to know physical love was a possibility, judging by her body's reaction to William's touch and she was certain William felt nothing but lust. She decided on a safe answer that might arouse Margaret's sympathy, for she absolutely wanted to be with the man again.

"I love him, *madonna*, but I do not think he loves me that much. It makes me sad," she admitted. "Maybe when he comes here, he will learn to love me." She busied herself tidying Margaret's pile of letters so that her mistress could not see her eyes. "You must not worry for me anymore, your grace. Now, excuse me, I must find Beatrice." She curtseyed and hurried away, leaving Margaret to smile to herself.

Little baggage, she has no intention of giving him up. And in truth, I cannot blame her.

15

Autumn 1469

"*E*dward captured by Warwick! Surely you jest," Margaret cried, when Thomas Rotherham, Bishop of Rochester, gave her the news in her audience chamber at Ten Waele. She knew Anthony must not have received her letter in time to warn Ned. "But how could such a thing have happened, my lord bishop? The people followed Warwick? 'Tis not possible."

The bishop chose his words judiciously. "There were several rebellions in the north and Midlands, and the king went to flush out the leaders. Now we know they were instigated by my lord of Warwick and"—he paused, looking at the floor—"your brother of Clarence."

"George! Oh, that foolish boy. Why would he oppose Edward?" she thought out loud. "Why?"

" 'Tis only a rumor, your grace, but 'tis said the earl offered Clarence the crown." Seeing Margaret's stunned expression, he hurried on, "For, as you must know, your brother and Isabel Neville were wed in July. We—the councilors—believe Warwick intends to make his new son-in-law king in Edward's place."

Margaret exploded. "What nonsense is this you speak, my lord bishop! Edward expressly forbade George to marry Isabel."

The bishop spread his hands. "'Tis a fait accompli, my lady. It happened in Calais in the middle of July. As soon as the wedding was celebrated, your brother and the earl embarked for England with the intent of ridding the country of Earl Rivers, his wife Jacquetta, and the whole Woodville family."

"Anthony," she whispered fearfully under her breath. Louder she said, "Pray continue, my lord. I can hardly credit what I am hearing." And yet she was not surprised. Had not Warwick told her himself he would rid England of Woodvilles?

"There was a battle in a place called Edgecote, and the rebels won. A few days later, Warwick disposed of two of the Woodville family as well as the earls of Pembroke and Devon."

Margaret gasped, her face ashen. "Which two Woodvilles?" she heard herself ask as if she were floating somewhere above the scene.

"The father and son, your grace." Again Margaret's heart lurched, but the bishop continued, "Earl Rivers and Sir John Woodville were executed at Coventry. I came here on behalf of your brother to enlist your help."

Handsome John, she thought sadly, he was the same age as me. His only crime was that he had married above himself at the queen's instigation and endured the smirks of the court on the arm of his seventy-two-year-old duchess wife. But rather him than Anthony! Her relief was palpable, but in as calm a tone as she could, Margaret heard herself asking, "And my Lord Scales, is he taken, too?"

"Nay, the king had commanded him to return to his wife's estates in Norfolk until the rebellion had died down. He thought Lord Anthony would be safer there. He is now, however, Earl Rivers, your grace."

Margaret nodded. "Certes, the title passed from his father. 'Twill be difficult to style him thus after all these years. He was my escort here last year, my lord bishop, as no doubt you remember, and he discharged his duty to me with utmost honor and courtesy. I believe I can count him as my friend." Margaret you wanton, she chided herself, the bishop does not need to know this. You are merely talking about him for your own selfish reasons. Speaking his name keeps him and his love alive for you. The bishop smiled politely.

. . .

LATER THAT AUTUMN she learned that Warwick had indeed captured Edward and was keeping him in confinement at his own castles of Warwick and Middleham. However, the earl had not taken full control of the government, preferring to let Edward be his mouthpiece, to which Edward was unusually agreeable. At least the rumor that Warwick was planning on crowning his son-in-law, George, in Edward's place was just that, a rumor, Margaret thought, relieved. She even hoped Edward would come to terms with the earl and they could once again be friends.

It was puzzling, therefore, that nothing came of the coup, neither an uncrowning nor a reconciliation. Instead, a complete loss of control ensued up and down the country, with Londoners rioting and violence breaking out even in quiet backwaters. Margaret had sent a frantic appeal to Charles in Holland, where he was administering his Dutch territories, to give aid to Edward. Charles sent a threat to London that it should remain loyal to Edward and the Burgundian alliance or London would expect his retaliation. Warwick's power was negligible without the crown behind it, and more than once Margaret questioned why the earl did not take it for himself. He was the wealthiest and thus the most powerful noble in England, and yet he stopped short of taking the crown. Perhaps he has honor after all, Margaret decided.

And by the middle of September, it appeared she was right. Edward was allowed to go free, but not before a force put together by Will Hastings, Richard of Gloucester and Jack Howard had begun to move north and threaten Warwick. The earl capitulated and bowed once again to his sovereign lord, Edward.

Margaret breathed a sigh of relief for her brother without a thought for her own position, which could have been an embarrassing one, as the Burgundian alliance had been made with Edward and no one else. And Edward had still not paid her dowry.

She got down on her knees that night and thanked God the head of her family was once again safe on the throne of England.

16

Spring 1470

*M*ary gave Margaret a bouquet of marguerites for her birthday on that chilly third day of May. Margaret was disappointed in having to spend it traveling from Louvain to Brussels, but she was charmed when Mary asked to get down from her horse to gather the early daisies for her stepmother. Margaret promised that they would celebrate soon at Coudenberg.

Traveling always tired Margaret, and so she was sleeping still when Mary ran into her bedchamber in Brussels two days later, followed by an embarrassed Jeanne, and jumped on the bed.

"*Belle-mère*, please wake up! You promised we would celebrate, and Madame de Halewijn and I can wait no longer to spoil you, and here you are still in bed!" she cried, as Margaret opened her eyes to see her stepdaughter's sweet face smiling at her. She rose up on one elbow and rubbed the sleep from her eyes. The sun was already filtering through the pretty stained glass windows in her chamber, and her maids had lit a cheery fire to take the chill off the room. Margaret retied the strings of her nightcap and reached out her arms to embrace Mary. Margaret caught Jeanne's look of apology and smiled it away.

"I did not hear the cock crow, my dove," Margaret said, using the term of endearment she had chosen not only "because your eyes are the color and softness of one, but because in English dove rhymes with love," she had told Mary not long after they arrived at Coudenberg the year before. Mary had clapped her hands and declared she was delighted to have a *surnom*. "Papa calls me child, and *grandmaman* just calls me Mary. My mother," she had said, her eyes sad, "called me her treasure."

Now she reminded Margaret of a rabbit as she hopped up and down on the colorful carpet beside the bed.

"What do you have in mind?" Margaret asked, laughing at her step-daughter's enthusiasm. "Let me see if I can guess." She pretended to think hard. "I wonder if it has anything to do with a horse, a dog and a bird."

Mary clapped her hands. "Aye, *belle-mère*, you are so clever!" she cried. "We are going hunting. Madame de Charny's husband has arranged every-thing. So please hurry."

Everyone laughed at her eagerness, knowing full well that the dressing of a duchess was not a hurrying matter. But Margaret threw off her bedcov-ers, put her feet into her satin slippers and tripped off to the privy in the garderobe next door. The chamber became a hive of activity as the duchess's toilet was readied. Astolat and Mary's favorite greyhound, Doucette, added to the commotion by tussling on the flagstone hearth while Marie did her best to quieten them. Margaret reappeared to laughter and Fortunata's fly-ing skirts as the dwarf performed some tumbling feats for Mary's delight.

Mary chattered on from her perch on the bed while Margaret's ladies prepared their mistress's wardrobe for the day. Over her lawn chemise, they laced her into a simple scarlet gown with a modest square-cut neck, dropped waistline and a long girdle loose about her waist. At the end of the silver and leather belt hung a velvet purse, in which she carried her rosary, her bone-handled table knife, a kerchief and a few coins for beggars or pilgrims she might encounter. As she was dressed, she tested Mary's English and then tried out her Flemish. She pointed to each item. "Belt—*de ceintuur*. Knife—*het mes*. Table—*de tafel*." Her vocabulary was increasing, and she enjoyed practicing the gutteral sounds. Mary nodded vigorously each time Margaret found the correct word, and Margaret's gentlewomen encouraged her with applause.

She had told Ravenstein during the ride to Brussels that she would spend her birthday in leisurely pursuits with Mary. She would not hold any audiences and gave permission for many of her servants to visit their families in the town or enjoy a walk in the Warende. Marie sniffed, but she turned it into a fake sneeze when Margaret swiveled round in her saddle to look at her. "I realize it is breaking with etiquette, Messire Ravenstein, but it was a tradition in my family to spend our birthdays thus, and I intend to continue it." Ravenstein bowed his head. He was glad of the time to check on the progress of his new town house being built in the shadow of the palace.

Today it was Marie's turn to brush Margaret's fair hair. Margaret dreaded those days, but she refused to change court etiquette by forbidding the countess to do it. It was an honor to dress the duchess's hair, and Margaret was sensitive to the fact. But she also knew Marie had not forgiven her for requesting Pierre be assigned to her household, thus ruining her dalliance with Guillaume, and the woman liked to take out her resentment by pulling none too gently on any knot she encountered in the duchess's waist-long hair. She grimaced once or twice, but because of young Mary's presence, she did not reprimand Marie. Once her thick tresses were in coiled braids and a fetching cap and jeweled headband were arranged on top, she studied herself in the silver mirror Beatrice held for her. She nodded her satisfaction, and the two women curtseyed and stood aside.

Fortunata stepped forward, made obeisance and offered her gift. "For you, *madonna*." She held up a kerchief embroidered with a daisy and two initials. "You see, I made the M this way and then"—she turned the kerchief upside down—"M from this way." But from Margaret's angle, all she saw was an M and a W: Margaret and Woodville. Margaret looked quickly at Fortunata, now innocently studying the ceiling, but the servant tilted her head to one side when she lowered her gaze to Margaret's laughing eyes. "Do you like it, *madonna*?"

"Aye, *pochina*, I like it very much," she said, kissing the monogram and tucking the gift well up into her long sleeve. "Thank you." She turned to Mary and held out her arms. "Let us break our fast and then ride like the wind, my dove."

Pierre de Bauffremont, Count of Charny, had organized a splendid day of riding and hunting with falcons. Although only twelve, Mary was such an accomplished horsewoman that she had her own mount, a small palfrey that pranced on delicate legs, ready for some exercise. Margaret's jennet was more sedate, she was happy to note, for although comfortable on horseback, she was afraid of falling.

"'Tis such a long way down for me," she said to Mary as they trotted on the path through the vast forest. "Not only is my horse bigger, but my head is much farther from the ground than yours."

"Cowardly custard, Mistress Longneck!" Mary cried, loving the English term for a faint heart. "I shall teach you how to gallop, for 'tis the most exciting feeling in the whole world."

"Hmmm, I am quite certain it is," Margaret replied, adjusting her knee around the sidesaddle pommel. "But not today, Mary. I am not in the mood today."

"Then watch me!" the girl cried, and urged her horse into a canter. Her bright blue skirts billowed out over the horse's back, and her flapping short mantle gave the impression she was flying.

Jeanne de Halewijn gave a frustrated groan and took off after her, as did several squires. The rache hounds put their noses to the ground and, long ears flopping, followed the horses at a safe distance. Astolat never strayed far from Margaret, and she enjoyed his company on these outings. It was as though Anthony was with her, she thought, ashamed of herself for such a silly fantasy. She longed for a letter from him, but none had arrived for months now. He was at sea, she knew, and there was no way to reach her.

A falcon-caught hare and several quails later, the hunters were ready to fill their stomachs. Pierre de Charny did not disappoint them, and they followed the horn to a clearing where an al fresco banquet of cold pies, fowl, jellies, tarts, fruits and nuts were set out in a brightly colored pavilion in the middle of the forest. They were glad of the tent, as the breeze was chilly and very little sun penetrated the newly leafed-out trees. The horses grazed on the forest grass nearby, and Margaret stretched out on cushions after all had had their fill and slaked their thirst. Mary picked up a plate of figs and Jeanne a pomegranate and they knelt by Margaret, feeding the fruit to her one by one and making them all laugh. Margaret loved the shiny pink pomegranates that came from the eastern Mediterranean and could be kept fresh for many months in the cool northern winters.

"I feel like Caesar's wife!" Margaret exclaimed at one point. "'Tis the way the Romans feasted, in truth."

"You *are* Caesar's wife, your grace," Jeanne said softly, "if Duke Charles would have his way."

Margaret frowned but put her finger to her smiling mouth. "Soft, Jeanne, you do not want Marie to hear you. She will tell my husband, mark my words." Then she clapped her hand over her smile. "See, I truly am becoming my husband's mouthpiece. I am even speaking like him." Mary did not understand the conversation, but as Jeanne laughed merrily, so did she.

A distant horn interrupted their pleasant bantering, and an answering one from their little encampment led two horsemen to Margaret's tent a few minutes later. They were Lord Ravenstein and his squire.

"I would not spoil such a pleasant day, Madame la duchesse, but I thought you should hear the news."

Margaret let Jeanne and Fortunata help her to her feet, and she brushed pomegranate seeds from her skirts and straightened her cap.

"I am obliged to you, Messire Ravenstein, for coming all this way. It must be important. What is your news?"

"The earl of Warwick and your brother of Clarence have fled England and are, if our intelligence is correct, making their way at this moment along the French coast to Honfleur. As Captain of Calais, the earl thought he would be safe there, but the garrison refused to allow him to land, so it is said, as word of his probable arrival as a traitor to King Edward had already reached them. 'Tis said his wife and two daughters are with him and even that the Lady Isabel, your sister-in-law, I think, was delivered of a dead child on board the earl's ship."

"I did not even know she was with child, my lord, but no matter. I am sorry for her." Margaret dismissed the Lady Isabel for she could not believe her ears. "George a traitor!" she groaned and paced about the pavilion. "'Tis incomprehensible. What can he gain from it?" Then she raised wide eyes to Ravenstein, who was already nodding. "The crown! Warwick must have promised him the crown. What wickedness!"

Ravenstein grunted his assent. "And on the way to France, the earl captured many of our own ships and has kept them as booty. The duke will not be happy when he hears this news. 'Tis said there was quite a sea battle between Lord Warwick and King Edward's admirals, the new Earl Rivers and Sir John Howard."

For a few seconds Margaret's heart was warmed when she thought of these two favorites of hers fighting together to defeat Edward's new enemy. In ten short years, who would have conceived that Edward's king-maker would turn his coat? And George! She could not bear to think of George at this moment. To turn traitor to one's brother—'twas a heinous crime. What must Cecily think? She was angry and humiliated, no doubt. Poor Mother!

Ravenstein waited patiently while she processed the information, shifting his weight off his painful leg.

"The earl has always favored France, Messire Ravenstein," Margaret said finally. "Why, even during the negotiations for my own marriage with Duke Charles, Warwick was still trying to push me—and thus Edward—into Louis' clutches. Louis will treat with Warwick, I promise you."

"I fear you are right, your grace, although with Burgundian booty in his waters, he must have a care he does not break the Treaty of Péronne with us."

Margaret snorted. "Certes, Warwick will find a way out of that little problem. Or Louis. They are both as wily as each other."

Ravenstein had called for pen and parchment, and his squire appeared with them as if by magic. Margaret saw him glance at her right hand and take note that she was wearing her signet ring.

"You came prepared, messire," Margaret said, amused. "You are right, we must inform my husband immediately of this state of affairs. Do we know where he is?" Margaret found this question slightly embarrassing. She had long since decided that she did not care where her husband was once he left her after his infrequent visits. "I crave pardon, but with the excitement of the arrival here and my birthday, I have lost track of him," she said hurriedly.

Ravenstein coughed over a chuckle. "'Tis understandable, your grace. We have news he is in Zeeland, and as soon as we have a letter, I will dispatch it there at once."

In ten minutes he was gone. Margaret sank down heavily onto the cushions, moistening her inkstained finger with saliva and wiping it on the grass, all the joy in the day gone. Whatever Warwick was planning with Louis, it did not bode well for Ned.

MARGARET HAD TO admit Charles had done his best to help Edward, and her journey to the great castle at Middleburg in June to beg for his support was in vain. He had even been pleased to see her, calling her his love and his dearest wife. The castle was across a narrow stretch of water from Sluis, guarding the harbor into Bruges, and almost completely covered half of the island it sat upon. The vast North Sea filled the view from her window in the great keep, and she spent many solitary moments gazing across its gray expanse and hoping for a glimpse of her homeland through the mist.

Fortunata complained of aches and pains every morning, and Margaret had to admit the ancient fortress was drafty and unwelcoming. But she had come for a purpose, and she was determined to arouse Charles to action against Warwick if she could. She knew she was Edward's only hope, as in his heart Charles was still loath to favor the York cause. I cannot be too direct, she reasoned, but maybe—just maybe—he might be lured into acquiescing if she caught him at a vulnerable moment. She chuckled to herself as she lay in bed plotting her strategy. Vulnerable was not a word a fighting machine would ever like attributed to himself, but she knew he was susceptible to flattery, and so she decided on a plan of attack.

She invited him to her chamber on two occasions during the week she was there, the first one yielding no satisfactory results. On the second, she fed him tempting delicacies herself, including oysters, a known aphrodisiac, and poured his wine while he lay comfortably on velvet cushions in only his gipon, shirt and hose. At least he is a handsome man, she thought, as she expertly shucked another oyster. She could at least pretend she loved him enough to seduce him, and he was not immune to her advances, when he was in the mood.

"Come to bed, my love," she urged, feeling the moment was perfect—her monthly course was about to start and she was convinced she was at her most fertile. "'Tis the right time for conception, and I would so dearly love to give you a son, a son who will look just like you and carry on your glorious mission." She held out her hand. "Come."

Charles was flattered and feeling pleasantly amorous. He did not usually respond to female artfulness, but Margaret had broken her resolve with Fortunata and asked the dwarf to lace Charles's hippocras with an aphrodisiac, in case the oysters didn't work. Whatever the combination of perfume, revealing gown and herbal helpers she used, Charles was like dough in her hands that night. He even allowed her to mount him and be in control of his body. To her surprise and pleasure, she reached a sustained climax at the same time as Charles, who immediately fell fast asleep and stayed with her all night. The next morning, he eyed her with new awe but said nothing until he quit her chamber, his gentlemen fussing around him.

"I will be discussing the Warwick situation this morning, my dear, if you care to be present."

Margaret was overjoyed. It worked, it worked, she told herself! "Nothing would give me greater pleasure, Charles. Thank you," she said coyly from the bed. He grunted, and jutting his head forward and waving his hand in salute, he strode from the room.

"My most severe gown today, Marie," she ordered, throwing off her false coyness with the fur bedcover. "I would have the councilors know I am a serious person."

Fortunata giggled, and Marie frowned. "Quite right, your grace. 'Tis unusual for Charles to include his wife in matters of state," she said.

The lords of Humbercourt and Hugonet flanked him during that morning's judicial meeting, and as she couldn't tell them apart, Margaret resolved to refer to these most important of Charles's advisers in her mind as The Henchmen. Both were about Charles's age, had black hair and favored long, colorful houppelandes.

However, their speaking styles were so different that Margaret thought she might finally be able to distinguish them. That of Guy de Brimeu, Seigneur of Humbercourt, was short and to the point, but when it was Guillaume Hugonet's turn to speak, she was not prepared for an almost two-hour oration filled with references to Ovid, Sully and Homer. Charles leaned forward in his usual fashion, and his eyes shone with pride for his favored adviser, the man who was so hated in Ghent for his harsh dealing with the rebels in the mid-Sixties. Hugonet's erudition pleased him, especially when it came to flattering him with the usual comparisons to

Charlemagne, Alexander and Caesar. He even applauded a few times, startling some courtiers out of napping on their feet.

"And therefore, your graces," Hugonet concluded, pushing back a lock of coal-black hair that had escaped from under his bright red velvet hat during a particularly dramatic moment, "as Menelaus set forth from Troy with a thousand ships to recapture his wife, Helen, so shall Burgundy set forth to recapture her treasure—the booty stolen from us by the traitor Warwick."

Margaret was not sure the simile worked very well, but she was more than satisfied that Hugonet was advocating an attack against Warwick, and this time it was she who applauded. A gasp went up from the watching court. Charles and The Henchmen turned to look at her as her smile faded and she quickly gripped her hands in her lap, lowering her eyes.

"Madame la duchesse is quite right," Charles announced after a pregnant pause and began some applause of his own. "This is a righteous act for Burgundy, and we shall ready the fleet with all haste to prevent Warwick from escaping back to England to cause our dear brother-in-law trouble."

Margaret raised her eyes and closed her lids once to him in silent thanks as the other courtiers shouted, "Long live Burgundy."

PART THREE

A Dutiful Duchess

Burgundy 1470–1477

17

1470–1471

Despite the best efforts of the Burgundian and English fleets—and Margaret credited Charles with at least a halfhearted effort—Warwick and George eluded them and landed in England later that summer. It was as though Edward had forgotten the lessons of the year before, for he did not heed the warnings from his spies and ambassadors. Edward could not believe his one-time mentor had made a pact with Margaret of Anjou and her warmongering son through Louis and was intent on reclaiming the crown for Henry, who was still languishing in the Tower.

Margaret worried more about where George fitted into Warwick's plans now. George could not be happy, she surmised, after being promised the throne. More to the point, however, was that Edward was caught in Coventry between two armies, those of Warwick and his brother, Lord Montagu, the earl marching from the south and Lord Montagu, who had finally deserted Edward, from the north. Edward, Richard, Anthony, Will Hastings and two hundred adherents streaked for the coast, found whatever ships they could at King's Lynn and fled the country on the second of October, Richard of Gloucester's eighteenth birthday.

"Edward is fled? You say he is in Holland? How can this be?" Margaret was in tears, and Ravenstein was taken aback. He had credited the duchess with too much sense to resort to weeping. He gestured behind his back to signal to her ladies that their mistress needed them, but Fortunata was already there, pouring her some newly pressed cider from the palace orchard and soothing her.

"Drink this, *madonna*. It is good apple juice. It will calm your belly. You must thank the Virgin Mary for giving a good landing to your brothers—and his friends," she emphasized, meaning Anthony. "Maybe you will see them soon, *madonna*. 'Tis not so bad."

Margaret raised her red eyes. "Aye, 'tis true, I should thank God for their safe delivery." She sniffed loudly and crossed herself. "I shall ask my husband if they may come here."

Ravenstein doubted that Charles would allow the exiles to travel wherever they chose, especially in view of Edward's lack of funds. It was said that he arrived near the small port of Alkmaar after being chased by Hanseatic pirates and getting stuck on a sandbar and could only offer the captain of the ship that rescued him a fur cloak as payment for the voyage of two hundred stranded Englishmen.

"Your brother is lucky he landed in that part of the duchy where Louis de Gruuthuse is governor, your grace. Gruuthuse has always been a supporter of your house, and King Edward will find a safe haven in The Hague with him," Ravenstein said, relieved that Fortunata had succeeded in stemming the flow of tears down Margaret's cheeks. "I promise I will add my voice to yours to suggest that Duke Charles might allow your brothers to visit you, but I cannot promise he will agree, you understand. Politically, 'tis awkward for the duke to have them here. And without upsetting you further, I respectfully submit that you are in a rather embarrassing position."

He had Margaret's attention now, and he shifted from one leg to the other, trying to ease his gouty foot.

"I beg of you sit, messire," Margaret said, seeing him grimace. "Guillaume, fetch Messire Ravenstein a chair, and Fortunata, put a stool close so that he can rest his leg." She waited until the grateful adviser was comfortable before firing off her next question, her tears forgotten. "What embarrassing position do you mean?"

"You are the sister of a penniless exiled king, your grace," Ravenstein said softly. "Charles's councilors will remind him of this, and they will remind him that Edward has not yet paid your dowry. I would not make too many demands at present, 'tis all," he finished nervously.

Margaret slumped back in her chair and stared up at the canopy above her, where her own marguerites and device, *bien en aviengne*, were woven into the heavy fabric. "Good will come of it" was the motto she had chosen when she first came to Burgundy, and she knew she must believe in it now of all times.

"I am grateful for your honesty, messire. In truth, I had not grasped my precarious position because of concern for my brothers." And Anthony, she stopped herself from saying. She gave a short laugh. "Life is never dull, is it?"

"I have not found it so, your grace," Ravenstein said, relieved that the duchess had found her sense of humor once more. "And never, it seems, around you."

"You are a brave man, Messire Ravenstein," she chuckled. "And so how should we proceed from here?"

It was three months before Margaret was once again enfolded into Edward's ample embrace. She patted his belly. "Why, Edward, what have you been doing since I have been gone? Or is this extra padding a new English fashion?" she teased, her excitement at seeing him overstepping the bounds of court courtesy. His gown appeared shabby beside the Burgundian courtiers, but she assumed that with little money at his disposal he must have done the best he could to replace the clothes he had landed in. What a sorry mess, she thought.

Edward was equally happy to see his little sister and merely laughed at her remark. "It seems I no longer have the power to cut off your head even if I wanted to, Meggie. You, on the other hand, are a sight for sore eyes, as I have said many times. Jack Howard was right. You are magnificent." He held her away from him and inspected her from the top of her two-foot hennin with its gold filigree decoration to the tips of her elongated red crakows that protruded beneath the sable hem of her velvet gown. Her face had lost its young plumpness, and he had to admit she was fair. He immediately spotted the rose brooch pinned proudly to the center of her gown and smiled. He knew he was truly among friends.

Despite his increased girth, Margaret noticed that Edward's face reflected the heavy burdens he had had to bear in the past year, and she put her hand up to stroke his cheek.

"You look tired, Ned. Come and sit by the fire. I would hear how Lord Gruuthuse has been treating you."

Charles had allowed his wife a private audience with her brother at Hesdin during the frozen month of January, and Edward was grateful to have the chance to speak English alone with Margaret. He filled her in on his exile and how Gruuthuse had welcomed him and Richard with all courtesy. They were now guests in his town house in Bruges.

"And have you heard," he exclaimed, a grin spreading over his handsome face, "that Bess gave me an heir in November? Young Edward is healthy, it appears, and looks like his mother."

"Aye, I heard, Ned. You must be relieved and happy. How I wish I was able"—She broke off and changed the subject. "How is Anthony?" she asked nonchalantly.

"Rivers remained in Bruges to deal with some shipowners," Edward replied, unsuspecting. "'Tis vital we get a fleet together and go and reclaim the throne. Your dear husband seems to be dragging his feet on this. I was hoping you had used your womanly wiles on him," he chortled.

"Ha! You jest, Ned. Charles has not the slightest interest in me as a woman, nor in any woman, it seems. But he does seem to appreciate my brain, big brother. Something you never did," she retorted.

"Not interested in women?" Ned sat up in the cushioned settle. "Do not tell me Charles is a sodomite, Meg?" He groaned. "What have I sent you to? No wonder you have not produced an heir."

"Nay, he is not that . . . hideous word," she said, and chose to ignore his final remark. "He does not seem to need to bed anyone. He is happier to be in a tent, on a battlefield, riding fully armed on a horse and with his precious soldiers than at home with his wife and daughter, 'tis all. There is no love between us, but he respects me, in truth."

"I am sorry for you, Meg. But now I understand why the man received me in Aire wearing the most elaborate suit of armor I have ever clapped eyes on. All but the codpiece sparkled with jewels. I was glad of my six feet three inches, otherwise I swear to you I might have felt small." They both laughed, and Edward asked, "So have you taken a lover?"

He was so matter-of-fact that Margaret laughed again. "'Tis your way, I know, and it is not that I do not crave love, I do, but I am the duchess, in case you have forgotten. I must set an example to my ladies and most of all to Mary." She paused, apparently sizing him up for a second. He was intrigued; she was about to reveal something, he was sure. But she said nothing.

He suddenly remembered he had something for her. "I almost forgot," he said, pulling a letter from the pouch on his belt. "I promised to give you this. 'Tis from Rivers, who—" He got no further, for Margaret had snatched the missive away from him. "God's bones, Meggie, you are behaving like a bitch in heat!" Then his eyes widened. "So that is the way of it. You and Rivers did finally rumple the bedsheets before you left our shores. Certes, I should have guessed."

"You guessed nothing, Ned," Margaret retorted, but she was blushing. Edward studied his nails and waited, amused. "Anthony and I . . . well, we . . . well, we love each other," she finally blurted out. "But that is all! We have never consummated that love, I swear to you. I came to Charles a virgin. Just ask him!"

"Meggie, Meggie, calm down." Ned laughed. "I believe you, although I trust you now regret not giving in to Anthony when you had the chance."

"He is an honorable man, Ned, and you would do well to emulate him," Margaret replied. "He believes in his marriage vows, unlike some I know." She raised an eyebrow and grinned at him. "But enough about me. What is the news of home—of England." She said the word wistfully, and Edward reached over and patted her hand.

"There is some hope for us, Meg. Warwick released poor mad Henry from the Tower and set the crown back on his head. Then he waited for her high and mightiness, Queen Margaret, to appear from France with an army. I believe he still waits. The people are not happy being governed by a puppet king, I am told, so as soon as I can get some ships, we shall return and take back what is ours. I know not what keeps the She-Wolf in France, but I pray daily she dallies with Louis until I can leave here."

"And George?" Margaret had dared not say his name till then. "That foolish boy."

Edward exploded, leaping to his feet and startling Astolat from his warm spot near the fire. The dog barked and frolicked around Edward, expecting him to play.

"Down, Astolat!" Fortunata commanded, appearing from nowhere and grasping the hound around its neck. "Lie down."

Edward strode about the room, his hands locked behind his back and his face grim. "George has committed treason, Margaret. He was prepared to overthrow me and have Warwick put him on the throne. Foolish boy? Nay, I am ashamed to say my brother is a measly-mannered *man*, more's the pity. And to think Dickon is the younger. Why, he has more strength of character in his little toe than George. I know he is your favorite, Meg—no, do not deny it—but I fear your loyalty is misplaced. I have given him everything, the ingrate."

"Except a role to play, Edward," Margaret said quietly. "I do not condone his treachery, but all of us have contributed to his dissatisfaction with his lot. I can see that now from a distance. He was spoiled by our mother and by me and by all who admired his good looks and charm. But he had no role to play in your court. Warwick took advantage of that and offered him a chance for glory. I suppose I cannot blame him."

Edward stopped pacing and looked at her. "You certainly do have all the brains in the family, Meg. Your explanation is so simple and yet so true. I believe that with Henry on the throne and no chance left for George, his family ties may yet bind him to me. Let us all work together on that. Will you write to him? He will always listen to you. And Mother is trying to turn him back to me. Sweet Virgin, I hope we succeed. I would dearly love both my brothers by my side when I rout the Lancastrian rebels out of England once and for all."

"Amen to that, Ned, amen," Margaret nodded.

SHE OPENED THE heavy oak door into the private chapel and stepped inside. It was cold and dark at the back where she and Fortunata were standing. The altar at the other end of it was illuminated, as she had hoped, and wrapping her mantle around her, she dipped her finger into the holy water, genuflected and signed herself before moving forward into the candlelight. Fortunata stood guard at the door.

"*Salve Virgo virginum,*" she began to intone, glancing towards the vestry door near the altar. There was no sign of a chaplain and it being long after Compline, she suspected the holy fathers were all abed, as was the rest of the ducal household. She prayed to St. Margaret that Charles would not take it into his head to visit the chapel at the same time, because she would not want him to catch her reading another man's love note. "St. George, saint of England and Charles's own favorite, pity this poor woman in sin. But I have need of your protection for just a few minutes. Let me not be disturbed, I pray you." All was silent.

"Marguerite, I must see you. I cannot bear to be so close and not have the chance to see you in the flesh. Say you will meet me. I will be wherever and whenever you wish. But hurry, my love, Edward will soon have ships enough to return to England and I must away with him."

A familiar verse ended the letter and Margaret remembered reading *Love for a Beautiful Lady* one rainy day in Greenwich and being much moved.

> *"So fair she is and fine,*
> *A lovely neck she has to hold,*
> *With arms and shoulders as men wold,*
> *And fingers fair for to enfold.*
> *Would to God that she were mine."*

" 'Tis my devout wish, Anthony," she whispered and kissed the words. Her heart pounded, and she looked around, wondering if Fortunata could hear it. The dwarf was on her knees in prayer as well, and it seemed only Margaret was aware of her noisy heart. Seeing Anthony was all she fantasized about every night before she fell asleep. When she had knowledge he was indeed escaped to Holland with Edward, she imagined a meeting, a joyous reunion. Only in your dreams, Margaret, she told herself. Not for the first time she cursed that her life was not her own, that she could not go and come as she pleased. But now he was asking her to arrange a meeting. She thought quickly and then called to Fortunata.

"*Pochina,* I need your help." As she relayed Anthony's message, she took a taper from the altar and held the flame up to the letter. As soon as the parchment caught fire, she let it drop to the floor and watched it disintegrate into ashes. "Next month we go to Lille and then to Ghent. I need you to find a suitable place en route where I can meet Anthony. It must be in secret, you understand, and I think 'tis easier for me to escape when we are on the road and not at Lille or Ten Waele. The most difficult problem is escaping from Marie. I cannot allow her to suspect anything. She is like a coiled snake, waiting to sink any poison into Charles that will lower me in his eyes."

Fortunata nodded. "*Madonna,* do you know de Charny's mother is dying?" Margaret shook her head, but then she saw the possibility.

" 'Tis perfect, *pochina*! I will be the kind duchess and allow her leave to go and visit her dying mother. You are so clever," Margaret exclaimed, clapping her hands. Then, remembering where she was, she looked around nervously. "Come, let us go to bed, and in the morning you will fetch Master Caxton—you will not be unhappy to do that, I imagine—and I will send him to Bruges to take care of my business."

"And you will send a letter to Lord Anthony with him, milady?"

"Aye, Fortunata, he shall indeed have a letter for Lord Anthony." Her heart singing, Margaret took Fortunata's hand, and they hurried back to the duchess's apartments.

A FULL MOON guided the small party on horseback through the flat countryside along the Leie River shimmering with moonglow as it flowed towards Ghent. Margaret prayed she could count on the discretion of the three people in her company. She had spent many hours on her knees praying to St. Valentine to intercede for her with God for the sin she was contemplating.

Once her mind was made up, Margaret enlisted Fortunata's help in setting her plan in motion, and now there was no turning back. Fortunata was the only one of the three she knew would die before betraying her mistress, and she had to believe the dwarf's assurances that William Caxton could be trusted as well. She turned back in her saddle to look at him, and he raised his hand in salute.

Out of sight of the little village of Peteghem, William's eyes scanned the meadows for any sign of ruffians. The hard life inside the cities had made outlaws of many a poverty-stricken man, and in the dead of night, a traveler was doubly at risk. He had been surprised one evening a fortnight before when Fortunata had asked him to receive the duchess in his little scriptorium. He assumed she wanted to see his progress on the *Recueil* translation and so, after asking a servant to sweep out and replace the old rushes in his sparsely furnished room, he had laid out several pages for her perusal. He changed into his best pourpoint, ran a comb through his curly hair and checked to see there were no holes in his hose. Not long after, Fortunata had knocked on the door and Margaret swept in. Marie had already left the palace to go to her mother's deathbed, and no one else in Margaret's train would ever have questioned any of her movements, let alone a private visit to her English adviser.

William had bowed and then knelt on the floor as was customary, but Margaret told him to rise while she walked slowly around the table, inspecting the manuscript. "You have a neat hand, Master Caxton, and I look forward to reading this at my leisure, but I confess this is not why I came." She had then proceeded to ask for his help.

William stared at Margaret's back now as they galloped towards Ooidonk Castle, a stronghold of the lords of Nevele a few miles from Peteghem, where the duchess had stopped for the night. He grinned to himself. He had not been an adventurer all those years for nothing, and they were most certainly on an adventure tonight. He hadn't asked for any details except those concerning Margaret's safety, and he was happy to put himself at her grace's disposal. The duchess had given him a new lease on life when she asked him to join her household, and it was a dream come true to be able to delve into his beloved writing with the blessing of his patron. In addition, she was his rightful sovereign's sister, he reminded her that night in his chambers; therefore he would ride anywhere and do anything she desired. He had been rewarded with a smile that charmed him.

The one Margaret most worried about was Guillaume, who rode beside her with Fortunata in the pillion saddle clinging on for dear life. Guillaume de la Baume, Lord of Irlain, and member of a noble Franche-Comté family, had been married to Henriette de Longwy in Margaret's and Charles's presence in the private chapel at Hesdin a little before the Christmas celebrations.

Margaret was pleased with her choice for him. Henriette was sixteen and one of her own maids of honor, a pretty young woman who had all but swooned when the match was proposed. Guillaume was grateful that

Margaret had not dismissed him over the Marie de Charny affair nor had ever mentioned it again, and he was ready to do anything she asked. Henriette was descended from the old counts of Burgundy and would bring a substantial dowry to the marriage. In return, the girl fulfilled her fantasy of attracting and winning the most desirable young man at court.

But had Margaret really bought his loyalty? "How much farther, Guillaume?" she now called to him, her breath a vapor in the cold air. "I thought it was only two or three miles."

"You will see the turret through the trees in a few minutes, your grace, never fear. I know my way. I have a wo—I mean, cousin here, madame."

Margaret hid her smile in her beaver-lined hood. "I am sorry we will not have time to see your *cousin*, sir. You will have to look him up the next time we come this way."

"Aye, your grace," Guillaume said, relieved that he had caught his blunder. He pointed right. "There, now you can see the slate roof shining in the moonlight."

They left the main path, and soon Guillaume reined in his horse under the first group of trees. Margaret and Caxton drew alongside him, and the horses pawed the ground, their flanks heaving. Guillaume put his finger to his lips, and they continued quietly through the trees, the sound of hooves muffled by the mossy ground. They skirted the walled garden and came to an orchard. Taking their cue from Guillaume, Margaret and William dismounted, and they all led their horses, Fortunata still on Guillaume's, through the apple trees to a field beyond. There they could see a charming cottage that was reflected eerily in a small lake.

"'Tis beautiful," Margaret exclaimed, drawing her cloak more tightly around her, "but I would warm my poor feet. Let us go inside."

The house had been built for the children of the lord to play in. It had two small rooms with furnishings that were in a sad state of repair.

"A fire!" Margaret cried, as she stepped into the larger of the two rooms. "Come, Fortunata, warm yourself with me."

"My cousin, your grace," Guillaume murmured, explaining the fire, and Margaret raised an eyebrow and replied, "Ah."

The four chilled travelers stood companionably around the hearth, and in the strange circumstances, they all forgot their positions for a moment. Margaret was dressed in a plain woolen gown that was too short for her, her braids were coiled up under a simple linen coif and she had removed all her jewelry. Only her fur-lined cloak would have given away her status if they had been stopped on the road, but she had counted on her escorts to keep everyone away from her in such a situation. They were to be a merchant family caught after curfew far from their home in Ghent had anyone asked, although both Guillaume and William were necessarily armed.

William went back to his horse and returned with a leather flask of wine that he thought would be welcome, and Guillaume went to a dresser and found some child-sized cups. He certainly has been here before, Margaret thought to herself, but said nothing.

"Soft, I think I hear someone," Guillaume said, moving into the first room, his hand on his shortsword. He returned in a flash. "There are two horsemen, your grace. I pray 'tis your friend. I am not in the mood for a fight."

"Take my cloak and keep Fortunata warm," Margaret commanded, her color rising and her pulse racing. "I pray you indulge me once again, my trusted friends. You must be outside this room and not try to know my visitor. 'Twill serve me and you better if you are ignorant of his identity. Do I have your word on this?"

They all nodded their assent and filed out, passing the closely hooded man who was hurrying in the direction of Fortunata's pointing finger.

Margaret was in Anthony's arms before Guillaume had barely closed the door on them. Without saying a word, Anthony threw off his heavy gloves and took her face in his hands. He carefully caressed it as if to remind himself of every precious part: the curve of her mouth, the soft hair on her cheek, the finely plucked brows, the dark gray of her eyes and her delicate skin glowing in the firelight.

Margaret wilted under his intense gaze, love flowing from her eyes as she took in every inch of that handsome face. She touched the scarred ear as if it were something holy and then let her fingers entwine themselves in his long, soft hair. She could feel the whole length of his body through her gown as he pulled her face to his and kissed her, gently at first and then, feeling her lips part, with a passion that took her breath away. She thought she would faint in the heat of their desire. She felt his hand on her breast and she took it and guided it under her bodice so that he could touch her skin and her hardened nipple. He moaned into her mouth, and she knew he needed more.

"Anthony, my love," she said, gently pulling away, but still holding his hand to her breast. "Should we do this?" she asked, although she already knew the answer. "I thought we would spend the night talking," she said with a chuckle. "How foolish was that?"

"'Twas foolish, Marguerite," he whispered, kissing her again. He untied the ribbon under her chin and drew off the coif. The thick braid toppled and began to unwind, just as Fortunata had hoped it would when she had only used a single pin to secure it. "I knew when I saw you I must have you," he told her as he combed his fingers through the braid and let it loose. He stood back to look at her. "Before God, I thought I would never break my marriage vow, but before God, I know I love you more than any vow I have ever taken, and everything tells me 'twould be a sin to deny this love. What say you, my heart, my dearest love? Do not deny me, I beg of you, for we may never have this chance again."

Margaret gasped and put her hand on his mouth. "Do not say so, Anthony. I could not bear it." He took the hand and one by one caressed the fingers with his tongue, causing her knees to wobble and a wetness between her legs. She told him, "I, too, have prayed for divine guidance in this, my love, and if He has brought you to me here, then I cannot deny you."

Slowly he undressed her by the fire, kissing each part of her as it was revealed until she stood naked in front of him, her lithe body exactly as he had pictured it those years ago in London when, dressed in her clinging robe, she had fainted in his arms. He stroked her flat belly and then ran both hands over her hips and around to her buttocks. She stood there mesmerized by his touch, unashamed of her nakedness while he was still fully dressed. How different from Charles, who had not cared what she looked like dressed or undressed.

"Anthony." She whispered his name as though it were a prayer. "Let me disrobe you, too."

His body was beautiful, she thought, touching the auburn hairs on his chest, the well-defined muscles of his arms, and the hard abdomen. Her eyes lowered to his groin, and with infinite care she took him in her hand, gently moving back and forth, and felt him grow. Anthony fetched a moth-eaten coverlet from the little bed and laid it on the floor in front of the fire as though it were made of the finest velvet, covered it with his fur-lined cloak and drew her down. Their bodies threw strange shadows on the wall when they came together as though they were Adam and Eve or the first lovers upon the earth, exploring and discovering each other with wonderment and delight.

Neither thought of their respective spouses that night. There was no need. They both knew God had made the one for the other, and in that lost place and time, their places in the real world were forgotten as they became as one for a few fleeting hours.

THE THREE HORSES and their cargo galloped hard for Peteghem to arrive before the cock crowed. A few early risers at the stables glanced at them curiously, but when they recognized Guillaume, whose size was difficult to disguise, one of the ostlers quipped, "Monsieur le chevalier has been out hunting again! Did you find any game birds, monseigneur?" He spotted Fortunata, her face buried against Guillaume's broad back. "Ah, I see you brought one back with you."

"Silence, you measle!" Guillaume snapped. "My passenger is but a child and a sickly one at that. Enough of your insolence. Now take the horses and wipe them down, sirrah."

The groom bowed low, hat in hand, until Guillaume had helped Margaret down, her hood hiding her face, and William had also dismounted. Then Guillaume carried Fortunata, who took her cue from him and groaned in pain, into the palace kitchens. Within a very few minutes, William was once again ensconced in his chambers, and Guillaume had seen Margaret and Fortunata to theirs. For such a big man he is remarkably nimble, Margaret thought, watching him sprint catlike along the passageway to his quarters. The guards Fortunata had drugged the night before were still sleeping peacefully as she quietly lifted the latch and opened the door to Margaret's chamber. The two women slipped inside, and Fortunata quickly undressed Margaret and then threw off her own gown and slipped into the bed with the snoring Beatrice. *Santa Maria,* but I am happy I was gone, she thought, putting her hands over her ears, although she had no trouble falling asleep as soon as her head hit the mattress.

Margaret shut herself into the privacy of her curtained bed and was too pent up to sleep. She could still smell Anthony's scent through her shift and feel his seed on her legs. Her body tingled at the thought of him as she tried to remember every thrilling moment of their illicit encounter. She was afraid to sleep in case she woke up and found it had all been a dream. But nay, she had another gift from him to reassure her it was not, and it lay under her pillow, waiting to be read night after night. He had written his own *Chanson d'Amour* to her and had had the pages beautifully illuminated with flowers and birds, with their secret M and W a recurring emblem through the little book.

She wondered if she would be with child from the night of passion, but she did not need to worry if she were, she realized. She had lain with Charles at Hesdin only a few weeks before, and there were enough members of her family with red-brown hair and blue eyes should the child resemble Anthony. A child! Anthony's child, she dared to imagine. She hugged herself, and curling up into a ball and tucking her cold feet into her chemise, she finally fell asleep.

She awoke from a dream in a sweat of fear. She was with Anthony in front of the fire, but they were in her castle of Male, not at Ooidonk. A year before, a conflagration in her chambers there had frightened her more than she would admit. She had lost some of her precious belongings from home, including many of her clothes and jewels as well as the book of prayers Richard had given her on her departure from England. In her dream, the flames surrounded her and Anthony's naked bodies, and a voice so terrible it could only have been the Devil shrieked at them, "These are the fires of hell you will know for your sin this night." Dear God, Margaret thought, rising to her knees behind her bed curtains. Look down upon us and forgive us our trespass, she begged.

ANTHONY HAD BEEN right. He and Margaret were not destined to see each other again during Edward's enforced exile in Burgundy. Although Charles promised publicly not to aid his brother-in-law and allowed the Lancastrian dukes of Exeter and Somerset to return to England thinking he was on their side, Charles in fact sent Edward fifty thousand florins and turned a blind eye to the fleet his brother-in-law was mustering.

Anxious for any news of the English party, Margaret was happy to see

Louis de Gruuthuse's ovine countenance in her audience chamber at Ten Waele a month to the day after she had lain with Anthony.

"Messire Louis, we greet you well." Margaret's voice was warm as she extended her hand for him to kiss. "What news of my brothers? I understand you have housed them these past few weeks together with others of their entourage, and for that you have my deepest gratitude."

Gruuthuse's black velvet houppelande swamped his slight form, but he carried himself with immense dignity and was never without the collar of the Golden Fleece about his shoulders. Ravenstein always spoke of him with utmost respect and had told Margaret that Messire Louis had one of the best minds and libraries in Europe.

"Your grace," Gruuthuse began, his voice surprisingly deep for his small body, "I bring happy tidings. King Edward has left our shores for his own kingdom. I left him on board my father-in-law's ship, the *Antony*, in Flushing earlier this month. He was well provisioned and had a goodly number of ships, thanks to the diligence of Earl Rivers—."

"Another Anthony!" Margaret interrupted excitedly. Seeing several of her courtiers looking askance at her outburst, she attempted to explain with more nonchalance than she was feeling. "Earl Rivers is Anthony Woodville, King Edward's brother-in-law. Do you see, my friends. My brother's ship is now the *Antony* and—" She stopped, seeing several people nodding and giving her false, patronizing smiles. She cleared her throat, for once embarrassed in front of her household. "Excuse me, messire, I did not mean to . . ."

Gruuthuse came to the rescue and smiled brightly at her. "No need for apology, your grace. 'Tis indeed a happy coincidence of names. I had not thought on it until you so astutely connected them." He turned and raised his voice so that all could hear. "Let us all now beseech St. Anthony that her grace's brother has a fair wind for England!" The court all signed themselves earnestly. "A fair wind," they echoed.

Margaret could have kissed the little man for his diplomacy and kicked herself for her foolishness. Since her night at Ooidonk, she was certain her adultery was visible to all, and so any moment of behavior that was not usual for her must surely add fuel to any fire of scandal that might be whispered about her. She glanced around the room, searching faces for signs of suspicion, but no one was boring holes in her and many of them were looking bored instead. Part of her wanted to cry out to them, Can you not see I am different? Can you not see I am finally fulfilled? Can you not see I have experienced the ecstasy only poems can convey?

She brought her wandering focus back to Gruuthuse, who was looking questioningly at her.

"What say you, your grace? Would it please you to come and enjoy my library when next you are in Bruges? Our mutual friend, William Caxton, used to come often until you whisked him away from us." His round eyes studied her as she gathered her wits.

"Your library, messire?" she managed. "Certes, I have heard much about your library. Of all things, I would like to see it. Master Caxton shall advise you when next I am in Bruges. My brother of Gloucester spoke enthusiastically of your collection, and Edward I know has plans to enlarge the one at Windsor and Westminster now that he has seen yours." A kind man and intelligent. I wonder if he and Anthony spent time in the library, she mused. Anthony, Anthony! All she thought of these days was Anthony. Suddenly she realized Gruuthuse was waiting for dismissal. "*Adieu*, Messire de Gruuthuse. I am in your debt, in truth, for my brothers' safe keeping and for your good news." Gruuthuse bowed his way from the dais, and she watched as he stopped to greet some of his acquaintances.

Her joy at hearing that Edward was on his way to England was dampened by despair of ever holding Anthony again. And as if to seal their ill-fated love, she had awakened not long after their tryst to find she would not bear his child after all.

As soon as she heard the news from England, Margaret ordered celebrations and fireworks in the city of Ghent. Other cities and towns followed suit in honor of their duchess's family.

> *"To her grace, the right worthy and beloved dowager duchess Isabella, my dear mother-in-law, I give you greetings. Today I received the happy news that my brother's enemies are at last vanquished and he sits again on the throne of England."*

Margaret paused, nibbling the top of her quill as she pondered the next sentence.

Isabella had Lancastrian blood in her veins. Margaret did not wish to offend her mother-in-law, knowing that it was she who had championed

Charles's marriage with a York princess. During the week at Sluis, when Isabella and Mary had visited her every day, Margaret had discovered that the dowager had no love for Queen Margaret. So she decided to write about the She-Wolf's downfall and not dwell on poor Henry. Margaret was determined, however, that Isabella should receive the news by her hand alone, so she knew she could not tarry in her task.

"As I have heard, Edward and his company became separated during the voyage to England but all were safely landed along the coast of Yorkshire and eventually gathered together. My brother George of Clarence was in the west country."

She stopped again, lifted her head and studied the wall hanging in front of her, barely noticing the finely woven thread in so many glorious colors.

George had finally come to his senses, it seemed, though not without much fence-sitting on his part. Once he knew Warwick's new plan to ally himself with Queen Margaret and put Henry back on the throne, he must have given up his dream of becoming king, she thought. She hoped that some of his decision to return to Edward's side was also due to the three impassioned written pleas she had sent him at Edward's behest. She was not to know that George had also been influenced by several visits from Cecily during those months Edward was in exile, and, as everyone knew, Cecily was a matriarch whose influence was hard to ignore.

"But when he heard of Edward's arrival and that men were flocking to him, he was determined to reunite with Edward, praise be to God. 'Tis said he fell on his knees when he approached Edward and Richard, and the king raised him up and they embraced."

Margaret dabbed at her eyes upon imagining the scene of her three brothers together once more and wished she could have been there to witness it.

"Edward now had an army to be reckoned with, although sadly, ma chère belle-mère, you will remember that Warwick's brother, the once faithful Lord Montagu, was now Edward's enemy, having reunited with his brother in the autumn. Edward was marching south towards London, and those citizens were much afraid. War-wick commanded the mayor to parade the feeble King Henry through the streets to give them courage, but I fear it had the opposite effect. As Edward approached, the

magistrates and other leaders opened the gates to him, and he rode in triumph with George, Richard, Lord Rivers and Will Hastings by his side."

Margaret frowned, wondering if she would bother to go into detail about Edward's meeting with Henry, and how Henry had embraced the surprised Edward and with a warm welcome had said he knew he had nothing to fear from his cousin of York. Putting Henry and his advisers in the Tower "for safe keeping" might not reassure Isabella when she read the letter further. But she decided to be honest and related the incident faithfully.

She dipped her pen in the inkwell and continued.

" 'Twas then that Edward proceeded to Westminster sanctuary, where Elizabeth and her children were residing still, and held his son for the first time. What a happy moment that must have been for them all, belle-mère, and I pray little Edward will prove a worthy heir to the throne. Every great leader needs a son to follow him."

Nay, I should not write thus, seeing that I seem unable to bear Charles one, she thought grimly, and she crossed the words out with bold strokes until they were illegible.

"Edward, fearful that Queen Margaret was to land from France with another army, knew he must fight the two Neville brothers as soon as he could. Fortunately, Warwick and Montagu followed Edward to London, and you should know that a battle was fought on Easter Sunday at a place called Barnet, a few miles north of the city. My brother's army was now twelve thousand strong, and I am proud to say my little brother Richard, at only eighteen, led the vanguard for Edward. It was a great victory for us, but it is tempered by the knowledge that two noble English brothers met their ends there. Because my lord the king and brother had heard that no one in the city believed that Warwick and his brother Montagu were dead, he had their bodies brought to St. Paul's, where they were laid out and uncovered upwards from the chest in the sight of everybody."

Margaret decided to leave out the disturbing news that for the first time in any battle that Edward had led, he had given the commoners no quarter. Unlike Charles, who thought nothing of massacring whole towns in punishment for rebelling against him, Edward's treatment of the common people had always given her heart that not all leaders were cruel. She looked up at the tapestry again, its bucolic hunting scene a world away from the slaughter that must have been witnessed at Barnet. God rest their souls, she prayed. She sighed, reread her words and continued.

"Even so, the danger was not over for Edward, for news of Queen Margaret's and her son's arrival from France sent him chasing after her army. They met on the field of Tewkesbury, and this time all was lost for young Edouard, the hope of the house of Lancaster, who was killed while fleeing the battle. Queen Margaret and her new daughter-in-law, Anne Neville, were found hiding in a convent nearby and taken prisoner."

She did not think it was of interest to Madame la Grande, as the dowager was now styled, that Anthony Woodville had been wounded at Barnet, as had Richard of Gloucester. Neither wound was mortal, but Anthony had not gone with Edward to Tewkesbury. She learned that he had been ordered to stay behind and defend London from an attack by another Neville, known as the Bastard of Fauconberg, with a rabble army of Kentishmen. Anthony and his men had fought off the assault and chased the rebels from the city.

Margaret suddenly shivered. A cold draft told her she was no longer alone, and she turned to see Beatrice curtseying to her.

"What is it, Beatrice?" she asked, smiling at her attendant. "I will be finished with this letter soon."

"'Tis Fortunata, your grace, and Azize. That monkey . . ." Beatrice held out her hands in despair.

"Sweet Jesu," Margaret said, exasperated, "Fortunata will not be happy until she has her own monkey, in truth. I will be there anon, Beatrice, I promise. In the meantime, pray ask Guillaume to attend me. I will need someone to carry this letter to Aire."

Beatrice curtseyed again and hurried out.

Margaret penned her final sentence.

"The strangest happening of all, belle-mère, was that when King Henry was advised of his son's death and his wife's capture, he fell into a deep melancholy and died within a day."

I hope 'twas simply a happy coincidence, she thought, as she dripped wax on the folded letter and used her heavy gold signet ring to seal it.

By the Holy Cross, I pray Edward had nothing to do with his death. She shook off the unpleasant thought and replaced it with one of rejoicing in the happy change in her family's fortune.

"Now to deal with duelling dwarfs and a monkey," she muttered to herself. She met one of Guillaume's men-at-arms at the door, a sturdy fellow with an ear missing and a scar across one cheek, and gave him instructions to proceed at once to the Duchess Isabella. As she watched him go, she realized with a pang that she had not had very much contact with the old woman since those festivities in Bruges three years before, and she resolved to ask Charles if they might visit her that summer.

CHARLES FINALLY MADE time for his mother in October after a summer of campaigning on his borders with France. Margaret joined him for part of the month of August, and she took advantage of Le Crotoy castle's position near the fishing village on the bay of the Somme by taking daily walks or rides on the south-facing beach and filling her lungs with fresh sea air. She loved going barefoot, digging her toes into the warm, fine sand with Astolat gamboling beside her and her ladies dabbling their feet in the cold English Channel. It was a happy time—unless Charles was with her. If he noticed a change in her he said nothing, but he left her to her own devices after one night of indifferent intimacy.

"I see you are bored with me already, my dear," he said sarcastically, after mounting her and finding her limp and uninvolved.

"I have a headache, Charles. Pray forgive me. I shall feel better on the morrow, I promise," she said without enthusiasm. Charles grunted and, losing his erection, he called for his gentlemen and quit her chamber. He did not return, and Margaret was relieved but guilt-ridden. She spent many hours on her knees and even visited the tiny new church in the village to confess her longings for her lover. The priest, who had heard many such admissions in his years behind the screen, yawned and gave her absolution. He had no idea the duchess of Burgundy was unburdening her soul to him.

Unusually, Charles came hurrying into her chamber just as she had finished her morning toilette. Her attendants flung themselves on the floor in obeisance.

"Up! Up! And out!" he shouted to them. "I would speak privately with my wife."

Margaret waited until the door was closed. "What is it, Charles? You look as though you have seen a ghost."

She was horrified to see him crumple on his knees in front of her and put his arms around her legs like a little child.

" 'Tis Mother!" he whimpered. "Mother is ill. They tell me she will not last, and I do not know what I shall do if she dies." He was crying now. Speechless, Margaret stared down at her almost forty-year-old husband with his head buried in her gown. His behavior never ceased to confound her. She let him cry for a few minutes and then began to stroke his graying hair. She could not imagine any of her brothers collapsing like this at any news of Cecily's illness, even Richard, who was half Charles's age. Her touch seemed to calm him, and when he eventually looked up at her, his eyes were dry and his look sheepish.

"I beg your pardon, Margaret. Have I offended you?"

Margaret looked down more kindly at him. "Nay, Charles. I know how fond you are of your mother. But until you tell me the nature of her illness, I cannot assess whether she is as near to death as you seem to imagine. Perhaps 'tis merely a *grippe.* Her physicians will soon have her humors set to rights, you will see. But you must pay her a visit. I understand it has been some time since you have been to Aire."

Charles stood up and strutted to the window, the thick muscles on his bowed legs not shown to advantage by the tight hose and short pourpoint.

"Aye, too long," he admitted. "She does not deserve such an unkind son as I am."

"You are guilty of not showing her your devotion, not of having none, Charles. There is a difference. Mayhap this sickness of hers is a blessing for her if it shows you the error of your ways."

He let her talk, and her reasonable words penetrated his guilt-ridden mind and made him nod his head. "You are right, Margaret." He looked across at her, standing tall in her favorite yellow and black gown, simple gold cauls holding her tightly braided hair on either side of her head. Her expression showed no judgment, and so he repeated, "You are always right, my dear. I shall make arrangements to visit my mother this very day."

In that moment, husband and wife looked at each other and understood the relationship they would have from then on. In that one incident between them, Margaret knew she would take Isabella's place, should the old duchess die, and Charles had tacitly acknowledged that a mother was the only female figure he needed or wanted in his life. Margaret's spirits rose. No more pretense of conjugal love would be a blessing for them both, in truth, other than occasional attempts to give Burgundy a male heir, she thought.

Charles walked back to her, picked up her hand and, bowing, pressed it long and hard to his lips. *"Merci, madame,"* he said humbly, turned and left the room.

WILLIAM CAXTON GALLOPED into the castle yard one windy day, the long liripipe on his chaperon streaming behind him and his horse kicking up clouds of sand and dust.

"I crave an audience with her grace, the duchess, sir," he informed the chamberlain, who eyed his dusty cloak and boots with disdain. "Don't fret, I shall make myself look respectable for the meeting," he said. "But I would see her grace as soon as she will receive me."

"Master Caxton, you may avail yourself of the scriveners' chamber over the bathhouse across the yard," the chamberlain said, scratching his groin and adjusting his heavy belt. "Your groom will be housed in the stable. I will inform the duchess you are here."

William bowed slightly and walked away, clutching his leather saddle-bag to his chest.

An hour later he was ushered into Margaret's presence. Her face lit up when she heard his name called.

"Master Caxton, this is a suprise! Come, tell me the reason for your visit." She held out her hand for him to kiss, and he came to kneel before her. She looked down on his kindly face with its black and gray beard and was again reminded of a badger. "Judging from your expression, sir, and from the way you are holding your purse, you have something to show me. Am I right?"

Her heart was racing. She had not had a word from Anthony since he had returned to England and helped Edward secure his throne. Caxton must have a letter for Elaine, she surmised, for him to have left Bruges. But what he brought out of the bag was a good deal larger than a letter. The courtiers crept closer, hoping for a glimpse of the gift the Englishman was presenting.

"Certes, you have finished the History of Troy!" Margaret cried delightedly when she beheld the book, beautifully bound in tooled leather. She rose and eagerly put out her hands to take it, lovingly caressing the binding and breathing in the smell of new leather.

Caxton was beaming and nodding. "Aye, your grace, I have. But I could not have finished it without your guidance and superior French," he said, bowing awkwardly over his knee. "You were truly the inspiration for the work, Lady Margaret," he murmured.

Margaret was amused. "Pshaw! I know not whether you are a mere toady or an inspired diplomat, in truth. 'Tis no wonder my brother employs you as an emissary on occasion." She turned the neatly scripted pages and rejoiced in reading the English words Caxton had so painstakingly copied. She read his preface out loud, even though only a few in the room understood.

"*'My pen is worn, my hand weary and not steadfast, mine eyes dimmed with overmuch looking on the white paper and my courage not so ready to labor as it hath been. Age creepeth on me daily.'*"

She looked at him, her eyebrow lifting. "How old are you, Master Caxton? Nay, you need not answer, but I fear you will have many more white hairs after copying this tome many times. For you will, you know. 'Tis very fine indeed, and there are those who will pay you dearly for a copy in our mother tongue," she told him, smiling. "You must stay awhile so I may read some of it before I will relinquish it."

"I am at your grace's service," he replied. "And yet I have a boon to ask. Will you grant me leave to journey to Cologne to learn the art of the new printing invention? My friend in the Guild of St. John, Master Mansion, has tasked me to learn what I can. He is the finest scribe in Bruges and with your blessing, we may set up in business together. I shall see to it that this book is the first English book to be set in type."

William's earnest face and impassioned plea made Margaret lean towards him and raise him to his feet. She felt a thrill of excitement at his words. A printing machine! She and Anthony had spoken of such long ago at Reading Abbey. The thought of her patronage enabling the first books in English to be set for posterity was exhilarating yet humbling.

"Certes, you have my blessing, Master Caxton. Take as much time as you need in Cologne and keep me informed at all times. In truth, I am as passionate—" She got no further. A small brown creature had flung itself at William and pulled off his feathered bonnet, running off with it and chattering with delight. It ran among the musicians and one tried to knock it over the head with his lute, but the little monkey was too fast. Dropping the hat, it jumped onto a chess table and sent the ivory pieces flying, eliciting curses from the player about to pronounce "check."

"Cappi! Ritorno qui, pronto!" Fortunata cried, emerging from her spot behind Margaret's chair, where her new pet had slipped out of its leash. The animal had no intention of returning, however, and eluding capture for ten more minutes, it scrambled up tapestries, swung from a wrought iron chandelier, and perched precariously on the sloping chimney vent before scampering back across the floor and seating itself jauntily in Margaret's throne.

Margaret did not know whether to laugh or to lambast Fortunata, and she tried to look stern. But seeing the monkey sitting so comfortably in her seat, its bright eyes looking enquiringly at her, she could not forbear to smile. She turned to see William still on one knee with tears of merriment rolling down his face, and, following his lead, the rest of the court gave way to mirth.

Margaret found herself laughing heartily, too. "You have brought the sun into my heart with your visit, sir, and I thank you for it," she said, holding out her hand and ending the audience.

As he bent over her hand again, he whispered, "I believe your grace will especially enjoy the chapter about the Trojan horse. Do not delay in reading it, I pray you." And replacing his hat on his head, he bowed out of the chamber.

MARGARET COULD NOT wait to escape from her duties and spend a few minutes with Master Caxton's book. Her fingers trembled as she turned the pages to find the passage he had alluded to and was not disappointed when the book naturally fell open to reveal a different piece of parchment. Her heart was in her mouth as she broke the seal and read:

"My fair Elaine, you are not forgotten. How could I forget our night together? I fall asleep each night with the memory of your lips on mine, our bodies entwined

and warmed by the fire in the hearth and the flames of our passion. Sweet lady, I have never known such a love could exist and for all I have read every romance ever written! One day, we shall write our own, I swear.

"The turmoil that was April and May has softened into summer and your brother is once again very much in the saddle."

Margaret knew that was code for being securely on the throne.

"His wife is once again with child, and we all pray for a brother to be a playmate for young Edward."

You mean another boy to ensure the succession. Aye, I will say an Ave for that, she thought.

"Your other brother—your favorite, 'tis rumored—and his wife are guardians of her sister, Anne. As you know, her husband was killed at Tewkesbury. She is a prize, and your brother guards her jealously. 'Tis a cause of much anxiety for all, due to young Dickon's interest in the girl."

So Richard wants to marry little Anne Neville, Margaret thought. That would mean George and Richard would share the massive Warwick inheritance. Aye, I think there might be cause for concern. She remembered well the constant quarreling between the brothers in their youth, but those were childish quarrels. What would come of adult quarrels? She frowned.

She looked down at the page again and ran her fingers over the script, imagining her lover dipping his pen in the ink and carefully wording his text. She pressed the vellum to her cheek and whispered his name. "Anthony. My love. How I long for you." She felt the familiar ache in her belly when she thought of him and their night together. At least I have that, she consoled herself. No one can take that from me. She smoothed the letter out on her knee and read the closing words.

"I trust this finds you well, my dearest Elaine, and still in love with your Lancelot."

Aye, Anthony, for ever, she vowed.

A WEEK BEFORE Christmas, with Charles, Margaret and Mary by her side, Isabella of Burgundy, princess of Portugal and granddaughter of John of Gaunt, passed away peacefully at her palace of Aire at the age of sixty-six. Although Margaret knew the dying woman had loved her, Isabella's parting words to her daughter-in-law, spoken in labored whispers from her enormous canopied bed, chilled Margaret.

"You must bear Charles a son, my dear, or all will be lost. Too many hate and misunderstand my son for his search for glory, and Louis will think naught of overrunning our lands if Charles"—she paused, a tear escaping from her rheumy eyes—"should Charles die before you can give him a male heir. France's Salic law does not recognize a woman as a ruler, as you know." She took another shallow breath between the almost transparent lips. "This will place little Mary in great danger. Promise me, Margaret, promise me you will do all you can to give Burgundy a son," she rasped, her eyes boring into Margaret's worried ones. "Swear on the life of St. Waudru, savior of barren women, that you will not fail in your duty to your husband, even if 'tis distasteful to you." Seeing Margaret's surprise, and with every breath an effort, she wheezed on, "I love my son, but I am not blind to his faults, in truth. Isabelle told me how neglected she was in matters of the flesh."

Margaret was horrified that this woman who had lived her life with such excruciating attention to etiquette was talking to her of such intimate matters. She stared at the wizened old dowager, who was holding the cross around her neck for Margaret to swear upon, and she did not know how to respond. She prayed she could be saved from a vow she had no intention of keeping. Dear St. Jude, rescue me, she begged the saint of desperate situations.

Watching Margaret's face, Isabella attempted another comment, but instead a spasm of coughing overcame her as Margaret reached out her hand to touch the crucifix, and three doctors appeared as if by magic, gently forcing her aside to minister to their patient. Margaret gratefully made her obeisance to the pathetic figure gasping for breath in the bed and hurriedly left the room. An hour later, Isabella breathed her last, with Charles holding her hand and a bishop anointing her with holy oil.

18

1473

*M*argaret thought of the dowager's words as she lay half sub-merged in a copper bathtub full of soothing hot, herbal water, a tented screen around her. She ran her hand over her white belly and fancied she could feel the new life inside her. A green woodpecker's laughing call outside the window of her chamber was a welcome spring sound. Knowing herself with child, she had chosen to come to St. Josse-ten-Noode to spend a few weeks at the charming hunting lodge, built by Duke Philip for himself and his family, before the responsibility of carry-ing Charles's child became a public matter.

She had been cheered when she passed the point at which she had begun to be so ill during her first pregnancy, and other than an occasional cramping in her belly, she felt well. The first experience had made her wary, however, and she would not tell a soul until she felt the baby was really safe in her womb.

Her bathing had become a weekly ritual that she looked forward to. It was the only time she had a modicum of privacy, for she let only Beatrice and Fortunata wash her, and even then she would ask them to let her soak by herself for a while. She did much of her thinking and planning there, hoping her cares would be washed away along with the week's grime. Unlike the larger of the ducal residencies, St. Josse-ten-Noode did not have water piped into the house, so Fortunata and Beatrice took turns replenishing the bath with ewers full of hot water, making the steam rise around her and shutting Margaret into her own blissful state. *It will be a boy, Madame la Grande,* she smiled to herself, *and I will have fulfilled your wish—if not the vow,* she admitted ruefully, remembering well the night she must have conceived.

Charles had spent most of the autumn campaigning in the south and east, keeping his borders strong against France, and Margaret had been greatly relieved by this after his rather frequent presence all that year. He missed his mother, she knew, and more than once he had broken down and cried with her. Twice his mercurial temperament had turned his tears into a tirade against his father and his own lot and then into a need to be loved. And twice Margaret found herself drenched in his tears as he failed to achieve a climax at the end of these humiliating scenes. Far from distancing her from him, he seemed to seek her out for counsel even more, calling her his *sage femme* and laughing ruefully at his poor choice of pun.

And then at the end of January, he had joined her in Ghent to welcome Edward's ambassador and old friend, William Hastings, to the court. It was then that Margaret found out that Anthony's wife, Eliza, was ill, and Anthony was talking of a pilgrimage to the Spanish shrine of St. James of Compostella to pray for her. *Will Hastings had no time for Woodvilles after their land dispute,* Margaret knew, and she was puzzled as to why he even mentioned Anthony.

"He seems to be much changed, your grace," Will told her. "I heard a rumor Rivers may have had something on his conscience. He believed it might send his wife to her grave and that he should atone for his sin. I wonder what it might have been." He was staring straight at her and could not fail to have seen the blush that wended its willful way up her neck and into her face. *You weasel,* she thought, *you know exactly what it was, knowing my brother's wagging tongue. Damn you, Ned, a family secret is a family secret.* And once again, the memory of the scene between Ned and Eleanor Butler came into her mind, although Ned had no idea she had witnessed it, 'twas true.

Responding to Hastings, she had somehow managed to announce, "Lord Anthony is a pious man, my lord; I cannot think his pilgrimage has aught to do with any untoward behavior. I am surprised you listen to such rumors, especially when you, too, are the subject of one, and 'tis fortunate Edward does not employ a court chronicler, as we do here," she said, pointing to a small man at a nearby table, whose beady eyes were taking in everything he could see or hear and occasionally putting pen to parchment. His predecessor, Philippe de Commynes, who was Jeanne de Halewijn's cousin, had left Charles's service overnight and gone over to Louis the previous year. The scandal had rocked the court, Charles was furious and Jeanne had been worried for her own safety.

Margaret paused for effect before driving her point home. "The poor fellow would have a hard time distinguishing who at the English court has not had their way with Mistress Shore." She was satisfied to see Will wince. "Aye, we hear rumors, too, Lord Hastings—all the way from London." She arched her brow and dared him to respond.

Will had clammed up immediately, taken aback that Margaret would refer to his liaison with Elizabeth Shore, the beautiful wife of a merchant, who had also enjoyed Edward's favors.

In her deliciously warm bath, Margaret chuckled now, easing her long body into a new position. Her smile turned to a grimace as she remembered Charles demanding that he share her bed that night of Hastings' visit. Knowing Will's reputation, perhaps Charles was worried that he might attempt to fondle her, too. She was surprised by her own laugh as she thought back on that ridiculous insinuation. But 'twas true that her whole mood had shifted when she had been certain she was pregnant. Her joy then was unimaginable. The thought of motherhood helped her with the pain of losing touch with Anthony. She had not heard from him for many months, but now she knew he must have been caring for Eliza and, knowing Anthony, he must surely be concerned about his wife, even if he did not love her truly. If she dies, he will be free, she thought resentfully, but I shall not. As one of the most eligible men at the English court, she could not imagine he would remain unmarried for long.

She slapped the water in frustration, and Fortunata, thinking she was being summoned, appeared at her side. After washing Margaret's long, wavy hair with saponaria, she combed it, searching for nits, before adding a shine with an infusion of rosemary and nettle.

"I have said nothing, *madonna*, but I am certain you are with child," she whispered in Margaret's ear, taking a clean piece of lawn and gently drying the heavy tresses.

Fortunata was not overly fond of bathing, so when Margaret sat up suddenly, sloshing water over the edge of the bath and all over the dwarf, she shrieked and jumped away. Why, the woman is uncanny, Margaret thought. How could she know? But, she admitted, since Fortunata's life was so wrapped up in hers, it should not have come as a surprise.

"Do not say a word to anyone, *pochina*, or 'tis a dungeon and torture for you," she admonished, and Fortunata smiled and nodded, not believing a word.

TWO DAYS LATER, Margaret knew something was wrong. An odorous discharge had been soiling her chemise since her bath, and the occasional cramp was becoming more frequent and painful. Dear St. Margaret, she prayed to her namesake and protector of pregnant women, do not let me lose this child. I am near to my twenty-eighth year and still I do not know the pleasure of motherhood. I know I should have stayed and made my solemn vow to Isabella that day, but intercede for me with our sweet Virgin that I not be punished for that omission. I have given gifts to many holy houses in penitence since, and I cannot think I have not atoned for that one little sin.

She lay on the soft mattress that had been freshly stuffed with down and sweet grasses, trying to sleep and forget the pain in her belly. Eventually the cramping subsided, and she sank into a deep sleep.

She could smell burning, and then she heard the unmistakable crackling of flames licking wood not far from her. She leapt out of bed, but the floor was red-hot, and so she jumped back onto the bed only to find it was now on fire. A searing pain shot through her body as her nightgown became engulfed in flames, and she heard herself screaming, "Fire! Fire! Help me! Oh, dear God, help me!"

The curtains around her bed were flung back. Fortunata and Marie were shaking her awake. Margaret's eyes flew open, and she realized she had been dreaming about the fire at Male again. She looked from Fortunata to Marie with relief until another searing pain made her scream again. This was no dream; it was very real. Flinging back the bedcovers, she saw the telltale red stain between her legs and instinctively knew she was losing the child. She began to sob and put her arms out to Fortunata, who held her close, whispering soft Italian words in her ear.

"*Cara madonna, non ha paura. Eccomi.* I am here, do not be afraid."

More cramping bent Margaret double, and calling for someone to fetch Doctor Roelandts, Marie set about helping Margaret to the little garderobe. For the next few hours until dawn broke, Margaret's chamber was a hive of activity. Her ladies took turns with her in the privacy of the tiny space, where she sat on the padded seat of the privy, expelling the precious contents of her womb, while sleepy servants brought in the copper bath and others followed with warm water and armfuls of clean drying cloths. Roelandts and his assistants stood around the bed inspecting the sheet and shaking their heads, waiting for the duchess to return so that they could examine her. Fortunata eyed the lancets and bowls that were being set out for the ritual of fleeming. Surely her mistress had lost enough blood, even though her body humors might indeed need re-establishing.

"There is too much blood. 'Tis not a good sign," Roelandts said to Marie, adjusting his hastily donned robe and scratching at his scalp through the sparse gray hair under his nightcap. "Something is wrong. Is this the time for her courses?"

Marie thought for a second. She was genuinely worried, as she was Margaret's chief attendant and so should anything happen to her mistress, she could be called to account by Charles. She nodded; she did not want the doctors to think she did not take note of her mistress's cycles. "Certes, her grace must be with child again." Then she remembered. "Ah, yes, Ghent," she muttered. Louder she said, "And perhaps this is a repeat of the first . . . experience?" she said for want of a better word. "Or," she suddenly thought, "do you think she is dying?"

Roelandts rounded on her. "I was not aware the duchess was with child, my lady," he said testily. "No one sought to inform me. But 'twould appear she is losing it, if that is the case." He sniffed and stared resentfully at the door of the garderobe. "It appears her grace has no need of me," he complained. "When you have bathed her and put her to bed, I will

send in a tincture and visit her in the morning. Good night, mevrouwe."
Yawning loudly, he bowed to Marie and left the room, followed closely by
his colleagues.

Another hour candle guttered and went out before Margaret, supported by Beatrice, emerged from the garderobe, her face white and her
eyes frightened.

"Where is Doctor Roelandts, Marie?" she asked. "Surely someone sent
for him."

"Aye, your grace, he was here for a spell, but he decided you did not
need him and so he left." Marie took pleasure in putting Roelandts in a
bad light after the Fortunata disaster. She had not forgiven him for bun-
gling the matter and giving her away. Serves him right if he is dismissed,
she thought spitefully.

Margaret was too exhausted to demand his presence again, and she
allowed herself to be lowered into the warm bathwater, soft towels protecting her from the hard copper sides. Only Fortunata worried that the
warm water might make Margaret's blood flow faster, but Marie silenced
her objection with a hiss and a painful pinch on her arm. But soon the
water turned bright pink, and Fortunata hurried forward to insist Margaret be taken out. Blood was still dribbling down her legs and Margaret
was so weak she could hardly stand as she was dried. With a bundle of
clean rags between her thighs, she was almost carried back to the bed,
which had been changed and freshened for her.

She stayed in the darkened room for two days while the cramps still
plagued her. The doctors finally decided her womb was infected and so
treated her with a decoction of garlic, burdock, liquorice roots and the
expensive powder from a ground unicorn's horn. Much to Fortunata's
relief, the doctors decided against any bloodletting this time.

On the eighth day of April, Margaret was transported in a litter to the
abbey of Dendermonde, where the Cistercian nuns helped her pray for
the soul of her lost child and praise God for her recovery.

As she lay prostrate in front of the gold-leafed crucifix in the abbey's
stone church, she let her tears flow onto the cold flagstones as she tried to
accept what Roelandts had told her.

"'Tis our belief you may be incapable of bearing a child, your grace,"
he had said, unable to look her in the eye. "But we should all pray to

the Virgin that God is merciful and a miracle may happen." And he had bowed and fled before he could be dismissed, leaving her with his awful prediction.

"What is a woman without a child?" she wept. "Have I been so wicked to deserve this?" And try as she may, she could not get the night of sweet but illicit love with Anthony out of her mind.

IT WAS AN early summer like none she could remember. The heat was already intolerable, and even the thick stone walls at Ten Waele seemed to burn from the inside out. It did not bode well for the harvest that year. Already, in May, the earth was bone dry.

Charles had invited her to take part in the festival of the order of the Golden Fleece in Valenciennes beginning on the second day of May, and reluctantly she set out with a small entourage, leaving Mary behind in Ghent. Not only did she hate being separated from her stepdaughter but she also missed Jeanne's company. Guillaume was a dull companion, albeit a loyal and hardworking protector. Even Lord Ravenstein had asked to stay on in Ghent, and Margaret had reluctantly acquiesced.

After four days of excruciatingly slow progress, some in the litter and some on horseback, and some stilted conversation with Marie de Charny, she called upon William Caxton to ride with her. She decided it was cooler on horseback than in the curtained litter, and she fanned herself with one hand while the other controlled her sturdy palfrey.

"Tell me of your time in Cologne, Master Caxton. You have learned much, I understand from Fortunata. I regret I have been unable to speak with you of late, but let us make use of this bothersome journey, shall we?" She tightened the ribbon of her wide-brimmed straw hat under her chin and wished she could throw off her clothes and jump in the Escaut River along which they were riding. She could feel beads of perspiration running down her back. Flies were buzzing around her, and she swatted at them with her fan.

As they passed through a hamlet between Condé and Valenciennes in the province of Hainault, several ragamuffin children ran up to her, begging pitifully. She threw them a few coins and watched as they scrabbled in the dust for them. Guillaume barked an order at one of his sergeants, and several men-at-arms hurried to remove the children from Margaret's path, but Margaret waved them away. She looked kindly at the dirty little faces that gazed up in awe at her, and William was dismayed to see tears rolling down her cheeks. Why, for all her wealth and power, she is unhappy, he thought. He was not used to displays of emotion and so looked away. He was even more startled by her next statement.

"I have been told I shall never bear a child, Master Caxton, so forgive me for becoming maudlin when I see one. 'Twas indulgent of me," she said. "I had no right to discomfit you."

William coughed. "Nothing to forgive, your grace. Quite understandable," he stammered. His embarrassment had been overridden by an intense feeling of respect for this magnificent woman who had humbled herself in front of a mere merchant. "I am at your service always," he said, giving her a steadfast look. "For anything."

Margaret smiled. "I believe you, sir. And now, tell me of the new invention I am hearing so much about. Will you set one up here? I trust you know you have my support in this, providing the first book you print is in English," she said, chuckling.

"Aye, your grace, I have spoken with my colleague at St. Donatian's—where all the scriveners in Bruges are employed, you understand—and we will form a partnership. He is the finest scribe in the land, and I will bring my knowledge of the new machine and my business skills to the enterprise. Your support will guarantee its success, I promise you!"

"'Tis good news, Master Caxton. Perhaps one day you will return to London and set up a machine there. My brother will be happy to give you his patronage, I am sure. And I can promise you, Lord Scales—I mean Earl Rivers—will be one of your first customers.

"But come, sir, I cannot be so selfish as to command your intelligent conversation all morning. I believe Fortunata would enjoy your company for a spell." William was startled once again when Margaret winked at him.

Grinning, he bowed in his saddle and wheeled his horse round to canter back along the ranks until he found Fortunata riding pillion behind one of Guillaume's henchmen.

"Your mistress sent me to entertain you, Fortunata," he said in English so that the escort would not understand. "I did not tell her you had entertained me all night, little wanton!"

Margaret heard Fortunata's merry laughter all the way from the back of the procession, and she smiled.

During the first ceremony's feasting, Margaret sat in a room all by herself and was served by the wives of several of the order, including Marie. She listened to the loud laughter of the men in the hall and called to Fortunata to perform some magic tricks for her ladies.

"Madame de Charny, come quickly," a page cried, running into the room and seeking out Marie. "Your husband has been taken ill."

"Go with him, Marie," Margaret commanded. "Take him to the ducal apartments and have Charles send his physician to tend him. We will await news here. Go."

Marie's face was pale. She called Guillaume's wife to go with her, and they hurried out. Henriette was Marie's pet, Margaret knew, and it had concerned her to see the two women always in each other's company, whispering behind their hands and sniggering together. She turned to see Fortunata gazing at the disappearing figures and was saddened to see the look of relief on the dwarf's face. They are unkind to you, my *pochina*, she realized. How can I stop them? Perhaps if I told Henriette of her husband's wild nights with Marie, it might put distance between the women. But, certes, I cannot stoop so low, although I would dearly love to rid myself of Marie. I am convinced she has hurt Fortunata, but I have no proof. She gave an audible sigh, and Fortunata came to her side.

"Are you unwell, *madonna*?"

Margaret smiled at the little woman's cocked head and dark eyes watching her mistress with concern. She shook her head. "Nay, I am merely sleepy," she said, longing for the seclusion of her downy bed. "It has been a long day."

She did not expect Charles that night and so was unprepared when he was suddenly announced. He strode into the room, his head and shoulders stooped as usual, and the ladies dropped to their knees in courtesy. Without Marie there to chastise him, which, as his stepsister, he tolerated, none of Margaret's ladies dared point out that their mistress was tired and did not want to be disturbed.

Beatrice stepped forward timidly and opened her mouth, but her fear of the duke was evident in her eyes, and he enjoyed roughly pushing her aside. "Out of my way, English lady," he snapped. "And the rest of you, get out!" he growled as he approached Margaret, who was sitting on the side of the bed.

Margaret rose in front of him, and, as always, her height disconcerted him. He turned away and addressed a figure in the tapestry on the wall instead. "I have much to tell you, Margaret, but my time with you here is short. I pray you, give me an hour." The knowledge that her extra inches rankled with him always cheered her. It was the only time in her life that she thanked God for them. His tone was more conciliatory, Margaret noted, and briefly wondered if he might have a kind word to say for the loss of her child.

"My duty is all to you, my lord," she responded, shrugging on her red and black fur-lined bed robe and curtseying briefly. "But I could wish you were more charitable to my ladies. Lady Beatrice is elderly and yet you mistreated her. There was no need." She walked across the tiled floor to pour wine for him. "Sweet Jesu," she muttered, as she felt the familiar itch of flea bites on her ankle. The residence was not large, and much of the household was lodged in the town. Margaret had noticed upon her arrival a few days before Charles that the place was less than clean and had admonished her chamberlain to spruce it up before the duke arrived. The fur trim on the hem of all her gowns was no match for the infestation here. In the morning, she would ask Fortunata to collect some plantain leaves to rub directly onto the bites. All this flitted through her mind as she concentrated on the task at hand and took Charles a goblet of wine.

"Come and sit, Charles. 'Twas a long but successful day. I was much moved by the ceremonies—"

"I came to tell you of Pierre de Bauffremont," he interrupted, and Margaret immediately felt guilty because she had not asked first.

She invited him to sit next to her on the settle. "What is the word? I was about to ask."

"'Tis serious, Margaret. An apoplexy, so I was told, with a paralysis on his right side," he said, shaking his head and sitting down. "They dare not move him for a few days. But when they can, I hope you will send both of them back to his estates. I cannot think he will last long, and Marie must be with him."

Margaret nodded; her prayer had been answered. Marie would go away! She was elated, but turned somber gray eyes to him. "I am sorry for them both, although he is past seventy-five years, Marie tells me." She didn't add that Marie was not kind about her husband and used a limp finger to describe his sexual capabilities. "He has lived a long life."

"Aye, and a noble one. His prowess as a jouster was never called into question. I am certain you have been told of the *pas d'armes,* the tournament he fought during my father's reign."

Margaret quickly interjected, "Certes, she must accompany him home and care for him. I shall go on very well without her, have no fear, Charles. I am not lacking attentive ladies, I can assure you." Sometimes too attentive, she thought, quaffing her wine to hide her grimace. "I shall have Ravenstein appoint another captain of my guard. You should not worry about me. You have enough to concern yourself with. I do not plan on being . . . ill again for a long time." She thought she would give him an opening, but it was not to be. Charles merely grunted. She gritted her teeth into the semblance of a smile. "Where to next, Charles?" She hoped talking about his campaigns would lighten his mood. And it did.

"Now that I have taken Alsace, Guelders and Zutphen, I shall attempt to conquer the Rhinelands and claim more territory for my duchy," he announced airily. This did not surprise Margaret, but his next statement did. "You are the first to know—after my council, of course—that I will soon change the name of Burgundy to Lotharingia and I have every expectation that the Emperor Frederick will crown me king of the Romans in the not too distant future. What say you, Margaret? You will be a queen!"

Margaret was speechless. The man's ego was beyond belief. Charles rubbed his hands together and chuckled. "My clever wife has nothing to say for a change," he said, but the sarcasm was lost on Margaret, who was too tired to respond. "Perhaps I should tell you why this is possible, my dear." Not waiting for an answer, he began regaling her with his achievements, and as Margaret listened politely, she wondered how she could prop open her eyelids to look as though she were still awake. When he came to describing how he had remodeled his army, Charles's eyes blazed with fierce pride. "It is divided into numbered companies of about nine hundred men, and within each company are four squadrons," he enthused. Margaret mouthed "oh" as many times as she felt were necessary to sound interested. "I have put twenty-five men-at-arms, valets, coustiliers—light horsemen, you know—archers with crossbows and archers on horseback, pikemen and gunners in each squadron. It is brilliantly conceived, don't you think? And I must have the only army with bowmen who can fire their weapons at the same time as dismounting their horses," he said proudly. "And you should see the uniforms I have designed. Am I boring you, Margaret?" he frowned as he saw her stifle a yawn.

"Nay, my lord," she protested unconvincingly. "'Tis fascinating, but it has been a long day." She was too tired to recognize the pout and the flushing up his neck that signified his choler mounting. She rose, stretched up her arms languidly and yawned again. "Does the bed not look inviting, my lord? Fortunata has warmed it," she said, removing the copper box full of embers. "Would you not like to rest your—"

She got no further, for Charles had leapt out of his chair, his fists clenched and his blue eyes bulging. "You dare to rise before I give you permission," he shouted. "Do you know my subjects now must address me as 'most dread lord'? Perhaps you should do the same, lady. I perceive you need another lesson in wifely duty."

Margaret froze in her tracks. "Nay, Charles, I beg of you. Let us not quarrel," she tried to sound calmer than the rising panic she felt. She might be taller than he, but she knew she was no match for his brute strength, as she had found to her cost on more than one occasion. He advanced towards her, and she put up her hands to fend him off. "Forgive me if I offended you, my lord, please—" But her words fell on deaf ears. She found herself once more flung on the counterpane, her wrists pinned to the bed. As he sat astride her, staring down into her terrified face, he grinned in triumph.

She tried to appeal to his noble birth. "Please, Charles, let me be," she gasped. She tried flattery. "You are a great leader—one of the greatest the world has ever seen—but surely you demean yourself with such behavior." She protested loudly as in one swift movement, he turned her over on her belly and pulled her towards the bottom of the bed. Sweet Jesu, what will he do to me? she thought, as she tried to grasp the sheets and heave herself forward and out of his grip. He immediately pinned her arms down again and lifted her chemise, exposing her bare buttocks. Reason with him, she thought desperately, bile rising in her throat.

"What would your soldiers think, treating your wife this way? Is this how you behave with them?" Far from mollifying him, it enraged him further.

"My soldiers?" He gave his short bark of laughter as he untied his codpiece. "They warm me well on a cold night in the field—just like this." And without further ado, he attempted to demonstrate what he meant. Her piercing scream was muffled by the pillow.

Her arms still pinned, she turned her head painfully and pleaded, "Stop! Stop! I beg of you, in the name of the blessed Virgin!" She could not move and she could not breathe. I must have died and gone to Hell, she thought, and she moaned helplessly. *Dear God, are you punishing me for my one night with Anthony?*

"I cannot breathe," she tried to tell him, as she felt herself going limp. *I am going to die. But perhaps t'would be better to die now than live with this humiliation every time, even though our meetings are blessedly few and far between. God help me. Somebody help me!*

Her passivity robbed Charles of his triumph and his climax—and saved her life, she was later convinced. He released his hold on her and slid off the bed and onto the floor panting, while Margaret turned on her side and lay still, breathing freely again. It took all her strength to raise herself up, carefully tie her cap back on her tangled mass of hair, and rearrange her nightgown. She stared down at her fully clothed husband, with his privates limply exposed out of their cloth harness, and her heart hardened.

"I have heard tales of your cruelty, my lord. How you threw men tied together off the ramparts of Dinant. How you massacred the innocent of Liège and set fire to the city. How you hanged the men of Nesle on a tree you bought for the purpose. I have refused to believe these stories because I did not want to. Now I know that they are the truth and that I am married to a monster.

"Most dread lord," she taunted him. "As a princess of England and daughter of York, I order you to leave my room and"—she paused for effect—"never return!"

Charles was dumbfounded at her speech. But with his characteristic change of mood after a fit of violence, he mumbled an apology, got to his feet and walked slowly to the door, holding the points of his codpiece in one hand and his hat in the other.

He took a deep breath. "God's good night to you, Margaret. I will see you for the final Fleece ceremony on the morrow, I trust," he said, as he turned the heavy handle. "You have a duty to me."

"I know my duty, Charles. Burgundy will not lack my loyalty, I swear to you. But any love that was possible between us is lost forever. Do you understand?"

He nodded, made her a curt bow and left the room.

Margaret ran to the door and turned the key in the lock and after blowing out the candles, climbed back into bed, bruised and angry. Gradually anger turned to despair and tears began to fall. She heard the watch call out the midnight hour. *My birthday,* she realized with a pang of self-pity. She buried her head under the pillow and wept, thinking back to happier Mays when she had been carefree and her parents had spoiled her on her special day. *Dear God, what do I have to live for? I am wife to a cruel madman who does not love me, nor I him. I cannot have or even see the man I love. I cannot bear a child. My family has surely forgotten me. Oh, sweet misery, why was I put on this earth?*

Suddenly Cecily's beautiful face floated through her mind, and her sobs began to subside. She had not thought of her mother for a long time. Now the memory of their tearful farewell came flooding back, and she remembered worrying that she would forget all of their faces. Then Cecily's words came to her with startling clarity. "God will give you strength to bear whatever fate has in store. Have faith, Margaret."

She thought of the shrines she had visited to pray that she might not be barren, the charity she had provided to the poor and the sick, and the relic she had given to St. Ursmer's Church at her dower town of Binche, and yet still God was not pleased with her. *I do have faith, Mother,* she reasoned, *but it does me no good.* She pummeled her pillow in frustration. *What else did you tell me, Mother?* She tried to remember.

"You should know, Margaret, that your children are the most precious things you have." *Ah, such cruel reminder. But I have no children, Mother,* she wanted to scream, *no children at all . . . except Mary.*

"Mary!" she cried, sitting up and calling the name into the darkness. "I do have a child. A dear, dear child, and I have selfishly forgotten all about her."

. . .

MARY RAN DOWN the palace steps at Ten Waele to meet her stepmother as soon as she heard the cavalcade ride through the gate and into the courtyard. She was surprised by the intensity of Margaret's embrace and laughed delightedly as she pulled away.

"You missed me as much as I did you, *belle-mère*," she cried, her eyes dancing. At sixteen, although still petite, her maturity and womanly curves meant she could no longer be considered a child. But to Margaret she would always be her gentle dove, and Mary was content to love Margaret as a child would her mother.

"You have no idea, Mary," Margaret said softly. It was hard to imagine this sweet thing was possibly born of a night similar to one she had experienced with the father. She shook the thought from her head. She would not denigrate Mary thus.

"And I you, my dove." She had been gone only a month and yet she felt she had aged a year. She had visited Notre Dame au Bois on her way back to Ghent and had begged forgiveness of the Virgin for her lack of faith. The solitude in the beautiful little church had allowed her time to think how to proceed with her life. Reconciling herself to barrenness, she recognized it was imperative that Mary find a good husband so that she could produce a male heir for Burgundy. She wondered if Nicholas of Lorraine was the man. Charles had betrothed his daughter to him that summer. But the alliance was tenuous at best. In the meantime, to ensure the safety of the duchy, she resolved to work hard to keep Charles alive until an heir was born.

"Look who has come to visit me, *chère belle-mère*," Mary now said, pulling Margaret up the palace stairs and into her private solar.

Philip of Cleves stood waiting to greet the two women, bowing low over Margaret's hand. Lord Ravenstein's son had virtually grown up with his cousin, Mary. His stepmother, Anne, another of the late duke of Burgundy's bastards, had been in charge of Mary's governance until Jeanne de Halewijn had assumed that role. Philip was just like his father: tall, aristocratic and blessed with the same hawk nose. A year older than Mary and a baronet, he would have made an excellent match for the heir of Burgundy but for their close kinship. Margaret felt sorry for Philip, because she could see the young man was head over heels in love with her stepdaughter. Mary, on the other hand, looked up to Philip as a big brother and adored him in quite another way.

"Philip, how good to see you," Margaret said. "What brings you to Ghent?"

"My uncle of Cleves is taking me to join the duke's army at Maestricht in a few days, your grace," Philip said pleasantly, "and I thought I would visit my father along the way."

Ghent is not exactly on the way to Maestricht, my lad, Margaret thought, amused, and I doubt 'twas your father you came to visit, but never mind. "I have yet to know my husband's intentions in Germany, Philip." She gave a false laugh, which perplexed Mary. "Perhaps you could enlighten me."

Before Philip could answer, a yelp of excitement heralded the entrance of Astolat, who, upon hearing Margaret's laugh had pushed open the door with his large hairy snout and bounded into the room to greet his mistress.

"Astolat!" Margaret cried, going on her knees and hugging the hound. "You naughty dog, how did you escape?"

A squire knocked and entered, panting, his face almost as purple as his livery. "I crave your pardon, your grace," he mumbled, when he saw Margaret, and he immediately went down on one knee. "He was too quick for me."

Margaret laughed and relinquished her hold on the dog to the young man, who quickly attached the leash. As she got off her knees, she happened to glance at Mary and was astonished to see her stepdaughter's eyes cast down to the floor and her cheeks as red as the young squire's. So that is the way of things, she thought. Poor Philip! I wonder how far this has progressed. 'Tis high time Mary and I had a talk, she decided, thanking and dismissing the squire.

"What is your name, young man?" she asked as he held open the door.

"Jehan de Mazilles, your grace," the squire said, effecting a bow.

"Mazilles? Aye, I remember, your father is the duke's cupbearer, is he not?"

Jehan's cherubic face glowed with pride. "He is, your grace. He is at present with the duke's army, and I hope one day to fight alongside him."

"Do not be too much in a hurry, Jehan. Fighting is not the only way to win an argument." Margaret could not resist lecturing the youth, whose beard wasn't even tough enough to scrape as yet. "Now, I pray you take Astolat outside for a walk."

She turned back to Mary, who was fiddling with the silver brooch on her belt. She has grown up so quickly, Margaret thought, noting proudly how the rich blue overdress showed off the young woman's creamy skin. "Come, children," she addressed Philip, who could not take his eyes off Mary. "Let us sit awhile. I see I interrupted your game of fox and geese," she said, walking to the table on which sat the cross-shaped board. "Who is winning?"

"NICHOLAS IS DEAD!" Mary's anguished cry echoed through the palace rooms, causing courtiers and servants to stop in their tracks and eye one another meaningfully.

"How can he be dead, *belle-mère*? He was only twenty-five!" Mary was confused, and Margaret held her tightly and let her cry. The young Duke Nicholas of Lorraine and Mary had been promised to each other for a year, and Margaret had helped Mary compose a sweet letter upon the betrothal declaring she would have no other husband but him. It was not the first time Charles had promised Mary to someone, and Margaret doubted the young woman had even known of some of the others. History is repeating itself, she thought grimly, as she well remembered her own list of suitors and her reaction to hearing of Dom Pedro's death. True, neither she nor I knew these intended, Margaret admitted, but at least we felt we had a future. Now Mary must adjust to yet another direction.

They were alone in an antechamber, where Margaret had broken the news to her stepdaughter.

"Hush, my dove," she soothed. "I was told once that crying is a sign of weakness in a great lady. You do not want the servants to disrespect you, do you? 'Twould not do." She smiled to herself as she knew she must have sounded exactly like Cecily.

Mary sat up. "But I have seen you cry, *belle-mère*. Do not deny it," she said indignantly. "Besides, I have every right to cry!" Her tears began again. "My true love is dead!" she wailed, and she buried her head in her stepmother's lap, her little greyhound trying to lick the salt on her face.

"Nonsense, child. I know your true love is not dead. I saw him only a few minutes ago tilting in the castle yard."

Mary froze and her crying ceased. Two huge gray eyes, a little red and puffy, stared up at Margaret, and a blush to rival Margaret's own flamed from her neck to her hairline.

"Wha-what . . . what are you saying, belle-mère? How could you know about Jeh—" She clapped her hand over her mouth.

"Jehan de Mazilles. 'Tis what you were about to say, Mary?" Margaret arched her brow and attempted a serious tone, but her lip was trembling, which made Mary take her hand from her mouth and giggle.

"Is he not the handsomest man you have ever seen, madame?" she asked, her face alight with happiness now.

Margaret's eyes softened. "I can think of one more handsome," she said.

"Father, yes?" Mary exclaimed and was surprised to see her stepmother wince. "No?"

"It does not matter, little one. What matters is that you do not lose control of your feelings for Jehan." What a hypocrite, Meg, she thought. But she heard herself pontificate, "You are the heir to Burgundy, Mary, and 'twould not do for you to go to a husband . . . let me say . . ."

"You mean, unchaste. Not a virgin," Mary blurted out. "I am not so boil-brained! But, certes, a little kissing does not count, does it?"

"I suppose not, Mary." Margaret could not lie. She could not bear to think that this lovely young woman might end up in a hateful marriage, as she had. How could she not encourage Mary to experience the joy of real love that she and Anthony knew? But it was her duty to protect Mary as a valuable asset to Burgundy, even though every fiber in her being revolted against it. Those kinds of emotions always made her think of her brothers. Ned had been able to marry for love, as had George. She had heard Dickon and little Anne Neville had tied the knot that spring. But remembering the light in his eyes when he watched the lovely young singer at Langthorne Abbey who, she was told, had borne him two children, she felt sure that his, too, was a marriage of state.

Mary dried her eyes, got up from the little footstool and sat down next to Margaret on the high-backed settle. "Now I am free, am I not? Perhaps Father would allow me to marry Jehan." She looked so hopeful, Margaret hated to burst her bubble.

"Nay, sweetheart," she said gently. "You are too important to waste on a nobody like Jehan, handsome though he may be." She weighed whether she should tell the girl that her father had high hopes of being offered a crown by the Holy Roman Emperor Frederick.

She remembered her tutorials from Ravenstein in those first months after her marriage. "Burgundy is not a nation, a kingdom, like England or France, your grace. 'Tis a jumble of duchies, counties, lordships and towns that were all independent at one time. Each has its own political tradition, economy and language. Most are surrounded by hostile nations, such as France, Lorraine and Germany. Often we must cross through those hostile territories when we go from one of ours to another. Your husband is determined to join them all together." He hoped he had made it simple for her, for there were days when he did not understand it either. Margaret had sat quietly, trying to assimilate the information.

"Do you believe the emperor will give Charles a crown, messire?" she said during their latest conversation a few days previously. "Would Charles not then have a kingdom within the borders of the Holy Roman Empire? 'Twould seem to me Frederick might be placing himself in a dangerous situation, knowing my husband's penchant for expanding his boundaries," she said almost to herself.

Ravenstein was impressed, although he did glance over his shoulder to make sure this treasonous remark had not been overheard. "My thoughts exactly, your grace," he murmured, "although perhaps not politic to broadcast to the world," he finished with a smile. Margaret had smiled fondly back at him. "Perhaps not, Messire Ravenstein."

No, she thought, returning to the matter at hand, Mary does not need to know something that might never come to pass. Emperor Frederick's other promise was to unite his son, Archduke Maximilian, with Mary as part of the bargain. Poor Mary, she thought, Maximilian had been the first of Mary's intendeds, when she was only six! If he did indeed become Mary's husband, the wheel would have turned full circle. How complicated our lives are, she mused, and not for the first time did she wish she had been born outside the palace walls.

She came out of her reverie to find Mary gazing expectantly at her. Margaret's heart went out to the girl. She reached over and unhooked a corner of the starched gauze that was caught on one of the metal prongs of Mary's elegant butterfly hennin.

" 'Twould seem we will be at Ghent for several months more, my dove. My duties are growing more time-consuming, and therefore you and Jehan might have some opportunities to talk," she said. "I cannot guarantee Madame de Halewijn's turning a blind eye, however. You may tell her that I have asked you to spend more time riding in the fresh air. Astolat needs exercising a lot these days, does he not?" And she winked.

Mary fell into her arms again. "You are the best stepmother a girl ever had," she cried. Then she gave a secret smile and whispered, "I wish you knew how wonderful it is to feel love like this!"

Ah, but I do, Mary, I do, Margaret thought, kissing the soft cheek offered her and watching her diminutive figure skip out of the room. How long ago Ooidonk seems now.

19

Autumn 1473

The hottest summer anyone could remember finally turned to fall. On that September day, Fortunata was admiring the huge carp in the lake inside the palace walls when she saw the horseman admitted at the gate. She instantly recognized the badge of scallop shells on the messenger's sleeve and ran to her mistress, who was enjoying a quiet read on an excedra in the pretty rose garden. Cappi clung to his mistress's back, and Fortunata admonished the monkey for digging his little toes uncomfortably into her shoulder.

"*Madonna,*" she cried breathlessly, when she reached Margaret's grassy seat, "a man has come from Lord Anthony! I saw him going to the stable."

Margaret jumped up, almost dropping her book on the ground. She instinctively straightened her turbaned headdress and smoothed her skirts.

"Are you sure, *pochina*? How do you know?"

"I am not boil-in-the-brain," Fortunata answered indignantly, and Margaret hid a smile. She loved it when Fortunata attempted idioms. "I am right, *conchiglia* is the sign of Lord Anthony, no?"

"Aye, it is!" Margaret nodded, and draping the train of her gown over her arm, she hurried down the path and into the palace, Fortunata close on her heels.

She was calm and collected when Francis, Anthony's squire, was ushered into her presence chamber, followed by curious courtiers and Guillaume. She waited patiently until everyone had quietened before speaking, pleased with her nonchalance.

"We give you welcome to Ten Waele, sir. I trust all is well with your master, Lord Rivers."

The man had been instructed to go down on both knees to the duchess, and he looked up in awe from his lowly position at the regal woman standing on the dais under the richly embroidered canopy. He was relieved to be addressed in English and broke into a smile. "Aye, your grace. My master is returning from Compostella and has made the journey overland from that place of pilgrimage."

Don't tell me Anthony is here! Her heart was in her mouth. Dear St. Margaret, what a joyous thought.

She continued coolly, however. "Is the earl nearby? He is right welcome to lodge with us if he is."

"He travels with the duke's safe-conduct through Burgundy on his way to Calais and merely wished to send greetings." He paused and pulled a missive from his belt. "And to give you this. I am instructed to wait for a response, your grace."

Margaret had to use every bit of self-control to prevent herself from snatching the letter from the squire's hand. Instead, she waved to Guillaume, who took the letter and bowed.

"Pray see to it that this good squire is fed and refreshed," she called to her chamberlain. "I thank you for your good offices, Francis. I will send my chevalier with a response anon."

Francis rose and bowed backwards from the room, taking in the lavish surroundings with wide eyes. Margaret called for music from her favorite gemshorns, and two musicians harmonized skillfully with the polished bones. The haunting sound always soothed her, and she was able to regain her composure and hear a petition from a merchant who thought he had been taxed too highly on his tiny shop.

Margaret was aware that the people of Ghent hated Charles and the outsider councilors such as Hugonet and Humbercourt, who taxed them unbearably to fund the wars and put rebellions down with undue harshness. Charles had instructed her many times not to give in to "those trouble-making Gantois," but today she was so impatient to read Anthony's letter that she was the soul of brevity and magnanimity. Astonished, the merchant's mouth fell open, revealing only six teeth left in his mouth. The guard standing beside him pulled him roughly to his feet, and the man stumbled to the door, bowing and babbling his thanks.

" 'Tis enough for the day," Margaret announced, descending the two steps of the dais, and taking the ever-present Guillaume's arm. "I will see the other petitioners on the morrow. My letter, Guillaume."

At her desk, she broke open the familiar seal and frowned as she read the greeting.

> *"To the high and gracious duchess of Burgundy, Margaret of England, I greet you well."*

Then she smiled. Certes, this was not a secret letter. She read on eagerly.

> *"The Lord our God has blessed this humble pilgrim upon his way to the shrine of St. James in Spain, and my spirit is much lifted."*

I am happy for you, Anthony, but this is not what I want to hear.

> *"I am in need of your counsel, if you would grant it. I am resting at Halle before continuing to Calais and home to England."*

Margaret nodded. She herself had prayed at the Church of Notre Dame there, which housed the Virgin's thighbone.

> *"I have much to tell you that is overlong for this message. I must continue straight, but if you can come to Enghien at week's end, I will tarry there until you do. Send word with Francis, my squire, and I shall know your mind.*
>
> *Your humble servant, A. Rivers."*

Margaret looked up at the paneled wall in front of her and stared at the painting by Meester van Eyck that graced it. Something was wrong, she could sense it. The words were dull and lifeless, even if they had to be formal. And why would he not pay his respects in Ghent? Her heart told her it was because he wanted a repeat of their last meeting; her head told her he did not want the court to wonder why he would make a detour to see her. He was not on a diplomatic mission, and he had no business in Ghent.

She picked up a quill, trimmed it and dipped it in her favorite sepia ink. She wanted to see him. But how to escape the trappings of her usual journeys? She could not leave Ghent without informing Ravenstein, and if she did, he would insist on traveling with her. She chewed the end of the quill and contemplated the tapestry on the far wall.

"*Lord Anthony, we greet you well,*" she began as formally as he. What next? she thought, looking back up at the bucolic scene in the wall hanging. It gave her an idea. She rang the little silver bell next to the inkwell on the green and red woven table covering, and Fortunata appeared before she could put down her pen.

"Is it good news, *madonna?*" she asked, a twinkle in her eye.

"I know not, *pochina.* Lord Anthony speaks like another man, but he wants to see me. We must, however, be clever, because no one must know 'tis he I will go and see. I have come up with a plan and you must help me."

"Certes, I will help!" Fortunata said, rubbing her hands and making Margaret laugh.

Francis was dispatched without delay with a verbal response for his master. "I hope no one tries to torture it from him," Margaret whispered to Fortunata as they watched the squire leap gracefully into his saddle and canter back through the palace gate and onto the road to Halle.

THE SMALL ENTOURAGE that escorted Margaret from Ten Waele the next day included Guillaume de la Baume and Fortunata. Mary stood at the window of her chamber and waved them off.

"Why can't I go?" she had asked Margaret that morning. "I have come with you to Notre Dame of Halle before." Her mouth was turned down and her eyes were resentful.

"I will travel faster without you, my dove. And my reason for visiting the shrine is very personal. Besides, you are old enough to understand why you must stay in Ghent as much as you do."

"Aye, I am a sort of hostage to these ghastly Gantois!" she retorted. "Father explained. Someone of the family must always be here."

"Ten Waele is your favorite residence, Mary, do not deny it. I shall only be gone three days, I promise. Then perhaps we can go apple-picking or hunting," Margaret conceded, and was happy to see Mary's eyes light up. "And perhaps you will find time to see Sir Galahad," as she had nicknamed Jehan. "Now, give me a kiss and wish me God speed."

Mary smiled to herself as she watched the last of the group trot through the courtyard, the sun glinting on the escorts' halberds. She would find ample excuse to spend time with Jehan, she thought gleefully. Who would want to go all that way for a few hours at a shrine and then on to Enghien to talk to a tapestry master, even if the tapestry was to be part of an elaborate canopy Margaret was planning to send to Charles? Nay, she was content to stay behind, she decided.

WHEN THE DUCHESS's little cavalcade trotted into the marketplace of the ancient town of Enghien, just ten miles from Halle, the citizens ran out of their houses, shops and stables to catch a glimpse of Margaret. She was riding a white jennet, her mantle of crimson and black spread over its rump and almost down to the ground.

Guillaume led the way to an official-looking man in a green gown and enormous hat, assuming he was the mayor. He was right. As the man bowed low, Guillaume waved his hand grandly and announced Margaret's wish to be taken to the workshop of Maître Jean Lanoue, weaver of Enghien. The mayor's eyes started from his head. This was an honor indeed for the duchess to choose a lesser known tapestry workshop to patronize. It was well known that Tournai and Brussels offered the largest and the best choice of weavers in the duchy. He positively groveled as he pointed the way, and then, to Margaret's amusement, he decided to lead her to the workshop himself. Soon the riders were being followed by all the children in the town, some pushing hoops, some riding hobbyhorses and others carrying younger siblings. A visit from the nobility was rare indeed in this out-of-the-way place.

Someone had run on ahead to warn Maître Lanoue that her grace, the duchess of Burgundy, was coming, and the old man laughed himself silly.

"*Taisez-vous*, Georges. Why would the duchess visit my humble workshop?" he asked between laughs. And then the words froze on his lips when he saw the blond giant on the magnificently caparisoned horse turn the corner of their street followed by a woman in the colors of Burgundy and looking every inch a queen.

"Mother of God!" he stammered. " 'Tis no jest."

He turned to his weavers and told them to work twice as hard.

"Pedal that loom, Jacques. Wind that hank, Michel. Pick up those bobbins, Madeleine," he cried. Then he noticed a stranger was in his shop, looking through the finished work that was spread on the counter in front of the opened shop shutters.

"Messire, you must leave, I pray you. Her grace, the duchess, will be visiting my shop any second. You may return when she is gone, and I will give you good service then." He was dismayed when the tall, handsome man ignored his words and continued inspecting the tapestries. "Messire, please!" Before he could physically push Anthony out of the door, Guillaume was handing Margaret down from her horse, and Jean had to hurry to welcome her into his humble workshop. Behind him, his weavers and apprentices scurried about obeying his orders.

Margaret had to bend her head at the low doorway and was therefore surprised to be in such a large room. She looked about her with interest. She had no idea that the looms were so big or that pedals were used to separate the warp from the weft, and she exclaimed with delight at the myriad colored threads that the *lissiers* had to choose from. Maître Lanoue enthusiastically described in minute detail the process of weaving a tapestry, and far from being bored, Margaret was fascinated. She knew she would never again look at the many beautiful wall hangings in her palaces in the same way. She loved the weaver's passion for his work and determined that even though the visit was a ruse to meet Anthony, she would commission this little man to make the canopy for Charles to use while on campaign.

She had seen Anthony disappear behind one of the looms and into the back of the shop as soon as she had entered. Even though he was dressed soberly, she recognized every inch of that proud figure, and her knees buckled for a second. She wished she could have dispensed with the business at hand and run after him instead.

After the tour, she gave Maître Lanoue her design ideas for the canopy, then turned and asked Guillaume to arrange the contract with the *lissier*.

"Maître Lanoue, do you have a garden where I might sit awhile with my servant Fortunata here," she asked, gently putting her hand on the dwarf's shoulder. "I think it must be the heat or the smell of the dye, but I am feeling a little faint. Nay, nay, Guillaume, you stay here as I asked, and I shall seek some fresh air. It will not be for long, but I do not want to be disturbed until I send Fortunata to find you, do you understand? Let the rest of the party visit the town and take refreshment at that pleasant-looking tavern in the marketplace. Now do as I say, Guillaume, I beg of you." Her voice was imperious, and Guillaume, although puzzled by her odd behavior, inclined his head in acquiescence. Thank heaven he is too dim to recognize a lie when he hears one, Margaret thought.

Maître Lanoue escorted Margaret through to the back of the house and into a pleasant garden scented with late roses. He seated her on a stone bench and gave her a cup of ale. Then, bowing almost to the ground, he went back inside and called to his wife to bring pen and parchment. This commission would be the making of them, he felt sure, and he thanked his patron saint, Anastasia, for the good luck.

As soon as the door hasp had clicked shut, Margaret stood up and looked around anxiously. Was this a fool's errand? she wondered.

"Fortunata, you did see Lord Anthony, did you not? I am certain he came this way."

"You were correct, my lady," a pleasant voice said behind her, making her jump. "I did come this way."

Margaret spun round, her eyes shining and her arms outstretched. "Anthony, my love, my love!" she cried. Fortunata discreetly tiptoed away and kept watch.

Anthony stiffened as Margaret reached him. "Nay, I cannot, my dear Marguerite." His voice broke as he said her name, and she could see a change had come over him. His cheeks were hollow and his mouth unsmiling. But it was his eyes that gave away his melancholy and something else too that she could not name. It was as though they had seen a great suffering that had burned to his very soul.

"What is wrong with you, Anthony. Are you ill?" she whispered, putting her hand up and stroking his cheek. He moaned as if in pain, took the hand and pressed it to his lips.

"Don't, Marguerite, I beg of you. Do not touch me. I do not deserve it." He stood gazing at her anxious face, and then could not help himself. He enfolded her in his arms and wept as if his heart would break.

"Speak to me, my love. What is it?" she said, holding him close and breathing in the familiar mixture of rosewater and leather. They stood thus for a few minutes until he pulled away and led her to the bench. For the next half hour, Anthony told her of Eliza's terrible illness—from a cancer, which gave her so much pain that she screamed day and night—and of his descent into the hell of guilt. Her dream of the fire flashed through Margaret's mind, and she inhaled sharply.

"In her agony, she has forsaken her faith, Marguerite. She called God a tormenter and swore she hated him. Then she called me an adulterer—nay, I do not know how she knew, and I did not ask her but, God pity me, I denied it. She said her sickness was a sign that I must lose all that is dear to me because of my sin. I knew not how to help her, but I knew what I must do."

"What was that, Anthony?" Margaret's tortured whisper told him she knew already.

"That you and I should never again . . ." He did not finish, for she stopped his words with her mouth. He pushed her away, signing himself as he did so. "Nay, I beg of you, do not tempt me. I have spent twelve weeks on this pilgrimage atoning for my sin against God—and Eliza. You should do the same," he said vehemently.

Unexpected anger flared in her when she realized that he had run away from his ailing wife to soothe his soul. It was a flaw in her lover she had not recognized before, and she fought the urge to raise her voice.

"You left Eliza when she most needed you. I trust you added that to your list of transgressions when you reached Compostella," she said harshly. Seeing him grimace did not make her feel better, and she instantly regretted her words. "I crave your pardon, Anthony."

"You are angry with me, Marguerite, and I cannot blame you. But if there was a chance that my pilgrimage would heal Eliza and at the same time save my soul, I had to take it. I do not believe Eliza will survive, but I did find peace. Santiago de Compostella is truly a holy place," he finished, staring off into the distance, and it was then that she recognized the other look in his eyes that she had not been able to name before. It was fanaticism.

And she understood. He had been visited by the Holy Spirit, and there was nothing she could do about it. She put her head in her hands, and it was her turn to weep. Thus they sat side by side, unable to touch or comfort each other, until Anthony stood up and said he must go.

"Tell me, my love, did God give me any hope?" she asked, feebly grasping at any straw. How could they never again experience the ecstasy they had enjoyed that night in the miniature castle in front of the fire? She had relived it night after night in her waking dreams, certain that one day they could steal another tryst. After all, that hope was all she lived for, if the truth be known. Otherwise her life was meaningless.

Anthony hesitated, and she looked up at him quickly. A flicker of his former self showed in his face, and her heart leapt.

"If we were both free, I cannot believe He would not grant us a little pity," he murmured, and then his face lit up with humor. "Nay, Marguerite, do not even think it. God would not condone the murder of your husband!"

"How did you know I was thinking exactly that?" Margaret said, reluctantly laughing. As they looked at each other for one long moment, they both understood it was because their souls were somehow bound together.

"Farewell, Marguerite," Anthony spoke first. "I know not if you still have my attempts at poetry, but if you do, then remember your Lancelot by them. I fear he is no more."

"They are in my heart, Anthony," she whispered, "as are you—always." He turned and walked away as she said, "I shall never give up hope."

He did not look back.

CHARLES, IN THE meantime, was expecting one of the greatest triumphs of his life. He was fresh from capturing Guelders' main cities and had entered into a treaty with the duke of Lorraine that allowed him free movement of his troops through that duchy whenever he needed to cross between his northern and southern territories. Now he had succeeded in persuading the Habsburg Emperor Frederick III to meet him at Trier. He was expecting Frederick to give him a crown.

Two-thirds of the Burgundian lands were part of the Holy Roman Empire, and Frederick recognized that Charles was now a dangerous man.

Charles was certain that by offering Mary—and thus all the Burgundian territories upon Charles's death—to young Maximilian, the emperor's son, Frederick would bestow a crown and title of king of the Romans upon him—or at the very least, king of Burgundy. Not satisfied with the promise of a crown, Charles was also proposing that Frederick name him heir to the empire. Their meetings lasted more than a month, many of them purely ceremonial as each ruler tried to outdo the other in lavish show and politeness. But while he acquiesced to the marriage alliance and made a few minor concessions, Frederick granted no kingship and no coronation took place.

In fact, one misty morning in late November, Frederick rose early and sailed away down the Rhine. Dismayed, Charles sent his man after him in a rowboat, to no avail. The emperor had had enough of all the posturing and did not trust Charles's motives. It was a bitter blow and made Charles all the more resolved to show the world he could build his own empire.

"MASTER CAXTON, YOU do not know how happy this book makes me," Margaret enthused, turning the pages and studying the even print. There were smudges and in places the type had not been lined up correctly, but she was overcome with awe at beholding the first book ever to have been printed in the English language.

William's grin split his usually serious face in two. His eyes are always merry, Margaret had noticed, but with his lack of teeth, 'tis no wonder he does not smile more. She had lost one of her bottom teeth recently due to the toothworm and could not stop exploring the new gap with her tongue. Experimenting in front of her mirror one day, she had discovered that unless she laughed or yawned widely, it was not noticeable. Poor Beatrice had lost nearly all her teeth, despite chewing mallow and rinsing with vinegar, as they all did.

"May I draw your attention to the introduction, your grace," William said. "I trust you will approve."

She skimmed the lines, reading here and there, " '. . . meekly beseeching the bounteous Highness of my said Lady'—Master Caxton, you flatterer," she teased him. " '. . . that of her benevolence . . . to accept . . . this simple and rude work here following.' Ah, have a care, I helped with the translation, sir," again she teased, not wishing to show how moved she was by his words of dedication. "'And if there be anything written or said to her pleasure, I shall think my labor well-employed.'" Despite her best efforts, however, she could not stop the tear that fell onto the parchment, and she hurriedly brushed it away. "I know not what to say, Master Caxton. I think you must see how truly humbled I am."

"I thank you, your grace. 'Twas a labor of love, albeit a difficult one."

"You have my profound gratitude, sir. Now walk with me and tell me what you hear in the streets of Bruges." She handed the book to Henriette de la Baume, and as she did so she noticed for the first time that the young woman was with child. She would be losing Henriette for a time before long, she knew. The girl had blossomed since Marie de Charny's departure the year before, and the mood among her company of ladies had also improved markedly. She was sorry when the news had come that Pierre, Lord of Charny, had succumbed to his apoplexy after several months of careful nursing, because he had been a good man and a pillar of Burgundian society. But in a letter to Charles she had been firm that Marie was no longer welcome at her court. Charles had not dared to contradict her, although if the truth were told, he was now far too occupied with acts of aggression by the Swiss to worry about his half sister's hurt feelings.

"What news from England, Master Caxton?" Margaret asked, choosing a piece of sugared galingale and nibbling on it as they began walking around the hall. She was pleased to be back in Bruges after all this time, despite the rain bucketing down outside. She had forgotten how pleasant the Prinsenhof was. It was not as large as the other ducal residences but more sumptuously decorated.

"I have been so engrossed with this book, my lady, I do not have much to tell you."

"Then tell me what your intentions are to Fortunata, Master Caxton." Margaret chuckled as she watched the man's face blanch and both eyebrows shoot heavenward. "She is dear to me, as you must know, and I cannot have her appearing before me red-eyed and mope-faced as she has done this week."

"Your gr-grace, you have taken me off guard," William stammered, hoping a hole would appear in front of him and he could conveniently disappear. "What has Fortunata told you?"

Clever man, Margaret thought, he has thrown the ball back to me. Now I must reveal how much I know.

"She tells me you have plans to quit Bruges and indeed Flanders and return to London and that you intend to find a wife there. Is this correct? As your patron, I hope you would inform me of your plans to leave my service."

Caxton's mouth dropped open. He had no idea that the dwarf shared such confidences with the duchess. He wondered what else the little minx had divulged. True, he was no longer an adventurer and as such had no obligation to remain celibate, but he had never dreamed that his pleasant dalliance with Fortunata would lead to her falling in love with him. Much as he enjoyed her most unusual attributes—and possibly Margaret would be generous with a dowry for her favorite servant—he had no intention of taking her to wife. He hoped to have children, and he was certain it would be impossible with a dwarf.

"My plans are but dreams at present, your grace. Certes, I would not make them until I had begged your leave to do so." He paused, searching for the right thing to say. "But in the matter of Fortunata, in truth, she and I have become . . . ah . . . close," he began. 'Twas a good choice of word, he thought. "But I did not promise her anything, and 'twas my understanding that she is bound in service to you, and therefore could not return to England with me—if indeed you gave me leave to return," he added hastily, "if any mention of marriage had arisen. 'Tis true she is bound to you, is it not, your grace?"

Margaret sighed. If the man had expressed any feeling for her *pochina,* she would have reluctantly released her from service and given her over to William. But she accepted William was no different from other men of his rank: he would not consider a low-born dwarf a suitable marriage partner. Poor Fortunata, she thought, she has no more luck than I when we give our hearts.

"I will speak to Fortunata, Master Caxton. We shall be leaving Bruges soon, and perhaps it is well that you remain here. And if you do return to London, I will commend you to my brother and Lord Rivers, as I promised." Margaret stopped and turned to him. "It is a small way of showing my appreciation for the other services you performed for me, sir." She smiled, the pain of Anthony's change of heart no longer so piercing. "I do not think the Lady Elaine has a need to correspond further with Sir Lancelot."

"I quite understand, your grace, and I thank you for the chance to serve you." He bowed over her hand. "Should you have any other printing requests, I am at your command."

She watched him limp away, his stubby legs shown to no advantage under his short robe. She smiled to herself: those legs are only good for reaching the ground. She felt a tug at her skirt. She turned and saw Fortunata's expectant face looking happily up at her. Her heart lurched, but she smiled fondly at the dwarf.

"You and I have much to talk about, *pochina*. I think we should go and pray in the chapel for a while."

This time it was Margaret who was able to console Fortunata in her pain.

IT WAS HARD to believe that Charles was still besieging the small city of Neuss on the Rhine.

He had set up his camp on two islands in the river facing the city. The rest of his army encircled the walls on the land side. He had begun the offensive on the last day of July the previous year, and there he sat through the warm autumn and into a bitter cold winter that eventually turned to spring, a spring that brought flooding and caused Charles to remove his two-room tent to the mainland. But still he threatened the starving people even into May. His wife continued the work of ruling the duchy with the help of councilors such as the Lords Ravenstein, Gruuthuse, Humbercourt and Hugonet. Margaret knew about duty and loyalty, and none was lacking from this daughter of York.

However, Charles seemed blissfully unaware that other enemies were beginning to conspire against him and form alliances to attack his territories far to the south, not the least of whom was Louis of France.

"Earl Rivers is at Neuss, your grace," Ravenstein told Margaret one day in early May. "It seems your brother, King Edward, is heeding the duke's call for aid against France. The earl is the king's emissary. We expect him in Ghent as soon as he and the duke have consulted."

At the mention of Anthony's name, Margaret felt the heat in her face and knew she was blushing. *Sweet Jesu, it has been a year and a half since*

Enghien, and I have prayed to every saint every night to remove this love for a man who is lost to me. Ravenstein winced as he concentrated on shifting his weight off his bad leg, allowing Margaret a moment to take her kerchief from her belt and fan herself with it.

"Fortunata," she called. "Have a page open the window. 'Tis warm in here."

She almost laughed out loud when she saw Fortunata's incredulous expression. The last few days had seen a return of the cold north wind, and Margaret had ordered that fires be kept burning in all her rooms to ward off the chill. The dwarf curtseyed and summoned a page loitering near the door to open a window. Ravenstein noticed nothing—or if he did, his face remained impassive.

"We must see to it that we welcome the king's emissary with all due respect, my lord. I happen to know Lord Anthony is particularly fond of venison. I will instruct the cook accordingly. And we must have music—I shall ask Meester Busnoys for a special anthem. His choir is something the earl will enjoy. Let us invite Seigneur de Gruuthuse. He and Lord Anthony have books in common." In her excitement to organize the banquet, Margaret rose without thinking, causing all those present in the audience chamber to fall to their knees. She quickly sat down, silently cursing court etiquette.

"Meester Busnoys and his choir are unfortunately with the duke at Neuss, your grace," Ravenstein reminded her. "'Tis said they do much to relieve the soldiers' tension there. But I will make sure Lord Anthony has music, never fear," he added warmly. He and his wife, Anne, another of Philip's bastards, were great lovers of music, and Anne had been the one to talk of Charles's skill on the harp. Ravenstein could have sworn Margaret's mouth dropped open when this had been revealed.

Margaret gave him one of her lovely smiles, and once again Ravenstein thanked heaven and Charles for allowing him to be in constant attendance upon the duchess. If not, I'd be freezing in a tent on the banks of the Rhine, he thought, rubbing his gouty leg.

"And so you believe my brother will finally bring an invading army over the Channel?" Margaret asked. "I have written to him reminding him of his pledge to Charles several times, but Edward is not as good a correspondent as my younger brother George. Sending Lord Anthony is perhaps a good sign."

• • •

I N   A   G O W N of satin brocade, its murrey and blue pattern of roses and marguerites proclaiming her ancestry, with shimmering gold silk floating over a jeweled heart-shaped headdress, Margaret watched as Anthony came towards her in the great hall at Ten Waele accompanied by his squires and several knights. To one side of her Mary sat in a gold and brown brocade overdress, crimson silk beneath. Her dark hair was coiled around her head and a little gold chapelet encircled the braids. Behind them stood Guillaume de la Baume, hovering like a guardian angel.

Clothed all in white but for a crimson gipon and shoes, with a jeweled collar draped over the ermine about his shoulders and the glittering order of the Garter clasped on his thigh, Anthony drew every eye in the room. Margaret noted that the padded doublet tapering to his trim waist showed off his physique to better advantage than the circular journade fashionable in Burgundy, which Margaret thought unmanly. And she especially hated the way the young dandies carried their tall hats on the end of a cane. "*C'est à la mode,*" Jeanne had shrugged. "It will pass, I dare swear."

Trumpets blew a fanfare as Anthony approached the dais and bowed low over his extended leg, and Margaret thought her heart would burst with love. How could she have imagined her feelings for him had dimmed? As the fanfare's last notes died away, he raised his eyes to hers, taking her breath away. In the past day and a half she had pondered this moment. How would she receive him? How would he treat her? Would she know in an instant whether love endured or had died? On his return to England and following Eliza's death that September, he had written one poem to her, which had brought her to tears.

> "*I saw my lady weep*
> *And Sorrow proud to be advanced so*
> *In those fair eyes where all perfections keep*
> *Her face was full of woe:*
> *But such a woe, believe me, as wins more hearts*
> *Than Mirth can do with her enticing parts.*"

Before his signature, he had written cryptically, "*Verba volant, scripta manet.*" She did not know why he was stating the obvious—everyone knew that words spoken disappear and only written ones remain—but she prayed he was telling her that what he had said in the *lissier's* garden was not forever.

Now she knew she was right, for his eyes today told her he loved her still. She gripped the arms of her chair to steady herself. Who is speaking, she wondered resentfully, and breaking this spell. Then she realized it was she who was intoning the usual high-flown greeting.

"You are welcome at our court, Lord Rivers. We trust your meeting with Duke Charles was mutually satisfactory." Her voice sounded calm, she thought, but how can that be when my mouth is parched and my throat in a vise?

Anthony was smiling. Margaret panicked. Sweet Jesu, what have I said? I know not what I said!

"I bring you greetings from your husband, the duke, your grace," Anthony said in his clear, pleasant voice. "I trust I find you well." His eyes said, "You are the most beautiful creature here, and I want you."

She gasped, and then she quickly looked around to see if anyone had noticed. On her stool, half hidden by Margaret's ermine-trimmed train, Fortunata gave an imperceptible smile. She had read those eyes as well.

Margaret held out her hand for Anthony to kiss and hoped he would notice that his gift was adorning her belt that night. She reluctantly withdrew her hand in the requisite amount of time and presented him to Mary, who blushed and stammered a welcome in English. Mary had not seen Lord Rivers since the marriage, when she was a child, and she had certainly not realized how handsome her stepmother's presenter was at that time. Even Jehan might be eclipsed by this knight, Mary thought.

"Lady Mary, 'tis indeed a pleasure to see you again," Anthony said. "May I say you are far lovelier than I remember. Your eyes are the color of a dove's wing—"

"Lord Anthony," Mary cried, interrupting and earning a stern look from Jeanne de Halewijn, "'tis also how *belle-mère* is telling me and why she is calling me her dove!" She looked excitedly from one to the other, and then, remembering her manners, put her hand out for Anthony to kiss, said shyly: "I thank you, sir, for your compliment."

"Your English is excellent, Lady Mary, but I think you have a good teacher," he said, stepping away and smiling at the young woman. He was charmed by her dimpled prettiness.

Later, seated next to Margaret at the banquet with Madame Ravenstein on his left, Anthony, with his long, fashionable sleeves tied behind him to avoid trailing them in the food, listened as Margaret plied him with questions about the English invasion. She told him she was certain that once the year-long truce with Louis ended in June, that wily king would not hesitate to attack Charles wherever he felt Charles was vulnerable.

"How many men will Edward bring?" she asked eagerly, making Anthony smile.

"Enough, your grace," he said loudly and then whispered, "'Twould not do to reveal too much at this time, you understand." He glanced around at their immediate neighbors and seeing they were engrossed to the right and left said, "May I see you in private, Marguerite?"

The silver goblet trembled in her hands and she set it down for fear of spilling the contents. "Mary and I will take you hunting tomorrow, Anthony. We can arrange to become separated, I have no doubt." Her eyes were shining.

He avoided them. "Then we shall speak tomorrow." Raising his voice again, he said, "May I present my compliments to your chef, your grace. This meat is the finest I have ever eaten, and I consider myself a connoisseur of venison."

Margaret caught Ravenstein's eye and smiled her thanks.

HER BIRTHDAY DAWNED gray and cold, but Margaret was determined nothing would deter her from riding out with Anthony. Fortunata splashed her with rosewater and Margaret rubbed a liquorice root on her teeth to remove the taste of sleep from her mouth. She dressed against the chill. The gray vair lining of her cloak would protect her from the wind and a large velvet hat, its liripipe wrapped around her neck, would keep her head and ears warm. Mary joined her just as Henriette and Beatrice were helping Margaret into her soft leather boots, and Margaret nodded in approval at Mary's sensible clothing.

A little while later, both women were hoisted into their sidesaddles and Mary was given her falcon. The bird sat quietly on her gloved hand, its little cap blinding it until that moment when it would be let free to hunt its prey. Mary attached a leather string with a bell around its leg and to the ring on her glove. Margaret watched admiringly. She had never taken to falconry, although she had ridden out many times with Dickon at Greenwich. She felt sorry for the smaller birds the hawks preyed upon, she decided, and preferred hunting with the hounds. Astolat was getting old, his whiskers graying around his face, but he was still game to accompany Margaret into the woods and had learned to flush out the birds for the falcons.

Anthony strode into the stable yard calling an apology for being late. "I was searching for a word to finish a poem," he told Margaret as he swung easily up into his saddle. Pegasus danced around, impatient to be off, but Anthony reined him in, and the beautiful animal responded immediately. Anthony's black felt bonnet sported an egret feather pinned in place by an elaborate ornament. When Margaret moved closer, she was alarmed to see that it was her gift to him from her marriage necklace.

" 'Tis a W, your grace, for Woodville," he teased her, knowing Mary was listening. "What did you think it was?"

"It is handsome, Lord Anthony," Mary called. "I like it. Now, we go, please?" She clicked her tongue, kicked her horse's flank and set off at a fast walk with her escort.

Following behind, Margaret arched her eyebrow at Anthony, and he grinned. "I had it arranged so that I could wear it," he said in a low voice. "Say you do not mind, Marguerite."

She laughed gaily. She had not felt so happy for years, she realized. She encouraged her horse, and soon the group was cantering along the river, followed by three grooms, leaving Ghent behind. They passed dozens of fishermen casting their lines in the gentle river; several paniers were already filled with trout and bream.

Margaret had told Jeanne that Lord Anthony and her grooms would be ample escort for that day.

"My mother once told me that if the wind changed when one's face was in an unpleasant expression, it would stay that way. Surely you do not want to go through life looking disapproving, Jeanne." Jeanne laughed. "That is better, my friend. I promise to look after Mary. I know what you are thinking, and do not deny it. Lord Anthony may soon be free, and we do not want any scandal to mar Mary's betrothal to Maximilian, do we? Certes, that is why I am along for the day. To keep an eye on them. And

Guillaume has given us that odd-looking fellow Hugues for extra protection, so do not fret."

Margaret chuckled now, thinking back on the conversation. If only Jeanne knew her guilty secret, she thought. It was the one thing she had kept from her friend.

The woods were carpeted with bluebells, which always reminded her of England. The horses slowed as they wove in and out of the trees, disturbing a small herd of deer and several highly nervous squirrels. Anthony regaled the ladies with stories about his charge, the Prince of Wales, for whom he had now been appointed governor at Ludlow Castle. Mary got bored listening to the daily life of young Edward Plantagenet and felt sorry for him.

"Sermons and schooling and sleep is all you speak of, Messire Anthony," she said in more comfortable French. "Does he have a companion other than old men? Poor boy." She was longing to get to her favorite hill, free of trees, where larks and pigeons, quails and warblers were easy prey for her merlin, and she spurred her horse onward. Hugues and the two other grooms seemed unconcerned about leaving Margaret and Anthony as they cantered after the young heir of Burgundy, all intent upon the hunt.

Skirting the hill, Margaret led the way to an abandoned hermit's hut, its roof suspect and the door long since broken off its hinges. They could hear Mary's high-pitched laughter in the distance. Margaret hoped she and Anthony would not be missed for a quarter hour. The thought of being alone with him for even that short a time was exhilarating, and feeling his arms around her as he lifted her from her horse wreaked havoc on her senses. She hoped he would kiss her, but he did not. He took her hand and led her inside the ramshackle shelter, dusted off a stone ledge and invited her to sit down with him.

"Anthony," she whispered, leaning close, but he put his finger to her lips.

"Nothing has changed for us, Marguerite," he began and felt her body sag with disappointment. "I cannot hide my love from you, that I know, but I cannot demonstrate that love and still be a humble servant of God. Call me a coward, if you will, but I fear the hellfire more than my miserable life can bear. Although I have committed the sin of adultery once

with you—nay twice, for I sinned against Eliza and condoned your sin-
ning against Charles—I cannot repeat it."

Margaret moaned and put her head in her hands. "I must have led a
sinful life to warrant this much pain," she said. "And yet I believe the love
we share is God-given, not Hell-bent." She had been so hopeful last night.
She had knelt by her bed and prayed to the infant Jesus to forgive her if
Anthony made love to her again. Aye, she knew it was wrong, but so was
her marriage to Charles.

"Marguerite, you must be content to know I love you and want to be
your friend. What pain is it, other than me, that you speak of? You are
possibly the wealthiest woman in Europe and have everything you could
ever wish for in land and treasure. More than this, you have your wits
and your health.

"'Tis true your husband is a belligerent man who spends most of his
time at war, but he seems to respect and cherish you. He told me three
times how delighted he was with your gift of the canopy, and in fact I
was privileged to see him walking among his troops in his jeweled armor
underneath it. A truly regal picture, but *un peu trop*, don't you think?" he
said, chuckling. "However, I deduced from my short time with him that
he could not respect you more highly." He paused, moderating his tone.
"So other than this pain of ours, what afflicts you so?"

Margaret had been listening to Anthony's observations with cynicism
and gave an unattractive bark of laughter. "Cherish? Respect? Aye, he
respects my brain and he cherishes my brother's aid, but there is an end
to it."

She got up and paced the few steps to the door and back, telling
Anthony of Charles's cruelty to his subjects, and then boldly described
his abuses in the bedroom. Anthony was outraged by the latter and full
of compassion for her, but he was not surprised by the cruelty. He had
seen Charles throw a mailed gauntlet in a fit of rage at a squire who
had disturbed him and a moment later smile pleasantly at Anthony as if
nothing had occurred. Anthony had been curious about Charles's distaste
for those who used God and His saints in their cursing when the man
thought nothing of using violence.

"I think I could bear all this if God would see fit to grant me children.
I have none, and it appears I will not have them." Margaret looked at him.

"You have no children either, Anthony. Does it not pain you?" She could have bitten her tongue when she saw him redden. Certes, she had forgotten about his bastard daughter, also named Margaret. It was so long ago, and he was so young, she wondered if he even saw the woman.

"We shall be missed, Anthony," she said, changing the subject. "Let us join the others. Only God knows what is to become of us." When he cupped his hands for her foot and she was ready to mount, she held his eyes with hers. "Will you keep to your promise of the *New Ellen* that you will come to me should we both be free?"

He hoisted her into the saddle, and his mood lightened. "Or you come to me," he retorted, his eyes twinkling up at her. "Lady, I know your worth, and there is naught that would keep you from me if the Fates are kind."

With that modicum of hope planted in her heart, Margaret kicked her horse into a canter. Another ruined birthday, she grimaced, calling Mary's name.

20

Summer and Autumn 1475

S t. Omer straggled along the last hillside beside the River Aa before miles of marshes and sand dunes led down to the sea and the English-held port of Calais. The new tower on the cathedral commanded the countryside and could be seen by the English in their territory around the staple town. It was in the small town that Margaret waited for Charles to come and meet Edward.

With Emperor Frederick threatening Charles in nearby Cologne, he had finally given up the siege of Neuss after the better part of a year, and Edward was expecting him to arrive with his full army at any time to honor their treaty of July 1474. The main aim of this treaty was to unite against Louis in combat, have Edward reclaim his French lands—lost to England by Edward's predecessor—and thus lessen Louis' ability to attack Charles's borders along the Somme. In fact, Edward was angered that Charles was not now waiting for him. He must have ignored the strongly worded message Edward had sent with Anthony to Neuss telling Charles to give up the siege and join him against France. Edward knew that Charles was peeved because he should have honored their alliance sooner. Charles had demanded that Edward land in Normandy and attack Louis directly. Edward had no intention of putting his smaller army in such danger; Calais was the safer landing choice. It seemed things did not bode well for a successful campaign.

Margaret wasted no time in traveling the few miles to Calais to greet her brother. He was surprised to learn that it was Margaret, not Charles, who had ordered Burgundian ships to England to carry the English force over the Channel. Margaret knew she must soothe Edward upon his arrival and hoped that her smiling face and beautiful gifts would mollify him. Edward was pleased to see his sister and embraced her fondly when they met, although he groused at the absence of Charles and his troops.

"We have been waiting for you for two years, Ned. What took you so long?" she teased, once they were ensconced in the chamber set aside for the king in the massive castle.

Edward growled. "Christ's nails, Meg, don't push me." Then he laughed. "You still have your wits about you, Meggie, in truth. Anthony told me that power and wealth had not changed you."

Margaret colored and turned away. "Is that all he said?" she said flippantly. "I went to a great deal of trouble to entertain him royally. Did he not even mention the venison?"

"I see my little sister is still lovelorn. You are not the only one, my dear. He is now the most eligible bachelor in all of England after my little Edward," he chuckled. "Fathers are positively throwing their daughters at him! But he does not seem to be disposed to take another wife. Have you bewitched him, Meg?"

"Don't be ridiculous, Ned. We have seen each other three times in the past five years, 'tis all." She didn't count their midnight adventure or the meeting at Enghien, only the ones the chroniclers would record. "'Tis hardly the stuff of a great romance," she joked. "Now, tell me how Mother is? She has not written of late."

"Mother is lost to us, I fear. She is now firmly cloistered at Berkhamstead and is content to give her life to God. I miss her sound advice, but in truth, she will always be able to make me feel small." Edward's laugh turned into a wheezing fit and Margaret regarded him with concern.

He continued, "George and Richard are here with me, as you know, and they will wait upon you at St. Omer in a few days. I thought you would prefer to see them away from this busy scene. Both are responsible for parts of the army and are now supervising the billeting of such a large force. 'Tis said no king of England has ever brought so many dukes and earls over the Channel to invade before."

"You trust George with your soldiers, Ned? My sources have informed me that he is still a thorn in your side and that he and Dickon have not forgotten how to squabble. Both have inherited fortunes in house and land from their Neville brides. Can they not be happy with their lot?" she asked.

"They are happy enough with their wives, it seems, and Richard is a tower of strength for me in the north, Meggie. He is much loved and respected there, and he eschews the court these days. He and Anne have a son—aye, another Edward! All three of us York brothers have given the same name to our heirs."

"Ah, but doesn't Dickon have a bastard son from the young woman with the harp? I thought his name was John."

"You are well informed, Meg," Edward said. "Kate Hautc is her name. Even though Dickon chose to hide his leman away in the country—close to Jack Howard, I might add—he has treated his two children by her honorably." He paused, studying his hands. " 'Tis George who has surprised us recently."

Margaret saw Edward was weighing what to say next. "What is the surprise, brother? Do not talk in riddles, I beg of you," she urged him.

"Perhaps I should not tell you, Meg, but you two are close. I know 'twill go no further." He saw Margaret cross her heart and continued, averting her gaze: "It seems George sired a bastard on a Flemish girl one wild night in a tavern favored by those weavers. Aye, you may look astonished, as was I when a wine-sodden George confessed his guilt to me not long afterwards. He does drink to excess, Meg, and then his temper and his tongue run away with him."

"And his prick, by all accounts," Margaret said, chuckling. More seriously she said, "I hope he provides for the babe at least."

Edward shrugged. "How should I know? 'Tis his problem, not mine," he said, and again Margaret noticed he avoided looking at her. "I doubt not he sends Frieda a coin or two on occasion, and it seems her merchant parents have arranged to wed her to a man in Tournai so she can disappear and not shame them."

For someone who had just declared this affair was not his problem, Edward seemed extremely well informed, Margaret thought fleetingly, but she did not doubt he had his spies.

"I pray Isabel is ignorant of the bastard," Margaret said. "She so dotes on George."

Edward nodded, pulling his ring on and off—a habit Margaret knew he only did when he was nervous. Why would George's infidelity cause Ned's unease, she wondered?

"He will no doubt tell you himself, Meg," Edward, said sighing. "The two of you have always had a special bond, although I am puzzled by it. You could not be more different. He has never understood the meaning of loyalty. But God's truth, he can be a charmer with his looks and disarming ways." He shifted in the chair and it groaned. "I would have thought you would be closer to Dickon. But he was so much younger than you, I suppose." As he stretched his legs out, the chair suddenly collapsed under his weight, leaving him sprawled on the floor in a most unkingly heap.

Margaret laughed and went to help him up. "Ned, why do you not look after yourself? If the truth be told, I am shocked by your girth. And you sound as though every breath is your last. Has Mother seen you thus?"

"'Tis not for you to comment on my person, Meg. Have a care," he warned, and Margaret, recognizing the signs of anger in him, brought the conversation to a close.

"Shall we walk around the ramparts, Ned? 'Tis overly warm in here. I want to tell you about the gifts I have brought for you. The tapestry is from one Maître Lanoue in Enghien."

"Do you think I don't know stalling tactics when I hear them, Meg? Even though your company is right welcome, my anger against your husband is rising by the minute. Not only has he failed to keep his end of the bargain here, he has behaved despicably to my favorite sister. I have half a mind to treat with Louis instead of him."

Margaret's eyes flew wide with dismay, and Edward threw back his head and laughed. "Do not fret, my dear, I know my duty."

And that is to do what is best for England, he did not add aloud.

RICHARD HAD GONE to see to his horse, which had thrown a shoe on the sandy road to St. Omer. "He does not trust anyone with his horse,"

George whispered to Margaret. "'Tis why we have grooms and smiths, Dickon," he called after his brother, who shrugged and continued to the stables, his stride purposeful.

Margaret led the way to the herb garden beside the monastery. They could hear monks chanting inside the old stone building. She plucked a sprig of rosemary and crushed the leaves between her fingers, inhaling the pungent aroma.

"I am glad we are alone for a few minutes, George. We have much to talk about."

George smiled and put his arm about her shoulders as they walked. A hedgehog was caught unawares as they trod softly along the dusty path, and it curled itself into a ball, daring anyone to come near its spiny form. Margaret bent close to inspect it, but observing the fleas that infested the little animal, she hurriedly moved away and unconsciously scratched at an old bite on her leg. She must remember to tell Fortunata to gather more tansies to hang in the garderobe to ward off the pests, she thought. 'Tis too hot to wear fur now.

"It has been a long time, Meg, has it not," George said, as they strolled between the immaculately manicured beds. "At Canterbury before your departure, I believe. You are still as tall as ever!" He ducked, laughing, as Margaret attacked him with the rosemary stalk. "How does marriage treat you? Rivers tells me Charles is a bullheaded man prone to temper tantrums. You would be enough to try a saint," he teased again. "But there has been talk in the family about your lack of progeny. Are you barren, Meg?"

Margaret bit her tongue. 'Tis useless. George has still not learned to be diplomatic, she thought. She wanted to divert attention from herself and could not resist asking, "How are all your babes, George?"

George looked sheepish. "You know about my bastard, don't you Meg? 'Twas folly on my part, I admit, but Isabel was pregnant and would not let me near her—I was very drunk."

"And you needed a woman. I understand, George. But I hope Isabel is none the wiser. She would be heartbroken. I hear she dotes on you. What have you done for the child—a boy, no?"

George nodded. "Aye, a boy, John or Jehan in Flemish. I only saw him once before Frieda was sent to be married. He has a remarkable likeness to me—or even Ned," he said. "To answer your question, I have sent the woman money. Unlike Dickon, who talks incessantly about his bastards and intends to have them at court when they are old enough, I am determined this shall remain a secret for Isabel's sake. I can only imagine Ned or Will Hastings told you about my child. Ah, I am right," he said, seeing her nod. "Ned is one to talk," he scoffed. " 'Tis common knowledge than he has left bastards the length and breadth of England, and none has been invited to court except for Arthur. I beg of you to keep all this to yourself, Meg. I love Isabel, and she is having great difficulty this time. Her humors are causing the physicians concern. Not to mention the dire predictions my astrologer is giving me. I am afraid if she found out about Jehan, 'twould kill her."

Margaret said nothing but watched a monk, his black robe proclaiming him a Benedictine, tend a bed with his hoe. She had more on her mind than George's bastard, but she did not know how to begin. Seeing her distracted, George gratefully changed the subject, giving her the opening she needed.

"You truly have not changed a speck, Margaret," he said, hoping she would respond to his usual flattery. "In truth, I have missed you. You are the only one who understands me."

"You have not missed me enough to write or to come and see me before now," she retorted. "At least I have seen Dickon and Ned since my marriage."

"Certes, Dickon and Ned saw you in Seventy-one—" He stopped, remembering why he had not been in exile with them.

Margaret seized her opportunity. "Aye, you realize what havoc you caused then, do you not," she said, pushing him towards a bench and away from the monk. "And as I understand it, you did not learn your lesson after Edward welcomed you back into the fold. I know of your quarreling with Dickon over the Neville estates. The two of you should be ashamed. Edward was most generous, especially with you after your . . . your wicked alliance with Warwick," she snapped, finally speaking her mind. "I have warned you before, George, and I will warn you for the last time. 'Tis well you do not continue to anger Ned. I sense his patience is running out where you are concerned."

George rounded on her. "What has Ned been saying about me? I have conducted myself well on this occasion, have raised more than my fair share of money and men for this infernal invasion," he said fiercely.

"What is his complaint about me now? I tell you, Meg, I am beginning to hate him. And sanctimonious Dickon."

"Do not say so!" Margaret cried, shaking him. "They are your brothers. We are all one family, and I do not have to remind you that our father and mother taught us that almost from birth. Oh, why can't you remember this? Are you so foolish as to think you will one day wear the crown?"

"Here comes Dickon. Why don't you ask him that question? He will be glad to tell tales about my so-called treachery. Lies, all lies!" George's blue eyes shone with tears of anger, and Margaret was immediately contrite.

"Pray forgive me, George, I should not have been so harsh. I just worry about you, 'tis all." She turned and pulled him to her, and she felt him melt.

"Ah, Meggie, I do miss you" was all he could stammer, and he quickly wiped his eyes with the back of his hand. Then he brushed past Richard. "I'm going fishing," he called. "The river is full of trout. I will see you at dinner."

"Was George crying?" Richard asked, a mischievous grin spreading over his face. "What did you say to him, Meg?"

"We were reminiscing, Richard, 'tis all. I was reminding him of our childhood and our choices in life. But come, let us not be morose. You have filled out, my lad, and are quite handsome now," she said, appraising him. "Come and sit by me and tell me about your children."

"Would that not pain you, Meg? I know from our time together in Bruges that you long for a child. But with Charles besieging every city he comes upon, 'tis no wonder you have not been able to conceive," he said, trying to keep the conversation lighthearted. "But as you ask, I will tell you that little Edward is the apple of Anne's eye. He is a happy boy, and everything one could want in a son. He is two now, and we have hopes that he will outlive us both. As for my other two, Katherine is the image of her mother, beautiful and willful." He paused as a wistful smile crossed his face. "And John, I believe, takes after Kate's father. Nay, Meg, I see your question. I have not been with her since I wed Anne. Do you think me very sinful?"

"I am not your mother nor your confessor, Richard," Margaret said, patting his arm. "I am no saint either. But we do the best we can, little brother. All will be judged in the end, praise be to God."

The brother and sister sat contemplating this truth and enjoying the shade of the St. Bertin Abbey until the bell of the cathedral nearby signaled Matins.

WHEN CHARLES ARRIVED a few days later, he came with only a small group of men, which Margaret knew would infuriate Edward. The king and his nobles were entertained a day later, and after polite conversation at dinner, angry voices could be heard behind the closed doors of Charles's private council chamber. Charles was surrounded by his chief councilors, Hugonet, Humbercourt, Ravenstein and the lord of Chimay. Jack Howard, Anthony, Will Hastings, George and Richard were behind Edward.

"God damn you to Hell, Charles!" Edward railed, the vein standing out from his forehead. "We had an agreement. Where is your army? Christ's nails, Louis must be wetting himself."

Charles's eyes were blue-black and glittering as he faced the irate king of England. Seated on a window seat, Margaret was watching the two and forgotten by most. Anyone else but Edward, she thought, and Charles would have struck him. She was keenly aware of Anthony's presence in the chamber and once or twice had caught him eyeing her. In those instances, they both quickly looked away.

Edward towered over the stocky Burgundian by almost a foot, but Charles was unafraid. "I do not tolerate anyone taking God's name in vain in my presence, Edward," he shot back, staring up at Edward's flushed face. "But 'tis well known, you Englishmen have the manners of pigs. If it were not for the respect I bear your sister, I would dismiss you from my sight forthwith."

Edward threw back his head and laughed in derision. He stood, arms akimbo, and stared down at Charles. "A duke dismiss a king?" he roared. "Only in your dreams, you, you"—Edward lapsed into English to properly convey his feelings—"bat-fowling, lily-livered skainsmate!"

"Enough! Edward, Charles, I beg of you!" Margaret was on her feet and forcing herself between the two men. "You are both behaving like pribbling brats." Her hennin poked Edward in the eye, and he yelped and jumped back. Charles's mouth dropped open as he felt Margaret give him a manlike shove in the chest that made him totter backwards. "You are both unworthy of your office," she cried.

She was vaguely aware of George's and Richard's amusement as they stood together observing this unusual scene. She glowered at them, and they stopped laughing.

"Come and help me, you craven clotpoles!" she called to them in English. "If word gets to Louis that England and Burgundy are at each other's throats, then all is lost. Certes, if only men had our common sense," she opined, "perhaps we would not have so much fighting."

Her dignity and voice of reason calmed the two leaders, who stood stock-still listening to her. In that moment, Margaret was quite unaware that she had fulfilled her wish of long ago, in another time of crisis, to one day be like her mother.

"Come both of you, make a plan to defeat Louis, not each other," Margaret entreated them. "Together you can do it." She took the right hand of each man and looked from one sheepish face to the other. "I beg of you, shake hands." When they had effected the gesture, she sighed. "Now, pray forgive me for leaving you and seeking some solace by the sea. And you, messires," she swept the room with her gaze, "are stalwart enough to take charge in my absence, I dare swear."

Eleven pairs of admiring eyes followed her progress out of the room; the twelfth pair watched her go with longing.

EVENTUALLY THE TWO rulers came to an agreement: Edward would attack Louis in Champagne and march towards Rheims to be crowned, and Charles would invade Lorraine, where Louis had regained a stronghold. They agreed to keep each other apprised of any dealings with Louis, which Edward dutifully did some weeks later.

Later that night at a banquet given by Charles in honor of the English king and princes, Margaret found her way to George's side. He gave her one of his charming smiles and lifted her hand to his lips.

"You are still a beauty, Meg, no mistake about that," he murmured. "But I think Charles has his hands full. You were a tigress at that meeting. Dickon and I were impressed. As for Edward, I have never seen him so cowed."

"Sweet Jesu, George, 'twould not have taken a genius to see we were getting nowhere. If Charles wants Edward here to fight Louis, and Edward wants Charles to help him regain his lands, then quarreling about it is mere folly. They are both big bullies, 'tis all. Are you primed for this invasion, brother? I can see Richard is."

Clarence grimaced. "Aye, Dickon is always ready for battle." His iris-blue eyes clouded over, and he frowned. "I would be game for a fight except—"

"Except what, George?"

"My astrologer read my charts last night, and his prediction was unnerving. He said I will return to my beginnings when I die—in other words, I will have a watery end," he told her, gripping her hands in his. "And we are going to the Somme—the river, Meggie. I have never been afraid in battle, but now I fear I am riding to meet my fate."

Margaret talked reason to him. She said beginnings meant he would die a doddering old man toothless and hairless as a babe in its mother's womb, and she dismissed the astrologer as a probable charlatan. As always she was able to calm him, although she could not stay the icy fingers that tightened around her heart.

Happily, the music had struck up a *piva* and she boldly asked him to lead her out, hoping to take his mind off his troubles. After all those years, brother and sister had not lost their step, and after demonstrating the intricate leaps and turns with flair, they were the toast of the gathering that night. Then Charles had astonished the English guests with some fine playing on his harp.

Edward leaned over and whispered to Margaret, "I did not know he possessed a sensitive bone in his body. The only strings I thought he was capable of playing were bowstrings. Certes, he is very skilled." His eyes came to rest on his favorite brother, Richard, sitting riveted in his chair, and he chuckled, causing Margaret to follow his gaze. "Our little brother is still pining for his Kate, methinks. 'Tis the harp has given him thoughts of her, I dare swear."

And judging from the faraway look in Richard's eyes, Ned was right.

CHARLES WAS COLD to Margaret following the altercation with Edward at St. Omer, and they spent the last few days avoiding each other. Margaret was relieved Charles had not taken his humiliation out on her in the bedroom again, but with her brothers near, she assumed he did not dare take the chance. They bade each other farewell in the small castle of

Fauquembergues, from which Charles was riding with Edward some way south towards the Somme and Louis before returning to his own troops. He kissed her on the mouth in front of the courtiers present in the room and was quite respectful. She, in her turn, wished him God speed and a swift return, although she knew he was never happier than with his soldiers.

Margaret stood on the steps waving her kerchief as Charles and Edward rode side by side, both magnificent in their own way. They were followed by George, Richard and Anthony, who had been invisible during the meetings at St. Omer, preferring to avoid compromising her duty to Charles. Richard's eyes were on Edward's back, and he did not see her. She called George's name, and when he turned to acknowledge her, something in his face sent a shiver down her spine. It was the face of a man doomed, and she tried not to think about the astrologer's strange prediction earlier that week as she watched the mile-long army snake its way past her.

Anthony, his chestnut hair gleaming in the sun, turned to look at her and lifted his mailed hand in salute. She blew a kiss. George, thinking it was for him, finally smiled and blew one back.

UPON RETURNING TO Ghent, Margaret found a letter from Anthony waiting for her. Someone—she assumed it was Fortunata—had put it on top of the pile that was ready for her attention. She glanced at the dwarf, who was innocently studying her nails. She must have recognized his script, she thought, amused.

"Henriette, I pray you sing something for us," Margaret said, hoping her voice sounded weary. "What do you sing to your little Guillaume? I should like to hear something soothing, for I have a headache. Fortunata, Beatrice, help me with my gown. I would lie down for a while."

Henriette picked up her lute, and in her low husky voice began:

> "La flours d'iver sour la branche
> Me plais tant a remirer
> Que nouvele ramembrance
> Me doune amours de chanter . . ."

The curtains on one side of Margaret's bed allowed her some privacy. She lay on the embroidered satin coverlet and propped herself up on the pillows, soothed by the music. She broke the seal on the letter, brushing the crumbs off her undergown.

"As I write this, you are entertaining your brothers at St. Omer. I chose to stay and keep vigil at the garrison. I cannot bear to see you with that man who has so defiled you. I fear I would humiliate us all by spitting him on my sword if he so much as looked at you cross-eyed. I know not what the campaign in France will bring, but I need you to know your silver scarf will ride with me in the field, as my heart rides with you wherever you are. Pray for me, my dearest love.

> *"Have a good day now, Marguerite*
> *With great love I thee greet*
> *I would we might often meet*
> *In hall, in chamber and in the street*
> *Without blame of the contrary*
> *God giveth that it so might be."*

He did not sign it, for with the seal destroyed, it could have been from anyone. She lay staring at the curtains decorated with her daisies and white roses and imagined a day when she might learn of Anthony's death. She saw his body mutilated on a battlefield and cringed. Then she imagined him old and gray, holding her hand as he lay peacefully dying, and that was the thought she had in her head when she fell asleep.

A FEW DAYS later, she sat in her favorite audience chamber at Ten Waele and waited for Ravenstein to give her the latest news.

"The duke informs us that your brother has treated with Louis, your grace," Ravenstein told her, his sharp eyes watching for her reaction. "Louis has offered the king a truce of seven years, a large pension and a marriage contract with the Dauphin for the Princess Elizabeth. In return, the English will leave France." His disgruntled tone showed he believed Edward had betrayed Burgundy.

Margaret's English hackles rose. "Certes, Messire Ravenstein, my brother had no choice," she retorted. "Why, pray, did the duke refuse to open the gates of any of his cities to Edward? What was the English army supposed to exist on during the campaign and into the winter? Grass? Nay, 'twas Charles who betrayed Edward, and I will not hear otherwise. Besides, my brother acted honorably by securing a truce for Charles as well, should he choose to treat with Louis within three months. Nay, you and I will have to disagree on this, messire." Margaret was firm, and Ravenstein bowed stiffly and left her presence, followed by his squires.

She slumped back into her chair and drummed her fingers on the arm. If the truth be told, she was disappointed in her big brother. He had been bought off without letting loose a single arrow. The two kings had met on a bridge at Picquigny and signed a peace treaty on the twenty-ninth day of August, and now Edward was on his way home. She had heard that only Richard had balked at turning tail without a fight and had refused the pension. Even he, however, did not say no to some other gifts from Louis. What will Mother say? Margaret groaned out loud. And Father would be ashamed. She remembered Edward's jesting with her at Calais and groaned again. He deceived me, she realized, and scowled.

THE BELL FOR Matins rang, and Margaret called for her prayer book. On her knees in front of the Virgin and Child, she prayed that Charles would take Louis' offer of a truce.

"Let there be peace, dear God. Burgundy has lost too many of her sons since Charles decided to become Caesar. If you give him the sense to accept what he has and be content, then I swear I will be a good wife to him." She did not go as far as to promise to give up her love for Anthony, which she realized left the door open for her prayer to be unanswered. As she always did when speaking to God, she ended her private meditation with an Ave Maria and "May the Mother of God have mercy on Anthony, my one true love, and me, a lowly sinner." Today she added, "And please, sweet Jesu, protect my brother George as he crosses back to England." His fear of dying in the Somme had been for naught, but there was danger still in the unpredictable waters of the Channel.

LESS THAN A fortnight later, one of her prayers was answered. Charles did indeed sign a nine-year truce with Louis. Among the terms was permission for Charles to move his troops from north to south or vice versa on the most direct road in a peaceable fashion. The other piece of news, which five years ago might have given Margaret pause for thought, was that Louis had paid a handsome ransom for the return of Margaret of

Anjou from England, and that lady would live quietly with a small pension at her father's court.

However, the terms did not directly affect Margaret's and Mary's life in Ghent, except that Lord Ravenstein was appointed lieutenant-general in Charles's northern territories and he was no longer to be Margaret's chief councilor.

"It has been my honor to serve you, your grace, and I shall miss your intelligence and sense of humor," Ravenstein told Margaret, bowing over her hand, his eyes twinkling. "You have taught me much about a woman's mind, something I never thought to understand in all my days on earth."

"Then my work has not been in vain," Margaret replied, laughing. "And I hope it has pleasant consequences for your dear wife. I shall miss her also when you move back to Brussels. I understand your house is magnificent."

"Aye, Anne will enjoy being mistress there, but she may be lonely. I will travel a great deal, but," he added hastily, "never think I am abandoning you, madame. I hope we shall correspond and keep each other abreast of the duke's business. Our good friend, Lord Gruuthuse, will take my place, and I know the two of you have much to talk of—his library for one. I was never able to keep pace with your knowledge of books in truth."

"I trust Gruuthuse with my life, my lord. I shall not forget his kindness to my exiled brothers, and I look forward to knowing him better. Thank you for your valuable service to me. If it weren't for you, I would not understand anything about this duchy I am helping to govern."

Ravenstein chuckled. "I do remember thinking I had a difficult task ahead of me in those first few months. My explanation of the estates general particularly sticks in my mind. Once I said the word 'parliament' it was as though a gauze had been lifted from your eyes. That was a long time ago now. If I may say, your grace, Burgundy never had a more able duchess."

Margaret blushed. "'Tis praise indeed from you, messire. I shall make sure Mary learns all there is to know about governing. My one concern is that Charles has not wed her to Maximilian yet. Should anything happen to the duke, God forbid"—she crossed herself quickly—"she would be putty in Louis' hands."

"If you have any power to persuade Duke Charles, I strongly urge you to do so, madame. 'Twould be a disaster for Burgundy if we had no man as a leader—although you, your grace, would be a worthy combatant."

"You are kind, Messire Ravenstein. I do hate to see you go, but God speed you in your new office." She rose from her chair, bringing the audience to an end. He bowed over his swollen leg and backed away from the dais. When he glanced up at her, he was astonished to see that her eyes were full of tears. He was touched beyond belief.

LOUIS VAN GRUUTHUSE was ushered into Margaret's presence chamber not long after Ravenstein's departure. The sandy-haired Dutchman could not have been more different from his predecessor. Whereas Ravenstein was tall, aloof and grave, Gruuthuse was slight, mild-mannered and talkative. Margaret had met him on many occasions and noticed that he seemed at ease with everyone in the room. He had a ready smile, which lit up his heavy-lidded large eyes. He still reminded Margaret of a sheep, although there was nothing of the sheep in the way he conducted the affairs of state. He was well respected for his intelligence and fairness throughout Burgundy, and Margaret knew she could not ask for a more honest councilor. He was styled Lord of Bruges, Prince of Steenhuse and was a knight of the order of the Golden Fleece. He had governed Holland ably for Charles, and Edward had bestowed the title earl of Winchester on him for his services to the English crown during Margaret's marriage negotiations and Edward's exile. From the moment she met him at Reading Abbey, Margaret had taken a liking to him.

"Your grace," he began, his deep voice always surprising her, "it is a great honor for me to serve you. I have taken the liberty of bringing a gift with me, in case this meeting did not go well and I could not live up to Lord Ravenstein's high standards."

Margaret arched her brow. "A bribe, Heer Lodewijck?" she said, favoring him with some Dutch. "Certes, I do not think Heer van Ravenstein would stoop to a bribe, but then it was perhaps because he thought I would be above taking one. As I see you are holding a book," she said, her eyes devouring the beautifully tooled leather cover embossed with gold letters, "I think I am about to accept one."

They both laughed, and he presented her with a copy of *La Roman de la Rose*, a book she had admired in his library on the one occasion she had visited his splendid house adjacent to the Church of Our Lady.

"First, may I compliment you on your Dutch, madame," Gruuthuse said, reverting to French, the court language, flattered the duchess had made the effort in his native tongue. "I know you would be pleased to know that Collard Mansion copied it for you, duchess. He and Master Caxton are in partnership, as you know."

Margaret snatched the book from his hands. She reverently opened the pages and marveled at the beautiful script by one of the masters of Europe, fluttering her fingers over the gold leaf and many-hued illuminations throughout the book.

"It is beautiful, Messire Louis. You are very kind, and I shall treasure it always," she said, smiling. "I believe you and I shall go along very well together."

"I have never had a doubt, your grace," the diplomat replied. "I have taken the liberty of including my device on the frontispiece."

"Ah, I see it. *Plus est en vous,*" she read.

"Aye, your grace, I thought it was most appropriate, for I have always known there is more in you, in truth," he said, smiling.

21

1476

Without Louis harassing him on his borders, Charles could turn his back on France and look to further aggrandizement in Alsace and Lorraine. Back in May, Duke René of Lorraine had already broken an agreement for safe passage to Charles's troops through his territory, and so Charles used this as an excuse to invade. By the first of the year, Lorraine was added to the Burgundian territories through two months of brilliant campaigning by Charles and the subsequent siege of its capital, Nancy.

Margaret heard the news from Chancellor Hugonet in one of his hourlong orations about Charles's prowess as a soldier and great conqueror. In Charles's absences, Margaret had always presided over the council at Gravensteen Castle, making decisions and passing judgment, but in those early months of the year, she was aware that the burghers of Ghent were grumbling at the taxes being levied on them to fund Charles's campaign, and she felt a few twinges of alarm at the dissent.

A messenger arrived at the end of February to give news of Charles's conquest of Grandson, a garrisoned Swiss town on the banks of Lake

Neuchâtel. Margaret had been horrified to hear that Charles had hanged many of those left alive on walnut trees outside the town, several to a tree. The rest, the messenger said with shameful nonchalance, had been thrown in the lake and drowned. The councilors had cheered at the victory, but Margaret had sunk into an even deeper melancholy. What little respect she had left for Charles was being eroded by the day.

In early March, another messenger cantered into the courtyard at Ten Waele, his horse white with lather and his Burgundian blue-and-white surcoat and cloak covered with mud and blood. Grooms sprang from nowhere to help him from the saddle and take the horse to the stables.

Guillaume escorted him to the duchess, who had just returned to the presence chamber from the prie-dieu in her chamber. She now spent many hours on her knees, telling her rosary. Several courtiers were playing chess and cards, and a quartet of recorders was playing a piece by their countryman Binchois. The messenger's disheveled appearance and hurried entrance was in stark contrast to the pleasant, leisurely scene.

"Your grace, the duke's messenger," Guillaume announced urgently.

Aye, Guillaume, I can see who he is, she thought unkindly. She clapped her hands and the music stopped abruptly. Guillaume went to her side as the messenger fell on his knees in front of her.

"My master and dread lord, the duke of Burgundy, has suffered a grievous defeat at Grandson on the shores of Lake Neuchâtel at the hands of the Swiss and their allies."

A gasp of horror went up from the assembled company. Everyone moved around the bringer of bad news. Margaret stared at the man in disbelief. Charles has never lost a battle, she wanted to tell him, but she was speechless.

"You must be mistaken," Gruuthuse said, breaking the silence. "Duke Charles took Grandson not a sennight ago. Explain yourself, sir."

The messenger did his best with the little information he had, but it seemed Charles had been lured out of his fortified camp at Grandson to help defend another town and, not knowing the allied army was so close, did not have time to set up for a battle and was trapped. The Burgundians turned and fled, several hundred losing their lives.

"A greater disaster was the loss of our entire baggage train, tents, artillery, plate, clothes and arms, your grace. The duke's jewels and tapestries, holy reliquaries, money and books—all plundered and scattered." Another gasp went up from the onlookers. "Duke Charles told me to tell you he was especially saddened by the loss of your gift, duchess. And," he remembered, "of his jeweled hat."

Margaret wanted to laugh; how she had hated that hat! She bowed her head in acknowledgment. Now perhaps you will stop your greedy warring and senseless killing, husband, she thought. On the other hand, if he abandoned his ambition, he would come back to her.

"We shall endeavor to send him replacements, have no fear," she assured the soldier. "But now, pray go and rest. I thank you for your good offices."

MARGARET SENT OUT a summons for a meeting of the estates general, and for days the members from all over Burgundy came riding into Ghent.

Seated on Charles's throne in the great hall of Gravensteen, Margaret addressed the representatives. She put forth the case for raising funds to cover the financial losses and for the necessity of recruiting thousands more soldiers. Charles had also demanded that Mary be sent to him, although Margaret was at a loss to know why. As she concluded reading Charles's demands, she was dismayed to hear the dissent in the hall. Finally, after loud arguments, the spokesman for the estates rudely rejected them all. Chancellor Hugonet leapt to his feet, his sharp, angry face reminding Margaret of a weasel.

"Then you shall know the duke's wrath, sirs," he thundered, his lock of black hair stuck firmly to his forehead from the sweat that was pouring down his face. "You will not go unpunished, I swear! And those of you Gantois who remember Sixty-seven can educate your fellows as to how terrible the duke's wrath can be."

"Shame on you!" called one voice from the midst of the company, and his cry was taken up by many. Margaret was afraid. The mood was ugly and a fistfight had broken out at the back of the hall. She rose and looked about for Guillaume. At times like these, she did not care about his brain; she was grateful for his brawn. He was there to take her arm and lead her through the archway behind her throne and into a private anteroom. Gruuthuse followed them. Margaret begged him to go back, round up the most prominent of the members and bring them to her immediately. Hugonet could still be heard bellowing at the top of his lungs.

"A faithful councilor, Guillaume," she murmured, "but Messire de Hugonet should curb his temper. I liked not the ugly tone of the discussion out there."

Guillaume nodded but had nothing to add.

Greeting the dozen or so delegates graciously as they filed in one by one, she invited them to sit at the large table to talk reasonably with her.

"'Twas a mob out there, sirs, and my feeble voice would not have been heard in such a din. I thank you for giving me your attention in more pleasant surroundings." She gave one of the smiles that had won over Ravenstein, and the men responded by sitting quietly, all eyes on her.

Within two hours of hearing each delegate one by one and considering each argument fairly, she finally won their confidence and more troops to send to Charles. The only concession she made was to agree not to send Mary to her father. Hugonet stood in the back of the room, finally subdued and admiring of the duchess's resolve, and Gruuthuse could not stop smiling.

"BELLE-MÈRE, WAKE UP! Father has been defeated again, and they think he is dead!" Mary cried, running into Margaret's chamber one sunny day in late June, making Astolat bark with alarm. The old dog now slept on Margaret's bed, keeping his mistress company, as Fortunata had suggested during one of her mistress's bouts of melancholy.

Margaret was sleeping soundly, despite a disturbing dream of Fortunata changing into a giant monkey, swinging from tree to tree in a forest with that hideous death grin of her other dreams on its face. She awoke with a start. Mary's words filtered through to her, their full implication making her scramble out of bed and call for her bed robe.

"Dead? What are you saying, child?" she asked, as Fortunata and Henriette helped her into the robe. "Where is Gruuthuse? Where did you hear this news?"

Jeanne hurried in, a worried frown on her usually calm face and her blue eyes pale with fear. "I was taking the air early, your grace, and I saw the messenger ride in. 'Tis true, there has been another defeat." She turned to Mary, who was standing beside Margaret, a frightened expression clouding her face. "There is no proof your father is dead, Mary. Let us not believe the worst until we hear the truth."

Margaret was now fully awake. She started to pace, tying and untying the knot of her belt. Charles dead? 'Tis impossible, she thought first. Then she considered the possibility. She had not seen him since Fauquembergues, almost a year ago, and he had been campaigning ever since. Certes, 'tis possible he's dead. That would mean—she swung round to face her stepdaughter, and Jeanne knew instantly what she was thinking: Mary is now the duchess! Little did Jeanne know that Margaret's thoughts were of widowhood, freedom and Anthony.

Margaret walked forward calmly and took Mary's hands in hers. She did not think the girl had yet considered the implications. "My dove, Jeanne is right. We must not give up hope until we know for certain your father is dead. Let us go and pray for the souls of those lost and for the return of the duke."

A few days later they received word that Charles was safe, and the three women breathed a sigh of relief.

"I am not ready to be duchess, *belle-mère*," Mary confessed in a whisper as they sat on their favorite excedra in the rose bower. "I am only twenty and have no husband."

"Certes, you are ready," Margaret retorted more confidently than she felt. "But you are right, we must expedite your marriage to Maximilian. I shall write to your father at once." She knew the papers were still pending, as was the papal dispensation. "You do understand your position, Mary."

"Aye, I know Louis does not acknowledge me as heir to the duchy because I am a woman. 'Tis hard to understand. He is still our liege lord, and yet my father fights him."

"I will send Messire Louis to you to explain it all to you, sweeting. I find it hard, too," she admitted ruefully, eliciting a giggle from Mary. "Now let us look forward to seeing your father ride through the gate. I am certain he must return now. His army has been so reduced."

MARGARET WAS NOT prepared to see the man who did ride through the palace gate and into the courtyard a few days later as she and Jeanne were walking arm in arm along the wide, white path by the lake.

"Anthony!" she whispered, recognizing his livery, and she gripped Jeanne's arm.

Jeanne said nothing, but she knew passion when she heard it. The duchess and the handsome earl! Certes, how blind I am, she thought. How delicious! They were made for each other.

Margaret became aware that she had given herself away with her exclamation, and with a blush mounting quickly on her cheeks, she begged Jeanne to ignore what she had heard.

Jeanne smiled and arched her brow. "Heard what, your grace?" she quipped, staring straight ahead. Margaret looked at her friend's profile with its cherubic retroussé nose and rosebud mouth belying the wicked twinkle in her eye and laughed. No one but Fortunata knew of her love for Anthony—although Edward probably guessed—and she did not trust anyone else. But perhaps Jeanne . . .

They hurried into the palace. Margaret changed her dress for one of green and gold damask, its plunging neckline trimmed with gold filigree and tiny pearls. Within the hour she was receiving Anthony and his companions in her presence chamber. After the courtly pleasantries, she suggested the court take the late afternoon air, and they processed to the gardens.

"What brings you here, Anthony?" she asked. "I was expecting Charles to return after the disaster at Murten. I was not expecting you. 'Tis a happy surprise."

" 'Tis not exactly on my way home, in truth, Marguerite, but this time I knew Charles was occupied elsewhere, and he had given me a safe conduct through his territories."

"You have seen Charles?" she shot back. "How is that possible?"

"I was with him a few days before the battle on my way back from a visit to the shrines of Italy. At first, out of courtesy, I offered him my services, but within a very short time we found we did not see eye to eye." He paused. "In truth, Marguerite, I do not think you would know your husband. He looks ill. He has grown his beard. 'Tis long and unkempt. He drinks tonics, potions and wine like water. And his ill humor has increased. 'Twas dishonorable how he treated his servants and his men." He shook his head. "He has painted himself into a corner with the Swiss, the Germans and Louis forcing his hand. I liked not his prospects, and I admit I left without fulfilling my duty to him. History will think ill of me, I am sure, but I saw no reason to die in an unknown land for an unknown cause. So I left. Besides, I had suffered the loss of a great deal of money and jewels from highwaymen in Venice, and I did not want to linger on my journey home."

"Except to see me," Margaret whispered, hardly hearing what he said. "Oh, Anthony, not a fortnight ago, I thought myself a widow. We were told by the first messenger that Charles had died at Murten, and, God help me, I rejoiced. In that moment, I thought we had a chance together, you and I. You have not changed your mind, have you, Anthony?" She turned her head to him and murmured, "How I long to be touched by you again."

She felt him stiffen by her side. "Despite the eight thousand others massacred, Charles is very much alive, Marguerite, although," he admitted grimly, "I came very close to throttling him several times. As for changing my mind, you know I cannot and stay true to the vow I made at Santiago de Compostella." He was acutely aware that they were the focus of attention, although no one could hear their conversation except perhaps Fortunata, but he was used to that. "You should put me out of your mind. I know I am only causing you pain."

She rounded on him then. "Then why did you come?" she said between clenched teeth as loud as she dared. "Each time I see you, the hope in my heart is allowed to flourish." She turned back to keep step with him and hoped they had not caused any gossip.

"Forgive me, Marguerite. 'Tis pure selfishness that keeps me coming back. You are what feeds my dreams, my musings and my life. Forgive me." He sounded so dejected that she moved her hand off his arm and onto his hand, squeezing it gently. "I think I have been to Hell and back these past few years. Edward has shunted me off to Ludlow to care for the Prince of Wales, and although I like the solitude there, I know he is displeased with my behavior of late. 'Too many pilgrimages, Anthony, too much melancholy' is what he says." He sighed.

"'Tis said I, too, am prone to melancholy. Fortunata despairs of me."

Anthony patted her hand. "Let us not dwell on it. I must confess," he said, changing the subject, "I am again taken with little Mary. She is a fine young woman."

Margaret gave him a sideways look. "Now that I am thirty, Anthony, are you looking at younger women?" she asked mischievously and was rewarded with a look of disbelief from him. She did not tease him any longer but poured out her concern for the duchy should Charles die before Mary was safely married. She told him of her meeting with the estates general, of her fear of the hatred for the chancellor, and of her growing reliance on Gruuthuse.

"He is a good man, Marguerite. Trust in him and Lord Ravenstein. If you are in dire straits, I have no doubt Edward will help you, too. I understand he has finished paying your dowry."

"Not before time," she retorted, and laughed.

"HE DID WHAT?" Margaret exclaimed. "Ah, now I know he has lost his mind."

Gruuthuse shook his head in sympathy. "'Tis indeed hard to contemplate, your grace. The Duchess Yolanda had given him shelter following Murten. As regent of Savoy, she was well disposed towards us, as you know. Astonishing, because she is Louis' sister."

"But kidnapping her! What folly was that?" Margaret paced up and down the red and white tiled floor, her swirling skirts sweeping up the fresh rushes. "Now Savoy is our enemy, and Louis will take this excuse to break the truce, I have no doubt."

Gruuthuse nodded. "Louis effected a daring rescue of his sister, and she is now safely with him, I understand. But we stand alone, and I fear greatly for Burgundy."

"Why does my father not simply come home, my lord? Lorraine is still ours," Mary said, from the settle next to the fireplace. Margaret had begun to include her stepdaughter in her meetings with Gruuthuse and Hugonet. Mary needed to be as informed as them all. "He can cross through to Luxembourg and then home."

"Aye, that is what he should do," Margaret agreed, smiling her approval at Mary.

Although she had no wish to spend another day under a roof with Charles, Margaret could not wish him dead. She could not envision what would be in store for her or Mary if he died. They would be at Louis' mercy, she knew. He had called her all manner of unkind names because of her resolve and influence over Charles, and she had been highly amused when she had learned of this. Now she feared its consequences. Louis would not treat her kindly, she was certain. Although, she thought, I am Edward's sister, and Louis wants to keep on Ned's good side. That could save me.

"Your grace?" Gruuthuse was looking quizzical, and Margaret realized he had spoken and she hadn't been paying attention.

"I crave pardon, messire. My thoughts were flying about like bats in a summer night's sky. You were saying?"

"Our latest intelligence is that the duke of Lorraine has taken heart after helping defeat us at Murten and believes he can claim back his duchy. He is moving to recapture Nancy." Margaret and Mary both stifled a gasp. "Duke Charles needs reinforcements or he will never get out of there alive."

Margaret continued her pacing, muttering to herself and frowning at the floor. She suddenly stopped and snapped her fingers.

"We shall go north, Messire Louis!" she announced. "North to Holland. We have not drawn on the province for men or money. What think you?"

Mary grimaced. "And sacrifice more young men to satisfy my father's lust for power," she exclaimed, startling Margaret with the vehemence of her condemnation. "But if it will save Burgundy, then you must go with Messire Louis, belle-mère, and Messire de Hugonet and I will stay here and manage things."

Gruuthuse nodded approvingly. "Duchess, Madame Mary is right. You and I will go north. My governorship there means I am well known and, I hope, trusted. We can safely leave Flanders in Hugonet's hands."

Margaret did not voice her concern for Hugonet in front of Mary. Instead she asked Gruuthuse to arrange their visit to Holland as soon as possible.

BEFORE SETTING OUT for Holland, Margaret and Mary spent a few days in September at the Prinsenhof in Bruges. The sun shone on the tall slate roofs of the houses for the six days of their visit, and for the first time, Margaret was invited to the Gruuthuse mansion she had heard so much about. Its imposing stone Gothic exterior rose three stories, a decorated turret at each end of the front that faced the courtyard. She admired the main hall's carved wood ceiling and the minstrels' gallery, reached by a carved stone spiral stairway.

Gruuthuse and his stout wife, Margaretha, stood at the base of the staircase to greet Margaret, who was escorted by Guillaume with Henriette a step behind them. The host first led Margaret to the *salle d'honneur,* which was hung with glorious tapestries, and offered her some sweet wafers and wine. Margaret noted the sheaves of barley carved into the ceiling acknowledging the family's fortune acquired over several generations from a beer monopoly. The house was full of light from the many windows that gave tranquil views over the little Arents river with its humpback bridges and the gardens that surrounded the back of the house. She read Gruuthuse's motto over the massive fireplace, *"Plus est en vous,"* and smiled to herself. Aye, faithful Louis, there is more in you than any of us knows, I warrant.

Gruuthuse led Margaret across the gallery over the front hall, through a bridge room to the most recent addition to the house: a small oratory, the vaulted wooden beam ends of it decorated with tiny cherubs, was actually inside the church of Our Lady next door. Cleverly, the mason had lowered the ceiling of a side chapel in the church to create a room above. Kneeling in front of the leaded windows, the party could look down on the altar below and take part in the service without leaving the house. Margaret was intrigued. She thought perhaps this was how God felt looking down on his bishops and all the people assembled to worship.

After Mass, Gruuthuse showed her his renowned library, which Margaret had wanted to see since her arrival in Burgundy. She spent an hour carefully taking books down from the shelves and admiring the illuminations, the beautiful script and the embossed leather bindings. Another visitor was announced, and Margaret was delighted to see William Caxton bowing before her. She had suggested to Gruuthuse that he might be made welcome that day, and the councilor had readily agreed. She saw Fortunata disappear into the shadows as Caxton nodded a greeting to her. His eyes are kind, Margaret noted, but it is sympathy not love in them.

"Master Caxton, 'tis a pleasure to see you again. I thought we had lost you to London until Messire Louis told me otherwise. I trust your new venture is thriving."

William's brown eyes were bright as he extolled the success of his new press and presented her with a printed book in English on the rules of chess. Margaret took it eagerly, but then she had an idea.

"I would like you to approach my brother George on your return to England for patronage, Master Caxton. And as an introduction, I shall send this to him as a gift from me. He has much to learn about the game," she said, chuckling. "He will see the humor in the gift, I promise you. I thank you for your indulgence. Shall we take a turn in the garden?" He offered her his arm immediately, and she turned to Gruuthuse. "Will you permit me to steal him for a few minutes? I know not when I may see him again."

OTHER THAN MIDDELBURG Island, Margaret had not set foot in Holland since she had been duchess, and by the time her small cavalcade rode into The Hague, she had uncharitably given the low-lying country a two-word description: soggy bog. It had started to rain in mid-October as they crossed the border with Brabant, and the sun had not reappeared until she rode through the city gate of The Hague five days later.

Preferring to use her carriage to shelter from the winds that blew unimpeded across the miles of bleak flat fenlands relieved only by the occasional windmill, Margaret, Fortunata and Beatrice were able to keep dry. She had left Henriette behind to be near her infant. Two younger attendants rode in a smaller chariot behind hers. Guillaume, too, had remained, sending his captain, Olivier de Famars, to provide armed escort. She lost count of the number of rivers they were ferried across, including the Diep. The mud made for slow going, and thus she had hours to ponder on the gloomy state of affairs in Burgundy, which the climate outside did not help to diminish. Although the rain persisted during her time there, she did not let it dampen her resolve to persuade the Dutch to provide Charles with support. She left a few days later with Gruuthuse's praises ringing in her ears and was satisfied she had done her duty.

MARY REJOICED IN her stepmother's homecoming in November, and Lord Hugonet was impressed by the number of men she had been promised from Holland. Four thousand troops were sent to join Charles's army in Lorraine, where he was laying siege to Nancy. Margaret was delighted

to learn that Charles had finally listened to her. Mary's wedding arrangements and papal dispensation were now almost complete. Mary and Maximilian would be wed the following spring in Aachen or Cologne.

As the household prepared for the Yuletide season, an optimism
buoyed all their spirits and as the year came to an end, so too, they hoped,
would all of Burgundy's woes.

PART FOUR

A Widow in Waiting

Burgundy and England,
1477–1480

22

Burgundy, 1477

"Fortunata!" Margaret screamed, coming out of another nightmare. The dream always came to her as the old year came to an end, when she would pray for her father's soul who died on the thirty-first of December sixteen long years before. The head on the Micklegate was still as vivid as ever, and each year, the horror of it gripped her imagination for days afterwards.

Holding a candelabrum, Beatrice hurried to Margaret's bedside and pulled the heavy curtains aside. Soothing Margaret's forehead with her cool hand, she spoke calmly. "Your grace, 'tis but a dream. Wake now, 'tis I, Beatrice, who will comfort you. Lady Margaret, wake up!"

Margaret sat up abruptly, her eyes wide open now. "Where is Fortunata?"

"She is . . . well . . . indisposed," Beatrice lied, knowing she was probably with Caxton.

"Oh," Margaret said, but then she clutched Beatrice's arm. "Ah, Beatrice, how glad I am to see you. 'Twas the usual dream, as you have guessed. I should be used to it by now, but it shocks me still." She drew the fur blanket up to her chin and rested her chin on her bent knees.

"You knew my father. Tell me about him," she begged, patting the side of the bed and inviting the older woman to sit. Despite her fondness for Margaret, Beatrice still could not lower her strict standards of etiquette and so remained standing, although she put the candelabrum down and wrapped herself in Margaret's fine woolen bed robe.

"I knew my cousin Cecily better than your father, your grace, when we were growing up. Your father was sent to their house at Raby as a young man to train, as you do know. Cecily told me she loved your father when she was only thirteen, but I did not think he was very handsome or strong. Your brother Richard reminded me of him, in truth. But I was wrong about him, Lady Margaret. He was strong and able to win people to him with his courage and charm. He used to call me Beet." She smiled, remembering. "I suppose 'twas because I blushed a lot when I was young."

"Beet! 'Tis a splendid name for you." Margaret had forgotten the nightmare and was watching this old friend of her parents with love. "I have been truly blessed to have you serve me all these years, Beet. You remind me of home." She looked wistful. "I wonder if I shall ever return to see them all again."

"As soon as the duke returns and Lady Mary is married, I think you should plan to visit, duchess. Certes, after all the tireless work you have done on your husband's behalf, you deserve to go and see your family." Beatrice was firm. "Surely you have but to ask."

Aye, she is right, Margaret thought. But when do I ever see Charles to ask him such trivial questions? One snowy afternoon at her desk a few days earlier, she had idly gone back over the events of the past two years in her accounts and discovered to her surprise that she had last seen Charles for five days in 1475, almost eighteen months ago. She could hardly credit that it had been that long. And the year before that, why, only twice for a few days at a time. This was not the marriage she had dreamed of all those years ago in her bed at Greenwich. She sighed.

"Certes, he will be back for the wedding, and then we shall think about England, Beet. I am sorry I woke you. 'Tis cold, and you should go back to bed. God keep you tonight, and God keep the duke and his army encamped in weather like this," Margaret murmured.

"Amen," Beatrice replied, crossing herself and padding back to her bed.

. . .

Margaret was reading a passage from her new book to Mary and Jeanne in the cosy solar at Ten Waele a few days later when a commotion downstairs broke her concentration. Margaret called to one of her attendants to go below and chastise whoever was spoiling the tranquility of the afternoon. The young woman did not have time to rise and put away her needlework when the door was flung open and two guards hurriedly stood to attention to let Lord Hugonet and Lord Gruuthuse pass.

"Pray forgive the intrusion, your grace," Hugonet said, bowing. "We must speak urgently and in private." Hugonet's thin face was pinched with worry as he straightened.

"Certes, messire," Margaret replied, concerned. "Ladies, pray leave us at once. Nay, Mary, you should remain." Margaret put out her hand and gentled Mary back into her chair. She waited until the room was empty before urging Hugonet to speak. "What is it, messire? You are looking peaked."

For once Hugonet came straight to the point. "'Tis the worst news, your grace. It would seem the duke has been defeated at Nancy and the army is in retreat." He paused. "Moreover, there is a rumor Duke Charles has perished."

Both Margaret and Mary leapt to their feet, faces ashen. "Charles dead?" Margaret managed to say. Mary was on the verge of tears. Margaret took and squeezed her hand. "I am sure 'tis a mistake, Mary. Who says this, messire?" she demanded. "How can we be sure 'tis not a repeat of the news from Murten?"

"We cannot as yet, in truth. But the soldiers who have ridden here to tell us of the disaster are speaking of a massacre by the Swiss and Lorraine troops such that 'tis nigh impossible for the duke to have survived."

Mary trembled. "*Belle-mère*," she whispered, "what will become of us?"

"I believe we must maintain order until these rumors can be confirmed or denied. Am I not right, Messire de Hugonet?" Margaret replied, before the chancellor could launch into one of his diatribes. "This means that you must write to your father's central administration in Malines to make sure the Treasury functions as usual."

"Me?" Mary's eyes were wide. "Why would they listen to me? 'Tis you who knows how to govern, *belle-mère*."

"Madame Mary has a point, duchess. If the letter comes from both of you, and you both use your present titles, then perhaps we may start a rumor of our own that Duke Charles is still alive." Gruuthuse had not said a word since entering, but now all three turned to him.

Hugonet's shrewd eyes crinkled in appreciation. " 'Tis well said, Louis. We will write at once. May we convene in my office, madame?" he said, looking at Margaret.

"Aye, messire. We shall be there directly." She and Mary acknowledged their bows and watched them leave with mounting anxiety. Mary sank into her chair and stared into the vast unknown of life without her father. Margaret paced and pondered and planned in her usual fashion. She and Mary were helpless without a powerful man behind them, especially as French law did not recognize a female line of inheritance. As soon as Louis hears that Charles is dead, he will not waste a minute in breaking the truce and reclaiming what he thinks is his, she admitted grimly. The question was: where would he attack first? She had not spent nine years as duchess and years before that with Edward without taking the measure of the Spider King. Her mind jumped all over the place as her soft leather shoes padded through the rushes, eventually stopping in front of the protruding chimneypiece where her eyes focused on her device: Good will come of it. She suddenly laughed. If Charles is dead, then I am a widow, she realized. If I am a widow, then I am free.

"Belle-mère, what is so amusing?" Mary interrupted Margaret's train of thought and made her jump guiltily. Had she said something about Anthony aloud? She turned and hurried to Mary's side, kneeling down and taking her hands.

"Nay, I was not laughing. 'Twas more of a cry for help, my dove. Or maybe 'twas because I realize that you are now the duchess. I should be making you obeisance, you see. And that made me laugh." I am not making things better, she realized, watching Mary's pinched face. "Oh, I know not. My mind for once is as muddled as a badly spun spindle of wool."

There was a long pause as both women sat with their own thoughts of Charles.

"How old were you when your father died in battle, chère belle-mère?" Mary surprised Margaret with her question. "I remember you telling me about those nightmares once and how you cried when you heard of his death. I ask because I feel no sadness, only shock. Is it because I am near twenty that I do not cry?"

Margaret put her arms around her. "I was fifteen, Mary. Much younger than you, 'tis all." She did not add that she had adored Richard, duke of York, who had been a loving father, interested in all his children, unlike Charles, who had never had more than a five-minute conversation with Mary in her whole life. "Come, sweeting," she said, using the English endearment Mary enjoyed, "let us rejoin the councilors. At least we shall be doing something instead of sitting and brooding." She rose and offered Mary her hand. When the younger woman stood, Margaret impulsively took her in her arms and they clung to each other for comfort for a few moments before gathering up their trains and walking to the door.

MARGARET HAD BEEN right. King Louis received the accurate report of Charles's death several days before Ghent did and attacked and captured the town of Saint-Quentin in Margaret's dowerlands the very next day. Several more attacks took place in the next week before Margaret and Mary learned definitively of the duke's demise. *He believes any former French lands revert to him because there is no male heir,* Margaret thought angrily. *How foolish Charles was not to try for a son with her or ensure Mary was safely married to a strong lord.*

"He was found frozen in a pond, your grace," Lord Ravenstein told Mary, after being received back in Ghent with Lord Humbercourt, who had come directly from the remnants of the army. Ravenstein did not upset the grave young woman now seated on the ducal throne by describing how the naked, half-submerged body had been known by one of his *valets de chambre,* who had returned to search the battlefield, only because of the scar across the duke's chest and his extraordinarily long nails. The face had been gnawed beyond recognition by wolves, it seemed. "Pray accept my deepest condolences, duchess," he said sadly. Then he bowed to Margaret, who was seated on a smaller chair next to Mary. "Duchess, I am sorry to be the bearer of such news, but all of us"—he turned to include Hugonet, Humbercourt, Gruuthuse and those other members of Charles's inner circle who had not been killed, taken prisoner or, as in the extraordinary case of Antoine, Bastard of Burgundy, turned their coat—"are ready to serve you both in this time of crisis."

"Thank you, messires," Mary said in a clear, strong voice, making Margaret proud. "Tomorrow we shall begin the mourning period for my father, informing our people that he is indeed dead. Duchess Margaret and I are in your hands, ready to hear your counsel."

If only the world outside this room could remain as civilized as within it, Margaret thought, listening as the experienced politicians discussed the facts and choices before them. Louis had already asserted his sovereignty over Dijon and threatened to overrun the northern territories as well if Burgundy refused to bow to his rule. Louis had promised to protect his godchild Mary's rights, but out of the other side of his mouth he threatened Burgundians who did not accept him as absolute ruler. He also offered his seven-year-old son, Dauphin Charles, in marriage. This would mean Burgundy would revert to French rule. All the Flemish and Dutch provinces would balk at such an idea. Already the people of Ghent were grumbling. They did not trust the Frenchmen, Hugonet and Humbercourt, who were counseling Mary.

With Ravenstein's help, Mary rejected the Dauphin in a letter to Louis.

"I understand that the duke, my father, may God pardon him, consented and agreed to the marriage between the son of the Emperor and me, and I am determined to have none other but the son of the Emperor."

Louis responded by sending his army into the duchy as far as Dijon, and in the north, he captured the town of Arras.

THE FIRST MARGARET heard that George's wife, Isabel, had died was when a rumor reached her that she herself was planning to marry the newly widowed George to Mary.

"Poor, fragile Isabel," she said to Jeanne. "I believe she truly loved George, in truth." She fiddled with her ring and shook her head. "You say the rumor comes from England and France? Although it would please me greatly, I cannot think Edward would sanction the marriage. You see, through Duchess Isabella, Charles—and now Mary—had a certain right to the English throne. A child of theirs would be a threat to Edward's children. He would be foolish to contemplate it, even to spite Louis." She had to admit to her chagrin that it was probably George himself who had started the rumor. He would enjoy the power and wealth that being Mary's husband would bring.

A few days later, as consequence of an urgent appeal made to Edward by Margaret, an embassy from England arrived to treat with the emperor's ambassadors there in Ghent to safeguard an earlier peace. Margaret was glad to see it was William Caxton who escorted the English emissaries, Dr. John Morton and John Donne, into the presence chamber. She was not prepared for the second English proposal of marriage for Mary, however.

"My sovereign lord King Edward, offers his brother-in-law, Anthony, Lord Rivers, as husband to the Duchess Mary," Morton announced to her, Mary and the assembled councilors.

The blood drained from Margaret's face, despite her pounding heart. What was Edward thinking? Before Mary or anyone else could say anything, Margaret heard herself speak in an unnaturally high voice.

"Lord Rivers!" she cried. "Pah! He is a mere earl and not of royal blood, a nobody and not worthy of our beloved duchess. I pray you, messires," she appealed to them, "reject this ridiculous proposal out of hand. Dr. Morton, are you certain you have your facts right?"

William Caxton suddenly knew who had met Margaret in the middle of the night at Ooidonk Castle. Christ's nails, 'twas Rivers, he thought. Poor lady, she loves him still.

"Aye, your grace. Those were the king, your brother's instructions," Morton replied. "And if Duchess Mary accepts, an English army will be at her disposal."

"The Duchess Mary will *not* accept," Margaret exclaimed vehemently, and even Lord Ravenstein raised an eyebrow.

Mary was also staring at Margaret. She could not remember her stepmother being so angry before. But then all tempers had been stretched to the fraying point in the past two weeks, and this proposal was ridiculous, even she could see that.

"The Duchess Margaret speaks for me, Dr. Morton. I am to marry the emperor's son and shall have none other. Archduke Maximilian has written of his intention to marry me as soon as possible. I pray you thank the king for his offer, but I must refuse." Mary gave a sign to Ravenstein, who stepped forward, bowed to the three Englishmen and indicated the door.

William bowed solemnly to Margaret. When she caught his eye, she could read sympathy in his look. Damn, she thought ruefully, he knows.

"MY LORD," MARGARET addressed Anthony formally, following his wish for them to temper the contents of their letters.

> "I write in this time of crisis of a matter far closer to my heart. It saddens me to tell you that Astolat, your precious gift to me of many years ago, has gone to his rest after nine years of devotion to me. He died peacefully in his sleep two nights ago at the foot of my bed."

Margaret paused, tears wetting her cheeks as she thought of how she held the big dog's head in her lap in those last few hours. Astolat had been ill since Margaret's return from Holland, sleeping most of the day and eating little. That night in early March, his breathing was labored and he lay with his eyes wide open, and Margaret knew the dog was suffering. At one point Margaret nodded off, and when she jerked awake, Astolat was whimpering. She saw Fortunata stroking the soft ears and whispering endearments to the dog.

"Do you remember, *madonna*, when I went under the table in King Edward's chamber? I was so frightened by that big dog. But Astolat, he has been my friend. And now I shall lose my friend." Her big eyes were full of sorrow as she moved to make room for Margaret, who sat up and let her tears fall freely onto Astolat's face.

"Aye, I fear we are both losing a friend today, *pochina*. I thank God we still have each other." Margaret put out her hand and wiped a tear from Fortunata's face. She looked down at Astolat, who was as still as a stone, trying to conserve what little energy he had left—for what, Margaret knew not. It was as though part of Anthony was dying, too, she thought morbidly. The dog seemed to sense her sorrow and struggled to lift his head to lick the salt from Margaret's cheeks. The effort proved too great, the big heart gave out and he sank down, exhaling one last time. Margaret lay next to him for some time, wallowing in her loss, and had finally fallen asleep, her hand held tightly in Fortunata's.

Now she wiped her cheeks and picked up her pen again, dipping it in the sepia ink. "I have now lost one of the best friends I have had in this life," she wrote. "I pray our friendship will last longer. Pray for us here in Burgundy." She paused again. Should she remind him she was now free? If anyone read the letter, it might prove a juicy piece of gossip, she admitted, and, sighing, she began to sign her name.

"*Belle-mère*, they have taken my councilors!" Mary cried, running into the antechamber, Jeanne close behind. Margaret threw some sand over the parchment to blot the ink, and rose to curtsey to her stepdaughter.

"What do you mean, child, taken my councilors?" Margaret exclaimed. "Who are 'they' and where have they taken who?"

Events had moved quickly since Charles's death had been confirmed, and Mary had called an assembly of the estates general and promised to be counseled by them. She had named Ravenstein as her lieutenant, which was circumspect, Margaret thought, given the unpopularity of the French councilors in Ghent. But a joint impassioned letter to Louis from both women asking for his protection during the first days of chaos had, in the Spider King's usual twisted way, been used against Mary and had caused the Gantois to distrust her subsequent pledge to be ruled by the estates. Unfortunately, the other signers of that early letter were Ravenstein, Humbercourt and Hugonet. It looked to her subjects as though Mary was dealing in secret with Louis while also promising to be governed by her councilors. She had been confronted with a copy of the letter and, horrified, she had desperately tried to explain the situation. From that day, demonstrations and parades by townspeople, burghers, craftsmen, merchants and apprentices took place daily outside the palace walls, and finally, Mary had been made to sign the Great Privilege, which restored all the rights to the towns that the dukes of Burgundy had taken away for more than a hundred years.

Mary was shaking. "Messires Humbercourt and Hugonet and two others, madame. Oh, please, what shall I do? They have taken them to the dungeons at Gravensteen. They have been accused of treason. They said the two had plotted to kidnap me and force me to marry the Dauphin. 'Twas not true, *belle-mère*, was it?"

Margaret paled. "Certes, it was not! And Messire de Ravenstein, did they take him?" she asked, knowing that he had signed that all-important letter.

Mary shook her head. Margaret assumed that the highest noble in Burgundy was too powerful to imprison, but she feared for the others. The two Henchmen were the most hated men in Ghent, she knew.

"But we are not permitted to leave," Mary told her fearfully. "We are as prisoners. And . . ." Mary looked at the floor, poking a patch of rushes with the toe of her blue satin shoe. It was obvious she was holding back some information.

"And what, Mary? Tell me," Margaret urged.

"Those people," she grimaced, "said that because you tried to marry me to your brother, George, you are guilty of treason, too."

Margaret exploded. "What?" she sputtered. Mary started nervously and watched Margaret begin the customary pacing. "'Tis laughable," Margaret snapped. "They have no proof, because 'tis a falsehood!"

"What will they do to us?" Mary said, wringing her hands.

"They can do nothing, Mary," Margaret said, hoping she sounded braver than she felt. "You are the duchess. They have no right to touch you." But on the other hand, they can do with me as they will, she thought. "Go back to your apartments, my dear, and I will be there anon. I must finish my letter."

Mary acquiesced and hurried from the room. Jeanne hesitated at the doorway. Margaret put her finger to her lips.

"I am a danger to Mary," she said in a low voice. "I must leave Ghent at once. But I do not want to frighten her. I pray you, Jeanne, send Monsieur de la Marche here and have Beatrice attend me immediately."

Jeanne curtseyed and left her.

Aye, I must go, she thought, signing her letter and folding it. But where? She thought briefly of fleeing to England to beg Edward for help, but she knew she must help Mary from within Burgundy. And if the Burgundians were accusing her of a treasonable act, they would doubly believe the story if she left the country. Nay, she must stay. Many of her dower lands were occupied by Louis' troops, and she dared not fall into their hands. Oudenaarde was far enough from Louis as well as being one of her own properties. It seemed a good choice.

Olivier de la Marche waddled in not long afterwards, and within an hour he had his orders and had agreed to accompany the dowager out of Flanders. As a close associate of Charles's, Margaret had no doubt the little Frenchman would also be treated with suspicion if he stayed. She invited him then and there to become her chamberlain as dowager, and he readily agreed.

"I have no wish to stay here with the temper of the Gantois at boiling point, your grace." He grinned, his bulbous nose almost meeting his chin and reminding her of a gargoyle she had seen recently. "I can have your household ready to leave within a day. I am better at planning happier events, such as your wedding celebrations, madame, but the same skill can be put to good use in a fleeing situation, I dare swear."

Margaret was cheered. Here was someone she could rely on, and one with a sense of humor. And with Guillaume giving her protection, she was sure she could move out of harm's way in short order.

"Thank you, sir. I will alert my ladies, and we shall leave the day after tomorrow."

She called to Fortunata, whom she assumed was listening at the door. "We are in danger, *pochina,* and I need you to tell Beatrice and the others to pack everything. We are not wanted here."

Fortunata gasped but ran to do her bidding.

THE WIND BLEW winter through the courtyard that morning in March as Margaret's attendants traipsed down the palace steps into carriages, onto horses or heaved furniture, plate, tapestries and other baggage onto carts. Her household was much reduced as dowager, but as La Marche pointed out, a smaller meinie made for faster traveling. However, Mary had insisted that her stepmother be accompanied by three hundred English archers who had returned from her father's disastrous campaign and were still in the pay of Burgundy.

Margaret watched the progress of the preparations from her window, the many colored panes sometimes casting the scene in a rosy, sunny or blue light. Servants below were scurrying from the palace to put hastily assembled belongings into the baggage carts, a sense of urgency in their step. Jeanne stood beside her, and neither woman wanted to voice their fear that they did not know when they would be together again. Margaret's and Mary's lives had been woven together for most of Margaret's time in Burgundy, which meant that Jeanne was always there for her as a friend. Both were thinking on times shared, crises overcome, concerns discussed, and neither wanted to be the first to say farewell. A small hand found Margaret's on her other side, and she started, although she would have known Mary's touch anywhere. She squeezed it, and it was then she quietly began to cry.

"We must all be brave, *belle-mère*." The now confident Mary spoke for all three. "'Tis cruel that we must be parted, but as Messire Louis told me, your life could be in danger if the crowd out there turns ugly. I shall keep you informed of all that happens, and one day, I promise you, we shall be together again."

Margaret was shamed by the young woman's courage and wiped her eyes. "The people love you, Mary. Do not forget that," she said. "You represent a new era for them, but I will always represent the old. I pray your councilors will soon be released to you, but in the meantime lean on Messire Louis. He is a good and loyal man."

She saw La Marche hurry down the steps to ready her carriage, barking orders to the coachmen and waving his expressive hands. With Cappi on her shoulder, Fortunata scurried along behind him, making certain the tussie-mussie and foot warmer were in place inside. It was time to go. With a sigh, she turned to embrace Jeanne and then, kissing Mary's forehead, she took the heart-shaped face in her hands and smiled into those serious gray eyes.

"May God bless you and give you strength and guidance to weather this storm, my dove. I shall work tirelessly to have Maximilian here as soon as the emperor allows it. You will be a bride before the summer is over, I promise you." She was gratified to see Mary's tension ease and a smile replace the seriousness.

A little cough told them they were not alone. Lord Louis stood on the threshold as the women turned. Margaret drew herself up to her full height and walked to him with a smile. He bowed low.

"I trust you will look after things here, messire. The duchess must count on you—and I must count on you."

"You have my solemn word, your grace. Your pupil has learned well," Gruuthuse said, smiling at Mary. "We shall prevail, I promise." Turning to Margaret, his tone gave away his mounting concern. "And now, I must wish you God speed and a safe journey to Oudenaarde, duchess. I fear the people are angrier than ever today. I hope you will have no trouble proceeding through them."

He was right. The clamor outside the palace gates did seem louder, but she was not going to delay their leaving any longer. On her way down the massive stone staircase to join La Marche waiting in the marble hall below, she made up her mind.

"Monsieur de la Marche, we shall process from the palace to the square, and there I will speak to the people."

La Marche's face fell. "'Tis too dangerous, your grace. I beg of you, reconsider."

But he knew the reputation of this indomitable daughter of York and was not surprised when she ignored him.

The ten-foot-high gates of Ten Waele swung open into the mass of people crowding the palace walls, and a fanfare announced the departure of the dowager. The English archers, well able to fend off the unarmed townspeople, soon made a path for the cavalcade to pass through, although the growls and grumbles from the mob were disheartening. As her chariot rumbled to the middle of the square, Margaret commanded her coachmen to stop. Guillaume dismounted and helped her out of the cumbersome vehicle as a hush came over the throng.

"'Tis the dowager, Duchess Margaret," one man shouted to those craning their necks to see. The information was passed back like a whisper of wind in pines.

"'Tis the English dowager—another bloody foreigner!" screamed a woman atop the shoulders of her husband. "Down with the foreigners!"

Before the cry could be taken up, Margaret mounted the few steps to the Gothic cross in the marketplace, her legs trembling and palms sweating, and held up her hands.

"Nay, good people—*my* people," she answered, praying her Dutch was good enough to say what she wanted. "I was born a stranger, 'tis true, but I am not one in my heart and courage. I have never forgotten your welcome in Flanders those many years ago and from that moment swore to become one of you. My friends, I pray that you will protect and uphold your duchess, Mary. She is ready to serve you, and you can have no better ruler, in truth. Go back to your homes. She is no threat to you."

The mood had not lightened, even though the spectators' silence spoke eloquently of their respect for her. Margaret wondered if she had said too much. She held her breath, her knees knocking, as she scanned the sullen faces before her. If they attacked, she would be killed, she had no doubt. Only now was she understanding how cruel Charles had been to his subjects, especially in Ghent, and how they hated the harsh rule of his councilors.

Suddenly a voice called from the back. "She speaks our language! The Englishwoman speaks our tongue. Let her go in peace."

Ayes and nodding heads followed the statement, and Margaret quickly knelt on the rough stone, crossed herself and gave thanks to God. Many of the onlookers signed themselves, too, and Guillaume took the quiet moment to urge Margaret to her feet and back into the carriage. He closed the door firmly and told the coachman to ride on without delay. The carriage was hemmed in on all sides, and Beatrice and Henriette were white with fear as leering faces appeared at the window and several thumps were heard on the wooden frame. Then as if moved by some unseen hand, the quiet crowd slowly parted to let the duchess and her train pass.

Margaret sank back on her cushions, her hands shaking and her heart racing. She did not know why she suddenly thought of her mother's brave stand against Queen Margaret at Ludlow's Market Cross all those years ago, but she was sure she knew now how Cecily must have felt.

WHEN MARGARET RECEIVED word of the horrors that had taken place following her departure, she spent hours on her knees. She blamed herself for leaving Mary and leaving Ghent. Together she and Mary must have represented a united force to the people, and when she was finally forced to flee, Mary was helpless to stop the Gantois wreaking revenge on the councilors.

"Hugonet, Humbercourt and the two others were accused again of treason in a mockery of a trial," Jeanne wrote in her neat script.

"As soon as she heard the verdict, my dear duchess went herself to the people on the very spot you spoke to them last month. If you could have seen her, you would have been so proud. She pleaded with the mob to spare her loyal councilors and she did not hide her tears. Such a picture she made—tiny, plainly dressed in gray with a simple black velvet cloth covering her hair. But the people's hearts have turned to stone. 'Twas heartrending and Messire Louis hurried her away before she could be harmed.

"The rest is almost too dreadful to tell, madame, but I know you would like the truth. In those dungeons underneath Gravensteen, they tortured Humbercourt and Hugonet horribly. 'Twas not seemly for Mary to be present for their executions, but I went in her place at noon so that Chancellor Hugonet would know that she cared. I have never witnessed such a ghastly sight. There was no possibility for the poor man to give one of his long speeches, he could not even open his mouth, for

they had broken his body so completely. They were forced to tie him to a chair in order to cut off his head. If I had not promised Mary that I would stay, I would have run from the scene. The mob howled for his blood in a hideous manner and they cheered as his beaten head was severed from his body. I must admit, I was forced to vomit upon the platform. I still have nightmares about the death, and I pray God and his angels have taken the loyal lord to his rest. He had none here on earth those last few days."

Margaret's hand was at her throat through this vivid description, and she found she was too shocked to cry.

"I am ashamed to say, I could not bring myself to return later in the day for the execution of Messire de Humbercourt, but I am told he died with dignity and 'Long Live Burgundy' on his lips. Mary is very low and misses you so much. She talks of nothing but Maximilian, and together with Messire Louis, wrote him a letter begging him to hasten to her side and lend her aid. It seems others in the council are not convinced Maximilian is the right choice for her."

Margaret looked up and groaned. Poor Mary, will she ever be a bride? she wondered.

"They are putting forth other candidates, including her cousin and dear friend, Philip of Cleves."

Sweet Philip, how he would love to be her husband, Margaret thought, but there is no doubt our strongest chance of saving Burgundy from France is Maximilian.

"'Tis said Louis has abandoned the effort of marrying Mary to the Dauphin, and as he continues to raid our borders, he is offering other princes under his sovereignty. The Dauphin, it seems, is now dangled before your brother, King Edward, for his little Elizabeth."

Aye, Edward would dearly love that match, she thought. So Louis continues to spin his webs.

Kneeling at her prie-dieu, she finally wept for the souls of The Henchmen, feeling guilty about the fun she used to make of them but knowing they were loyal patriots and had been harshly treated by the Gantois. She begged the Virgin, Mary's namesake, to guide her stepdaughter through this morass, although she had been cheered to hear that after the deaths of the councilors and sixteen more of Charles's servants, the tide was turning and the people had finally had enough of vengeful bloodshed. Any love they might have had for Louis went up with the flames of the plundered villages and fields the French troops were leaving in their wake as they continued to invade Burgundian lands. Picardy and the duchy of Burgundy were already his. Margaret felt so helpless away from the center of things. But she had worries of her own, for Louis was encroaching farther and farther on her property and had already burned her favorite village of Binche, a little too close to Oudenaarde for comfort, and so she removed her court to the Brabant city of Malines northeast of Brussels, which was to become her main residence for the rest of her life.

"ANTHONY!" SHE BREATHED when she saw the letter awaiting her after her weekly visit to the poorhouse. She continued to minister to the sick, and Malines was beginning to revere their dowager duchess. Fortunata always accompanied her mistress, and Margaret cherished the wise little woman's advice to some of the patients in the many beds she circulated among.

"I like helping these people, because they are good people. Poor, like me in Padua," Fortunata had told Margaret once.

Margaret called for the dwarf and Beatrice to accompany her to the garden, which was full of roses in the blazing July sun. Wearing their wide-brimmed straw hats, the three women, followed at a discreet distance by a couple of menservants, wandered along the scent-laden paths to a stone seat under a tree by the River Dyle. A kingfisher darted away at their arrival, its bright blue wings flashing danger to other birds along the banks. A couple of coots scooted away, and a majestic great heron took to the air in effortless motion from the midst of some yellow flag irises on the opposite bank of the river. The spot reminded Margaret of Shene, and she had sought it often during the long days of that troubled summer.

Beatrice was showing her age. She had lost some inches because of her permanently stooped shoulders, and her hands, once elegantly long, were now reminiscent of a bird of prey's talons. Even a short walk such as they had taken tired the faithful attendant, and Margaret took her arm and helped her onto the seat.

"Forgive me, ladies, but I would read my letter in private. You will not mind if I walk alone a pace?" She expected the pout from Fortunata and watched her with amusement as she flounced off to pick watercress along the river bank.

Beatrice was grateful. "I am content here, your grace. I shall not want for company." She indicated the coots and a squirrel that had timidly wandered near them, twitching its bushy red tail and keeping its beady eye on them.

"I was sorry to read from your letter that Astolat had died. I hope you find another pup to replace him soon." Astolat was not merely another dog, Anthony, Margaret thought indignantly, he was my link to you. How can you think I could replace him? *"You are in my thoughts at this difficult time, and we are kept abreast of events in Burgundy weekly through our embassies."* Spies more like, Margaret thought.

"There is a storm brewing here that should concern you personally, madame. My lord of Clarence"—Dear God, not George again, she thought. *"My lord of Clarence has much displeased the king, your brother, and this time Edward has imprisoned him in the Tower."*

Margaret gasped and glanced quickly at Beatrice. But she had nodded off in the sunshine. What is Edward thinking? But more to the point, what has George done now? She read on, a worried frown creasing her brow.

"You will hear the many reasons from a closer source than I, I have no doubt, but one of them involved you, your grace."

Margaret frowned. She had been feeling guilty about her lack of correspondence with her family in the last six months, but she hoped they would understand, given the circumstances. So she could not fathom why she could be a cause of George's incarceration.

"A rumor reached us that you were planning to wed the Duchess Mary to George, and he was mightily pleased." Damn Louis' eyes, she seethed. *"Edward dismissed the idea as ridiculous, and I fear this turned George against the king. Then another marriage proposal with James of Scotland's sister was received, and—this will make you smile I have no doubt—a double wedding proposed with you and James's brother, Albany!"* Margaret laughed out loud. *"Edward rejected them on the grounds that you were both too recently widowed and your period of mourning was not yet over."*

Certes, Margaret reminded herself, I am in mourning. But then she grew angry with Edward, who had not even asked her opinion of the match. "Such gall," she muttered. "I am no longer his to bandy about."

She continued reading.

"George has asked me to appeal to you to write to Edward and beg for his release. My lady, I do not think Edward will listen to you. Clarence has overstepped his bounds, so Edward tells me, and must learn his lesson better this time.

"I trust you are in a safe place and are keeping well. The death of your husband must have been a shock and I extend my deepest sympathies."

Hah! Don't be such a hypocrite, Anthony, Margaret thought, but she knew he was maintaining a facade in case the letter fell into other hands. It was then that she noticed the odd signature, and color flooded her cheeks. On one line he had written M followed on the next by his motto, *Nulle la Vault*, and signed it *ARivières*, with his usual capital letters. If I am reading this correctly, she exulted, the M must be for Marguerite. "Thus, *Marguerite: None is worth her*," she murmured, ecstastic. He had communicated his continued feelings for her, she believed, and twirled around, lifting her face to the sun in the first carefree gesture of the past six months.

Fortunata, who had been surreptiously watching her mistress, clapped her hands in delight and startled poor Beatrice from her little nap.

MARGARET DID BEG for clemency from Edward for George, but the king was unheeding. Then events in her own purview took precedence over fighting a losing battle with her brother as word came to her that Maximilian was nearing the end of his two-month journey from Vienna. A marriage agreement had been signed in May, Margaret was happy to learn, and Maximilian was coming to claim his bride.

In imperial splendor, the eighteen-year-old prince rode his white horse into Malines to meet the dowager duchess, who was to accompany him on the final leg of his journey to Mary. Margaret was impressed. Malines was impressed. And Burgundy rejoiced at the savior who seemed like a young god coming to send Louis packing back to Paris. He approached, dismounted at the steps of the ducal residence and bowed over Margaret's hand. She sank into a deep obeisance until he raised her up and gave her a lovely smile. Margaret thought Mary would be entranced by the elegant young man with his flowing blond hair, handsome face dominated by the long, aquiline nose, prominent Habsburg chin and sensuous mouth. She prayed he was also kind. It was too soon to ascertain that characteristic, she knew, but his looks and bearing were far from the youth of the little portrait Mary had under her pillow. He was every inch a man and worthy of her dove. They would make a beautiful couple, she decided.

Maximilian, on his part, was surprised that he stood eye to eye with the dowager. No one had warned him how tall she was. He hoped she was not as intimidating as her height made her seem and thus was gratified to see a warm smile given in return.

"Come, your highness, we have prepared a feast for you. My chamberlain will show you to your rooms," Margaret said, cheerfully accepting the proffered arm. "I will tell you all about Mary when you are refreshed and ready to dine."

MARY AND MAXIMILIAN fell head over heels in love the moment they met. He greeted her in Dutch and Jeanne in French. The court was impressed with his language abilities. He had even practiced some bad English on Margaret on their journey to Ghent, and she had enjoyed his company despite her dismay with his feeble grasp of politics. *He is young,* she reasoned.

Ghent cheered his arrival loudly, a very different sound from the angry shouts of six months ago, Margaret thought. She smiled and waved and fancied her reception was warm as well. The eight hundred horsemen who accompanied the prince did not allow for crowds in the square in front of Ten Waele that day. But the townspeople had plenty of chances to witness their duchess's bridegroom as, clad in silver armor, he sat on an enormous chestnut destrier, his golden hair crowned with a pearl diadem, leading the procession through the streets to Ten Waele. Mary stood at her second-story window and stared in wonder at this vision of the perfect knight as he rode into the courtyard below.

Later Margaret and Jeanne brought the two young people together in Margaret's solar. Maximilian was mezmerized by the dainty woman in a scarlet overdress lined in white satin who stood gazing admiringly at him.

"At last you have everything that you have desired for so long," Margaret whispered to Mary, urging her forward towards the bashful young man. She winked at Jeanne. "Your highness, Mary has a token of her willingness to wed you upon her person, should you choose to find it. 'Tis a symbol of marriage, and you should not hesitate to look."

The conspirators chuckled as Maximilian, his face as red as the magnificent ruby ring on his thumb, gingerly put out his hand and unloosed the gillyflower that was pinned to Mary's breast. Then he bowed solemnly and offered it back to her. Mary giggled. "I accept, your highness," she murmured seductively. She turned to the amused Margaret. "You are cruel, *belle-mère*, poor Maximilian is tongue-tied, and I do not blame him. Come, let us sit and talk."

Margaret was delighted with Mary's handling of the situation, and perceived that her absence all these months had provided Mary with a new sense of independence. She had indeed grown into her duchess role.

Fortunata was not so bowled over by the handsome young prince. As she tucked Margaret into bed that night and removed the warming stone, she gave her own opinion. "He is handsome, *si*, but his eyes are"—she searched for the word—"ah, *si*, weak."

"Weak?" Margaret repeated. "How can you say that, *pochina*? You hardly saw him."

"I saw enough. He is soft and weak. But handsome," she admitted, nodding to herself. "They will have beautiful children together," she predicted.

For the first time, she believed, Margaret disagreed with her little confidante. "I think you are wrong, *pochina*. Maximilian is the answer to all our troubles."

Fortunata harrumphed before sharply drawing the curtains and saying good night.

WITHIN A VERY few days, the wedding was celebrated, and as the bells rang out at St. Bavo's and at every other church in Ghent, there was hope in the air that the tribulations of the past year could be put behind the beleaguered Burgundians.

Unfortunately, they had only just begun.

23

Burgundy, 1478

*B*y the time Lent began, Mary was radiant in her pregnancy. Margaret's emotions rocketed between intense jealousy and immense joy. That Mary and Maximilian had fallen in love was the only glimpse of sunshine throughout the tumultuous year since Charles's death.

"*Belle-mère,* I am the happiest woman on earth!" Mary had told Margaret one day in late December when she knew she was with child. Margaret did not have the heart to say Mary was being tactless. Instead she smiled and kissed the young woman, noting the bloom on her cheeks and the new swell of her bosom. Briefly she remembered that day in her bath at Josse-ten-Noode, when she rejoiced in her own changing body. It was too late for her, she knew, and as a barren woman, she had no expectation of being married again. If the truth were known, she had no intention of even entertaining such an idea, unless, of course, it was with Anthony.

"Have you told Maximilian, my dear?" Margaret asked, one dreary day in late February as the two women sat for the artist Hans Memling. She had temporarily moved back to Ghent at Yuletide, as extensive renovations to her new residence in Malines were being undertaken. She had abandoned the old palace that Charles had used when the judicial branch of the Low Countries was moved to the city, which, as the richest of Margaret's dower towns, gave her financial security. In November, she had purchased the house from John, Bishop of Cambrai, another of Duke Philip's bastards, and planning the rebuilding had taken her mind off the constant French incursions that still plagued several areas along the Burgundian borders.

Mary nodded, smoothing the wool dress over her still-flat stomach. "He is very pleased with me, madame."

"Mary, my dear. Don't you think you could call me Margaret now? We have always been friends, have we not? When you were a child, it seemed appropriate that you call me stepmother, and I did my best to be a mother to you. But after all, you are twenty-one now, and I am hardly an old lady," Margaret said, laughing. "Although your son will look at me that way, in truth."

"So what will little Philip call you, *belle*—Margaret," Mary said, dimpling at the first use of the older woman's name. "Aye, I am certain 'tis a boy, and Maximilian has agreed he shall be named for my grandfather. It would be prudent to give the heir of Burgundy a name with happy associations for our people."

"Very wise," Margaret said, remembering with a shudder the grisly events of March in Ghent. "Let Philip call me *grandmère*, I beg of you. It would please me greatly."

"Madame la Grande, may I request that you not move so much at this time," a voice called from the back of the empty audience chamber.

It took Margaret a second to realize that the artist was speaking to her. She wondered if she would ever get used to her new title. She knew Isabella had been styled thus when Charles became duke and married her, and so as a widow she had accepted it was to be hers now Mary was the duchess. Fortunata had laughed when she had first heard about it. "If milord duke dies, *madonna*, you will have the same name as his mother, yes? But it is perfect, you see. You are *une grande madame*," and she clapped her hands with delight at her own witticism.

Margaret, on the other hand, had glowered at her. "Do not poke fun at my height, *pochina*, or I will poke fun at yours!" Will we ever get over this feeling of being stared at? she wondered. "Neither of us can change the way we are, so we must not jest about it, you and I." Fortunata had nodded and hung her head in mock shame.

Margaret smiled now. Aye, my beloved *pochina*, you are quite right. Madame la Grande is appropriate. She called out, "Forgive me, Meester Memling, I had forgotten all about you, so quiet back there. How much longer must we sit here? When can we see the painting? When will it be finished?"

Mary laughed at her. "You sound like I did a dozen years ago."

Hans Memling was one of Burgundy's preeminent artists, and he had asked the two duchesses to be models for a large work commissioned by one of Bruges' weathiest merchants, Johannes de Doper, to be given to the St. John Hospital church. He came out from behind his easel, on which he was making sketches for the enormous wood-paneled tryptich that was three-quarters complete. Mary and Margaret would be depicted as St. Catherine of Alexandria and St. Barbara respectively, two saints particularly revered in Bruges. The work would portray the mystical marriage of St. Catherine to the infant Jesus.

"Madame, 'tis well known you have a love of books. May I respectfully suggest that if you are finding sitting still . . . ah, how should I put it? . . . troubling, perhaps I should draw you with an open book in your hands. A book, I trust, would make this ordeal more pleasant," Memling said, smiling sweetly. Margaret was struck by the artist's youthfulness despite his more than forty years. His untidy brown hair showed no intention of turning gray, and the prominent dimple in his chin gave him a cherubic air. She looked at him sheepishly.

"I fear I am become impatient of late, meester. Aye, a book would keep me quiet," she said. "I shall read from Lord Rivers' English translation of *The Dictes and Sayings of the Philosophers,* which he has been kind enough to send me. 'Tis a copy from our old friend William Caxton's press. You remember Master Caxton, meester?" The artist nodded. Before Margaret could rise, Fortunata was there to thrust the book into her hands. Margaret laughed. "As you see, 'tis never far from me, Mary," she said, stroking the brown leather cover lovingly. "I am learning much," she hurriedly added, waving Memling off. "I shall be a model model now, meester, have no fear."

Memling bowed and returned to his work, while Margaret chose a passage to read. Mary gave her left arm a shake to ward off stiffness after holding it up to receive a betrothal ring from an invisible source. The Virgin and infant Jesus with the ring had already been painted on the wooden panel at the workshop.

"*Belle-mère*—I mean, Margaret, you look very demure reading your book. A perfect St. Barbara. She was also very beautiful, I believe, and that is why her father locked her up while he was gone, if I remember the story correctly."

Margaret was touched. Mary had never commented on her appearance before. "Do you think I am beautiful, my dove? With my long neck and hair the color of hay, I think myself ordinary at best."

"Aye, I think you are beautiful! And you cannot say you do not notice the way others look at you." Mary chuckled. "No false humility, my dear Margaret, I beg of you."

"'Tis not at my beauty they stare, Mary," Margaret protested. "They stare at my extraordinary height, 'tis all. Just as they stare at Fortunata. Am I right, *pochina*?" She turned to look at Fortunata, who nodded vigorously from her perch on the window seat behind them. "But enough of this nonsense. Let me read you the passage on falsehoods, sweeting, lest you confuse flattery with one," she said. "Besides, I must keep my promise to Meester Memling to be still and stave off the pangs of hunger. My belly growls, and I smell something delicious wafting from the kitchens."

Later, as the two women devoured oysters, skate-and-cod pie, a custard and some dates and nuts, Henriette hurried in with a letter for Margaret.

"'Tis from Calais, your grace," Henriette said, curtseying and handing her the letter. "Is that not the king of England's seal?"

Margaret's heart beat faster. She saw that Henriette was correct. "Ned never writes to me. What can he want now?"

"Perhaps he is informing you that he intends to send us help against Louis, Margaret," Mary suggested quietly. "You have begged enough."

"Aye, and I am the fairy queen!" Margaret retorted. "I have given up on that, Mary. My brother likes his pension from Louis too much, in truth."

She had broken the seal and spread out the vellum. Having no secrets from Mary now except in the matter of Anthony, Margaret began to read Ned's usual opening, "*Right honorable and well beloved sister, we greet thee well,*" out loud. Her eyes skimmed ahead, and, before she could open her mouth to read again, the room went black and she slipped off her chair, fainting onto the red and blue carpet.

Mary leapt to her feet, her needlework falling forgotten off her lap, and, commanding one of her ladies to fetch the physician, she hurried to Margaret's side. Jeanne ran to the popinjay, which was minding its own business on its perch, and waved her arms wildly, making the poor bird squawk and flap its wings in an effort to escape its tether. The result was what Jeanne was hoping for, and, retrieving a fallen green feather, she thrust it into the fire and then held the burnt quill up to Margaret's nostrils. Margaret moaned and, opening her eyes, wrinkled her nose in disgust.

"Pardon me, your grace," Jeanne said, apologizing. "But praise God 'twas naught but a simple swooning. Come, I beg of you take some wine."

Margaret took a draught, coughed and eased herself back into the chair.

"What is it, *belle-mère*?" Mary said, her worried eyes huge in her blanched face. "Was it something in the letter?"

Margaret remembered and gave an anguished cry. "George, my dearest brother George." She stopped, not wanting to say the words, and when she did, they mirrored her overwhelming melancholy. "He is dead!" Not taking her glazed eyes off the crackling fire, she downed her wine.

Both Mary and Jeanne gasped at the news, and at that moment the doctor appeared, followed by a page carrying a box of potions and instruments. Mary waved him away. "Thank you, doctor, but Madame la Grande has recovered. She swooned, 'tis all."

The doctor bowed gravely but insisted on examining the patient. He left a few minutes later after giving Margaret a tincture to take before she retired for the night.

"My dear Margaret, may I read the letter to you? I will stop whenever you ask me to." Mary knelt beside her stepmother and gently removed the letter from the rigid fingers. Margaret absently nodded her willingness to listen, and Jeanne pulled up a stool to sit by and hold her hand.

"*I regret to inform you that our brother George is dead,*" Mary read.

Margaret moaned again. That was as far as she had gone, but Mary read on.

"It came to my notice that even from the Tower he was plotting against me, spilling vile lies about me, my wife and her family and even our mother. He was brought to trial for treason . . ."

Mary stopped, drawing in a sharp breath as she read ahead, not wanting to distress Margaret further.

Margaret sat ramrod-straight in her chair, her grip on Jeanne's hand like a vise. "Go on, Mary," she said, her voice cracking.

" . . . for treason, as you may have heard. Before Parliament I accused George of plotting to take the throne. Some of these efforts will be well known to you, but lately there were more that came to my ears. In truth, Margaret, one of them involved you and your alleged wish that George be wedded to Mary."

Mary looked up in surprise. "Is this true, *belle-mère?*"

Margaret drew a deep breath. "Before I was betrothed to your father, there was some talk of marrying you to George," she admitted, "but Edward could not take that risk, Mary. George was disappointed because it would have meant he and I could stay together always. But that was many years ago. I swear to you, there is no truth to George's story." In a flash of insight, she guessed George must have known that she would support him in a match with Mary had it been offered. *Ah, George, your ambition and pride had no bounds, in truth, and look what it has brought you,* she thought sadly. To Mary she said, "I pray you, continue. I am ready."

"Only mother begged me to spare him, Meg. All others deserted him. Richard believed my soul would rot in Hell if I took my own brother's life and cautioned me to rescind the sentence, but he also believed in George's guilt. No one came forward to speak in his defense at the trial, and he was forced to defend himself. Had he shown remorse for all his past transgressions towards me or had he pleaded with me for his life, I might have relented, but he was arrogant until the end. As long as he lived, my throne was in jeopardy. His request that the execution be private was honored, and as you know he was drinking heavily, I ordered a butt of his favorite malmsey to be delivered to him that night, and even though the poison was administered in a cup of it, I do not think he suffered greatly in his death. He is now lying in Tewkesbury with Isabel, God rest his soul. Pray for me, Margaret, I beg of you. This decision was the most difficult of my life, and I know it will not be looked on kindly by history."

Mary whispered his farewell and signature and gazed with love and sympathy at her stepmother. "I am so sorry, Margaret." With her new self-confidence, she raised her voice. "Come, let us all pray for Clarence's soul and," she added, although she did not much feel like it, "for Edward." She fell on her knees and signed herself and was followed in quick succession by Margaret and Jeanne.

Margaret's thoughts had flown back to England and her childhood. She saw herself playing chess at Greenwich with George, which made her wonder if he had received her gift of the book from Caxton. She heard again the silly squabbles he and Dickon had engaged in daily. She felt his hand in hers as he led her in a dance. And she remembered the last time she had seen him—at Fauquembergues in Seventy-five, looking back at her from his horse. Her eyes flew wide and she slumped back onto her heels.

"Sweet Mary, Mother of God," she whispered, causing Jeanne to look at her anxiously. "The prediction! George's astrologer told him he would have a watery end. The malmsey! Do you think they drowned him in it?" she asked of no one. She shuddered, imagining George's last look on the world, his blue eyes open, his sweet smile still upon his face, and his elegant blond hair spread out like a halo in the amber wine. She crossed herself again and tried to concentrate on her prayers, but her family's faces kept appearing one by one, each one frozen in the time of her girlhood. Gone were her father, her brother Edmund, her sister Anne, her cousin of Warwick, and now George. And then, because she could not help it, Charles's face manifested itself in her vision. She suddenly remembered that she had also seen Charles for the last time that morning in late July at Fauquembergues as he rode off with Edward to deal with Louis. Unlike George, he had given her nary a backward glance.

And then Fortunata flitted into view, her dark eyes prominent as they surveyed Margaret with love and sympathy. "*Madonna,* I am sorry you are sad," she said quietly. "Where is your kerchief? The one I gave you. Weep into it, and you will feel better."

Margaret smiled through her tears. "'Tis always with me, Fortunata," she told her servant, taking the well-worn embroidered kerchief from her sleeve as if to prove it. "It will always remind me of you."

"I am always here with you, *madonna*. I remind you of me every day," Fortunata said indignantly, which at any other time would have made Margaret laugh.

"*BELLE-MÈRE,* TAKE THE pain away!" Mary screamed from her elaborate canopied bed, her petite form racked by labor. "Christ's bones, but it hurts!"

Margaret and the midwife raised eyebrows at the unaccustomed swearing, but Margaret took Mary's hand and stroked it rhythmically to reassure her. "'Twill be over soon, I promise, my dove. And you will have a fine son, I predict. Remember, our pilgrimage to St. Collette. She will answer our prayers for an heir."

Mary turned her perspiring face to her stepmother and gave a wan smile. "Aye, 'twas right that we went. But I am so hot, Margaret. Is it me or is the weather warm outside?"

"Both, sweet Mary," Margaret smiled at her, and then another labor pain overtook more conversation. Every muscle in Mary's body and face went rigid as she gritted her teeth and tried not to scream, while the dumpy Flemish midwife fussed and tut-tutted around her, her chilblained hands none too gentle.

The room was overcrowded, Margaret thought, but not having gone through childbirth, she did not like to dismiss anyone in case the attendant might have a role about which she was ignorant. But so many people contributed to the heat in the room. She finally dismissed three of the ladies who seemed to be merely bystanders. The birthing chair was ready for Mary as soon as she felt the urge to push, and Margaret pondered on her emotions at this extraordinary moment. Witnessing the birth of her first grandchild—Mary had begged Margaret to think on the babe as her own flesh and blood—was a thrill, but it was tinged with bitterness that she had never known what it was like to watch a child of her own enter the world. There was an ache in her heart for the loss of that knowledge and joy, and she swallowed hard a few times to suppress the lump in her throat.

Mary's grip on her hand tightened again, and Margaret realized the pains were closer together and more intense. A spotless pile of swaddling bands lay ready to encase the baby when it breathed, and near the fireplace several buckets of hot water were being constantly exchanged when they cooled. Behind the bed curtains by the window, Margaret knew, Mary's physicians and her astrologer were quietly standing by in case of any emergency. This was no ordinary birth—during which men were not usually present—but an event of great political and historical importance involving the greatest heiress in Europe. Nothing must go wrong. In her anxiety, Margaret had reluctantly agreed to ban Fortunata from the scene because the astrologer had deemed the dwarf's presence did not align properly with Mary's stars that day.

Margaret vaguely wondered how townsfolk and peasants dealt with the process. She had visited many a house and even hovel in her tireless work among the poor and pitied the mothers who could barely suckle their infants for sickness and lack of sustenance. Thank God, this child would know no such deprivation, she thought, although the Christ child had been born of humble parents and in less than ideal surroundings. In her waking moments alone in her huge bed, she had often dreamed of adopting a poor child and giving it a chance in life. Perhaps she would one day, she thought.

"Help me with her to the chair," the buxom midwife barked to her two assistants, who jumped to attention. Margaret let go of Mary's hand, smiling cheerfully.

"'Tis not long now, my dove. Just do as Vrouwe Jansen tells you, and all will be well." She watched as Mary, her chemise up over her distended belly, was helped out of bed and onto the awkward-looking chair.

The child was reluctant to make an entrance, and poor Mary grunted and groaned during pushing efforts for more than an hour before Vrouwe Jansen's coaching changed from stern to encouraging. "I see the head, your grace. Now, one, two, three, push. Aye, 'tis good! Only a few more."

Mary was tiring. Her small frame did not lend itself to easy childbearing, so her breaths were labored and mingled with screams and prayers to every saint she could conjure up. Finally the head and shoulders were freed and the rest of the slippery body fell into the midwife's waiting red hands. Margaret heard an excited gasp from the three birthing attendants.

"'Tis a fine baby boy, duchess!" Vrouwe Jansen proclaimed. "You have a son."

Margaret could not suppress a whoop of joy. Going to Mary's side, she put her arm around her stepdaughter, and both stared in wonder at the wrinkled form that was being held up and smacked into life. A lusty cry emanated from the heir of Burgundy, and for the first time in several hours, Mary's face broke into a smile.

"I have a son, Margaret," she whispered. "And he appears healthy."

"Aye, my dove, you are a clever girl!" Margaret exulted. "A boy at the summer's solstice must be a good omen."

"Maximilian and I have agreed to name him Philip, after my much beloved grandfather," Mary said to the midwife, taking the now swaddled babe and holding him to her breast. "I hope that is another good omen."

Margaret noted the absence of the Habsburg jutting jaw, which was a prominent feature of his father's face, and told Mary her son would be handsome.

Mary smiled adoringly at her child, suckling happily at her tit. "Philip the Handsome," she murmured to him, "I am the luckiest mother in the world."

As was traditional, the baby's baptism took place within a week of his birth, and it was Margaret who carried the child to St. Donatian's Cathedral through the streets of Bruges that bright June day.

A few days before, a disturbing rumor that the child was a girl had infiltrated the walls of the Prinsenhof, and when it reached Margaret's ears, she flew into a rage.

"Who started this?" she railed at poor Lord Louis. "There was no secrecy around the birth, and all of us in the bedchamber saw the baby was a boy. 'Tis cruel, and I pray the vicious lie never reaches Mary."

Gruuthuse nodded. "I would not doubt Louis of France's hand in this, your grace. He has stooped to lower lies." He did not need to voice them. Margaret knew all too well those Louis had spread about her, including that she had already borne a child before her marriage to Charles.

Margaret did not respond. She was thinking. The councilor recognized the familiar pacing and furrowed brow and watched her silently as she glided up and down the red and white tiles.

"I have an idea, messire," she had said turning to him triumphantly. "We shall extinguish the spark of this story before the flames have a chance to kindle."

Flanked by Lord Ravenstein and the count of Luxembourg, with Anne of Ravenstein holding the christening robe's train of crimson cloth of gold, Margaret came out of the cathedral on the square, the organ thundering behind her in a joyful anthem. They were an impressive sight, and for a moment the crowd stared, awestruck. Margaret saw her chance and stepped out in front of her two escorts.

"Your grace?" Ravenstein began, and then was astonished to see Margaret carefully disrobe the baby, who was showing his displeasure at being awakened by lusty exercise of his lungs. "Your grace, what are you doing?" Ravenstein spluttered.

"Extinguishing a fire, messire," she whispered. Releasing the final piece of clothing from the child and tossing it to Lady Anne behind her, whose mouth was also agape, Margaret held the baby aloft and cried, "Good people of Burgundy, I present to you your heir, Philip, baptized here today in the name of the Father and the Son and the Holy Ghost."

"Amen," chanted the crowd in rote. As if to prove the point, baby Philip chose the moment to spout a fountain from his maleness, causing a great cheer to erupt. Someone shouted, " 'Tis indeed a boy! Long live Philip of Burgundy!" and the rest followed suit.

Then a big brute of a man up front called out, "God bless Madame la Grande!" and another cheer went up, as did a couple of gleefully thrown hats.

Ravenstein smiled and then he laughed, his eagle eyes lively with amusement. "How I have missed your mind, your grace. Counseling was never so stimulating as when I had the honor to serve you."

"Burgundy is fortunate to have such a loyal servant, messire," Margaret replied, helping Anne of Ravenstein dress the baby again. "And," she added, shaking Philip's water from her sleeve, "I pray this fire is well and truly snuffed out."

Back in her apartments and resting on her bed, the windows wide to let in what breeze there was on that warm day, Margaret suddenly felt tired and unaccountably sad. Holding Philip in her arms for so long had been bittersweet. She turned her huge betrothal ring on her finger and for the thousandth time wished she had a child. She had thought long and hard about remarrying, now that her year's mourning for Charles was over, but her barrenness was well known, and she doubted she was a useful marriage tool for anyone now. Certes, if Anthony had come to her and offered it, she would have run into his arms. But he had never written even of the possibility, although a poem he had sent recently had struck a chord and given her hope. She reached under her sweet-smelling pillow and pulled it out.

> *"I was as blithe as a bright bird on a briar*
> *When I saw that maiden in the hall.*
> *She is white of limb, lovely, true,*
> *She is fair and flower of all.*
> *Might I have her at will,*
> *Steadfast of love, lovely, true,*
> *Of my sorrow she might save me,*
> *Joy and bliss were e'er to me new."*

"Of my sorrow, she might save me," she repeated. "And I wish that you might save me from mine, my love."

But it was Edward, not Anthony, who changed her life.

A week after she had carried little Philip to his baptism in St. Donatian's, she left Bruges to supervise the renovations to the residence in one of her favorite dower towns, Binche in Hainault, about forty miles south of Brussels. The old castle at the northwest corner of the impressive wall around the small city had suffered in the fires during Louis' attempt to push his boundaries north, and she was supervising its restoration. The decoration took her mind off continued aggression by Louis in many other parts of the duchy, but she felt relatively safe here.

It was another warm day, when, with a simple cap covering her head and her overdress tucked up in her belt, she consulted with the mason on improvements to the chapel and reception room. She had asked for the windows to be enlarged so that she could look out on the terrace garden and pleasant meadows on the hill beyond the wall. She was not expecting a visitor and was somewhat dismayed when Olivier de la Marche hurried in and announced Will Hastings. She hastily pulled her skirt down over her chemise and straightened her cap.

"Certes, my lord Hastings, this is a surprise. Please forgive my appearance," she said, smiling and stepping gingerly over some masonry on the floor. "To what do I owe the pleasure of your presence here in my humble house?"

Margaret never ceased to astonish Will with her ability to adapt herself to any situation, and he went forward with an answering smile and low bow. He waited for her to put out her hand to kiss.

Instead she laughed. "Let us dispense with the usual formalities, my lord. My hand is filthy, as you can see."

His eyes twinkled with amusement, and he offered his arm to lead her out to the garden. A true Englishwoman, Margaret insisted that roses be a mainstay of all of her gardens, and the scent from the myriad blossoms was almost overpowering. She breathed it in with a sigh of pleasure.

"May I say you are as lovely as ever, your grace," Will murmured. "I always find your company intoxicating."

Knowing all too well his reputation as a seducer, she did not take the compliment seriously. "'Tis the roses have intoxicated you, my lord, and addled your wits. You cannot fool me, for I see myself daily aging in my mirror. You, on the other hand, do not look a day older," she rejoined but quickly changed the subject. "Let us forego the false flattery and agree that time is not kind, shall we? I would far rather know how Lady Hastings is liking Calais?"

She felt him stiffen. *Sweet Jesu, did he really believe I might fall for his flattery? She almost laughed. What utter foolishness! Surely, she thought, this is not why he came, although he has only brought a squire and a groom with him.*

"My wife looks on Calais as an outpost, your grace," he replied, dropping the unctuousness from his voice so suddenly that Margaret was disconcerted. "We shall return to London shortly, and I believe she is counting the days."

Ah, his lady's displeasure was what caused his distemper, she thought with relief, not the reminder that he was married. She relaxed and again asked him the reason for the unexpected visit.

Will wanted to say "a hare-brained scheme of your brother's," but of course he did not. He looked about them and saw he could speak freely. Then he turned to face Margaret and gave her Edward's message. He watched her face change from benign smile to outright astonishment, and he was amused that he had rendered her speechless by the end.

"The little boy's mother has been sworn to secrecy, and she is waiting for my message with her husband in Tournai and will be close by in case . . . well, in case . . ."

"In case I cannot fulfill my duty as a surrogate mother or in case I die? I understand, my lord," Margaret was finally able to say.

"Something to that effect, your grace."

"And you say George sanctioned this? It seems hard for me to imagine he had a conversation about his bastard with Ned before . . . when under sentence of death," she finished, lowering her eyes to the dusty path. "Was it George's idea?"

"Nay, your grace. Edward—I mean, the king's grace—was in such torment over Clarence's imminent death that I believe he wanted to make some atonement. He said Clarence was grateful and that you should know he could not think of anyone better to whom he would entrust his son. I understand the mother will be paid handsomely and will ready the boy— Jehan is his name—should you agree to the plan. 'Tis necessary that he remain in seclusion for obvious reasons and because 'twas my lord of Clarence's last wish that history not know he had dishonored his wife on one night."

"Certes, George's honor did not desert him completely, I am happy to know," Margaret said sadly. "In matters marital, he was far more moral than Ned and Dickon." Or you and I, she almost said, but stopped herself.

Will had the grace to color beneath his graying beard. "Aye, he was," he agreed. They walked on in silence, Will giving Margaret time to digest the extraordinary plan Edward had concocted. Margaret was touched beyond belief when Will told her Ned thought George's son would fill the void of her own childlessness as well as provide a permanent link to her favorite brother. Her heart glowed and her excitement mounted. Why not? she thought. As they turned at the ten-foot-thick wall that separated them from the sheep in the field beyond, she gazed up at the warm bricks of her house and made a decision.

"He shall live here!" she exclaimed, her joy not lost on Will. "'Tis far away from court and prying eyes, and no one will look for him here. I shall appoint a chaplain to tutor him, and he shall be brought up properly—but quietly. One day, I shall tell him about his father," she said, her step quickening. She was already making plans and wanted to talk to the mason again. "You may tell Edward that I am very agreeable and that he can count on my discretion. I shall write my thanks to Ned and have you send the letter from Calais."

"Nay, your grace. 'Twas the king's express wish that no written trace mark this exchange. I will tell him when I return to London next week. He will be delighted, believe me."

"Not as much as I am, Lord Hastings," she cried, and she ran up the steps. As she reached the door into the house, she turned. Just as quickly as enthusiasm had bubbled, her mood changed, and her voice was suddenly tinged with doubt. "But his mother. The little boy's mother—how can she bear to let him go? How can I be happy when I am taking another woman's child?" Dejected, she waited for Will to mount the stairs to her side.

With a kindness she had not seen before, he took her hand and kissed it.

"It seems the mother is pleased to divest herself of her bastard, your grace. She and her boatman husband have trouble enough feeding the two they have had since being wed and they welcome the money. Your concern is misplaced, I can assure you."

She was all smiles again. "Then we shall prepare a palace for a prince, my lord," she cried, happily.

Margaret felt like a young, adventurous woman again as Fortunata and Henriette helped her into a plain kersey gown. Despite the fine lawn of her chemise underneath, the scratchy material irritated her skin, and she pitied the women who had to wear these clothes every day. Her tailor had produced a light mantle and hood that would conceal her face from all but prying eyes, and she wore a widow's wimple with folds that hung from her chin and completed the picture of an ordinary townswoman.

Only three people in her residence at Oudenaarde knew of her mission: Fortunata, Guillaume and Henriette. Seeing the tears in Henriette's eyes when the plan was revealed, she was deeply moved.

"Certes, Henriette, why the sad face?"

"Your grace, they are tears of happiness. Every time you speak to my little Guillaume, I know how you have longed for a child." Henriette curtseyed as she spoke.

Margaret thanked her and turned away. There was a time, she thought, when only Fortunata would have understood. Disguising herself as she was doing today took her mind back to that May Day at the Wardrobe when she and her ladies had sneaked away for a day of anonymous entertainment. She remembered Fortunata attacking the young man who had taken the liberty of kissing her mistress, and she could not forbear a chuckle.

"Guillaume will meet you at the stable, your grace," Henriette whispered conspiratorially. "He looks like a farmer today. You will not know him." She giggled.

Margaret had explained to Fortunata that it was imperative that she and Guillaume not be recognized. "You are well known, *pochina*, and would give me away."

"I understand," the dwarf had answered. "I will make the room ready for the child."

Margaret and Guillaume traveled as though brother and sister on two hackneys, with one of his soldiers dressed as a groom on another. On dry roads along the River Schelde they were able to cover the eighteen miles in one day, reaching Tournai at Compline. The unusual five-towered cathedral of Notre Dame was ringing its bells for the final service of the day. Inside the city wall, they crossed the river and rode up the hill and past the famous belfry, making their way to a respectable hostelry by the episcopal palace recommended to Guillaume. For the first time in her life, Margaret lay on a crude wooden pallet padded with fresh straw. Guillaume was to sleep on another but first he covered her with a blanket he had brought for the occasion, knowing she would not touch any bedding provided by the inn. They also shared the room with a merchant and his wife on their way to Santiago de Compostella.

"How do you know that is where they go, Guillaume?" Margaret asked while they were eating the meager fare of the penny-pinching landlord. Margaret had stared hard at the trencher on which sat a large lump of fatty beef and a slab of cheese. The ale was good, and the cheese robust, so she chewed as much of the beef as she could stomach and hoped the gravy-sopped trencher would satisfy her hunger along with the cheese.

"Do you see the tin shell-shaped badge pinned to his tunic?" Guillaume said quietly, as they sat at the other end of a long refectory table opposite the couple. "That proclaims a pilgrim, and it serves as a sign that the wearers should be respected on their journey south. 'Tis also a keepsake, proving you have made the pilgrimage. Do you not have such a badge in England, your grace?"

Margaret now remembered seeing pilgrims on the road to Canterbury with similar pins, but it had not occurred to her they were connected to their journey. Compostella made her think of Anthony, and it was his face that haunted her dreams that night. She saw the scarred ear, his clear blue eyes and fine chestnut hair. And then she touched him and his clothes miraculously vanished and they were once again naked together stretched out on the hard floor. He gently ran his finger up her calf as he kissed her mouth. This time, though, there was no fire in the hearth, and she was shivering. She woke up with a start, forgetting where she was but knowing she was cold and indeed something was moving up her leg. She kicked off the blanket and slapped at her calf.

"What is it, Margaretta?" Guillaume whispered into the pitch black room. He had been instructed to use the name to avoid recognition, but it came hard after years of using her title. He need not have worried, for the pilgrim couple snored in the exhausted sleep of those who have walked all day. "Are you unwell?" He fumbled for his tinderbox and used the spark to light a taper he had by his pallet. Margaret held up a bedbug in her pinched finger and thumb and flung it from her. "Ugh!" was all he heard. He was dismayed. The dowager was getting quite a lesson in humility, he thought, but would she blame him for his choice of shelter? He had spent many a night bedded thus during his heyday as a philanderer. He now preferred his feather bed and soft Henriette next to him.

"I am cold, Guillaume. May I share your pallet?" the duchess asked, as if she was asking him to help her dismount or open a door. Guillaume blanched in the darkness. "I promise to be good," she added, chuckling to herself at her audacity.

"I . . . I do not . . . what did you say?" Guillaume stammered.

Margaret did not bother to reply but crawled towards him dragging her blanket with her. "'Tis no time to be high-minded, Guillaume. Your mistress is cold," she muttered, losing patience. "I pray you make room for me."

Bowing as best he could from his position on the straw, he managed to remember his manners, much to Margaret's amusement. "I would be honored, Margaretta," he said. Regretfully, humor was not something that came easily to Guillaume, she knew, so she lay down beside him, her back to him, and wished him good night. A few minutes later, she felt him turn towards her and put his arm over her in a protective gesture that warmed her in more ways than one.

THE NEXT DAY, storm clouds threatened to burst over them, and Margaret was almost regretting she had come. Several fleas and bugs had gnawed her delicate skin all night, and when she rose to take a piss in the jakes by the window, she was so stiff that she could hardly stand up straight.

The groom was ordered to stay with the horses, and Guillaume escorted Margaret to Notre Dame so that she could visit the precious relics of St. Eleftheria and recite her prayers at Prime with the townspeople. It was her first time in the huge cathedral, and she looked about her in awe. She was not used to being jostled, and when one man rudely pushed her aside to make his reverence before the holy shrine, it took all her self-control to not demand he go down on his knees to her. As if he would believe I am who I am, she realized, chiding herself for her arrogance. She made the sign of the cross and prayed for forgiveness.

They wended their way through the streets and over the bridge, to the Quai St. Brice, on the east side of the Escaut river, which faced the fish market on the opposite bank. From the busy market a cacophony of raucous voices almost drowned the coarse calls of the boatmen on the river. The scene was colorful and alive. Margaret sat down on a wall, Guillaume standing by her, and watched fascinated as ordinary people went about their daily tasks. Farther up the river she saw a group of washerwomen, skirts tucked up to their knees, bent over in the river rinsing their laundry, others slapping wet clothes on the rocks or rubbing them with lumps of lard soap. They were laughing and gossiping and occasionally called to a child too near the water to move to safety. The river near the Pont des Trous ran so swiftly that Margaret could see the fortified bridge was not the only way the Tournois kept unwanted visitors out.

"'Tis time for us to find our charge, Guillaume. You have the address, do you not?"

"Aye, your grace. 'Tis not far from this *quai,* I am told, in the *quartier* St. Jean de Caufours."

This side of the river was less populated, and they saw only a few people in the maze of narrow alleys. There was slime on the walls, and the smell of human waste, some of it trickling down the path, assailed their nostrils and made Margaret clamp her kerchief over her nose and mouth as she carefully picked her way along.

Eventually, Guillaume stopped at a one-story house, boasting only a small window covered with oilskin and a sturdy wooden door. The top half of the door swung open when he knocked, revealing a young woman, who, Margaret was happy to note, had on a clean coif and apron. She was blond and might have been pretty if not for a sickly appearance, and Margaret assumed this was Frieda, the mother of George's bastard. Frieda thrust out her breasts when she saw Guillaume and gave him a seductive smile. She did not immediately see Margaret standing a little way off.

"My husband be not here, mijnheer. He won't be home for hours." She emphasized the last word and winked. "Do you want to come in?"

Margaret knew that in a former time, Guillaume would not have hesitated, but today he was affronted, and looking pointedly at Margaret, he told the woman, "I believe you are expecting us, mevrouwe. We come from the bishop to fetch the boy."

They had practiced this scene on the journey from Oudenaarde. It had been arranged that the transaction would take place in the name of Margaret's friend the bishop of Tournai, and little Jehan's mother would not be told that her son would be taken into Duchess Margaret's care. This way, the woman or her new husband would not cause trouble later. Simple folk did not question a bishop's command. Margaret was pleased that Guillaume seemed to have retained his instructions well. She inclined her head to the woman, who gave her a cursory glance but turned her pale blue eyes back to Guillaume's handsome face.

"Come in," she said, unlocking the bottom half of the door and swinging it open. "The boy is in here. I am his mother."

Margaret had a hard time adjusting to the gloom inside the house. There was not enough money for rushlights during the day, she guessed. The beams were so low that Guillaume had to bend over. The floor was the usual dirt, and a rough table and bench in the center of the room could seat a family of six. A curtain of nondescript color concealed a second room, but the stench of animal hides and excrement from it told Margaret that the family goat or cow was penned there. Perhaps an ordinary life was not so enticing after all, she mused.

Sitting quietly on a bed on one side of the wall were three children ranging in age from five to a baby in a little girl's arms, all gazing in awe at the enormous man standing in their kitchen. Frieda waved an arm at them. "My children," she explained, not very enthusiastically. "Pierre, come here to meet this man," she said to the eldest child.

"Pierre?" Margaret said, concerned. "We thought the boy's name was Jehan."

"It was," replied the woman, giving Margaret short shrift after noting the less than perfect Dutch. "But he's a bastard, and my husband's name is Jehan. He did not want the neighbors to think the boy was his." Her tone was matter-of-fact, and Margaret looked at the little boy, who lowered his eyes at this pronouncement.

Frieda jerked her head at her son, who slipped off the bed and stood quietly on spindly legs, unsure of what to do next.

"Come here, boy!" his mother commanded, pointing to a spot in front of Guillaume. As he came towards them, the light from the open door fell on his face, and Margaret gasped. Of his lineage there was no doubt. He was every inch a York. The curious high bone over his right eye reminded her of Edward, and his blond curls of George. He gave a stiff little bow.

"*Goedendag*," he said solemnly.

Margaret smiled at him. "*Goedendag*, Pierre. Do you speak French?" The boy nodded. "My Dutch is not very good."

"My husband speaks French," Frieda said proudly. "He taught the boy. And I have secretly taught him English. Say something in English, Pierre."

"I good boy," the terrified five-year-old stammered in barely recognizable English. This made Frieda laugh cruelly, which resulted in a paroxysm of coughing. Without a word, Pierre ran to the table, dipped a cup in the pitcher of ale and carried it to his mother. Snatching the cup and taking a gulp, Frieda said, "Pardon me, it be damp here. I seem to cough when it's damp." She picked up a corner of her apron and wiped her mouth and nose. Margaret noticed the red streak in the sputum and for the first time felt pity for the woman. Perhaps she would mention to her friend the bishop that this family might be in need of assistance. It was the least she could do for little Pierre's mother, she thought, although then she remembered the money they would receive and dismissed it.

"I think it be best you take him quickly," Frieda told Guillaume haughtily. "His sister will miss him, and the sooner they get used to it the better for all of us. I have no tolerance for whiners." She lifted her arm and threatened the girl, who cowered, clutching the baby more tightly. "She knows her place," she said with a short laugh and coughed again. "And Pierre does, too; he will do as he is told as long as you have a good belt nearby. And now, where is my money?"

Guillaume took a pouch from his belt and gave it to Frieda, and her eyes lit up. Little Pierre was forgotten.

Margaret took the boy's hand, and as soon as she felt the small fingers curl around hers, she was lost in an emotion she had never before experienced. Tears filled her eyes, and she hurried from the house so that no one would notice. Once in the alley, she expected that Frieda would coming running out to give her son a last hug, but instead, the woman slammed both doors behind Guillaume and yelled, "*Opgeruimd staat netjes.*"

"And good riddance to you, too, you unnatural mother," Margaret muttered.

At that moment the skies opened and a cloudburst soaked the three of them as they ran back to the river and found some shelter under a tree. Margaret knelt down to be on the same level as the child and asked in English if he was all right.

"Aye, mevrouwe," he replied shyly, staring at the kind woman with the warm smile. "I be happy not in that house." He pointed back down the alley. "I be happy with you now?"

"Aye, Pierre, you will be happy with me, I promise you." Margaret kissed him on the forehead and wrapped her skirts around him to keep him warm. "Guillaume, when it stops raining, why don't you carry young Pierre on your shoulders so he can see everything."

Pierre's eyes were wide with astonishment when the giant lifted him as though he were naught but a leaf and set him on his back. Then he unexpectedly threw back his head and laughed, and Margaret's hand flew to her mouth. It was her father's laugh, loud and exuberant, and her heart leapt for joy.

ON THE JOURNEY back to Binche, she made up her mind that the boy would be known by his original name, hoping it might help him soon forget his dismal beginnings, so she told Pierre he must get used to a new home, a new mother and a new name.

"Do you think you can do all that, my dear?" she asked him in English. "And although I will speak to you mostly in French, we shall make sure, when we are alone, that you don't forget your English. The name you used to have, Jehan, is a good one, and I shall call you that. 'Tis like John in England."

Pierre's eyes were wide. "But that be my father name, mevrouwe. He not want me to be same. He call me Pierrequin."

"You are with me now, Jehan, and Mijnheer Warbecque will never know. 'Twill be our little secret. *You* will be my secret. Would you like that?"

"Aye! I love secrets. I be good at keeping them." And he put his grubby finger to his lips. Surprisingly unafraid, the boy chattered from his perch in front of Guillaume, exclaiming at being on horseback for the first time in his life. "I so high, mevrouwe. Like a bird."

His use of the word for mistress reminded Margaret that she must tell him about the biggest change of circumstances. "You must call me Duchess Margaret, sweeting. That is what everyone calls me."

He frowned. "Duchess? What it mean?"

"'Tis a different way of saying mevrouwe or mistress, but as you will see, little Jehan, I do not live in a house like your mother."

"It be not like that one?" and he pointed back to Tournai. "I have bed with my baby brother and sister. Will I have new brother and sister to play with at your house, duchess?" he asked, eagerly.

Margaret shook her head and sighed. "I have no other children, Jehan. You will be my only one, but I shall love you all the more, you see, because I don't have to share you."

Jehan digested this and in a matter-of-fact tone, he pronounced, "Is good."

"But there is Fortunata, who plays magic tricks, and she will let you feed her monkey," Margaret promised.

The boy's eyes lit up happily. "Is good!" he repeated. "Very good."

By the time they rode through the gates at Binche and up to the palace, Margaret was calling the boy Jehan Le Sage—John the good.

In French, she told Guillaume why. "When I came to my wedding ten years ago." She paused. Was it only ten years, she thought. So much has happened, it seems like twenty. "Edward took pity on his little sister who was sailing off by herself to live in a strange country. He sent his favorite jester with me to entertain me on the voyage. It was a thoughtful gift. The jester's name was Jehan Le Sage. It seems fitting that this second gift from Edward should have the same name, in truth."

Guillaume nodded thoughtfully. "Aye, 'tis quite appropriate," he said. "And he does seem to be a good boy, despite the currish mother."

Once inside the palace, Jehan looked about him, speechless. His eyes took in the beautiful tapestries, the brightly painted ceilings and walls, as Margaret led him to his own room underneath the chapel. He gasped when he saw the window giving out onto the garden below. He had never seen glass in a window before except in church, and he ran to it to tap the panes. Margaret laughed.

Cappi scampered in followed by Fortunata, and the boy stared at both of them. Fortunata picked up the monkey and put him in Jehan's arms. The boy held the animal out stiffly from him, a look of panic on his face, but Cappi's chattering and curious eyes made Jehan laugh, and soon he was chasing the monkey around the room.

"I live here?" Jehan asked, when he stopped. "Only me in this big room?"

Margaret nodded. She was not prepared when little Jehan threw himself at her and squeezed her knees. When Beatrice came to tell her mistress that Messire de Montigny was here to begin his governance of the new resident of the palace, she came upon a scene that warmed her heart. Margaret was seated on the bed, cradling the sleeping boy against her breast, her chin resting on his flaxen curls and a serene smile softening her face.

"At last, your grace," Beatrice whispered, "your wish has come true."

MARGARET WAS UNABLE to stay long with little Jehan, but by the time she left to return to Malines, a routine had been established and she had formed a bond with the boy. She decided he should be allowed to call her Aunt Margaret, although she pointedly explained to everyone that it was only to make him more comfortable. Within a short time, he was the darling of the household, and Margaret felt only the heartache of giving up her newfound inspiration and did not worry for his well-being. Pierre de Montigny was a kind and learned man, and he told Margaret that Jehan was soaking up new knowledge with the ease of a sponge.

The boy was happily playing with a wooden sword when she went to wish him farewell, and he barely noticed her. It was just as well, for she was needed in the north, and her duties always came first.

AT YULETIDE, MARGARET and Mary were together at Ghent once more, but because Margaret had not told either Mary or Jeanne about Jehan, she had to be content with sending the boy gifts and a letter telling him he was in her thoughts daily. The fewer people who knew about George's bastard, the better, she thought. She looked forward to the time when she could tell him about his father and their whole family. But he would have to be older, much older, she decided.

"Margaret, I do not think you have heard a word I said," Mary said, laughing. "What are you daydreaming about?"

"Certes, my dear one, you are right. You now have my full attention," Margaret replied, ignoring Mary's question.

"Cousin Philip has been promoted by Maximilian to lead his cavalry. Messire Ravenstein is very pleased with his son," Mary said, beaming. "Is that not wonderful news?"

Margaret could not imagine why placing someone so near and dear to her heart in a position of such peril would be wonderful news, but she nodded and smiled. She remembered the last time she had spoken to Philip of Cleves and wondered if Mary would be so enthusiastic now if she knew how much in love with her the young man was.

He had the look of his father: tall, rangy and with the same hawk nose. He would make someone an admirable husband, Margaret had thought, as they sat together in her newly furbished palace at Malines in the late autumn.

"Has your father arranged a marriage for you yet?" Margaret had teased him. He was the most eligible bachelor at court and seemed to prefer it that way.

Philip looked down at his long, thin hands, and Margaret could see the question had given him anguish.

"You still love Mary, in truth," she said kindly. "How cruel of me to raise marriage when your lady is no longer available to you. Forgive me, Philip."

He had looked up at her then, and she was again struck by the likeness to his father. "God forgive me, your grace, but I hate Maximilian. I know you believed he was the strongest candidate for Mary's hand, but I trust him not." Margaret caught her bottom lip as she recalled Fortunata's similar verdict on the man.

Margaret looked at Mary's radiant face now and knew she would keep Philip's secret. Even though he was an impetuous youth and surprisingly inept in matters politic, Maximilian made Mary happy, and Margaret would never do anything to jeopardize that. She had a good rapport with the young prince, although he exasperated her frequently. Thank heaven he had good counsel from the lords Ravenstein and Gruuthuse, although she had caught them pursing their lips at a few of his puerile suggestions. She was still convinced that she had made the right choice for Mary.

AND IT SEEMED Margaret was right, because by August of 1479, Maximilian's army had forced Louis into battle at Guinegatte in Artois and succeeded in driving the French armies back across the Somme.

The annual procession of the Holy Blood in Bruges two days later was a particularly significant occasion. The city watched as Mary and Margaret took their places to witness it and give thanks for the victory. Hundreds of clergymen, nuns and monks wove their way behind the bishop, who carried a small rock-crystal vial between his hands for all to see. It contained a fragment of bloodstained cloth said to have been used by Joseph of Arimathea to wipe Christ's body. Crusaders had brought it back to Bruges. Margaret was very moved, and when it was her turn to kneel and kiss the relic inside the small but magnificent basilica, her knees trembled and she became light-headed.

"*Laudate Dominum, omnes gentes,*" she whispered in her praise of God, her eye following the lofty pillars that supported the painted ceiling of the Romanesque church. It did not have the immensity of other cathedrals she had prayed in, but she thought it was the most beautiful because of the colors. She truly felt blessed in that place of worship, and she prayed fervently upon her little cushion.

"I have much to praise you for, dear Lord, but I must ask that you show your love and favor to Mary and Maximilian, little Philip and the new child that Mary carries within her. I pray they govern the good people of Burgundy with justice and mercy." Not like Charles, she found herself adding. "I also ask that you bless my own little Jehan and that one day you will show me why I was sent to rescue him from a cruel life. I pray for humility and strength to do my part in the governance of this duchy. And as always, I pray for forgiveness and compassion for my illicit love for Anthony. May you bless and keep him safe always. In our savior Jesu Christ's name, amen."

She closed her eyes and thought she heard Anthony's voice murmur, "I thank you, Marguerite." She opened them quickly, but saw only the bishop raising his hand in a blessing over her head.

She signed herself, rose and genuflected in front of the massive gold crucifix and slowly made her way down the church to her escort waiting outside. The solemn part of the occasion over, the crowd in the Burg began to cheer the two duchesses as they walked down the covered Gothic staircase and onto the cobblestones below. Margaret wore black and gold. Mary was in a splendid overdress of Burgundian purple and black, with an underdress of crimson. Her train was carried by Anne of Ravenstein, and her three-foot-high hennin sparkled with jewels under the gauze. Despite her daintiness, she was the epitome of a great ruler.

"Imagine, Margaret," Mary said, as she waved to her subjects, whose voices had found their exuberance after years of gloom under Charles, "in a week, I will have been married two years. And in that short time, we have come from near disaster to this triumph. And much of it I owe to you, my dear stepmother."

"Pah!" Margaret exclaimed, waving with her. "'Tis you who should take the credit, my dove. You and Maximilian have given Burgundy hope. Just listen!"

THE MOOD WAS jubilant at the feast following the procession. Servants set platters of peacock, swan and heron before the guests, and the musicians piped merrily on hautboys and recorders.

Fortunata was eager to show off a new trick she had been practicing in secret, and Mary gave her permission to enact it during one of the entremets. First she began turning cartwheels around the room and then she clapped her hands and called for Cappi. The little jackanapes ran to her, and Margaret watched with half an eye as he imitated Fortunata's acrobatics until, taking a flying leap, he landed on his owner's head. Margaret had to smile at the picture the two made.

"Did you like our trick, *madonna*?" the dwarf asked, encouraged by the smile. She and Cappi performed some other feats, and the guests applauded with enthusiasm. "I am good, *non*?" she asked everyone, before running behind Margaret's chair and reappearing carrying a man's high hat. She placed it on her head and then quickly removed it, taking bows left and right as a magician might.

"Will you pay to see some more?" she asked the diners cheekily. "Only a little money, plis." And she walked around the room with the upturned hat begging for a coin or two. Margaret frowned. What was the scamp up to? she wondered. She did not ever ask to be paid for her tricks—she did not need to, she won enough from the cup game to spoil herself with new ribbons for Cappi or a comb for her hair. A few of the courtiers indulged her by dropping a coin into the hat. Then, in front of Margaret again, she took the pennies from the hat one by one, and the next time she put her hand in the hat, she brought out a wriggling baby rabbit. A gasp of astonishment went up, and Margaret applauded loudly.

"*Pochina*, you are a marvel! Where did you learn to do that?" she cried.

She opened the embroidered bag on her belt and brought out a florin. Fortunata's eyes lit up with excitement. She was about to step up and claim her prize when Cappi decided he did not care for his mistress holding another animal, and springing from nowhere, he plucked the poor rabbit from Fortunata's fingers and proceeded to kill it in front of the horrified audience. Some of the women swooned as blood splattered on the tiled floor and rushes. Fortunata blanched and tried to get hold of Cappi's leash. He lashed out and bit her hand, his razor-sharp teeth sinking deep into her flesh, and she screamed. Two guards rushed over, halberds at the ready, but when they saw what was happening they began to laugh.

" 'Tis not amusing, gentlemen," Mary said, rising from her chair and glaring at them. "Take the dead rabbit away, if you please!" The men bowed, cowed by the young duchess's stern command, and one picked up the little carcass from the floor by one foot, holding it out in front of him as though it would come back from the dead and attack him, earning jeers from the men in the room.

Margaret asked Henriette and Beatrice to tend to Fortunata's bleeding hand, and Mary sent for the physician. Begging the guests to continue their enjoyment of the feast, Margaret followed her attendants into the antechamber. Doctor Roelandts came in panting, a few minutes later, carrying his bag of potions, tinctures and bandages. Margaret sat the dwarf down and stroked her glistening forehead. The little woman was obviously shocked and in pain. Margaret fed her some wine while the doctor examined the wound. He spread salve on it and bandaged up the hand, none too gently, Margaret noted. He still remembers her transgression, she thought sadly. He was a good doctor, otherwise she might have let him go. He always made her think of Marie de Charny, and she wondered how the spiteful woman had taken Charles's command that she not return to Margaret's household. Margaret had discovered from Henriette that Marie had been physically cruel to Fortunata on several occasions, which had answered some of the questions about Fortunata's puzzling behavior in those days. Marie deserved to be banished, she had decided.

Now she looked fondly on her little servant, who was nursing her hurt hand and scolding Cappi. Her face was twisted in such an ugly frown that she would have frightened off a hardened villain, much less a trembling monkey. I am too indulgent with her, Margaret concluded. That monkey is dangerous and should go, but 'twould break Fortunata's heart. Besides, she had only been trying to cheer me up. Nay, I cannot punish her.

THE SUN WAS low in the sky and a flock of starlings chattered and screamed at one another in the trees on the other side of the palace wall. Margaret and Jeanne were walking arm in arm around the island in the lake, Fortunata close behind. The six-sided island was only there as ornamentation, the small geometrical beds offering heartsease and gillyflowers in the summer among low manicured hedges, but in late September, the garden was cleared. The island's isolation always gave Margaret a sense of freedom from the confines of the palace, and she and Jeanne enjoyed an intimacy there unknown in the busy, crowded court inside. From one side they could look over the fish-filled lake to the little zoo, where lions paced in a cage along the water.

Margaret pulled her mantle around her shoulders against the brisk late-afternoon breeze and lifted her soft wool skirt over a puddle.

"Jeanne, do you think Mary is happy with Maximilian? I could not bear to think she was forced into . . ."

"Certes, she is happy, your grace. Think no more on it," Jeanne replied, hugging herself against the chill. "Ever since she set eyes on the man, she talks of no one else."

"I am satisfied then. Whatever happened to Sir Galahad?" Margaret asked, remembering the young Jehan.

"He went with his father to join the army at Neuss and that was that, I believe. Mary pined for a time, but once Maximilian came, she had eyes for no one else."

A little cry interrupted their conversation. Margaret turned to the sound and was dismayed to see Fortunata clutching at her neck.

"What is it, *pochina*? There are midges out, I fear. Did you get bitten?" she asked, pointing to the tiny insects that hovered over the lake in small swarms. "Let me see."

Fortunata could not answer her. Her cheek and jaw were in spasm and she could not open her mouth. She allowed Margaret to feel the area, but her eyes told the story of pain under the fingers.

"Jeanne, would you alert the boatman that we should return immediately," Margaret said. "We should get Doctor Roelandts to look at Fortunata."

When she heard the physician's name, Fortunata scowled and managed to shake her head. Margaret tut-tutted and shooed her along the path to the steps, where Jeanne was waiting in the stern of the little boat. The man handed both women to the middle seat and rowed the short way to a staircase and door into the palace. Mouthwatering aromas were coming from the kitchens behind the great hall as the three women hurried to the chambers beyond the chapel and oratory. Margaret made Fortunata sit in her big chair and plumped up the cushions around her, feeling her forehead and holding her hand. Fortunata winced as Margaret's thumb put pressure on the place where the monkey's bite had pierced the skin two months before. Margaret felt a spasm under her fingers and looked closely at the wound, which had healed tolerably well. Beatrice came into the room, her well-lined face now creased in a frown. The door banged behind her, and Fortunata jumped.

"My head hurts very much, *madonna*," Fortunata said irritably. She reached her good hand up to rub her neck and shoulders. "And I am so stiff."

"Never fear, *pochina*, the doctor will be here anon." Margaret was at a loss as to how to help her little friend, but she kept holding her hand and reassuring her.

A few minutes later, Doctor Roelandts bustled in and rolled his eyes when he saw the dwarf thus pampered. Servants did not belong in the duchess's chair, he grumbled to himself, and especially not this ugly creature.

"What seems to be the trouble, your grace? It looks to me like an ill humor," he said. "Are you not able to find the cause yourself, Fortunata? I thought you were all-knowing in sickness and medicine," he added, smirking.

"Enough of your barbed tongue, doctor," Margaret snapped. "Pray examine the patient. She seems to have a stiffness in her neck and face, and I felt her hand go rigid a few minutes ago."

Roelandts' curiosity got the better of him and he put his hand out to feel Fortunata's jaw. She writhed away in pain. The doctor frowned, which did not escape Margaret's notice. Then he picked up Fortunata's hand and scrutinized the bite wound.

"Has it been two months since the monkey bit you, Fortunata?" he asked more gently. "And did you keep the bandage on, as I instructed?"

Fortunata pouted. "I had to clean Cappi after he killed the rabbit. He was very afraid and so he . . . you know . . . dirtied himself," she explained. "I took the wet bandage off."

"What is it, doctor? The wound seems to have healed, in truth. 'Tis her neck and cheek that pains her."

He motioned Margaret to the other side of the room. "The two are related, your grace. 'Tis an ailment that I have only heard of before now. And I know not how to treat it, madame." Then he lowered his eyes and his voice. " 'Tis said it is painful, and I fear 'twill get worse."

"And then what happens?" Margaret barked. "Will she get over it? Answer me plainly, sir!"

Roelandts dared not lie. He shook his head. "I am told 'tis incurable, duchess."

Margaret's hand flew to her mouth to stop her cry of anguish. Beatrice and Jeanne were tending to the patient, who had not moved since she was put in the chair. Cappi was curled up in her lap and made odd little chirping noises. Margaret held herself erect and began to question the doctor more thoroughly. She was afraid his resentment of Fortunata might have caused him to paint a blacker picture than was necessary. He answered her as best he could, but it was clear he did not know how to proceed.

Margaret finally brought herself to ask, "Is she going to die? Tell me the truth."

Roelandts nodded slowly, rubbing his big nose. "In those cases I have heard about, they did."

"Pah!" she spat at him in her rising fear. " 'Twas because those other cases did not have the benefit of the best doctor in Burgundy with all the best medicines at his disposal. A tight neck and jaw cannot be that serious. Use your skill to cure Fortunata, and perhaps there will be a fine reward for you if you do." She saw the doctor's eyes light up, so she was quick to add, "But if she dies, you will be dismissed. Do you understand?"

Margaret turned away, not wanting the doctor to see her tears. Do not cry in front of servants, Margaret. 'Tis the sign of weakness and they will not respect you. Aye, mother, but perhaps you have never been told you might lose your best friend, Margaret thought wretchedly.

Roelandts was dumbfounded. He had never seen the duchess this angry except perhaps during the kidnapping catastrophe. And once again it was merely out of concern for this servant, a deformed, interfering witch of a servant at that. It was not to be believed. But he bowed and returned to the patient, feeling again the stiffness in the dwarf's neck muscles. Fortunata groaned and tried to move her head away from his probing fingers.

"Hush, *pochina*, the doctor is only trying to help," Margaret soothed her.

"Where else does it hurt?" Roelandts asked. Fortunata tapped her forehead and her hand. The doctor nodded. "We must also rid her body of the ill humors that were thrown off balance from the bite. We must bleed her, then the neck may loosen. I must go and fetch my cups. If your ladies could prepare Fortunata, I can apply them immediately, duchess," he said, bowing, and hurried away. He returned with a colleague and their bag of bloodletting instruments.

Seated on a stool, her upper back exposed, Fortunata readied herself for the ritual of cupping. First Roelandts nicked a small vein on one shoulder blade with his fleem, which made Fortunata wince, and then deftly applied a thick glass cup to it, asking his assistant to press the rim firmly to the skin. Then the doctor lit a taper with the tinderbox and heated the glass. As he began the process on a vein on the other shoulder, the changing temperature in the first glass created a vacuum within it and thus a gentle suction with the shoulder. The blood began to drain into the glass and when the second cup was in place, the doctor removed the first, leaving a round welt on the shoulder. The two physicians examined the color of the blood, held it up to the candlelight to check for impurities and nodded sagely. After removing the second cup, Roelandts wiped Fortunata's back and called for someone to help her dress.

"She should recover her spirits by the morning, your grace," Roelandts told Margaret, smiling more cheerily than he felt. "I will give her a sleeping potion. She needs rest."

Indeed, Fortunata seemed better the next day, and Margaret breathed a sigh of relief, as did Doctor Roelandts.

A FEW DAYS later, Beatrice knocked on Margaret's door and entered. She opened the shutters to reveal a gray winter day, but there was enough light to see the grotesque grimace on Fortunata's face as she still lay sleeping at the foot of Margaret's bed. Beatrice and Fortunata had forged a bond over the years as the only two attendants who had come with Margaret from England. They often ate together and they shared a bed. Beatrice had known of Fortunata's affection for William Caxton and knew the dwarf had spent nights with him. She did not approve, but she was a kind woman and recognized it might have been a once in a lifetime love for the unfortunate dwarf.

Fortunata's eyes flew open when she felt Beatrice's presence near her truckle bed and she tried to move. "I overslept, Beatrice. I am sorry."

"How do you feel today?" Beatrice asked, wondering why Fortunata did not wipe the grin off her face.

Fortunata frowned. She knew her heart was beating too fast and she could feel her face was taut, but she did not want to frighten Beatrice, who, now in her fifties, might be prone to seizures. "I feel better," she lied, gingerly standing up, "Shall we wake *madonna* Margaret now?"

"*Si*, I mean aye," Beatrice said, helping Fortunata lace up her overdress and covering her braids with a cap.

Margaret was terrified by Fortunata's face, which reminded her of her recurring nightmare. Fortunata saw her mistress's fear and judged something was badly wrong with her face. She went to the silver mirror and fell to her knees when she saw her reflection. A searing pain ripped through her back and she fell sideways to the floor. Margaret was by her side in a moment, and Beatrice ran to the door to call for help. Guillaume was not far away and hearing the call, ran into the room. Margaret was kneeling beside the dwarf, who was rigid with pain and fear.

"Carry her to the bed, Guillaume, I beg of you. I know not what else to do for her," Margaret said, her voice a monotone. "Then go and fetch Roelandts."

By the time the doctor arrived, followed by several curious attendants, Margaret had been quickly dressed, a simple velvet turban encasing her hair. Roelandts tried leeches this time. Margaret shuddered when he removed the slimy creatures engorged with blood from Fortunata's skin. The muscle pain in Fortunata's back had subsided, but her face was still stretched into a grin. Margaret forced some wine between her clenched teeth, but Fortunata had trouble swallowing it.

"Come, little one, try to drink this," Margaret urged, holding the dwarf's head up and tipping a little more of the sweet liquid into her mouth. How would she eat, she asked herself? There must be a way to open her mouth enough for food. The leeching had done some good, she thought, feeling the small body relax a little into the mattress. She then became aware of the number of people crowded into the room and stood up, her eyes blazing. "Leave!" she cried, advancing on them with purpose. "All of you, leave!"

The room was emptied within seconds, even Beatrice reluctantly closing the door behind her.

"*Pochina*, I am here and I shall nurse you through this. You must fight, my dearest little friend, for I cannot imagine you anywhere but by my side." Her eyes were filled with tears, but she tried to sound brave. "Tell me what I can do for you. Do you want to pray? Is there some medicine you think will help you? Oh, speak to me, *pochina*, please say something."

Fortunata put her hand out and stroked Margaret's cheek. In any other circumstance, she would never have dared to touch the duchess thus. Margaret was past caring about etiquette and only wanted to ease her little friend's suffering.

"I love you, *madonna*," she whispered, her words hard to understand. "You are the finest lady in the world. I am sorry I must leave you, but you must promise me one thing."

"Do not talk of leaving me, Fortunata. I command that you stay." Margaret could not stop the tears now. "What is it you want me to do?"

Fortunata fumbled beneath her gown and pulled out the long chain on which Margaret's gift of long ago still hung. She kissed the ring, and despite the locked muscles, her face and eyes softened. "This is for William. I want to give this to William, because he gave me love, too, *madonna*. He is a good man." A tear escaped down the side of her face, but she did not take her eyes off Margaret. "You promise?"

"Certes, I promise. He will be proud to take it, I warrant. Do you want him to see you? I will send a messenger to England," she said, knowing it to be pointless.

Fortunata shook her head as best she could. "I am not pretty today," she said.

Margaret had to chuckle. "Aye, I have seen you prettier, *pochina*."

Margaret stayed by her servant all day, cooling her hot forehead with wet towels, aching with sadness at every shallow breath Fortunata managed to take and wincing with every spasm that attacked different parts of her body. During the morning hours, they prayed together and Margaret told her servant of the joy that she had brought into her lonely life in Greenwich. Margaret reminisced about their times together and thanked her for her devotion. They both cried and laughed in between the increasing bouts of pain. At some point, Beatrice came in with some food and ale, but neither Fortunata nor Margaret could eat.

"You will take care of Cappi? Be kind to him, *madonna*. He was only jealous of the rabbit. He is not a bad monkey, in truth."

Margaret nodded briefly, but she had every intention of locking up her *pochina's* killer in the Ten Waele zoo.

Fortunata had much to get off her chest. She knew she was dying. "I am sorry you never had a child, *madonna*. I hated Duke Charles for what he did to you. I know he hurt you badly one night, and I wanted to kill him."

"How did you know, Fortunata? In truth, I do not remember telling anyone but my brother about that night."

"I was under the bed, *madonna*. The duke did not see me when he came in, and I was afraid of him, so I hid under the bed. I heard—" She broke off and again she reached up to touch Margaret's face. "One day you will find Anthony, *madonna cara*. I know this to be true in here," and she tapped her heart.

"Perhaps," Margaret sighed. "Now you must sleep. I will be close if you need something."

Margaret sat quietly by the bed until it was dark, when Beatrice came in to light the candles. Fortunata heard her and put out her hand. At the same time a spasm made her arch her back and scream with pain. Beatrice ran to her and held her hand, looking anxiously at Margaret. "What is it, your grace? What would cause this? I am afraid for you to be here. Perhaps you will contract the same sickness."

"I do not care, Beatrice. I cannot leave her to die by herself."

"Die?" Beatrice gasped. "I did not—" She let go of Fortunata's hand and knelt to pray. "Dear God, save this good woman. She means so much to us, and especially to my mistress. Why must you take her now?"

"God gives and God takes away," Fortunata said, her breathing an effort now. "Do not be sad, Beatrice. Only now you must care for *Madonna* Margaret, *si?*"

"*Si*, I mean aye," Beatrice said, indulging the dying woman in their little game.

"That is good. I am happy." Again her back arched and she gasped for breath, her stomach muscles rigid.

She is suffocating, Margaret suddenly realized. She cannot have long now.

"I will stay by her and keep vigil, Beatrice, thank you. Stay close, and I will call if I need you." She walked with Beatrice to the door and murmured, "Pray fetch my chaplain." Beatrice left the room, her nose buried in her kerchief.

As the Belfort's great bells rang for vespers over the city of Ghent, Monseigneur de Clugny droned the last rites and anointed Fortunata's burning forehead with oil. Margaret helped Fortunata hold a cross between her hands as the dying woman's rasping breaths came farther and farther apart.

"Farewell my sweet *pochina*, may the angels carry you to your rest," she whispered. "Watch over me from your heavenly home and never forget you were loved by a grateful duchess."

A slight pressure on her hand told Margaret that Fortunata had understood. With one more anguished effort she tried to inhale, but the body she had so cursed all her short life dealt her one last cruel blow, and she expired without a sound. The chaplain gave Margaret a blessing, closed Fortunata's eyes and left the room to supervise the burial.

Fortunata's fingers were still entwined with Margaret's when Jeanne de Halewijn hurried in to console her friend. When she tried to gently pry Margaret away, Margaret cried out as if in pain, "Leave me alone, I beg of you! Oh, God, I want to die," she wept, as Jeanne softly closed the door. Margaret gazed at the lifeless figure on her lap. "You promised you would be here always. *Pochina*, ah, my little one, what shall I do without you?"

24

Burgundy, 1480

*M*argaret presided over the Yuletide celebrations that year at Coudenberg, as Mary was in seclusion awaiting the birth of her second child. But it seemed to her immediate circle that she just did not care about anything. And they were right. She missed Fortunata on a daily basis, glancing behind her every few minutes to make sure the dwarf was really not in her shadow or kneeling beside her at the prie-dieu, where they had exchanged such secrets. The world did not seem real without Fortunata in it, and she felt like a sleepwalker drifting through the days.

Not long after the Twelfth Night feast, Margaret was teaching Maximilian some words of English when Jeanne was announced and came hurrying into Margaret's chambers.

"Forgive the intrusion, your graces, but the baby is coming," she said breathlessly. Maximilian looked concerned but let Margaret ask the questions. Childbirth was a mystery to him, although he thoroughly enjoyed his participation in the cause. He was a lusty young man, Margaret had found out when she asked Mary not long after the marriage if all was well behind the bedchamber door. Mary had dimpled, blushed and stammered an assent, so she had not pressed for details but merely smiled and changed the subject. Lucky Mary, she thought.

"How soon do you think, Jeanne?" Margaret said, rising and smoothing out her green and red damask gown. Seeing Maximilian at a loss for words, she excused him to seek amusement elsewhere and called for help in changing into something more practical to attend the birth. Mary had begged her to be there again. Beatrice carefully removed the elaborate butterfly hennin, noticing not for the first time that Margaret's hair was losing its youthful luster and there were new lines on her brow. She replaced the concoction with a simple veil on a velvet headband and laced Margaret into a plainer overdress, tucking a gorget across her chest and under the square neck of the gown.

"Thank you, Beet," Margaret said affectionately. "I pray you send Henriette or one of the younger ladies to attend me later. I want you to go to bed early and rest those old bones of yours. I shall brook no protest. 'Tis an order."

Beatrice was grateful and curtseyed her thanks. "In truth, your grace, I do tire quickly these days," she said. "May the Virgin protect the young duchess in her labors this night."

"Amen to that," Margaret said, removing her rings and dropping them into her silver casket. "I shall not need these tonight either."

The Brussels midwife found to assist in the birth was a complete contrast to the rough and ready Vrouwe Jansen. Vrouwe Smit was obsequious in the extreme, bowing and wringing her hands at every question Margaret had.

"Doctor de Poorter, where did you find this woman?" Margaret asked, finding the physicians and the astrologer behind a screen, consulting charts. The old doctor bowed and told her Vrouwe Smit had come highly recommended. The astrologer was looking pleased with himself, waving his volvelle vigorously, and Margaret raised an eyebrow.

"If the birth takes place before midnight, your grace, I foresee a bright future for the child," he beamed. "He or she shall be a ruler."

Margaret frowned. If this child was to rule, it would mean Philip might not live long. She adored her godson and refused to believe in the man's prediction. A cry from Mary cut short any response she was forming, and she gratefully returned to her stepdaughter's bedside.

An hour later, causing more pain, it seemed to Margaret, than Philip had, Mary's second child, a girl, wriggled into the world. Vrouwe Smit smiled and bowed with pride in her handiwork before she turned the child upside down and lightly spanked the little buttocks. Margaret heard a satisfied grunt from behind the screen when the baby cried and so knew it was not yet midnight. The midwife placed the tiny baby into Mary's arms and then efficiently helped to expel the afterbirth, while Margaret watched, fascinated.

"The duchess must sleep now," Vrouwe Smit pronounced with another bow and wringing of hands. "'Twas not an easy birth. 'Twould be wise to have the wet nurse immediately and let the mother rest."

Mary reluctantly gave the baby back to the woman and gingerly got off the birthing chair with Margaret's help.

"A boy and a girl, Mary, a king's choice," Margaret said, tucking her into the freshly made bed.

"Aye," Mary said sleepily. "Max and I hoped for a girl, my dearest Margaret. We want to name her after you. In Dutch she will be Margaretha."

"Do you think Burgundy is big enough for two of us?" Margaret asked, bursting with pride. "This is indeed an honor I was not expecting, but you have made me very happy. A thousand thanks, my dove." She bent and kissed the wet forehead, smoothing the disheveled hair from Mary's face. "Sleep well, and may God watch over you and little Margaretha."

As she passed the men behind the screen, she briefly wondered if the astrologer's foretelling would come true but then dismissed it and went to tell Maximilian that he had a daughter.

THE PROBLEMS WITH France were by no means over, and the euphoria in Flanders after Guinegatte did not extend to the other Burgundian provinces. There were uprisings in cities, pirates attacked the herring fleets, and Maximilian was accused of using some of the ducal treasure to fund his war chest. Margaret spent many weeks traveling to her dower towns raising money for troops and weaponry so that the young archduke could put down the rebellions.

She was able to spend two weeks in Binche. The meadows were full of hawthorn and apple blossoms, and white clouds scudded across the sky, creating a natural backdrop for house swallows and martins swooping to gather materials for their nests in the city walls or under the eaves of houses. She wondered if little Jehan would remember her. The last time she had visited had been in November, and the boy had greeted her with such enthusiasm that it had taken her breath away. She need not have worried, for Jehan, upon seeing her cavalcade ride into the courtyard, disobeyed his tutor and ran helter-skelter through the palace to greet his aunt on the front steps. He flung his arms around her, and she picked him up and covered his face with kisses. His rosy cheeks were soft as silk, and she was once again elated to hear his laugh so like her father's.

"I love you, Aunt Margaret," he whispered as he wrapped his little arms around her neck. "You bring me a present?"

So this is what it is like to have a child, she thought, hugging him and feeling his fragile body warm against her.

" 'Tis ill-bred to ask such questions, Jehan. You should never expect anything. Expectations may lead to disappointment," she chided, but she winked at him as she carried him into the house. Soon he was whooping across the great hall on his new hobbyhorse, thrusting his wooden sword at all who came near him. Margaret was glad La Marche was not with her. He had frowned his displeasure when she had brought Jehan to Binche last year. It was not that he was unkind to Jehan, but the boy interfered with La Marche's ordered way of running Margaret's household. " 'Tis good for both of us to have a child in the house, monsieur," she had told him once. "We forget too easily what it was like to be young, do we not." La Marche had grunted but nodded in agreement. "You are probably right, your grace," he acknowledged, "but I still do not approve."

The Binche steward had readied her apartments, and she took Jehan there, asking what he had learned from de Montigny. He was proud to be able to recite his numbers in French and then in Dutch.

"Clever boy," she said, clapping her hands. "But now that I am here, we shall speak English together." And she began to correct the lazy speech he had picked up from his Flemish-born mother. They spent leisurely days wandering through the garden, and one day he was put on a small jennet and walked around the courtyard with a groom holding him firmly on the saddle. The pleasure on the boy's face as he had his first riding lesson put a smile on the faces of everyone watching. De Montigny declared he was an apt student, and Margaret was satisfied the boy had forgotten his hideous former circumstances, although he did ask for his sister one night after saying his prayers.

Margaret's smile faded. "I regret I cannot bring her here, sweeting, but perhaps one of the household knows of a boy in the town who can come and play. Would you like that?" The sister was forgotten as an excited Jehan clambered onto the high bed and snuggled up under the fine wool blanket.

"Tell me a story, Aunt Margaret," he begged. Margaret could see he was not at all sleepy.

She took the plunge and told Jehan all about a rich and noble family in England whose name was York. It took all her resolve not to tell him it was his story, too.

DESPITE MAXIMILIAN'S SUCCESSFUL campaign of the previous summer, Louis still would not go away.

Margaret returned to Malines from Binche to find Maximilian waiting for her, having returned from troubled Guelders province.

"Madame Margaret," Maximilian began. He had come up with that name as a way of incorporating her new title with the more personal first name. He did not care to call her stepmother, he had told Mary. "We need your brother's help to bring Louis to his senses. We need him to forge a new alliance with us. Do you think he will agree?"

"Why do you not ask him, Maximilian? He can but deny you." She was flattered that he had sought her out. It meant she was still important to Burgundy. She was not being put out to pasture.

"What the archduke is trying to say, your grace, is would he deny *you?*" Ravenstein interrupted, making Maximilian frown. Margaret was dismayed. It was the first time she had noticed any dissension between them, and she hoped Maximilian was not demonstrating a thirst for autonomy. He could not rule Burgundy without the understanding of those men who had lived and breathed it all their lives. Maximilian was an outsider, and he should tread lightly.

She kept her tone even and smiled at them both. "Are you asking me to negotiate on your behalf, Maximilian? Do you wish me to write to Edward?"

"No, Madame Margaret. I wish you to go to England and speak with

Edward directly. I believe—and Messire de Ravenstein believes," he added, realizing he must keep on the councilor's good side, "that a personal visit by you to England would make Louis sit up and take notice."

Margaret began to pace and think, earning a smile of recognition from Ravenstein. Puzzled, Maximilian watched her.

"Well?" he asked a little impatiently, but Margaret kept walking.

Then she turned and nodded slowly. "If Louis believes we are making a strong alliance with England, he may withdraw from our borders." Ravenstein chuckled. He knew she would understand. She frowned and stabbed the air with her finger, finding a flaw in the idea. "Ah, but will Edward want to give up his French pension? And the Dauphin? The betrothal with my niece Elizabeth was part of their bargain," she thought out loud. "He is mightily fond of that pension. We would have to make some monetary compensation, I fear, which we can ill afford."

"The economic benefits to England would be great, your grace," Ravenstein reminded her. "Since the treaty in Seventy-five, the English merchants have suffered in their trading with us. We could perhaps offer a new prosperity."

"Our immediate need is for archers to reinforce my army, madame," Maximilian added. "If you make Edward agree to sending those at least, it would give Louis pause for thought. But an alliance is the true goal."

Margaret's excitement was beginning to mount. Go to England! How could she refuse? And she could see the wisdom in the argument. Edward, Richard, Hastings, Howard, Bishop Morton—they all would listen to her. She was a York, a Plantagenet princess.

"Aye, messires," she exclaimed. "I will go to England!"

MARGARET'S RETINUE ARRIVED at the Prinsenhof a month later. The city of Bruges was quiet after an outbreak of plague that hot summer. She hoped the ship Edward was sending for her would arrive soon, so that they could be on their way before any of her household contracted the disease. She ordered that none of her retainers be allowed into the streets and that the palace gates should be closed to anyone coming from the infected areas of the city. During the few days she was sequestered there, her new doctor, John de Wymus, gave her a daily regimen to keep her humors in balance. Doctor Roetlandts no longer gave her confidence.

"Do not sleep during the day, your grace. Do not walk after a meal, and if you must walk, I pray you avoid the noontime sun—oh, and when there are clouds as well or it is too hot or too cold." Margaret thought that he had hedged on all weather eventualities but took his advice anyway. She drank the unappetizing potions he concocted, which included feverfew and marigolds, and sadly avoided eating her favorite cheeses.

"The *Falcon* is in Calais, your grace," Gruuthuse informed her a few days later, coming into her presence chamber in his usual somber black velvet gown. He never seemed to get overheated, Margaret had observed when he first began serving her. In summer and winter, he wore black velvet, his collar of the Golden Fleece proudly around his neck. At state occasions, he was transformed into a peacock-tail of colors and jewels, and Margaret had exclaimed at his extravagance, making him smile—sheepishly as usual.

"Sir Edward Woodville is your escort, duchess. 'Twas his elder brother who presented you to Duke Charles, was it not? You remember Lord Anthony, I trust. A magnificent jouster, but I must confess I admire his literary knowledge more than his skill with a lance."

"Aye, I remember him well." Margaret was certain she was blushing, but she hoped Gruuthuse might blame the heat. "We shall start for Calais in the morning, messire. I shall instruct Chamberlain La Marche to make the arrangements. Look after Mary in my absence, Messire Louis. I know I can count on you."

"You are gracious, duchess." He offered her his arm. She always knew that this meant he wanted to speak with her privately. "I would I could accompany you on this difficult visit, your grace. I do not doubt your negotiating skills, but I would protect you from some of its more unpleasant machinations."

Margaret gave a peal of laughter. "But messire, I shall merely be talking to my family. We have had plenty of experience with family squabbles. I am truly looking forward to renewing those skills. Do not fret for me, my dear Heer Lodewijk," she affectionately used the Dutch, "I can hardly contain my excitement."

"May I say how much you will be missed, your grace. Your intelligent diplomacy is much needed at present," he said meaningfully.

Margaret frowned. "What are you implying, messire? I pray you do not play me for a green girl now."

"I would not spoil your anticipation of the visit with your family by worrying you, if I did not think it important," Gruuthuse said, pulling nervously at his lower lip. "I would only warn you that while we councilors are devoted to our duchess, the prince is another matter . . ." He trailed off. "Sweet Jesu, I have said too much."

"Nay, messire," Margaret assured him, knowing now that Maximilian had won no friends in Burgundy. "Forewarned is forearmed. When I return, I will speak to my stepdaughter and her husband. Thank you for your honesty."

Gruuthuse bowed, relief in his eyes. Before he could say his farewells, Henriette came running through the doorway, dismaying the usher who should have announced her.

"Madame la Grande, come quickly, 'tis Beatrice," she cried, her headdress askew.

Margaret paled. Beatrice had worked tirelessly in preparing Margaret's wardrobe for the voyage to England and had been heard singing like a girl in anticipation of seeing her homeland once more. Pray God she does not have plague, Margaret thought. She bade a hurried farewell to Gruuthuse, and picking up her train, she followed Henriette along the corridor to the ladies' chamber.

"Beatrice, dear Beatrice," Margaret murmured as she bent over the old woman lying so still in the bed. Beatrice's face was as gray as a cold November morning, and her breathing was so shallow that Margaret could hardly detect it. "What happened, Henriette? She was well a few hours ago and singing happily."

Beatrice opened her eyes and put her hand to her meager breast. "Your grace, dear cousin Cecily, I will be well tomorrow, I promise."

"Cecily?" Margaret gasped, looking wildly at Henriette, who shrugged.

"She keeps calling me Marie, your grace. She is living in the past but seems to know we are leaving tomorrow. 'Tis strange."

"Have Doctor de Wymus come immediately. She has obviously had a spasm." Margaret looked down at her faithful attendant. She felt guilty. I should have sent her home a year ago when I first noticed how old she was, she admonished herself. How selfish I am. She reminded me of Mother and home. That is why I kept her by me, but now I may have killed her.

De Wymus bustled in on his short, stumpy legs, out of proportion to his long torso. He clicked his tongue when he saw the patient and loosened the tight ribbon around the neck of Beatrice's chemise. Her breathing eased when he gave her a foxglove tincture.

Relieved, Margaret gave the old woman a bright smile. "There now, Beet. I pray you listen to the doctor and get better." She felt as though she were addressing a child, but it seemed to soothe Beatrice.

Suddenly her hand reached out and grabbed Margaret's gown. Her eyes were desperate. "England! I must go home to England! Please do not leave me behind, my lady. Swear to me you will not leave me behind!"

Margaret looked at the doctor. He shrugged and turned his hands up in a gesture of helplessness.

"I promise you shall go home to England, my dear Beet." She did not add that it might be in a shroud. "Now let us pray for your swift recovery."

Beatrice was sleeping peacefully when she left, and the next morning astounded Margaret by appearing as usual to help her dress.

"You frightened us all, Beatrice. I am pleased you are better," Margaret said. "Are you certain you can travel? We have to go to Calais today, and it will be a tiring two days. But you can rest in the carriage and will be relieved of your duty to me."

As she left the room to say good-bye to Mary, she did not see Beatrice sink onto the settle, fatigued by the hour of playacting. She was determined to return to England, and nothing was going to stop her.

SIR EDWARD WOODVILLE and Sir James Radcliff were the first to greet her on the quay beside the *Falcon*. The many mariners and soldiers that manned Edward's impressive ship had all been specially decked out in new purple and blue velvet jackets and provided an honor guard for the duchess and her party from the harbor yard to the gangplank. Sir Edward bowed gracefully and took her hand from Guillaume's to lead her up the sturdy plank to the rough, hardened grasp of Captain William Fetherston on the main deck. Her pulse had quickened when she first saw Sir Edward, having forgotten how like Anthony this youngest Woodville brother was.

"Thank you, Sir Edward," she said, and turned to the weatherbeaten face of the captain. "I greet you well, Captain. I pray we have calm seas, for I am not a good sailor."

Fetherston grinned. Margaret was dismayed to see that he had not a tooth left in his head. "If the wind holds, we shall have smooth sailing to Dover, your grace. Our sovereign lord commanded it so," he said boldly and gave her a broad wink.

Margaret chuckled. For some reason, he reminded her of Jack Howard, and then she remembered he was another old friend she would see again. She breathed in the sea air, hearing the gulls crying overhead as they watched for fish in the murky harbor water or quarreled over a dead one on the dock. She felt the gentle rocking of the boat beneath her feet, and her dread of the *mal de mer* resurfaced.

"Doctor Lambert has prepared this for you, Margaret," Mary had told her when Margaret had gone to bid her stepdaughter farewell at the Prinsenhof. She gave Margaret a vial and explained it was advisable to take it before the ship set sail. "'Tis ground galingale, and you must take it in water or ale." Margaret thanked her gratefully.

Mary had the two children brought in to say good-bye to their godmother, and Margaret found she was almost more loath to leave them than Mary. Philip at almost two was an engaging child, and he lisped a farewell prettily. Then it was time for her to say good-bye to Mary, and the two women embraced tearfully. Both thought back on that fateful day in Ghent when they had wondered if they would ever see each other again.

"I am so afraid something will keep in you England, Margaret. I have worried that Edward will find you a new husband and you will never return to us. I have prayed to the Virgin to bring you back safely. Your home is here with us. We could not live without you. You must believe this." Mary was gripping Margaret's arms as she looked deep into her stepmother's eyes. She really could not imagine life without this rock in her life. "Promise me you will return!" she entreated.

Margaret shook her gently. "Certes, I shall be back and bothering you, my dove. What could possibly keep me in England now?" she said. Anthony, she thought guiltily. I would stay for Anthony. "Now kiss me and let me go. Farewells are so final." And Mary had kissed both cheeks and held Margaretha up to receive her godmother's blessing.

"Your grace, would you like to go below?" Sir Edward interrupted her thoughts. "The captain thinks we can catch the tide and a fair wind for Dover."

Margaret laughed. "Nay, I shall stand on deck and watch the horizon as the captain of the *New Ellen* taught me. Oh, sweet Jesu," she said, as it dawned on her. "'Twas exactly the same day of June but a dozen years ago. Do you remember?" Sir Edward grinned and nodded. "'Tis a good omen, I hope, and bodes well for my mission. And now I should like some ale to go with my magic potion, Sir Edward, if 'tis possible. Your brother and I share a sad lack of sea legs."

25

England, Summer 1480

The cliffs of Dover shone white in the sun. This time the wind was stiff and fair and they made the crossing in only a few hours. Margaret and Beatrice hung over the rail of the quarterdeck and gazed in silence at the place of their birth.

"Not too tired, Beet?" Margaret asked after a moment.

"Tired but happy, your grace," Beatrice replied. "I prayed all night when I was struck down that I would see you safe in London and with your family. It seems our blessed Lord heard my prayer." She sighed as she turned back to look at the magnificent chalk cliffs rising above them as the captain brought the ship safely past the treacherous Goodwin Sands and into the harbor, where the castle dominated the town.

Margaret's party was rowed ashore and spent the night in the castle. The next day, they continued their sailing along the Kentish coast and around the headland on the Isle of Thanet, past Margate—the port of Margaret's long-ago departure—and into the Thames estuary as far as Gravesend. The ginger powders had done their work, and Margaret enjoyed the voyage. But she was ready to land and begin her diplomatic task.

The last leg of the journey took place on the royal barge. The two dozen bargemen, in York murrey and blue jackets decorated with white roses, pulled them easily up the Thames past banks of wild celery, meadowsweet and yellow iris. Margaret's eyes misted when she recognized the lime-washed walls of Greenwich Palace and saw her brother waving at the top of the water steps with Will Hastings by his side. She took out her kerchief and waved back as the oarsmen deftly pulled in their oars in unison and held them upright to form an honor guard for her.

"Welcome! Welcome, Meg," Edward called from his perch above her. "Careful now, those steps are slippery."

Guillaume de la Baume, Lord of Irlain, was not about to let the dowager duchess of Burgundy slip into the Thames, and Margaret caught a look of annoyance on his face.

"He is merely being helpful, Guillaume. I pray you show these English how you can smile." They negotiated the six steps without mishap, and then Margaret found herself enveloped in Edward's embrace, the breath almost squeezed from her.

"My dearly beloved sister, we greet you well!" he exclaimed once he had let go. "Will, you were right, she hasn't changed a whit. What think you, Jack? Still the same dignified lady, I would say. Every considerable inch a duchess, every inch a York!" Edward was in his element, his booming voice including the whole gathering on the quay. "What say you, sirs? Shall we give my sister of Burgundy a whooping London greeting?"

Margaret was warmed by his exuberance and those present were enthusiastic in their hurrahs. She bowed this way and that, acknowledging the smiling faces. And then the cry went up "A York, *á* York!" and she felt the familiar swell of pride.

"Home!" she thought, exultant. "I'm home."

A BOATMAN TOLD his customer, who told the fishwife, who told her neighbor, who passed on the news in the tavern that night: Margaret of York was to arrive in the city the next day. When the royal barge landed at Haywharf near Coldharbour House, which Edward had refurbished for his sister's visit, hundreds of people lined the lane and Thames Street, along which Margaret had to walk to enter the residence.

"God bless you, duchess!" they cried, waving and cheering her. A little girl ran out and shyly gave her a few buttercups she had found near the river, and Margaret stopped to talk to her. Awed, the crowd watched quietly as the duchess in her patterned gold and black silk gown and her high headdress took one of the flowers and held it under the girl's chin. "I see you like butter, child," she said softly. "I do, too." She turned to Guillaume and asked him for a candied ginger she knew he always carried with him and gave it to the girl. "I thank you for the flowers," she said, watching the enjoyment on the little face as the first bite of the sweet was taken. "What is your name?"

"Mary," pronounced the girl boldly. "Mary, an it please you."

"A good name, in truth," Margaret said, sighing for her own Mary far away.

She moved on, and the applause was enthusiastic. "She be one of us," someone called after her. "She ain't forgotten us."

Margaret gave them a smile before disappearing inside Coldharbour. *Nay, I have never forgotten, and you are in my heart always,* it said.

She exclaimed with pleasure at each room in her temporary home. Edward had ordered new beds with red and green curtains and hangings. Tapestries adorned the walls, and she was especially taken with one depicting the history of Troy. It reminded her of William Caxton.

"Certes," she told Beatrice and Henriette as soon as the ladies had unpacked Margaret's personal effects, "we must pay a visit to Master Caxton. I should like to see him again."

Like a child on spree, she had to explore every nook and cranny in the house that had once belonged to Warwick's father. She climbed the turret steps and looked out from the top window, where she had a magnificent view of London Bridge and could hear the boatmen calling "rumbelow, furbelow" as they picked up their rhythm after shooting under it. Opening the other window, she leaned out over the roofs and spires spread before her. A glow suffused her as she remembered the time she and Fortunata had done the same thing at the Wardrobe the night before she left. *London,* she called to the city, *I never thought to see you again.* Her only regret in this homecoming was that Fortunata could not share it with her.

Edward had sent her a pipe of his own wine, and she invited Guillaume to sit and enjoy it with her that first night. He was turning out to be pleasant company, she had to admit, and decided that Henriette had been good for him. Maximilian had even sent him alone on a diplomatic mission to the English court the year before, so he was becoming more appreciated.

In one corner of the room, a trio of musicians were playing lute, rebec and recorder. Beatrice and Henriette were talking quietly under the arras. She sometimes wondered what had become of Marie de Charny, but she was certainly not a subject she would ever discuss with her chevalier. Her lips twitched now as she thought of the scene in Marie's room, and she gave Guillaume a sidelong glance of appraisal. Aye, he still is a handsome devil, she decided.

Edward had allowed her a few days to get settled before her official visit began, and she chose a fine one to take the royal barge to Westminster to find Caxton's print shop. Walking near the great abbey brought back so many memories for her, and it gave her a thrill to hear the English language all around her again. It was music to her ears.

"We are to seek the sign of the Red Pale," Margaret told Guillaume. "Ah, 'tis over there," she said, pointing to a wooden board on which was painted a shield with a thick red stripe down the center hanging from a wrought-iron arm over the door. Guillaume had the small escort wait outside while the duchess paid her visit.

William Caxton could not believe his eyes when he saw the duchess and Guillaume stooping to enter his premises. Smiling broadly as he came towards her, his limp a little more pronounced than before, William bowed over Margaret's hand.

"I never thought to see you here, your grace. Let me show you my press and how it works, if you will allow." And for the next hour, Margaret listened and watched, enthralled, as William had his workers print a page especially for her from the setting of the letters to the inking process, to the pressing and finally to pulling the paper away carefully from the type. Margaret read the words:

"The women of this country be right good, wise, pleasant, humble, discreet, sober, chaste, obedient to their husbands, true, secret, steadfast, ever busy and never idle, temperate in speaking and virtuous in all their works. Or, at least, should so."

She burst out laughing. "And where are these paragons, Master Caxton, for I know of none such as these." William uncharacteristically blushed, intriguing Margaret. "Ah, you have taken a wife," she exclaimed.

William nodded. "Aye, your grace, and I have a daughter."

"My felicitations, sir."

"But perhaps you would like to know the real reason I chose this for you, your grace," William said, indicating the paper. Seeing Guillaume talking to his foreman, he continued softly, "'Tis my own little joke on Earl Rivers." He saw her start at the mention of Anthony and knew he had been right about the two of them. "'Tis the preface in this edition of the earl's *Dictes and Sayings of the Philosophers*. When his lordship gave me his translation to print, I was careful to study the original French for discrepancies. Imagine my astonishment when I found Lord Anthony had failed to include the unkind passage about women written by Socrates. 'Twas the only passage omitted." He paused, letting this sink in. "I came to the conclusion that my lord held women—and perhaps one particular woman—in very high esteem and did not want to dishonor her—I mean, them. 'Twas a gallant gesture, don't you think?"

Margaret looked William straight in the eye and smiled brightly. "I could not begin to understand the earl's motive, Master Caxton, but I will ask him when I next see him. I thank you for your choice." She folded the paper and tucked it in her belt. She looked around and made sure they were out of earshot of Guillaume and Caxton's employees before saying, "There is another reason for my visit."

William was curious. What could the duchess have to say to him of a private matter? She did not beat about the bush.

"I have something to give you, sir, and I trust you will hold it as dear as the person who willed it to you was to me." She pulled a small velvet pouch from the bag at her waist and offered it to him, noticing his somber expression. "Aye, I feel certain you heard about Fortunata's death. This was her last wish, and I did not want to put her gift into anyone else's hands but yours."

William stammered his thanks. His eyes were sad as he opened the pouch and tipped the lovely ring onto his palm. He was astonished. "This was Fortunata's?" he asked. "Are you certain 'twas I she willed it to? 'Tis very valuable, in truth."

Margaret nodded. "I gave it to her many years ago for her faithful service to me. You must have meant much to her, sir." Her gaze was intense. "I hope you were kind."

Caxton lowered his eyes. "Not as kind as she was to me, your grace. I did not deserve her love, I know that." He looked up. "I should have liked her to know that in as much as I am capable of love, I felt some for her, too. But in truth, there was no one she loved more on this earth than you, duchess."

Margaret was moved. "Then keep the ring safe, Master Caxton, and every time you look on it, pray for Fortunata's soul." Caxton nodded and reverently placed the token back in its velvet pouch and tucked it inside his pourpoint.

As she was leaving and William was bowing over her hand again, she murmured, "Thank you for holding a secret, Master Caxton. You are a good man."

"Tell me how your little charge is faring, Meg," Edward asked one day as they rode out together in the pleasant park that climbed the hill behind Greenwich to the tower built by a former owner of the land, Duke Humphrey of Gloucester. Margaret and Richard had explored the building many times during their years at the palace, rudely snatched from Humphrey's possession by a spiteful Margaret of Anjou soon after her wedding to Henry. The view from the crenelated watchtower had never failed to awe Margaret, and today was no exception. She and Edward stood by a crenel in a short wall that afforded them a perspective on London ordinary people could never have. In twelve years, Margaret could see the city had expanded farther beyond its walls and was creeping towards the Isle of Dogs.

Edward had noted the light in her eyes when she spoke glowingly of her little Jehan. "I named him for your other gift to me, Ned, remember?" she said, winding her flapping liripipe around her neck. Ned's hair was windswept into a golden halo about his bare head. He had almost lost his soft velvet hat to the strong breeze. Two of his squires stood at the opposite side of the tower looking towards the estuary and the fields of Kent, and Margaret was certain they were out of earshot. "You sent Jehan Le Sage with me to Flanders."

Edward frowned and then laughed. "Aye, so I did," he said. "I seem to recall that Fortunata . . ." He paused, remembering. "I was sorry to hear about Fortunata, Meg. She was a dear little thing—quite ugly, but amusing."

"With you, all women must be startlingly beautiful to be interesting, Ned," Margaret retorted. "Many of us who are not so believe we have more to offer than rosy lips, blue eyes and flaxen hair, not to mention tits as large as musk melons. 'Tis true, Elizabeth is not well endowed, but she seduced you with her beauty, you cannot deny it."

Edward demurred with a grin. "There are those who think you are striking, my dear sister, therefore no false modesty from you, pray," he chided her. "Those I have in mind include the now rather pompous Anthony Woodville. He will be joining us here soon, you may like to know." She did like to know, and she hugged herself in anticipation. "As you know, he governs my son at Ludlow, and admirable work he is doing, I will admit. But the fellow bores me now with his piousness and poetry."

Margaret said nothing. After witnessing his current lifestyle during the short time she had been in London, it did not surprise her that Edward was unimpressed. He had now taken a new mistress, one Elizabeth—sometimes called Jane—Shore, and she had also seen Will Hastings dally with her. The two cronies egged each other on, seeming to revel in revelry, the more debauched the better. Margaret felt sorry for the queen, who, although not in the first flush of youth, was still very beautiful. What puzzled Margaret was that Edward obviously still loved his wife. How can he love her and yet dishonor her so? she asked herself. He was not even discreet about it.

"I cannot blame Lord Anthony, my dear Ned," Margaret said quietly. "Your court has no morals that I can see. I do not consider myself a prude, but I cannot approve of it. Does Mother ever visit? No, I did not think so." She chuckled. "Imagine the lectures you would have to endure."

"You will have the chance of hearing one next week, Meg, when she comes for a splendid banquet I am planning for your homecoming. Dickon is even leaving his beloved Yorkshire to attend in your honor. Do keep him off the subject of George, though. He still hasn't forgiven me."

"I am not sure if I have, Edward," Margaret said softly. "And every time I see my little Jehan I am reminded of my lost brother."

"'Lost' is a good word for George, Margaret. He lost his way, his loyalty and his conscience, in truth, and found himself standing on a precipice of his own making. I had no alternative but to gentle him over. I hope you believe I made it as painless as possible."

Margaret heard the regret in his voice and reached out her hand to his puffy one resting on the crenel stone. "I believe you, Ned. I pray daily to God to forgive you and to our Lord Jesus that He eases George's entry into the kingdom of heaven."

Edward removed his hand and gave a short, sharp laugh. "Now you sound like Anthony, Meg. I did what was right for England, nothing less." But more gently, he whispered before walking to the spiral staircase, "It pleases me that you are taking care of George's bastard. It is a small atonement, don't you think?"

"Aye, Ned," Margaret said. "And one day, when Jehan is ready, I will tell him only of George's attributes, have no fear." She tucked her arm in his to be guided down the steep, narrow steps. "And now tell me who else is invited to the Banquet of the Age."

MARGARET'S DAYS WERE spent in close counsel with Edward and his advisers, and her negotiation skills on behalf of Maximilian and Mary were the talk of the council chamber. One hot July day, a familiar figure greeted her at the start of that day's session.

"Sir John! Your pardon, I mean Lord Howard," Margaret cried upon seeing Jack, his hair a good deal grayer than she remembered. "I greet you well, my lord. I have missed your wisdom and knowledge in this chamber and I know Edward has. Where have you been?"

Jack Howard bowed over Margaret's outstretched hand. She felt his mustache tickle her fingers. His smile was quizzical as he told her, "I have been on a diplomatic mission of my own, your grace. Were you not apprised of my whereabouts?"

"I asked, but I regarded the answer as vague."

"Ah, out of sight, out of mind, I'll warrant," he smiled, now wondering why his mission to France had not been discussed with Margaret. He did not tell her he had returned with Edward's annuity and a promise of fifteen thousand more crowns to sweeten the proposed marriage with Louis' heir. "How are the negotiations, your grace?" he asked, deflecting her questions. "The king is driving a hard bargain, I have been told."

"Certes! He has us—I refer to Burgundy, my lord," she said, seeing an eyebrow raised in query, "between the Devil and the deep sea. He wants Maximilian to compensate him for his French pension should he choose to support us, which I can understand, but now he wants one of his daughters betrothed to my little Philip, the heir of Burgundy, and not pay a penny's worth of dowry. I cannot see Maximilian agreeing. And I am curious to know how Ned expects Louis to sanction a marriage between the Dauphin and his own Elizabeth if he is negotiating with us. He is playing with a two-edged sword, Lord Howard, and I like it not."

Jack chuckled at her vehemence. "Always thinking, duchess. We should never have let you go to Burgundy. You are right, in truth, although I should not say anything so treasonous here in this palace," he said, lowering his voice though his eyes still twinkled.

Margaret grinned. "This was the very room where you gave me Fortunata all those years ago." Her tone softened then. "You heard that she died?" Jack nodded and offered his condolences.

As they talked, Margaret's eyes wandered to a group of courtiers talking quietly in a far corner. One of the men seemed familiar to her although his portly figure in its padded pourpoint and the graying hair over a once-handsome face did not immediately trigger a memory. She gently nudged Jack and nodding in the man's direction, asked if he knew who it was.

"The one in green, duchess? 'Tis John Harper, loyal servant to your brother. Why? Do you wish to meet him?" He was astonished to see Margaret's head shake vehemently and her merry eyes laugh over the hand on her mouth.

"We have already met, Lord Howard when we were much younger," she said, not adding "and very foolish." Jack understood the implication immediately, stroking his gray mustache to hide his amusement. He tactfully changed the subject.

On their way to the next council meeting, Jack's conscience got the better of him. He knew Edward would be using the information brought from Louis to bargain with Burgundy at the session. "I confess I have not been—well—straight with you, your grace. I am returning from France with a small delegation to persuade the king to refuse your son-in-law's requests for aid. That is all I can say at present," he finished hurriedly as he nodded to the guards to open the chamber door and let the indignant duchess of Burgundy pass through. God's bones, but Edward puts me in precarious places, he thought.

But Margaret never batted an eyelid during the morning discussions. Her face was calm and serene while underneath she seethed and planned Burgundy's next move.

ELIZABETH WOODVILLE HAD made Greenwich her favorite palace since Margaret left for Burgundy, and her taste was exquisite, Margaret had to acknowledge. Ned had grumbled to his sister when she first arrived, "I will have to go begging in the streets to pay for her furnishings," but then he had winked.

Edward clearly still adored his wife, despite the presence of his mistress, Jane Shore, at court, which Margaret could not condone. You are such a hypocrite, Meg, she told herself, for ever since Edward had told her Anthony was on his way from Ludlow, she found herself constantly glancing out of windows to the river like a moon-struck young girl in case she might see her own lover coming. She took a bath every day now just in case, exasperating her ladies, whose duty it was to sprinkle her favorite rosemary into the water, sponge their mistress, wash her hair, dry her and smooth her skin with fragrant oil of almonds and rosewater. The whole process of washing and dressing Margaret often took two hours or more, and Henriette asked Beatrice what had caused this sudden change in the weekly bath routine. Beatrice shrugged. She had guessed many years ago that her charge had given her heart to Anthony Woodville, but she had never spoken about it to anyone except God.

Following Mass one drizzly day not long after Margaret's arrival, Ned and Elizabeth and a small company of close advisers were assembled in the queen's watching chamber, the largest of the royal family's private rooms, to spend family time with Margaret. The queen kissed her warmly. "God's welcome to you, Margaret. You have not changed at all," she said.

Margaret laughed. "You were always a bad liar, Elizabeth. But thank you for the kind words. Certes, but your beauty still eclipses all others," she said loudly enough for the favorite, Jane, to hear. "And I see you are again with child." Ned had told her Elizabeth had been devastated when their third son, George, died soon after his birth the year before. Margaret did not comment on the name but knew Ned was unable to forget his brother, traitor or no. She was glad.

Elizabeth sighed. "Aye, we are hoping for another boy." She leaned towards her sister-in-law. "There is nothing worse than seeing your baby wither before your eyes, Margaret." Her expression of sorrow revealed her softer side, and Margaret took her hand and pressed it. Elizabeth suddenly remembered that Margaret had not ever known the pleasures of motherhood and whispered, "I am so sorry you were unable to bear a child, Margaret. It must have caused you untold heartache."

Margaret nodded, grateful for the queen's concern. Her glance fell on the small boy at Elizabeth's elbow and her eyes widened in astonishment. Sweet Jesu, George was right, she thought, Jehan could have been Ned's judging by this child's features. Covering her confusion, she said cheerfully, "And this is . . ."

"Richard, duke of York," the little boy told her gleefully and without guile. "And I will be theven in . . ." He carefully counted his fingers and then his face fell. "Mother, when will I be theven?"

"On the seventeenth day of August, child. Soon," Elizabeth said sweetly. Ah, here is the favorite, Margaret thought, seeing the affection on Elizabeth's face.

"Then I shall be here to celebrate your birthing day, Richard," Margaret said, taking in every inch of the tow-haired, blue-eyed boy with his bold manner. "We shall have to do something special." Richard grinned up at her, showing the gap where his baby front teeth had fallen out and given cause for the lisp.

Ned waved his son away. "Go and play with your puppy, Dickon, there's a good boy. The dog needs to learn when not to relieve himself in here," he said, pointing to where a wolfhound pup was taking a piss in the rushes. The boy ran off. Margaret was introduced to her nieces, Elizabeth, Cecily, Mary, Anne and Catherine, as yet none as comely as her parents, although fourteen-year-old Elizabeth showed a quiet charm and promise of beauty that pleased her. She also met George's and Isabel's two little orphans and gave them a special kiss each.

There was activity at the doorway to the chamber, and those nearby stood aside as newcomers entered.

"His grace, the Prince of Wales," announced the usher, "and Lord Rivers."

Margaret's heart sang when she heard Anthony's name.

"Edward!" cried Queen Elizabeth, holding out her arms to her elder son, who, under the watchful eye of his governor, walked stiffly to his mother. Changing her demeanor to match his, she put out her hand to be kissed and accepted his formal bow. "How you have grown, my dear child," she murmured. "Has he not grown, Ned?" she turned to ask the king, who was observing the scene from his comfortable chair in the center of Elizabeth's private watching chamber.

"Certes, he has grown, Bess, we have not seen him for months," Ned responded. "Here, boy, let me take a look at you."

The pale prince flamed red at being thus addressed. "Aye, your grace," was all he said, however, as he approached his huge parent, who was resplendent in a purple satin doublet trimmed with ermine that need not have been fashionably padded.

"Do you know who this is?" Ned asked, pointing a fat finger at Margaret seated on his other side.

"My Aunt Margaret, Father," the boy responded, turning his limpid blue eyes on the imposing figure with the tallest hennin he had ever seen. "My Lord Rivers has told me all about her."

Now it was Margaret's turn to blush, and to cover it, she bent forward with outstretched arms to take nine-year-old Edward's shoulders and pull him towards her. "No bows for me, Edward. I should like a kiss," she said, giving him an encouraging smile. "Your brother has given me several since I arrived in England, and I hope you will oblige your old aunt."

She was dismayed to see the boy eye her with suspicion.

"I fear you must blame me, your grace," said the voice that always sent the blood galloping through her veins. "Young Edward has recently learned correct court manners, and kissing strange women is certainly not correct." Anthony bowed, but he kept his eyes on her from under his lashes.

"Edward," he said to the boy, "her grace, the duchess of Burgundy, should receive a bow and a brush of the lips on her hand, like this." He bowed again as Margaret extended her hand. Neither was prepared for the shock they both received when he took it, making Anthony clutch it in a most incorrect fashion before he pressed it to his mouth. The sensuality of his touch was so unmistakable that Margaret thought she would faint. Instead she managed a clear, though a little high, "Lord Anthony, it is a pleasure to see you again."

She was horrified to hear Ned's imperceptible "I'm sure it is," said on stifled laughter. She withdrew her hand quickly, and Anthony stepped aside, recovering his composure. She turned her attention to the boy in front of her, who mimicked his uncle in all but the seductive touch.

"Good boy," Ned said approvingly. "Now you may give your aunt a proper kiss."

Still the boy stood straight as a pike, a flush suffusing his thin face. His black satin gipon hung on him like an old man's skin, and his patterned hose drooped on scrawny legs. He does not look healthy, Margaret decided, and he certainly has no intention of kissing me. She was reminded of George's and Dickon's return from Duke Philip's court and how George was embarrassed to be kissed. It must be common with boys turning into young men, she thought, so patted Edward's hand and winked at him. "'Tis no matter, Edward. I am happy to meet you, Richard and all your sisters. I pray you, go and greet them, for I am sure they are anxious to hear about Ludlow." The boy bowed and walked off, relieved.

Anthony stood by awkwardly for once, not knowing where he belonged. Ned rescued him by inviting him to pull up a stool, and then stood, offering Elizabeth his arm to "see what the children are doing. Certes, you two must have much to talk over," he said, grinning. Elizabeth looked puzzled but joined her husband to wander over to where the children were playing marbles and fox and geese. No one in the room was aware of the charged atmosphere that seemed to Margaret must be visible. She forced herself to look into Anthony's eyes and swam in the emotion she saw there.

"I must first say how sorry I am for the loss of your husband, Marguerite," he said. "A bully and a warmonger, but your husband nevertheless. Your life must have changed in a moment, and a day does not go by that I do not think of you and pray for you. But I was sorrier to hear about Fortunata. She must leave a large hole in your life."

Margaret nodded sadly. "Many times larger than her dear little body took up on earth." She took a deep breath. "What next, Anthony?" she asked. "What is there for us?"

"For us? 'Tis your decision, my dearest Elaine, not mine. You are a dowager duchess and a princess of England, and I am a mere earl. Your brother may not like it."

"My sister Anne was allowed to divorce her traitorous husband and wed her lover, Thomas, may God rest her soul," she said, signing herself. She had not mourned Anne's passing four years before as she had hardly ever seen her eldest sister. "You and I are free to wed, Anthony. And now Mary has Maximilian—" She broke off and said as loud as she dared, "Are you saying that if I desired it, you would agree?" She could not believe she was actually speaking these words and that they were not part of one of the many waking dreams she had had alone in her curtained bed since becoming a widow. And so calmly were they talking about marriage that she laughed at the release of her pent-up hopes.

"His grace, the duke of Gloucester!" The announcement cut off any more conversation, and all eyes were on the door as Richard walked into the room, his long leather boots covered in the dust of travel and his spurs ringing on the flagstones. The courtiers gave him reverence as he came purposefully to Margaret, his smile broad and his hands outstretched.

"Margaret!" he cried. "I did not believe my eyes when I read Ned's letter summoning me to a banquet in your honor. What brings you back to England?"

"Duty, Dickon." Margaret had risen when she saw him and stayed Anthony's answer with her hand on his arm. She went to her youngest brother and embraced him fondly. She was taken aback at the change in him. New lines creased his sharp features, his mouth was hard, and his shoulders stooped a little. She had the impression the weight of responsibility that Edward had put on him in the north had aged him. But when he smiled, it still brightened his dark features and reached the eyes whose color matched hers. Ned came forward to greet him, and they grasped forearms and clapped each other on the back.

"Uncle Richard!" cried Ned's eldest, as young Elizabeth ran unheeding into his arms, earning a frown from her mother. "Uncle Richard, I am so happy to see you."

"And I you, my poppet." Richard kissed the top of her head, while Ned smiled benignly on them. "Now let me greet my sister properly, child, and I hope you will look after Johnny while we are here."

Margaret had noticed a youth follow Richard into the watching chamber and thought he was a page. Now she saw Richard take the boy gently around the shoulders and lead him to her for inspection.

"This is my son, John," Richard said proudly. "Anne was not feeling well when I left and begs to be excused," he told Ned, "and my little Ned is too young to come without his mother, so I thought I'd introduce you to another member of the family, Meg. John, this is your Aunt Margaret, my sister, who lives over the sea in Burgundy."

"I am honored to make your acquaintance, my lady," the sturdy youth said, unafraid. He gave a little bow over an extended leg, also encased in long leather boots. "John of Gloucester, an it please you."

"Why, it does please me, John of Gloucester!" Margaret exclaimed. She gave him her hand to kiss and bent to ask, "Tell me, do you sing as well as your mother?"

Richard coughed nervously, but he had forgotten his wife was not there. John furrowed his brow, obviously thinking hard. "I do sing, my lady, but no one sings as well as my mother," he finished earnestly, reminding Margaret so much of Richard as a boy that she chuckled. He turned to Richard, gray eyes expectant. "Will Katherine be here, Father?"

"'Tis his sister," young Elizabeth explained to Margaret. "She lives with our other aunt in Suffolk. I like Katherine, she's amusing."

"Willful is how I would describe her," Ned said, returning to Margaret and laughing. "But then she's very like her mother, n'est ce pas, Dickon." He still loved to tease his little brother, and his eyes danced when he saw Richard's telltale flush.

Margaret marveled at the growth of her family in twelve years—so many children she had never seen before. A warmth suffused her at being in their midst. It appeared the York succession was safe and, barring her concern for young Edward, strong.

Now if she could only bring the diplomatic negotiations to a fruitful conclusion and finish her conversation with Anthony, she would be as content as she had ever been in her life.

THE ROYAL BARGE came for her at midmorning on the day of the banquet, and the people of London came to wave to her from the wharves and houses on both banks of the river. St. Paul's dominated the London skyline, its great belltower topped by a gilded eagle, and Southwark's mighty St. Mary Overie towered over the gabled roofs of the south bank community, where the stews and taverns attracted those seeking solace with prostitutes and ale. The bells of London rang for Matins, and Margaret was proud she could still distinguish the carillon from St. Paul's, the bright tones of All Hallows, and the big, booming bell of St. Mary-le-Bow.

She found herself holding her breath as she always had as the barge navigated the treacherous waters under London Bridge, and then, in no time on a waning tide, she was pulled up to Elizabeth's favorite Palace of Pleasaunce. The river at Greenwich in front of the gleaming white building was teeming with boats and barges of all sizes, and liveried boatmen maneuvered their craft into vacant spaces along the pier to discharge their passengers. The king's guests had arrayed themselves in brilliant silks and satins, and nary a somber black gown was to be seen.

A cheer went up when the royal barge approached the water steps leading to the royal apartments. Guillaume had begun vicariously to enjoy the attention given his mistress, and he waved before helping Margaret reach the doorway to the tower. He was proud of the duchess in her purple and silver gown, the deep revers of the bodice and slashed sleeves showing the crimson silk of her underdress, and the train trailing many feet behind her. Her enormous butterfly hennin, on which floated a transparent golden gauze, was embroidered with gold thread and sewn with pearls. Around her neck was a ruby and amethyst collar from which hung a sparkling diamond as big as a robin's egg.

Guillaume's considerable height was amplified by his high silk hat, and he was the only man there to show off the floor-length gown preferred by the most fashionable court in Europe. It was split from floor to waist in front and belted, exposing his long, muscular legs clad in creamy hose, and sported enormous padded shoulders and sleeves. A heavy triple gold chain necklace adorned his barrel chest, and his shoe points preceded him by a foot or more. He was the perfect escort for the tall, elegant duchess, and many on the pier stood and stared at the picture of Burgundian opulence in front of them before the couple turned and disappeared up to the great hall.

The quiet hum of voices belied the number of people who had gathered to honor Edward's sister, and when she was announced, she was surprised to see so many crowded into the king's watching chamber. The conversation ceased as she waited for Guillaume to present her to the king, who was seated at the other end of the room with Elizabeth beside him.

Then she saw Cecily, regal in black satin, her widow's wimple white against her face, its folds tucked neatly into the high bodice. She almost forgot herself and called out "Mother!" but instead, to a fanfare of trumpets, she walked sedately on Guillaume's arm between the bowing guests, amused by the awed glances she and her chevalier were attracting. She could not wait to be with Cecily, but she knew she must play her part first in this courtly charade. And besides, her mother of all people would never condone a public show of emotion.

"Lord Hastings," she murmured as she passed Will, who grinned in open admiration. "Lord Howard . . . Sir Edward . . . Bishop Morton . . ." she remembered them all and finally she was at the low dais making her obeisance in front of the king. Edward was standing, his hand held out to her in a welcoming gesture. She took it and bowed to Guillaume, who bowed in turn and went to take his place behind her chair. Edward turned her and boomed, "We are here to honor my dear sister, Margaret of York, dowager duchess of Burgundy. Let us give thanks for her visit to us and for a safe return when she leaves us."

"Thanks be to God," muttered the crowd, crossing themselves. Edward nodded to the musicians, who began to play quietly, signaling for the guests to resume their chatter.

"Mother, dear Mother. How I have longed for this moment. Give me your blessing," Margaret said, on her knees in front of Cecily and kissing her hand. Cecily lightly touched her daughter's forehead and murmured a blessing. Margaret rose and took her seat between Cecily and Edward. "I was afraid you would not come. 'Tis a long way from Berkhamsted for some oysters, flampayns and porpoise."

"So you remember my favorite dishes, Margaret," Cecily said, pleased. "Certes, I would not miss a chance to see you, my dear. Yet you should feel honored, for you must also remember how much I hate long journeys." Margaret nodded, memories of long days on the road to Fotheringhay flooding back. "I must say, daughter, you wear your office well." She leaned sideways to whisper in Margaret's ear. "You are the envy of every woman here today, aye, even the beautiful Elizabeth." Cecily had never really approved of her daughter-in-law, and Margaret suspected Edward's choice had been one of the reasons why her mother had withdrawn from the court.

"You exaggerate, Mother," she answered. "But I will take a compliment from you gladly," she said. She was amazed at how clear Cecily's skin still was. Her face was lined a good deal more, and her hands showed the bumps and knobs of joint stiffness, but no one would guess she was born on the third of May in the same year Agincourt was fought, sixty-five years ago. It always seemed to Margaret that sharing the same birthday with her mother was important. A good omen perhaps. Now it was her turn to whisper, "I know not how Ned has grown so corpulent. He worries me, in truth. Listen to him breathe. I have heard better in the sick wards of St. John's hospital in Bruges, where I minister."

Cecily shook her head sadly. "I know not. And his court is dissolute, Margaret. I am shocked to see that harlot Jane Shore is invited here. I cannot understand why Elizabeth allows it."

"The Duchess Isabella had it worse, Mother. My father-in-law had twenty-three bastards by various mistresses, and they were all in positions of power at court when I arrived."

Cecily pursed her lips in disapproval. "I hope you did not have to consort with any of them. But now I remember, Antoine, who fought Scales, was one of them, no? I hope your husband was more circumspect, Margaret. You were happy, dear?" she asked, not observing that Margaret almost choked on her wine. She was disappointed Margaret had borne no children but had the tact to say nothing. "I was sorry to hear of his untimely death—like your father's."

Margaret mumbled something unintelligible in response to the query but immediately began to extol the virtues of her two step-grandchildren. And then she turned the subject to Dickon's bastards. Cecily shrugged. "John is a nice boy. And Katherine over there is a beauty. I never saw the mother, but then I believe Richard has been faithful to little Anne since he married her."

Margaret did not like to tell her mother that indeed she had seen Richard's mistress, Kate, right under her nose at Stratford Langthorne. She followed her mother's gaze to a group of the royal children talking animatedly to each other. A petite young woman, perhaps twelve or

thirteen judging from her sprouting breasts, was the center of attention, her long chestnut hair a crowning glory above a sweet but mischievous face.

"They do not look at all alike, the brother and sister, I mean," Margaret said. "But it seems Richard is very proud of his son."

Cecily nodded. "And the dark-haired boy next to John is Arthur,
Edward's bastard. The Wayte wanton was discarded soon after his birth,
I remember, but no one speaks to me of such gossip. There are others, I
assume, but Ned at least has the decency not to parade them here. I hear
the queen does not care for that boy, though," she sighed, shaking her
head as she looked at her son's growing brood. "Arthur, I mean."

"Certes, I am having a difficult task absorbing so much in such a little
time," Margaret said, scarcely believing she was having this conversation
with her proud parent. Bastards, mistresses, dissolute court—these were
not topics she thought Proud Cis would even mention, let alone speak
about to her youngest daughter. She suppressed a laugh.

"What are you two whispering about," Edward interrupted them. "I
have just been given the signal that our dinner awaits. Mother, will you
let Margaret's elegant escort take you in? As the guest of honor, Margaret
must go with me. Are you ready, sister?" He stood and offered his arm,
and the court watched in silence as the king and the duchess led the way
into the great hall to a fanfare of trumpets.

And thus began the banquet of the era, as Margaret was to dub her
family reunion.

The tables were set with spotless white linen, the king's table covered
by crimson cloth of gold. The sunlight streamed in through the two-story
windows, glinting off the silver plate and cups on the head tables. After
the ritual handwashing and grace said by Bishop Morton, the first of the
three courses was brought in to the sound of smacking lips and whispers
of anticipation. Elizabeth relaxed her silence at meal rule on this occasion,
which made for a convivial ambience. The servers were clothed in murrey
and blue from their soft bonnets to their parti-colored hose.

Soon the messes were filled with mouthwatering delicacies. Neighbors
shared the food, spearing fish and fowl onto their own trenchers, sop-
ping gravy with hunks of bread and quaffing quantities of wine. Each
course began with a soup, and then it was a choice of roasted exotic game

birds such as crane, egret, bittern and heron; fish—bream, carp and pike wrapped in paper-thin gold foil; followed by custards and flampayns.

Edward was happy to see the haunches of venison, mutton and beef appear and swamped them generously with rich sauces. Margaret was not surprised her brother weighed as much as a small horse as she watched him devour dish after dish, helped down with half loaves of bread and cups of wine. At one point he belched so loudly that the room went silent, thinking he was saying something important. He guffawed when he realized he had everyone's attention, not caring that he had a mouthful of food and had dribbled gravy down his magnificent purple gown.

"Eat! Eat!" he bellowed, thoroughly enjoying himself. Elizabeth's smile never faded, but her eyes were hard.

Cecily, who was given a place of honor on his left side, lost her temper. She rapped his knuckles with her spoon when the conversation resumed and spoke in a lowered but threatening voice. "Edward, your eating habits are reprehensible. I should visit you more often and then perhaps you would curb your appetites—all your appetites. Your court could benefit from some good Christian guidance, my boy." She glared at him and dared him to respond. Margaret bit the inside of her cheek so that she would not laugh and waited to see what Ned would do.

He stared dumbfounded at his elderly mother. No one ever spoke to him this way. He wiped his mouth on the back of his hand, leaving a stringy piece of meat dangling from the ermine trim of his sleeve, and gulped down more wine. Margaret could have sworn she heard him mutter, "Aye, Mother," but she could not be certain. He did, however, put down his knife, wipe his hands and push away his plate.

"I have had enough," he called to Jack Howard, who was serving him that night. Cecily looked smug until he added, "I need to leave room for the roast swan I know we have been promised." Jack bowed and removed his gold plate, and immediately a clean one was placed before him.

"Christ's nails, Meggie, she still reduces me to a puling boy," he murmured to Margaret on his other side. "Thank God she has found another calling in Berkhamsted." He belched again, more subtlely this time, and asked how she was liking Coldharbour. He was carefully avoiding her mission. Besides, he had just noticed a pretty young thing who could not have been more than his daughter's age talking to Anthony Woodville. "Ah, yes, Maria Fitzlewes, Bess's new lady-in-waiting."

Margaret sighed, despairing of him. "She is but a child, Ned. Be sensible."

Later, when the tables had been cleared and the musicians had taken up their instruments at the far end of the hall, they were joined by Richard, who had headed up another table. He asked Edward permission to lead their sister out and begin the dancing for the evening. Edward, who found dancing difficult these days, waved his hand, happily passing off the duty to his little brother. For her part, Margaret was glad to stand up after hours of eating.

"I am no George, Meg," Richard said with regret as they took their places for a *basse danse*. "You must miss him in the family gathering. I know I do."

"And yet you did not come to his defense," Margaret said more harshly than she intended. Certes, she missed George, and she had been dismayed that no one spoke of him except for one brief mention by Ned when she had first arrived. It was as if he had never existed.

She felt Richard tense. "I could not in all good conscience, Meg. He was a traitor to Ned, to our family, for all I loved him. Mother was the only one who tried, but even she gave up on him. But I do fear for Ned's soul—to put one's own brother to death . . ." He trailed off sadly.

Margaret was keeping her eyes on the ground, as was the custom, but she was startled into looking up when Richard passed her to a new partner in the second part of the dance. Anthony took her hand, and they moved in unison down the brown and white marble floor.

"I fear we shall never finish our conversation," Margaret told him, trying to concentrate on the steps and not on his fingers entwined in hers. "Edward has me kept me on my toes and in his presence constantly. I cannot return to Burgundy without knowing what is to become of us." As all she could look at were his feet, she was pleased to see he did not affect the ridiculously long shoes favored by Guillaume. Rather, he wore soft boots with short cuffs that draped around his ankles.

"I return the prince to Ludlow on the morrow, Marguerite, but I have been given leave to see to my estates in September. Will you come to The Mote when your diplomatic mission is over? You must almost ride by Maidstone on your way back to the coast. I shall invite Edward as well. I have no doubt he will wish to accompany you as far as he can."

Margaret lightly squeezed his hand, and he knew, as the music brought them to the final bow, that she would come to him in Kent.

IN THE DAYS following the banquet, Margaret kept in close proximity to her comfortable quarters at Coldharbour. She spent hours reading under a spreading chestnut or strolling through the herber, a straw hat protecting her face from the sun and her overdress tucked up in her belt while she deadheaded roses and gillyflowers with her small knife.

Beatrice and Henriette worried that their mistress was slipping into melancholy, but in fact Margaret delighted in the peacefulness of the time away from Edward's council chamber and from her usual busy routine in Malines. It gave her an opportunity to savor the few days she had spent with her family before one by one they disappeared back to their own lives.

Richard left first, receiving word that another skirmish on the border with Scotland meant his presence was required there at once. He galloped off with his small entourage, his son proudly settled in the saddle before him, and waved his cap at Margaret, shouting "God speed."

She had not been at the pier when the Prince of Wales and his governor were rowed away on the start of their long journey back to the Welsh border. She did not want to say good-bye to Anthony.

Parting with her mother was not as heart-wrenching this time, even though she and Cecily had formed a bond she had not experienced as a young princess at court. They spent several hours together discussing Margaret's attempts to reform the permissive religious orders in Burgundy, and Cecily was pleased her daughter was involved with so many charitable works. " 'Twill bring you to God and his Heaven in the end, Margaret. Your salvation is certain, and I will go to my grave knowing that at least one of my children has lived a virtuous life."

Margaret had stabbed her finger with her needle at the remark and hoped Cecily's eyes were sufficiently old and dim not to notice. She kept silent and let her mother speak her mind. She hoped Cecily could not read her mind or her heart.

A few days later, she thought the whole palace of Greenwich had heard the argument Cecily and Edward had about Mistress Shore.

"How dare you flaunt that harlot in front of me, and more to the point, in front of your wife, who is carrying your child. Have you no pride, no sense of decorum, no common sense at all? I am ashamed of you, Edward, and your Father would have surely horsewhipped you."

From her room three doors away, Margaret heard Edward's fist crash down on a table, and she wondered if he had broken it.

"Enough, Mother! I am no longer a child, and I will not be spoken to as though I were one. You are here as my guest, but unless you cease with your lectures, I will call for your carriage and ship you back to Berkhamsted without delay." Then Margaret heard the door slam behind him.

Cecily had spent the rest of the day with her two daughters, her composure remarkable and her smile bright. But she left Greenwich the next day. Margaret chuckled as she remembered the scene, and she was glad there was no council meeting that day or she would have got nowhere with Edward.

She pondered how well her bargaining skills were advancing Maximilian's cause. So far, Edward had not agreed to anything concrete. She had been dismayed to learn the nature of Jack Howard's diplomatic mission to Louis. Edward was clearly loath to fall off the fence one way or the other. On the one hand, he wanted good relations with Burgundy. Burgundy had great economic value for England, and therefore keeping Burgundy strong against France was imperative. He was also well disposed to help Margaret reclaim her dower lands from Louis, she knew. But marriage of his daughter with the Dauphin and the continuing generous French pension was much too tempting to forego.

She was waiting with bated breath to see if Maximilian would accept Ned's latest proposal that in exchange for six thousand archers and Edward's support of Mary's and Maximilian's claims to territories seized by Louis, her stepson-in-law would agree to betroth little Philip to Anne of York. She was so certain her diplomacy would win Edward over that she had even commissioned a goldsmith in Cheapside to craft a ring with eight diamonds and a central rose of pearls for the princess. Now she had to wait for Maximilian's answer.

Staring unseeing at the newly printed first page of William Caxton's most recent book, *Chronicles of England*, Margaret's mind was not on "*When Albyne with his susters first entered into this isle*" but on her tantalizing conversation with Anthony during the *basse danse.* It had been arranged that Edward would indeed escort his sister into Kent and that a stay at The Mote was sanctioned. Ever since she had heard, she chafed at having to stay in London longer.

In the early part of August, Edward finally agreed to several points of the mission, and Coldharbour became a hive of activity as Margaret began to make the arrangements to recruit and transport the English archers that were promised. She was exultant. Her Burgundian advisers helped identify ships' captains to sail the soldiers across to the Low Countries, and she began to look forward to her journey home.

ONE BUSY MORNING, as her ladies put the final touches to Margaret's intricately wound turban, Beatrice gave a shriek of pain and fell to the ground in a heap. One of the English attendants told Henriette later, "The hale old goes as do ellum boughs." She translated, "The branches of the elm are known to snap off even when they seem healthy."

"Sweet Mother of God," Margaret cried, pushing Henriette aside and kneeling on the carpet beside the old woman. "Don't just stand there, someone fetch the physician and the chaplain!" A page ran off to do her bidding while Margaret cradled Beatrice's head in her lap, willing her to open her eyes. "Dearest Beet, can you hear me? Is she still breathing, Henriette? Fetch a looking glass."

Henriette handed her a little copper mirror, and Margaret held it to Beatrice's mouth, hoping to see a telltale mist from her breath. There was nothing, and in a very few moments, Margaret knew she had lost the person who had served her the longest.

"Go!" she commanded everyone in the room. "Leave me with her. We can do nothing more for her. I would see the priest when he comes, but that is all." She did not need to tell them twice. They all crossed themselves and scurried from the room. Margaret did not want them to see her cry, but as soon as the door closed, she allowed her tears to fall on the now calm but cold face of Lady Beatrice Metcalfe. She had been a surrogate mother to Margaret, and despite her quiet manner, Margaret knew Beet had loved her like a daughter.

"Ah, Beet, at least you saw England again," she wept. "You shall be buried here, and English roses will grace your grave."

She prayed for the old woman's soul to rest in peace, and then she asked St. Margaret to buoy her own spirits at the closing of yet another chapter in her life.

"YOUR GRACE, MY lords," Margaret cried, dismayed. "I pray you believe me when I say I was not informed of Maximilian's intentions." She was on her feet and appealing to the fixed stares of an angry Edward and his equally vexed councilors. "When did this happen?"

"Your stepson signed a treaty with Louis not three days ago, duchess," Jack Howard told her, regretting it was he who had to give her the news. He knew how hard she had worked to secure terms, and he knew she had been blindsided by both Edward and Maximilian, and he felt sorry for her. No man could have achieved as much as she had at Edward's court at this point in time, and all present had gained an enormous respect for her. "A seven-month truce is assured and peace negotiations are to be worked out in October."

"Well, then," she replied, shrugging her shoulders and turning to Edward with a smile. "'Tis obvious to me that Maximilian was forced into the truce because he had not received your latest terms, your grace. I do not believe he did it to deceive you. He did it because he thought he had no alternative."

Inside she knew this was not true, and her bile rose and her anger grew. She felt betrayed by Maximilian and was reminded of Lord Louis' warning. For her dearest Mary's sake, she could not allow these councilors to know that or to suspect her of wasting their time.

Edward's narrowed eyes bored into her own. "Does this mean that Burgundy, as an *ally* of France"—he emphasized the word to drive home the odd suggestion—"will support Scotland's war against us?" He paused and then deliberately added a snide "duchess?"

Margaret swallowed hard. So that was it: Scotland was the issue. She did not feel Maximilian had even given it a moment's thought, but she promised to write to Maximilian and ask for his support for Edward's campaign. To her intense relief, that seemed to satisfy her brother, although there was some muttering among the councilors. How she missed Ravenstein. He had been right, this was more difficult than she had imagined. She caught Jack's eye and was astonished when he gave her an imperceptible bow. Praise indeed, she thought a little more happily.

AND THEN IT was time to go.

While her household readied itself for the journey back to Ghent, Margaret was feted once again by the city of London in heartfelt farewell. The merchant guilds gave her a purse of gold in thanks for her negotiating new trade terms for them and their Burgundian counterparts.

She took almost the same route as she had taken from Stratford on her first journey. This time Edward's barges joined her at Tilbury, and the flotilla made its slow way out of the Thames estuary and into the mouth of the River Medway. Wheeling flocks of gulls and terns accompanied them in the air, while grebes, teals and ducks paddled alongside. Rochester was Kent's largest city after Canterbury and not long after a deep bend in the river, the Norman castle with its many keeps and the twin-towered cathedral came into view.

"On to The Mote, Meg?" Edward said after lingering two days in the city.

Margaret had received yet another missive there from Maximilian requesting that Edward join in a peace conference in October. Margaret showed her impatience with a terse reply that outlined her successes, which included a betrothal ring for Philip, but concluding,

> *"I have to point out to you that during these negotiations you have left me and your ambassadors very troubled."*

She was truly beginning to understand Gruuthuse's parting remarks to her. Maximilian needed to be taken in hand. She had quickly folded the letter and used her heavy betrothal ring to seal the wax before she changed her mind about sending it. She said nothing to Edward.

"To The Mote," she murmured, savoring the thought. "Have you sent word to Anthony?"

"What do you think, O innocent one?" Edward laughed down at her. "Certes, he has been expecting us this sennight. I plan on voiding his forest of game, and I do not expect to be entertained every minute of our stay. I accepted to come only because 'tis a chance for me to rest apace and I knew it would please you, Meg. As I told you, I find Rivers much changed of late, and I shall be happy to leave you two to your books and prayers." A chuckle was followed by a sigh of resignation. "Then I suppose I must join Dickon in the north." He grunted. "Although he does not seem to need my help anymore. Certes, I would trust that lad with my life, Meg."

Margaret nodded, but for once her mind was on what she would be wearing when she and Anthony spent time with their books and prayers.

THE ROAD FROM Maidstone led through woods, past the hamlet of Grove Green, its fields under the plough, and on towards Otham. Trotting the final mile, the riders caught glimpses of The Mote's fanciful turrets beckoning in the distance between the trees like so many fingers.

Margaret was riding with Guillaume, seated upon her new blue and violet cloth of gold pillion saddle, a gift from Edward. They rode side by side with Edward, and Margaret badly wanted to kick her palfrey into a gallop. Behind them trailed a small retinue of servants and several horses stacked high with baggage. The rest of the Burgundian entourage had moved on to Canterbury, where Margaret would join them later.

She turned back to look at the train and sadly noted Beatrice's absence. She had arranged for burial in the little churchyard of All Hallows, a stone's throw from Coldharbour, where Beatrice had taken to attending Mass. A white rose was planted over her grave, as Margaret had promised. Henriette saw her mistress's sorrowful face gazing at the place Beatrice usually had behind one of Guillaume's squires and smiled in sympathy. I shall have to rely on Henriette now, Margaret thought with a sigh and nodded her thanks.

Margaret realized this was to be the first time she would see Anthony in his own element. These were his lands and this was his magnificent house, its warm sandstone walls protected by a narrow moat and gate tower. Standing on the short steps leading to the entry into the great hall, Anthony, his steward and squires waited to welcome the king and his sister.

"God's greeting to your graces!" Anthony called. "You honor us with your gracious presence. I bid you most welcome to my humble house."

"Humble, my arse," Edward murmured, but smiled and waved.

"Hush, Ned. I pray you behave yourself whilst we are here for my sake," she begged. " 'Tis of great importance to me, as I know you are aware."

Ned harrumphed as two burly squires helped him dismount and watched as he stretched up his arms and bent his back this way and that to relieve the stiffness from the ride. In contrast, Anthony ran nimbly down the steps and came to kneel before his king.

"Up, Anthony, up!" Ned said impatiently. "This is not an official visit. As soon as I have dined, I shall be seeking some sport in your forest. We saw a herd of bucks along our path. Have your master of the hunt attend me soonest. Messire de la Baume will accompany me but you must stay so that we do not all abandon Margaret."

Guillaume looked pleased, Anthony surprised and Margaret amused. Guillaume had handed Margaret down from the palfrey, and she was receiving Anthony's obeisance, her hand trembling as he bent over and kissed it.

"Whatever your grace desires," he said pleasantly. "I shall enjoy showing Duchess Margaret the house and garden, although," he apologized, "since Eliza's death, the garden has been sadly in need of a woman's touch."

Margaret's heart leapt. Was this an overture? Should she read anything into the otherwise flippant remark? She smiled into his sapphire eyes and said for the benefit of Edward and the others who were watching them, "Perhaps I can speak to your gardener while I am here, Lord Anthony. It would be the least I can do to thank you for your kind hospitality."

Tucking her arm into his, Anthony led the way into the house. It was lavishly furnished and Edward raised an eyebrow. "It seems I may have been rewarding Bess's family a little too generously, Anthony," he remarked. The smile left Anthony's face, and for a second Edward let him stew before laughing uproariously. "I am jesting with you, Rivers, you addle-pate. Pay me no mind."

Anthony grinned in relief and invited the guests to enter his private solar, where a table mounded with food awaited. Edward's piggy eyes lit up greedily, and he immediately snatched up a tempting duck drumstick and began chewing on it.

"How long will you stay, Marguerite?" Anthony whispered to her while Edward was in enthusiastic consultation with the master of hunt.

"A precious three days, Anthony. We are expected in Canterbury on Sunday and will sail for Calais on Monday. God willing, the negotiations are concluded and I have fulfilled my part of the bargain. It has not been easy. But I do not wish to talk of diplomacy with you."

"Anthony, by your leave," Edward called out. "De la Baume here and I will hunt immediately. Master Simpson has the hounds ready, and we can fend for ourselves. We shall be gone a few hours. I beg of you do not bore Meg with too many of your moral philosophies." He laughed and strode from the room, followed obediently by Guillaume and Master Simpson.

Anthony led Margaret into the garden, which was looking rather neglected, she admitted, and on the pretense they were in search of the head gardener, the two evaded Margaret's attendants and disappeared into the small maze. Without a word, Anthony took Margaret into his arms and crushed his mouth on hers like a man desperately seeking to find his life's breath in her. She moaned as the familiar sensation in her breasts traveled down to her loins and made her knees give way.

"We cannot . . . we should not . . . not here," she tried to say, but she did not stop his fingers unlacing her gown and reaching into her bodice to fondle her. She could hear voices not far from them but not near enough to understand words. They might be discovered at any moment, she knew, but what did she care? For the first time in almost ten years, she was again knowing what it was like to be desired—to feel herself drown in the scent, the touch, the essence of the man she had always loved.

Gently Anthony pushed her to the ground, the thick untended grass cushioning her underneath him. He kissed her nipples hard under her chemise and she writhed in pleasure, arching her back and willing him to come into her. He knelt between her legs, her skirts high and exposing the soft hair of her pubis, and relinquished his hold on her as he swiftly untied his codpiece to loose his prick. Then he was in her, both muffling their groans of pleasure but moving in unison to the natural rhythm of love. Both had waited so long for this moment that they could not savor the sweetness slowly enough, and as one they climaxed in an ecstasy Margaret could never have imagined possible.

"My dearest love, my Marguerite, you are my life, my love, my soul. In truth, I know I must be dreaming, but let me not wake and find that I was right." Anthony held her face in his hands, their bodies still throbbing together, and poured his love into her eyes. "Say I am not dreaming."

"You are not, my love. I am here and we are real." She reached up and kissed him, teasing his mouth with her tongue.

"Madame la Grande!" Henriette's voice was clear as a bell. "Are you lost in there?"

The lovers stopped kissing. Anthony rolled off Margaret and pulled her skirts down. With nimble fingers they retied their loose clothing. Margaret called out, "Aye, we were lost but are no longer. Lord Anthony believes he knows the way. We shall be there anon, do not fret." To Anthony she whispered, "Do you know the way out of this, Anthony? And I am not talking about the maze."

He hesitated. "Not here, not now, Marguerite. This must wait for a more circumspect moment. We cannot decide a lifetime in a moment in a maze." His eyes twinkled, and the tiny misgiving she had experienced just then vanished as soon as it had appeared. She smiled and allowed him to help her to her feet. He straightened her simple headdress—a veil on a jeweled band—and tucked a wayward blond tendril beneath it, kissing her nose as he did so.

A minute or so later, they emerged from the labyrinth as they had gone in, Margaret sedately on his arm, and reassured their anxious attendants that they had only been lost for a little while.

Henriette, however, noticed a grass stain on the back of Margaret's gown that had not been there when her mistress had walked out of the house earlier. She could not wait to tell Guillaume that his suspicions had been correct. She smiled to herself, happy for her mistress that she, too, knew the love of a handsome man.

EDWARD WAS SNORING in his wing of the house within minutes of finishing supper. He and Guillaume had killed a buck between them and returned highly satisfied from the hunt. The conversation during the meal had been pleasant enough until a truth emerged that had taken Margaret off guard.

"You mean you did not know that Anthony was promised to James of Scotland's sister—ha, ha!" he laughed, remembering, "another Margaret. Were you disappointed James withdrew the offer, Anthony? I suppose Dickon's successful skirmishes on the border put a burr under James's saddle. 'Twas only recently Anthony was let off the hook. 'Twas quite a blow for all of us, was it not?" Anthony gave a curt nod.

"I did not know, Ned," Margaret said quietly, and was gratified to see Anthony's sheepish look. "It would have been a fine match, and I am truly sorry for you, my lord."

Neither Anthony nor Edward knew if she really meant it, but to be safe, Edward changed the subject.

In her bed, the red and white sarcenet curtains pulled around her, Margaret dared to relive the enchantment in the maze. She touched herself reverently, trying to understand fully how her body had responded. She heard whisperings in the room and thought it was Henriette instructing the other lady who would share the truckle bed and attend her. The room went silent, and she heard the door click shut.

"Henriette?" she called, hoping she had not made any sounds of pleasure as she imagined Anthony's hands upon her skin. In answer, the curtain was quietly drawn aside, and Anthony himself said, "I sent her away, Marguerite. I hope you don't mind."

She squealed her delight and reached her arms out to him in the faint glow of the night candle. Her hair caressed his skin as she pulled him down to her and then rolled on top of him. He stroked it as though it were pure gold. Her face was in shadow, but he knew she was smiling in triumph. Straddling him, she took her time arousing him, kissing his neck, his scarred ear, and the base of his throat. He could feel her soft breasts brush lightly on his stomach and loins as she worked her way slowly down his body. When she felt he could stand no more, she mounted him and with the astonishing skill of a more practiced lover she brought him to heights he was helpless to resist.

Lying together in a bed for the first time, Margaret's happiness knew no bounds. She snuggled into the crook of his arm, and as lovers will, they whispered of their joy to each other. Margaret then propped herself up on an elbow and ran her fingers lightly through the curly hair on his chest. She had noticed white in his chestnut head hair when they arrived the day before, but although he and Edward were close to forty, Anthony was far more youthful.

"Will you stay with me all night, Anthony?" she asked, not daring to hope he would agree.

"'Tis your bed, Marguerite. I am at your command," he teased her, tucking a long strand of her hair over her ear so that he could see her face better. They talked until the candle guttered and went out, and only in the dark did she venture to bring up the future.

"And what of us now, Anthony? Do you think God will sanction our union now? I need permission from Mary and Maximilian but do you need permission? I cannot think Edward would deny us, do you? He has practically pushed me into your arms since the first day we met. However, I was somewhat dismayed to learn that you could have gone north to Scotland any day. I wonder if you would have told me? I did not think you a dissembler."

She felt him stiffen and take a deep breath before saying, "As brother to the queen, my life is not my own, Marguerite. You of all people must know this. Edward viewed me as a prize to offer James, just as he tried to give you to James himself a few years ago." He was relieved when Margaret giggled.

"Would that not have been comical—both of us married to a brother and sister in Scotland?"

"Comical, aye," Anthony agreed, "but neither of us would have been free to love as we are now. And you do know that I love you, don't you?"

Margaret sighed. "I think you do, but I cannot get you to offer me marriage. You could come to Burgundy and your position as my consort would give you more than you have now, Anthony. And then there is little Jehan, who is so in need of a father."

It was out. In her eagerness to involve her love in all aspects of her hopes, dreams and reality, she had forgotten he was not aware that she had taken charge of George's bastard.

"Jehan?" Anthony's interest was piqued. "Who is little Jehan, pray? I believed that you were barren, dearest Elaine."

Hell's bells, Margaret said to herself followed by Forgive me, Lord, for she was about to lie. "Ah. Jehan is not mine, Anthony. He is a boy from Tournai whom I have adopted in secret. He lives in my residence at Binche in southern Brabant. He has brought joy into my life since Charles's death, but with all the rumors that Louis has circulated about my indiscretions, I could not add wood to the fire. He has a tutor-chaplain and my servants at Binche spoil him horribly. You will see, he will love you, too." She was sitting up now, her arms hugging her knees as she thought of the three of them together at Binche. "And you can teach him to hunt and to joust and to write beautiful poems . . ." She trailed off, sensing a reticence in darkness. "Shall we be married, Anthony?" she whispered again. "I think I shall die if I cannot have you."

"Then, my love," Anthony suddenly decided, "I cannot deny you." He pushed her down a little more roughly this time. "And I can no longer deny myself." He made love to her with an ardor that in her mind was tantamount to signing a contract.

THE LITTLE CAVALCADE trotted out of The Mote's estates during the afternoon of the third day towards the road to Canterbury. As she held onto the pillion handle and gazed happily at the countryside they were passing, she burst into song.

> "*Sumer is icumen in*"

"A bit late for that, my dear Meg. The bracken is turning gold, and the fields are brown with turned earth. Is there not a song for autumn?" Edward laughed at her. "But I am glad to see you in good spirits. I thought that leaving England—and a certain person—you might lapse into melancholy again. You were a torrent of tears the last time you left us, I seem to remember."

Just you wait until next week, Edward, Margaret thought merrily, when Anthony declares his intention to marry me. Then you'll know why I am singing, and she continued:

> " . . . *loudly sing Cuckoo.*
> *Groweth seed and bloweth mead*
> *And springeth the wood anew.*
> *Sing Cuckoo.*"

The lovers had agreed to wait until she was back in Burgundy and could present the idea to Mary and Maximilian at the same time as Anthony approached Edward. He had promised a ring would follow as soon as he could prevail upon his favorite goldsmith to make one. True to his word, Edward had left them in peace for much of the visit and turned a blind eye to the *grande passion* he imagined was all these two were indulging in.

"You will love Malines, Anthony," Margaret had enthused not long before she had to mount up and ride away. "And we can spend some of the year in England here at The Mote or on your other estates, and I shall be so happy to come back and forth."

Anthony had laughed at her childlike excitement and stopped her mouth with a kiss. "That is to seal the bargain," he told her, "but nothing formal until we have broached both our sovereigns!"

"Sealed with a kiss," Margaret murmured happily.

ARMED WITH TREATIES for Maximilian to ratify and the promised archers, Margaret's party finally arrived at Dover six days later than planned. Thanks to her impassioned persuasion, Edward had also sent letters to Maximilian agreeing to meet with him and Louis at a location convenient to the prince. He could not have been more conciliatory, Margaret exulted, when she rode into Dover just as the tide was turning. Her diplomatic mission a success and her future happiness all but assured, her leaving England was a very different affair from the last.

"Ned, I pray you remember me kindly," Margaret said to her brother as they stood together on the quay, a cacaphony of grating, clanking, shouting and whinnying making long conversation difficult. "I give you my word I will keep England's best interests at heart while serving my dear Mary. I thank you for these"—she tapped the precious pouch of parchments that Edward had signed at Canterbury—"and I thank you for your generous hospitality."

"Meg, before you go, I want to tell you how sorry I have always been that I sent you to a monster in Burgundy. If I can ever make it up to you . . ." His face was serious for once, and she reached up and planted a kiss on his mouth.

"You may have cause to remember that remark, Ned, and I pray you to consider it if you do," she said cryptically, turning and putting out her hand for Guillaume to help her up the short plank to the ship. Edward stared after her puzzled, but then he smiled and called, "In truth, you are a fine ambassador, duchess! God speed, Mistress Nose-in-a-Book."

Brother and sister laughed heartily, enjoying the childhood memory and masking a fear that they might never meet again. Indeed, Edward's laughter soon turned to wheezing and then into a full blown fit of cough-

ing, which caused many around him to look concerned. The noise, coupled with the dockside din, muffled the sound of a horse's hoofs on the
cobblestones, and Edward's attendants turned in alarm, fearing an attack
upon their king when they saw the horseman almost upon them. Margaret could see it was naught but a messenger and waited for him to alight
and present himself to Edward before calling her final farewells.

But whatever it was, it was not for Ned. The man loudly addressed
the captain instead, waving frantically. "I have an urgent missive for her
grace, the dowager duchess of Burgundy."

Margaret groaned. Not another letter from Maximilian, she hoped.
Surely her work in England was finished—and besides, she had already
taken her ginger-root powder. She would wait until she could not turn
back and then she'd read it, she decided. She watched Guillaume stride
down the gangplank to take the letter, but she was distracted by a sailor
retrieving a line near her feet and, and when she looked up, Guillaume
was safely back on board.

"All hands on deck!" the captain cried. "Cast off, cast off! The tide is
turning."

"Farewell, Ned!" Margaret cried, as the slip of water between them
widened into a gulf, and the ship was gradually pulled by the tide and
wind into the open sea. "I will see you in October."

"I cannot hear you, Meggie," Edward shouted back. "Farewell and may
God go with you," adding "my beloved sister" in a whisper. He was surprised to find he had tears in his eyes.

WATCHING THE MAJESTIC white cliffs that protected the harbor slide by
on either side of the *Falcon* on that golden day in late September, Margaret
climbed the few steps to the forecastle and this time did not find the need
to look back over the stern.

The coast of Flanders was a line upon the horizon when she remembered the letter the messenger had delivered. Turning to look for Guillaume, she saw Henriette cradling a puppy in her arms. She frowned.
Where did that come from? she wondered. She waved at her attendant,
who immediately climbed the stairs to Margaret's vantage point in the
bow. The prow cut through the gentle waves, sending spray up occasionally and creating a rainbow in the sunlight. For the time being, Margaret
thought gratefully, her stomach was behaving.

"Who gave you the puppy, Henriette? I do not remember you receiving it or even seeing it until now. 'Tis adorable and reminds me of Astolat when I first—" She stopped when she saw the secret smile on Henriette's face.

"Did you not see the messenger give it to Guillaume?" she asked. " 'Tis from my Lord Rivers for you—together with this letter," she added, passing the pup to Margaret so that she could retrieve the letter from her belt. "What will you call him?"

Margaret's face was being washed with dog kisses, and she was laughing happily. "Anthony sent him?" she cried. "Then I shall have to call him Lancelot. Lancelot du Lac—not really of the lake, but of the water," she said, indicating the English Channel. She hugged the wriggling wolfhound and took a deep breath. "I want to thank you for your discretion, Henriette. You and Guillaume are loyal and trusted friends." She lowered her voice. "You will be pleased to hear I may never have a fit of melancholy again, if my dream comes true. Nay, I cannot tell you more. Now go and see the younger maids are behaving themselves."

Henriette curtseyed and left Margaret standing on the forecastle looking towards Burgundy, her hood and cloak standing out behind her in the stiff wind, Lancelot in her arms. There were tears of joy on her lashes and a desire in her heart to return to Mary, her grandchildren and little Jehan. When Anthony came, they would be one happy family, and maybe she could reveal her secret boy to all.

With trembling fingers, Margaret broke the seal on her letter and read:

> *"My heart, my soul, you left me to burn*
> *Musing upon my love to return*
> *Should I let thee go? Oh no, dear God, no!*
> *Or fly to thee fast on the tide's next turn?"*

"Fly, my love, fly," Margaret whispered into the wind. "To Burgundy!"

Author's Note

The vast domain held by the four Valois dukes of Burgundy for little more than a century collapsed within two decades of Charles the Bold's death at Nancy. Joseph Calmette in *The Golden Age of Burgundy* states, "The last of the great dukes, because of his impulsive and impetuous nature, brought the whole structure crashing down. . . . The powerful State of Burgundy, which had appeared like a blinding flash across the horizon of history, suddenly, and for ever, vanished, on the fatal day of the Nancy disaster." If my readers have a hard time understanding the intricacies of Burgundian politics, which I have tried to whittle down and make palatable here for historical fiction aficionados, then I hope they may appreciate the research and editing that went into that whittling down.

Margaret of York's early life in London is not well documented other than a few mentions of her appearances in public places such as at Elizabeth Woodville's coronation and her declaration of willingness to marry Charles the Bold at the Great Council at Kingston. Twenty-two was considered old for a royal princess to make a marriage alliance, but her unwed status was not for lack of suitors. Edward was otherwise occupied with keeping himself safe on the throne during those first years of his reign, and so Margaret's marriage necessarily took a back seat. It is odd, too, that her father, Richard of York, never betrothed her as a child to another noble family, which was common in medieval times. It seems the Yorks also allowed all their sons to reach late teens without matching them with heiresses. And all three sons chose their own wives for one reason or another.

Although I have walked over almost all the ground covered in the book, I had to resort to a few virtual walks through villages in northern France. Sadly, the palaces of Greenwich, Ten Waele, Coudenberg, Binche and Prinsenhof no longer exist in their medieval splendor, but I was able to step inside part of Margaret's palace at Mechelen (Malines), which is now a theater, thanks to the timely exit of the artistic director from the closed building. She kindly showed me into what must have been the great hall, and I felt Margaret's presence for the first time in my tour. Also seeing the house in Damme where Margaret and Charles were married was especially poignant. Likewise, imagining Margaret's visit to Louis de Gruuthuse's magnificent house—which is intact and now a museum not to be missed in Bruges—was a highlight of my trip.

I was lucky that nowhere are the names of Margaret's ladies recorded, except for Marie de Charny, Duke Philip's bastard daughter. We know who traveled with Margaret to her wedding, but we do not know who stayed with her in Burgundy, if anyone. As the only girl left in the York household from an early age, Margaret must have lacked for sisterly companions. I chose to invent Fortunata because I needed Margaret to have someone to confide in, someone with intelligence and humor who would not have been chronicled and who could bridge the great divide for Margaret between her life in England and on the Continent.

William Caxton continued to translate and print books at the Red Pale, aided by his foreman Wynkyn de Worde, until his death in 1491. It is thought that close to a hundred books were printed by him. We know he had a daughter, Elizabeth, who survived him, because her ex-husband, Gerard Croppe, filed claims against William's will in 1496. We do not know, however, who his wife was.

My other invention is the love story of Margaret and Anthony Woodville. It is not beyond the realm of possibility, given that Anthony was the queen's brother and at court constantly. He shared Margaret's love of books, and they must have had much to talk about. I am not the only person who thinks an *affaire de coeur* is plausible. Margaret's most recent biographer, Christine Weightman, and another Margaret expert, Ann Wroe (*Perkin, The Perfect Prince*), have told me they believe it was a possibility. Both Margaret and Anthony were pious people, Margaret even more so in her old age (she lived to age fifty-nine), when she was resigned to widowhood and did not seek to remarry. History tell us that she did not marry Anthony, though I leave the reader anticipating the marriage at the end of the book. In fact, a month after Margaret left England, Anthony married the heiress Maria Fitzlewes, hence my brief mention of the young woman during Margaret's last few days at Greenwich in 1480. We do not know if Maria was Anthony's personal choice or one thrust upon him.

History also tells us that Margaret did indeed stay with Anthony at his estate in Kent (The Mote) before returning to Burgundy at the end of that summer. It was this little piece of information that set me on the path of a possible love between them. I hope the reader will forgive me for allowing Margaret to end her precious visit to England on a positive note! As for Anthony, it has been my experience that men have a hard time facing conflict in a romantic relationship, and I imagined he was no different. I like to think he had her best interests at heart by letting her go back to Burgundy full of happy anticipation. Perhaps this deception and guilt was the reason he was wearing a hair shirt under his doublet when he was undressed for his execution three years later. As a novelist, I can only imagine! Here is the poem he wrote the night before his death at Pontefract on orders of King Richard III:

> "My life was lent,
> To what intent?
> It is near spent,
> So welcome Fate!
> Though I ne'er thought
> Low to be brought,
> Since she so planned
> I take her hand."

I have taken a few dramatic liberties in the book, which I hope the reader will forgive. I do not like to play with facts, believing strongly that in the best historical fiction, history is the skeleton and the author merely puts flesh on the bones. We do not have an exact date for Caxton's return to England, but we know he had set up his shop under the sign of the Red Pale by 1477. We know from the above-mentioned poem and from his love of poetry that Anthony Woodville tried his hand at the art; certainly his prose can be read in several books that Caxton printed. None of his poetry except the above has survived, and so with the help of some fifteenth- and sixteenth-century anonymous verse, I have put the pen in Anthony's hand. The last poem in the book, however, is my own modest attempt at the form.

Margaret did have a "secret boy" at Binche from 1478 to 1485 (the time of Bosworth), when he and his tutor-chaplain disappeared from Margaret's accounts. Fellow author and historian Ann Wroe has written extensively about the boy in the Richard III Society's quarterly, *The Ricardian*, and in her biography of Perkin Warbeck (or was he Duke Richard, who disappeared from the Tower in 1483 with his brother, Edward?). Even though we know Jehan existed, we do not know Margaret's reason for taking him in or why he disappeared from her accounts.

Edward IV's death in April 1483 set off a series of events that culminated in Richard of Gloucester becoming king, setting aside Edward's two sons, who have become known through history as the princes in the Tower. A few weeks following King Edward's death, Bishop Stillington came forward to admit he had been witness to a "pre-contract" of marriage, which was deemed binding in those days, between Edward and Eleanor Butler before Edward married Elizabeth Woodville. This has never been proven, but the story has persisted, and it proved catastrophic for the house of York in the mid-1480s. I chose to include this story in case a reader might want to discover the consequences as told in my first novel, *A Rose for the Crown*.

As a novelist, I found that the hardest feature of my storytelling came in the guise of an exact itinerary of Charles the Bold and Margaret's and Mary's whereabouts throughout Charles's ten-year rule. When I wanted Margaret in Bruges, she was in Ghent, and when I wanted her to meet Anthony secretly, I had to do it on one of her many travels to evade the eagle eye of the court chronicler! Herman Vander Linden was very assiduous in his archive-combing back in the 1930s, but he was a thorn in my side as a fiction writer! However, I have to confess his publication proved invaluable on most occasions.

The five years of Margaret's life after her return to Burgundy were so full of tragedy that I hesitate to burden the reader. For those of you who care, she suffered through her dear Mary's tragic death from a riding accident in 1482, Anthony's beheading by Richard III in 1483 and the fall of her beloved house of York at Bosworth in 1485. Maximilian of Austria was never accepted by the Flemish people, even spending seven months as a prisoner in Bruges a few years after Mary's death. He was a man of ambitious ideas, proud and brave, but he was unstable and egotistical, leading Margaret's and Mary's faithful councilors, Ravenstein and Gruuthuse, for example, to abandon him.

Margaret did, however, soldier on to bring up her step-grandchildren, following Mary's death, and see Philip the Handsome become duke of a much smaller state of Burgundy and Margaretha regent of the Netherlands. Philip married Joan of Spain and in 1506 became Philip I of that country, thus founding the Spanish Habsburg family. His son became the Holy Roman Emperor Charles V. All had Margaret to thank for her love and influence.

Cecily of York died in 1495 at the age of eighty and was outlived by only two of her twelve children (some Web sources say thirteen): Elizabeth, duchess of Suffolk, who died in early 1503, and Margaret, duchess of Burgundy, who died November 24, 1503.

Anne Easter Smith
Newburyport, Mass.

Glossary

all-night—snack before bedtime served to the king by one of his lords.

arras—tapestry or wall hanging.

attaint—imputation of dishonor or treason. Estates of attainted lord often forfeited to the crown.

avise—to look closely, study.

bailey—outer wall of a castle.

bavière—part of armor that protected lower face.

basse danse—slow, stately dance.

buckler—small round shield.

burthen—refrain or chorus of a song.

butt—barrel for wine.

butts—archery targets.

caravel—medieval sailing ship.

catafalque—funeral chariot.

caul—mesh hair covering, often jeweled or decorated, often encasing braids wound on either side of the head.

chaperon—elaborate soft hat, often with a liripipe attached.

chevalier—knight of honor.

churching—first communion given to a woman following the period of
    seclusion after giving birth.

clarion—a horn.

coif—scarf tied around the head.

caparisoned—ornamental cloth covering over a horse's armor.

conduit—drinking fountain in a town or city with piped-in water.

coney—rabbit or rabbit fur.

cote—(or *cotehardie*) long gown worn by men and women.

coustilier—cavalry soldier.

crakows—fashionable long-pointed shoes, said to have originated in
    Krakow, Poland.

crenellation—indentation at top of battlement wall.

ewerer—water-pourer and holder of hand-washing bowls at table.

excedra—low, grass-covered garden wall.

fewterer—keeper of the hounds.

flower of sovenance—flower (real or jeweled) to serve as a reminder or to
    encourage a knightly enterprise.

galingale—an aromatic root of the ginger family.

garderobe—inside privy. Often used to store clothes.

gemshorn—musical instrument of polished, hollowed goat's horn.

gipon—close-fitting padded tunic.

gittern—plucked, gut-stringed instrument similar to a guitar.

groat—silver coin worth about fourpence.

hennin—tall conical headdress from which hung a veil. Steepled hennins
    were as much as two feet high. Butterfly hennins sat on the head like
    wings with the veil draped over a frame.

houppelande—full-length or knee-length tunic or gown with full sleeves
    and train.

jakes—privy or pisspot.

jennet—saddle horse often used by women.

jerkin—jacket.

journade—short, circular unbelted gown for men, popular in Burgundy.

jupon—see *gipon*.

kersey—coarse woollen cloth.

kirtle—woman's gown or outer petticoat.

leman—lover, sweetheart, usually mistress.

liripipe—long scarf attached to a hat or chaperon.

malmsey—kind of wine.

meinie—group of attendants on a lord.

merchant adventurers—English cloth merchants living and trading abroad.

mess—platter of food shared by a group of people.

murrey—heraldic term for purple-red (plum).

obit—memorial service for the dead.

osier—willow shoot used for baskets.

palfrey—small saddle horse.

patten—wooden platform strapped to the sole of a shoe.

pavane—slow, stately dance.

pennon—triangular flag attached to lance or staff. Often rallying point during battle.

pibcorn—horn pipe.

pillion—pad placed at the back of a saddle for a second rider.

pipkin—earthenware or metal pot.

plastron—gauzy material tucked for modesty into the bodice of a gown.

points—lacing with silver tips used to attach hose to undershirt or gipon.

puling—whining; crying in a high, weak voice.

quintain—target.

readeption—name given to the government that was formed following Henry VI's reemergence from captivity in 1470.

rebec—three-stringed instrument played with a bow.

sackbut—early form of trombone.

sanctuary—place of protection for fugitives. Safe haven usually for noble women and their children, who paid to stay.

sarcenet—fine, soft silk fabric.

seneschal—steward of a large household.

sennight—week (seven nights).

settle—high-backed sofa.

shawm—wind instrument making a loud, penetrating sound. Often used on castle battlements.

shout—sailing barge carrying grain, building stone or timbers, common on the Thames.

solar—living room often doubling as bedroom.

squint—small window in wall between a room and a chapel. Often women would participate in a service through it.

stewpond—private pond stocked with fish for household use.

stews—brothel district.

Staple Town—center of trade in a specific commodity (e.g., Calais for wool).

stomacher—stiff bodice.

subtlety—dessert made of hard spun colored sugar formed into objects or scenes.

sun-in-splendour—heraldic badge name for full sun with rays.

surcote—loose outer garment of rich material, often worn over armor.

suzerain—feudal overlord.

tabard—short tunic bearing the coat of arms of a knight worn over chain mail.

tabor—small drum.

trencher—stale bread used as a plate.

trictrac—game.

tun—barrel.

tussie-mussie—aromatic pomander.

verjuice—sour fruit juice used for cooking and medicines.

viol—stringed instrument, ancestor of the viola da gamba.

Bibliography

Calmette, Joseph. *The Golden Age of Burgundy.* Trans. Doreen Weightman. London: Phoenix Press, 1962.

Clive, Mary. *This Sun of York.* New York: W. W. Norton and Co., 1962.

Commynes, Philippe de. *Memoirs, The Reign of Louis XI 1461–83.* Trans. Michael C. Jones. London: Penguin Books, 1972.

Gairdner, James, ed. *The Paston Letters.* Stroud, Gloucestershire, U.K.: Sutton Publishing, 1986.

Giles, John Allen. *The Chronicles of the White Rose of York.* London: J. Bohn, 1845.

Hammond, P. W. *Food and Feast in Medieval England.* Stroud, Gloucestershire, UK: Sutton Publishing, 1993.

Kendall, Paul Murray. *Warwick the Kingmaker.* London: Phoenix Press, 2002.

Leyser, Henrietta. *Medieval Women: A Social History of Women in England 1450–1500.* London: Weidenfeld & Nicolson. 1989.

Myers, A. R., ed. *The Household of Edward IV.* Manchester University Press, U.K., 1959.

Newman, Paul B. *Daily Life in the Middle Ages.* Jefferson, N.C.: McFarland & Company, Inc., 1961.

Norris, Herbert. *Medieval Costume and Fashion.* London: J. M. Dent & Sons, 1927.

Reeves, Compton. *Pleasures and Pastimes in Medieval England.* New York: Oxford University Press, 1998.

Richardson, Geoffrey. *The Popinjays.* Shipley Yorks, U.K: Baildon Books, 2000.

Ross, Charles. *Edward IV.* London: Eyre Methuen Ltd., 1974.

Scofield, Cora L. *The Life and Reign of Edward IV* (2 vols.). London: Frank Cass & Co. Ltd., 1967.

Speed, J. *The Counties of Britain: A Tudor Atlas* (pub. 1611). London: Pavilion Books, Ltd., 1995.

Tyler, William R. *Dijon and the Valois Dukes of Burgundy.* Oklahoma: University of Oklahoma Press, 1971.

Uden, Grant. *The Knight and the Merchant.* New York: Roy Publishers, 1966.

Vaughan, Richard. *Charles the Bold.* Woodbridge, Suffolk, U.K: The Boydell Press, 1973.

Weightman, Christine. *Margaret of York.* Stroud, Gloucestershire, U.K.: Sutton Publishing, 1989.

Wroe, Ann. *The Perfect Prince.* New York: Random House, 2003.

Summary

Daughter of York traces the tumultuous life of Margaret of York, whose family was thrust into prominence in 1461, when Margaret's brother Edward defeated the warring Lancastrian faction and was declared king of England. At the tender age of fifteen, Margaret discovers that her dear brother Ned has political power and authority that depend, to some extent, on her own value as a young woman of marriageable age.

As Margaret grows in her role as Edward's confidante and awaits being promised to some far-flung groom on the Continent, she discovers her own fascination with the complex world of politics and international affairs. Her developing friendship with Anthony Woodville, a courtier who shares her intellectual pursuits and is charmed by her high-born beauty, leads her to seek more time in the inner circle of her brothers' court. But in an effort to thwart Louis of France and to ally Britain with Burgundy, Edward promises Margaret to Duke Charles, and she finds herself on a ship with her most trusted servant, the dwarf Fortunata, and her other ladies-in-waiting, escorted by Anthony to her new homeland.

Margaret's childless marriage to Charles proves frustrating and disappointing, as her new husband travels for months at a time, and does not seem to be truly in love with his young wife. Margaret throws herself into getting counsel from her advisers at court and learning the ways of her new country, all the while pining for her beloved Anthony. Through the intercession of Fortunata and the printer William Caxton, Anthony and Margaret communicate their love through a series of secret missives. These communiqués keep Margaret's hope alive, even as she faces challenges to her authority as a foreign duchess. Through triumph and tragedy, Margaret never forgets that she is in her heart an English princess and a daughter of the House of York.

Discussion Questions

1. How do the deaths of Margaret's father, Richard, and her brother, Edmund, impact the political fortunes of the York family? What might Margaret's recurring nightmares of the Micklegate symbolize? To what extent is Margaret's mother, Cecily, responsible for holding the family together in the aftermath of Richard's death, and what does her absence from Edward's court suggest about her feelings about her son's rule?

2. How would you characterize Margaret's relationships with each of her brothers—Edward, Richard, and George? Whom does she most trust, and whom does she most love? In what respects does Margaret act as a surrogate mother to her siblings, and to what extent are her fears for them realized?

3. "Each time she was with Edward in public, her eyes would scan the groups of courtiers for Anthony Woodville. . . . [s]he had tried to put him from her mind in the two years since Edward was crowned." What initially draws Margaret to Anthony

Woodville, and how does the fact of his marriage to Eliza Scales impact Margaret's feelings about him? Given that Edward seems to encourage the flirtation between his sister and one of his most trusted advisers, why do Margaret and Anthony go to such lengths to conceal their mutual attraction?

4. How does the arrival of Fortunata change Margaret's opinion of court life? Why does Fortunata succeed in becoming Margaret's most trusted confidante in Burgundy, and how does she disappoint her mistress most grievously? In what respects does their relationship seem to deviate from the typical one between mistress and maid, and how do others at court register their feelings about this breach of custom?

5. How does Margaret feel about her arranged marriage to Charles of Burgundy compared to her former intended, Dom Pedro? Why does Edward assign Anthony Woodville to escort Margaret on her journey to her new home? How is Margaret's marriage important to the growing political power of England? In what way is Margaret's wedding night predictive of the nature of her physical relationship with Charles?

6. How does the court at Burgundy compare to Edward's court in England? Why does Margaret feel especially alienated in her new home? How does her stepdaughter, Mary, help Margaret adjust to her new responsibilities and duties as duchess of Burgundy? To what extent do Margaret's feelings of unhappiness seem to stem from her inability to bear a child to term?

7. How is literature—and poetry in particular—significant to the characters in *Daughter of York*? With their frequent allusions to Arthurian characters like Lancelot and Elaine, how are Margaret and Anthony able to redefine their largely unrequited romantic relationship?

8. What does the end of the novel imply about Margaret and Anthony's future together? Why do you think the author chose to end the novel on this note? What do you think sustained Margaret's interest in Anthony over the course of so many years?

9. Of the many scenes in *Daughter of York*, which did you find most moving or memorable? Why? Which of the characters in the novel did you find most intriguing or compelling? Why?

Q & A with Anne Easter Smith

Q: *How did you first become interested in Margaret of York? What historical details from her life enabled you to envision her as a character in a fictional context?*

A: All during my research on Richard III and his family for my first book, *A Rose for the Crown,* I kept finding out little tidbits about Margaret that intrigued me. For instance: that she, even though a useful royal marriage tool, was unmarried for so long; that it was she who commissioned William Caxton to print the first book written in English; that she had a passion for rose-petal jam; and on a more personal note, that she was very tall for her era—something that, at just over six feet, I could relate to.

Q: *Can you describe your process for incorporating historical facts with fictional scenes in your novels?*

A: This is the most difficult aspect of my work. I have come up with a method that works for me. I have a large display chart on which I make a grid, running dates down the side and characters along the top. Every time I find a chronological fact about one of my factual characters, I enter it in the grid. That becomes my framework, and then I can weave my fictional characters around those facts.

Q: *You mention in your author's note that you were able to walk almost all the ground covered in the book. Which historical sites from Margaret of York's life did you find most fascinating and why?*

A: There are so many! I have to say Belgium (Burgundy) was a revelation. Of course, Bruges is special and I especially enjoyed walking through Louis of Gruuthuse's magnificent house (now a museum) because I could see Margaret there. My traveling companion and I also biked up the canal/river from Bruges to Damme to see the actual house where Margaret and Charles were married. It made her *joyeuse entree* into Bruges from there so real for me. But I think Ghent and Malines (or Mechelen) were the highlights of my footstep-following. What is so sad is how many of the wonderful medieval towns were devastated first by World War I, with artillery fire, and then World War II, with bombs. I've saved my favorite place till last: Binche, where Margaret kept her secret boy and which still has an intact city wall—the only one in Belgium.

Q: *You've written that no incontrovertible evidence exists of the romantic relationship between Anthony Woodville and Margaret. To what extent might such an extramarital liaison have been likely in that era?*

A: Very likely. Most marriages in the medieval period—even in the lower-born—were business arrangements. Finding love outside the marriage bed was commonplace until Victorian times (and even then it went on in secret). The more I read about Margaret and Anthony, the more I think they would have enjoyed each other's company intellectually and that it could have blossomed into love and an affair. When I suggested this to Christine Weightman, who has written the latest biography of Margaret (upon which I relied heavily), and her friend Ann Wroe, who researched extensively in the Burgundian archives for her book *The Perfect Prince,* they both endorsed my supposition, convinced that "something went on" between the two.

Q: Margaret's inability to conceive a male heir does not in any way jeopardize her marriage with Charles. Given the intense focus in that era on the transfer of power through male lineage, why is that the case?

A: To be honest, I don't know. He enjoyed the alliance with England that his marriage forged to help stave off Louis of France, but I don't think he cared about having another wife, per se. In all the research I did on Charles, it seemed he was convinced he was invulnerable and believed in his own destiny alone. Mary did succeed him because Burgundy was a duchy and there were no laws against a female inheriting. It does seem odd that he had three wives (the first albeit very brief) and only one offspring. This also led me to believe he was not really interested in women. Of course he should have secured the dukedom with a male heir, but I'm not sure he cared about what happened after he died.

Q: You portray Margaret as a savvy politician in her own right. To what extent is this characterization based on historical evidence?

A: Mostly because Charles left her in charge so many times when he went off to war trying to add to the Burgundian lands. And I gleaned from Richard Vaughan's excellent biography of Charles that after Charles's mother died, he turned to Margaret for advice. It was Margaret's tireless work, after the shock of Charles's death and the uprisings culminating in the terrifying executions of Humbercourt and Hugonet, that finalized the marriage between Mary and Maximilian, bringing stability back to the Lowlands.

Q: You examine the feud between the Yorkists and the Lancastrians in Daughter of York. To what extent does Margaret feel her first and most powerful allegiance is to the house of York?

A: I loved the fact that Margaret would often sign herself Marguerite d'York before she signed herself Marguerite de Bourgogne! It spoke volumes to me. After Bosworth, Margaret funded two attempts to unseat the Tudors and put a Yorkist king back on the throne: Lambert Simnel in 1487 and Perkin Warbeck (who will be a focus of my third book) in the 1490s. She never let Henry forget that there was still a Yorkist ready to oust him from the throne until the day she died in 1503! No wonder he called her "this Diabolicall Duches" (sic).

Q: How much of your book is fact and how much is fiction?

A: What is difficult, for a novelist, is being able to tell the reader which is fact and which is not. No footnotes for us! But I would say that, if we had them, almost all the pages of my book would have a surprising number of footnotes.

Q: If Daughter of York were produced as a film and you were its director, whom would you choose to play some of the principals?

A: What a delicious dilemma! Even though she is dark and Margaret had fair hair, I would like to see Emily Blount play Margaret, Damien Lewis as Edward and Alfred Molina as Charles. As for Anthony, he lives only in my dreams! But it would not be Brad Pitt.

Q: *Why did you decide to end your chronicle of Margaret of York's life where you did?*

A: Had I been writing a biography, of course it would have ended with Margaret's death and included all the sad things that happened to her after her visit to England in 1480. Would you, as a reader, have liked to wallow in her misery over dear Mary's untimely death, Anthony's execution (not counting the devastation she might have had upon learning of his marriage to Maria Fitzlewes not three months after her departure), Edward's unexpected death, and the demise of the House of York at Bosworth? Margaret's life, after her return to Burgundy, was actually one of quiet piety and charitable works, coupled with caring for her step-grandchildren. Not exactly exciting novel reading! I wanted the reader to take away a picture of a vibrant, joyful Margaret full of hope for the future. And that's how we should remember her!

Q: *Do you expect to explore any more of Margaret's life in future novels?*

A: Margaret will feature as a peripheral character in my next novel about Perkin Warbeck, a pretender to the throne, and in my fourth one about Cecily of York, in which Margaret will be a young girl again.

Enhance Your Book Club

1. Would you like to know more about Anne Easter Smith, the author of *Daughter of York*? Visit her official website, http://www.AnneEasterSmith.com/default.html, to learn more about her commitment to both the performing arts and historical fiction. If your book club is interested in connecting with Anne for a telephone conference call, send her an email at anne@AnneEasterSmith.com to check her availability, or just to let her know your thoughts about *Daughter of York*.

2. When Margaret returns from her years in Burgundy and is received at her brother's court, Edward arranges for a royal feast that includes some of the family's favorite foods, including his mother's beloved oysters, flampaynes, and porpoise—not forgetting Margaret's own favorite rose-petal jam. What foods would your family reunion include, and which dishes would especially satisfy the most finicky members of your family? Your book club might want to discuss favorite family recipes and share them at a future gathering.

3. Are you intrigued by the lavish region of Burgundy described in *Daughter of York*? Did you know that the lands encompassed by Burgundy in the medieval era now include France, Belgium, and the Netherlands? If you're considering making a trip to tour medieval Burgundy, you will want to visit http://www.inenuitmechelen.be/en/ to read more about Mechelen (Malines), the city where Margaret of York lived following Charles's death, and where she died in 1503.

4. If you would like to research further into Margaret's family and the people and events around the Wars of the Roses, visit the Richard III Society's website at: www.r3.org.

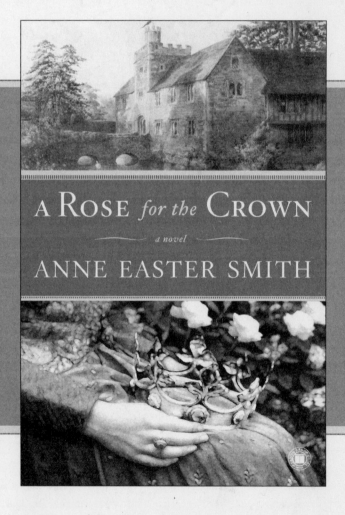